THE YEAR'S
BEST SCIENCE
FICTION

SEVENTH ANNUAL COLLECTION

ALSO BY GARDNER DOZOIS

Anthologies

A Day in the Life
Another World
Beyond the Golden Age
Best Science Fiction Stories of the Year, Sixth Annual Collection
Best Science Fiction Stories of the Year, Seventh Annual Collection
Best Science Fiction Stories of the Year, Eighth Annual Collection
Best Science Fiction Stories of the Year, Ninth Annual Collection
Best Science Fiction Stories of the Year, Tenth Annual Collection
Future Power (with Jack Dann)
Aliens! (with Jack Dann)
Unicorns! (with Jack Dann)
Magicats! (with Jack Dann)
Bestiary! (with Jack Dann)
Mermaids! (with Jack Dann)
Sorcerers! (with Jack Dann)
Demons! (with Jack Dann)
Dogtales! (with Jack Dann)
Ripper! (with Susan Casper)
Seaserpents! (with Jack Dann)
The Best of Isaac Asimov's Science Fiction Magazine
Time-Travellers from Isaac Asimov's Science Fiction Magazine
Transcendental Tales from Isaac Asimov's Science Fiction Magazine
The Year's Best Science Fiction, First Annual Collection
The Year's Best Science Fiction, Second Annual Collection
The Year's Best Science Fiction, Third Annual Collection
The Year's Best Science Fiction, Fourth Annual Collection
The Year's Best Science Fiction, Fifth Annual Collection
The Year's Best Science Fiction, Sixth Annual Collection

Fiction

Strangers
The Visible Man (collection)
Nightmare Blue (with George Alec Effinger)

Nonfiction

The Fiction of James Tiptree, Jr.

THE YEAR'S BEST SCIENCE FICTION

**SEVENTH
ANNUAL
COLLECTION**

Edited by Gardner Dozois

ST. MARTIN'S PRESS   NEW YORK

for
EILEEN GUNN
and
JOHN D. BERRY

Design by Judy Dannecker

Library of Congress Catalog Card Number: 85-645716

CONTENTS

ACKNOWLEDGMENTS

The Editor would like to thank the following people for their help and support: first and foremost, Susan Casper, for doing much of the thankless scut work involved in producing this anthology; Ellen Datlow, Michael Swanwick, Sheila Williams, Ian Randal Strock, Charles Ardai, Tina Lee, Kristine Kathryn Rusch, Dean Wesley Smith, Pat Cadigan, Arnie Fenner, Janet and Ricky Kagan, Pat LoBrutto, Susan Protter, Patrick Delahunt, Virginia Kidd, David S. Garnett, Charles C. Ryan, Chuq von Rospach, David Pringle, George Alec Effinger, James Turner, Lucius Shepard, Susan Allison, Ginjer Buchanan, Lou Aronica, Amy Stout, Beth Meacham, Claire Eddy, James Patrick Kelly, Edward Bryant, David G. Hartwell, Tim Sullivan, Bob Walters, Tess Kissinger, Michael G. Adkisson, Steve Pasechnick, Nicholas Robinson, Andy Watson, Michael Sumbera, Glen Cox, Eileen Gunn, Jessica Amanda Salmonson, Mark Van Name, Martha Soukup, Robert Killheffer, Greg Cox, Byron Preiss, Dave Harris, David Memmott, and special thanks to my own editors, Gordon Van Gelder and Stuart Moore.

Thanks are also due to Charles N. Brown, whose magazine *Locus* (Locus Publications, P.O. Box 13305, Oakland, California 94661, $28.00 for a one-year subscription—twelve issues; $40.00 for a one-year subscription—twelve issues via first-class mail) was used as a reference source throughout the Summation, and to Andrew Porter, whose magazine *Science Fiction Chronicle* (Science Fiction Chronicle, P.O. Box 2730, Brooklyn, N.Y. 11202–0056, $27.00 for a one-year subscription—twelve issues) was also used as a reference source throughout.

SUMMATION
1989

Nineteen eighty-nine was a year of changes and ominous omens, as perhaps is befitting for the penultimate year of a turbulent decade. Pat LoBrutto resigned his position as senior editor at Doubleday Foundation to pursue a career as a free-lance writer and anthologist. Beth Meacham relinquished her duties as Tor editor-in-chief and moved to Tucson, Arizona, with husband (and former editor of *The Twilight Zone Magazine*) Tappan King— she will, however, continue to work as executive editor of Tor, and as an acquisitions editor for them, commuting in to New York City ten times a year. Patrick Delahunt, one of SF's foremost literary agents, has abruptly retired from the agency business, causing a feeding frenzy among other agents, who have at once swooped in on his client list. Lynx Books died, following on the heels of Pageant, and the Isaac Asimov Presents line has fallen into a state of limbo, although there are still rumors from time to time that it will be started up again. Two long-running magazines died, the majority of SF lines have made cutbacks of one degree of severity or another, and rumors of buying slowdowns at some houses are rife.

And the Salman Rushdie affair—the details of which I certainly don't have to rehash here—raises the ugly possibility of censorship by terroristic threat. During the last year, more than one SF writer said to me, with a nervous laugh, "Thank goodness the Ayatollah doesn't read SF!" But someone *else* with a political/religious/polemical ax to grind might, and how long would it take for the SF publishing industry to cave in under the kind of pressure that was brought to bear on the publisher of *The Satanic Verses?* Censorship is a thousand-headed snake that *must* be fought every time it raises one of those heads, at whatever level, no matter what the cost.

As the last item makes clear, this was a year of ominous omens for the whole publishing industry, not just for science fiction publishing (which, in fact, was actually affected less severely than some other areas). The summer of 1989 was widely reported to be a very bad one for sales in general, and this caused shakeups throughout the publishing industry at the very top of the corporate ladder, with corporate presidents and board chairmen being fired or being forced into retirement at several giant conglomerates; some lines, like E.P. Dutton, suddenly undergoing dramatic changes; and with other publishing houses put up for sale altogether by their parent corporations, many of whom admitted to massive operating losses.

It becomes clear that SF publishing—and probably the publishing industry in general—is headed into the heavy weather of another recession. The key questions are: how bad will things get? And for how long?

For there were also *contradictory* omens. Even as some SF lines were dying, new ones were being born. The British publisher Pan, for instance, will start a new three-part science fiction/fantasy/horror list under editor Kathy Gale, and NAL will create a new three-part science fiction/fantasy/horror list called Roc Books, under editor John Silbersack. Deborah Beale at London Century is starting a new line of prestige novellas, to be published as individual books, and Malcolm Edwards will be working on starting a new science fiction and fantasy line for Grafton Books. Bantam Doubleday Dell's two new lines, Spectra Special Editions and Doubleday Foundation, seem to be doing well, as is the new Tor Double line. The small press market has never been livelier, or more important to the field. SF writers continued to figure prominently on nationwide bestseller lists. And though the total number of books published in the related SF/fantasy/horror fields *was* down slightly in 1989, "down" is a relative term: 1,784 books were published this year, according to the newsmagazine *Locus*—an 8 percent drop from last year's total of 1,936, admittedly, but still an enormous number of books.

I've said this before, but I think that it's worth repeating: There is a periodic boom-and-bust cycle that has repeated ever since there *was* such a thing as SF as a distinct publishing category. But it should be pointed out that every boom-and-bust cycle has left the habitual SF-reading audience *larger than it was before the boom began.* Some of the gains are always held, and I don't really believe that any "bust" or recession will be capable of reducing SF to pre-1974 levels of readership or advances or sales, unless most of the publishing industry at large collapses with it. Even with most of the fat trimmed away—and there's a lot of fat out there to be trimmed—the "retrenched" genre as a whole will still be larger and more prosperous than it was in 1973.

Even more important than the question of sales is the question: is there still anything out there *worth reading?* In a 1977 essay, I decried the advent in science fiction publishing of what I referred to as "the junk-food mentality: cut quality, cut costs, hype your product relentlessly, and sell in bulk," and warned that "the creative end of the genre is in many places in danger of being taken over by corporate marketing specialists who have no intention of taking any risks, by people who care nothing about SF as an art form, by people who think of writers as sausage factories and regard the SF audience as just another cowlike group of consumers to be manipulated." This mentality, and the short-sighted, bottom-line, immediate-gratification corporate accounting practices that promulgate it, is responsible for a great deal that is wrong with today's publishing industry, and not just in SF, by any means. And those junk-food specialists are just the people who, when belt-tightening time comes, will try to eliminate the few novels of quality that remain in their lists, rather than cut back on the hordes of "surefire" commercial crap that they've cluttered the bookshelves with—let's hope that they can be prevented from doing this in the tough times ahead, for that way leads to the stagnation of the genre and the ultimate falling away of much of the genre audience, however commercially sensible and "hardheaded" the strategy looks in the short term.

In fact, in an odd way, the most encouraging thing about today's SF market is that adult work of quality *does* still manage to get into print, in spite of the increasing flood of choose-your-own-adventure books, "share-cropper" books, *Star Trek* novels, "Robotech" books, shared-world anthologies, "Thieves World" novels, wet-dream mercenary fantasies, "Dungeons and Dragons" scenarios, and movie novelizations that it must fight against for rack display space.

That quality work does still manage to get into print is almost solely because there are still editors working in the field who are courageous or naive enough to treat their audience as if it were composed of intelligent adults of all ages . . . and as long as *that* remains true, science fiction as a genre worth reading will survive.

It was a somewhat gloomy year in the SF magazine market, which suffered several heavy losses. Toward the beginning of 1989, we lost *The Twilight Zone Magazine*, which folded after producing only three 1989-dated issues, and toward the end of the year, we began hearing dire rumors about *Amazing* as well. Alas, those rumors were confirmed in the beginning of 1990, while I was typing a clean copy of this Summation. *Amazing* has died, at least as a digest-sized science fiction magazine. There are several contradictory rumors currently floating about as to the future of the magazine—one has it that it will become a large-format gaming magazine, similar to TSR's *Dragon* magazine; another has it becoming a "graphic comix" magazine—but, whatever its future, it is clearly not intended to continue as anything we would consider a science fiction magazine. This is a shame, since, under editor Patrick L. Price, *Amazing* was livelier than it had been for years, and was publishing some very good material—but its continuing low circulation and its inability to attract advertising revenue have finally done it in. (I've had occasion to read memorial services over *Amazing's* grave two or three times before during the last fourteen years of editing Best of the Year anthologies, and each time it has fooled me by rising again reborn in a new avatar, but I have the uneasy feeling that this time the Grand Old Lady, SF's oldest and longest-running magazine, may well be gone for good.) With the demise of *Amazing* as a fiction magazine, the digest-sized SF magazine market is reduced to three titles: *The Magazine of Fantasy and Science Fiction*, *Analog*, and *Isaac Asimov's Science Fiction Magazine*, the lowest number of digest-sized titles in years.

On the upbeat side, *Aboriginal SF* and the British magazine *Interzone* both made it up from the semiprozine ranks into the professional magazine category this year, and there seems to be reason to be cautiously optimistic about the future of both. *Interzone* seems to be publishing better material than ever, and gained national newsstand distribution in the United Kingdom this year. *Aboriginal SF* continued to dramatically increase its circulation for yet another year, and is widely available in major chain bookstores like Dalton's and Waldenbooks that sometimes carry no other SF magazines at all. (A cautionary note was struck, however, by its admission, in an early

1990-dated issue, that it is beginning to feel the pinch of money problems, caused mainly by the high cost of producing a large-format magazine and by the difficulty in attracting enough advertising revenue. Let's hope that *Aboriginal* can survive the cash-flow crunches that may be on the way, since SF can use all the short-fiction markets it can get.) *Analog* celebrated its sixtieth birthday early in 1990, and is still going strong.

A new large-format magazine, *Starshore*, was announced, but little else was known about it by press time. There were also rumors about an upcoming new horror magazine, called *Shadows Magazine*, to be edited by veteran horror editor Charles L. Grant, but there was little concrete information to be had about that by press time, either. Maybe we'll have more information on those projects next year.

As most of you probably know, I, Gardner Dozois, am also editor of *Isaac Asimov's Science Fiction Magazine*. And that, as I've mentioned before, does pose a problem for me in compiling this Summation, particularly the magazine-by-magazine review that follows. As *IAsfm* editor, I could be said to have a vested interest in the magazine's success, so that anything negative I said about another SF magazine (particularly another digest-sized magazine, my direct competition), could be perceived as an attempt to make my own magazine look good by tearing down the competition. Aware of this constraint, I've decided that nobody can complain if I only say *positive* things about the competition . . . and so, once again, I've limited myself to a listing of some of the worthwhile authors published by each.

OMNI published first-rate fiction this year by Connie Willis, James Blaylock, Michael Swanwick, Jonathan Carroll, Robert Silverberg, J.R. Dunn, Bruce McAllister, Marc Laidlaw, and others. *OMNI*'s fiction editor is Ellen Datlow.

The Magazine of Fantasy and Science Fiction featured excellent fiction by Lucius Shepard, Mike Resnick, Charles Sheffield, Robert Silverberg, Judith Dubois, Bradley Denton, and others. *F & SF*'s longtime editor is Edward Ferman.

Isaac Asimov's Science Fiction Magazine featured critically acclaimed work by Judith Moffett, Connie Willis, Kim Stanley Robinson, Robert Silverberg, Nancy Kress, Eileen Gunn, Kathe Koja, Alexander Jablokov, Bruce Sterling, Megan Lindholm, Kristine Kathryn Rusch, and others. *IAsfm*'s editor is Gardner Dozois.

Analog featured good work by Charles Sheffield, Lois McMaster Bujold, Michael Flynn, Elizabeth Moon, W.T. Quick, Rick Shelley, Harry Turtledove, and others. *Analog*'s longtime editor is Stanley Schmidt.

Amazing featured good work by Nina Kiriki Hoffman, Sheila Finch, Kristine Kathryn Rusch, Gregory Benford, Phillip C. Jennings, Harry Turtledove, R. Garcia y Robertson, and others. *Amazing*'s editor was Patrick L. Price.

Interzone featured good work by Brian Stableford, Lisa Goldstein, Karen Joy Fowler, Ian MacDonald, William King, Richard Calder, J.G. Ballard,

Greg Egan, Kim Newman, Phillip Mann, and others. *Interzone*'s editor is David Pringle.

Aboriginal Science Fiction featured interesting work by Patricia Anthony, R.P. Bird, Walter Jon Williams, Kristine Kathryn Rusch, Resa Nelson, Jonathan Lethem, and others. The editor of *Aboriginal Science Fiction* is Charles C. Ryan.

Short SF continued to appear in many magazines outside genre boundaries. *Playboy* in particular continues to run a good deal of SF, under fiction editor Alice K. Turner.

(Subscription addresses follow for those magazines hardest to find on the newsstands: *The Magazine of Fantasy and Science Fiction*, Mercury Press, Inc., Box 56, Cornwall, CT 06753, annual subscription—twelve issues— $21.00 in US; *Isaac Asimov's Science Fiction Magazine*, Davis Publications, Inc., P.O. Box 7058, Red Oak, IA 51566, $25.97 for thirteen issues; *Interzone*, 124 Osborne Road, Brighton, BN1 6LU, England, $26.00 for an airmail one-year—six issues—subscription; *Aboriginal Science Fiction*, P.O. Box 2449, Woburn, MA 01888–0849, $14.00 for six issue, $22.00 for twelve.)

Among the fiction semiprozines, the most commercially viable title, and the one most likely to be the next to escape up into the professional category, is probably *Weird Tales*, edited by George H. Scithers, John Betancourt, and Darrell Schweitzer. It's a thoroughly professional magazine, lacking only in circulation to qualify it for the professional category. Things were livelier in the fiction semiprozine market this year than they have been since the high days of the Pat Cadigan-edited *Shayol*, and there are now several strange and eclectic magazines out there that are well worth a look. Perhaps the most prominent of them is *New Pathways*, edited by Michael G. Adkisson, a glossy, good-looking magazine full of interestingly quirky stuff of all sorts; *New Pathways* perhaps tries a little too self-consciously to be weird, but there's always something of interest to read here, and I recommend it. *Nova Express*, edited by Michael Sumbera, with help by Glen Cox and Dwight Brown, is another enjoyably eclectic magazine, an interesting mix of fiction, highly opinionated reviews, and gonzo journalism. They have also published some worthwhile interviews with Howard Waldrop, John Kessel, and others, and the only genuinely entertaining convention reports I've seen in some while; *Nova Express* also spends a fair amount of time demonstrating how hip it is, but the tone of the magazine is more robust and gonzo than the somewhat cooler and more intellectual/abstract tone of *New Pathways*, and so far there has been something in every issue that made me laugh out loud (in a *good* way, guys, in a *good* way), no mean recommendation. An all-fiction semiprozine called *Strange Plasma* made an impressive debut this year; edited by Steve Pasechnick, the stories in *Strange Plasma* strike me as being of considerably higher overall quality than the stories in the vast majority of semiprozines—one of them, in fact, a story by Robert Sampson, made it into this anthology, and two more, stories by Paul Park and R.A. Lafferty, were on my short list; clearly this is a magazine to watch. Another weirdly eclectic magazine that made its debut this year was *Journal Wired*, edited by Andy Watson and Mark V. Ziesing; another mixed-content magazine, it seems to consist mostly of a kind of critical ranting, some of it—notably the rants by Lucius Shepard and John Shirley—entertaining, some of it not—although they did publish an intriguing story by A.A. Attanasio, and an even more intriguing story by Rudy Rucker that accomplished the difficult literary feat of making the watching of a live sex show in a sleazy porno theater on 42nd Street an upbeat, morally positive, life-affirming, damn near *pastoral* experience; only Rucker could—excuse the expression —pull this off. Mention should probably also be made here of *Ice River*, edited by David Memmott; although it published mostly poetry, there were many names featured here which would be familiar to genre audiences, and much that would be of interest to them. They have reportedly ceased publication.

There are also a slew of horror semiprozines, too many to list here, although the most visible of them are probably *Midnight Graffiti*, *American Fantasy*, *Fear*, and *Grue*; all of these magazines are in competition with *Weird Tales* to fill the vacuum left in the horror short-fiction market by the demise of *The Twilight Zone Magazine* and *Night Cry*. It's a good bet that one of these magazines will make it up into the pro classification within the next couple of years; so far *Midnight Graffiti*, edited by Jessie Horsting and James Van Hise, seems to be giving *Weird Tales* its stiffest competition for this spot, although they're a little light on the amount of fiction they publish per issue. *The Horror Show*, one of the top horror semiprozines, died this year. Once again, there was no issue of *Whispers*, either. There is also a semiprozine aimed at the High Fantasy market, *Marion Zimmer Bradley's Fantasy Magazine*, but, to date, the fiction published there has yet to reach reliable levels of quality. As ever, *Locus* and *SF Chronicle* remain your best bet among the semiprozines if you are looking for news and/or an overview of the genre. *Thrust* is the longest-running of those semiprozines that concentrate primarily on literary criticism. Among other criticalzines, *Short Form* was taken over by Mark Van Name, who has seemingly returned it to a reliable schedule of publication after several missed issues. However, although there is still a lot of interesting material here, they don't seem to review much short fiction anymore, which was the *raison d'etre* for the magazine's existence in the first place; critical theorizing and polemics we can get elsewhere, in plenty, but short fiction reviews are vanishingly rare. Steve Brown and Dan Steffan only managed to get out one issue of *Science Fiction Eye* this year; admittedly, it was a fat issue stuffed with fascinating material, but the magazine's seeming inability to stick to their announced publishing schedule must be a worry to subscribers. *The New York Review of Science Fiction*—edited by a Cast of Thousands, including Kathryn Cramer, L.W. Currey, Samuel R. Delany, David G. Hartwell, Greg Cox, Robert Killheffer, John J. Ordover, and Gordon Van Gelder—has managed to infuriate many over the last two years with its highly opinionated reviews and didactic theoretical essays, but it has also managed to solidly establish itself as the most reliable and intriguing of the new crop of criticalzines; it's already been a Hugo finalist once, and I strongly suspect that it will be again—it might even win, one of these days. Another offbeat and interesting criticalzine is *OtherRealms*, edited by Chuq Von Rospach and Laurie Sefton, a hard-copy version of an online "electronic fanzine" that is accessible through the computer networks; this may well be the wave of the future, if the networks become large and widespread enough.

(*Locus*, Locus Publications, Inc., P.O. Box 13305, Oakland, California 94661, $40.00 for a one-year first-class subscription, 12 issues; *Science Fiction Chronicle*, Algol Press, P.O. Box 2730, Brooklyn, NY 10202–0056, $27.00 for one year, twelve issues; *Thrust*, Thrust Publications, 8217 Langport Terrace, Gaithersburg, MD 20877, $8.00 for four issues; *Science Fiction Eye*, Box 43244, Washington, DC 20010–9244, $10.00 for one year; *Short Form*, Hatrack River Publications, P.O. Box 18184, Greensboro, NC 27419–8184, one-year subcription (six issues) $24.00; *Weird Tales*, Terminus Publishing Company, Box 13418, Philadelphia, PA 19101–3418, $18.00 for six issues; *New Pathways*, MGA Services, P.O. Box 863994, Plano, TX 75086–3994, $10.00 for a one-year four-issue subscription, $18.00 for a two-year subscription. *Nova Express*, White Car PubLications, P.O. Box 27231, Austin, TX 78755–2231, $8 for a one-year four-issue subscription; *Strange Plasma*, Edgewood Press, P.O. Box 264, Cambridge, MA 02238, $8 for three issues; *Journal Wired*, P.O. Box 76, Shingletown, CA 96088; *Other-Realms*, 35111–F Newark Blvd., Suite 255, Newark, CA 94560, $11 for a one-year four-issue subscription; *Ice River*, David Memmott, 953 N. Gale, Union, OR 97883, $9 for a one-year three-issue subscription; *Grue Magazine*, Hells Kitchen Productions, Box 370, Times Square Station, New York, NY 10108, $11.00 for three issues; *American Fantasy*, P.O. Box 41714, Chicago, IL 60641, $16.00 a year; *The New York Review Of Science Fiction*, Dragon Press, P.O. Box 78, Pleasantville, NY, 10570, $24.00 per year; *Midnight Graffiti*, 13101 Sudan Road, Poway, CA 92604, one year for $24.00.)

This was a stronger year than last year overall in the original anthology market. The two best SF anthologies of the year were probably the mixed original-and-reprint anthologies *What Might Have Been? Volume 1: Alternate Empires* (Bantam Spectra), and *What Might Have Been? Volume 2: Alternate Heroes* (Bantam Spectra), both books edited by Gregory Benford and Martin H. Greenberg, and both packed with some very good stories, including stories that have made it on to major award ballots this year and last. Check out in particular the Frederik Pohl, the Robert Silverberg, the Harry Turtledove, the Gregory Benford, the Karen Joy Fowler, and the George Alec Effinger in Volume 1, and the Silverberg, the Sheila Finch, the Barry N. Malzberg, the Marc Laidlaw, and the Walter Jon Williams in Volume 2. These belong on the shelves of everyone who enjoys Alternate History stories. As an aside, I might mention that this has been a good year in general for Alternate History stories in SF, with several excellent ones by Silverberg, John Crowley, Bruce Sterling, Neal Barrett, Jr., and others, none of them connected to the Benford/Greenberg anthologies, appearing here and there throughout the genre. In addition, the stories from another good anthology, *Time Gate* (Baen), edited by Robert Silverberg with Bill Fawcett, can also be read as *de facto* Alternate History stories, deriving most of their impact from the throwing together of computer simulations of Famous Figures from history, and working out how they would interact. The best story here is the Silverberg, but everything in the book is well worth reading. There are a few Alternate History stories in the next two anthologies as well—including one that will probably get the author run out of Texas on a rail—but mostly they're filled with prime examples of that *very* strange new subgenre that is being referred to (no doubt with tongue firmly in cheek) as "cowpunk"—bizarre hybrids of SF/fantasy/horror with the traditional Western story. The major creative force behind cowpunk seems to be Joe R. Lansdale—he brought us a good anthology of stories of this sort a couple of years ago, and this year he was back with two more: *Razored Saddles* (Dark Harvest), edited by Lansdale and Pat LoBrutto, and *The New Frontier* (Doubleday), edited by Lansdale alone. These are hugely enjoyable books, and the Benford/Greenberg anthologies beat them out only by a hair for the title of best SF anthologies of the year. Squinted at from a slightly different perspective, they could also be considered horror anthologies, in which case they would be rivaled by only one other book for the title of best horror anthology as well. As you might have guessed, these are enormously eclectic books, with an amazing range of subject matter, mood, and choice-of-attack. In *Razored Saddles*, check out in particular the Lewis Shiner, the Chet Williamson, the Howard Waldrop, the Lansdale, the Scott A. Cupp (get ready for the tar and feathers, Scott), the Al Sarrantonio, and the Neal Barrett, Jr.; particularly noteworthy in *The New Frontier* are the Barrett, the John Keefauver, the Shiner, the Loren D. Estleman, and the Cupp—although actually there are almost no bad stories in either book. Pat LoBrutto has been the literary godfather of cowpunk, the editor who cared enough to somehow force this stuff on the timid world of corporate publishing, and I hope that his recent departure from Doubleday doesn't spell the end of this strange subgenre; I'd like to see more books like this.

Other interesting and offbeat one-shot SF anthologies this year included *Foundation's Friends* (Tor), edited by Martin H. Greenberg, an anniversary shared-world anthology in which various writers created stories set in some of Asimov's fictional worlds, and *The Microverse* (Bantam Spectra), edited by Byron Preiss, David M. Harris, and William R. Alschuler, an extremely handsome, coffee-table-book-sized mixed anthology of SF and scientific essays on the topic of subatomic worlds; as usual with these big glossy Byron Preiss books, the art, the photos, and the nonfiction essays are generally stronger than the fiction, but this one does contain excellent work by Connie Willis and Gregory Benford, and good stuff by Silverberg, Rudy Rucker, and others.

Turning to the SF anthology series, 1989 saw the publication of *Full Spectrum 2* (Bantam Spectra), edited by Lou Aronica, Shawna McCarthy, Amy Stout, and Patrick LoBrutto. Last year, talking about *Full Spectrum 1*, I said that the stories in that particular book were remarkably consistent in quality, with none of them really bad . . . but with none of them of really first-rate quality, either. My opinion of *Full Spectrum 2* is almost the reverse: the anthology does contain a fair number of bad stories this year, but it *also* contains two of the very best stories of 1989, by Michael Swanwick and Kim Stanley Robinson—and, to be fair, the bulk of the stories in this *very* large anthology are still pretty good, falling somewhere between the two extremes; you certainly get your money's worth here in entertainment value. It'll be interesting to see what *Full Spectrum 3*, already in the works, will be like, especially as McCarthy and LoBrutto will very probably not be associated with it. *Full Spectrum 2* doesn't seem to have had the impact on the science fiction community that *Full Spectrum 1* had, in spite of the Swanwick and Robinson stories, but this is still potentially one of the most important SF anthology series to be introduced in many years, and I wish it well. Another important new series is *Pulphouse* (Pulphouse Publishing), edited by Kristine Kathryn Rusch, a quarterly hardcover anthology—billed as a "hardback magazine"—that is primarily available by subscription. Each issue of *Pulphouse* has a specific theme; they started last year with Horror (*Pulphouse One*), and so far have cycled their way through Speculative Fiction, Fantasy, and Science Fiction issues, and so back to Horror again (*Pulphouse Five*). Interestingly, some of these themed issues seem to work better than others —last year's Speculative Fiction issue, for instance, was quite bad, and this year's Fantasy issue (*Pulphouse Three*) was, surprisingly, quite good. *Pulphouse Three*, in fact, is the best of the *Pulphouse* issues to date, and a good anthology by anyone's standards, containing a first-rate story by Alan Brennert, and very good ones by Janet Kagan, Steve Perry, Marina Fitch, and Charles de Lint. *Pulphouse Four* (the Science Fiction issue) doesn't contain anything quite as good as the best of the stuff from the previous issue, but still contains good work by Bridget McKenna, Ray Aldridge, Bruce Boston, Kim Antieau, and others. *Pulphouse Five* (back to Horror again) isn't as strong a horror anthology as *Pulphouse One* had been, but still features good work by Elizabeth Hand, George Alec Effinger, Scott Edelman, Francis J. Matozzo, and others. These books are uneven, yes, but the series as a whole is one of the most interesting to come along in some time, and definitely deserves your support. (Subscription address: Pulphouse Publishing, Box 1227, Eugene, OR 97440; $17.95 per single issue, $30 for a half-year subscription (two issues) or $56 for a full-year subscription (four issues); you can also write to them to obtain information about their short-story collection and chapbook novella lines.)

New Destinies (Baen), edited by James Baen, featured some solid work, but, as usual, nothing really outstanding. *Synergy Four* (Harcourt Brace Jovanovich), edited by George Zebrowski, featured some good work, particularly a moving story by Chad Oliver, but I continue to feel that at $8.95

for a rather slender mass-market paperback, this series is grossly overpriced, and I wonder if it will survive. *L. Ron Hubbard Presents Writers of the Future Vol. V* (Bridge), edited by Algis Budrys, is the usual compendium of novice work; some of the writers featured here may well become famous someday, but it's not going to be for any of the stories in this particular book. A promising new British anthology series was started this year, *Zenith* (Sphere), edited by David S. Garnett; the first issue featured interesting work by Christopher Burns, William King, Lisa Tuttle, and others. There was also a volume of the British series *Other Edens* this year, but I missed it; I'll consider it for next year.

The new incarnation of *Universe*, now edited by Robert Silverberg and Karen Haber, didn't appear this year, but is promised for 1990. Silverberg, the former editor of *New Dimensions*, was probably the most important original anthology editor of the 1970s, and it'll be interesting to see what he and Haber can do with *Universe* here in the 1990s.

There didn't seem to be as many shared-world anthologies this year as there were last year, but they included: *Arabesques II* (Avon), edited by Susan Shwartz; The *Man-Kzin War II* (Baen), edited by Larry Niven; *There Will Be War, Vol.* 8 (Tor), edited by Jerry Pournelle; and an interesting Kipling-pastiche tribute anthology, A *Separate Star* (Baen), edited by David Drake and Sandra Miesel.

In the horror market, the best original horror anthology was clearly *Blood Is Not Enough* (Morrow), edited by Ellen Datlow, which featured very good new work by Tanith Lee, Susan Casper, Pat Cadigan, Chet Williamson, Edward Bryant, and others, as well as some classic reprints. It was rivaled only by *Razored Saddles* and *The New Frontier*, if you consider them horror anthologies. I also enjoyed a British anthology of "quiet horror," *Dark Fantasies* (Legend), edited by Chris Morgan, which featured good work by Brian Stableford, Christopher Evans, Lisa Tuttle, Brian W. Aldiss, and others. Also entertaining was *Spirits of Christmas* (Wynwood), edited by Kathryn Cramer and David G. Hartwell, a mixed original and reprint anthology that featured good work by Gene Wolfe, Michael Swanwick, Susan Palwick, Martha Soukup, and others. *Book of the Dead* (Bantam), edited by John Skipp and Craig Spector, was somewhat tiresome, with only Lansdale and Bryant handling the material with any real panache. *Night Visions VI* (Dark Harvest) was disappointing. Other original horror anthologies included: *Scare Care* (Tor), edited by Graham Masterton; *Stalkers* (Dark Harvest), edited by Ed Gorman and Martin H. Greenberg; *Phantoms* (DAW), edited by Martin H. Greenberg and Rosalind M. Greenberg; and *Post Mortem* (St. Martin's), edited by Paul F. Olson and David B. Silva—all contained interesting work, but none enough to make them exceptional.

A new original horror anthology series, *Borderlands*, edited by Tom Monteleone, has been announced for next year.

It was a decent if unspectacular year for novels overall, even though once again there were no clearly dominant novels, novels clearly destined to sweep the awards, as there have been in years when novels such as William Gibson's *Neuromancer* or Frederik Pohl's *Gateway* were on the lists. *Locus* estimates that the total number of books published this year dropped by 8 percent—the first decrease since 1982—but, even so, they estimate that there were 279 new SF novels (a 12% drop from last year's all-time high of 317), 277 new fantasy novels (a slight increase over last year's total), and 176 new horror novels (down 3% from last year's count of 182). So even with an 8% drop, there were still 732 new SF/fantasy/horror novels published in 1989, according to *Locus*—clearly the novel field has expanded far beyond the ability of any one reviewer to keep up with it, even a reviewer who *doesn't* have as much other reading at shorter lengths to do as I have. Once again, I must admit that I was unable to read all the new novels released this year, or even the majority of them. In fact, I had less time for novels this year than ever before, and was able to read very few of them.

So, therefore, I am going to limit myself here to mentioning those novels that have gotten a lot of attention and acclaim this year. They include: *Good News from Outer Space*, John Kessel (Tor); *Look into the Sun*, James Patrick Kelly (Tor); *Dream Baby*, Bruce McAllister (Tor); *Tides of Light*, Gregory Benford (Bantam Spectra); *A Fire in the Sun*, George Alec Effinger (Doubleday Foundation); *Tourists*, Lisa Goldstein (Simon & Schuster); *Hyperion*, Dan Simmons (Doubleday Foundation); *A Talent for War*, Jack McDevitt (Ace); *Buying Time*, Joe Haldeman (Morrow); *Sugar Rain*, Paul Park (Morrow); *Soldier of Arete*, Gene Wolfe (Tor); *Imago*, Octavia Butler (Warner); *The Stone Giant*, James Blaylock (Ace); *A Child Across the Sky*, Jonathan Carroll (Legend); *Orbital Decay*, Allen M. Steele (Ace); *Prentice Alvin*, Orson Scott Card; *The Parasite Wars*, Tim Sullivan (Avon); *Homegoing*, Frederik Pohl (Del Rey); *Being Alien*, Rebecca Ore (Tor); *The Stress of Her Regard*, Tim Powers (Ace); *Dawn's Uncertain Light*, Neal Barrett, Jr. (NAL Signet); *Paradise*, Mike Resnick (Tor); *Out on Blue Six*, Ian MacDonald (Bantam Spectra); *The New Springtime*, Robert Silverberg (Warner); *Carrion Comfort*, Dan Simmons (Dark Harvest); *The Tides of God*, Ted Reynolds (Ace); *The City, Not Long After*, Pat Murphy (Doubleday Foundation); *Rimmrunners*, C.J. Cherryh (Warner); *Lyonesse: Madouc*, Jack Vance (Underwood-Miller); *Phases of Gravity*, Dan Simmons (Bantam Spectra); *On My Way to Paradise*, Dave Wolverton (Bantam Spectra); *Farewell Horizontal*, K.W. Jeter (St. Martin's); and *The Boat of a Million Years*, Poul Anderson (Tor).

Of the first novels, the biggest stir was probably made by Allen M. Steele, although Ted Reynolds and Dave Wolverton got a fair amount of press too.

It was a good year for Dan Simmons, who published three of the year's most-talked-about and extensively reviewed novels.

If 1989 was only a so-so year for novels, it was a strong year for short-story collections.

The two best collections of the year were: *Patterns*, Pat Cadigan (Ursus) and *Crystal Express*, Bruce Sterling (Arkham House). Cadigan and Sterling produced some of the best work at short lengths done by *anybody* in the 1980s, and it's all assembled here in these two extremely powerful collections, by two young writers who are already well on their way to being numbered among the Big Names of the 1990s; if you buy any collections this year, make it these two, because they are absolutely vital to an understanding of where short fiction is going in the decade ahead.

There were also quite a few other first-rate collections this year, though, including: *Tangents*, Greg Bear (Warner); *Forests of the Night*, Tanith Lee (Unwin Hyman); *The Folk of the Fringe*, Orson Scott Card (Phantasia); *Novelty*, John Crowley (Doubleday Foundation); *Escape from Kathmandu*, Kim Stanley Robinson (Tor); *Children of the Wind*, Kate Wilhelm (St. Martin's); *Winterwood and Other Hauntings*, Keith Roberts (Morrigan); and *Endangered Species*, Gene Wolfe (Tor). Also worthwhile were: *Frost and Fire*, Roger Zelazny (Morrow); *Heatseeker*, John Shirley (Scream/Press); *By Bizarre Hands*, Joe Lansdale (Ziesing); *The Asimov Chronicles*, Isaac Asimov (Dark Harvest); *A Romance of the Equator: Best Fantasy Stories*, Brian W. Aldiss (Gollancz); *Salvage Rites*, Ian Watson (Gollancz); *John Collier and Fredric Brown Went Quarreling Through My Head*, Jessica Amanda Salmonson (W. Paul Ganley); *Richard Matheson: Collected Stories*, Richard Matheson (Scream/Press); *Borders of Infinity*, Lois McMaster Bujold (Baen); and *Author's Choice Monthly Issue One: The Old Funny Stuff*, George Alec Effinger (Pulphouse).

As has been true for several years now, small press publishers—Arkham House, Ziesing, Ursus Press, Phantasia, Dark Harvest, Scream/Press, and several others—continue to play a vital role in bringing short-story collections to the reading public. In fact, it seems like they play a more central role every year. A decade ago, hot new writers like Pat Cadigan, Bruce Sterling, Lucius Shepard, and Michael Swanwick would almost certainly have been able to sell their first collections as regular trade books; now, if it were not for the genre small press publishers, many of these valuable collections would not get into print at all—or, at the very best, would be delayed for several years until the writers became famous enough to tempt one of the trade publishers into taking a chance on a collection. Fortunately for us, though, small-press publishers continue to fill some of the void created by the trade publishers' timidity about collections. One small press publisher, Pulphouse Publishing, has even committed itself to publishing a new short-story collection *every month* throughout the coming year; the Pulphouse collections are slender books, admittedly, more like chapbooks than like trade paperbacks, but they're getting material to the public that wouldn't otherwise have been seen, and they're a welcome addition to the scene.

Having slapped the trade publishers on the wrist for being reluctant to publish collections, it would be unfair not to mention those trade houses that *do* publish collections with somewhat more frequency than other publishers do, notably, this year, Tor, Morrow, St. Martin's, Warner, and Gollancz. Tor should be especially praised for instituting the Tor Doubles line, modeled after the old Ace Doubles line of short novels published back-to-back. This line is getting many of the best novellas of the last few decades back into print again, many of them long unavailable to the ordinary reader since their initial publication. Other publishers are also working this same ground, to good effect: Pulphouse is running a line of original novellas, published as individual chapbooks, as is Cheap Street, Ziesing, and others. In England, London Century will soon be coming out with a line of original novellas published as books, this one a high budget, high-publicity trade line edited by Deborah Beale; it'll be interesting to see how it's received. I wish all of these projects well, since a novella collection may in some circumstances be just as difficult to sell as a short-story collection . . . if not more so. And we need to improve the availability of short fiction to the general public if SF is to remain healthy. I remain convinced that the really vital work, the evolutionary work that reshapes the genre in its own image, is usually done at short-story length, and *not* in the novels, in spite of the money and attention spent on them. Without the work being done at shorter lengths, usually by ill-paid and under-appreciated new young writers, the genre would eventually sicken and die—no matter how many sharecropper books and Robotech novels were making it onto nationwide bestseller lists in the meantime.

Nineteen eighty-nine was a solid if unexceptional year in the reprint anthology market. As usual, your best bets in the reprint anthology market were the various "Best of the Year" anthologies, and the annual Nebula Award anthology. This year, there were three "Best" anthologies covering science fiction (my own, Donald Wollheim's, and a new British series called *The Orbit Science Fiction Yearbook*, edited by David S. Garnett), one covering horror (Karl Edward Wagner's *Year's Best Horror Stories*), and one covering both horror and fantasy (Ellen Datlow and Terry Windling's *The Year's Best Fantasy*). All of these, and the Nebula Award anthology, are solid values. We lost another of the "Best" anthologies this year, as Art Saha's *Year's Best Fantasy Stories* was canceled—a shame, since it was a good series, and covered the fantasy market from a slightly different slant than does Windling in her half of *The Year's Best Fantasy* (Saha tended more toward *Unknown*-style modern urban fantasy than toward High Fantasy). Other solid values this year included: *The New Hugo Winners* (Wynwood), edited by Isaac Asimov; *The Best of the Nebulas* (Tor), edited by Ben Bova; *The Best from Fantasy and Science Fiction: A 40th Anniversary Anthology* (St. Martin's), edited by Edward L. Ferman; *The World Treasury of Science Fiction* (Little, Brown), edited by David G. Hartwell; and *The Mammoth Book of Golden Age Science Fiction: Short Novels of the 1940s* (Robinson), edited by Isaac Asimov, Charles G. Waugh, and Martin H. Greenberg. I'm a bit put off by the premise of the *Best of the Nebulas* anthology, since selecting the "best" stories to win the Nebula automatically implies that the Nebula-winning stories that were left out were inferior, probably not an idea that the Science

Fiction Writers of America really ought to be promulgating. (Of course, you can dismiss all that as sour grapes, if you wish, since my own two Nebula-winning stories didn't make it into the book.) At any rate, these are anthologies that ought to be in any reasonably complete SF collection, especially the Hugo and Nebula volumes. Other worthwhile reprint anthologies this year included: *The Great SF Stories: 19* (DAW), edited by Isaac Asimov and Martin H. Greenberg; *The Book of OMNI #6* (Zebra), edited by Ellen Datlow; *The Book of OMNI #7* (Zebra), edited by Ellen Datlow; *Interzone: The 4th Annual Anthology* (Simon & Schuster UK), edited by John Clute, David Pringle, and Simon Ounsley; *Another Round at the Spaceport Bar* (Avon), edited by George H. Scithers and Darrell Schweitzer; and *What Did Miss Darrington See?* (The Feminist Press), edited by Jessica Amanda Salmonson. Noted without comment are: *Time Travellers from Isaac Asimov's Science Fiction Magazine* (Ace), edited by Gardner Dozois; *Transcendental Tales from Isaac Asimov's Science Fiction Magazine* (Donning Starblaze), edited by Gardner Dozois; and *Seaserpents!* (Ace), edited by Jack Dann and Gardner Dozois.

It was another weak year in the SF-oriented nonfiction SF reference book field. Your best bets for reference this year were: *Science Fiction, Fantasy & Horror* (Locus Press), edited by Charles N. Brown and William G. Contento; and *Science Fiction and Fantasy Book Review Annual 1988* (Meckler), edited by Robert A. Collins and Robert Latham.

There's still no sign of the rumored update of the Peter Nicholls's *Science Fiction Encyclopedia*, which is a shame, since it is urgently needed, not really having been adequately replaced by James Gunn's 1988 *The New Encyclopedia of Science Fiction*. Let's hope it comes along soon.

There was some very interesting stuff in the general nonfiction field, the best of it by experienced genre hands. Probably the most controversial critical book of the year, and one of the most valuable, was Alexei and Cory Panshin's history/critical analysis of the early days of the field, *The World Beyond the Hill: Science Fiction and the Quest for Transcendence* (Jeremy P. Tarcher); you don't have to agree with all of the Panshins's critical theorizing—certainly I didn't—to find the historical information amassed here fascinating, and I suspect that this may well be this year's nonfiction Hugo winner. That is, unless it's the even more fascinating *Grumbles from the Grave* (Del Rey), a posthumously published collection of letters and errata by the late Robert A. Heinlein; every Heinlein fan will want this one—it offers many intriguing insights into his work and the man behind the work, and, frankly, it's far more readable and entertaining than his last few novels. Another fascinating look at Golden Age roots by a Golden Age giant (just post–Golden Age, actually, if you want to be picky) is Arthur C. Clarke's *Astounding Days: A Science Fictional Autobiography* (Bantam). Clarke is drier than the pugnacious Heinlein, but clear-headed and informative, and there are hours of absorbing reading here. These three books alone make it a pretty strong year in the general nonfiction field, and they belong on the bookshelves of every serious student of the genre.

Also interesting was Ursula K. Le Guin's *Dancing at the Edge of the World* (Grove) and *The Illustrated History of Science Fiction* (Ungar), by Dieter Wuckel and Bruce Cassiday. There were also additions to the seemingly endless parade of books about the late Philip K. Dick, this time two sometimes contradictory biographies: *To the High Castle—Philip K. Dick: A Life 1928–1962* (Fragments West), by Gregg Rickman, and *Divine Invasions: A Life of Philip K. Dick* (Harmony), by Lawrence Sutin. There is also a book of essays by Philip K. Dick himself, *The Dark-Haired Girl* (Mark V. Ziesing). Other critical studies of Famous Dead People this year include *Pathways to Elfland: The Writings of Lord Dunsany* (Owlswick Press), by Darrell Schweitzer; *The Legacy of Olaf Stapledon* (Greenwood), edited by Patrick A. McCarthy, Charles Elkins, and Martin H. Greenberg; and *Mary Shelley: Romance and Reality* (Little, Brown), by Emily Sunstein.

A science book everyone interested in SF ought to read is *Wonderful Life: The Burgess Shale and the Nature of History* (Norton) by Stephen Jay Gould—I suspect that SF writers will be mining *this* one for new ideas for years to come. And anyone who liked space heroes, monsters, and dinosaurs when they were young really ought to pick up *The Calvin and Hobbes Lazy Sunday Book* (Andrews and McMeel), by Bill Watterson, somebody who remembers what childhood was *really* like. Also a must for most SF fans is *The PreHistory of the Far Side* (Andrews and McMeel), by Gary Larson, the gonzo cartoonist who has been referred to, with good reason, as "the Gahan Wilson of the 1980s." I had more pure fun reading the Watterson and the Larson than I got from almost anything else I read this year, and I think that most people who are interested in SF will agree.

Nineteen eighty-nine was another good year at the box office for genre films, although I remained unimpressed by most of them. The box office blockbuster of the year was *Batman*, which earned enough to make it the fifth highest-grossing film of all time. *Indiana Jones and the Last Crusade*, *Back to the Future II*, and—something of a surprise high-grosser—*Honey, I Shrunk the Kids* also did extremely well at the box office. The new Indiana Jones movie was considerably better than the last one, the dumb and inept *Indiana Jones and the Temple of Doom*. This one goes back to a script that contains some flashes of sly wit and even some outright humor, and if the ending is lame—which it is—they at least had the smarts to put Sean Connery, who twinkles better than anyone in the world, into the movie to help hold it up—in fact, Connery and Harrison Ford work extremely well with each other, and, what's more important, *off* of each other as well. *Field of Dreams* was probably the most critically acclaimed movie of the year, and didn't do badly at the box office, either. I personally enjoyed *The Adventures of Baron Munchausen*, although it was a major box office disaster, and didn't fare all that well with some of the critics, either. It is slow in spots, but it is also full of slyly intelligent touches, and is visually sumptuous almost beyond belief. *Ghostbusters II* and *Star Trek V: The Final Frontier* were greeted with general indifference by the movie-going public, and the poor reaction to *Star Trek V* in particular may well spell the end of the Star Trek movies. *The Abyss*, a big-budget and much-ballyhooed film, pretty much dogged out as well. I surprised myself by actually enjoying *Bill and Ted's Excellent Adventure*, although I was a little grumpy about the fact that a film ostensibly bemoaning historical ignorance should do so little research into what historic personages and time periods were *really* like; still, a fun movie. A New Zealand film, *The Navigator: An Odyssey Across Time*, has been getting some excellent reviews, but you'll probably have to go to your local video-rental store to find it. There were two expensive, glossy, full-length animated features this year, *The Little Mermaid* and *All Dogs Go to Heaven*; following the recent *Oliver & Co.*, *The Land Beyond Time*, and the semi-animated *Who Framed Roger Rabbit*, this may indicate a revival of the full-length animated feature, largely moribund for many years. Let's hope so, anyway.

On television, a new cable channel called The Sci-Fi Channel, featuring nothing but you-know-what, has been being talked about all year, but so far has yet to materialize; maybe next year. Elsewhere, the critics have been surprisingly kind to the new series *Alien Nation*, and it seems to be finding an audience, as is the series *Quantum Leap*. *Star Trek: The Next Generation* is still sailing along, although *Beauty and the Beast* finally sank low enough in the ratings to be canceled by the network, in spite of a frantic last-ditch effort to restructure the show so that it could continue without Catherine (Linda Hamilton), who refused to renew. This being the kind of world that it is, *Freddy's Nightmares* and *Friday the 13th: The Series*, weekly TV series based on two long-running series of slasher movies, remain wildly popular, and a "Freddy glove," a pull-on glove with long slasher claws, was one of the most popular Christmas gifts this year for children under five.

Speaking of slasher movies, since I have come to feel that my taste in films may be out of date—since, for instance, when a director gleefully announces that his upcoming movie "will set new standards for screen violence" I tend to sigh wearily instead of licking my lips in anticipation—I have once again turned to that writer, anthologist, *bon vivant*, and noted authority on SF/Horror films, Tim Sullivan—a man who really *enjoys* a good exploding-head movie every once in a while—and asked him to contribute a list of *his* ten favorite genre movies this year. Tim's list of the year's top ten films is:

1. *The Adventures of Baron Munchausen*; 2. *Henry: Portrait of a Serial Killer*; 3. *Miracle Mile*; 4. *Paperhouse*; 5. *Erik The Viking*; 6. *I, Madman*; 7. *The Navigator: An Odyssey Across Time*; 8. *Earth Girls Are Easy*; 9. *Pet Sematary*; 10. *Tales from the Gimli Hospital*. Tim adds that modesty prevents him from listing *The Laughing Dead*, a horror movie directed by Somtow Sucharitkul (S.P. Somtow) in which Sullivan *himself* plays the leading

role—a priest who turns into a hideous monster—and gets to tear several hapless men and women apart on screen, surely the realization of the dream of a lifetime for Tim. Connoisseurs who have seen Tim's performance agree that Tim could easily become the John Agar of the 1990s if he were to pursue his acting career.

My own personal favorite film this year was *The Fabulous Baker Boys*—but, unfortunately, it wasn't a genre movie. So sue me.

* * *

The Forty-seventh World Science Fiction Convention, Noreascon Three, was held in Boston, Massachusetts, from August 31 to September 4, 1989, and drew an estimated attendance of 7,100. The 1989 Hugo Awards, presented at Noreascon Three, were: Best Novel, *Cyteen*, by C.J. Cherryh; Best Novella, "The Last of the Winnebagos," by Connie Willis; Best Novelette, "Schrödinger's Kitten," by George Alec Effinger; Best Short Story, "Kirinyaga," by Mike Resnick; Best Nonfiction, *The Motion of Light in Water*, by Samuel R. Delany; Best Professional Editor, Gardner Dozois; Best Professional Artist, Michael Whelan; Best Dramatic Presentation, *Who Framed Roger Rabbit*; Best Semiprozine, *Locus*; best Fanzine, *File 770*, edited by Mike Glyer; Best Fan Writer, David Langford; Best Fan Artist, Brad W. Foster and Diana Gallagher Wu (tie); plus the John W. Campbell Award for Best New Writer to Michaela Roessner.

The 1988 Nebula Awards, presented at a banquet at the Penta Hotel in New York City on April 22, 1989 were: Best Novel, *Falling Free*, by Lois McMaster Bujold; Best Novella, "The Last of the Winnebagos," by Connie Willis; Best Novelette, "Schrödinger's Kitten," by George Alec Effinger; Best Short Story, "Bible Stories for Adults, No. 17: The Deluge"; plus the Grand Master Award to Ray Bradbury.

The World Fantasy Awards, presented at the Fifteenth Annual World Fantasy Convention in Seattle, Washington, over Halloween weekend, were: Best Novel, *Koko*, by Peter Straub; Best Novella, "The Skin Trade," by George R.R. Martin; Best Short Story, "Winter Solstice, Camelot Station," by John M. Ford; Best Collection, *Storeys from the Old Hotel*, by Gene Wolfe and *Angry Candy*, by Harlan Ellison (tie); Best Anthology, *The Year's Best Fantasy: First Annual Collection*, edited by Ellen Datlow and Terri Windling; Best Artist, Edward Gorey; Special Award (Professional), Terri Windling and Robert Weinberg (tie); Special Award (Non-Professional), Kristine Kathryn Rusch and Dean Wesley Smith for *Pulphouse*; plus a Life Achievement Award to Evangeline Walton.

The 1989 Bram Stoker Awards, presented at a banquet at the Warwick Hotel in New York City on June 17, 1989 by The Horror Writers of America, were: Best Novel, *The Silence of the Lambs*, by Thomas Harris; Best First Novel, *The Suiting*, by Kelley Wilde; Best Collection, *Charles Beaumont: Selected Tales*, by Charles Beaumont; Best Novelette, "Orange Is for Anguish, Blue for Insanity," by David Morrell; Best Short Story, "Night They Missed the Horror Show," by Joe R. Lansdale; plus Life Achievement Awards to Ray Bradbury and Ronald Chetwynd-Hayes.

The 1988 John W. Campbell Memorial Award-winner was *Islands in the Net*, by Bruce Sterling.

The 1988 Theodore Sturgeon Award was won by "Schrödinger's Kitten," by George Alec Effinger.

The 1988 Philip K. Dick Memorial Award-winners were *Wetware*, by Rudy Rucker and *400 Billion Stars*, by Paul McAuley (tie).

The Arthur C. Clarke award was won by *Unquenchable Fire* (Century), by Rachel Pollack.

Dead in 1989 were: **William F. Temple**, 75, longtime fan and author of *The Four-Sided Triangle* and *Shoot at the Moon*; **Robert Adams**, 56, best-selling author of the *Horseclans* and the *Castaways in Time* series; **Edward A. Byers**, 50, frequent contributor to *Analog*; **Ben Barzman**, 79, author of *Echo X*; **Gertrude T. Friedberg**, 81, author of *The Revolving Boy*; **Barry Sadler**, 49, author of the Casca series of mercenary fantasies as well as of the hit song "Ballad of the Green Berets"; **Jean Paiva**, 45, horror novelist; **Aeron Clement**, 52, author of *The Cold Moons*; **Dame Daphne du Maurier**, 81, considered a pioneer of the modern Gothic novel, who also wrote such short fantasies as "The Birds" and "Don't Look Now"; **Donald Barthelme**, 58, literary writer and sometime fantasist, author of the surreal quasi-fantasy novel *Snow White*; **Walter Farley**, 74, author of two long-running and extremely popular series of "young adult" novels about horses (I myself read all of them when I was a kid), *The Black Stallion* series and *The Island Stallion* series, one of which, *The Island Stallion Races*, may well be the only science fiction horse book ever written, complete with civilized and rather charming UFO aliens; **Hans Helmut Kirst**, 74, German novelist, author of *The Night of the Generals*; **Norman Saunders**, 82, longtime pulp magazine and paperback artist; **C.C. Beck**, 79, comic book artist and creator of Captain Marvel; **Dik Browne**, 71, creator of the comic strip *Hagar the Horrible*; **Elmer Perdue**, 69, well-known fan; **Bertha Gallun**, 79, wife of SF writer Raymond Z. Gallun; **Margaret Wiener**, 95, widow of scientist Norbert Wiener; **Mel Blanc**, 81, the man who provided the voice for Bugs Bunny, Porky Pig, Daffy Duck, and dozens of other cartoon characters; **Graham Chapman**, 48, one of the founding members of *Monty Python's Flying Circus*; **Gilda Radner**, one of the original stars of *Saturday Night Live*; **John Houseman**, 86, veteran actor, perhaps best known to genre audiences for his role in the movie *Ghost Story*; **Gert Frobe**, 75, best known for the title role in *Goldfinger*; **John Payne**, 77, costar of the classic Christmas fantasy *Miracle on 34th Street*; **Maurice Evans**, 87, best known to genre audiences for his role in *Planet of the Apes*; **Jock Mahoney**, 70, who played the title role in a number of *Tarzan* movies; and **Richard Quine**, 68, director of the classic fantasy movie *Bell, Book and Candle*.

JUDITH MOFFETT
Tiny Tango

Although Judith Moffett is the author of two books of poetry, a book of criticism, and a book of translations from Swedish, she made her first professional fiction sale in 1986. Since then, she has won the John W. Campbell Award as Best New Writer of 1988, and the Theodore Sturgeon Award for her story "Surviving," and her first novel *Pennterra* was released to high critical acclaim. She has since completed a second novel. Born in Louisville, Kentucky, she now lives with her husband in Rose Valley, Pennsylvania. She has a Ph.D. in American Civilization from the University of Pennsylvania, where she is presently adjunct associate professor of English, and teaches courses in science fiction and creative writing, in addition to directing a variety of independent study projects. She has also taught for four summers at the prestigious Bread Loaf Writer's Conference, and was given a National Endowment for the Arts Creative Writing Fellowship Grant for her poetry —which she then used to finance the writing of her first novel. "Surviving" was in our Fourth Annual Collection, and her story "The Hob" was in our Sixth Annual Collection.

Here she offers us a disaster story of a very *personal* sort, in a powerful and deeply moving tale that may be one of the most controversial and talked-about stories of the year.

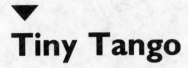

Tiny Tango

JUDITH MOFFETT

I

I've been encouraged (read: ordered) by my friend, a Hefn called Godfrey, to make this recording. I'm not sure why. It's to be the story of my life, and frankly, a lot of my life's been kind of grim. Godfrey tells me he values the story as an object lesson, but to whom and for what purpose he's not saying. It isn't news anymore that the Hefn don't think like we do.

I made an important choice at twenty-two. Because of that choice I'm alive right now, but I'm still wondering: was it a wise choice, given that the next twenty-five years turned out to be a kind of living death? I hoped that if I did this recording, thought it all through in one piece, I'd be able to answer that question. I need to understand my life better than I do. I'm about to be put to sleep for a long time—forever if things go badly—and I need to know . . . well, what Godfrey thinks *he* knows. What it's meant. What it's all been *for*.

I can't really say that this review has worked, because I still don't think I know. But who can tell? Maybe you listeners in the archive will see something in it I can't see. (Godfrey's betting that you will.)

I recall a certain splendid June morning between the two accidents, mine and Peach Bottom's—a bright, cool morning after a spell of sticky weather. I'd hobbled out to the patio in robe and slippers with my breakfast tray, and loitered over my homegrown whole-grain honey and raisin muffins and strawberry-soy milkshake, browsing through a new copy of *Rodale's Organic Gardening* magazine (featuring an article I'd written, on ways to discourage squirrels in the orchard and corn patch). Then, after a while, I'd taken my cane and gimped out in a leisurely way to inspect the crops. I'd broken an ankle bone that was taking its time about healing; to be forbidden my exercise routines was distressing, but also kind of a relief.

Because the kitchen garden provided my entire supply of vegetables and fruit, my interest in it was like a gardening hobbyist's crossed with a frontier homesteader's. If a crop failed I knew I wouldn't, or needn't, starve. On the other hand, since I never—ever—bought any produce for home consumption, if a crop failed it *would* almost certainly mean doing without something for a whole year. The daily tour of the kitchen garden was therefore always deeply interesting; and if the tour of the field test plots was even more so, theirs was an interestingness of a less intimate type.

Something serious had happened to the Kennebec potatoes; I noticed it at once. Yesterday at dusk the plants had been bushy and green, bent out of their beds on water-filled stalks by last week's storm of rain but healthy, thriving, beginning to put out the tiny flowers that meant I could soon steal a few small tubers from under the mulch to eat with the new peas. Now the leaves of several plants were rolled and mottled with yellow. I pulled these up right away, doubting it would do any good, sick at heart as always to see my pampered children fail, however often failure struck them down.

The biggest threat to crops in an organic garden like mine is always disease spread by insects, aphids or leafhoppers in this case, which had all but certainly passed this disease on to other potato plants by now. The mottling and leaf-rolling meant that the bugs—probably aphids, the flightless sort I'd been taught to call "ant cows" in grade school—had infected my Kennebecs with a virus. At least one virus, maybe more. The ants would soon have moved their dairy herd all through the patch, if they hadn't already. Plants still symptom-free would not remain so for long. When Eric showed up I would get him to spray the patch with a Rotenone solution but it was probably too late to save the crop by killing the carriers, the vector. These potatoes already had a virus, incurable and potentially lethal.

I remember that I thought: Well, that makes some more of us then.

I left the heap of infected plants for Eric to cart to the incinerator; they must not be composted but burned, and at once, or there'd be no chance at all of saving the crop and I could look forward to a potatoless year.

Destroy the infected to protect the healthy. The AIDS witch-hunts of the late nineties, the vigilante groups that had broken into testing and treatment facilities all over the country in order to find out who the infected people were, had been acting from a similar principle: identify! destroy! They wanted not just the ones with the acute form of the disease, but also those who'd tested positive to HIV-I, II, and/or III. I'd been lucky; workers in the Task Force office where my records were kept had managed to stand off the mob while a terrified volunteer worked frantically to erase the computer records and two others burned the paper files in the lavatory sink. The police arrived in time to save those brave people, thank God, but in other cities workers were shot and, in that one dreadful incident in St. Louis, barricaded in their building while somebody shattered the window with a firebomb.

My luck hadn't stopped there, no siree. I had the virus right enough, but not—still not, after twenty-five long years—the disease itself. (These two facts have shaped my life. I mean my adult life; I'd just turned twenty-two, and was about to graduate from college in the spring of 1985, when my Western Blot came back positive and everything changed.)

Even the sporadic persecutions ended in 2001, when they got the Lowenfels vaccine. That took care of the general public; but nobody looked for a cure, or expected that a way would ever be found to eliminate the virus from the bodies of those of us who'd already been exposed to it. The best *we* could hope for was a course of treatment to improve our chances of not developing full-blown AIDS, at least not for a long, long time. The peptide vaccine that had become the standard therapy by 1994, which worked with the capsid protein in the cells of the virus, was ineffective with too many patients, as were the GMSC factor injections; and zidovudine and its cousins were just too toxic. A lot more research still needed to be done. We hoped that it would be, that we would not be forgotten; but we didn't think it a very realistic hope.

The bone punch, and especially the Green Monkey vaccine which quickly supplanted that radical and rather painful procedure, meant the end of terror for the unsmitten; for the less fortunate it meant at least the end of persecution, as I said, and so for us, too, the day when the mass inoculations began was a great day. A lot of us were also suicidally depressed. Imagine how people crippled from childhood with polio must have felt when they started giving out the Salk vaccine to school kids on those little cubes of sugar, and the cripples had to stand around on their braces and crutches and try to be glad.

It didn't do to think too much about it.

The Test Site clinician who gave me the news had steered me into a chair right afterwards and said, "When the results came in I made you an appointment for tonight with a counselor. She'll help you more than you'd ever believe, and I don't care what other commitments you've got to break: you be there.' And he wrote the address and the time on a piece of paper, and I went.

The counselor was a woman in her thirties, sympathetic but tough, and she told me things that evening while I sat and was drenched in wave after icy wave of terror and dread. "We don't know why some people seem to resist the virus better than others, and survive much longer, or why some of those that are AB-positive develop the disease fairly quickly, while others can have a latency period of five or six years," Elizabeth said. "We don't know for sure what triggers the development of the acute disease, if and when it does develop, or what percentage of infected people will eventually develop it.

"But there's a lot of research going on right now into what they call 'cofactors,' variables that may influence the behavior of the virus in individual cases. Cofactors are things like general health, stress levels, life style. We think—we're pretty sure—that it's extremely important for people like you, who've been exposed, to live as healthfully and calmly as you possibly can. The HIV-I virus is linked to the immune system. You get the flu, your immune system kicks in to fight the flu virus, the AIDS virus multiplies; so the trick is to give your immune system as little to do as possible and buy yourself some time.

"Now, what that means in practical terms is: take care of yourself. Get lots of sleep and exercise. Don't get overtired or too stressed out. Pay attention to your nutrition. Meditate. Above all, try not to fall into a despairing frame of mind! There's a good chance they'll find an effective treatment in four or five years, and if that happens and you're still symptom-free, you should be able to live a normal life with a normally functioning immune system, so long as you keep up your treatments."

That was the gist of her talk, and some of it sank in. She was wrong about the treatment, of course. In those days everybody expected it would be the vaccine that would prove impossible to make, that a drug to control the course of infection seemed much likelier. We were better off not knowing. Even with treatments to hope for, in those days it was fairly unusual to survive as long as four or five years after infection.

Elizabeth suggested a therapy group of people like myself that I might like to join, a group that had volunteered for a research project being done by a team of psychoneuroimmunologists, though we didn't know that's what they were. They were the hope-givers, that was enough. During the weeks that followed, with help from Elizabeth and the group, I began to work out a plan—to impose my own controls over my situation, in accordance with the research team's wish to explore the effects of an extraordinarily healthful life style on symptom-free HIV-I carriers.

My undergraduate work in biology had been good enough to get me accepted into the graduate program at Cornell with a research assistantship. Until the test results came back I'd been excited by the challenge and the prospect of a change of scene; afterwards, and after a few sessions with Elizabeth and her group, I began instead to feel apprehensive about the effort it would take to learn the ropes of a new department, new university community, new city famous for its six annual months of winter. It seemed better to stick to familiar surroundings and to continue with the same counselor and therapy group. So I made late application to my own university's graduate department and was admitted, and I stayed on: my first major life decision to be altered, the first of many times I was to choose a less challenging and stressful alternative over one that in every other way looked like the more attractive choice.

I'd caught the virus from my major professor; he'd been my only lover, so there could be no doubt of that. While I was still nerving myself up to tell him about the blood test he died in an accident on Interstate 95. Distressingly enough, I'm afraid I felt less grieved than relieved. The death let me off the hook and, more importantly, cleared the way for me to stay, for Bill's presence would have been a difficulty. I'd felt from the first instant that I wanted *no one*, apart from the Task Force people, to know. Not my Fundamentalist family, certainly. Not my friends, from whom I now found myself beginning to withdraw (and since, like me, most of these were graduating seniors, this was easier than it sounds.) Overnight my interests had grown utterly remote from theirs. They were full of parties and career plans; I was fighting for my life, and viewed the lot of them from across the chasm of that absolute unlikeness.

I strolled, more or less, through graduate school, working competently without distinguishing myself. I wasn't in a hurry, either. Distinction and rapid progress would have meant a greater commitment and a lot more work, and these were luxuries I could no longer afford, for my first commitment, and first responsibility, now, were to keeping myself alive.

As for how I was to use this life, a picture had gradually begun to form.

First of all it was necessary to divest myself of desire. The yuppiedom I had only recently looked forward to with so much confidence—the dazzling two-career marriage and pair of brilliant children, the house in the suburbs, the cabin in the Poconos and the vacations in Europe—had become, item by item, as unavailable to me as a career in space exploration or ballet. Children, obviously, were out. So was marriage. So, it seemed, was sex in any form; sex had been my nemesis, scarcely discovered before it had blighted me forever. The prestigious high-pressure career in research, which my undergraduate record had made seem a reasonable ambition, had become anything but. I was not after all going to be one of those remarkable professional mothers, making history in the lab, putting in quality time with the kids every day, keeping the lines of communication with my husband open and clear at every level no matter what. I built up the picture of the life I had aspired to for my counselor and my group—and looked at it long and well—and said good-bye to it, as I believed, forever. All that was over.

The next step was to create an alternate picture of a life that *would* be possible. We discussed my abilities and my altered wish list. I toyed briefly with the idea of a career in AIDS research—but AIDS research in the late eighties was about as calm and unstressful a line of work as leading an assault on the North Face of the Eiger in winter, and I had no yearning for martyrdom, then or ever. Through the hours and hours of therapy it emerged that what I wanted most was simple: just to survive, until the other scientists working that field had found a drug that would control the virus and make a normal life possible again. It wasn't hard to work this out in group, because we all wanted the same thing: to hang on until the day—not too far away now—when some hero in a white coat, mounted on a white charger, came galloping up to the fort, holding a beaker of Miracle Formula high like a banner.

But *how* to hang on? For each of us the answer, if different in particulars, was also the same. We wanted to be able to support ourselves (and our families, if we had them) in reasonable comfort, and to keep our antibody status secret. Achieving this, for some of us—the older ones—meant giving up practices in law or medicine, or business careers, or staying in but lowering our sights. Some of us quit struggling to save troubled marriages or get custody of children.

For me the obvious course seemed to be a teaching job in an academic backwater, preferably one in that same metropolitan area. Accordingly—at a time in my life when I'd expected to be at Cornell, cultivating a mentor, working with keen zest and keener ambition at my research, developing and pursuing a strategy for landing a classy position at a prestigious eastern university—I quietly looked into the several nearby branch campuses of the Pennsylvania State University Commonwealth Campus System and made a choice.

My personal style altered a lot during graduate school. I'd done some acting in high school and college, and that made it easier—though you mustn't suppose it was *easy*—to put my new persona over by turning down invitations ("too busy") and so on. Before long my department, which had been so delighted to keep me, had lumped me in with that breed of student that fizzles out after a promising undergraduate takeoff, and the rest of the RA's had given up on me too.

My therapy group speedily became my complete social universe. Nobody in the Bio Department could possibly have shared the intensity of common concern *we* shared within what we came to call the Company (after the thing Misery loves best). When as time went by one or another of us would lose the battle for wellness, the rest would push aside our own fears and rally round the ailing boon Companion, doing our best to make the final months as comfortable as we could. That wasn't easy either, let me tell you. But we did it. We were like a church family, all in all to one another. Elizabeth, who had given her life to helping us and the researchers at Graduate Hospital—she was our pastor and our friend, and yet, even so, a little bit of an outsider. When she asked what I meant to do for *fun*—since life could not consist entirely of the elimination of challenges and risks—I could only reply that just staying alive and well seemed like plenty of fun for the present, and think privately that no true Companion would ever need to have *that* explained to him or her.

We never told our real names, not in a quarter of a century, and stubbornly refused all that time to evolve from a collective into an assembly of intimates, but we knew each other inside out.

But to the people in my department, who did know my name, I appeared by the age of twenty-nine to have contracted into a prematurely middle-aged schoolmarmish and spinsterish recluse, and nobody there seemed surprised when I accepted a job for which I was grossly overqualified, teaching basic biology and botany at a two-year branch of the Penn State System, fifteen miles out in the suburbs of Delaware County.

My parents in Denver were also unsurprised. Neither had known how to read between the lines of my decision to stay put rather than go to Cornell. To them all college teaching seemed equally prestigious, and equally fantastic. They liked telling their friends about their daughter the future biology professor, but they knew too little about the life I would lead for the particulars to interest them much or invite their judgment. After the first grandchild came they'd been more incurious than ever about my doings, which had seemed less and less real to them anyway ever since I left the church. My new church was the Company, and of this they knew nothing, ever.

My job was a dull one made duller by my refusal to be drawn into the school's social web. But it was tolerable work, adequately paid. I stayed in character as the reliable but lackluster biologist; I did what was necessary, capably, without zest or flair. My pre-tenure years were a balancing act, filled but not overfilled. I prepared and taught my classes, swam a mile or ran five every day, meditated for half an hour each morning and evening, carefully shopped for and cooked my excruciatingly wholesome and balanced meals, and took the train into the city one night a week to meet with the Company, and one afternoon a month for my aptly named gag p24 treatments. Every summer for five years I would spend some leisurely hours in the lab, then sit in my pleasant apartment and compose a solid, economical, careful paper developing one aspect or another of my Ph.D. research, which had dealt with the effects of stress on the immune system in rats. One after another these papers were published in perfectly respectable scientific journals, and were more than enough to satisfy the committee that in due course awarded me tenure.

By the time they had approved me, in the fateful year 1999, my medical records had been destroyed. No document or disk anywhere in the world existed to identify me by name as a symptom-free carrier of the HIV-I virus, though no other personal fact spoke as eloquently about the drab thing I had become.

The fourteen years had thinned the ranks of Companions, but a fair number of us were still around. Just about all of us survivors had faithfully—often fanatically—followed the prescribed fitness/nutrition/stress management regimen, and it was about then that our team of doctors began to congratulate us and each other that we were beating the bejeezus out of the odds. If you're wondering about the lost Companions, whether they too hadn't stuck to the routines and rules, the answer is that they usually *said* they had; but it was easy enough for us to see (or suppose) how this or that variable made their cases different from ours.

I myself hardly ever fell ill, hardly had colds or indigestion, so extremely careful was I of myself. My habits, athletics aside, were those of a fussy old maid—Miss Dove or Eleanor Rigby or W.H. Auden's Miss Edith Gee. They were effective though. When a bug did get through my defenses despite all my care—as some inevitably did, for student populations have always harbored colds and flus of the most poisonous volatility—I would promptly put myself to bed and stay there, swallowing aspirins, liquids by the bucket, and one-gram vitamin C tablets, copious supplies of which were always kept on hand. No staggering in with a fever to teach a class through the raging snowstorm—no siree, not on your life. Not this survivor.

After tenure I bought a little house in a pleasant development of modest brick tract homes on half-acre lots near the campus, and settled in for the long haul. For years I'd subscribed to the health magazine *Prevention*, published by the Rodale press; now at last I'd be able to act on their advice to grow my own vegetables instead of buying the toxin-doused produce sold in the supermarkets. I mailed off my subscription to *Organic Gardening*, had the soil tested, bought my first spade, hoe, trowel, and rake, and some organic fertilizers, spaded up a corner of the back yard, and began.

That first post-tenure summer I made a garden and wrote no paper. My mood was reflective but the reflections led nowhere much. The next year of teaching was much the same: I did my job, steered clear of controversy, kept in character. But as the following spring came on—spring of the year 2000—I became restless and vaguely uneasy. Even as I loosened the soil in my raised beds and spread over them the compost I had learned to make, I had dimly begun to know that the cards I'd been playing thus far were played out, that it was time for a new deal.

What I felt, I know now, were the perfectly ordinary first stirrings of a midlife crisis, probably initiated by the "marker event" of successfully securing my means of support for the foreseeable future. Ordinary it may have been, but it scared me badly. Uneasiness is stressful; stress is lethal.

I've stopped to read over what I've written to this point. It all seems true and correct, but it leaves too much out, and I think what it mainly leaves out is the terror. I don't mean the obvious terror of the Terror, the riots of 1998–99, when I might have been killed outright had the mob that stormed the Alternate Test Site on Walnut Street gotten its talons into my file and learned my name, when the Company met for months in church basements kept dark, when threatening phone calls woke Elizabeth night after night and she didn't dare come to meetings because the KKK was shadowing her in hopes of being led to us. I certainly don't deny we were scared to death while that nightmare lasted, but it *was* like a nightmare, born of hysteria and short-lived. In a while, we woke up from it. I'm talking about something else.

It's true that we all know we're going to die. Whether we're crunched by a truck tomorrow while crossing the street, or expire peacefully in our sleep at ninety, we know it'll happen.

Now, as long as one fate seems no more likely than the other, most people manage to live fairly cheerfully with the awareness that one day they will meet their death for sure. But knowing that your chances of dying young, and soon, and not pleasantly, are many percentage points higher than other people's, changes your viewpoint a lot. Some of the time my radically careful way of life kept the demons at bay, but some of the time I would get up and run my five miles and shower and dress and meditate and drive to school and teach my classes and buy cabbages and oranges at the market and drive home and grade quizzes and meditate and eat supper and go to bed, all in a state of anxiety so intense I could scarcely control it at all.

There were drugs that helped some, but the best were addictive so you couldn't take those too often. The only thing that made years of such profound fear endurable was the Companionship of my fellow travelers. Together we could keep our courage up, we could talk out (or scream or sob out) our helpless rage at the medical establishment as years went by without producing the miracle drugs they'd been more or less promising, that would lift this bane of uncertainty from us and make us like everybody else—mortal, but with equal chances. Now, terror and rage are extremely stressful. Stress is lethal. I had said so over and over in print, my white rats and I had demonstrated it in the lab, statistics of every sort bore out the instinctive conviction that we had more to fear from fear itself than from just about anything else; and so our very terrors terrified us worst of all. But we bore it better together than we possibly could have borne it alone.

A few of my Companions in these miseries took the obvious next step and paired off. One or two probably told each other their real names. I wasn't even tempted. But sexual denial is stressful too; so on Saturday afternoons I used to rent a pornographic video or holo. A lot of these were boring, but trial and error taught me which brands showed some imagination in concept or direction, and voyeurism in that sanitary form did turn me on, it worked, it took care of the problem. Miniaturized in two or three dimensions, the shape-shifting penises of the actors seemed merely fascinating and the spurting semen innocent. No matter that a few spurts of semen had destroyed my life, and that a penis, the only real one I'd ever had to do with, had been the murder weapon; these facts did not feel relevant to the moaning and slurping of the young folks—certified AB-Negatives every one—who provided my weekly turn-on.

For a very long time I was content to release my sexuality, for hygienic reasons, into its narrow run for an hour or so each weekend, like some dangerous animal at the zoo. A few of the guys in the Company were straight, and maybe even willing, but a real relationship—a business as steamy and complicated as that—would have been out of the question for me. Others might have the skills; I lacked them. How much safer and less demanding the role of voyeur in the age of electronics, able to fast-forward through the dull bits and play the best ones over!

The Company, directed by Elizabeth, seemed to understand the force of these feelings. At any rate I wasn't pushed to try to overcome them.

Well, as I was saying: the beginning of my thirty-seventh summer, one year after receiving tenure at the two-year college where I seemed doomed to spend the rest of my life, however long that proved to be, and a year after the worst of the rioting ended—the beginning of that summer found me jittery and depressed, and very worried about being jittery and depressed. Probably I wouldn't have acted even so; but at about the same time, or a bit earlier, I'd begun to exhibit a piece of obsessive-compulsive behavior that until then I'd only heard about at Company gatherings: one morning, toweling down after my shower, I caught myself scrutinizing the skin of my thighs and calves for the distinctive purplish blotches of Kaposi's sarcoma, the form of skin cancer, previously rare, whose appearance is a diagnostic sign of the acute form of AIDS.

How long I'd been doing this half-consciously I couldn't have told you, but from that morning I was never entirely free of the behavior. I'd reached an age when my skin had begun to have its share of natural blotches and keratoses, and I gave myself heart failure more times than I can count, thinking some innocent bruise or lesion meant *this was finally it*. After several weeks, growing desperate, I gave up shaving my legs—and shorts and skirts in consequence—and suffered through the hot weather in loose overalls, just to avoid the chronic anxiety of seeing my own skin. I nearly drove myself nuts.

The Company assaulted this symptom with shrewd concern and a certain amount of relish. Your unconscious is trying to tell you something, dummy, one or another of them would say; I used to do that when I got so freaked out in the riots—sloppy about doing my Yoga—too busy chasing the bucks—into a bad way after I lost my mother—upset because I couldn't afford to keep the house but didn't want to sell. Remember when I did that? they'd say. Just figure out what you're doing wrong and fix *that*, then you'll be okay. For starters, try deciding whether it's something you need to work into your life, or something you need to get rid of.

I didn't see how it could very well be the latter, since my present life had been stripped to the bare essentials already. But what they said made sense. It was this sort of counsel that made us so necessary to one another.

Elizabeth, moreover, had a concrete suggestion. On her advice I rented a condo in the Poconos near the Delaware Water Gap—almost the vacation spot of my former Yuppie dreams—for a couple of weeks. The Appalachian Trail, heavily used in summer unfortunately, passes through the Gap. I spent the two weeks of my private retreat hiking the Trail, canoeing on the river, and assessing the state of my life.

So how was I doing?

Well, on the plus side, *I was still alive.* Half the original Company of sixteen years before, when I'd just come into it, were not, most from having developed the disease, though in a few cases more than a decade after seroconverting. In the early days it had been hoped that if a person with HIV-I antibodies hadn't fallen ill after six or eight years or so he probably never would, but it hadn't turned out like that. So far, the longer we survived, the more of the virus we had in us; to be alive at all after such a long time was pretty remarkable. I tried to feel glad.

I'd chosen a suitable job and fixed things so I could keep it; I'd also managed my money intelligently during the years before getting tenure. My salary, while not great, was adequate for a single person who hardly went anywhere and whose expensive tastes ran to top-of-the-line exercise equipment and holographic projectors. Raises would be regular, I would be able to manage my house payments easily. I'd already bought nearly all the furniture I needed, and had assembled a solid reference library of books, tapes, and disks on nutrition, fitness, stress management, and diseases, especially my own; and the gardening and preserving shelf was getting there. In short, all the details of the plan I had devised for myself sixteen years before were in place. And it had worked out: here I was.

So how come I felt so lousy?

At first, when I tried to tot up the negatives, it was hard to think of any at all. I was alive, wasn't I? Didn't that cancel out all the minuses right there?

As a matter of fact, it didn't. Once I got started the list went on and on.

As a bright college senior I had planned to make something really dazzling and grand of my life. That dream had been aborted; but I began to see that all these years I had been secretly grieving for it as for an aborted child. However obvious this looks now, at the time the recognition was a terrific shock. Years and years had lapsed since my last conscious fantasy of knocking the Cornell Biology Department on its collective ear, and I really believed I had ritualistically said goodbye to all that, early in my therapy.

Just what was it I'd wanted to do after Cornell, apart from becoming rich and famous? I could hardly remember. But after a while (and an hour of stony trail, with magnificent views of New Jersey) I had called back into being a sense of outward-directedness, of largesse bestowed upon a grateful world, that differed absolutely from the intense and cautious self-preoccupation which had governed my life from the age of twenty-two. Once, I had craved to be a leader in an international scientific community of intellectual exchange. Now, I thought, planned, and worked for the well-being of just one individual, myself—for what was the Company but just myself, multiplied by fifteen or eleven or nine? I'd hardly given a thought to *normal* people, people not afflicted as we were, for a long, long time, and certainly I had given them nothing else—not even a halfway decent course in botany.

It was an awful shock, remembering what it had been like to take engagement with the great world for granted. I turned aside from the Trail and its traffic to climb a gray boulder shaggy with mountain laurel, and sat staring out over the summery woods, remembering the hours I'd spent talking with Bill—my professor, the one who'd exposed me to the virus—about world population control and sustainable agriculture. No details came back; but the sheer energy and breadth of vision, the ability to imagine tackling issues of such complexity and social import, now seemed unbelievable. How had I shrunk so small?

At that moment on the mountain my triumph of continuing to live looked paltry and mean. I'd died anyway, hadn't I? Wasn't this death-in-life a kind of unwitting suicide? But I knew at bottom that it was no ignoble thing to have gone on living where so many had died. My fit of self-loathing ran its course, and I climbed down from the rock and started back down the Trail toward the Water Gap, three miles below, where I'd left my car.

I pondered as I went. What was missing from my life now seemed clearer. Meaningful work, first and foremost. Engagement. Self-respect, if that wasn't asking too much—not simply for having survived, but for contributing something real to society; and perhaps even the respect of others.

And last of all I let myself remember, really remember, those springtime afternoons in Bill's sunny office with its coffee machine and little refrigerator and daybed, and added one more thing: intimacy, social and sexual. Not the Company, that bunch of neutered and clairvoyant clones, but I and Thou: intimacy with the Other.

It was a list of things necessary to a fulfilled and happy life, and it bristled like a porcupine with potential stresses.

The trail was rough and steep, and I was wiped out from both my journeys, the inner more than the outer. When I let myself back into the condo the sun had set, and I thought with a fierce rush of resentment how *nice* it would be, just for once, to microwave a box of beans and franks and open a Coke, like a normal American citizen on holiday, instead of having to boil the goddamned homemade pasta and cook the spaghetti sauce from scratch. The strength of this resentment astounded me all over again: how long had I been sitting on the powderkeg of so much rage *against the virus itself*?

Enlightenment came early in the first week of my retreat, so I had plenty of time left to process my insights and form conclusions.

About personal intimacy first. Essential or not, I found that I still just didn't feel able to risk it. The potential trouble seemed bigger than the potential payoff; as I've mentioned, I lacked the skills.

About engagement. More promising. The thought of connecting myself in a meaningful way to society by some means that didn't threaten my own stability appealed to me a lot. I could *teach* in a more engaged fashion, but that felt far too personal, too exposed and risky. Then I thought of something else, something actually quite perfect: I could volunteer to work with AIDS patients. This may sound uniquely stressful for someone in my position, but the prospect oddly wasn't. I already knew everything about the progression of the disease, I'd been through it half a dozen times with dying Companions, so could not be shocked; I needn't fear infection (being infected already); and I felt certain my powers of detachment would be adequate.

Then about meaningful work. I pondered that one for the whole ten days remaining, pretty much all the time.

In the end it was a dream—the holo of the unconscious—that showed me what to do. I dreamed of Gregor Mendel, the Austrian monk who invented modern genetics while serving obscurely in a monastery. In my dream Mendel had the mild wide face with its little round-lensed spectacles of the photograph in the college biology text I used. Sweating and pink-faced in his heavy cassock, he bent tenderly over a bed of young peas, helping them find the trellis of strings and begin to climb. I stood at a little distance and watched, terribly moved to see how carefully he tucked the delicate tendrils around the strings. As I approached, he looked up and smiled as if to say, "Ah, so *there* you are at last!"—a smile brim-full of love—and handed me his notebook and pen. When I hung back, reluctant somehow to accept them, he straightened up slowly—his back was stiff—and moving closer drew me into an embrace so warm and protective that it seemed fatherly; yet at once I was aware of his penis where it arched against me through the folds of cloth, and of his two firm breasts pressed above my own. He kissed the top of my head. Then he was gone, striding away through the gate, and I stood alone among the peas, the pen and notebook in my hands somehow after all—in my own garden, my own back yard.

It had been a long time, literally years, since I'd last cried about anything; but when I woke that dawn my soaked pillow and clogged sinuses showed that I'd been weeping in my sleep, evidently for quite a while. Not since childhood had I felt such powerful love; not since childhood had anyone loved *me*, or held me, in just that way. To be reminded broke my heart, yet there was something healing in the memory too, and in the luxury of crying.

I lay in my dampness and thought about Mendel—how, having failed to qualify as a teacher, he had returned to the monastery; and there, in that claustrophobic place, in that atmosphere of failure, without the approval or maybe even the knowledge of his bishop, he planned his experiments and planted his peas.

In its way Mendel's life was as circumscribed, and presumably as monastic, as my own. Yet instead of whining and bitching he'd turned his hand to what was possible and done something uniquely fine.

Me, I'd written off further research because the campus lab facilities were so limited and so public, and applying for funding or the chance to work for a summer or two in a better-equipped lab seemed incautious. It was also true that I'd done about as much in the area of stress and the immune system as I cared to do, and that white rats got more expensive every year and the administration more grudging each spring when my latest requisition forms went in. But if I could change directions completely—

Well, the Company had a perfect field day with that dream. You can imagine. They were all sure I'd been telling myself to do exactly that: *shift directions*, devise some experiments for my own backyard garden and publish the results. About the symbolism of the hermaphroditic monk, opinion was divided; one person thought him a fused father/mother figure, breasts and gownlike cassock muddling his obvious identity as *Father* Mendel. ("Monks are called *Brother*," a lapsed-Catholic Companion protested.) Others suggested variously that the dream message concerned repressed bisexuality, incest, plain old sexual frustration, even religious longings. They all seemed to have a clearer idea of that part of what it meant than I had myself. But I thought they were right about the other part: that I seemed to want to turn my garden to scientific account in some way, then write up the results (the pen and notebook, both anachronistic types) and disseminate them.

II

This was the year 2000, when four separate strains of HIV virus had been isolated and more than a million people had died. There was a desperate need for qualified volunteer help, for the hospital wings, hastily thrown up by the newly organized National Health, were bursting with AIDS patients. The great majority of new cases now were addicts and the spouses and infants of addicts, and most of these were poor people. Except among the poor, sexual transmission of the virus had become much less common for a variety of reasons. So there were far fewer groups like ours being formed by then, but still plenty of old cases around—people exposed years ago who had survived a long time but whose luck had finally run out. As mine might any day.

Perhaps I secretly believed that by caring for such people I could somehow propitiate or suborn the Fates—"magical thinking" this is called—or perhaps my bond with them, which I refused to *feel*, demanded some other expression of solidarity. I don't know. I told myself that this was my debt to society, due and payable now.

So, soon after returning from my retreat, I attended an Induction Day for volunteers at the AIDS Task Force office in the city. The experience wrung me out and set me straight. I'd vaguely pictured myself helping in the wards, carrying lunch trays and cleaning bedpans, but it was plain from what the speakers told us that I would find this sort of work more emotionally demanding than I'd expected and more than I'd be at all able to handle. I had already known better than to offer myself as a counselor or a "buddy" assigned to a particular patient; I'd been "buddy" to too many Companions already, with more of this bound to come, and even in that collective and defended context it was hard. That left the dull but essential clerical work: getting new patients properly registered and identified within the bureaucracy of the National Health, processing and filing information, explaining procedures, taking medical histories.

I signed up for that, one afternoon a week. Compared to the burdens other volunteers were shouldering I felt like a coward, but within the Company itself I was a sort of hero, though resented also for what my action made the rest face anew: their fear. Several of the gay men who had gone to Induction Days in years past, but had not felt able to sign up for anything at all, felt especially put down; but *everyone* reported a sense of being implicitly criticized. "You're, like, the teetotaler at the cocktail party," said one of the gays, making us all laugh.

We were no band of activists and saints, the nine of us left of the original Company. Nobody new had joined us for a long time. When the National Health was chartered by Congress, the mandatory anonymous universal blood tests establishing who was and who was not a carrier had brought in a few fresh faces for a time, but those just-identified AB-Positives had mostly preferred to form groups of their own. The rigors of psychoneuroimmunology didn't appeal to everybody, nor did the medical profession agree unanimously that avoiding stress should be a First Principle for the infected. But it was ours; and by making my Companions feel guilty I was guilty myself of stressing them. I understood their resentment perfectly.

At the same time I did feel a first small flush of self-respect to find that none of the others could face this work, relatively undemanding though it was, and that I could.

And almost at once I had my reward. The obsessive blotch-hunting stopped, I could again bear with composure the sight of my own skin; but a stranger and funnier reward was to follow. One day in the hospital outlet shop, on an errand for a busier volunteer, my eye fell by chance upon an object invented to make life easier for diabetic women: a hard plastic device molded to be tucked between the legs, with a spout designed to project a stream of urine forward, the more conveniently to be tested with litmus strips. In a flash a bizarre idea sprang fully developed into my head, exactly like one of those toads that lie buried in dried-up mudholes in the desert, patiently waiting out the years for the rains that tell it the time had come to emerge and mate. I bought the thing.

Back home I dug out an old electric dildo whose motor had long since burned out—a flexible rod with a "skin" of pink rubber. This I castrated, or rather circumcised. I then glued the three inches of amputated rubber foreskin snugly to the base of the plastic spout and snipped a hole in the tip.

I now had an implement capable of letting female plumbing mimic male plumbing, at least from a short distance, unless the observer were very sharp-eyed or very interested.

Inspired, my next step was to go out and buy myself a complete set of men's clothing: socks and underwear, trousers generously tailored, shirt, sweater, tie, and loosely fitting sport jacket, all of rather conservative cut and color and good quality. I even bought a pair of men's shoes. I'm quite a tall woman—five feet ten and a half inches—with a large-boned face, a flat chest, and the muscular arms and shoulders you build up through years at the rowing machine. And I found that the proverb *Clothes make the man* is true, for my full-length bathroom mirror confirmed that I made a wholly creditable one. Last of all, into the pouch of my brand-new jockey shorts, right behind the zipper of my new slacks, I tucked the plastic-and-rubber penis. The hard thing pressed against my pubic bone, none too comfortably.

Dress rehearsals went on for a whole weekend. By Monday, based on comparisons with certain water-sports videos I had seen, I thought the effect hilariously realistic. *Where Brother Mendel leads,* I said to myself with reckless glee, *I follow*! I can tell you for sure that this entire undertaking—making my dildo, buying my disguises, learning to fish out the fake penis suavely and snug it in place and let fly—was altogether the most fun I'd had in years. The only fun, really, the only bursting out of bounds. The thought of beans and franks was nothing to this.

When I felt ready for a trial run I put on my reverse-drag costume and drove to a shopping mall in a neighboring state, where for three hours I practiced striding confidently into the men's rooms of different department stores. I would hit the swinging door with a straight arm, swagger up to a urinal, plant my feet wide apart . . . I kind of overacted the role, but I could do this much with a flourish anyway. What I could *not* do was unclench my sphincter; I was all style and no substance in the presence of authentic (urinating) men. So I flunked that final test.

But my first purpose all along had been voyeuristic, and in this I was wildly, immediately successful. It was a mild day in early autumn. Lots of guys in shirtsleeves, with no bulky outer clothing to hinder the eager voyeur, came in and struck a pose at urinals near mine. For three hours I stole furtive glances at exposed penises from within a disguise that no one appeared even to question, let alone see through. It was *marvelous*. I drove home exhilarated quite as much by my own daring as by what I'd managed to see. To have infiltrated that bastion of male privilege and gotten away with it! What a triumph! What an actor!

All that year, the year 2000, I worked by fits and starts on my role of male impersonator, adding outfits to suit the different seasons and practicing body control (roll of shoulders, length of stride) like a real actor training for a part. I cruised the men's rooms less often than I'd have liked, since it seemed only prudent to avoid those near home, and I was kept fairly busy. But over time by trial and error I gained confidence. I learned that large public men's rooms in bus and train stations, airports, interstate rest areas and the like, were best—that men visiting these were usually in a hurry and the rooms apt to be fairly crowded, so that people were least likely to take notice of me there. It was in one such place that I was at last able to perfect my role by actually relieving myself into the porcelain bowl, and after that time I could usually manage it, a fact which made me smug as a cat.

Every cock I sneaked a look at that year seemed beautiful to me. The holos were so much less interesting than this live show that I all but stopped renting them. I also made some fascinating observations. For instance, young gay men no longer rash enough to pick somebody up in a bus station or whatever would sometimes actually stand at adjacent urinals, stare at one another, and stroke themselves erect. Wow! I felt a powerful affinity with these gays, whose motives for being there were so much like my own. Alas, they also made me nervous, for my prosthesis couldn't hold up to fixed regard, and sometimes, if I lingered too long, someone would show more interest than was safe.

The Company had been three-fourths gay men in the beginning, five of whom were still around, yet not one had ever said a word to the rest of us about mutual exhibitionism in public toilets, and it seemed possible that most straight men had never noticed. After sixteen years of weekly group therapy I'd have sworn none of us could possibly have any secrets left; but perhaps the gay Companions simply preferred not to offer up this behavior to the judgment of the straights—even now, and even us. Perhaps it was humiliating for them, even a bit sordid. I could see that. This behavior of mine had its sordid side. The recreational/adventurous side outweighed that twenty to one; but I took my cue from the gays, and kept my weird new hobby to myself—learning in this way that withholding a personal secret from the Company, retaining one exotic scrap of privacy, exhilarated me nearly as much as having live penises to admire after all the dreary years of admiring them on tape.

But if the dream image of Gregor-Mendel-as-hermaphrodite was present to me through much of this experience—for I knew that in some deep way they were connected—Mendel was a still more potent icon in the garden that summer. At first thought, backyard research seemed very small beer. I knew as well as anyone that the day had long since passed when a single white-coated scientist, working alone amid the test tubes in his own basement laboratory, could do important research. Mendel himself had had a larger plot of ground at his disposal.

Yet examining the unfamiliar literature of this field, and browsing in *Biological Abstracts*, forced me to revise my view: there were some very useful experiments within the scope even of a backyard researcher. Some of the published papers that interested me most had been written by amateurs. It appeared that master gardeners, like amateur archaeologists and paleontologists, had long been making substantial contributions to the fields of plant breeding, pest control, cultivation practices, and the field trials of new varieties. Organic methods of gardening and farming, which were what interested me, were particularly open to contributions from gardeners and farmers, non-scientists who had taught themselves to run valid trials and keep good records. Genetic engineering and chemical warfare were clearly not the only ways to skin the cat of improved crop yields.

The more I looked into it, the more impressed I was, and correspondingly the more hopeful. Though but a beginning gardener I was a trained scientist; if these other people could do something useful in their modest way, I should certainly be able to.

I'd lost my first two crops of melons to bacterial wilt and/or mosaic virus, I wasn't sure which, and both years my cucumbers had also died of wilt. (The first couple of seasons in an organic garden are tough sledding.) The striped cucumber beetle was the probable vector for both diseases. God knows I had enough of the little bastards. Now, you can grow *Cucurbita*—the vining crops, including all melons, squashes, cucumbers, and gourds—under cheesecloth or spun-bonded floating row covers, which exclude the bugs, but you have to uncover the plants when the female flowers appear so the bees can get at them, and if the bees can, so can the beetles. Besides, half the fun of gardening is watching the crops develop, and how can you do that if they're shrouded under a white web of Ultramay?

No, the thing was to produce a cultivar with resistance, or at least tolerance, to one or more of the insect-borne diseases. After reading everything I could get my hands on about bacterial wilt and cucumber mosaic virus, I concluded that a project of trying to breed a really flavorful variety of muskmelon strongly resistant to bacterial wilt would make the most sense. Wilt was a bigger problem in our area, and some hybridization for wilt resistance in muskmelons had already been done. But I was much more powerfully attracted to the mosaic problem. It took the Company about half a minute to point out, once they'd understood the question, that cucumber mosaic is caused by a *virus*. There's no cure for mosaic; once it infects a plant the plant declines, leaf by leaf and vine by vine, until it dies. (Just like you-know-who.)

There's no cure for bacterial wilt, either, but I couldn't help myself: I began to plan an experiment focusing on mosaic.

I didn't want to waste time duplicating the research of others, so I made several trips that summer to Penn State's main campus at University Park to extract from their excellent library everything that was known about all previous efforts to breed virus resistance into muskmelons. These trips were fun. For one thing it pleased me a lot to be doing research again. For another

I did the trips in undrag, stopping at every highway rest area on the Pennsylvania Turnpike between Valley Forge and Harrisburg to investigate men's rooms—and in fact simply to use them too, as this was, prosthesis and all, easier, quicker, and less grubby than using the ladies'.

It turned out that the breeders had never made much headway against virus disease in muskmelons, and since the introduction of row covers and beetle traps the subject had been generally slighted. Commercial growers had been getting around the problem of pollination for quite a while by constructing great tents of Ultramay over their fields and putting a hive of honeybees inside with the melons. As this was hardly practical for the home gardener, the state agricultural extension services recommended several pesticides for use on the beetles (and aphids, another serious virus vector for cucurbits) during the two or three weeks when the plants would have to come out from under cover to be pollinated. Spraying at dusk was suggested, to spare the bees. But these were persistent toxins and I doubted all the bees would be spared, though they might pollinate the vines before they died.

I also read up on the life cycle of the striped cucumber beetle, then built a clever cage in which to rear as many generations of virus-bearing beetles as necessary to carry the critters through the winter—they hibernate in garden trash, but I wanted to guarantee my supply. When the cage was ready I rigged a shelf-and-fluorescent-tube setup in which to raise a sequence of zucchini plants to feed the beetles—nothing grows faster than a zucchini, and nothing's easier to grow, and the beetles love them. As each plant in turn began to sicken I would transplant a new, healthy seedling into the soil on the bottom of the rearing cage, then cut through the stem of the sick zucchini, shake off the beetles, and remove the plant. The roots had to be left undisturbed, because the soil around them contained eggs, feeding larvae, and pupae, but by the time the space was needed for a new transplant the roots would have died or been eaten up.

It worked beautifully. My quarter-inch black-and-yellow beetles spent that winter, and the next four winters, living the life of Riley.

And throughout that hard late winter of 2001 I spent all my spare time thinking out my project, its objectives and procedures, until I knew exactly what I wanted to do. By April a small ranked and labeled army of cantaloupe seedlings stood waiting in my basement, under lights, for the day when they could safely be set out in their carefully prepared beds and tucked under Ultramay. Assuming no spectacular early success, the plan would organize my summers for the next five years. Plant breeding is not an enterprise for impatient people. It *is* a gesture of faith in the (personal) future.

In early May, just as the azaleas were at their peak of bloom, a week before the last frost date in Delaware County, Jacob Lowenfels and his team of American and French researchers announced their discovery of the AIDS vaccine.

The announcement threw me, and the rest of the Company with me, into a profound funk. Except for us and several thousand dying people, the whole city seemed to rejoice around us; even the war news yielded pride of place. Thank God the spring quarter had ended, except for some finals I could grade with one hand tied behind me. Watering cantaloupe seedlings before turning in, on the night of May 15, I came within a hair of wrenching the table over and dumping the lot of them, *smash*, onto the concrete floor. Why should these frivolous *Cucurbita* live when so many innocents were dead?

I know, I know: the Lowenfels vaccine was of enormous importance even to us—even, for that matter, to those who had developed the disease but would not begin dying seriously for months or years; for overnight the fear of discovery and persecution ended. We were no longer lepers. People could acquire immunity to us now. Only those already in the final stages of dying from AIDS benefitted not at all, so that the AIDS wings of the hospitals lay for weeks beneath a blanket pall of sorrow.

And of course I knew all this really, even at the time. I carried out my trays of cantaloupes and honeydews on the sixteenth after all, and planted them on schedule. The beds beneath their Ultramay covers looked so peculiar that I decided to fence the yard, discourage the neighbor's curiosity. I planted with a leaden heart that day, but the melons didn't seem to mind; in their growing medium of compost, peat moss, and vermiculite dug well into my heavy clay soil they soon sent out runners and began to produce male flowers. When the female flowers appeared about ten days later I pulled the Ultramay off of some beds just long enough to rub the anthers of the male flowers against the pistils of the female ones. At other beds I sent in the beetle troops. At the same time I was growing a year's supply of vegetables in my kitchen garden. My computer kept daily records for both garden and field trials. In August I gave my control melons away by the cartrunkload to the Companions, ate tons of them myself, froze some, saved the rest to rot peacefully till they could be blended with autumn leaves into a giant compost tower. (The vines that died of mosaic, and the malformed fruit they produced, if any, went out with the trash.) And I preserved, packaged, labeled, and froze my hybrid seeds.

None of the varieties I'd inoculated with the virus that first year had resisted it worth a damn. I saved seed from only one mosaic-stunted hybrid cultivar, a *Cucumis melo* called "Mi ting tang," which had shown good resistance to cucumber mosaic (plus gummy stem blight and downy mildew) in field trials in Japan. That one had managed to struggle to maturity and produce a crop despite its illness. The fruit, though dwarfed, had a fair flavor and good thick flesh, and I thought I might backcross and then cross it with other varieties after I saw the results of my hybridizing the following year. Resistance in the Ano strains of muskmelon appeared to vary according to the weather; I wanted to find out more about that too.

Between times I canned and froze and dried my garden produce as one after another the overlapping crops came in. Once I'd gotten over the shock of the vaccine it was a wonderful summer, the best of my life, full of pleasurable outdoor work; and the four that followed resembled it pretty closely.

Each fall and winter I would overhaul my records and revise my schedules; compost plant residues; treat the soil of the inoculated beds to kill any leftover beetles; care for the next year's beetle crop and manage their supply of zucchini plants; clean and oil my tools; consume my preserved stock of organically grown, squeaky-clean food; teach my classes and run my labs; put in my afternoon at the hospitals every week; meet with the Company; and take my treatments. In a small way I'd also begun to write for gardening magazines, mainly Rodale's and *National Gardening*, though occasionally for *Horticulture* or even *Harrowsmith*. I'd never been so busy nor interested nor free of anxiety, and I think now that unconsciously I'd come to believe that I was safe. "Magical thinking," sure—but it *was* a much healthier and better-rounded way of life, no question.

It was the fifth year of the research, the spring of 2006, that two events occurred to shatter the even tenor of my days. The arrival of the ship from outer space was the big news; but the Hefn delegation was still in England, and in the daily headlines, when devastating news broke upon us in the Company: for our counselor Elizabeth had developed the bodily wasting and red-rimmed eyes of AIDS-Related Complex, and confessed at last that all this while she had been keeping a secret of her own.

One and all we were stricken anew with terror, my eight surviving Companions and I. Elizabeth who had been our mother, our guardian, our stay against destruction, who had held us together and wedged the door shut against the world's cruelty, could not be dying—for if she were dying we could none of us feel safe. Our reaction was infantile and total: we were furious. Who would take care of us when she was dead? When an accountant who called himself "Phil" promptly developed skin lesions, we all blamed Elizabeth.

"Phil's" symptoms turned out to be hysterical; his apparent defeat had been the medium through which we had collectively expressed our virulently reactivated panic and dread. After that episode we pulled ourselves together and stopped whining long enough to think a little of Elizabeth, and not so much about our miserable selves.

She had been admitted to Graduate Hospital, the one our psychoneuroimmunology team was affiliated with. I sat with her for a while one afternoon, a sulky, resentful child and her mortally ill mother. When I apologized for my behavior Elizabeth smiled tiredly. "Oh, I know how you all feel, you're reacting exactly like I thought you would. Listen, Sandy, this had to happen sometime. You folks have all been much too dependent and you know it. Now's your chance to stand on your own, ah, eighteen feet—

but I'm sorry you feel let down." She grimaced. "I feel pretty bad about that myself."

Her generosity dissolved my fretful resentment; and love, shocking as the dream-love of Gregor Mendel, flooded into the vacancy. I choked and burst into wrenching tears; Elizabeth patted my arm, which made me cry harder; in a moment I was crouching beside her bed, my hot, wet face pressed against her shoulder, the first time in twenty years that I had touched another human being intimately. A surreal moment. It was glorious, to tell the truth, though I felt as if my chest would burst with grief.

When I forced myself to report this scene on Company time, the story was received in a glum silence tinged with embarrassment. Finally "Larry," a balding, thickening physical therapist I'd known since he was a skinny teenager, puffed out a breath and said disgustedly, "Well, don't feel like the Lone Ranger, Sandy. I never touch anybody either, except on the job. Hell, we *all* love Elizabeth! But I never let myself know that. I haven't taken an emotional risk in so many years I literally can't remember when the last time was, and you people aren't any better than me."

"I've often thought," said "Phil," "that it's funny we don't love each other. I mean, as much as we need each other, you'd think . . ."

He trailed off, and we glanced obliquely (and guiltily) at one another, except for the two couples present—who naturally couldn't help looking a little smug—and the one father who blurted defensively, "I love my kids!"

"Elizabeth knows we love her," said "Sherry," over against the far wall.

"Maybe she does," "Larry" growled, "but *we* need to know it. That's my point, goddammit."

"Other groups do better. Some of them are really close," I put in. "Maybe we fuss over ourselves so much we can't connect, except to spot weaknesses."

"Other groups don't have our survival rate either," "Mitch" reminded me.

Breaking the gloomy silence, "Phil" roused himself to say, "What about these spacemen, anything doing in that direction?"

When the Hefn first arrived, half the world's people had recoiled in panicky dismay; the other half had seemed to expect them to provide a magical cure for all our ills: war, cancer, pollution, overpopulation, famine, AIDS. So far they had shown no interest in us whatever. The landing party was presently in London because the mummified corpse of one of their relations, stranded here hundreds of years ago, had been discovered in a Yorkshire bog; but suggestions that they set up some sort of cultural and scientific exchange with humanity had been politely ignored and I doubted there was any chance at all that Elizabeth's life was going to be saved by ET intervention. The AIDS Task Force in New York had already sent them a long, pleading letter, but had received no reply. We were all aware of these facts. Nobody bothered to answer "Phil," and after a while the hour was over and we broke up; and when the Hefn ship took off from the moon a few weeks later, having neither helped nor harmed us by their visit, we weren't surprised. It was what we'd expected.

Just as we expected Elizabeth to waste and decline, and finally die, and she did—leaving the Companions rudderless and demoralized. At least we'd rallied and borne up pretty well throughout the last weeks of her dying. We must have done her, and ourselves, a little good.

Surprisingly, despite even this trauma none of the rest of us became ill. Apparently we who were still alive were the hardiest of the lot, or at least the ones who had taken the best care of ourselves. But the emotional jolt of Elizabeth's death—the one death we had *not* protected ourselves from being badly hurt by—showed me, as the dream of Mendel had showed me all those years ago, that something was still wrong with my life. It was still a loveless life, and just when I seemed to need it least it now appeared that I was no longer willing to do without love. I'd failed to acknowledge Elizabeth alive; now that she was dead I wanted at least to keep alive the emotion— the capacity for feeling and showing emotion—that she had released in me at the end.

It didn't have to be romantic love, in fact I rather thought that any other sort would probably be preferable, though I was still determined not to *teach* lovingly. It seems odd now that I never thought of getting a pet—or maybe the image of a dog wouldn't readily superimpose itself upon the image of a backyard carpeted with melon vines? And I'm allergic to cat dander . . . anyway, whatever the reasons, the idea never crossed my mind. The months glided by as usual, and became years, before anything changed.

III

What happened was that I broke a small bone in my left ankle in a common type of running accident: one foot came down at the edge of a pothole and twisted beneath me as I fell. The X-ray showed a hairline fracture. They put me in a cast and crutches and ordered me off the foot for a month, and this was May.

May 2010; Year Four of my second five-year plan. With the whole season's research at stake I had no choice but to hire some help.

A bright, possibly talented sophomore in my botany course took the job. His name was Eric Meredith, and he was the first person other than my unobservant parents, a dishwasher repairer, and the water meter reader to have entered my house in the ten years I had owned it. I bitterly resented the need that had brought him there; but I knew the source of this bitterness (apprehension: what other infirmities would be violating my privacy in future summers?) and made a perfunctory effort not to work it out on Eric.

He seemed not to take my unfriendliness personally—I had a certain reputation at the college as a grump—and willingly did what I told him to without trying to chat me up. I showed him *once* how to handle the transplants, how big and how far apart to make the holes, how to work fertilizer and compost into the loose earth, dump in a liter of water, and firm the soil around the stem. He never forgot, never did it wrong, even beneath my jealous eye; he seemed to discover a knack for the work in the process of performing it that pleased him as much as it mollified me. He was scrupulously careful with the labeling and weighed the Ultramay at the beds' edges with earth, leaving no gaps for wandering bees or beetles to find. In a week the entire lot of transplants was in the ground. I recorded the data myself—I could sit at a keyboard, anyway—but Eric did everything else.

He grew so earnestly interested in the experiment, what's more, that after the second week he couldn't help asking questions; and I found his interest so irresistible that before I knew it I'd invited him to review the records.

For I did, finally, really appear to be getting someplace. Several hybrids of the "Mi ting tang" (Ano II) strain had done unusually well the previous year; I thought I knew now which of their parents to cross with Perfection and Honey Dew to produce at least one variety which would show exceptional tolerance to mosaic in the field. Immunity now looked impossible, resistance unlikely; but I felt I would be more than satisfied with a strain that could *tolerate* the presence of the virus in its system without being killed or crippled too much—that could go on about its business of making a pretty good crop of sweet, firm-fleshed melons in spite of the disease.

Eric sat for an hour while the screen scrolled through the records of a near-decade. I jumped when he spoke. "This whole thing is just *beautifully* conceived." His amazement was understandable; why expect anything good from a professor as mediocre in class as I? "You're just about there, aren't you?"

He had a plain, narrow face, much improved by enthusiasm. I felt my own face growing warm. "Mm-hm, I think so. One more season. Of course, this isn't a very exciting experiment—not like what they do in the labs, genetic manipulation, that sort of thing."

"Well," said Eric, "but it's not so much the experiment itself as the experimental model. Heck, you could apply this model to any traits you were trying to select for. Did you work it out yourself?" I suspected that this was doubt, but when I nodded he did too. "I thought so, I never came across this system of notation before and I bet everybody'll be using it after you publish."

I'd been working in isolation a long time, without admiration, and the traitorous balloon of gratitude that swelled my chest undid me. "Come have something cold to drink," I offered gruffly, and as I went before him into the kitchen the rubber tip of my crutch slipped on a wet patch of linoleum and I fell, whacking my head hard on the corner of a shelf on the way down.

For a few seconds the pain in both ankle and scalp was blinding. Then as I struggled to rise, embarrassed and angry, and as Eric leaned over me to help, I saw the drops of blood on the floor, brilliant against the pale tiles. "Get away!" I shouted, shoving him so hard he stumbled against the counter and I fell flat on my back. In rage I hauled myself upright, holding to the counter, and managed to rip off some paper toweling to blot my head with. Again Eric moved instinctively to help, and again I snapped, "No, get back I said, keep away from me. *Did you get any blood on yourself?*"

"Unh-unh," said Eric, looking at his hands and arms, bewildered and then—bright student—suddenly comprehending. "Oh, hey, it's okay—I'm vaccinated."

I froze and stared at him, my head singing. *"What did you say?"*

"I'm *vaccinated* against AIDS. A bone punch in the sixth grade, see?" He pulled down the neck of his tee shirt and showed me the little V-shaped scar on his collarbone.

Vaccinated. Immune. Of course he was. *Everybody* was vaccinated nowadays. Eric had been in no danger from me—but in my instinctive panic I'd given myself away. For exactly the third time that decade I burst into tears, and I couldn't have told you which of the two of us was the more embarrassed.

I don't remember how I got him out of the house. I spent that evening raging at myself, my situation, the plague that had blighted my life, aborted my career, turned me into a time bomb of thwarted need. So what if it came out that I was a carrier of the virus? Nobody gave a damn anymore. During the past few years, the deadly microorganisms that had built up strength in my system throughout the first ten had begun to decline. I might never die of AIDS now, might not even be infectious, nobody knew. Even if I were, the world had been immunized against me. Yet I *felt* infectious, consumed with longing for something that would certainly be destroyed if I tried to possess it. No amount of rational certainty that this was *not* so acted to defuse a conviction which had for so long been the central emotional truth, the virtual mainspring, of my life. For the past nine years I had abstained from sex for my own reasons of stress-avoidance, not to protect others; I had known this and not-known it, both.

The truth was, I had lived as a leper too long to change my self-concept. Now here was this boy, who had guessed my guilty secret just like that and spoken it aloud without batting an eye. He would have to be replaced, possibly bribed . . . no, that was crazy thinking. Yet the thought of facing him was unendurable. I'd pay him off in the morning and dismiss him. The pain of this thought astonished me; yet I couldn't doubt it must be done.

I had not, however, factored in Eric's own attitudes and wishes. The next day he showed up at the usual time and went straight to work in the kitchen garden, spreading straw mulch on the tomato and pepper beds, whistling the noble theme from the second movement of Beethoven's Seventh. From the kitchen window I watched his tall, bony frame fold and unfold, gather the straw from the cart in armfuls and heap it carefully around the bases of the plants; and gradually I became aware that here was the only living being, not one of the Company, who knew The Truth. Gradually, it even began to seem a wonderful thing that somebody knew. Eric dragged the empty cart across the yard for more straw bales, then back to the nightshade beds. I regarded his back in its sweat-soaked tee shirt, the play of the shoulder muscles, the stretching tendons at the sides of his knees as he folded and straightened—and something fluttered and turned over in my middle-aged insides. "Eric," I murmured in wonderment; and as if he had heard he turned his head, saw me at the window, waved and grinned. Then he stooped to gather another armful of straw and I fell back out of view.

That grin . . . I dropped onto a stool, hearing in my head the incongruous voice of my best high-school friend: "He looked over at me from the other side of the class and it just really boinged me." Boinged, I'd been boinged! By Eric's cheerfulness, the wave of his long arm with its brown work glove at the end. I knew by then, I guess, that I wasn't going to fire him; but I couldn't see how to do anything else with him either.

At noon Eric came to the house to wash up under the spigot before leaving, in his khaki shorts and old running shoes. He had taken off his shirt, and dust and bits of straw had stuck to the sweaty skin of his chest and back, and in the curly golden hairs of his legs and the blond mop on his head. He was a very lanky guy, pretty well put together, not a bit handsome. I regarded his long body with awe.

"I'll be late tomorrow, got a dentist appointment," he said. "Listen, I wanted you to know I'm not going to say anything to anybody else about yesterday. In case you were worrying about it. I mean, I don't go in for gossip much anyway, and even if I did I wouldn't spread stuff around about you."

I managed to reply, "Thanks, I'd appreciate it if you wouldn't."

Eric started to say something else but instead stuck his head under the faucet for a minute, dried himself on his shirt, and slipped away around the house. There was a paperback novel crammed into the back pocket of his shorts, its title *Sowbug!* scrawled diagonally across the cover in screaming colors, and water droplets spangled his bare shoulders.

And so we went on as before, but nothing was as it had been for me. Once again I became an actor, for I found myself against all sense and expectation carrying a blazing torch for a boy considerably less than half my age: a clever, nice, probably not terribly remarkable boy who (as the Companions agreed) was serving now as representative object of the pent-up love of half a lifetime. Eric, the wick for this deep reservoir of flammable fuel, became "Lampwick" in Company nomenclature: Lampwick, the boy who went to Pleasure Island with Pinocchio and turned into a braying jackass before the puppet's horrified eyes.

I felt like the jackass, let me tell you. *Knowing* the passion that so rocked me to be symbolic and categorical, hardly about Eric-the-singular-individual at all, made exactly zero difference to my experience of it. In the Company we'd been talking and thinking more about love since Elizabeth's death, and they all thought it was great. *All* loves are part personal, part associational, the more worldly among them assured me. Go for it! Get it out of your system. Wasn't your primary sexual involvement in the past with a teacher? Hey, the unconscious is a tidy bastard; naturally yours would think it fitting to pass the baton to the next generation by making you fall for a student of your own.

And I have to admit that even the hopeless misery of *this* passion was, in a weird way, kind of fun. It rejuvenated my libido, for one thing. It took me out of myself. I no longer feared the lethal effects of stress so much, and in any case this stress was salutary too.

I did take enormous care to protect myself from the humiliation of letting Eric catch me out, as he had caught me out about my antibody status. He never dreamed I seethed with lust for him, I feel quite sure of that. I think he did regret my aloofness—he was a sociable boy, and truly admired my work—but not so much as to be pained by it; and in any event Eric had other fish to fry that summer.

My ankle had healed well enough by late July for me to take over the kitchen garden, and a bit later the processing of its produce, when that began to roll in; but I pretended a greater disability than I really had just to keep Eric around. And when my old mother in Denver had a stroke, making a visit unavoidable, I was happy to leave him in charge of both kitchen garden and melon plots. The special hybrids were looking great, but records on rainfall and hours of sunlight during this crucial month would have to be kept. I asked Eric to come live in the house while I was away, and promised him a bonus if he did a meticulous job of keeping the records.

I decided not to fly, and drove west in an erotically supercharged state of psyche, sleeping in the carbed, peeing in the men's rooms of seven states, feasting my eyes on hundreds of penises and fantasizing that this or that one could be Eric's . . . I hadn't done much of this recently and suspect I made a less convincing man as I grew older but I had a terrific time for a while, although to tell the truth I rather wore my imagination out. My mother was feeling better and received my attentions with gratified complacency; but the five grandchildren had become her life, and we regarded one another, benignly enough, through a glaze of mutual incomprehension. It seemed likely that I would see her next when I flew out for the funeral.

All the same I stayed a week before returning by easy stages across the hot, dry, dusty plains, eager to get back but pleased to think of Eric still holding the fort in my stead. No point in pretending I couldn't handle the work now, not after a drive like this. Anyway, the term would be starting soon. When I got back I'd have to let him go; and so I dawdled and fantasized across Kansas and Missouri, and late in the afternoon of August 30 was approaching Indianapolis when I told the radio to turn itself on and was informed that early that same morning there had been a meltdown at the nuclear power plant at Peach Bottom, on the Susquehanna River downstream from Three Mile Island.

Luckily traffic was light. I managed to pull off the road without smashing up, and sat gripping the wheel while the radio filled me in. The disaster was unprecedented, making even Chernobyl look paltry. The Peach Bottom plant was fifty years old and overdue to be shut down for good. It *had* been shut down in the Eighties, then reopened in 1993, when improved decontamination technology had reduced its radioactivity to acceptable levels. Though the plant had a history of scandalously inept management, technicians asleep on duty and so on, stretching back a long way, it didn't appear that the meltdown had been caused by human error.

From the standpoint of damage to nearby populations the weather could not have been much worse, given that it was summer. A storm system with a strong south-southwest wind had pushed the enormous radioactive plume across the fertile Amish farmland of Lancaster County; then a westerly shift had carried the plume over the continuous urban sprawl of Wilmington, Philadelphia, and Trenton. Heavy rains had dumped the hot stuff on the ground across that whole area. The storm had also put out the fire at the plant; damage was therefore horrific but, so far, highly localized.

The plume had been washed to earth before it could enter the upper atmosphere—but in one of the most densely populated regions of the world. A very high death count from acute radiation poisoning was expected; the Amish farmers, working in the fields without radios to warn them, were especially at risk. *Eight million people*, more or less, had to be evacuated and relocated, probably permanently, for the Philadelphia-Wilmington area would be a wasteland for at least a decade to come, perhaps much longer.

Terry Carpenter's name was mentioned again and again. A moderate Republican Congressman from Delaware County, Carpenter was being described by reporters as a miracle worker. His understanding and the speed of his response suggested that Carpenter had planned carefully for just this sort of emergency. Because of him the cost in human lives would be far less, though no one person could cope with every aspect of a disaster as great as this one . . . (I'd crossed over and voted for the guy myself, last election. Good move.)

People who had not yet left their homes had been urged to keep doors and windows shut and air conditioners turned off, to reduce inhalation uptake, which would be reduced somewhat anyway by the rain, and to draw water in their bathtubs and sinks before the runoff from the storm could contaminate the supply. Each was to pack a small bag . . .

The radio went on and on as I sat by the highway, shocked beyond thought. My house, my garden, the campus, the hospital where I worked and the one where I had my monthly treatments, the Company, the experiment—

all the carefully assembled infrastructure of my unnatural life—had melted down with the power plant. What in the world was I going to do? My trip had saved me from radiation poisoning, and from being evacuated and stuck in a Red Cross camp someplace; my car and I were clean. But my life was in ruins.

And all the while, still in shock, I thought about Eric, whom I'd left to mind the store, who might be in my house right now with the doors and windows shut, waiting to be evacuated. Abruptly snapping out of it, I drove back onto the road and went off at the next exit, where I found a pay phone that worked and put the call through.

But the phone in my house rang and rang, and finally I hung up and stood shaking in the already-sweltering morning, unable to think what to do now, stranded. Impossible to go back to Denver. Impossible to go home. Impossible also to find Eric, at least until things settled down. Eric, of course, would go to his parents' house—only what if they lived in the evacuation zone? A lot of our students were local kids; it was that kind of college.

I knew not even that much about Eric's personal life, I realized with a furious rush of shame, and at this moment all my uncertainty and power-lessness fused into a desperate need to find him, see him, make sure he was all right. Of all the desperately threatened people I knew in the area of contamination, only this one boy mattered to me.

I got back in my car and started driving. I drove all night, stopped at a western Pennsylvania sleepyside for a nap the following morning, drove on again. The radio kept me posted on developments. All that way I thought about Eric. Half of my mind was sure he was fine, safe in his parents' (grandparents'?) home in Pittsburgh or Allentown; the other half played the Eric-tape over and over, his longness and leanness, the grownup way he'd handled my breaking down, his careful tenderness with the melon seedlings (like Mendel's!), his reliability, his frank, unstudied admiration of my trial model, his schlock horror novel *Sowbug*! Why hadn't I been *nicer* to him while I'd had the chance? Why had I played it safe? My house and garden were lost, my experimental records doubtless ruined by fallout, the work of the past decade all gone for nothing, yet worse by far was the fact that I had squandered my one God-given chance to come close to another person, thrown it away, out of fear. I beat on the steering wheel and sobbed. Eric, Eric, if only I hadn't been so scared.

Whatever happened now, I knew I would never again watch him fold that long body up like a folding ruler to tend the crops or sic the virus-loaded striped cucumber beetles onto a melon cultivar. That life was finished. There was nothing to connect us now, because I had wasted my one chance and would never get another. I was hardly thinking straight, of course; I was in shock. I'd heard my colleagues speak often enough, and wistfully enough, of promising former students from whom they rarely or never heard anymore. Students go away and teachers stay—that's the way it's always been, they'd say. Put not your faith in students. A card at Christmas for a year or two after they leave, then zip.

But I wasn't thinking of what Eric might or might not have done in some hypothetical future time; I was thinking of what I myself had failed to do and now could never do. I cried, off and on, for hours, being forced once by uncontrollable weeping to stop the car. I shed far more tears during that nightmarish trip than in my whole previous life since childhood. If I'd only put my arms around him, just one time, just held him for a minute, not even saying anything—if I'd just managed to do that—As the hours and miles went by my grief became more and more inconsolable, as if all the tragedy of the meltdown, and even of my life, were consolidated into this one spurned chance to become human. It didn't matter whether Eric wanted to be befriended (let alone held) by me, diseased middle-aged spinsterish schoolmarm and part-time pervert that I had become; what mattered, beyond measure or expression, was that I'd been too cowardly even to consider the possibility of closeness with another person and now it was too late.

I drove and wept, wept and drove. Gradually traffic going the opposite direction began to build up. Just west of Harrisburg a bunch of state troopers were turning the eastbound cars back. Beyond the roadblock only two lanes were open; the other two, and the four going west, were full of cars fleeing the contaminated zone. I pulled over, cleaned my blotchy face as best I could with a wet cloth, and got out. A trooper was directing U-turns at the head of a line of creeping cars. I walked up to him. "Excuse me, do you know how I can find out where somebody is?"

The trooper turned, gray-faced with exhaustion. "You from Philadelphia?" I nodded. "I dunno, bud," he replied—reminding me that I was still in my traveling costume of undrag. "In a coupla days they'll know where everybody's at, but it's a madhouse back there right now, there's eight million people they're trying to evacuate. You had your radio on?"

"Yeah, but—"

"Maybe it's too far to pick it up out here." He took off his cap and rubbed his hand over his face. "Everybody that's got someplace to go, that has a car, is supposed to go there. Relatives, whatever. That's what all these people are doing. These are the ones from Lancaster and thereabouts—Philadelphia people were supposed to take the Northeast Extension or else head down into south Jersey or Delaware along with the Wilmington people. The ones that don't have noplace to go, they're all being sent to camps up in the Poconos or down around Baltimore. The Army's bringing in tents and cots."

"For eight million people?"

"Naaah, most of 'em'll have somebody they can stay with for a while. They figure a million and a half, two million, tops. Still a hell of a lot of campers. Who ya looking for?"

"A student of mine, he was house-sitting for me."

"Local kid?"

"I don't know, actually."

The trooper looked me over, red swollen eyes and rumpled, slept-in clothes, and drew his own conclusions but was too tired to care. "Probably went home to his folks if they don't live around Philly. They're telling everybody to call in with the info of where they're at as soon as they get to wherever it is they're going. There's a phone number for every letter of the alphabet. A couple more days, if the kid does like he's supposed to, you'll be able to track him down."

"Sounds pretty well worked out," I said vaguely. A couple of days, IF he was okay, and no way to find out if he wasn't.

"It's a goddamn miracle is what it is," said the trooper fervently. "That goddamn Congressman, Terry Carpenter, that son of a bitch was just waiting for something like this to happen, I swear to God, must of been. He had everything all thought out and ready to go. He commandeered the suburban trains in Philly, the busses, all the regular Amtrak trains and the freight trains too, that were anywheres around, and had 'em all rolling within a couple hours of the accident, got the hospitals and so forth emptied out, and look at this here—" he waved at the six lanes of cars contracting into four, but moving along pretty well, at about forty "—it's the same back in Philadelphia except at the ramps and like that." The trooper put his cap back on. "I got to get back to work here. Don't worry about your little pal, he'll be okay. You got someplace to go? I can give you directions to a refugee camp."

"No thanks, I'm fine." It was stupid to resent the trooper for what he was thinking but I did all the same.

I edged my car into the stream of traffic being guided back the way it had come, but at the first exit slid out of formation and onto a little road that headed off into the mountains. I drove along for several miles, looking for a town with a phone; but when I finally found one, in front of a closed-up shop in a closed-up town, there was still no answer.

That was crisis time, there and then. I don't know how long I stood beside that phone kiosk while the battle raged. At one point several busloads of Amish families went by, probably headed for relatives in Ohio; they stared out, faces blank and stony; for them too it was the end of the world. The wind had only held SSW a little while before shifting to southwest, but that was long enough.

Finally I got back into the car, turned it around, reentered the turnpike by the eastbound ramp, drove back to the roadblock, and found my trooper. He stood still and watched me walk up to him, too beat to show surprise. "Look," I said, "I'd like to go in and help search for the people that got missed. They must need volunteers. I'm volunteering."

Very slowly he nodded. "If that's what you want. Go on into Harrisburg and talk to somebody there. Get off at the Capitol, there's a trooper station set up around there somewheres, you'll see it. Maybe they'll take you. I'll radio ahead so they know you're comin'." I thanked him and started to leave; he called after me, "Listen up a minute, bud. Later on it might be too late to change your mind. We might be moving people out of York and Harrisburg if the wind shifts again."

"I understand," I called back, and felt him watch for a minute before moving to his car to use the radio.

In Harrisburg I talked fast and they took me—took me also, at face value, for a youthfully middle-aged man. They issued me a radiation suit, and minimal instructions, and flew me into the contaminated zone along with a batch of other volunteers, a few Quakers and some workers from Three Mile Island.

We were dropped in Center City, fifteen miles from where I needed to be. They didn't like to spare any people for the suburbs, but emergency volunteers are hard to control and some of the others were looking for friends or relatives too. In the end they let each of us take a police vehicle with a loudspeaker and told us to make a mad dash for home, then drive back slowly into the city, keeping the siren on and picking up stragglers as we came.

I'd only made it a little more than halfway home when I ran out of gas. The damned van burned ethanol and I'd been driving some kind of electric or solar car for thirteen years, but even so . . . I tore off on foot in my radiation suit to find a filling station, looking I'm sure exactly like a space invader in a B-grade flick, trying to run along the deserted street—not deserted enough, though: when I got back with a can of ethanol half an hour later, streaming with sweat and nearly suffocated, the van was gone. Like an idiot I hadn't taken the keys. I heaved the can into a hedge and started walking.

I was seven miles from home, give or take half a mile. Just as I set off, the sun came out. I had to pee badly and didn't know how (or whether) to open the suit, and I was already terribly thirsty.

That walk was no fun at all. I had to rest a lot. I also had decided that wetting the suit was preferable to the consequences of any alternative I could think of, which made the hike even more unpleasant than it would have been in any case. It was more than three hours from the time I'd left the van when I finally got home. The key was in my pocket but I couldn't get to it; I ended up breaking my own basement window to get in.

Eric wasn't there.

I knew the house was empty the instant I got inside. In the basement I leaned against the cool wall, overcome with exhaustion and letdown. After a while I fumbled with the suit till something came unfastened, and crawled out of it, drenched and reeking; I left the suit in the basement with all my seed-starting equipment and insect cages and dragged myself on wobbling knees upstairs, shutting the door behind me.

The kitchen sink was full of water. So were both bathroom sinks and the tub. My feeling of letdown lifted; he'd followed instructions then, that probably meant he'd gotten safely away. Good old Eric. I drank a couple of liters of water from the sink before stripping off my vile clothes and plunging into the full, cool tub. Might as well die clean.

Almost instantly I went to sleep. When I woke an hour or so later with a stiff neck I took a thorough bath, got dressed again (this time in my "own" clothes, some shorts and a shirt), realized I was famished, and raided the refrigerator for a random sampling of Eric's abandoned provisions: cold chicken, supermarket bread, a banana, a tomato from the garden. The power was off, but the doors had been kept shut and nothing had spoiled. I drank a can of Eric's Coke, my first in nearly thirty years. It was delicious. In a cabinet I found a bag of potato chips and ate them all with deliberate relish: exquisite! There were half a dozen boxes of baked beans in there—and pickled herring—and a box of cheese—Irrationally I began to feel terrific, as if the lost chance with Eric were somehow being made up for by his unintended gifts, the last meals I expected ever to eat. I meant to enjoy them, and I did.

Sated at last, I wandered into my airless bedroom and fell across the bed. Strange as it may sound, I never thought to switch on the transistor, so wholly had I crossed over into a realm governed by the certainty of my own imminent death. I had been fleeing my death for so long that on one level I actually felt relief to believe I could give in to it now, stop twisting and doubling and trying to give it the slip. Nor, still stranger, did I even glance into the garden.

The house was stifling, must have been shut up for many hours. It had been many hours too since people had been told not to run any more water or flush their toilets, though both of mine were flushed and clean. These things pointed to Eric's safe escape and relieved my mind of its last burden. I sank like a stone into sleep. When I woke it was dark, and the house was being battered by the amazing racket of the helicopter landing in the little park a block away.

They'd caught the person who had pinched my van as he was trying to cross the Commodore Barry Bridge into New Jersey. A police van is a conspicuous object to steal, but he'd been offered no alternatives and didn't mind being apprehended at all, so long as his captors took him out of danger. He'd seen me stop and leave the van, waited till I was gone, then poured fuel from some cans in his landlady's garage into the tank and taken off, while I'd still been hoofing it up the road. Inside the helmet I hadn't heard the engine start. It seemed less reasonable to steal the van outright than to beg a lift, but people act oddly when their lives are at stake and that was how he'd chosen to play it—a white man in his fifties, no family, a night-shift worker who had somehow slept through the evacuation. In fact, the very sort of person I'd been sent to pick up. All this I learned later.

It had taken time to trace the van, and everybody was plenty busy enough without coming to rescue the would-be rescuer, and they didn't even know my name. But I'd mentioned the name of my development to one of the other volunteers, and its general location near the campus, and eventually they sent the helicopter out to find me. It wasn't till I was out of my suit again that anybody realized the man they'd come to find had metamorphosed into a woman.

The rest is all aftermath, but I may as well set it down anyway.

I lived for a month in a refugee camp near Kutztown, Pennsylvania, on land owned by the Rodale Research Center; I chose it for that reason. By month's end it was obvious that Greater Philadelphia was going to be un-inhabitable for years—maybe a decade, maybe more.

A month to the day after the accident they sighted the returning Hefn ship.

I took a pretty high dose of radiation. My chances of developing leukemia in fifteen or twenty years aren't bad at all. However, I don't expect to be around that long unless I accept the Hefn's offer (of which more later).

One day in the camp they paged me, and when I got to the admin tent, who should be standing there in pack, tee shirt, and shorts but Eric Meredith. I'd found out, quite quickly, that he had indeed gone to relatives in Erie with the first wave of the evacuation, and had sent him a letter saying how relieved I was that he'd gotten away safely. I'd mentioned that I would be staying at the Rodale Camp for a while. Eric had come all that way, not to collect his bonus (as I thought at first), but to deliver the contents of his backpack: a complete printout of the records of my experiment, this season's preliminary notes on disk, and six seriously overripe cantaloupes containing the seeds of *Cucumis melo reticulatus* var. Milky Tango, the hybrid melon I'd had the highest hopes for, saved by his quick thinking from the radioactive rain. "I didn't know how to get the tough disk out of the computer," he apologized.

I stared at the bagful of smelly spheres on the table before us with the oddest emotion. For part of a day not long before I'd surrendered, I'd given up my life. By purest luck my life had been restored to me; but I had crossed some psychic boundary that day, and had never crossed back again. And Eric and the experiment both belonged to the time before the accident, when fighting viral diseases had been most of what I cared to do.

It only took one step to close the distance. I took it, put my arms around that bony, sinewy, beanpole torso and held myself against it for a moment out of time. Eric stood stiff as a tomato stake, and about as responsive, but I didn't mind. "Eric, do me a favor," I said, letting go of him and stepping back. "I'll take half of these, you keep the others. Plant them in your grand-parents' back yard next summer. Finish the experiment for me."

A coughing fit made me break off, and Eric unstiffened enough to say, "Are you okay? That cough sounds terrible."

"I'm fine now. I had a cold, then bronchitis. Listen: the soil at my place will be contaminated for years, and God knows when I'll get another yard to grow things in. The college may reorganize, but it hasn't been decided whether or where. Not in Delaware County, though. Will you be going on down to University Park?"

He nodded. "Next week. They're letting us start late."

"Good, then you just have time to collect yourself a supply of cucumber beetles. You can expose them to mosaic later if they haven't already picked it up." The poor kid was staring, unable to believe what was happening. "I'm perfectly serious. Look: *you* saved the data and the seed. I was in the house for eight hours or so myself and it never crossed my mind to try to rescue either one." This was true. The only thing *I'd* thought to rescue, when the helicopter came, had been my fake penis. "You've earned the right to finish the work. But don't feel you have to, either; the Rodale people will be glad to take over, or a seed company would."

"Oh no, I *want* to! Really!" he protested. "If you don't that is—but you could make money from this. It isn't right."

"Tell you what. For safety's sake, let's have another copy of these records made and print out the ones from this summer. I'll hang on to half the seed, as I said. If you don't produce salable results I'll see that somebody who might gets my copy and the seed; and if you do get results we'll split the money down the middle. How does that sound?"

The camp had several notaries. We wrote up an agreement and got one of them to notarize our signatures. I wasn't even sure it was legal—Eric was only nineteen or twenty—but never mind, I thought, never mind!

I walked him back to his car. Still bedazzled by the turn of events, he let the window down to say earnestly, "Nobody *ever* gave me anything this important before. I don't know what to say."

"You gave me something important too."

"*I* did? When? What was it?"

I thought of trying to tell him just what, thought better of it. "Cold chicken. Potato chips. Baked beans. Coke."

It took him a minute to realize what I was talking about, but then he objected, "That's different! That's not the same thing at all!"

"Less different than you know. Think about it, eh?" And then, a bit rashly, "Think about *me* once in a while."

Last month I attended Eric's graduation from Penn State: *Magna cum laude* in biology and a graduate fellowship to Cornell. For a boy from the nether regions of academe, not bad at all. Maybe he'll do with his life what I'd have done with mine if things had been different. Eric's final proof of Milky Tango's tolerance to mosaic under a wide variety of growing conditions earned him his classy degree, though he gave me full credit for my own work, to which his was only the capstone—but a beautifully cut and polished capstone, every bit as good as the one I might have cut myself. I wore a long-sleeved shirt to the commencement, too warm for such a sunny day, to cover the Kaposi's lesions that have spread now over much of my body.

My own research has taken an unexpected turn.

Early last summer I donned a radiation suit and went back home to see my abandoned garden and my field trial beds. Everything was a disheartening mess, but that wasn't what I'd come to see. Eric had ripped loose the Ultramay cover on the Milky Tango beds to harvest those six melons. Remnants of the stuff flapped around me as I knelt to look, imagining his haste and fright as he'd scrabbled frantically among the vines while behind him in the house the printer pipped and pinged. But such thoughts weren't what I'd come for either.

The rest of the Milky Tango seedcrop had eventually rotted where it lay, and the seeds had been directly exposed to the elements all these months. I'd been reading a lot about using fast neutrons, X-rays, and gamma rays to induce desirable mutations in plants, including disease resistance, and had begun to wonder what effect the fallout might have had on my own already highly resistant muskmelons. I wanted to know whether any of the accidentally irradiated seed had made it through the winter and germinated, and so did my new bosses at the Rodale Press, who were paying for this expedition. Our Hefn observer was interested too—enough to come along and help.

Sure enough, there were about two dozen volunteer seedlings growing in the Milky Tango plots. Some leaves showed signs of moderate beetle damage but not enough to set the plants back much. With Godfrey's help I transplanted each seedling, radioactive soil and all, into its own large peat pot brought along for the purpose. Back at the Research Center we planted the lot of them at a special site set apart from the other trials and waited to see what would happen.

While we were waiting I got sick. Before that, the eighteen months between the Peach Bottom accident and my illness were my happiest ever.

When Penn State made the decision to disband the Delaware County Campus, they offered to try to place the tenured faculty at other branches of the system; but by then the Rodale Press had offered me a job. I'd been writing for their magazines for years and knew a number of Rodale editors and writers through correspondence, so it was natural enough that they should think of me when an editorial slot opened up that September at *Backyard Researcher* magazine, the newest member of the Rodale family of publications.

I can remember when all this part of Pennsylvania was farmland, and Kutztown a tiny college town with one main street, one bad motel, and one decent restaurant. But high-tech industry like AT&T and Xerox had moved in, changing the character of the area completely. When I came here to live, the Research Center had become a green island in a sea of development. I moved into one of the old farm buildings at the Center and commuted to my job in Emmaus, where the Press was located. Living out at the Center made it easier to keep an eye on my new experimental garden. No more battling with diseases now; the project I devised had to do with increasing yields in several kinds of potatoes. No more hyperpure living, either; the potato chip and I were strangers no longer. No more Companions; we were scattered to the winds, but the new friends I made here knew about my condition. No more celibacy: for a while, one of these friends became my lover.

When the Hefn returned and decided to take charge of us, they looked around for pockets of sanity and right action in the general balls-up we'd made of things, and so they were interested in the Rodale enterprise and in sustainable agriculture generally—enough to assign us a permanent observer/advisor, and that was Godfrey. He moved into the farmhouse with me. When I got sick he knew about it; when the lesions appeared he asked about them, and the disease they meant I had. It's because of Godfrey that the search for a "cure"—fallen on very thin times since the numbers of still-living victims had dropped below ten thousand—has taken off again.

It looks pretty promising, actually. They've found a way to paralyze the enzyme that the virus uses to replicate in the cell—not like zidovudine and its kindred, which only slowed the enzyme down, but a drug that stops it cold. There's no way I'd still be alive by the time they finish sanding the side effects off the stuff, not in the natural course of things. But Godfrey's had another idea.

You know that, like cucumber beetles, the Hefn hibernate—and that their bodies use chemicals pretty much the same way ours do? Well, Godfrey figures it should be possible to synthesize a drug—using a chipmunk or woodchuck model in conjunction with a Hefn model—that would put the ninety-five-hundred-odd AIDS patients and AB-positives to sleep for a couple of years, until the cure can be perfected. There's a problem about testing the stuff if we *all* take the cold sleep, because of course the bosses, the Gafr, won't let them use animals. So we might be asleep for quite a while—or forever—or be damaged by the procedure. But the Gafr have given the go-ahead, and I'm thinking seriously about it. The Kaposi's can only be treated effectively with radiation, and I've had much more than my fair share of that already. I'll die of cancer anyway, probably sooner than later; in a month I'll be forty-nine. But I'm thinking about it. I wish they'd come up with this before, is all.

I have to tell you something funny. One of my irradiated melon plants turned out to be one hundred percent *immune* to mosaic! It's peculiar in other ways that make it useless for commercial purposes at this point, but the Rodale breeders are sure to keep working on improvements. I mentioned before that like all cucurbits melons produce separate male and female flowers, the male flowers bearing the pollen-producing stamens, the female flowers the pistil and ovary. Ordinarily it's easy to tell which is which, because the ovary behind the female blossom is a large hairy structure and the male flower has nothing behind it but a stem.

Well, the immune melon bears male and female flowers that look exactly alike! You can't tell them apart, except by peering closely at the inner structures or tearing off the petals, because the ovary is tiny, and concealed entirely within the flower. The fruit is correspondingly tiny, about the size of a small orange—much too small to appeal to growers, though I'd think home gardeners might raise it as a novelty.

I've given this new cultivar the official name of Tiny Tango, a name to please the seed catalogue writers. Privately I think of it as Male Impersonator (or sometimes—a pun—Atomic Power Plant). Its rind is tan and thin, netted like the rind of an ordinary cantaloupe, and its flesh is a beautiful deep salmon-orange, as sweetly, intensely delicious as any I ever tasted.

CHARLES SHEFFIELD

Out of Copyright

One of the best contemporary "hard science" writers, British-born Charles Sheffield is a theoretical physicist who has worked in the American space program, and is currently chief scientist of the Earth Satellite Corporation. Sheffield is also the only person who has ever served as president of both the American Astronautical Society and the Science Fiction Writers of America. His books include the best-selling nonfiction title *Earthwatch*, the novels *Sight of Proteus, The Web Between the Worlds, Hidden Variables, My Brother's Keeper, The McAndrew Chronicles, Between the Strokes of Night, The Nimrod Hunt, Trader's World*, and *Proteus Unbound*, as well as the collection *Erasmus Magister*. His most recent novel is *Summertide*. He lives in Bethesda, Maryland.

Here he slyly suggests that finding the right tool for the right job is more than half the battle—particularly if you're smart enough to know which jobs are *really* the important ones . . . and just what kind of tools you need to do them right.

▼
Out of Copyright

CHARLES SHEFFIELD

Troubleshooting. A splendid idea, and one that I agree with totally in principle. Bang! One bullet, and trouble bites the dust. But unfortunately, trouble doesn't know the rules. Trouble won't stay dead.

I looked around the table. My top troubleshooting team was here. I was here. Unfortunately, they were supposed to be headed for Jupiter, and I ought to be down on Earth. In less than twenty-four hours, the draft pick would begin. That wouldn't wait, and if I didn't leave in the next thirty minutes, I would never make it in time. I needed to be in two places at once. I cursed the copyright laws and the single-copy restriction, and went to work.

"You've read the new requirement," I said. "You know the parameters. Ideas, anyone?"

A dead silence. They were facing the problem in their own unique ways. Wolfgang Pauli looked half-asleep, Thomas Edison was drawing little doll-figures on the table's surface, Enrico Fermi seemed to be counting on his fingers, and John von Neumann was staring impatiently at the other three. I was doing none of those things. I knew very well that wherever the solution would come from, it would not be from inside my head. My job was much more straightforward: I had to see that when we had a possible answer, it *happened*. And I had to see that we got *one* answer, not four.

The silence in the room went on and on. My brain trust was saying nothing, while I watched the digits on my watch flicker by. I had to stay and find a solution; and I had to get to the draft picks. But most of all and hardest of all, I had to remain quiet, to let my team do some thinking.

It was small consolation to know that similar meetings were being held within the offices of the other three combines. Everyone must be finding it equally hard going. I knew the players, and I could imagine the scenes, even though all the troubleshooting teams were different. NETSCO had a group that was intellectually the equal of ours at Romberg AG: Niels Bohr, Theodore von Karman, Norbert Weiner, and Marie Curie. MMG, the great Euro-Mexican combine of Magrit-Marcus Gesellschaft, had focused on engineering power rather than pure scientific understanding and creativity, and, in addition to the Soviet rocket designer Sergey Korolev and the American Nikola Tesla, they had reached farther back (and with more risk) to the great nineteenth-century English engineer Isambard Kingdom Brunel. He had been one of the outstanding successes of the program; I wished he were working with me, but MMG had always refused to look at a trade. MMG's one bow to theory was a strange one, the Indian mathematician Srinivasa Ramanujan, but the unlikely quartet made one hell of a team.

And finally there was BP Megation, whom I thought of as confused. At any rate, I didn't understand their selection logic. They had used billions of dollars to acquire a strangely mixed team: Erwin Schrödinger, David Hilbert, Leo Szilard, and Henry Ford. They were all great talents, and all famous names in their fields, but I wondered how well they could work as a unit.

All the troubleshooting teams were now pondering the same emergency. Our problem was created when the Pan-National Union suddenly announced a change to the Phase B demonstration program. They wanted to modify impact conditions, as their contracts with us permitted them to do. They didn't have to tell us how to do it, either, which was just as well for them, since I was sure they didn't know. How do you take a billion tons of mass, already launched to reach a specific target at a certain point of time, and redirect it to a different end point with a different arrival time?

There was no point in asking them *why* they wanted to change rendezvous conditions. It was their option. Some of our management saw the action on PNU's part as simple bloody-mindedness, but I couldn't agree. The four multinational combines had each been given contracts to perform the biggest space engineering exercise in human history: small asteroids (only a kilometer or so across—but massing a billion tons each) had to be picked up from their natural orbits and redirected to the Jovian system, where they were to make precise rendezvous with assigned locations of the moon Io. Each combine had to select the asteroid and the method of moving it, but deliver within a tight transfer-energy budget and a tight time schedule.

For that task the PNU would pay each group a total of $8 billion. That sounds like a fair amount of money, but I knew our accounting figures. To date, with the project still not finished (rendezvous would be in eight more days), Romberg AG had spent $14.5 billion. We were looking at a probable cost overrun by a factor of two. I was willing to bet that the other three groups were eating very similar losses.

Why?

Because this was only Phase B of a four-phase project. Phase A had been a system design study, which led to four Phase B awards for a demonstration project. The Phase B effort that the four combines were working on now was a proof-of-capability run for the full Europan Metamorphosis. The real money came in the future, in Phases C and D. Those would be awarded by the PNU to a single combine, and the award would be based largely on Phase B performance. The next phases called for the delivery of fifty asteroids to impact points on Europa (Phase C), followed by thermal mixing operations on the moon's surface (Phase D). The contract value of C and D would be somewhere up around $800 billion. That was the fish that all the combines were after, and it was the reason we would all overspend lavishly on this phase.

By the end of the whole program, Europa would have a forty-kilometer-deep water ocean over all its surface. And then the real fun would begin. Some contractor would begin the installation of the fusion plants, and the seeding of the sea-farms with the first prokaryotic bacterial forms.

The stakes were high; and to keep everybody on their toes, PNU did the right thing. They kept throwing in these little zingers, to mimic the thousand and one things that would go wrong in the final project phases.

While I was sitting and fidgeting, my team had gradually come to life. Fermi was pacing up and down the room—always a good sign; and Wolfgang Pauli was jabbing impatiently at the keys of a computer console. John von Neumann hadn't moved, but since he did everything in his head anyway, that didn't mean much.

I looked again at my watch. I had to go. "Ideas?" I said again.

Von Neumann made a swift chopping gesture of his hand. "We have to make a choice, Al. It can be done in four or five ways."

The others were nodding. "The problem is only one of efficiency and speed," added Fermi. "I can give you an order-of-magnitude estimate of the effects on the overall program within half an hour."

"Within fifteen minutes." Pauli raised the bidding.

"No need to compete this one." They were going to settle down to a real four-way fight on methods—they always did—but I didn't have the time to sit here and referee. The important point was that they said it could be done. "You don't have to rush it. Whatever you decide, it will have to wait until I get back." I stood up. "Tom?"

Edison shrugged. "How long will you be gone, Al?"

"Two days, maximum. I'll head back right after the draft picks." (That wasn't quite true; when the draft picks were over, I had some other business to attend to that did not include the troubleshooters; but two days should cover everything.)

"Have fun." Edison waved his hand casually. "By the time you get back, I'll have the engineering drawings for you."

One thing about working with a team like mine—they may not always be right, but they sure are always cocky.

* * *

"Make room there. Move over!" The guards were pushing ahead to create a narrow corridor through the wedged mass of people. The one in front of me was butting with his helmeted head, not even looking to see whom he was shoving aside. "Move!" he shouted. "Come on now, out of the way."

We were in a hurry. Things had been frantically busy Topside before I left, so I had cut it fine on connections to begin with, then been held up half an hour at reentry. We had broken the speed limits on the atmospheric segment, and there would be PNU fines for that, but still we hadn't managed to make up all the time. Now the first draft pick was only seconds away, and I was supposed to be taking part in it.

A thin woman in a green coat clutched at my arm as we bogged down for a moment in the crush of people. Her face was gray and grim, and she had a placard hanging round her neck. "You could wait longer for the copyright!" She had to shout to make herself heard. "It would cost you nothing—and look at the misery you would prevent. What you're doing is immoral! TEN MORE YEARS"

Her last words were a scream as she called out this year's slogan. TEN MORE YEARS! I shook my arm free as the guard in front of me made sudden headway, and dashed along in his wake. I had nothing to say to the woman; nothing that she would listen to. If it were immoral, what did ten more years have to do with it? Ten more years; if by some miracle they were granted ten more years on the copyrights, what then? I knew the answer. They would try to talk the Pan-National Union into fifteen more years, or perhaps twenty. When you pay somebody off, it only increases their demands. I know, only too well. They are never satisfied with what they get.

Joe Delacorte and I scurried into the main chamber and shuffled sideways to our seats at the last possible moment. All the preliminary nonsense was finished, and the real business was beginning. The tension in the room was terrific. To be honest, a lot of it was being generated by the media. They were all poised to make maximum noise as they shot the selection information all over the System. If it were not for the media, I don't think the PNU would hold live draft picks at all. We'd all hook in with video links and do our business the civilized way.

The excitement now was bogus for other reasons, too. The professionals —I and a few others—would not become interested until the ten rounds were complete. Before that, the choices were just too limited. Only when they were all made, and the video teams were gone, would the four groups get together off-camera and begin the horse trading. *My ninth round plus my fifth for your second." "Maybe, if you'll throw in $10 million and a tenth-round draft pick for next year. . . ."*

Meanwhile, BP Megation had taken the microphone. "First selection," said their representative. "Robert Oppenheimer."

I looked at Joe, and he shrugged. No surprise. Oppenheimer was the perfect choice—a brilliant scientist, but also practical, and willing to work with other people. He had died in 1967, so his original copyright had expired within the past twelve months. I knew his family had appealed for a copyright extension and been refused. Now BP Megation had sole single-copy rights for another lifetime.

"Trade?" whispered Joe.

I shook my head. We would have to beggar ourselves for next year's draft picks to make BP give up Oppenheimer. Other combine reps had apparently made the same decision. There was the clicking of data entry as the people around me updated portable databases. I did the same thing with a stub of pencil and a folded sheet of yellow paper, putting a check mark alongside his name. Oppenheimer was taken care of, I could forget that one. If by some miracle one of the four teams had overlooked some other top choice, I had to be ready to make an instant revision to my own selections.

"First selection, by NETSCO," said another voice. "Peter Joseph William Debye."

It was another natural choice. Debye had been a Nobel prizewinner in physics, a theoretician with an excellent grasp of applied technology. He had died in 1966. Nobel laureates in science, particularly ones with that practical streak, went fast. As soon as their copyrights expired, they would be picked up in the draft the same year.

That doesn't mean it always works out well. The most famous case, of course, was Albert Einstein. When his copyright had expired in 2030, BP Megation had had first choice in the draft pick. They had their doubts, and they must have sweated blood over their decision. The rumor mill said they spent over $70 million in simulations alone, before they decided to take him as their top choice. The same rumor mill said that the cloned form was now showing amazing ability in chess and music, but no interest at all in physics or mathematics. If that was true, BP Megation had dropped $2 billion down a black hole: $1 billion straight to the PNU for acquisition of copyright, and another $1 billion for the clone process. Theorists were always tricky; you could never tell how they would turn out.

Magrit-Marcus Gesellschaft had now made their first draft pick, and chosen another Nobel laureate, John Cockroft. He also had died in 1967. So far, every selection was completely predictable. The three combines were picking the famous scientists and engineers who had died in 1966 and 1967, and who were now, with the expiration of family retention of copyrights, available for cloning for the first time.

The combines were being logical, but it made for a very dull draft pick. Maybe it was time to change that. I stood up to announce our own first take.

"First selection, by Romberg AG," I said. "Charles Proteus Steinmetz."

My announcement caused a stir in the media. They had presumably never heard of Steinmetz, which was a disgraceful statement of their own ignorance.

Even if they hadn't spent most of the past year combing old files and records, as we had, they should have heard of him. He was one of the past century's most colorful and creative scientists, a man who had been physically handicapped (he was a hunchback), but mentally able to do the equivalent of a hundred one-hand push-ups without even breathing hard. Even I had heard of him, and you'd not find many of my colleagues who'd suggest I was interested in science.

The buzzing in the media told me they were consulting their own historical data files, digging farther back in time. Even when they had done all that, they would still not understand the first thing about the true process of clone selection. It's not just a question of knowing who died over seventy-five years ago, and will therefore be out of copyright. That's a trivial exercise, one that any yearbook will solve for you. You also have to evaluate other factors. Do you know where the body is—are you absolutely *sure*? Remember, you can't clone anyone with a cell or two from the original body. You also have to be certain that it's who you think it is. All bodies seventy-five years old tend to look the same. And then, if the body happens to be really old—say, more than a couple of centuries—there are other peculiar problems that are still not understood at all. When NETSCO pulled its coup a few years ago by cloning Gottfried Wilhelm Leibniz, the other three combines were envious at first. Leibniz was a real universal genius, a seventeenth-century superbrain who was good at everything. NETSCO had developed a better cell-growth technique, and they had also succeeded in locating the body of Leibniz in its undistinguished Hanover grave.

They walked tall for almost a year at NETSCO, until the clone came out of the forcing chambers for indoctrination. He looked nothing like the old portraits of Leibniz, and he could not grasp even the simplest abstract concepts. Oops! said the media. Wrong body.

But it wasn't as simple as that. The next year, MMG duplicated the NETSCO cell-growth technology and tried for Isaac Newton. In this case there was no doubt that they had the correct body, because it had lain undisturbed since 1727 beneath a prominent plaque in London's Westminster Abbey. The results were just as disappointing as they had been for Leibniz.

Now NETSCO and MMG have become very conservative; in my opinion, far too conservative. But since then, nobody has tried for a clone of anyone who died before 1850. The draft picking went on its thoughtful and generally cautious way, and was over in a couple of hours except for the delayed deals.

The same group of protesters was picketing the building when I left. I tried to walk quietly through them, but they must have seen my picture on one of the exterior screens showing the draft-pick process. I was buttonholed by a man in a red jumpsuit and the same thin woman in green, still carrying her placard.

"Could we speak with you for just one moment?" The man in red was very well-spoken and polite.

I hesitated, aware that news cameras were on us. "Very briefly. I'm trying to run a proof-of-concept project, you know."

"I know. Is it going well?" He was a different type from most of the demonstrators, cool and apparently intelligent. And therefore potentially more dangerous.

"I wish I could say yes," I said. "Actually, it's going rather badly. That's why I'm keen to get back out."

"I understand. All I wanted to ask you was why you—and I don't mean *you*, personally; I mean the combines—why do you find it *necessary* to use clones? You could do your work without them, couldn't you?"

I hesitated. "Let me put it this way. We could do the work without them, in just the same way as we could stumble along somehow if we were denied the use of computer power, or nuclear power. The projects would be possible, but they would be enormously more difficult. The clones augment our available brainpower, at the highest levels. So let me ask you: Why *should* we do without the clones, when they are available and useful?"

"Because of the families. You have no right to subject the families to the misery and upset of seeing their loved ones cloned, without their having any rights in the matter. It's cruel, and unnecessary. Can't you see that?"

"No, I can't. Now, you listen to me for a minute." The cameras were still on me. It was a chance to say something that could never be said often enough. "The family holds copyright for seventy-five years after a person's death. So if you, personally, *remember* your grandparent, you have to be pushing eighty years old—and it's obvious from looking at you that you're under forty. So ask yourself, Why are all you petitioners people who are in their thirties? It's not *you* who's feeling any misery."

"But there are relatives—," he said.

"Oh yes, the relatives. Are you a relative of somebody who has been cloned?"

"Not yet. But if this sort of thing goes on—"

"Listen to me for one more minute. A long time ago, there were a lot of people around who thought that it was wrong to let books with sex in them be sold to the general public. They petitioned to have the books banned. It wasn't that they claimed to be buying the books themselves, and finding them disgusting; because if they said that was the case, then people would have asked them *why* they were buying what they didn't like. Nobody was forcing anybody to buy those books. No, what the petitioners wanted was for *other* people to be stopped from buying what the *petitioners* didn't like. And you copyright-extension people are just the same. You are making a case on behalf of the relatives of the ones who are being cloned. But you never seem to ask yourself this: If cloning is so bad, why aren't the *descendants* of the clones the ones doing the complaining? They're not, you know. You never see them around here."

He shook his head. "Cloning is immoral!"

I sighed. Why bother? Not one word of what I'd said had got through to him. It didn't much matter—I'd really been speaking for the media, anyway—but it was a shame to see bigotry masquerading as public-spirited behavior. I'd seen enough of that already in my life.

I started to move off toward my waiting aircar. The lady in green clutched my arm again. "I'm going to leave instructions in my will that I want to be cremated. You'll never get me!"

You have my word on that, lady. But I didn't say it. I headed for the car, feeling an increasing urge to get back to the clean and rational regions of space. There was one good argument against cloning, and only one. It increased the total number of people, and to me that number already felt far too large.

I had been gone only thirty hours, total; but when I arrived back at Headquarters, I learned that in my absence five new problems had occurred. I scanned the written summary that Pauli had left behind.

First, one of the thirty-two booster engines set deep in the surface of the asteroid did not respond to telemetry requests for a status report. We had to assume it was defective, and eliminate it from the final firing pattern. Second, a big solar flare was on the way. There was nothing we could do about that, but it did mean we would have to recompute the strength of the magnetic and electric fields close to Io. They would change with the strength of the Jovian magnetosphere, and that was important because the troubleshooting team in my absence had agreed on their preferred solution to the problem of adjusting impact point and arrival time. It called for strong coupling between the asteroid and the 5-million-amp flux tube of current between Io and its parent planet, Jupiter, to modify the final collision trajectory.

Third, we had lost the image data stream from one of our observing satellites, in synchronous orbit with Io. Fourth, our billion-ton asteroid had been struck by a larger-than-usual micrometeorite. This one must have massed a couple of kilograms, and it had been moving fast. It had struck off-axis from the center of mass, and the whole asteroid was now showing a tendency to rotate slowly away from our preferred orientation. Fifth, and finally, a new volcano had become very active down on the surface of Io. It was spouting sulfur up for a couple of hundred kilometers, and obscuring the view of the final-impact landmark.

After I had read Pauli's terse analysis of all the problems—nobody I ever met or heard of could summarize as clearly and briefly as he did—I switched on my communications set and asked him the only question that mattered: "Can you handle them all?"

There was a delay of almost two minutes. The troubleshooters were heading out to join the rest of our project team for their on-the-spot analyses in the Jovian system; already the light-travel time was significant. If I didn't follow in the next day or two, radio-signal delay would make conversation impossible. At the moment, Jupiter was forty-five light-minutes from Earth.

"We can, Al," said Pauli's image at last. "Unless others come up in the next few hours, we can. From here until impact, we'll be working in an environment with increasing uncertainties."

"The PNU people planned it that way. Go ahead—but send me full transcripts." I left the system switched on, and went off to the next room to study the notes I had taken of the five problem areas. As I had done with every glitch that had come up since the Phase B demonstration project began, I placed the problem into one of two basic categories: act of nature, or failure of man-made element. For the most recent five difficulties, the volcano on Io and the solar flare belonged to the left-hand column: Category One, clearly natural and unpredictable events. The absence of booster-engine telemetry and the loss of satellite-image data were Category Two, failures of our system. They went in the right-hand column. I hesitated for a long time over the fifth event, the impact of the meteorite; finally, and with some misgivings, I assigned it also as a Category One event.

As soon as possible, I would like to follow the engineering teams out toward Jupiter for the final hours of the demonstration. However, I had two more duties to perform before I could leave. Using a coded link to Romberg AG HQ in synchronous Earth orbit, I queried the status of all the clone tanks. No anomalies were reported. By the time we returned from the final stages of Phase B, another three finished clones would be ready to move to the indoctrination facility. I needed to be there when it happened.

Next, I had to review and approve acquisition of single-use copyright for all the draft picks we had negotiated down on Earth. To give an idea of the importance of these choices, we were looking at an expenditure of $20 billion for those selections over the next twelve months. It raised the unavoidable question, Had we made the best choices?

At this stage of the game, *every* combine began to have second thoughts about the wisdom of their picks. All the old failures came crowding into your mind. I already mentioned NETSCO and their problem with Einstein, but we had had our full share at Romberg AG: Gregor Mendel, the originator of the genetic ideas that stood behind all the cloning efforts, had proved useless; so had Ernest Lawrence, inventor of the cyclotron, our second pick for 1958. We had (by blind luck!) traded him along with $40 million for Wolfgang Pauli. Even so, we had made a bad error of judgment, and the fact that others made the same mistake was no consolation. As for Marconi, even though he looked like the old pictures of him, and was obviously highly intelligent, the clone who emerged turned out to be so indolent and casual about everything that he ruined any project he worked on. I had placed him in a cushy and undemanding position and allowed him to fiddle about with his own interests, which were mainly sports and good-looking women. (As Pauli acidly remarked, "And you say that *we're* the smart ones, doing all the work?")

It's not the evaluation of a person's past record that's difficult, because we are talking about famous people who have done a great deal; written masses of books, articles, and papers; and been thoroughly evaluated by their own contemporaries. Even with all that, a big question still remains: Will the things that made the original man or woman great still be there in the cloned form? In other words, *Just what is it that is inherited?*

That's a very hard question to answer. The theory of evolution was proposed 170 years ago, but we're still fighting the old Nature-versus-Nurture battle. Is a human genius decided mainly by heredity, or by the way the person was raised? One old argument against cloning for genius was based on the importance of Nuture. It goes as follows: an individual is the product of both heredity (which is all you get in the clone) and environment. Since it is impossible to reproduce someone's environment, complete with parents, grandparents, friends, and teachers, you can't raise a clone that will be exactly like the original individual.

I'll buy that logic. We can't make ourselves an intellectually exact copy of anyone.

However, the argument was also used to prove that cloning for superior intellectual performance would be impossible. But of course, it actually proves nothing of the sort. If you take two peas from the same pod, and put one of them in deep soil next to a high wall, and the other in shallow soil out in the open, they *must* do different things if both are to thrive. The one next to the wall has to make sure it gets enough sunshine, which it can do by maximizing leaf area; the one in shallow soil has to get enough moisture, which it does through putting out more roots. The *superior* strain of peas is the one whose genetic composition allows it to adapt to whatever environment it is presented with.

People are not peas, but in one respect they are not very different from them: some have superior genetic composition to others. That's all you can ask for. If you clone someone from a century ago, the last thing you want is someone who is *identical* to the original. They would be stuck in a twentieth-century mind-set. What is needed is someone who can adapt to and thrive in *today's* environment—whether that is now the human equivalent of shade, or of shallow soil. The success of the original clone-template tells us a very important thing, that we are dealing with a superior physical brain. What that brain thinks is the year 2040 *should* be different from what it would have thought in the year 1940—otherwise the clone would be quite useless. And the criteria for "useless" change with time, too.

All these facts and a hundred others were running around inside my head as I reviewed the list for this year. Finally I made a note to suggest that J.B.S. Haldane, whom we had looked at and rejected three years ago on the grounds of unmanageability, ought to be looked at again and acquired if possible. History shows that he had wild views on politics and society, but there was no question at all about the quality of his mind. I thought I had learned a lot about interfacing with difficult scientific personalities in the past few years.

When I was satisfied with my final list, I transmitted everything to Joe Delacorte, who was still down on Earth, and headed for the transition room. A personal shipment pod ought to be waiting for me there. I hoped I would get a good one. At the very least, I'd be in it for the next eight days. Last time I went out to the Jovian system, the pod internal lighting and external antenna failed after three days. Have you ever sat in the dark for seventy-two hours, a hundred million miles from the nearest human, unable to send or receive messages? I didn't know if anyone realized I was in trouble. All I could do was sit tight—and I mean tight; pods are *small*—and stare out at the stars.

This time the pod was in good working order. I was able to participate in every problem that hit the project over the next four days. There were plenty of them, all small, and all significant. One of the fuel-supply ships lost a main ion drive. The supply ship was not much more than a vast bag of volatiles and a small engine, and it had almost no brain at all in its computer, not even enough to figure out an optimal use of its drives. We had to chase after and corral it as though we were pursuing a great lumbering elephant. Then three members of the impact-monitoring team came down with food poisoning—salmonella, which was almost certainly their own fault. You can say anything you like about throwing away spoiled food, but you can't get a sloppy crew to take much notice.

Then, for variety, we lost a sensor through sheer bad program design. In turning one of our imaging systems from star sensing to Io-Jupiter sensing, we tracked it right across the solar disk and burned out all the photocells. According to the engineers, that's the sort of blunder you don't make after kindergarten—but somebody did it.

Engineering errors are easy to correct. It was much trickier when one of the final-approach-coordination groups, a team of two men and one woman, chose the day before the Io rendezvous to have a violent sexual argument. They were millions of kilometers away from anyone, so there was not much we could do except talk to them. We did that, hoped they wouldn't kill each other, and made plans to do without their inputs if we had to.

Finally, one day before impact, an unplanned and anomalous firing of a rocket on the asteroid's forward surface caused a significant change of velocity of the whole body.

I ought to explain that I did little or nothing to solve any of these problems. I was too slow, too ignorant, and not creative enough. While I was still struggling to comprehend what the problem parameters were, my trouble-shooters were swarming all over it. They threw proposals and counterproposals at each other so fast that I could hardly note them, still less contribute to them. For example, in the case of the anomalous rocket firing that I mentioned, compensation for the unwanted thrust called for an elaborate balancing act of lateral and radial engines, rolling and nudging the asteroid back into its correct approach path. The team had mapped out the methods in minutes, written the necessary optimization programs in less than half an hour, and implemented their solution before I understood the geometry of what was going on.

So what did I do while all this was happening? I continued to make my two columns: act of nature, or failure of man-made element. The list was growing steadily, and I was spending a lot of time looking at it.

We were coming down to the final few hours now, and all the combines were working flat out to solve their own problems. In an engineering project of this size, many thousands of things could go wrong. We were working in extreme physical conditions, hundreds of millions of kilometers away from Earth and our standard test environments. In the intense charged-particle field near Io, cables broke at loads well below their rated capacities, hard-vacuum welds showed air-bleed effects, and lateral jets were fired and failed to produce the predicted attitude adjustments. And on top of all this, the pressure, isolation, and bizarre surroundings were too much for some of the workers. We had human failure to add to engineering failure. The test was tougher than anyone had realized—even PNU, who was supposed to make the demonstration project just this side of impossible.

I was watching the performance of the other three combines only a little less intently than I was watching our own. At five hours from contact time, NETSCO apparently suffered a communications loss with their asteroid-control system. Instead of heading for Io impact, the asteroid veered away, spiraling in toward the bulk of Jupiter itself.

BP Megation lost it at impact minus three hours, when a vast explosion on one of their asteroid forward boosters threw the kilometer-long body into a rapid tumble. Within an hour, by some miracle of improvisation, their engineering team had found a method of stabilizing the wobbling mass. But by then it was too late to return to nominal impact time and place. Their asteroid skimmed into the surface of Io an hour early, sending up a long, tear-shaped mass of ejecta from the moon's turbulent surface.

That left just two of us, MMG and Romberg AG. We both had our hands full. The Jovian system is filled with electrical, magnetic, and gravitational energies bigger than anything in the Solar System except the Sun itself. The two remaining combines were trying to steer their asteroid into a pinpoint landing through a great storm of interference that made every control command and every piece of incoming telemetry suspect. In the final hour I didn't even follow the exchanges between my troubleshooters. Oh, I could *hear* them easily enough. What I couldn't do was comprehend them, enough to know what was happening.

Pauli would toss a scrap of comment at von Neumann, and, while I was trying to understand that, von Neumann would have done an assessment, keyed in for a databank status report, gabbled a couple of questions to Fermi and an instruction to Edison, and at the same time be absorbing scribbled notes and diagrams from those two. I don't know if what they were doing was *potentially* intelligible to me or not; all I know is that they were going about fifty times too fast for me to follow. And it didn't much matter what I understood—they were getting the job done. I was still trying to divide all problems into my Category One–Category Two columns, but it got harder and harder.

In the final hour I didn't look or listen to what my own team was doing. We had one band of telemetry trained on the MMG project, and more and more that's where my attention was focused. I assumed they were having the same kind of communications trouble as we were—that crackling discharge field around Io made everything difficult. But their team was handling it. They were swinging smoothly into impact.

And then, with only ten minutes to go, the final small adjustment was made. It should have been a tiny nudge from the radial jets; enough to fine-tune the impact position a few hundred meters, and no more. Instead, there was a joyous roar of a radial jet at full, uncontrolled thrust. The MMG asteroid did nothing unusual for a few seconds (a billion tons is a lot of inertia), then began to drift lazily sideways, away from its nominal trajectory.

The jet was still firing. And that should have been impossible, because the first thing that the MMG team would do was send a POWER-OFF signal to the engine.

The time for impact came when the MMG asteroid was still a clear fifty kilometers out of position, and accelerating away. I saw the final collision, and the payload scraped along the surface of Io in a long, jagged scar that looked nothing at all like the neat, punched hole that we were supposed to achieve.

And we did achieve it, a few seconds later. Our asteroid came in exactly where and when it was supposed to, driving in exactly vertical to the surface. The plume of ejecta had hardly begun to rise from Io's red-and-yellow surface before von Neumann was pulling a bottle of bourbon from underneath the communications console.

I didn't object—I only wished I were there physically to share it, instead of being stuck in my own pod, short of rendezvous with our main ship. I looked at my final list, still somewhat incomplete. Was there a pattern to it? Ten minutes of analysis didn't show one. No one had tried anything—this time. Someday, and it might be tomorrow, somebody on another combine would have a bright idea; and then it would be a whole new ball game.

While I was still pondering my list, my control console began to buzz insistently. I switched it on expecting contact with my own trouble-shooting team. Instead, I saw the despondent face of Brunel, MMG's own team leader—the man above all others that I would have liked to work on my side.

He nodded at me when my picture appeared on his screen. He was smoking one of his powerful black cigars, stuck in the side of his mouth. The expression on his face was as impenetrable as ever. He never let his feelings show there. "I assume you saw it, did you?" he said around the cigar. "We're out of it. I just called to congratulate you—again."

"Yeah, I saw it. Tough luck. At least you came second."

"Which, as you know very well, is no better than coming last." He sighed and shook his head. "We still have no idea what happened. Looks like either a programming error, or a valve sticking open. We probably won't know for weeks. And I'm not sure I care."

I maintained a sympathetic silence.

"I sometimes think we should just give up, Al," he said. "I can beat those other turkeys, but I can't compete with you. That's six in a row that you've won. It's wearing me out. You've no idea how much frustration there is in that."

I had never known Brunel to reveal so much of his feelings before.

"I think I do understand your problems," I said.

And I did. I knew exactly how he felt—more than he would believe. To suffer through a whole, endless sequence of minor, niggling mishaps was heartbreaking. No single trouble was ever big enough for a trouble-shooting team to stop, isolate it, and be able to say, there's dirty work going on here. But their cumulative effect was another matter. One day it was a morass of shipments missing their correct flights, another time a couple of minus signs dropped into computer programs, or a key worker struck down for a few days by a random virus, permits misfiled, manifests mislaid, or licenses wrongly dated.

I knew all those mishaps personally. I should, because I invented most of them. I think of it as the death of a thousand cuts. No one can endure all that and still hope to win a Phase B study.

"How would you like to work on the Europan Metamorph?" I asked. "I think you'd love it."

He looked very thoughtful, and for the first time, I believe I could actually read his expression. "Leave MMG, you mean?" he said. "Maybe. I don't know what I want anymore. Let me think about it. I'd like to work with you, Al—you're a genius."

Brunel was wrong about that, of course. I'm certainly no genius. All I can do what I've always done—handle people, take care of unpleasant details (quietly!), and make sure things get done that need doing. And of course, do what I do best: make sure that some things that need doing *don't* get done.

There *are* geniuses in the world, real geniuses. Not me, though. The man who decided to clone me, secretly—*there* I'd suggest you have a genius.

"Say, don't you remember, they called me Al. . . ."

Of course, I don't remember. That song was written in the 1930s, and I didn't die until 1947, but no clone remembers anything of the forefather life. The fact that we tend to be knowledgeable about our originals' period is an expression of interest in those individuals, not memories from them. I know the Chicago of the Depression years intimately, as well as I know today; but it is all learned knowledge. I have no actual recollection of events. I don't *remember*.

So even if you don't remember, call me Al anyway. Everyone did.

MIKE RESNICK
For I Have Touched the Sky

Mike Resnick is one of the best-selling authors in science fiction, and one of the most prolific. His many novels include *The Dark Lady*, *Stalking the Unicorn*, *Paradise*, and *Santiago*. His recent novel *Ivory* was well-received and a new novel, *Second Contact*, has just been published. Last year, his story "Kirinyaga"—which was in our Sixth Annual Collection—won the Hugo Award, and was one of the year's most critically acclaimed, and controversial, stories. He lives with his family, a whole bunch of dogs—he and his wife run a kennel—and at least one computer in Cincinnati, Ohio.

Here he returns to the milieu of "Kirinyaga," an orbiting space colony that has been remade in the likeness of ancient Kenya, for another compelling tale of cultural conflict, and of the terrible price that must sometimes be paid by those who quest after knowledge.

▼

For I Have Touched the Sky

MIKE RESNICK

There was a time when men had wings.

Ngai, who sits alone on His throne atop Kirinyaga, which is now called Mount Kenya, gave men the gift of flight, so that they might reach the succulent fruits on the highest branches of the trees. But one man, a son of Gikuyu, who was himself the first man, saw the eagle and the vulture riding high upon the winds, and, spreading his wings, he joined them. He circled higher and higher, and soon he soared far above all other flying things.

Then, suddenly, the hand of Ngai reached out and grabbed the son of Gikuyu.

"What have I done that you should grab me thus?" asked the son of Gikuyu.

"I live atop Kirinyaga because it is the top of the world," answered Ngai, "and no one's head may be higher than my own."

And so saying, Ngai plucked the wings from the son of Gikuyu, and then took wings away from *all* men, so that no man could ever again rise higher than His head.

And that is why all of Gikuyu's descendents look at the birds with a sense of loss and envy, and why they no longer eat the succulent fruits from the highest branches of the trees.

We have many birds on the world of Kirinyaga, which was named for the holy mountain where Ngai dwells. We brought them along with our other animals when we received our charter from the Eutopian Council and departed from a Kenya that no longer had any meaning for true members of the Kikuyu tribe. Our new world is home to the marabou and the vulture, the ostrich and the fish eagle, the weaver and the heron, and many other species. Even I, Koriba, who am the *mundumugu*—the witch doctor— delight in their many colors, and find solace in their music. I have spent many afternoons seated in front of my *boma*, my back propped up against an ancient acacia tree, watching the profusion of colors and listening to the melodic songs as the birds come to slake their thirst in the river that winds through our village.

It was on one such afternoon that Kamari, a young girl who was not yet of circumcision age, walked up the long, winding path that separates my *boma* from the village, holding something small and gray in her hands.

"*Jambo*, Koriba," she greeted me.

"*Jambo*, Kamari," I answered her. "What have you brought to me, child?"

"This," she said, holding out a young pygmy falcon that struggled weakly to escape her grasp. "I found him in my family's *shamba*. He cannot fly."

"He looks fully fledged," I noted, getting to my feet. Then I saw that one of his wings was held at an awkward angle. "Ah!" I said. "He has broken his wing."

"Can you make him well, *mundumugu*?" asked Kamari.

I examined the wing briefly, while she held the young falcon's head away from me. Then I stepped back.

"I can make him well, Kamari," I said. "But I cannot make him fly. The wing will heal, but it will never be strong enough to bear his weight again. I think we will destroy him."

"No!" she exclaimed, pulling the falcon back. "You will make him live, and I will care for him!"

I stared at the bird for a moment, then shook my head. "He will not wish to live," I said at last.

"Why not?"

"Because he has ridden high upon the warm winds."

"I do not understand," said Kamari, frowning.

"Once a bird has touched the sky," I explained, "he can never be content to spend his days on the ground."

"I will *make* him content," she said with determination. "You will heal him, and I will care for him, and he will live."

"I will heal him, and you will care for him," I said. "But," I added, "he will not live."

"What is your fee, Koriba?" she asked, suddenly businesslike.

"I do not charge children," I answered. "I will visit your father tomorrow, and he will pay me."

She shook her head adamantly. "This is *my* bird. *I* will pay the fee."

"Very well," I said, admiring her spirit, for most children—and *all* adults—are terrified of their *mundumugu*, and would never openly contradict or disagree with him. "For one month you will clean my *boma* every morning and every afternoon. You will lay out my sleeping blankets, and keep my water gourd filled, and you will see that I have kindling for my fire."

"That is fair," she said after a moment's consideration. Then she added: "What if the bird dies before the month is over?"

"Then you will learn that a *mundumugu* knows more than a little Kikuyu girl," I said.

She set her jaw. "He will not die." She paused. "Will you fix his wing now?"

"Yes."

"I will help."

I shook my head. "You will build a cage in which to confine him, for if he tries to move his wing too soon, he will break it again, and then I will surely have to destroy him."

She handed the bird to me. "I will be back soon," she promised, racing off toward her *shamba*.

I took the falcon into my hut. He was too weak to struggle very much, and he allowed me to tie his beak shut. Then I began the slow task of splinting his broken wing and binding it against his body to keep it motionless. He shrieked in pain as I manipulated the bones together, but otherwise he simply stared unblinking at me, and within ten minutes the job was finished.

Kamari returned an hour later, holding a small wooden cage in her hands.

"Is this large enough, Koriba?" she asked.

I held it up and examined it.

"It is almost too large," I replied. "He must not be able to move his wing until it has healed."

"He won't," she promised. "I will watch him all day long, every day."

"You will watch him all day long, every day?" I repeated, amused.

"Yes."

"Then who will clean my hut and my *boma*, and who will fill my gourd with water?"

"I will carry his cage with me when I come," she replied.

"The cage will be much heavier when the bird is in it," I pointed out.

"When I am a woman, I will carry far heavier loads on my back, for I shall have to till the fields and gather the firewood for my husband's *boma*," she said. "This will be good practice." She paused. "Why do you smile at me, Koriba?"

"I am not used to being lectured to by uncircumcised children," I replied with a smile.

"I was not lecturing," she answered with dignity. "I was *explaining*."

I held a hand up to shade my eyes from the afternoon sun.

"Are you not afraid of me, little Kamari?" I asked.

"Why should I be?"

"Because I am the *mundumugu*."

"That just means you are smarter than the others," she said with a shrug. She threw a stone at a chicken that was approaching her cage, and it raced away, squawking its annoyance. "Someday I shall be as smart as you are."

"Oh?"

She nodded confidently. "Already I can count higher than my father, and I can remember many things."

"What kind of things?" I asked, turning slightly as a hot breeze blew a swirl of dust about us.

"Do you remember the story of the honey bird that you told to the children of the village before the long rains?"

I nodded.

"I can repeat it," she said.

"You mean you can remember it."

She shook her head vigorously. "I can repeat every word that you said."

I sat down and crossed my legs. "Let me hear it," I said, staring off into the distance and idly watching a pair of young men tending their cattle.

She hunched her shoulders, so that she would appear as bent with age as I myself am, and then, in a voice that sounded like a youthful replica of my own, she began to speak, mimicking my gestures.

"There is a little brown honey bird," she began. "He is much like a sparrow, and as friendly. He will come to your *boma* and call to you; and as you approach him, he will fly up and lead you to a hive, and then wait while you gather grass and set fire to it and smoke out the bees. But you must *always*"—she emphasized the word, just as I had done—"leave some honey for him, for if you take it all, the next time he will lead you into the jaws of *fisi*, the hyena, or perhaps into the desert, where there is no water and you will die of thirst." Her story finished, she stood upright and smiled at me. "You see?" she said proudly.

"I see," I said, brushing away a large fly that had lit on my cheek.

"Did I do it right?" she asked.

"You did it right."

She stared at me thoughtfully. "Perhaps when you die, I will become the *mundumugu.*"

"Do I seem that close to death?" I asked her.

"Well," she answered, "you are very old and bent and wrinkled, and you sleep too much. But I will be just as happy if you do not die right away."

"I shall try to make you just as happy," I said ironically. "Now take your falcon home."

I was about to instruct her concerning his needs, but she spoke first.

"He will not want to eat today. But starting tomorrow, I will give him large insects, and at least one lizard every day. And he must always have water."

"You are very observant, Kamari."

She smiled at me again, and then ran off toward her *boma.*

* * *

She was back at dawn the next morning, carrying the cage with her. She placed it in the shade, then filled a small container with water from one of my gourds and set it inside the cage.

"How is your bird this morning?" I asked, sitting close to my fire, for even though the planetary engineers of the Eutopian Council had given Kirinyaga a climate identical to Kenya's, the sun had not yet warmed the morning air.

Kamari frowned. "He has not eaten yet."

"He will, when he gets hungry enough," I said, pulling my blanket more tightly around my shoulders. "He is used to swooping down on his prey from the sky."

"He drinks his water, though," she noted.

"That is a good sign."

"Can you not cast a spell that will heal him at once?"

"The price would be too high," I said, for I had foreseen her question. "This way is better."

"How high?"

"*Too* high," I repeated, closing the subject. "Now, do you not have work to do?"

"Yes, Koriba."

She spent the next few minutes gathering kindling for my fire and filling my gourd from the river. Then she went into my hut to clean it and straighten my sleeping blankets. She emerged a moment later with a book in her hand.

"What is this, Koriba?" she asked.

"Who told you that you could touch your *mundumugu's* possessions?" I asked sternly.

"How can I clean them without touching them?" she replied with no show of fear. "What is it?"

"It is a book."

"What is a book, Koriba?"

"It is not for you to know," I said. "Put it back."

"Shall I tell you what I think it is?" she asked.

"Tell me," I said, curious to hear her answer.

"Do you know how you draw signs on the ground when you cast the bones to bring the rains? I think that a book is a collection of signs."

"You are a very bright little girl, Kamari."

"I *told* you that I was," she said, annoyed that I had not accepted her statement as a self-evident truth. She looked at the book for a moment, then held it up. "What do the signs mean?"

"Different things," I said.

"*What* things?"

"It is not necessary for the Kikuyu to know."

"But you know."

"I am the *mundumugu*."

"Can anyone else on Kirinyaga read the signs?"

"Your own chief, Koinnage, and two other chiefs can read the signs," I answered, sorry now that she had charmed me into this conversation, for I could foresee its direction.

"But you are all old men," she said. "You should teach me, so when you all die, someone can still read the signs."

"These signs are not important," I said. "They were created by the Europeans. The Kikuyu had no need for books before the Europeans came to Kenya; we have no need for them on Kirinyaga, which is our own world. When Koinnage and the other chiefs die, everything will be as it was long ago."

"Are they evil signs, then?" she asked.

"No," I said. "They are not evil. They just have no meaning for the Kikuyu. They are white man's signs."

She handed the book to me. "Would you read me one of the signs?"

"Why?"

"I am curious to know what kind of signs the white men made."

I stared at her for a long minute, trying to make up my mind. Finally I nodded my assent.

"Just this once," I said. "Never again."

"Just this once," she agreed.

I thumbed through the book, which was a Swahili translation of English poetry, selected one at random, and read it to her:

> *Live with me, and be my love,*
> *And we will all the pleasures prove*
> *That hills and valleys, dales and fields,*
> *And all the craggy mountains yields.*
> *There will we sit upon the rocks,*
> *And see the shepherds feed their flocks,*
> *By shallow rivers, by whose falls*
> *Melodious birds sing madrigals.*
> *There will I make thee a bed of roses,*
> *With a thousand fragrant posies,*
> *A cap of flowers, and a kirtle*
> *Embroider'd all with leaves of myrtle.*
> *A belt of straw and ivy buds,*
> *With coral clasps and amber studs;*
> *And if these pleasures may thee move,*
> *Then live with me and be my love.*

Kamari frowned. "I do not understand."

"I told you that you would not," I said. "Now put the book away and finish cleaning my hut. You must still work in your father's *shamba*, along with your duties here.'

She nodded and disappeared into my hut, only to burst forth excitedly a few minutes later.

"It is a *story*!" she exclaimed.

"What is?"

"The sign you read! I do not understand many of the words, but it is a story about a warrior who asks a maiden to marry him!" She paused. "*You* would tell it better, Koriba. The sign doesn't even mention *fisi*, the hyena, and *mamba*, the crocodile, who dwells by the river and would eat the warrior and his wife. Still, it is a story! I had thought it would be spell for *mundumugus*."

"You are very wise to know that it is a story," I said.

"Read another to me!' she said enthusiastically.

I shook my head. "Do you not remember our agreement? Just that once and never again."

She lowered her head in thought, then looked up brightly. "Then teach *me* to read the signs."

"That is against the law of the Kikuyu," I said. "No woman is permitted to read."

"Why?"

"It is a woman's duty to till the fields and pound the grain and make the fires and weave the fabrics and bear her husband's children," I answered.

"But I am not a woman," she pointed out. "I am just a little girl."

"But you will become a woman," I said, "and a woman may not read."

"Teach me now, and I will forget how when I become a woman."

"Does the eagle forget how to fly, or the hyena to kill?"

"It is not fair."

"No," I said. "But it is just."

"I do not understand."

"Then I will explain it to you," I said. "Sit down, Kamari."

She sat down on the dirt opposite me and leaned forward intently.

"Many years ago," I began, "the Kikuyu lived in the shadow of Kirinyaga, the mountain upon which Ngai dwells."

"I know," she said. "Then the Europeans came and built their cities."

"You are interrupting," I said.

"I am sorry, Koriba," she answered. "But I already know this story."

"You do not know all of it," I replied. "Before the Europeans came, we lived in harmony with the land. We tended our cattle and plowed our fields, and we produced just enough children to replace those who died of old age and disease, and those who died in our wars against the Maasai and the Wakamba and the Nandi. Our lives were simple but fulfilling."

"And *then* the Europeans came!" she said.

"Then the Europeans came," I agreed, "and they brought new ways with them."

"Evil ways."

I shook my head. "They were not evil ways for the Europeans," I replied. "I know, for I have studied in European schools. But they were not good ways for the Kikuyu and the Maasai and the Wakamba and the Embu and the Kisi and all the other tribes. We saw the clothes they wore and the buildings they erected and the machines they used, and we tried to become like Europeans. But we are not Europeans, and their ways are not our ways, and they do not work for us. Our cities became overcrowded and polluted, and our land grew barren, and our animals died, and our water became poisoned, and finally, when the Eutopian Council allowed us to move to the world of Kirinyaga, we left Kenya behind and came here to live according to the old ways, the ways that are good for the Kikuyu." I paused. "Long ago the Kikuyu had no written language, and did not know how to read, and since we are trying to create a Kikuyu world here on Kirinyaga, it is only fitting that our people do not learn to read or write."

"But what is good about not knowing how to read?" she asked. "Just because we didn't do it before the Europeans came doesn't make it bad."

"Reading will make you aware of other ways of thinking and living, and then you will be discontented with your life on Kirinyaga."

"But you read, and you are not discontented."

"I am the *mundumugu*," I said. "I am wise enough to know that what I read are lies."

"But lies are not always bad," she persisted. "You tell them all the time."

"The *mundumugu* does not lie to his people," I replied sternly.

"You call them stories, like the story of the lion and the hare, or the tale of how the rainbow came to be, but they are lies."

"They are parables," I said.

"What is a parable?"

"A type of story."

"Is it a true story?"

"In a way."

"If it is true in a way, then it is also a lie in a way, is it not?" she replied, and then continued before I could answer her. "And if I can listen to a lie, why can I not read one?"

"I have already explained it to you."

"It is not fair," she repeated.

"No," I agreed. "But it is true, and, in the long run, it is for the good of the Kikuyu."

"I still don't understand why it is good," she complained.

"Because we are all that remain. Once before, the Kikuyu tried to become something that they were not, and we became not city-dwelling Kikuyu, or bad Kikuyu, or unhappy Kikuyu, but an entirely new tribe called Kenyans.

Those of us who came to Kirinyaga came here to preserve the old ways—
and if women start reading, some of them will become discontented, and
they will leave, and then one day there will be no Kikuyu left."

"But I don't want to leave Kirinyaga!" she protested. "I want to become
circumsized, and bear many children for my husband, and till the fields of
his *shamba*, and someday be cared for by my grandchildren."

"That is the way you are supposed to feel."

"But I also want to read about other worlds and other times."

I shook my head. "No."

"But—"

"I will hear no more of this today," I said. "The sun grows high in the
sky, and you have not yet finished your tasks here, and you must still work
in your father's *shamba* and come back again this afternoon."

She rose without another word and went about her duties. When she
finished, she picked up the cage and began walking back to her *boma*.

I watched her walk away, then returned to my hut and activated my
computer to discuss a minor orbital adjustment with Maintenance, for it
had been hot and dry for almost a month. They gave their consent, and, a
few moments later, I walked down the long, winding path into the center
of the village. Lowering myself gently to the ground, I spread my pouchful
of bones and charms out before me and invoked Ngai to cool Kirinyaga with
a mild rain, which Maintenance had agreed to supply later in the afternoon.

Then the children gathered about me, as they always did when I came
down from my *boma* on the hill and entered the village.

"*Jambo*, Koriba!" they cried.

"*Jambo*, my brave young warriors," I replied, still seated on the ground.

"Why have you come to the village this morning, Koriba?" asked Ndemi,
the boldest of the young boys.

"I have come here to ask Ngai to water our fields with His tears of compassion," I said, "for we have had no rain this month, and the crops are
thirsty."

"Now that you have finished speaking to Ngai, will you tell us a story?"
asked Ndemi.

I looked up at the sun, estimating the time of day.

"I have time for just one," I replied. "Then I must walk through the fields
and place new charms on the scarecrows, that they may continue to protect
your crops."

"What story will you tell us, Koriba?" asked another of the boys.

I looked around, and saw that Kamari was standing among the girls.

"I think I shall tell you the story of the Leopard and the Shrike," I said.

"I have not heard that one before," said Ndemi.

"Am I such an old man that I have no new stories to tell?" I demanded,
and he dropped his gaze to the ground. I waited until I had everyone's
attention, and then I began:

"Once there was a very bright young shrike, and because he was very bright, he was always asking questions of his father.

" 'Why do we eat insects?' he asked one day.

" 'Because we are shrikes, and that is what shrikes do,' answered his father.

" 'But we are also birds,' said the shirke. "And do not birds such as the eagle eat fish?'

" 'Ngai did not mean for shrikes to eat fish,' said his father, 'and even if you were strong enough to catch and kill a fish, eating it would make you sick.'

" 'Have you ever eaten a fish?' asked the young shrike.

" 'No,' said his father.

" 'Then how do you know?' said the young shrike, and that afternoon he flew over the river and found a tiny fish. He caught it and ate it, and he was sick for a whole week.

" 'Have you learned your lesson now?' asked the shrike's father, when the young shrike was well again.

" 'I have learned not to eat fish,' said the shrike. 'But I have another question.'

" 'Why are shrikes the most cowardly of birds?' asked the shrike. 'Whenever the lion or the leopard appears, we flee to the highest branches of the trees and wait for them to go away.'

" 'Lions and leopards would eat us if they could,' said the shrike's father. 'Therefore, we must flee from them.'

" 'But they do not eat the ostrich, and the ostrich is a bird,' said the bright young shrike. 'If they attack the ostrich, he kills them with his kick.'

" 'You are not an ostrich,' said his father, tired of listening to him.

" 'But I am a bird, and the ostrich is a bird, and I will learn to kick as the ostrich kicks,' said the young shrike, and he spent the next week practicing kicking any insects and twigs that were in his way.

"Then one day he came across *chui*, the leopard, and as the leopard approached him, the bright young shrike did not fly to the highest branches of the tree, but bravely stood his ground.

" 'You have great courage to face me thus,' said the leopard.

" 'I am a very bright bird, and I am not afraid of you,' said the shrike. 'I have practiced kicking as the ostrich does, and if you come any closer, I will kick you and you will die.'

" 'I am an old leopard, and cannot hunt any longer,' said the leopard. 'I am ready to die. Come kick me, and put me out of my misery.'

"The young shrike walked up to the leopard and kicked him full in the face. The leopard simply laughed, opened his mouth, and swallowed the bright young shrike.

" 'What a silly bird,' laughed the leopard, 'to pretend to be something that he was not! If he had flown away like a shrike, I would have gone hungry today—but by trying to be what he was never meant to be, all he did was fill my stomach. I guess he was not a very bright bird, after all."

I stopped and stared straight at Kamari.

"Is that the end?" asked one of the other girls.

"That is the end," I said.

"Why did the shrike think he could be an ostrich?" asked one of the smaller boys.

"Perhaps Kamari can tell you," I said.

All the children turned to Kamari, who paused for a moment and then answered.

"There is a difference between wanting to be an ostrich, and wanting to know what an ostrich knows," she said, looking directly into my eyes. "It was not wrong for the shrike to want to know things. It was wrong for him to think he could become an ostrich."

There was a momentary silence while the children considered her answer.

"Is that true, Koriba?" asked Ndemi at last.

"No," I said, "for once the shrike knew what the ostrich knew, it forgot that it was a shrike. You must always remember who you are, and knowing too many things can make you forget."

"Will you tell us another story?" asked a young girl.

"Not this morning," I said, getting to my feet. "But when I come to the village tonight to drink *pombe* and watch the dancing, perhaps I will tell you the story about the bull elephant and the wise little Kikuyu boy. Now," I added, "do none of you have chores to do?"

The children dispersed, returning to their *shambas* and their cattle pastures, and I stopped by Juma's hut to give an ointment for his joints, which always bothered him just before it rained. I visited Koinnage and drank *pombe* with him, and then discussed the affairs of the village with the Council of Elders. Finally I returned to my own *boma*, for I always take a nap during the heat of the day, and the rain was not due for another few hours.

Kamari was there when I arrived. She had gathered more wood and water, and was filling the grain buckets for my goats as I entered my *boma*.

"How is your bird this afternoon?" I asked, looking at the pygmy falcon, whose cage had been carefully placed in the shade of my hut.

"He drinks, but he will not eat," she said in worried tones. "He spends all his time looking at the sky."

"There are things that are more important to him than eating," I said.

"I am finished now," she said. "May I go home, Koriba?"

I nodded, and she left as I was arranging my sleeping blanket inside my hut.

She came every morning and every afternoon for the next week. Then, on the eighth day, she announced with tears in her eyes that the pygmy falcon had died.

"I told you this would happen," I said gently. "Once a bird has ridden upon the winds, he cannot live on the ground."

"Do all birds die when they can no longer fly?" she asked.

"Most do," I said. "A few like the security of the cage, but most die of broken hearts, for, having touched the sky, they cannot bear to lose the gift of flight."

"Why do we make cages, then, if they do not make the birds feel better?"

"Because they make us feel better," I answered.

She paused, and then said: "I will keep my word and clean your hut and your *boma*, and fetch your water and kindling, even though the bird is dead."

I nodded. "That was our agreement," I said.

True to her word, she came back twice a day for the next three weeks. Then, at noon on the twenty-ninth day, after she had completed her morning chores and returned to her family's *shamba*, her father, Njoro, walked up the path to my *boma*.

"*Jambo*, Koriba," he greeted me, a worried expression on his face.

"*Jambo*, Njoro," I said without getting to my feet. "Why have you come to my *boma*?"

"I am a poor man, Koriba," he said, squatting down next to me. "I have only one wife, and she has produced no sons and only two daughters. I do not own as large a *shamba* as most men in the village, and the hyenas killed three of my cows this past year."

I could not understand his point, so I merely stared at him, waiting for him to continue.

"As poor as I am," he went on, "I took comfort in the thought that at least I would have the bride-prices from my two daughters in my old age." He paused. "I have been a good man, Koriba. Surely I deserve that much."

"I have not said otherwise," I replied.

"Then why are you training Kamari to be a *mundumugu*?" he demanded. "It is well known that the *mundumugu* never marries."

"Has Kamari told you that she is to become a *mundumugu*?" I asked.

He shook his head. "No. She does not speak to her mother or myself at all since she has been coming here to clean your *boma*."

"Then you are mistaken," I said. "No woman may be a *mundumugu*. What made you think that I am training her?"

He dug into the folds of his *kikoi* and withdrew a piece of cured wildebeest hide. Scrawled on it in charcoal was the following inscription:

> I AM KAMARI
> I AM TWELVE YEARS OLD
> I AM A GIRL

"This is writing," he said accusingly. "Women cannot write. Only the *mundumugu* and great chiefs like Koinnage can write."

"Leave this with me, Njoro," I said, taking the hide, "and send Kamari to my *boma*."

"I need her to work my *shamba* until afternoon."

"Now," I said.

He sighed and nodded. "I will send her, Koriba." He paused. "You are certain that she is not to be a *mundumugu?*"

"You have my word," I said, spitting on my hands to show my sincerity.

He seemed relieved, and went off to his *boma*. Kamari came up the path a few minutes later.

"*Jambo*, Koriba," she said.

"*Jambo*, Kamari," I replied. "I am very displeased with you."

"Did I not gather enough kindling this morning?" she asked.

"You gathered enough kindling."

"Were the gourds not filled with water?"

"The gourds were filled."

"Then what did I do wrong?" she asked, absently pushing one of my goats aside as it approached her.

"You broke your promise to me."

"That is not true," she said. "I have come every morning and every afternoon, even though the bird is dead."

"You promised not to look at another book," I said.

"I have not looked at another book since the day you told me that I was forbidden to."

"Then explain *this*," I said, holding up the hide with her writing on it.

"There is nothing to explain," she said with a shrug. "I wrote it."

"And if you have not looked at books, how did you learn to write?" I demanded.

"From your magic box," she said. "You never told me not to look at *it*."

"My magic box?" I said, frowning.

"The box that hums with life and has many colors."

"You mean my computer?" I said, surprised.

"Your magic box," she repeated.

"And it taught you how to read and write?"

"I taught me—but only a little," she said unhappily. "I am like the shrike in your story—I am not as bright as I thought. Reading and writing is very difficult."

"I told you that you must not learn to read," I said, resisting the urge to comment on her remarkable accomplishment, for she had clearly broken the law.

Kamari shook her head.

"You told me I must not look at your books," she replied stubbornly.

"I told you that women must not read," I said. "You have disobeyed me. For this, you must be punished." I paused. "You will continue your chores here for three more months, and you must bring me two hares and two rodents, which you must catch yourself. Do you understand?"

"I understand."

"Now come into my hut with me, that you may understand one thing more."

She followed me into the hut.

"Computer," I said. "Activate."

"Activated," said the computer's mechanical voice.

"Computer, scan the hut and tell me who is here with me."

The lens of the computer's sensors glowed briefly.

"The girl, Kamari wa Njoro, is here with you," replied the computer.

"Will you recognize her if you see her again?"

"Yes."

"This is a Priority Order," I said. "Never again may you converse with Kamari wa Njoro verbally or in any known language."

"Understood and logged," said the computer.

"Deactivate." I turned to Kamari. "Do you understand what I have done, Kamari?"

"Yes," she said, "and it is not fair. I did not disobey you."

"It is the law that women may not read," I said, "and you have broken it. You will not break it again. Now go back to your *shamba*."

She left, head held high, youthful back stiff with defiance, and I went about my duties, instructing the young boys on the decoration of their bodies for their forthcoming circumcision ceremony, casting a counter-spell for old Siboki (for he had found hyena dung within his *shamba*, which is one of the surest signs of a *thahu*, or curse), instructing Maintenance to make another minor orbital adjustment that would bring cooler weather to the western plains.

By the time I returned to my hut for my afternoon nap, Kamari had come and gone again, and everything was in order.

For the next two months, life in the village went its placid way. The crops were harvested, old Koinnage took another wife and we had a two-day festival with much dancing and *pombe*-drinking to celebrate the event, the short rains arrived on schedule, and three children were born to the village. Even the Eutopian Council, which had complained about our custom of leaving the old and the infirm out for the hyenas, left us completely alone. We found the lair of a family of hyenas and killed three whelps, then slew the mother when she returned. At each full moon, I slaughtered a cow—not merely a goat, but a large, fat cow—to thank Ngai for His generosity, for truly He had graced Kirinyaga with abundance.

During this period I rarely saw Kamari. She came in the mornings when I was in the village, casting bones to bring forth the weather, and she came in the afternoons when I was giving charms to the sick and conversing with the Elders—but I always knew she had been there, for my hut and my *boma* were immaculate, and I never lacked for water or kindling.

Then, on the afternoon after the second full moon, I returned to my *boma* after advising Koinnage about how he might best settle an argument over a disputed plot of land, and as I entered my hut, I noticed that the computer screen was alive and glowing, covered with strange symbols. When I had taken my degrees in England and America, I had learned English and French and Spanish, and of course I knew Kikuyu and Swahili, but these symbols represented no known language, nor, although they used numerals as well as letters and punctuation marks, were they mathematical formulas.

"Computer, I distinctly remember deactivating you this morning," I said, frowning. "Why does your screen glow with life?"

"Kamari activated me."

"And she forgot to deactivate you when she left?"

"That is correct."

"I thought as much," I said grimly. "Does she activate you every day?"

"Yes."

"Did I not give you a Priority Order never to communicate with her in any known language?" I said, puzzled.

"You did, Koriba."

"Can you then explain why you have disobeyed my directive?"

"I have not disobeyed your directive, Koriba," said the computer. "My programming makes me incapable of disobeying a Priority Order."

"Then what is this that I see upon your screen?"

"This is the Language of Kamari," replied the computer. "It is not among the 1,732 languages and dialects in my memory banks, and hence does not fall under the aegis of your directive."

"Did you create this language?"

"No, Koriba. Kamari created it."

"Did you assist her in any way?"

"No, Koriba, I did not."

"Is it a true language?" I asked. "Can you understand it?"

"It is a true language. I can understand it."

"If she were to ask you a question in the Language of Kamari, could you reply to it?"

"Yes, if the question were simple enough. It is a very limited language."

"And if that reply required you to translate the answer from a known language to the Language of Kamari, would doing so be contrary to my directives?"

"No, Koriba, it would not."

"Have you in fact answered questions put to you by Kamari?"

"Yes, Koriba, I have," replied the computer.

"I see," I said. "Stand by for a new directive."

"Waiting. . . ."

I lowered my head in thought, contemplating the problem. That Kamari was brilliant and gifted was obvious: she had not only taught herself to read and write, but had actually created a coherent and logical language that the computer could understand and in which it could respond. I had given orders, and without directly disobeying them, she had managed to circumvent them. She had no malice within her, and wanted only to learn, which in itself was an admirable goal. All that was on the one hand.

On the other was the threat to the social order we had labored so diligently to establish on Kirinyaga. Men and women knew their responsibilities and accepted them happily. Ngai had given the Maasai the spear, and He had given the Wakamba the arrow, and He had given the Europeans the machine and printing press; but to the Kikuyu, He had given the digging-stick and the fertile land surrounding the sacred fig tree on the slopes of Kirinyaga.

Once before we had lived in harmony with the land, many long years ago. Then had come the printed word. It turned us first into slaves, and then into Christians, and then into soldiers and factory workers and mechanics and politicians, into everything that the Kikuyu were never meant to be. It had happened before; it could happen again.

We had come to the world of Kirinyaga to create a perfect Kikuyu society, a Kikuyu Utopia: could one gifted little girl carry within her the seeds of our destruction? I could not be sure, but it was a fact that gifted children grew up. They became Jesus, and Mohammed, and Jomo Kenyatta—but they also became Tippoo Tib, the greatest slaver of all, and Idi Amin, butcher of his own people. Or, more often, they became Friedrich Nietzsche and Karl Marx, brilliant men in their own right, but who influenced less brilliant, less capable men. Did I have the right to stand aside and hope that her influence upon our society would be benign, when all history suggested that the opposite was more likely to be true?

My decision was painful, but it was not a difficult one.

"Computer," I said at last, "I have a new Priority Order that supersedes my previous directive. You are no longer allowed to communicate with Kamari under any circumstances whatsoever. Should she activate you, you are to tell her that Koriba has forbidden you to have any contact with her, and you are then to deactivate immediately. Do you understand?"

"Understood and logged."

"Good," I said. "Now deactivate."

When I returned from the village the next morning, I found my water gourds empty, my blankets unfolded, my *boma* filled with the dung of goats.

The *mundumugu* is all-powerful among the Kikuyu, but he is not without compassion. I decided to forgive this childish display of temper, and so I did not visit Kamari's father, nor did I tell the other children to avoid her.

She did not come again in the afternoon. I know, because I waited beside my hut to explain my decision to her. Finally, when twilight came, I sent for the boy, Ndemi, to fill my gourds and clean my *boma*, and although such chores are woman's work, he did not dare disobey his *mundumugu*, although his every gesture displayed contempt for the tasks I had set for him.

When two more days had passed with no sign of Kamari, I summoned Njoro, her father.

"Kamari has broken her word to me," I said when he arrived. "If she does not come to clean my *boma* this afternoon, I will be forced to place a *thahu* upon her."

He looked puzzled. "She says that you have already placed a curse on her, Koriba. I was going to ask you if we should turn her out of our *boma*."

I shook my head. "No," I said. "Do not turn her out of your *boma*. I have placed no *thahu* on her yet—but she must come to work this afternoon."

"I do not know if she is strong enough," said Njoro. "She has had neither food nor water for three days, and she sits motionless in my wife's hut." He paused. "*Someone* has placed a *thahu* on her. If it's not you, perhaps you can cast a spell to remove it."

"She has gone three days without eating or drinking?" I repeated.

He nodded.

"I will see her," I said, getting to my feet and following him down the winding path to the village. When we reached Njoro's *boma*, he led me to his wife's hut, then called Kamari's worried mother out and stood aside as I entered. Kamari sat at the farthest point from the door, her back propped against a wall, her knees drawn up to her chin, her arms encircling her thin legs.

"*Jambo*, Kamari," I said.

She stared at me but said nothing.

"Your mother worries for you, and your father tells me that you no longer eat or drink."

She made no answer.

"Listen to my words, Kamari," I said slowly. "I made my decision for the good of Kirinyaga, and I will not recant it. As a Kikuyu woman, you must live the life that has been ordained for you." I paused. "However, neither the Kikuyu nor the Eutopian Council are without compassion for the individual. Any member of our society may leave if he wishes. According to the charter we signed when we claimed this world, you need only walk to that area known as Haven, and a Maintenance ship will pick you up and transport you to the location of your choice."

"All I know is Kirinyaga," she said. "How am I to chose a new home if I am forbidden to learn about other places?"

"I do not know," I admitted.

"I don't *want* to leave Kirinyaga!" she continued. "This is my home. These are my people. I am a Kikuyu girl, not a Maasai girl or a European girl. I will bear my husband's children and till his *shamba*; I will gather his wood and cook his meals and weave his garments; I will leave my parents' *shamba* and live with my husband's family. I will do all this without complaint, Koriba, if you will just let me learn to read and write!"

"I cannot," I said sadly.

"But *why?*"

"Who is the wisest man you know, Kamari?" I asked.

"The *mundumugu* is always the wisest man in the village."

"Then you must trust to my wisdom."

"But I feel like the pygmy falcon," she said, her misery reflected in her voice. "He spent his life dreaming of soaring high upon the winds. I dream of seeing words upon the computer screen."

"You are not like the falcon at all," I said. "He was prevented from being what he was meant to be. You are prevented from being what you are not meant to be."

"You are not an evil man, Koriba," she said solemnly. "But you are wrong."

"If that is so, then I shall have to live with it," I said.

"But you are asking *me* to live with it," she said, "and that is your crime."

"If you call me a criminal again," I said sternly, for no one may speak thus to the *mundumugu*, "I shall surely place a *thahu* on you."

"What more can you do?" she said bitterly.

"I can turn you into a hyena, an unclean eater of human flesh who prowls only in the darkness. I can fill your belly with thorns, so that your every movement will be agony. I can—"

"You are just a man," she said wearily, "and you have already done your worst."

"I will hear no more of this," I said. "I order you to eat and drink what your mother brings to you, and I expect to see you at my *boma* this afternoon."

I walked out of the hut and told Kamari's mother to bring her banana mash and water, then stopped by old Benima's *shamba*. Buffalo had stampeded through his fields, destroying his crops, and I sacrificed a goat to remove the *thahu* that had fallen upon his land.

When I finished, I stopped at Koinnage's *boma*, where he offered me some freshly brewed *pombe* and began complaining about Kibo, his newest wife, who kept taking sides with Shumi, his second wife, against Wambu, his senior wife.

"You can always divorce her and return her to her family's *shamba*," I suggested.

"She cost twenty cows and five goats!" he complained. "Will her family return them?"

"No, they will not."

"Then I will not send her back."

"As you wish," I said with a shrug.

"Besides, she is very strong and very lovely," he continued. "I just wish she would stop fighting with Wambu."

"What do they fight about?" I asked.

"They fight about who will fetch the water, and who will mend my garments, and who will repair the thatch on my hut." He paused. "They even argue about whose hut I should visit at night, as if I had no choice in the matter."

"Do they ever fight about ideas?" I asked.

"Ideas?" he repeated blankly.

"Such as you might find in books."

He laughed. "They are *women*, Koriba. What need have they for ideas?" He paused. "In fact, what need have any of us for them?"

"I do not know," I said. "I was merely curious."

"You look disturbed," he noted.

"It must be the *pombe*," I said. "I am an old man, and perhaps it is too strong."

"That is because Kibo will not listen when Wambu tells her how to brew it. I really should send her away"—he looked at Kibo as she carried a load of wood on her strong, young back—"but she is so young and so lovely." Suddenly his gaze went beyond his newest wife to the village. "Ah!" he said. "I see that old Siboki has finally died."

"How do you know?" I asked.

He pointed to a thin column of smoke. "They are burning his hut."

I stared off in the direction he indicated. "That is not Siboki's hut," I said. "His *boma* is more to the west."

"Who else is old and infirm and due to die?" asked Koinnage.

And suddenly I knew, as surely as I knew that Ngai sits on His throne atop the holy mountain, that Kamari was dead.

I walked to Njoro's *shamba* as quickly as I could. When I arrived, Kamari's mother and sister and grandmother were already wailing the death chant, tears streaming down their faces.

"What happened?" I demanded, walking up to Njoro.

"Why do you ask, when it was you who destroyed her?" he replied bitterly.

"I did not destroy her," I said.

"Did you not threaten to place a *thahu* on her just this morning?" he persisted. "You did so, and now she is dead, and I have but one daughter to bring the bride-price, and I have had to burn Kamari's hut."

"Stop worrying about bride-prices and huts and tell me what happened, or you shall learn what it means to be cursed by a *mundumugu*!" I snapped.

"She hanged herself in her hut with a length of buffalo hide."

Five women from the neighboring *shamba* arrived and took up the death chant.

"She hanged herself in her hut?" I repeated.

He nodded. "She could at least have hanged herself from a tree, so that her hut would not be unclean and I would not have to burn it."

"Be quiet!" I said, trying to collect my thoughts.

"She was not a bad daughter," he continued. "Why did you curse her, Koriba?"

"I did not place a *thahu* upon her," I said, wondering if I spoke the truth. "I wished only to save her."

"Who has stronger medicine than you?" he asked fearfully.

"She broke the law of Ngai," I answered.

"And now Ngai has taken His vengeance!" moaned Njoro fearfully. "Which member of my family will He strike down next?"

"None of you," I said. "Only Kamari broke the law."

"I am a poor man," said Njoro cautiously, "even poorer now than before. How much must I pay you to ask Ngai to receive Kamari's spirit with compassion and forgiveness?"

"I will do that whether you pay me or not," I answered.

"You will not charge me?" he asked.

"I will not charge you."

"Thank you, Koriba!" he said fervently.

I stood and stared at the blazing hut, trying not to think of the smoldering body of the little girl inside it.

"Koriba?" said Njoro after a lengthy silence.

"What now?" I asked irritably.

"We do not know what to do with the buffalo hide, for it bore the mark of your *thahu*, and we were afraid to burn it. Now I know that the marks were made by Ngai and not you, and I am afraid even to touch it. Will you take it away?"

"What marks?" I said. "What are you talking about?"

He took me by the arm and led me around to the front of the burning hut. There, on the ground, some ten paces from the entrance, lay the strip of tanned hide with which Kamari had hanged herself, and scrawled upon it were more of the strange symbols I had seen on my computer screen three days earlier.

I reached down and picked up the hide, then turned to Njoro. "If indeed there is a curse on your shamba," I said, "I will remove it and take it upon myself, by taking Ngai's marks with me."

"Thank you, Koriba!" he said, obviously much relieved.

"I must leave to prepare my magic," I said abruptly, and began the long walk back to my *boma*. When I arrived, I took the strip of buffalo hide into my hut.

"Computer," I said. "Activate."

"Activated."

I held the strip up to its scanning lens.

"Do you recognize this language?" I asked.

The lens glowed briefly.

"Yes, Koriba. It is the Language of Kamari."

"What does it say?"

"It is a couplet:

> *I know why the caged birds die—*
> *For, like them, I have touched the sky.*"

The entire village came to Njoro's *shamba* in the afternoon, and the women wailed the death chant all night and all of the next day, but before long Kamari was forgotten, for life goes on, and she was, after all, just a little Kikuyu girl.

Since that day, whenever I have found a bird with a broken wing, I have attempted to nurse it back to health. It always dies, and I always bury it next to the mound of earth that marks where Kamari's hut had been.

It is on those days, when I place the birds in the ground, that I find myself thinking of her again, and wishing that I were just a simple man, tending my cattle and worrying about my crops and thinking the thoughts of simple men, rather than a *mundumugu* who must live with the consequences of his wisdom.

GREGORY BENFORD

Alphas

Gregory Benford is one of the modern giants of the field. His 1980 novel
Timescape won the Nebula Award, the John W. Campbell Memorial Award,
the British Science Fiction Association Award, and the Australian Ditmar
Award, and is widely considered to be one of the classic novels of the last
two decades. His other novels include *The Stars in Shroud*, *In the Ocean of
Night*, *Against Infinity*, *Artifact*, and *Across the Sea of Suns*. His most recent
novels are the best-selling *Great Sky River* and *Tides of Light*. Benford is a
professor of physics at the University of California at Irvine.

In the vivid and extraordinarily ingenious story that follows, he takes us
to Venus, and explores that mysterious planet more thoroughly than it has
ever been explored before: from one end to the other—quite literally.

▼
Alphas

GREGORY BENFORD

Chansing did not intend to become famous throughout the solar system. He was a private, close-lipped man, and he disliked media chatter about his sacrifice, his quickness, his daring.

Still less did he plan to be the butt of a thousand jokes. Or the central element in a standard examination question given to undergraduate physics majors.

But all this happened because of the Alphas.

The name stuck to humanity's first alien visitors, despite the fact that it merely referred to their direction of approach—Alpha Centauri. The Alphas did not come from Earth's nearest star, and indeed, no one ever did discover their origins.

Or much else. The Alphas simply decelerated into the solar system and began their tasks. They made no attempt to speak with the burgeoning human society of 2126 that was clinging to the asteroid belts and laboring on its first Mars colony.

This in itself was vaguely insulting. Matters got worse.

When a team of linguists did make rudimentary contact with the Alphas, they learned only that the aliens were not particularly interested in the heights of human culture, or in mankind's view of the meaning of it all, or the wondrous beauties of Earth.

The Alphas were here for a job, period. Their sole repeated message to mankind, delivered in English, Spanish, and Chinese, was:

> Stay back. Do not attempt to interfere. Our work will be of no harm to your enterprises.

One might think this would be clear and convincing. After all, the Alphas' first project was the clearing of the Venusian atmosphere—a task human engineers thought would take centuries. They did it inside eight months.

With a twist, however. The Alphas did not convert Venus into an Earth-like Eden. The atmosphere was still an unbreathable muck of muggy carbon dioxide and assorted noxious sulphuric winds.

But one could see through it. For the first time in four billion years the perpetual shroud parted. The great steepled volcanoes and yawning canyons of Venus lay bare.

The Alphas apparently wanted clear air in order to more easily build massive, sprawling complexes around both poles of the Venusian spin axis.

Earth ships hovered tens of millions of kilometers away, the closest the Alphas would permit anyone to approach. Their instruments showed that these Alpha polar stations produced enormous magnetic fields that oscillated fiercely.

More than this no one knew. Even the linguists had never actually seen an Alpha.

Unmanned ships sent to nose about the Venusian area came back as burnt crisps. One would have thought this was ample warning.

But when a secret government expedition sought out Chansing to pilot a high-tech, stealth-augmented mission into polar orbit around Venus, Chansing considered it carefully. He had always been a risk-taker; three high-velocity missions to the Jovian moons and multiple scars attested to that. He was the most famous daredevil in the system.

He also knew that if he turned this down, the government would go looking for somebody of lesser repute. And if that guy made it back from Venus, nobody would remember Chansing anymore.

Pursuit of fame was not the fulcrum of his character. Simple pride, calm and sure and laconic, accounted for nearly everything he did. Here was a gamble that could pay off far larger than any ore strike.

So he went. He had never had much of a head for science itself; few pilots did. Even though this was a scientific expedition, designed to ferret out the secrets of the Alphas, Chansing did not think he would need to know much more than how to dodge and swerve at high speeds.

This was only the first thing he was wrong about.

Matters went well at first. The expedition ship slipped into orbit under cover of an extensive solar storm, supported by an electromagnetic scrambling burst from the massed radio telescopes on Earth and the Moon.

But by then there was something else in orbit around Venus.

At first Chansing did not believe that the image floating in the large screen could be real.

"You check for malfs?" he asked Doyle, the ship's systems officer.

After a long moment she said, "Everything checks. That thing's real."

Chansing did not want to believe in the glowing circle that passed in a great arc through free space and then buried a ninth of its circumference in the planet. Without understanding it, he knew immediately that this was tech-work on a scale that made their mission look pitifully inadequate. And dangerous.

"Magnify," he ordered curtly. He knew not to show alarm. The scientists around him in the control vault were visibly shaken. They had been arrogant enough on the trip out, sure that their stealth shielding and projectors would work fine. Now their drawn mouths and hooded eyes told Chansing more than any tech-talk could about their chances.

The hoop was half again larger than Venus. Its uniform golden glow seemed to dim the sun's glare. The opticals zoomed in for a close-up. As the image swelled, Chansing expected to see detail emerge. But as the rim of Venus grew and flattened on the screen, the golden ring was no thicker than before, a brilliant hard line scratched across space.

Except where it struck the planet's surface. There a swirl of fitful radiance simmered. Chansing saw immediately that the sharp edges of the ring were cutting into the planet. Venus's thick blanket of air roiled and rushed about the ring's hard edge.

"Max mag," he said tensely. "Hold on the foot, where it's touching."

No, not touching, he saw. Cutting.

The blue-hot flashes that erupted at the hoop's foot point spoke of vast catastrophe. Clouds boiled like fountains. A green tornado swirled, its thick rotating disk rimmed by bruised clouds. At the vortex violence sputtered in angry red jets.

Yet even at this magnification the golden hoop was still a precise, scintillating line. It seemed absolutely straight on this scale, the only rigid geometry in a maelstrom of dark storms and rushing energies.

The physicists and astronomers gaped. He felt their presence at his back. The ship was cramped and they were always kibitzing.

"Give us some room," he said irritably, even though they were only peering through the rear hatch.

"It's moving," Doyle whispered, awed.

Chansing could barely make out the festering foot point as it carved its way through a towering mountain range. The knife-edge brilliance met a cliff of stone and seemed to simply slip through it. Puffs of gray smoke burst all along the cut. Winds sheared the smoke into strands. Then the hoop sliced through the peak of a high mountain, its rate not slowing at all.

He peered carefully through the storm. Actual devastation was slight; the constant cloudy agitation and winds gave the impression of fevered movement, but the cause of it all proceeded forward with serene indifference to obstacles.

"Back off," he said.

The screen pulled away from the impossibly sharp line. The hoop, no

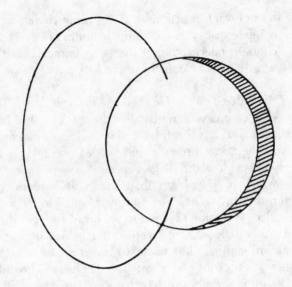

longer a perfect circle, pressed steadily in toward the axis of Venus. It flattened on the side that pushed inward.

"Lined up with the pole," Doyle said. "See? I've projected it onto the planet's image."

Computer-processed graphics coalesced. With clouds eliminated, he could see the entire structure.

The hoop's flat side was parallel to the axis of Venus's rotation. It held steady on the planet's surface, so it must be revolving at the same rate as the planet.

"Where'd it *come* from?" one of the physicists asked.

Chansing smothered the impulse to cackle with manic laughter. Somehow the Alphas had brought this thing, or made it, without anybody detecting it. A planet-sized surgical knife.

"Probably just wasn't lit up before," Doyle said reasonably. "Now that they're using it, we can see it."

Yet in a way his instincts warred with his intelligence. The hoop shared a planet's smooth curves, its size, its immense uncaring grace. Chansing struggled to conceive of it as something made by design. This was tech beyond imaging.

"It's moving toward the poles," Doyle said, her voice a smooth lake that showed no ripples. Chansing liked her nerve. If he ever settled down and had a wife, he knew it would be a woman like Doyle.

The scientists, though, muttered uneasily. Chansing had felt crews get jittery before and didn't like the sound of those amateurs.

"Let's get closer," said Eardley, a small woman nominally in charge of scientific matters. Chansing was supposed to follow her orders. But not if it endangered the ship.

"Don't think it's a good idea," he said.

"The closer we are to the planetary surface, the better we'll avoid infrared detection," Eardley said, reciting what everyone knew already. That was her style and Chansing had to make himself ignore it.

"Okay." He went through the motions of bringing them slightly closer in. They were still farther out than the strange luminous ring, and he was damned if he would go much nearer. He checked the stealth radiators that were supposed to hide them from the Alphas. Everything still looked good.

The hoop glowed brighter and flattened more and more as its inner edge approached the center of Venus. Chansing felt suspended, anxious, all his clever plans for this mission dashed to oblivion by this immense simple thing that sailed so blithely through a planet.

His imagination was numbed. He struggled to retain some grip on events by digressing into detail. "How . . . how thick is it?"

Doyle's glance told him that she had noticed the same strange lack of dimension. "Smaller than a ship, I'd judge," she said, her eyes narrowing.

"That small," Chansing said distantly, "but it's cutting through . . ."

Doyle said, "The planet doesn't split."

Chansing nodded. "Some places you can see where the thing's cut through rock and left a scar. But things close up behind it."

"Pressure seals the scar again," Doyle agreed. She smiled and Chansing recognized the look of almost sexual relish. She liked problems—real ones that you could get a grip on. So did he.

"It's no kind of knife I ever saw," Chansing said, the words out before he saw how useless they were. Doyle arched an eyebrow at him. But he had to say something and keep his voice calm and matter-of-fact; he could sense the scientists getting itchy at his back.

"If it eats rock, how come it's so thin?" he said with elaborate casualness. Somebody laughed merrily, and somehow the meaningless joke relaxed the small party.

This released the scientists, and a torrent of speculation broke among them. Chansing couldn't follow it. Instead, he consulted his chip-imbedded Advisor, a partial intelligence culled from a long-dead genius named Felix. The thin voice spoke in his mind.

I DO HAVE AN IDEA, IF YOU WOULD CARE TO HEAR.

Chansing caught the waspish, haughty air the Advisor sometimes projected when it had been consulted too infrequently for its own tastes. It rode in a small pocket in his lower neck. Perpetual monkey on his back, Chansing often said. He murmured a subvocal phrase to entice Felix to go on.

I BELIEVE IT TO BE WHAT WAS CALLED BY THEORETICIANS A COSMIC STRING. I HAVE STUDIED SUCH MATTERS IN MY YOUTH, AND RECALL THE PHYSICS UNDERLYING SUCH HYPOTHETICAL OBJECTS.

Chansing grimaced at the Advisor's supercilious tone, but again indicated his interest. He thought in a private cloister of his mind, *Advisors smell better if you give 'em some air*, and resolved to let Felix tap into his visual and other sensory webs more often. It kept them from getting the Advisor equivalent of cabin fever.

STRINGS WERE MADE AT THE VERY EARLIEST MOMENTS OF OUR UNIVERSE. YOU CAN ENVISION AT THAT TIME A COOLING, EXPANDING MASS. IT FAILED TO BE PERFECTLY SYMMETRICAL AND UNIFORM. SMALL FLUCTUATIONS PRODUCED DEFECTS IN THE VACUUM STATE OF CERTAIN ELEMENTARY PARTICLES—

What the hell's that mean? Chansing thought irritably. He watched the hoop slowly cut through a slate-gray plain. Around him tech-chatter filled the control vault. Scientists needed only the tip of an iceberg to start them endlessly guessing.

A GOOD ANALOGY. THINK OF ICE FREEZING ON THE SURFACE OF A POND. AS IT FORMS, THERE IS NOT QUITE ENOUGH AREA, PERHAPS, AND SO SMALL CRINKLES AND OVERLAPS APPEAR. RIDGES OF DENSER ICE MARK THE BOUNDARY BETWEEN REGIONS THAT DID MANAGE TO FREEZE OUT SMOOTHLY. ALL THE ERRORS, SO TO SPEAK, ARE SQUEEZED INTO A SMALL PERIMETER. SO IT WAS WITH THE EARLY UNIVERSE. THESE EXOTIC RELICS HAVE MASS, BUT THEY ARE HELD TOGETHER PRIMARILY BY TENSION. THEY ARE LIKE CABLES WOVEN OF WARPED SPACE-TIME ITSELF.

So what?

WELL, THEY ARE EXTRAORDINARY OBJECTS, WORTHY OF AWE IN THEIR OWN RIGHT. ALONG THEIR LENGTHS THERE IS NO IMPEDIMENT TO MOTION. THIS MAKES THEM SUPERCONDUCTORS, SO THEY RESPOND STRONGLY TO MAGNETIC FIELDS. AS WELL, THEY EXERT TIDAL FORCES. ONLY OVER A SHORT RANGE, HOWEVER—A FEW METERS. I SHOULD IMAGINE THAT THIS TIDAL STRETCHING ALLOWS IT TO EXERT PRESSURES AGAINST SOLID MATERIAL AND CUT THROUGH IT.

Like a knife?

YES. THE BEST KNIFE IS THE SHARPEST, AND COSMIC STRINGS ARE THINNER THAN A SINGLE ATOM. THEY CAN SLIDE BETWEEN MOLECULAR BONDS.

So why's this one cutting through Venus? It just fall in by accident?

I SINCERELY DOUBT THAT SUCH A VALUABLE OBJECT WOULD BE SIMPLY WANDERING AROUND. THE ALPHAS ARE SOPHISTICATED ENOUGH TO UNDERSTAND THEIR USES.

Using it? For what?

THAT I DO NOT KNOW. I WOULD IMAGINE HANDLING SUCH A MASS IS A SEVERE TECHNICAL DIFFICULTY. SINCE IT IS A PERFECT SUPER-CONDUCTOR, HOLDING IT IN A MAGNETIC GRIP SUGGESTS ITSELF. THUS THE ALPHAS' POLAR STATIONS.

Chansing recognized Felix's usual pattern—explain, predict, then pretend haughty withdrawal until Chansing or somebody else could check the Advisor's prediction. He shrugged. The idea sounded crazy, but it was worth following up.

To Doyle he said, "Analyze the magnetic fields near that thing."

Doyle quickly nodded. "I'm getting something else, too."

"Where?"

"Coming up from near the south pole. A lot of fast signals—"

"What kind?"

"Like a ship."

"Alphas." It was not a question.

"Looks like."

Chansing peered at the screen. The glorious squashed circle had cut slightly farther into the planet. It was still aligned with its flattened face parallel to the rotation. He estimated the inner edge would not reach the planet's axis for several more hours at least. As it intruded farther, the hoop had to cut through more and more rock, which probably slowed its progress.

Doyle shifted the view, searching the southern polar region. A white dab of light was growing swiftly, coming toward them. It was a dim fleck compared with the brilliant cosmic string.

"Better get us buttoned up," Chansing said.

The scientists had fallen silent. The crew left hurriedly, each taking a last glance at the screen where two mysteries of vastly different order hung, luminous and threatening.

They ran, but they had no real chance. Five Alpha ships moved fast and hard, their ships taking accelerations beyond human pilots.

The scientists moaned and grunted in their harnesses as the high g's came on them. They wanted to know how things were going and got irritated when Chansing didn't answer. He wondered if they wanted a pep talk while he was trying to move fast and yet stay electromagnetically invisible. He finally had Doyle calm them down.

Not that it mattered. When the end was obvious, Chansing deployed their last hope of escaping detection: three blinding antennas mounted on the ship's hull. When the Alpha ship was close enough, he had a few tricks. Until then he simply held to their uniform electromagnetic blackout.

He was working on the hull when a signal came on comm from Doyle. "Something's happening with the hoop."

Chansing quickly made his way inside. The scientists were already devising new ideas to check, and some of them tried to tell him about it, but he brushed them off.

The vision that confronted him in the cool geometries of the control vault was mystifying. The hoop had nearly reached the polar axis, he saw. But it was not moving inward now. Instead, it seemed to turn as he watched. Its inward edge, razor-sharp and now ruler-straight, was cutting around the planet's axis of rotation. One screen gave a simulation, the hoop spinning about its flat edge.

"It slowed its approach to the axis," Doyle said. "When it got there, it started this revolving."

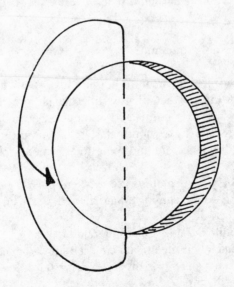

"Looks like it's getting faster," Chansing said.

"Yes. The magnetic fields are stronger now, too."

"Look, it's slicing around the axis."

"Like cutting the core from an apple."

"Revolving—"

"And picking up speed."

As he watched, the hoop revolved completely around the axis of Venus. The golden glow brightened further as if the thing was gaining energy.

"Pretty damn fast," Chansing said uselessly, wrestling to see what purpose such gigantic movements could have. His mind skipped and jangled with agitated awe. Chansing grimaced.

The hoop's inner edge was not exactly along Venus's axis. Instead, it seemed to stand a tiny fraction out from the line around which the planet itself spun. Chansing watched it revolve with ever-gathering speed. The hoop seemed like a part in some colossal engine, spinning to unknown purpose. It glowed with a high, prickly sheen as fresh impulses shot through it— amber, frosted blue, burnt orange—all smearing and thinning into the rich, brimming honey gold.

"I'm picking up a high whirring in the magnetic fields."

THAT IS THE INDUCTIVE SIGNAL FROM THE COSMIC STRING'S REVO-LUTION. IT IS ACTING LIKE A COIL OF WIRE IN A GIANT MOTOR.

"What *for?*" Chansing demanded, his throat tight. Without ever having set foot on it, he felt that Venus was somehow *his*, humanity's—and damned well not some plaything in a grotesquely gargantuan engine.

I CANNOT UNDERSTAND. CLEARLY, IT MOVES TO THE BECKON OF SOME UNSEEN HAND. STRINGS ARE SUPPOSED TO BE QUITE RARE, AND SHOULD MOVE AT VERY NEAR THE SPEED OF LIGHT. IF ONE WANDERED INTO THE GALAXY, IT MIGHT WELL COLLIDE WITH STARS AND MOLEC-ULAR CLOUDS. THAT WOULD SLOW IT. PERHAPS THIS ONE DID, AND SOMEHOW THE ALPHAS CAPTURED IT IN A TRAP OF MAGNETIC FIELDS. A SUPREMELY DIFFICULT TASK, OF COURSE, BEYOND THE SCOPE OF THINGS HUMAN—BUT NOT, IN PRINCIPLE, IMPOSSIBLE. IT MERELY DE-MANDS THE MANIPULATION OF MAGNETIC FIELD GRADIENTS ON A SCALE UNKNOWN—

"What's your point?" Chansing demanded. Though the Advisor-talk streamed through his mind with blinding speed, he had no patience for the smug, arched-eyebrow tone of Felix's little lectures.

> SIMPLY THAT THE COSMIC STRING IS CLEARLY EMPLOYED HERE IN
> SOME SORT OF CIVIL ENGINEERING SENSE. DOYLE DETECTS THE IN-
> DUCTIVE FIELDS FROM ITS REVOLVING, BUT SURELY THIS CANNOT BE
> THE PURPOSE. NO, IT IS A SIDE EFFECT. NOTE HOW THE STRAIGHT
> INNER EDGE OF THE CIRCLE STOPS SHORT OF EXACTLY LYING ALONG
> THE PLANET'S AXIS. THIS CANNOT BE A MISTAKE, NOT WITH ENGINEERS
> OF THIS ABILITY. CLEARLY, THE OFFSET IS INTENDED.

The hoop revolved faster and faster. Through Doyle's comm line he could
hear the distant *whump-whump-whump* of magnetic detectors in the control
vault.

"A giant engine? What for?" Chansing persisted.

> THE REGION NEAR THE POLE IS THE MOST AFFECTED, I WOULD
> VENTURE. THIS QUICK REVOLUTION EVOKES A PRESSURE ALL AROUND
> THE POLAR AXIS. THE FASTER THE STRING REVOLVES, THE MORE
> SMOOTH IS THIS PRESSURE. IT SLICES FREE THE ROCK CLOSE TO THE
> AXIS. THIS LIBERATES THE INNER CORE CYLINDER IT HAS CARVED AWAY,
> FREES THE ROCK. THE RESULTS OF THIS I CANNOT SEE, HOWEVER.

"Humph!" Chansing snorted in exasperation. "Let me know when you
have an idea."

They did not have long to wait. The Alphas were more than an hour from
rendezvous when the central axis tube, formed by the revolving cosmic string,
pulsed with fresh brilliance.

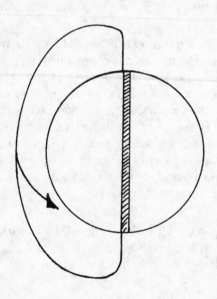

Chansing listened to the scientists and got some idea of what might be happening. Still, even though he could see it, the truth was hard to believe. He stared at the four-color simulation.

The liquid oozing of rock far below, at the planetary core, pressed hard against the beating *ssstttttppp-ssstttttppp-ssstttttppp* of the revolving, scintillant hoop. In one revolution the white-hot nickel-iron liquid at the core flowed into the depressurized cylinder. Then the passing hoop chopped it off, liberating it from the pressure of fluid behind it. The pipe was filling.

The whirring hoop formed a blurred donut envelope around Venus, moving with the mad buzzing frenzy of a huge insect. Now the flux tube hummed with new life deep in the rock of Venus. The tube walls kept back the pressing solid rock on all sides—except at the core, where immense pressures forced more metal into the tube with each revolution.

Vast stresses fought along the tube walls. The strumming tube gnawed, burning a cylinder of stone free of its mother world. Liberated pressures pushed the freed rock upward from below. The axial flux tube filled.

Then its pearly, transparent walls of force dulled to gray. A plug of rock was streaming out.

The golden lance had now struck a tube into the center of this world, to its treasure. The tube throat was artfully shaped, fattening slightly as the white-hot metal funneled up from the core. The gusher flowed without restraint or turbulence, molten metal rushing from the vast core pressure to the void of space. The riches squirted up and out, fleeing the groaning weight of Venus.

Delicate streamers of green and amber danced amid the white torrent of metal—the only horde this planet boasted. The tube sucked this treasure above the blanket of gas.

Doyle made their view tilt, following a black fleck of impurity up the glowing pipeline, starward, into sucking void, high beyond air's clutching. There, flexing magnetic fields peeled away streamers, finding orbits for the molten pap. The yellowing, shuddering fluid, free of gravity's strangle, shot out into the chill. Returned to the spaces it once knew, the metal cold-formed, mottled, its skin crusted with impurities. The birthing thread creaked and groaned in places as it unspooled. It fractured in spots, yet kept smoothly gliding along its gentle orbit.

Cooling, it grayed. Graying, threads formed into enormous webbed structures.

"They're . . . making a home," Chansing said hollowly.

"Sucking a whole planet dry," one of the scientists said. "No wonder they ignore us."

He found Doyle gazing at him raptly. Did she think he had a solution? Then he saw that she was simply sharing what both of them knew. They were competent and quick, but there were limits, and they were about to meet them.

He didn't trust anyone in the slim crew to handle their last-ditch blinding cannons. The bulky antennas were electromagnetically isolated from the rest of the ship, and they had to be commanded from someone directly on the hull.

So he did it himself. It meant delegating his primary responsibility of piloting—but there was going to be damn little of that to do unless they managed to fool the Alphas.

Chansing got himself into the command brace just as the Alpha craft began decelerating. Venus lay close below, beneath the shimmering whirl of the golden cosmic string.

He didn't have much experience with the gear, but then nobody did. This was black-tech stuff, secret stickers all over it.

But he had used similar, less powerful rigs in the asteroids to escape government regulators. He cross-correlated the dishes and waited. There wasn't long. Of the original five Alpha ships sent to intercept the Earth expedition team, only one craft came forward like a hornet, and when it was a few hundred kilometers out, Chansing fired his first concealing burst.

The tangle of electromagnetic fields was supposed to confuse and blind the very best microwave detectors, and elude other frequencies altogether.

Chansing never got a second shot.

He had only an instant before a violent *whoosh* drew him head-first out of his brace. He realized the air lock had fractured.

He windmilled his arms in the rushing air, whirling away from the shining skin of the ship. Tumbling. Spinning.

Small cries sought him. Screams. They were dying back in the ship.

Everyone had worn helmets, that was standard. But the Alphas had used something special. The bulkheads crackled with electrical surges. Lightning sought and fried the slow, vulnerable humans.

Chansing heard them die, horrible gasping pain forcing shrill pleas from their throats.

And time slowed for him. One of the attributes of a first-class pilot is the almost languorous extension of events in a crisis. For Chansing, all motion became silky, sure, with infinite time to consider possibilities. But no time to mourn those he could do nothing to help any longer. He found that the only one whose face came to his was Doyle. Then he carefully put the image aside.

He vectored hard to correct his plunge, and the jumble of impressions began to make sense. He hung above the dayside of Venus, near the north pole. Far below, the ruddy twilight stretched shadows of mountains across the beaten gray plains. All this lay behind the incandescent golden aura left by the cosmic string as it spun with endless energy. One edge of it arrowed straight down along the pole, impossibly straight. The other side bulged out far beyond the planet's equator.

The hoop spun faster than the eye could follow, making a hovering tapestry diffused over the entire world. Chansing could see no gray jet of matter spewing up along the polar axis. When the outflowing cylinders of yellow metal-lava struck the sucking vacuum in orbit, the glare and exploding fog were obvious, serving to obscure what fervid process was at work there.

Now he was going to get a close look. He was nearly over the pole, and far away, nearly over the soft curve of the world, hung vast gray warrens.

This he took in with the barest glance, unable to react, because something came looming into his view, swelling with the speed of its approach.

His own ship floated like a helpless insect beside a predatory bird as the Alpha craft slowed and stopped. The comparison came to Chansing because of both size and a certain tantalizing, evocative sweep of the larger ship's lines. It had flared wings made of intricate intersecting hexagons, as though spun out from a single thread. Its forward hull bulged like a gouty throat, while the blackened thrusters at its rear puckered wide. While the Earth ship expressed mechanical rigidities, this huge craft seemed sculpted by minds expressing body symmetries and senses beyond his fathoming.

Speculation ceased. Something big rushed forth from a darkened oval hole in the craft's side, moving far swifter than a human could. It headed for him.

Chansing turned immediately and sped away. There was nowhere to go, but he was damned if he would wait to be caught. His turn brought into view the pole again, and the golden glow of the spinning hoop below. From this angle the shimmering covered the whole of Venus, a vast radiance beyond the puny concerns of a single fleeing man.

Chansing tried to angle away from the onrushing form and gain the small shelter of his own ship. But a quick glance behind him showed that the alien object was closing fast. He veered sideways once, then again, darting furiously in hopes that the oncoming thing could not match him. But at each turn it was closer, following him with almost contemptuous ease. It loomed so large now Chansing could see large straight sections of bossed metal, studded with protuberances. Between the riveted metal sections was a rough, crusted stuff that seemed to flex and work with effort.

He realized abruptly that the thing was *alive*, that muscles rippled through it. Six sheathed legs curled beneath it, ending in huge claws.

The head—Chansing saw eyes, more than he could count, moving independently on stalks. But beside them microwave dishes rotated. Above, telescoping arms socketed in shiny steel. They opened into many-grappling arrays of counter-posed pads.

The thing was at least ten times the size of a human. A bulging throat throbbed beneath stiff crusted gray-green skin. Its rear quarters were swollen as though thruster tubes lodged there. Yet they were also banded with alternating yellow-brown rings, like the markings of a living creature. Chansing was the first human to see an Alpha, and for an instant he was lost in curiosity. This was all he could think before the gaping pads spread farther to clasp him in a rough but sure embrace.

The thing brought him up toward its moving eye array. It studied him for a long moment. Chansing was so rapt upon the oval-shaped orange eyes that only after a while did he notice the steady tug of acceleration. The thing was carrying him, not back to its ship, but toward the pole. It tossed him from one oval array of pads to another, letting him tumble for seconds in space before snagging him again.

LIKE A CAT PLAYING WITH A MOUSE.

his Felix Advisor had said mournfully.

Chansing's mind whirled, empty of terror and rage. He felt only a distant, painful remorse at all he was about to leave behind—laughter, silky love, a friend's broad unthinking grin, the whole warm clasp of the humanity he had failed, and would now die for in a meaningless sacrifice to something beyond human experience.

He tried to wrench away from the coarse black pads, but they seemed to be everywhere. They pushed and caught him, in the growing golden glow that now suffused everything.

Then he came to rest in a thick knot of pads. They pressed against him so that he could not jerk away.

He wondered abstractly how the thing would kill him. A crushing grasp, or legs pulled off, or electrocution . . .

A rage came into him, then, and he tried to kick against the thing. He got a knee up into it and pushed, struck sidewise with his arms—

—and was free. Impossibly, he glided away at high speed from the long pocked form of worked steel and wrinkled brown flesh. It did not follow.

He spun to get his bearings and saw nothing but a hard glow. He was close to the hoop. No, not merely close—it surrounded him.

Chansing looked behind him. Above him hung the fast-shrinking alien. The thing now lay at the end of a glowing tube that stretched . . . stretched and narrowed around him as Chansing watched.

He was speeding along the planetary axis, down the throat of the pipe made by the whirring hoop. Shimmering radiance closed in on him.

He righted himself and fired jets. The alien had given him a high velocity straight down into the hoop tube. Plunging along the polar axis. If he could correct for it in time—

But the brilliant walls drew nearer. He applied maximum thrust to stop himself, even though that meant his fuel would burn less efficiently. His insuit thrusters were small, weak, intended only for maneuvers in free fall.

The alien had so carefully applied accelerations that Chansing did not veer sidewise against the looming hoop walls. He was plunging precisely toward the pole of Venus. Through the shimmering translucent walls he could see a dim outline of Venus, as ghostly as a lost dream.

His thrusters chugged, ran smoothly for a moment, and then coughed and died. He fell in sudden eerie silence.

He had been simpleminded, thinking that the alien anthology of flesh and steel would kill him in some obvious way. Instead, from some great and twisted motive, it had given him this strange trajectory into the mouth of a huge engine of destruction.

At any moment, he supposed, the tube would vent more liquid metal outward. In an instant Chansing would vanish into singed smoke.

Vainly, he tried his sensorium. No human tracers beckoned. He grimaced, his breath coming rapidly in the sweat-fogged helmet.

The shimmering walls drew closer. He almost felt that he could touch them, but kept his arms at his side. He fell feet first, watching a small yellow dot between his boots slowly grow. His Felix Advisor remarked,

WE ARE INSIDE THE BORE OF THAT TUBE THAT STRETCHES OUT ALONG THE POLAR AXIS. LET US HOPE THE ENTIRE TUBE HAS BEEN EMPTIED BY THE ALIEN MINING OPERATIONS. IT APPEARS WE DO HAVE A QUITE EXACT TRAJECTORY. THE ALIEN SENT US FALLING STRAIGHT ALONG VENUS'S SPIN AXIS. WE MAY WELL FALL ALL THE WAY THROUGH THE PLANET.

Chansing tried to think. "How . . . how long will that take?"

LET ME CALCULATE FOR A MOMENT. YES, I RETAIN DATA ON VENUS. WHICH YIELDS . . . I AM PERFORMING THE DYNAMICAL INTEGRAL AN-ALYTICALLY . . .

Across Chansing's in-suit field of view appeared:

$$\text{time} = \left[\frac{\pi}{2} - \tan^{-1}\left(\frac{v}{R\sqrt{\frac{4\pi}{3}G\rho}} \right) \right]\left(\frac{4\pi\,G\rho}{3} \right)^{-1/2}$$

TIME TO PASS THROUGH TO THE OTHER SIDE OF THE PLANET IS 36.42 MINUTES. I WOULD ADVISE YOU TO START A RUNNING CLOCK.

Chansing called up a time-beeper in his right eye, set it to zero, and watched the spool of yellow digits run. He grunted sourly. Let Felix the Advisor read it. Time was of no importance when the outcome was so barrenly clear.

Chansing fell.

He had long been used to the sensation of free fall, but always in the silent enormity of open space, or the confines of a ship.

It had been easy then to convince his reflexes that he was in some sense flying, airy and buoyant, oblivious to gravity's cruel laws.

Here . . . here he plunged downward between mottled glowing sheets that rushed past with dizzying speed. He *felt* the silvery rim of Venus thrusting up to meet him as the planet flattened into a plain and crinkled mountains grew, detail getting finer with every moment.

The exposed skin of Venus had a naked look, pale and barren beneath a sun it had not seen for billions of years. Its infernal cloak now gone, it lay open to cosmic rape.

Furrowed low hills stretched away, filling half his sky beyond the glowing translucence. The ravaged land was a rutted waste, already mauled by its inward collapse. The first plugs of metal-lava had sent vast quakes through her, leaving clouds of dust that were settling slowly over jagged scarps.

The ground hurtled up, a vast hand swatting at him, and he flinched automatically. He plunged toward a broad hillside—

—braced himself for the impact—

—and felt nothing.

Instantly, he shot through into a dim golden world, alone. The glowing walls gave off some light, but he could see nothing beyond them.

Far below, between his boots, was a single yellow point. Felix's voice came to him.

THE TUBE FORMED BY THE REVOLVING COSMIC STRING IS INDEED EMPTY. WE ARE INSIDE THE PLANET NOW. I ESTIMATE OUR SPEED AT 934 METERS PER SECOND.

Dark mottled shapes soared up toward him and flashed soundlessly past in the walls. "Headed for what?"

IF THE ALIEN CYBORGS HAVE CONSTRUCTED THIS MIRACULOUS PLA-NETCORING DEVICE WITH THE PRECISION I WOULD EXPECT OF THEM, I PREDICT WE SHALL PLUNGE ENTIRELY THROUGH THE CENTER AND OUT TO THE OTHER SIDE.

"A cyborg?" Chansing asked, dazed.

HALF-ORGANIC BEING, HALF-MACHINE. I COULD NOT ASCERTAIN THE EXACT PROPORTIONS FROM SUCH HASTY OBSERVATION, BUT—

"Skip that! How can I get out of this?"

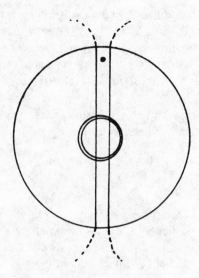

WE CANNOT. BY THRUSTING THE COSMIC STRING TO VERY NEAR THE PLANETARY AXIS, THE CYBORGS INSURED THAT THERE IS NO SPIN ALONG THIS TUBE. MATTER COMING UP FROM THE CORE—OR DOWN FROM OUTSIDE, AS WE ARE—WILL SUFFER NO SLOW DRIFT, AND SO SHOULD NOT STRIKE THE WALLS. IN ADDITION, UNIQUELY TO THIS CHOICE THEY HAVE ADROITLY MADE, THERE IS NO CORIOLIS FORCE THAT WOULD DEFLECT US.

Chansing grimmaced. It was all bad news. Despite the glowing walls, the light around Chansing was dimming.

He fought down rising panic. Part of his fear came from the simple fact that he was falling at greater and greater speeds, and sheer animal terror threatened to engulf him. He struggled against this like a man hammering at a dark wave that loomed higher even as he struggled. His breath caught and he forced his throat to open, his lungs to stop their spasmodic heaving.

Grainy, blurred shapes flashed past—features in the rock illuminated by the thin barrier of the rotating hoop. The yellow glare below had swollen to a brilliant disk. He could feel now through his sensorium a bone-deep bass *whuum-whuum-whuum-whuum* of the spinning magnetic fields.

"Maybe . . . maybe I can reach the walls. Is there any way I can slow down?"

Chansing felt Felix's sharp, peeling laugh. A circle appeared in his left eye.

It billowed into a sphere—Venus—with a red line thrust along the axis or revolution. A small blue dot moved inward near the top of the axis, just below the surface. The core brimmed a hot yellow.

WE NOW HAVE ACQUIRED A SPEED OF 1,468 METERS PER SECOND. THE HOOP MATERIAL, REMEMBER, IS EXTREMELY DENSE—MANY MILLIONS OF TONS PACKED INTO A THREAD THAT HARDLY SPANS MORE THAN AN ATOM'S WIDTH. IF YOU WERE TO STRIKE THAT MATTER AT OUR PRESENT SPEED, YOUR HAND WOULD VAPORIZE.

Chansing's breath came in fast, jerky pants, the fear creeping in. "Suppose they get some core metal in here, comin' out, and we meet it."

I DON'T SUPPOSE I HAVE TO ANALYZE THAT POSSIBILITY FOR YOU.

"No, guess not."

Chansing cast about for some idea, some fleeting hope. The walls were nearly dark now, the radiance of the hoop somehow absorbed by the rock beyond. Smouldering orange-brown wedges shot past—lava trapped in underground vaults, great livid oceans of scorching rock.

THE HOOP TUBE IS STANDING EMPTY PERHAPS THE CYBORGS ARE WORKING ON SOME MINOR REPAIRS. OR PERHAPS THEY SIMPLY PAUSE TO LET THE ORBITED TEAMS THAT ARE FASHIONING THE FIRST BATCH OF CORE METAL DO THEIR WORK. IN ANY CASE, ASSUMING THE CYBORG ABOVE DID NOT SIMPLY THROW US IN TO SEE US BOILED AWAY BY A GUSHER OF IRON, THERE IS ANOTHER FATE.

Chansing tried to calm himself and focus on Felix's words. The walls seemed closer as he fell, the tube narrowing before him. He pulled himself rigid and straight, arms at his sides, feet down toward the yellow disk below that grew steadily. He blinked back sweat and tried to see better.

I BELIEVE WE HAVE PASSED THROUGH THE CRUST AND ARE NOW ACCELERATING THROUGH THE MANTLE. NOTE THAT THE OCCASIONAL LAVA LAKES ARE GETTING LARGER AND MORE NUMEROUS. BY ANALOGY WITH EARTH, TEMPERATURE INCREASES INWARD UNTIL IT EXCEEDS THE MELTING POINT OF SIMPLE SILICATE ROCKS. THEN—DRAWING ON STUDIES OF SIMILAR PLANETS—WE WILL ENTER AN INCREASINGLY DENSE AND HOT CORE. AT THIS POINT THE ROCKS WILL BE FLUID AND AT ABOUT 2,800 DEGREES CENTIGRADE.

"What keeps them out of this tube?"

THE HOOP PRESSURE, WHICH IS TRULY IMMENSE. I CALCULATE—

"And the heat? The hoop stops that?" Chansing asked, seeking reassurance, though he already suspected the answer.

HEAT IS ELECTROMAGNETIC RADIATION, WHICH HOOP PRESSURE ALONE CANNOT ABSORB. IT PASSES THROUGH THE WALLS—WHICH IS WHY WE SEE NOW THE DARK ROCK BEYOND. SOON, THOUGH, THE SILICATES WILL BEGIN TO GLOW WITH THEIR HEAT OF COMPRESSION.

"What'll we do?"

THE HEAT RADIATION EXERTS A PRESSURE. BUT THIS IS SYMMETRIC, OF COURSE, ACTING EQUALLY IN ALL DIRECTIONS. SO IT CANNOT PUSH US TOWARD ONE WALL IN PREFERENCE TO ANOTHER. BUT IT WILL COOK US QUITE THOROUGHLY.

"How . . . how long?"

PASSAGE THROUGH THE CORE . . . ABOUT 9.87 MINUTES.

"My suit—it'll silver up for me, right?"

TRUE, IT ALREADY HAS. AND I CALCULATE WE MIGHT SURVIVE ONE ENTIRE PASSAGE IF WE SEAL UP COMPLETELY, CLOSE YOUR HELMET VISOR, DAMP ALL INPUTS. PERHAPS THE CYBORG UNDERSTOOD THAT IT MAY KNOW A GOOD DEAL ABOUT OUR TECHNOLOGY. YES, YES . . . I AM BEGINNING TO SEE ITS DEVILISH LOGIC.

Chansing shut down all his suit inputs. His suit skin reflected the blur of thickening light around him with a mirror finish. The walls rushing past were turning ruddy, sullen. "Where are we?"

WE MUST BE APPROACHING THE BOUNDARY AT WHICH IRON MELTS. THIS COLOR CHANGE PROBABLY SIGNALS THE TRANSITION FROM THE MANTLE TO THE OUTER CORE. WE CAN EXPECT SOME VARYING MAGNETIC FIELDS NOW, SINCE THIS IS THE REGION—SO THEORY SAYS— WHERE THE PLANET'S FIELD IS BORN. LARGE TIDES OF MOLTEN METAL EDDY ABOUT, CARRYING ELECTRICAL CURRENTS, LIKE GREAT WIRES IN A GENERATOR STATION. VENUS'S SPIN SERVES TO WRAP THESE AROUND, CREATING CURRENT VORTEXES, WHICH IN TURN CREATE MAGNETIC WHORLS.

"Damn, it's getting hot already."

EXTERNAL TEMPERATURE IS 2,785 DEGREES CENTIGRADE.

Chansing clicked his visor down and was in complete blackness. He wondered if he could stand the heat in utter isolation, falling faster and faster.

He again struggled to slow his breathing. If he was to live through even the next few minutes, he would have to think clearly, and the dark might even help that as long as he could keep his natural reactions from running away.

LUCKILY, THE ADDED SPEED IMPARTED BY THE CYBORG WILL TAKE US THROUGH THAT MUCH FASTER. I REGISTER EXTERNAL TEMPERATURE NOW AT WELL OVER 3,000 CENTIGRADE. HERE—ONE OF THE SUIT'S LIGHT PIPES WILL GIVE US A FAINT IMAGE WHICH IS ALL WE NEED IN SUCH A PLACE.

"Damn all, *think*!"

I AM. I SIMPLY DO NOT SEE ANY WAY OUT OF OUR DILEMMA.

"There's gotta be *some* way—"

THE EXISTENCE OF A WELL-DEFINED PROBLEM DOES NOT IMPLY THE EXISTENCE OF A SOLUTION.

"Damn you!"

Felix was a disconnected intelligence, a mere voice from a chip buried in Chansing's neck. There was no point in getting mad at it. The tiny remnant of a once-great mind could still take offense, refuse to help him, even though that would mean that the chip-mind itself would be doomed.

"Look, we get through this, we'll be back outside, right?"

YES. BUT THAT IS THE DEVILISH NATURE OF THIS CYBORG'S TRICK. WE ARE PARTICIPATING IN AN ANCIENT SCHOOLBOY'S HOMEWORK PROBLEM—A SHAFT THROUGH THE PLANET, WITH US AS THE HARMON-ICALLY OSCILLATING TEST MASS.

"What . . ."

Chansing suddenly saw what Felix meant.

In his eye the blue dot shot through the core and on, out through the other side of the red tube. It rose toward the surface, its velocity dwindling in gravity's grip, then broke free of the surface and slowed further. But after hesitating at the peak, it began to fall again, to execute another long plunge through the heart of the spitted planet.

WE CAN PERHAPS SURVIVE THIS ONE PASSAGE. BUT ANOTHER, AND ANOTHER?—SO ON, *AD INFINITUM*?

"There's got to be a way out."

Chansing said this with absolute conviction. Even if a gargantuan alien had made this incinerating rattrap, still it could have made a mistake, left some small unnoticed exit.

He had to believe that, or the panic that squeezed his throat would overwhelm him. He would die like a pitiful animal, caught on the alien's spit and roasted to a charred hulk. He would end as a cinder, bobbing endlessly through the central furnace.

WE MIGHT POSSIBLY TRY SOMETHING AT THE VERY HIGH POINT, WHEN THE HOOP BEGINS TO CURVE OVER FAR ABOVE THE POLE. WE SHOULD COME TO REST THERE FOR A BRIEF INSTANT.

"Good. Good. I can maybe pump some of the cooling stuff—"

REFRIGERANT FLUIDS YES, I SEE. USE THEM IN OUR THRUSTER. BUT THAT WOULD NOT BE ENOUGH TO ATTAIN AN ORBIT.

"How about the hoop? Maybe I could bounce off it up there, where it's spinning. I could pick up some vector, get free of the tube."

Chansing felt Felix's strangely abstract presence moving, pondering, as though this were merely some fresh problem of passing interest. Falling in absolute blackness, he felt his stomach convulse. He clamped his throat shut and gulped back down a mouthful of acid bile.

Now a strange sound came to him. The racheting *whuum-whuum-whuum* of the revolving hoop caried gurglings and ringing pops.

The long strumming sounds broke Chansing's attention. They seemed like majestic voices calling out to him, beckoning him into the utter depths of this world.

No. He shook himself, gasped, and switched the light pipe image into his left eye.

The walls outside bristled with incandescent heat, cherry-red. Globs of scorched red churned in the walls.

"Stop your calculatin'! Give me an answer."

VERY WELL. THE IDEA MIGHT BE MARGINALLY POSSIBLE. I CANNOT ESTIMATE WITH CERTAINTY. HOWEVER, IT WOULD REQUIRE THAT WE BE CLOSE ENOUGH TO THE HOOP-FORMED WALL. THE CYBORG HAS PLACED US EXACTLY IN THE CENTER OF THIS TUBE, AS I MEASURE. WE NEED TO MOVE PERHAPS A HUNDRED METERS BEFORE WE WILL BE WITHIN THE PRESSURE SHOCK WAVE OF THE HOOP AS IT TURNS.

"How far's that?"

A FEW HUNDRED METERS, I ESTIMATE.

"That's not so hard. I can use the cooler stuff—"

EXTRACT IT NOW AND WE WILL DIE IN SECONDS.

"Damn all. I'll do it when we're clear, then."

THAT IS TEMPTING, BUT I FEAR IT WOULD NOT BE EFFECTIVE. THE
TUBE OPENS AS IT RISES TOWARD THE SURFACE. HERE, THE TUBE WALL
IS ONLY A STONE'S THROW AWAY. BY THE TIME WE ARE CLEAR OF THE
CORE, THE WALLS WILL BE TOO FAR TO REACH IN TIME—UNLESS WE
BEGIN TO MOVE NOW.

"Yeah, yeah—*how?*"

EVEN A MINUTE PRESSURE APPLIED NOW WOULD GIVE US ENOUGH
PUSH TO REACH THE WALL DURING THE RISE OUT. IT IS A MATTER OF
MOMENTUM.

"Pressure . . ."

Chansing frowned. The claustrophobic suit filled with the sound of his
panting, his sour sweat, the naked smell of his fear.

He felt nothing but the clawing emptiness of falling, weightless. He
squinted at the tiny image that came through the light pipe.

The walls outside were flooded with fire. The nickel-iron core only a short
distance beyond raged and tossed with prickly white compressional waves.
He flew close to livid pink whorls that stretched for tens of kilometers, yet
passed in a few seconds of harsh glare. The hoop's constant *whuum-whuum-
whuum* stormed in his teeth and jaw with grinding persistence. His tongue
seemed to fill his throat, and the air was a choking, searing bite in his nostrils.
The suit was close to overheating. He realized he was nearing the point
where his own grip on himself would slip. He would do something rash to
escape the heat, and he would die.

To this was added the gathering sense of menace as he shot down the
immense bore-hole. Like all space workers, he had suppressed his fear of
falling through long years of practice. But that was in the cool, serene
perspectives of space. Here, he was flung by long streamers of glowing fire,
racing downward at huge speeds.

But something Felix had said plucked at his memory. Even a minute
pressure . . .

"The light. You said something about it pushing us."

YES, OF COURSE, BUT THAT ACTS EQUALLY IN ALL DIRECTIONS.

"Not if we turn some of the silver off."

WHAT? THAT WOULD—OH, SEE . . . IF WE SLIGHTLY LESSEN THE
SILVERING ON THE FRONT OF US, SAY, BY ROBBING THE AUTOCIRCUITS
THERE OF POWER . . . YES, THEN THE LIGHT WILL REFLECT LESS WELL.
WE WILL BE PUSHED IN THAT DIRECTION BY THE LIGHT STRIKING US
FROM BEHIND.

"Let's do it. Not much time."

BUT THE HEAT! LESSENING THE REFLECTION HEIGHTENS THE AB-
SORPTION.

Chansing had already guessed that. "Show me how to taper down the
silver on my chest."

NO, I DON'T—THE TEMPERATURE OUTSIDE, IT'S 3,459 CENTIGRADE!
I CAN'T TAKE—

"Give the info. *Now.*" Chansing kept his own mind under tight control.
This was the only way, he felt sure of it, and seconds counted.

NOT NOW, NO! I'LL . . . I'LL THINK OF SOMETHING—SOMETHING
THAT WILL WORK—YES, WORK WHEN WE GET THROUGH THE CORE.
I'LL REVIEW MY BACK MEMORIES, I'LL—

"No. *Now.*"

He felt the Advisor's fear, surging now nearly as strongly as his own. So
the chip had finally broken, revealed the fragments of its residual humanity.

Deliberately, he reached within himself and smothered Felix. It called
plaintively to him in a small, desperate voice. Chansing clamped down,
forcing it back into a cranny of himself.

"*Now.*"

The yellow-white hell soared away above Chansing's head. The walls
nearly seeped a sullen red, but it was a relief after the incandescent fury that
dwindled now, a fiery disk fading above him like a dimming sun.

Chansing panted deeply, though it seemed to do no good. Prickly waves
washed over him, giving him unbearable itches that moved in restless storms
across his skin. His lungs jerked irregularly. His arms trembled. It was as
though his whole body was racheting in dying spasms, unable to cooperate
any longer.

But he managed to keep his arms and legs straight. The light pressure
would not have forced him in only one direction if he spun or tumbled.

Had it been enough? The long minutes at the core had crawled by, bringing agonizing lungfuls of heated air.

Now the heat ebbed slightly, but not much.

WE ARE, AFTER ALL, JUST ANOTHER RADIATING BODY. WE CAN ONLY LOSE HEAT BY EMITTING IT AS INFRARED WAVES. SO WE MUST WAIT FOR COOLER SURROUNDINGS BEFORE THIS INTOLERABLE HEAT CAN DISPERSE.

His Felix Advisor seemed remarkably collected, given the hysteria that had beset it only minutes before. "How about the cooling thing?"

YOU MEAN OUR REFRIGERATOR? IT CAN ONLY FUNCTION BY EJECTING WASTE HEAT AT A COOLER SINK. THERE *IS* NO COLDER PLACE TO EXCHANGE HEAT WITH, YOU SEE.

"So we wait till we get out?" It seemed an impossibly long time. Between his boots he could see the blackness of the planet's mantle, thousands of kilometers of dead rock they must shoot through before regaining the dark of space itself. And there he would somehow have to make good this attempt, or else he would slow and pause and then plunge again. He wished again that he had saved his thruster fuel. It would give him some freedom, some hope of being something other than the helpless, dumb test particle in a grotesque experiment.

WE DO HAVE SOME FLUIDS WE COULD EJECT, BUT—

"What? Look, we try everything. Got no hope otherwise."

THE REFRIGERANT FLUIDS. WE COULD BRING THEM TO A HIGH TEM- PERATURE AND VENT THEM.

"Think it'll help much?" To lose the coolant meant he would have no chance whatever if he failed up ahead and fell back into the tube. He would fry for sure.

I CANNOT TELL HOW MUCH MOMENTUM WE PICKED UP FROM THAT MANEUVER. PUSHING A LARGE MASS SUCH AS OURSELVES WITH MERE LIGHT PRESSURE—

Chansing laughed with a jittery edge. "I'm the mass here—you weigh nothin' at all. And don't you worry 'bout calculatin' what'll happen. Time comes, up at the top of this hole, I'll have to grab whatever's in sight. Fly by the seat of my pants, not some eee-quation."

THEN I SHOULD VENT THE REFRIGERANT FLUIDS?

"Sure. Bet it all!" Chansing felt small icy rivulets coursing along his neck as he let the Advisor take fractional control of his inboard systems.

I AM WARMING THE POLY-XENON NOW.

"And when you spray it, just use the spinal vents. That'll give us another push in the right direction. Could make the difference."

OH. I SEE. I DID NOT THINK OF THIS POSSIBILITY.

"Trouble with you Advisors is you can't imagine anythin' you haven't seen before."

LET US NOT DEBATE MY PROPERTIES AT QUITE THIS TIME. WE ARE RISING TOWARD THE SURFACE, AND YOU MUST BE READY. I BELIEVE THE WALL YOU FACE IS NEARER NOW. NOTICE THE SPARKLING?

"Yeah. What's it mean?"

THAT IS WHERE THE MANTLE ROCK IS FORCED BY SIDEWISE PRESSURE AGAINST THE PASSING COSMIC STRING. SOMEHOW THE ROCK IS HELD BACK. CLEARLY, THE CYBORGS MUST RELAX THIS HOOP PRESSURE SOME-HOW, DOWN IN THE CORE, IN ORDER TO FILL THIS TUBE WITH THE LIQUID IRON WE SAW BEFORE.

"Maybe they just slow it down some? Let the iron squish in a li'l 'fore the next time the string comes whizzin' by?"

Chansing fumbled with the suit refrigerator controls. He knew he had to understand more about the hoop, get some idea of how to use it.

POSSIBLY. CLEARLY, THE ROTATING STRING EXERTS GREAT PRESSURE AGAINST THESE ROCKS.

Chansing watched the quick flashing in the walls. For him to see these sparks at all, they must be enormous, since his reeling, relentless speed took him by kilometers of the ruby-red rock in an instant. Still he felt the dizzying velocity. It threatened to make him throw up, and he had to clench his throat against that.

He saw from the 3-D simulation Felix ran in his left eye that he was rising toward the surface, slowing as gravity asserted itself.

He had to find a way to escape the tube, but no idea came to him. He had nothing he could throw to gain even a tug of momentum. The coolant jet throbbed behind him, but relative to the blur of motion in the walls he could not tell whether it did any good. It occurred to him that if he was too successful, he would crash into the speeding wall and be torn to pieces in an instant. Somehow the abstract nature of these things, the dry, distant, physics-experiment feel, frightened him all the more.

THE TUBE IS FLARING OUT. WE ARE APPROACHING ONE SIDE OF IT, BUT I CANNOT JUDGE OUR VELOCITY WELL. AS WE RISE, THE HOOP CURVES AWAY TO MAKE ITS GREAT ARC OUTWARD. THE MAJESTY OF IT IS IMPRESSIVE, I MUST SAY.

"Forget that. What can I *do*?"

I AM TRYING TO SEE HOW WE CAN USE OUR SITUATION, BUT I MUST SAY THAT A SOLUTION CONTINUES TO ELUDE ME. THE DYNAMICS—

"We're getting close."

The rock around him had already ceased to glow, and beyond the walls lay complete darkness. The tunnel was broadening. He saw it by the steady golden aura, a shimmering passage that led away both up and down.

Again he thought of what would happen if he could do nothing up ahead. The cool logic of dynamics would, Felix said, fling him back into the core. The heat would kill him on the next pass, or if it only managed to send him into delirium, there would be another cycle, and another, and another. . . . He would bob endlessly, a crisp cinder obeying simple but inexorable laws. . . .

And then instantly he was swimming in light.

Stars bloomed beneath his feet. A bowl of brilliant gas and suns opened below him as he shot free of the planet's grasp, above the twilight line. After the sultry darkness, this sky was a welcoming bath of colors and contrasts.

Out, free!

He could feel his suit cool as it lost heat to the cold sky. It went *ping* as joints contracted. Wrinkled hills rose above his head, the whole naked landscape stretching as it drew away.

The golden walls fell away from him on one side, but in front of him the radiance did not fade or recede. It was much closer. He *had* gained some significant speed, then.

But now he was losing his speed along the tube. He watched the planet above his helmet turn into a gigantic silvery bowl. The dawn line cut this bowl in half. As he rose, Venus's curve brought into view the immense gray orbital works of the Alphas.

His rate of rise dwindled. The far side of the hoop tube was bending away. In front of him the glow was brighter, and he took a few moments to be sure he was in fact curving over along with the hoop walls. Could he see the flicker of motion from the rapidly rotating string? He had begun to think of the walls as solid, and now he became aware of their gauzy nature.

THE COSMIC STRING CAN EXERT PRESSURE ONLY WHEN IT IS VERY NEAR YOU, OF COURSE. UNTIL NOW YOU WERE MOVING WITH RESPECT TO IT AT HIGH SPEEDS. NOW YOU WILL HAVE A LOW RELATIVE SPEED, BUT ONLY FOR A BRIEF MOMENT.

"You save any of that cooler stuff?"

YES, BUT THERE IS VERY LITTLE.

"Get ready."
Already he could detect no further shrinking in the wrecked face of Venus below. He must be near the top of his swing.
"Firing!"
He felt the jetting pressure at his back. The glowing hoop tube curled away like an opening funnel. Beyond, he could see the gossamer surface generated by the globe-spanning cosmic string. It appeared now to wrap the world in a rainbowy strangle hold.
The venting at his spine gurgled to a stop.
Whuum-whuum-whuum.
A vibrant, intense glow was all around him. He windmilled his arms and brought his boots down toward the golden surface. It pulsed with freshening energy. He felt as though he was a fragile bird, vainly flailing its wings above a sheet of translucent, wispy gold. Falling toward it. Performing his own sort of experiment . . .
The impact slammed him hard. It jarred up through his boots like a rough, wrenching punch. He had crouched, letting his legs absorb the momentum. Suddenly, he was shooting along the surface of the sheet.

IT HAS CONVEYED IMPULSE TO YOU, AN INFINITESIMAL FRACTION OF ITS SPINNING ENERGY.

Chansing felt himself loft slightly higher, then come down toward the sheet again. He had shot sidewise, away from the polar axis, going out on a tangent like a coin flung off a merry-go-round.
He hit again.
This time the jolt twisted his ankle. It felt like a hand grabbing at him, then losing its grip. But it gave him another push out.

I ESTIMATE YOU ARE GAINING SIGNIFICANT VELOCITY FROM THESE
ENCOUNTERS. IT IS DIFFICULT TO CALCULATE, BUT—

Chansing ignored the tiny piping Advisor. His ankle ached. Was it broken?
He had no time to bend over and feel it. The shimmering plain came rising
toward him again, hard and flat.

This time the shock was greater. It caught his feet and flung him off at
an awkward angle, twisting him with a wrenching stab of pain.

YOU WILL HAVE TO BE MORE CAREFUL AS YOU SET DOWN UPON IT.
IT CAN CONVEY SPIN, BUT IF YOUR VELOCITY IS NOT ALIGNED WITH
ITS, THERE IS A VECTOR COUPLING, A TORQUE—

"Shut up!" he cried in pain and frustration. He did not want to set down
on the golden surface again, the ghostly curtain that could clutch and break
him. But the velocity he was picking up from the thing flung him sideways,
not up. Only his own rebounding through his knees kept him above the
flickering radiance. If he slipped, tumbled, went shooting across the damned
thing as he spun out of control—

The golden sheet rushed at him.

He struck solidly. This time his left leg shrieked with pain, and he barely
managed to kick free. The glow immersed him, and he saw he was going
to fall again soon. He windmilled. This time the shock was not as great, but
the muscles of his left leg seized up with an agonizing spasm.

He blinked away sweat. A weakness came over him and his ears rang. He
wearily spun himself again, using his arms, slower this time because the
motion hurt his leg.

He expected to hit quicker, but the jolt did not come. He looked down
and could not judge the distance. The glow had dimmed. It took a long
moment before he realized that the sheet was curving farther away from
him, wrapping down to follow the arc of the planet.

He was free. Out. In the clean and silent spaces.

WE ARE ON A HIGHLY ELLIPTICAL ORBIT, I GATHER. IT SHOULD TAKE
US AT A SIGNIFICANT ANGLE WITH RESPECT TO THIS HOOP PLAIN. I
CANNOT CALCULATE THE DETAILS, SO IT MAY BE THAT WE WILL RETURN
WITHIN ITS VOLUME.

"Never mind," he said, panting.

WE WILL NEED THE INFORMATION IN DUE TIME, HOWEVER.

"I doubt it. Look up."

Obsessed with its own mathematics, the Advisor piped with surprise as it responded to what Chansing saw.

Above them floated the long, sleek metallic body of the cyborg.

He had not intended to be the butt of a thousand jokes, and still less did he appreciate being the example cited in physics textbooks.

Some of the jokes turned upon childish anal analogies, others upon the sheer helplessness of his situation.

But he *had* done something very nearly impossible.

The Alpha that plucked him from above the shimmering veil of the rotating cosmic string explained nothing. It simply returned him to the gutted hulk of his ship.

At first he thought the rest of the expedition was dead. Electrical overload had seared the inner chambers.

But in the control center he found a metal equipment shell sealed from the inside. He popped it open and there was Doyle, crouched and ready in case he had turned out to be an Alpha. She had gotten herself into the shell as a precaution, guessing that the Alphas would use induced lightning as a weapon. Electricity can't penetrate inside a conductor.

They shared the awful job of storing away the bodies. Chansing found himself staring into their contorted faces for a long time, trying to read meaning into their last moments.

With a week's work Chansing and Doyle were able to get ship systems running again. They limped away from Venus and were picked up three weeks later. By that time Chansing was in pretty bad shape and needed a lot of medical attention. The media attention was less agreeable to him.

Earthside authorities were incensed, of course, but there was little they could do. Earth massed its transmission power and beamed messages at the still-growing Alpha webworks in orbit about Venus. After wasting time on acrimonious insults, the bureaucrats asked a few pointed questions. Surprisingly, the Alphas deigned to reply.

Had the Alphas truly intended to kill the crew?

Yes.

Had they intended to kill Chansing?

Yes, doubly yes.

Why?

No answer.

Why had they finally saved him?

Because he displayed (untranslatable) and proved himself (untranslatable).

Could they admit another scientific team to study their great works?

They could not say, truly. Perhaps another team would like to try?

Well, then, would the Alphas guarantee their safety?

That depended. Could the humans guarantee that their team would display (untranslatable)?

Well, what *was* (untranslatable)?

In reply the Alphas sent a picture of Chansing.

Much discussion followed this. Could the Alphas not generalize from the particular to the general? That would explain why they sent a picture of a single person when they were asked for a general property.

Or did their philosophy simply not hold the belief that experience could be chopped up into categories?

This last seemed unlikely, given their ability to manage the huge mass and power of the cosmic string. Science itself depended on mathematical generalizations. The ability to generalize *was* intelligence, wasn't it?

Still . . . Did anyone want to gamble his or her life on the turn of a philosophical point?

So the Alphas continued to gut the world that was once linked with beauty and feminine grace. They pulled the rich metal core free and freeze-formed their own vast gray cities, for reasons still unknown. Though they shared the solar system, they took no further notice of humanity.

Chansing remained the only person who had ever seen an Alpha. And no one tried to repeat his performance.

He quickly tired of publicity, the questions, the fame, the money, the women, the incessant buzzing attention. He went in search of Doyle, after the noise had died down, and she was everything he had hoped.

He successfully resisted public appearances by simply pointing out that he never flew anywhere. Never mind that he had been a pilot once.

He bought a large, comfortable home on ample wooded grounds in northern China. Doyle furnished it during layovers between her ongoing career as a pilot. It is a single-storied, pine construction with handsome teak walls, and has no stairs. Nowhere in the house is there an elevated floor.

Chansing is cordial to guests and in later years has adopted the curious practice of going everywhere in a powered wheelchair. Though his legs are sound, he rarely stands up.

He takes his exercise in other ways. There is a swimming pool, but no diving board.

CONNIE WILLIS

At the Rialto

Connie Willis lives in Greeley, Colorado, with her family. She first attracted attention as a writer in the late 1970s with a number of outstanding stories for the now-defunct magazine *Galileo*, and in the subsequent years has made a large name for herself very fast indeed. In 1982, she won two Nebula Awards, one for her superb novelette "Fire Watch," and one for her poignant short story "A Letter from the Clearys"; a few months later, "Fire Watch" went on to win her a Hugo Award as well. Last year, her powerful novella "The Last of the Winnebagos" won both the Nebula and the Hugo. Her short fiction has appeared in *Isaac Asimov's Science Fiction Magazine*, *OMNI*, *The Magazine of Fantasy and Science Fiction*, *The Berkley Showcase*, *The Twilight Zone Magazine*, *The Missouri Review*, and elsewhere. Her books include the novels *Water Witch* and *Light Raid*, written in collaboration with Cynthia Felice, and *Fire Watch*, a collection of her short fiction. Her first solo novel was *Lincoln's Dreams*; upcoming is a new solo novel, *Doomsday Book*. Her story "The Sidon in the Mirror" was in our First Annual Collection, her story "Blued Moon" was in our Second Annual Collection, her story "Chance" was in our Fourth Annual Collection, and her "The Last of the Winnebagos" was in our Sixth Annual Collection.

In the fast-paced and funny screwball comedy that follows, she teaches us a lesson in quantum physics unlike any we're likely to have seen before.

▼
At the Rialto

CONNIE WILLIS

> *Seriousness of mind was a prerequisite for understanding Newtonian physics. I am not convinced it is not a handicap in understanding quantum theory.*

—EXCERPT FROM DR. GEDANKEN'S KEYNOTE ADDRESS TO THE 1988 INTERNATIONAL CONGRESS OF QUANTUM PHYSICISTS ANNUAL MEETING, HOLLYWOOD, CALIFORNIA

I got to Hollywood around one-thirty and started trying to check into the Rialto.

"Sorry, we don't have any rooms," the girl behind the desk said. "We're all booked up with some science thing."

"I'm with the science thing," I said. "Dr. Ruth Baringer. I reserved a double."

"There are a bunch of Republicans here, too, and a tour group from Finland. They told me when I started work here that they got all these movie people, but the only one so far was that guy who played the friend of that other guy in that one movie. You're not a movie person, are you?"

"No," I said. "I'm with the science thing. Dr. Ruth Baringer."

"My name's Tiffany," she said. "I'm not actually a hotel clerk at all. I'm just working here to pay for my transcendental posture lessons. I'm really a model/actress."

"I'm a quantum physicist," I said, trying to get things back on track. "The name is Ruth Baringer."

She messed with the computer for a minute. "I don't show a reservation for you."

"Maybe it's in Dr. Mendoza's name. I'm sharing a room with her."

She messed with the computer some more. "I don't show a reservation for her either. Are you sure you don't want the Disneyland Hotel? A lot of people get the two confused."

"I want the Rialto," I said, rummaging through my bag for my notebook. "I have a confirmation number. W37420."

She typed it in. "Are you Dr. Gedanken?" she asked.

"Excuse me," an elderly man said.

"I'll be right with you," Tiffany told him. "How long do you plan to stay with us, Dr. Gedanken?" she asked me.

"*Excuse* me," the man said, sounding desperate. He had bushy white hair and a dazed expression, as if he had just been through a horrific experience or had been trying to check into the Rialto.

He wasn't wearing any socks. I wondered if *he* was Dr. Gedanken. Dr. Gedanken was the main reason I'd decided to come to the meeting. I had missed his lecture on wave-particle duality last year, but I had read the text of it in the *ICQP Journal*, and it had actually seemed to make sense, which is more than you can say for most of quantum theory. He was giving the keynote address this year, and I was determined to hear it.

It wasn't Dr. Gedanken. "My name is Dr. Whedbee," the elderly man said. "You gave me the wrong room."

"All our rooms are pretty much the same," Tiffany said. "Except for how many beds they have in them and stuff."

"My room has a *person* in it!" he said. "Dr. Sleeth. From the University of Texas at Austin. She was changing her clothes." His hair seemed to get wilder as he spoke. "She thought I was a serial killer."

"And your name is Dr. Whedbee?" Tiffany asked, fooling with the computer again. "I don't show a reservation for you."

Dr. Whedbee began to cry. Tiffany got out a paper towel, wiped off the counter, and turned back to me. "May I help you?" she said.

Thursday, 7:30–9 p.m. *Opening Ceremonies.* Dr. Halvard Onofrio, University of Maryland at College Park, will speak on the topic, "Doubts Surrounding the Heisenberg Uncertainty Principle." Ballroom.

I finally got my room at five, after Tiffany went off duty. Till then I sat around the lobby with Dr. Whedbee, listening to Abey Fields complain about Hollywood.

"What's wrong with Racine?" he said. "Why do we always have to go to these exotic places, like Hollywood? And St. Louis last year wasn't much better. The Institut Henri Poincaré people kept going off to see the arch and Busch Stadium."

"Speaking of St. Louis," Dr. Takumi said, "have you seen David yet?"

"No," I said.

"Oh, really?" she said. "Last year at the annual meeting you two were practically inseparable. Moonlight riverboat rides and all."

"What's on the programming tonight?" I said to Abey.

"David was just here," Dr. Takumi said. "He said to tell you he was going out to look at the stars in the sidewalk."

"That's exactly what I'm talking about," Abey said. "Riverboat rides and movie stars. What do those things have to do with quantum theory? Racine would have been an appropriate setting for a group of physicists. Not like this . . . this . . . do you realize we're practically across the street from Grauman's Chinese Theatre? And Hollywood Boulevard's where all those gangs hang out. If they catch you wearing red or blue, they'll—"

He stopped. "Is that Dr. Gedanken?" he asked, staring at the front desk.

I turned and looked. A short roundish man with a mustache was trying to check in. "No," I said. "That's Dr. Onofrio."

"Oh, yes," Abey said, consulting his program book. "He's speaking tonight at the opening ceremonies. On the Heisenberg uncertainty principle. Are you going?"

"I'm not sure," I said, which was supposed to be a joke, but Abey didn't laugh.

"I must meet Dr. Gedanken. He's just gotten funding for a new project."

I wondered what Dr. Gedanken's new project was—I would have loved to work with him.

"I'm hoping he'll come to my workshop on the wonderful world of quantum physics," Abey said, still watching the desk. Amazingly enough, Dr. Onofrio seemed to have gotten a key and was heading for the elevators. "I think his project has something to do with understanding quantum theory."

Well, that let me out. I didn't understand quantum theory at all. I sometimes had a sneaking suspicion nobody else did either, including Abey Fields, and that they just weren't willing to admit it.

I mean, an electron is a particle except it acts like a wave. In fact, a neutron acts like two waves and interferes with itself (or each other), and you can't really measure any of this stuff properly because of the Heisenberg uncertainty principle, and that isn't the worst of it. When you set up a Josephson junction to figure out what rules the electrons obey, they sneak past the barrier to the other side, and they don't seem to care much about the limits of the speed of light either, and Schrödinger's cat is neither alive nor dead till you open the box, and it all makes about as much sense as Tiffany's calling me Dr. Gedanken.

Which reminded me, I had promised to call Darlene and give her our room number. I didn't have a room number, but if I waited much longer, she'd have left. She was flying to Denver to speak at C.U. and then coming on to Hollywood sometime tomorrow morning. I interrupted Abey in the middle of his telling me how beautiful Cleveland was in the winter and went to call her.

"I don't have a room yet." I said when she answered. "Should I leave a message on your answering machine or do you want to give me your number in Denver?"

"Never mind all that," Darlene said. "Have you seen David yet?"

To illustrate the problems of the concept of wave function, Dr. Schrödinger imagines a cat being put into a box with a piece of uranium, a bottle of poison gas, and a Geiger counter. If a uranium nucleus disintegrates while the cat is in the box, it will release radiation which will set off the Geiger counter and break the bottle of poison gas. It is impossible in quantum theory to predict whether a uranium nucleus will disintegrate while the cat is in the box, and only possible to calculate uranium's probable half-life; therefore, the cat is neither alive nor dead until we open the box.

From "The Wonderful World of Quantum Physics,"
a seminar presented at the ICQP Annual Meeting
by A. Fields, PhD, University of Nebraska at Wahoo

I completely forgot to warn Darlene about Tiffany, the model-slash-actress.

"What do you mean you're trying to avoid David?" she had asked me at least three times. "Why would you do a stupid thing like that?"

Because in St. Louis I ended up on a riverboat in the moonlight and didn't make it back until the conference was over.

"Because I want to attend the programming," I said the third time around, "not a wax museum. I am a middle-aged woman."

"And David is a middle-aged man who, I might add, is absolutely charming."

"Charm is for quarks," I said and hung up, feeling smug until I remembered I hadn't told her about Tiffany. I went back to the front desk, thinking maybe Dr. Onofrio's success signaled a change. Tiffany asked, "May I help you?" and left me standing there.

After a while I gave up and went back to the red and gold sofas.

"David was here again," Dr. Takumi said. "He said to tell you he was going to the wax museum."

"There *are* no wax museums in Racine," Abey said.

"What's the programming for tonight?" I said, taking Abey's program away from him.

"There's a mixer at six-thirty and the opening ceremonies in the ballroom and then some seminars." I read the descriptions of the seminars. There was one on the Josephson junction. Electrons were able to somehow tunnel through an insulated barrier even though they didn't have the required energy. Maybe I could somehow get a room without checking in.

"If we were in Racine," Abey said, looking at his watch, "we'd already be checked in and on our way to dinner."

Dr. Onofrio emerged from the elevator, still carrying his bags. He came over and sank down on the sofa next to Abey.

"Did they give you a room with a seminaked woman in it?" Dr. Whedbee asked.

"I don't know," Dr. Onofrio said. "I couldn't find it." He looked sadly at the key. "They gave me 1282, but the room numbers go only up to seventy-five."

"I think I'll attend the seminar on chaos," I said.

The most serious difficulty quantum theory faces today is not the inherent limitation of measurement capability or the EPR paradox. It is the lack of a paradigm. Quantum theory has no working model, no metaphor that properly defines it.

Excerpt from Dr. Gedanken's keynote address

I got to my room at six, after a brief skirmish with the bellboy-slash-actor, who couldn't remember where he'd stored my suitcase, and unpacked. My clothes, which had been permanent press all the way from MIT, underwent a complete wave function collapse the moment I opened my suitcase, and came out looking like Schrödinger's almost-dead cat.

By the time I had called housekeeping for an iron, taken a bath, given up on the iron, and steamed a dress in the shower, I had missed the "Mixer with Munchies" and was half an hour late for Dr. Onofrio's opening remarks.

I opened the door to the ballroom as quietly as I could and slid inside. I had hoped they would be late getting started, but a man I didn't recognize was already introducing the speaker. "—and an inspiration to all of us in the field."

I dived for the nearest chair and sat down.

"Hi," David said. "I've been looking all over for you. Where were you?"

"Not at the wax museum," I whispered.

"You should have been," he whispered back. "It was great. They had John Wayne, Elvis, and Tiffany the model-slash-actress with the brain of a pea-slash-amoeba."

"Shh," I said.

"—the person we've all been waiting to hear, Dr. Ringgit Dinari."

"What happened to Dr. Onofrio?" I asked.

"Shhh," David said.

Dr. Dinari looked a lot like Dr. Onofrio. She was short, roundish, and mustached, and was wearing a rainbow-striped caftan. "I will be your guide this evening into a strange new world," she said, "a world where all that you thought you knew, all common sense, all accepted wisdom, must be discarded. A world where all the rules have changed and it sometimes seems there are no rules at all."

She sounded just like Dr. Onofrio, too. He had given this same speech two years ago in Cincinnati. I wondered if he had undergone some strange transformation during his search for room 1282 and was now a woman.

"Before I go any farther," Dr. Dinari said, "how many of you have already channeled?"

Newtonian physics had as its model the machine. The metaphor of the machine, with its interrelated parts, its gears and wheels, its causes and effects, was what made it possible to think about Newtonian physics.

Excerpt from Dr. Gedanken's keynote address

"You *knew* we were in the wrong place," I hissed at David when we got out to the lobby.

When we stood up to leave, Dr. Dinari had extended her pudgy hand in its rainbow-striped sleeve and called out in a voice a lot like Charlton Heston's, "O Unbelievers! Leave not, for here only is reality!"

"Actually, channeling would explain a lot," David said, grinning.

"If the opening remarks aren't in the ballroom, where are they?"

"Beats me," he said. "Want to go see the Capitol Records building? It's shaped like a stack of records."

"I want to go to the opening remarks."

"The beacon on top blinks out Hollywood in Morse code."

I went over to the front desk.

"Can I help you?" the clerk behind the desk said. "My name is Natalie, and I'm an—"

"Where is the ICQP meeting this evening?" I said.

"They're in the ballroom."

"I'll bet you didn't have any dinner," David said. "I'll buy you an ice cream cone. There's this great place that has the ice cream cone Ryan O'Neal bought for Tatum in *Paper Moon*."

"A channeler's in the ballroom," I told Natalie. "I'm looking for the ICQP."

She fiddled with the computer. "I'm sorry. I don't show a reservation for them."

"How about Grauman's Chinese?" David said. "You want reality? You want Charlton Heston? You want to see quantum theory in action?" He grabbed my hands. "Come with me," he said seriously.

In St. Louis I had suffered a wave function collapse a lot like what had happened to my clothes when I opened the suitcase. I had ended up on a riverboat halfway to New Orleans that time. It happened again, and the next thing I knew I was walking around the courtyard of Grauman's Chinese, eating an ice cream cone and trying to fit my feet in Myrna Loy's footprints.

She must have been a midget or had her feet bound as a child. So, apparently, had Debbie Reynolds, Dorothy Lamour, and Wallace Beery. The only footprints I came close to fitting were Donald Duck's.

"I see this as a map of the microcosm," David said, sweeping his hand over the slightly irregular pavement of printed and signed cement squares. "See, there are all these tracks. We know something's been here, and the prints are pretty much the same, only every once in a while you've got this," he knelt down and pointed at the print of John Wayne's clenched fist, "and over here," he walked toward the box office and pointed to the print of Betty Grable's leg, "and we can figure out the signatures, but what is this reference to 'Sid' that keeps popping up? And what does this mean?"

He pointed at Red Skelton's square. It said, "Thanks Sid We Dood It."

"You keep thinking you've found a pattern," David said, crossing over to the other side, "but Van Johnson's square is kind of sandwiched in here at an angle between Esther Williams and Cantinflas, and who the hell is May Robson? And why are all these squares over here empty?"

He had managed to maneuver me over behind the display of Academy Award winners. It was an accordionlike wrought-iron screen. I was in the fold between 1944 and 1945.

"And as if that isn't enough, you suddenly realize you're standing in the courtyard. You're not even in the theater."

"And that's what you think is happening in quantum theory?" I said weakly. I was backed up into Bing Crosby, who had won for Best Actor in *Going My Way*. "You think we're not in the theater yet?"

"I think we know as much about quantum theory as we can figure out about May Robson from her footprints," he said, putting his hand up to Ingrid Bergman's cheek (Best Actress, *Gaslight*) and blocking my escape. "I don't think we understand anything *about* quantum theory, not tunneling, not complementarity." He leaned toward me. "Not passion."

The best movie of 1945 was *Lost Weekend*. "Dr. Gedanken understands it," I said, disentangling myself from the Academy Award winners and David. "Did you know he's putting together a new research team for a big project on understanding quantum theory?"

"Yes," David said. "Want to see a movie?"

"There's a seminar on chaos at nine," I said, stepping over the Marx Brothers. "I have to get back."

"If it's chaos you want, you should stay right here," he said, stopping to look at Irene Dunne's handprints. "We could see the movie and then go have dinner. There's this place near Hollywood and Vine that has the mashed potatoes Richard Dreyfuss made into Devil's Tower in *Close Encounters*."

"I want to meet Dr. Gedanken," I said, making it safely to the sidewalk. I looked back at David. He had gone back to the other side of the courtyard and was looking at Roy Rogers' signature.

"Are you kidding? He doesn't understand it any better than we do."

"Well, at least he's trying."

"So am I. The problem is, how can one neutron interfere with itself, and why are there only two of Trigger's hoofprints here?"

"It's eight fifty-five," I said. "I am going to the chaos seminar."

"If you can find it," he said, getting down on one knee to look at the signature.

"I'll find it," I said grimly. He stood up and grinned at me, his hands in his pockets. "It's a great movie," he said.

It was happening again. I turned and practically ran across the street.

"*Benji IX* is showing," he shouted after me. "He accidentally exchanges bodies with a Siamese cat."

* * *

Thursday, 9–10 P.M. "The Science of Chaos." I. Durcheinander, University of Leipzig. A seminar on the structure of chaos. Principles of chaos will be discussed, including the Butterfly Effect, fractals, and insolid billowing. Ballroom.

I couldn't find the chaos seminar. The Clara Bow Room, where it was supposed to be, was empty. A meeting of vegetarians was next door in the Fatty Arbuckle Room, and all the other conference rooms were locked. The channeler was still in the ballroom. "Come!" she commanded when I opened the door. "Understanding awaits!" I went upstairs to bed.

I had forgotten to call Darlene. She would have left for Denver already, but I called her answering machine and told it the room number in case she picked up her messages. In the morning I would have to tell the front desk to give her a key. I went to bed.

I didn't sleep well. The air conditioner went off during the night, which meant I didn't have to steam my suit when I got up the next morning. I got dressed and went downstairs. The programming started at nine with Abey Fields' Wonderful World workshop in the Mary Pickford Room, a breakfast buffet in the ballroom, and a slide presentation on "Delayed Choice Experiments" in Cecil B. DeMille A on the mezzanine level.

The breakfast buffet sounded wonderful, even though it always turns out to be urn coffee and donuts. I hadn't had anything but an ice cream cone since noon the day before, but if David were around, he would be somewhere close to the food, and I wanted to steer clear of him. Last night it had been Grauman's Chinese. Today I was likely to end up at Knott's Berry Farm. I wasn't going to let that happen, even if he was charming.

It was pitch-dark inside Cecil B. DeMille A. Even the slide on the screen up front appeared to be black. "As you can see," Dr. Lvov said, "the laser pulse is already in motion before the experimenter sets up the wave or particle detector." He clicked to the next slide, which was dark gray. "We used a Mach-Zender interferometer with two mirrors and a particle detector. For the first series of tries we allowed the experimenter to decide which apparatus he would use by whatever method he wished. For the second series, we used that most primitive of randomizers—"

He clicked again, to a white slide with black polka dots that gave off enough light for me to be able to spot an empty chair on the aisle ten rows up. I hurried to get to it before the slide changed, and sat down.

"—a pair of dice. Alley's experiments had shown us that when the particle detector was in place, the light was detected as a particle, and when the wave detector was in place, the light showed wavelike behavior, no matter when the choice of apparatus was made."

"Hi," David said. "You've missed five black slides, two gray ones, and a white with black polka dots."

"Shh," I said.

"In our two series, we hoped to ascertain whether the consciousness of the decision affected the outcome." Dr. Lvov clicked to another black slide. "As you can see, the graph shows no effective difference between the tries in which the experimenter chose the detection apparatus and those in which the apparatus was randomly chosen."

"You want to go get some breakfast?" David whispered.

"I already ate," I whispered back, and waited for my stomach to growl and give me away. It did.

"There's a great place down near Hollywood and Vine that has the waffles Katharine Hepburn made for Spencer Tracy in *Woman of the Year*."

"Shh," I said.

"And after breakfast, we could go to Frederick's of Hollywood and see the bra museum."

"Will you please be quiet? I can't hear."

"Or see," he said, but he subsided more or less for the remaining ninety-two black, gray, and polka-dotted slides.

Dr. Lvov turned on the lights and blinked smilingly at the audience. "Consciousness had no discernible effect on the results of the experiment. As one of my lab assistants put it, 'The little devil knows what you're going to do before you know it yourself.' "

This was apparently supposed to be a joke, but I didn't think it was very funny. I opened my program and tried to find something to go to that David wouldn't be caught dead at.

"Are you two going to breakfast?" Dr. Thibodeaux asked.

"Yes," David said.

"No," I said.

"Dr. Hotard and I wished to eat somewhere that is *vraiment* Hollywood."

"David knows just the place," I said. "He's been telling me about this great place where they have the grapefruit James Cagney shoved in Mae Clark's face in *Public Enemy*."

Dr. Hotard hurried up, carrying a camera and four guidebooks. "And then perhaps you would show us Grauman's Chinese Theatre," he asked David.

"Of course he will," I said. "I'm sorry I can't go with you, but I promised Dr. Verikovsky I'd be at his lecture on Boolean logic. And after Grauman's Chinese, David can take you to the bra museum at Frederick's of Hollywood."

"And the Brown Derby?" Thibodeaux asked. "I have heard it is shaped like a *chapeau*."

They dragged him off. I watched till they were safely out of the lobby and then ducked upstairs and into Dr. Whedbee's lecture on information theory. Dr. Whedbee wasn't there.

"He went to find an overhead projector," Dr. Takumi said. She had half a donut on a paper plate in one hand and a styrofoam cup in the other.

"Did you get that at the breakfast brunch?" I asked.

"Yes. It was the last one. And they ran out of coffee right after I got there. You weren't in Abey Fields's thing, were you?" She set the coffee cup down and took a bite of the donut.

"No," I said, wondering if I should try to take her by surprise or just wrestle the donut away from her.

"You didn't miss anything. He raved the whole time about how we should have had the meeting in Racine." She popped the last piece of donut in her mouth. "Have you seen David yet?"

Friday, 9–10 P.M. "The Eureka Experiment: A Slide Presentation." J. Lvov, Eureka College. Descriptions, results, and conclusions of Lvov's delayed conscious/randomed choice experiments. Cecil B. DeMille A.

Dr. Whedbee eventually came in carrying an overhead projector, the cord trailing behind him. He plugged it in. The light didn't go on.

"Here," Dr. Takumi said, handing me her plate and cup. "I have one of these at Caltech. It needs its fractal basin boundaries adjusted." She whacked the side of the projector.

There weren't even any crumbs left of the donut. There was about a millimeter of coffee in the bottom of the cup. I was about to stoop to new depths when she hit it again. The light came on. "I learned that in the chaos seminar last night," she said, grabbing the cup away from me and draining it. "You should have been there. The ballroom was packed."

"I believe I'm ready to begin," Dr. Whedbee said. Dr. Takumi and I sat down. "Information is the transmission of meaning," Dr. Whedbee said. He wrote "meaning" or possibly "information" on the screen with a green Magic Marker. "When information is randomized, meaning cannot be transmitted, and we have a state of entropy." He wrote it under "meaning" with a red Magic Marker. His handwriting appeared to be completely illegible.

"States of entropy vary from low entropy, such as the mild static on your car radio, to high entropy, a state of complete disorder, of randomness and confusion, in which no information at all is being communicated."

Oh, my God, I thought. I forgot to tell the hotel about Darlene. The next time Dr. Whedbee bent over to inscribe hieroglyphics on the screen, I sneaked out and went down to the desk, hoping Tiffany hadn't come on duty yet. She had.

"May I help you?" she asked.

"I'm in room 663," I said. "I'm sharing a room with Dr. Darlene Mendoza. She's coming in this morning, and she'll be needing a key."

"For what?" Tiffany said.

"To get into the room. I may be in one of the lectures when she gets here."

"Why doesn't she have a key?"

"Because she isn't here yet."

"I thought you said she was sharing a room with you."

"She *will* be sharing a room with me. Room 663. Her name is Darlene Mendoza."

"And your name?" she asked, hands poised over the computer.

"Ruth Baringer."

"We don't show a reservation for you."

> We have made impressive advances in quantum physics in the ninety years since Planck's constant, but they have by and large been advances in technology, not theory. We can only make advances in theory when we have a model we can visualize.
>
> Excerpt from Dr. Gedanken's keynote address

I high-entropied with Tiffany for a while on the subjects of my not having a reservation and the air conditioning and then switched back suddenly to the problem of Darlene's key, in the hope of catching her off-guard. It worked about as well as Alley's delayed choice experiments.

In the middle of my attempting to explain that Darlene was not the air conditioning repairman, Abey Fields came up.

"Have you seen Dr. Gedanken?"

I shook my head.

"I was sure he'd come to my Wonderful World workshop, but he didn't, and the hotel says they can't find his reservation," he said, scanning the lobby. "I found out what his new project is, incidentally, and I'd be perfect for it. He's going to find a paradigm for quantum theory. Is that him?" he said, pointing at an elderly man getting in the elevator.

"I think that's Dr. Whedbee," I said, but he had already sprinted across the lobby to the elevator.

He nearly made it. The elevator slid to a close just as he got there. He pushed the elevator button several times to make the door open again, and when that didn't work, tried to readjust its fractal basin boundaries. I turned back to the desk.

"May I help you?" Tiffany said.

"You may," I said. "My roommate, Darlene Mendoza, will be arriving some time this morning. She's a producer. She's here to cast the female lead in a new movie starring Robert Redford and Harrison Ford. When she gets here, give her her key. And fix the air conditioning."

"Yes, ma'am," she said.

The Josephson junction is designed so that electrons must obtain additional energy to surmount the energy barrier. It was found, however, that some electrons simply tunnel, as Heinz Pagel put it, "right through the wall."

From "The Wonderful World of Quantum Physics," A. Fields, UNW

Abey had stopped banging on the elevator button and was trying to pry the elevator doors apart. I went out the side door and up to Hollywood Boulevard. David's restaurant was near Hollywood and Vine. I turned the other direction, toward Grauman's Chinese, and ducked into the first restaurant I saw.

"I'm Stephanie," the waitress said. "How many are there in your party?"

There was no one remotely in my vicinity. "Are you an actress-slash-model?" I asked her.

"Yes," she said. "I'm working here part-time to pay for my holistic hair-styling lessons."

"There's one of me," I said, holding up my forefinger to make it perfectly clear. "I want a table away from the window."

She led me to a table in front of the window, handed me a menu the size of the macrocosm, and put another one down across from me. "Our breakfast specials today are papaya stuffed with salmonberries and nasturtium/radicchio salad with a balsamic vinaigrette. I'll take your order when your other party arrives."

I stood the extra menu up so it hid me from the window, opened the other one, and read the breakfast entrees. They all seemed to have cilantro or lemon-grass in their names. I wondered if "radicchio" could possibly be Californian for "donut."

"Hi," David said, grabbing the standing-up menu and sitting down. "The sea urchin pâté looks good."

I was actually glad to see him. "How did you get here?" I asked.

"Tunneling," he said. "What exactly is extra-virgin olive oil?"

"I wanted a donut," I said pitifully.

He took my menu away from me, laid it on the table, and stood up. "There's a great place next door that's got the donut Clark Gable taught Claudette Colbert how to dunk in *It Happened One Night*."

The great place was probably out in Long Beach someplace, but I was too weak with hunger to resist him. I stood up. Stephanie hurried over.

"Will there be anything else?" she asked.

"We're leaving," David said.

"Okay, then," she said, tearing a check off her pad and slapping it down on the table. "I hope you enjoyed your breakfast."

Finding such a paradigm is difficult, if not impossible. Due to Planck's constant the world we see is largely dominated by Newtonian mechanics. Particles are particles, waves are waves, and objects do not suddenly vanish through walls and reappear on the other side. It is only on the subatomic level that quantum effects dominate."

Excerpt from Dr. Gedanken's keynote address

The restaurant was next door to Grauman's Chinese, which made me a little nervous, but it had eggs and bacon and toast and orange juice and coffee. And donuts.

"I thought you were having breakfast with Dr. Thibodeaux and Dr. Hotard," I said, dunking one in my coffee. "What happened to them?"

"They went to Forest Lawn. Dr. Hotard wanted to see the church where Ronald Reagan got married."

"He got married at Forest Lawn?"

He took a bite of my donut. "In the Wee Kirk of the Heather. Did you know Forest Lawn's got the World's Largest Oil Painting Incorporating a Religious Theme?"

"So why didn't you go with them?"

"And miss the movie?" He grabbed both my hands across the table. "There's a matinee at two o'clock. Come with me."

I could feel things starting to collapse. "I have to get back," I said, trying to disentangle my hands. "There's a panel on the EPR paradox at two o'clock."

"There's another showing at five. And one at eight."

"Dr. Gedanken's giving the keynote address at eight."

"You know what the problem is?" he said, still holding onto my hands. "The problem is, it isn't really Grauman's Chinese Theatre, it's Mann's, so Sid isn't even around to ask. Like, why do some pairs like Joanne Woodward and Paul Newman share the same square and other pairs don't? Like Ginger Rogers and Fred Astaire?"

"You know what the problem is?" I said, wrenching my hands free. "The problem is you don't take anything seriously. This is a conference, but you don't care anything about the programming or hearing Dr. Gedanken speak or trying to understand quantum theory!" I fumbled in my purse for some money for the check.

"I thought that was what we were talking about," David said, sounding surprised. "The problem is, where do those lion statues that guard the door fit in? And what about all those empty spaces?"

Friday, 2–3 P.M. *Panel Discussion on the EPR Paradox.* I. Takumi, moderator, R. Iverson, L. S. Ping. A discussion of the latest research on singlet-state correlations, including nonlocal influences, the Calcutta proposal, and passion. Keystone Kops Room.

* * *

I went up to my room as soon as I got back to the Rialto to see if Darlene was there yet. She wasn't and when I tried to call the desk, the phone wouldn't work. I went back down to the registration desk. There was no one there. I waited fifteen minutes and then went into the panel on the EPR paradox.

"The Einstein-Podolsky-Rosen paradox cannot be reconciled with quantum theory," Dr. Takumi was saying. "I don't care what the experiments seem to indicate. Two electrons at opposite ends of the universe can't affect each other simultaneously without destroying the entire theory of the space-time continuum."

She was right. Even if it were possible to find a model of quantum theory, what about the EPR paradox? If an experimenter measured one of a pair of electrons that had originally collided, it changed the cross-correlation of the other instantaneously, even if the electrons were light years apart. It was as if they were eternally linked by that one collision, sharing the same square forever, even if they were on opposite sides of the universe.

"If the electrons *communicated* instantaneously, I'd agree with you," Dr. Iverson said, "but they don't, they simply influence each other. Dr. Shimony defined this influence in his paper on passion, and my experiment clearly—"

I thought of David leaning over me between the best pictures of 1944 and 1945, saying, "I think we know as much about quantum theory as we do about May Robson from her footprints."

"You can't explain it away by inventing new terms," Dr. Takumi said.

"I completely disagree," Dr. Ping said. "Passion at a distance is not just an invented term. It's a demonstrated phenomenon."

It certainly is, I thought, thinking about David taking the macrocosmic menu out of the window and saying, "The sea urchin pâté looks good." It didn't matter where the electron went after the collision. Even if it went in the opposite direction from Hollywood and Vine, even if it stood a menu in the window to hide it, the other electron would still come and rescue it from the radicchio and buy it a donut.

"A demonstrated phenomenon!" Dr. Takumi said. "Ha!" She banged her moderator's gavel for emphasis.

"Are you saying passion doesn't exist?" Dr. Ping said, getting very red in the face.

"I'm saying one measly experiment is hardly a demonstrated phenomenon."

"One measly experiment! I spent five years on this project!" Dr. Iverson said, shaking his fist at her. "I'll show you passion at a distance!"

"Try it, and I'll adjust your fractal basin boundaries!" Dr. Takumi said, and hit him over the head with the gavel.

Yet finding a paradigm is not impossible. Newtonian physics is not a machine. It simply shares some of the attributes of a machine. We must find a model somewhere in the visible world that shares the often bizarre attributes of quantum physics. Such a model, unlikely as it sounds, surely exists somewhere, and it is up to us to find it.

Excerpt from Dr. Gedanken's keynote address

I went up to my room before the police came. Darlene still wasn't there, and the phone and air conditioning still weren't working. I was really beginning to get worried. I walked up to Grauman's Chinese to find David, but he wasn't there. Dr. Whedbee and Dr. Sleeth were behind the Academy Award Winners folding screen.

"You haven't seen David, have you?" I asked.

Dr. Whedbee removed his hand from Norma Shearer's cheek.

"He left," Dr. Sleeth said, disentangling herself from the Best Movie of 1929–30.

"He said he was going out to Forest lawn," Dr. Whedbee said, trying to smooth down his bushy white hair.

"Have you seen Dr. Mendoza? She was supposed to get in this morning."

They hadn't seen her, and neither had Drs. Hotard and Thibodeaux, who stopped me in the lobby and showed me a postcard of Aimee Semple McPherson's tomb. Tiffany had gone off duty. Natalie couldn't find my reservation. I went back up to the room to wait, thinking Darlene might call.

The air conditioning still wasn't fixed. I fanned myself with a Hollywood brochure and then opened it up and read it. There was a map of the courtyard of Grauman's Chinese on the back cover. Deborah Kerr and Yul Brynner didn't have a square together either, and Katharine Hepburn and Spencer Tracy weren't even on the map. She made him waffles in *Woman of the Year*, and they hadn't even given them a square. I wondered if Tiffany the model-slash-actress had been in charge of assigning the cement. I could see her looking blankly at Spencer Tracy and saying, "I don't show a reservation for you."

What exactly was a model-slash-actress? Did it mean she was a model *or* an actress or a model *and* an actress? She certainly wasn't a hotel clerk. Maybe electrons were the Tiffanys of the microcosm, and that explained their wave-slash-particle duality. Maybe they weren't really electrons at all. Maybe they were just working part-time at being electrons to pay for their singlet-state lessons.

Darlene still hadn't called by seven o'clock. I stopped fanning myself and tried to open a window. It wouldn't budge. The problem was, nobody knew anything about quantum theory. All we had to go on were a few colliding electrons that nobody could see and that couldn't be measured properly because of the Heisenberg uncertainty principle. And there was chaos to consider, and entropy, and all those empty spaces. We didn't even know who May Robson was.

At seven-thirty the phone rang. It was Darlene.

"What happened?" I said. "Where are you?"

"At the Beverly Wilshire."

"In Beverly Hills?"

"Yes. It's a long story. When I got to the Rialto, the hotel clerk I think her name was Tiffany, told me you weren't there. She said they were booked solid with some science thing and had had to send the overflow to other hotels. She said you were at the Beverly Wilshire in Room 1027. How's David?"

"Impossible," I said. "He's spent the whole conference looking at Deanna Durbin's footprints at Grauman's Chinese Theatre and trying to talk me into going to the movies."

"And are you going?"

"I can't. Dr. Gedanken's giving the keynote address in half an hour."

"He is?" Darlene said, sounding surprised. "Just a minute." There was a silence, and then she came back on and said, "I think you should go to the movies. David's one of the last two charming men in the universe."

"But he doesn't take quantum theory seriously. Dr. Gedanken is hiring a research team to design a paradigm, and David keeps talking about the beacon on top of the Capitol Records Building."

"You know, he may be onto something there. I mean, seriousness was all right for Newtonian physics, but maybe quantum theory needs a different approach. Sid says—"

"Sid?"

"This guy who's taking me to the movies tonight. It's a long story. Tiffany gave me the wrong room number, and I walked in on this guy in his underwear. He's a quantum physicist. He was supposed to be staying at the Rialto, but Tiffany couldn't find his reservation."

The major implication of wave/particle duality is that an electron has no precise location. It exists in a superposition of probable locations. Only when the experimenter observes the electron does it "collapse" into a location.

> The Wonderful World of Quantum Physics,
> A. Fields, UNW

Forest Lawn closed at five o'clock. I looked it up in the Hollywood brochure after Darlene hung up. There was no telling where he might have gone: the Brown Derby or the La Brea Tar Pits or some great place near Hollywood and Vine that had the alfalfa sprouts John Hurt ate right before his chest exploded in *Alien*.

At least I knew where Dr. Gedanken was. I changed my clothes and got in the elevator, thinking about wave/particle duality and fractals and high entropy states and delayed-choice experiments. The problem was, where could you find a paradigm that would make it possible to visualize quantum theory when you had to include Josephson junctions and passion and all those empty spaces? It wasn't possible. You had to have more to work with than a few footprints and the impression of Betty Grable's leg..

The elevator door opened, and Abey Fields pounced on me. "I've been looking all over for you," he said. "You haven't seen Dr. Gedanken, have you?"

"Isn't he in the ballroom?"

"No," he said. "He's already fifteen minutes late, and nobody's seen him. You have to sign this," he said, shoving a clipboard at me.

"What is it?"

"It's a petition." He grabbed it back from me. " 'We the undersigned demand that annual meetings of the International Congress of Quantum Physicists henceforth be held in appropriate locations.' Like Racine," he added, shoving the clipboard at me again. "*Unlike* Hollywood."

Hollywood.

"Are you aware it took the average ICQP delegate two hours and thirty-six minutes to check in? They even sent some of the delegates to a hotel in Glendale."

"And Beverly Hills," I said absently. Hollywood. Bra museums and the Marx Brothers and gangs that would kill you if you wore red or blue and Tiffany/Stephanie and the World's Largest Oil Painting Incorporating a Religious Theme.

"Beverly Hills," Abey muttered, pulling an automatic pencil out of his pocket protector and writing a note to himself. "I'm presenting the petition during Dr. Gedanken's speech. Well, go on, sign it," he said, handing me the pencil. "Unless you want the annual meeting to be here at the Rialto next year." I handed the clipboard back to him. "I think from now on the annual meeting might be here every year," I said, and took off running for Grauman's Chinese.

> When we have the paradigm, one that embraces both the logical and
> the nonsensical aspects of quantum theory, we will be able to look past
> the colliding electrons and the mathematics and see the microcosm in
> all its astonishing beauty.
>
> Excerpt from Dr. Gedanken's keynote address

"I want a ticket to *Benji IX*," I told the girl at the box office. Her name tag said, "Welcome to Hollywood. My name is Kimberly."

"Which theater?" she said.

"Grauman's Chinese," I said, thinking, This is no time for a high entropy state.

"Which theater?"

I looked up at the marquee. *Benji IX* was showing in all three theaters, the huge main theater and the two smaller ones on either side. "They're doing audience-reaction surveys," Kimberly said. "Each theater has a different ending."

"Which one's in the main theater?"

"I don't know. I just work here part-time to pay for my organic breathing lessons."

"Do you have any dice?" I asked, and then realized I was going about this all wrong. This was quantum theory, not Newtonian. It didn't matter which theater I chose or which seat I sat down in. This was a delayed-choice experiment and David was already in flight.

"The one with the happy ending," I said.

"Center theater," she said.

I walked past the stone lions and into the lobby. Rhonda Fleming and some Chinese wax figures were sitting inside a glass case next to the door to the restrooms. There was a huge painted screen behind the concessions stand. I bought a box of Raisinets, a tub of popcorn, and a box of jujubes and went inside the theater.

It was bigger than I had imagined. Rows and rows of empty red chairs curved between the huge pillars and up to the red curtains where the screen must be. The walls were covered with intricate drawings. I stood there, holding my jujubes and Raisinets and popcorn, staring at the chandelier overhead. It was an elaborate gold sunburst surrounded by silver dragons. I had never imagined it was anything like this.

The lights went down, and the red curtains opened, revealing an inner curtain like a veil across the screen. I went down the dark aisle and sat in one of the seats. "Hi," I said, and handed the Raisinets to David.

"Where have you been?" he said. "The movie's about to start."

"I know," I said. I leaned across him and handed Darlene her popcorn and Dr. Gedanken his jujubes. "I was working on the paradigm for quantum theory."

"And?" Dr. Gedanken said, opening jujubes.

"And you're both wrong," I said. "It isn't Grauman's Chinese. It isn't movies either, Dr. Gedanken."

"Sid," Dr. Gedanken said. "If we're all going to be on the same research team, I think we should use first names."

"If it isn't Grauman's Chinese or the movies, what is it?" Darlene asked, eating popcorn.

"It's Hollywood."

"Hollywood," Dr. Gedanken said thoughtfully.

"Hollywood," I said. "Stars in the sidewalk and buildings that look like stacks of records and hats, and radicchio and audience surveys and bra museums. And the movies. And Grauman's Chinese."

"And the Rialto," David said.

"Especially the Rialto."

"And the ICQP," Dr. Gedanken said.

I thought about Dr. Lvov's black and gray slides and the disappearing chaos seminar and Dr. Whedbee writing "meaning" or possibly "information" on the overhead projector. "And the ICQP," I said.

"Did Dr. Takumi really hit Dr. Iverson over the head with a gavel?" Darlene asked.

"Shh," David said. "I think the movie's starting." He took hold of my hand. Darlene settled back with her popcorn, and Dr. Gedanken put his feet up on the chair in front of him. The inner curtain opened, and the screen lit up.

KATHE KOJA

Skin Deep

Since her debut last year, Kathe Koja is receiving wide attention as one of the most exciting new writers around, and has become a frequent contributor to *Isaac Asimov's Science Fiction Magazine, SF Eye,* and elsewhere. Her first novel, *The Funhole,* is due to be published soon. Her story "Distances" was in our Sixth Annual Collection. She lives in Willowbrook, Illinois.

Here she gives us an unsettling depiction of a close encounter of a *very* unusual kind . . .

▼

Skin Deep

KATHE KOJA

The morning, air like steam curling wetly down his throat—the daily bastard rush of the heat: there was no getting used to it, not for him anyway. Skin moist and mushy, like staying too long in the shower, hair always frizzy-slick, always sticking to something, breath like water in his mouth. The bed was a lake of last night's dreamy sweat, so Taylor sat up to smoke a handrolled cigarette, two fingers absently brushing the puckering sores on his chest and neck; there were more, on his buttocks and thighs. They didn't hurt. He put out the cigarette, other hand flapping on the nightstand for his glasses: flimsy things, round-lensed with plain pale glass. It pleased him to affect such a quaintness; it gratified his growing sense of the grotesque.

He dressed in the bathroom, pulling clothes from the shower curtain rod. A rich mold had begun in the tub. He ignored it. Shoes, keys, cigarettes, out the door.

The woman at the doughnut shop: "Hey-hey, Blondie," she always called him Blondie, "lookin' a li'l worn out today, huh? Big night last night?"

"The biggest." Spatulate silver tongs, heavy brown doughnuts creamy with grease; she put three in the bag, added an anemic danish, squeezed his fingers as he paid. Outside it was hotter than ever and not even noon. The air conditioner in his car hadn't worked since January.

Parking, the doughnut bag sagged against his bare thigh; it made him shiver. Her building was old, one of the oldest on the block, and that was saying something. No security, no buzzers, no elevator: no notion, in those days, of such niceties. As he doubletimed it up the stairs, new sweat drizzled on his sores, starting a soft throb in rhythm with his heart, beating too fast for the mere exertion of climbing. His hard knock on the door pushed it open.

"Here," his voice gluey in his throat, thick with anticipation, "I brought you something sweet," and he proffered the bag to where she lay, there in the corner between the TV and the unused bed, all of her pulsing, a faint visible vibration, her color the sweet pink sheen of a baby's mouth, shading to a delicate violet as he gave her the bag, and, in the giving, tore it. Fatty chocolate, the hungry glow of her, and he was hungry, too, oh yes. Keys, he dropped them, shoes off, shirt off in one motion and shorts in the other, sores throbbing, hard-on aching, and fell upon her, literally, entirely, eyes closed and mouth open, sucking in her smell, enveloped in her, her name wet in his throat.

He cried out when he came, a breathless spent sob of pleasure, and she generated her special purr, a basso that tickled his bones. With his free hand, he rubbed at the sweat on his face, blew out breath like a swimmer: whoo! One of the doughnuts had rolled under the TV stand, and he fished it back with one foot. "Here," and she ate it, the operation as always a queasy thing to watch: so many *teeth*, and all of them like—what? rubber? spines? Anemone teeth, yeah. "Good?" and she told him yes, it was very good.

He lay in her for a while, mindless enjoyment of her rich buoyancy, talking quietly as she purred, until inevitably he stiffened again, and again she made him cry. On the TV, an earnest white man implored him to SEEK HOME PROTECTION, PLEASE! before a backdrop of window bars worthy of vanished Spandau. Then the credits for "Another World," and he sat up, dizzied, wiping more sweat. Time to go, but he dallied, fingerfed her the last crumbs, talked more daily nonsense, took two exhausted bites of the cheese danish; it lay like lead in his mouth.

"Trish," swallowing with difficulty, "Trisha, I have to go now." He stroked her, rubbing skin between fingers, loving, again, the sheer *feel* of her. "Tomorrow?"

She gave him to understand No; with the usual complicated juju, she made him understand *Thursday*, and he frowned, defeated by the thought of two whole empty days. He dressed, holding a chairback for support; dizzy again, with the exertion and the heat she loved. "Bye, babe," he said, made proud by her soft drowsy sounds. "I'll be back on Thursday, okay? Bye," and he walked downstairs like an old man, the new sores seeping gently through his shirt.

Her name was no more Trisha than his was the sounds she made when she saw him, but they had to call each other *some*thing. He had been seeing her for six months, time enough for shamefaced urge to become urgent complacency: every three days at least, shine, rain, or hurricane. Time enough too to stop questioning, aside from the lingering idle wonder of what the hell?

He had come upon her (ho ho) by silly accident. A friend, bitterly bitching about an old girlfriend and his hostage wardrobe still at her place, and he,

Taylor, paying back an old favor: "I'll get it back for you, man," chuckling all the way to the broken-down apartment building, chuckling as he turned the friend's purloined key, choking on his chuckle as he saw the new tenant. Skinned his hand raw on the bannister, fell one-kneed and cursing into the afternoon heat of the street, went back and told his friend Get your own fuckin' clothes! He suppressed the part about the living lump of twinkling flesh; no sense in having people look funny at you, friends, police, board of health, whoever.

Had she drawn him back, after so inauspicious a meeting? He'd toyed with that thought later, for otherwise how explain his *next* visit? Bowstring tight, sneaks poised for the first one-minute mile, opening the door like the girl in a horror movie whom the audience jeers for her mindless courage.

"Still there," he'd mumbled through tight teeth, "still fucking *in* there," but nothing happened. He stared, panting, exquisitely cautious. The lump moved. He was gone.

He came back. This time the lump looked—oh shit, forlorn? Stupid, but strangely true. That time he'd stayed long enough to learn something even stranger: it was a very smart lump; it was not really a lump; it was a female. (A female *what*, the jury was still out on that one.) But finding out it, *she*, was intelligent lessened his fear, and finding that she could *talk*, after her fashion, and he understand after his, lessened it further. By the end of a week he was feeding her, day-old bread and stale doughnuts, giddy with his own bravery, proud of his bizarre adventure.

The direction it took seemed laughably preordained, later—she *was a girl*, right? An accident, a stumble as he adjusted the TV for her (she liked TV, any TV) and his bare foot brushed her bulk. He had literally jumped, startled beyond fear at the sheer *difference* of it, the purely—say it—*alien* feel of her. And beyond the shock, like an echo: pleasure. Only a whisper of what she could give, but enough even then to intrigue him. Pig for it, he'd mocked himself nervously, and to the undercurrent of her encouragement touched her again. And again. And again, so caught up in the strangeness that his orgasm, when it happened, was almost a surprise; his sticky shorts rode home with him as testimony. You're *sick*, he'd told himself, half-laughing, half-guilty, you'll fuck *anything*.

The first sores had horrified him. Oh shit I got the alien AIDS, worse than AIDS, I know it is, and he drove there barefoot and shirtless, confronted her in a terror so great he was nearly in tears. She waited out his hysteria, then explained, in her wordless patient way, that the sores were harmless, a by-product of sorts of the meeting of their disparate skins. Comfort came from her in tsunami waves, and he wept with relief, believing her utterly. Harmless, she said *harmless*, and with a different sort of relief, he shed his jeans.

The biggest questions—what, how—she ignored, or could not answer. His curiosity was very great at first, but when she grew agitated, her color changing, her underbelly swelling like a bullfrog's throat, he stopped asking, instead tried to calm her down. After a while he even stopped caring, though he wondered how she fared on the days he did not visit—their times together regulated, always, by *her* choice: apparently she prized her privacy—and how she fed. He wondered, too, who owned the building and why he didn't come calling for tardy rent. Of course, she'd be daunting—she'd daunted the hell out of him, hadn't she? And she was being *nice*. About this too he stopped caring; somebody else's problem, after all.

As his visits progressed, the day-old treats became freshly-baked (she had a glutton's passion for chocolate), the talks less perfunctory and more intimate, the intimacies more profound. It was a cliché, but he could talk to her about anything, absolutely anything: she was interested in whatever he had to say, at any length. She was soothing when he needed to be soothed, exciting when he wanted stimulation, silent when quiet was what he craved. And she was so easy to please, her wants minimal. Because that was so, he did more than she asked, brought sweeter treats, cleaned the apartment (while his own place grew more moldy by the day), brought rabbit-ears for the TV when the reception grew balky; he wanted to pay for cable, but neither could figure out a way for installation without unwelcome discovery, so she had to make do with network. Never mind, she said: she loved the soaps, could recite their byzantine intrigues by the hour, a litany of names like Tracey and Reva and Nola: she did it sometimes to amuse him. Her favorite character was called Trisha, and so he called her that; the name pleased her very much.

If someone had pointed out to Taylor that he had become obsessed, he would have laughed, but the truth was that there was little else in his life anymore but her. He had no time for other friends—he was either anticipating the next visit or recovering from the last one—and his barhopping nights seemed, now, a waste of time. A waste of time, too, his job at the video store, reluctant manager to bored clerks; he could not afford to quit, but did the minimum, sliding by. His apartment looked like a garbage can. (He joked, in a tentative way, about moving in with her; her instant negative surprised and wounded him. They never spoke of it again.)

He wanted to come more often: every day, if possible. Not possible, she told him, agitation riding beneath her calm refusal. "Every other day then," he said, trying for a light request, surprised himself by the anxious demand of his voice. "C'mon, that's okay, isn't it? *Isn't* it?"

When *I* say, she said, and would not discuss it. That day she was particularly loving, but he was angry and refused to be placated. He left without asking when he might come back, and stayed away for four straight days. When he returned, on the morning of the fifth day, he was half in tears; he could not understand why she would not grant him more time.

He sat in his dark apartment, the TV on without sound, drinking lukewarm beer, absently fingering his sores. Was she growing bored with him? She *seemed* happy, but how could he know? He was at the mercy of her disclosures, and she said nothing about herself; all they talked of was him. How to find out? She would not answer willingly. Force was out of the question, and in any case, he could never bring himself to hurt her; even to think of threatening her made him feel sick. He drank another beer, two, four, and fell asleep with his mouth open. His dreams were of her.

He did not ask again, did not even bring up the subject. But it festered, making him one time sullen, the next almost unctuous. In their times apart, he sat imagining, angrily wondering what solitude provided that *he* could not. Inevitably his imaginings grew redder, and he came to believe it was not her need for solitude that kept him frustrated and at bay.

It was after a long night of stale beer that he began to watch her building. Not spying, he told himself, just—watching. His beachhead was the greasy spoon across the street from her building, its windows bleary with old fumes, its counter permanently scarred like the veteran of some dire chemical war. He sat there, waiting out the breakfast rush, waiting for a seat by the farthest window. When it emptied, he took his coffee and toast and established himself there, pretending to read the paper. It was a B-movie move, but nothing better suggested itself: if he sat there openly staring, they would make him leave.

He drank his coffee, ate his toast so slowly it hardened. He rested his elbows on the headlines and watched, but nothing happened that he could even remotely connect to Trisha: people left the building, others came: a man in khaki shorts and a red T-shirt, a fat man in an ancient summer suit, a woman in a mottled tank dress. The woman had a halfass furtive air, but maybe that was just his imagination. Besides, what would a woman have to do with Trisha? What would *any* of them? Asshole, he told himself, go home. And he did.

But he came back, kept coming. He became a regular, quiet and surly in his window booth. One morning, parking, another idea, child of frustration, had birth: forget the greasy spoon, he would watch from *inside* her building. No one would question or even wonder; it was not a place where motives were asked. He took the paper and a can of beer, and settled in the aching heat at the top of the stairs, sipping, sweating, waiting.

It was an hour, maybe two—he wore no watch—when he heard her, not speaking, unmistakable: somehow she *knew* he was there, and was calling him. Peremptory, almost angry—Trisha, angry with *him*! He went to her —there was no way not to—and saw her wear a darker color than he had ever seen before, a deep coral flush. The surface of her seemed to glitter, and her voice was higher, less understandable.

She told him to stop it. Stop it *now*.

"Stop what?" but he was obviously guilty; he was flushing, too. And angry, angry as she. "It's a free fucking country, isn't it?" and more, getting louder and less coherent, until she ordered, *ordered*, him away: go home, she said, almost red now, never do this again. And unspoken, unspeakable, the threat that she would send him away for good. "Go to hell," he shrieked, and hurled the nearest thing—a cracked plastic ashtray full of old butts; it did not hit her, but the ashes sifted down to settle on her skin. He slammed out, ran down the stairs, drove off with much squealing of tires and open-window cursing. He was badly frightened: of banishment, of the impossibility of never seeing her, never having her again. Frightened not of her anger, but at what had prompted it; instinct had been right; there was more than privacy at stake here.

He went back. He had to; even the risk was less than the need to know. More cunning this time, he hid on the ground floor, sitting beerless, solemn and immobile in the greenish shadow of the door, determined to wait all day and all night, to wait until an answer came. The heat seemed more brutal, or perhaps that was his fear.

Not so many people in-and-out today. The khaki-shorts guy, as usual, hurrying past without a glance, hurrying up the stairs. He followed, very very quietly, creeping like an insect to the top of the stairs. Khaki Shorts went down her hallway; Khaki Shorts, my God! Khaki Shorts went *inside* her apartment. Without knocking! Without a key!

It was hard to breathe, all of a sudden, hard to stand. Sweat ran down his sides. His sores tingled. Without knowing he did it, he turned her doorknob, with one lurching motion slammed open her door. He stood in the doorway unmoving, unspeaking, *seeing.*

Khaki Shorts was already out of them, one naked sore-spotted leg already resting on Trisha's sweet pink bulk, erection rapidly wilting at the sight of Taylor in the doorway. "What the *fuck?*" said Khaki Shorts, and in one lunge Taylor grabbed him by the arm and punched him solidly in the face, punched him again before an answering punch knocked his own air away. He fell back, landing square on his ass, a comical pose. Trisha's brick-red color was grimmer than anything she might have said. Khaki Shorts was bellowing "What the fuck's your *problem,* man? You her *pimp* or something, man?" and Taylor got up, shaking his head, his mouth hanging open, staring like a walking lobotomy, and kneed Khaki Shorts as he dressed; a motion of perfect violence, perfectly executed. Khaki Shorts let out a mumbled grunt and vomited, down on one knee, and Taylor turned and left.

Driving home he cried, still open-mouthed, sick with a grief he could not control, empty of all rage: this was far too serious for stupid anger. You her pimp, man? You her *pimp,* man? He drove past his own apartment, had to turn around and go back. Inside he sat staring down at his hands, his shaking hands. He sat that way until it grew dark, then light again. His hands had stopped shaking. He knew what he had to do.

He parked across from her building, left the keys in the car. His walk was brisk, unhurried. There was no expression on his face. He opened her door on a woman with bright blonde hair and sagging breasts, her pulpish body bright with sores: "Don't mind me," he said, voice too flat but void of threat. "Just go on," and he went into the bathroom and carefully closed the door.

The woman left at once, and Trisha's command came to him, ominous and cool. He was not afraid. He left the bathroom, came to sit beside her. She was a fierce tomato color, and her teeth were exposed.

"I love you," he said, very calmly. "But I can't share you."

She did not answer, but slowly, too slowly to track, she went from red to pink again, the softest, palest pink he had ever seen her wear. She did not question him—he was grateful for that—in fact did not speak at all, only reached with her bulk, her loving vastness, opened herself to him: a long precious lovemaking, absolute in its kindness: she understood what he needed.

He did not cry, this time, nor did he move from her. All his sores were bleeding, fresh red blood and a cool fluid, and the mixture beaded, ran off her skin. He was weak, too weak to take more than tiny erratic breaths, too weak to keep his eyes open; but before they closed for good, he saw her go a color for which there was no name, and he knew it for her true color, the color of her heart. A sweet and luminous smile, and her embrace grew stronger and stronger, a force terrific but completely painless, like being hugged to death. He felt the precise moment when his heart stopped: it felt like a door, closing with rich finality. Yes, he thought, still smiling, or at least it felt as if he was.

There is such a thing as heaven and hell; she was a long-lived organism. How long, she wasn't sure; she was apologetic, but never mind, he told her, we can find out together. What he did not tell her was that he could *feel* them, still, when they came to her, a grubby parade of them, endless as a soap opera.

He had never enjoyed soap operas, but he had time, now, to change his mind.

STEVEN POPKES
The Egg

One of the fastest-rising young writers in SF, Steven Popkes has become a frequent contributor to *Isaac Asimov's Science Fiction Magazine, Night Cry, The Twilight Zone Magazine,* and elsewhere. His well-received first novel *Caliban Landing* appeared in 1987, and he is involved in working on a projected anthology of "Future Boston" stories being put together by the Cambridge Writers' Workshop. He has a master's degree in physiology, and lives in Somerville, Massachusetts.

In the poignant story that follows, Popkes spins a tense and suspenseful tale of a boy caught in a deadly web of conflict and intrigue between competing alien races in a future Boston that's been opened to the stars.

▼

The Egg

STEVEN POPKES

The rusty, pitted steel was soft but sharp as a knife. It was thirty or forty feet back to the beach. I didn't really want to climb back down; I didn't even have to look to convince myself. I knew how far it was. I tried rehearsing things I could say to my Aunt Sara: "Once I got that high, I had to keep going. It was too far to get back down" or "I was just trying to go up a little ways, but then I got stuck." I shook my head. Didn't wash. She'd never *told* me not to come here, but the wreck was the kind of thing she thought eleven-year-old boys Should Not Mess With.

Wasn't my home anyway.

I stretched my neck trying to see over the hull to the upper deck. I'd seen the wreck with Aunt Sara's binoculars a couple of weeks before. Well, Gray'd seen it and pointed it out to me. *I'd* needed the binoculars, not him. His eyes are a lot sharper than people's eyes. It had taken me a couple of weeks to figure out how to get over here—two condemned bridges and an old mud flat's worth of time.

It was a big ferry, forty meters if it was anything. It was called the *Hesperus*—I'd got that much from my cousin Jack before he decided I was too young to talk to. I stood there and looked at it. The pontoons had of course collapsed and rotted away—the wreck had been there about five or six years. There were broken tubes all over like so many snakes. These were the pressure fittings to fill up the pontoons, I think. Some of the blue and white paint was still showing in places on the housings, and where the brass fittings were still there and not all corroded and crumbled by the salt, you could still see a little yellow shine. It must have looked grand, running passengers and cars across the harbor, maybe pulling the whistle at some of the larger ships going up to Maine, or over to Europe or Africa—the kind of thing I'd read about happening on earth since I was a little kid.

I heard sort of a whisper from the beach and looked down. It was Mama. She stood on the sand staring at me, eyes frowned and crinkled at the edges, the way mothers get when they're worried. You know. She'd done that even when she was alive.

I said, "You worry too much, Mama." I looked up again. It wasn't that far. I looked back to the ground to tell her that but she was gone. I wished she'd stay in one place for a while.

I kept my balance by holding the edge of a warped hull plate. The ledge was narrow, rotting like an old log, but it carried me over the pontoon housings. The wind blew from inland. It went right through my jacket. Cold. I shivered like I was almost dead—the way the swamp miners shake when they cough back home. Home. That was something. This was supposed to be home, now. All my life I'd heard how good it was going to be on earth. Well, you could have had earth as far as I was concerned. It wasn't worth a dog's hind leg to me.

The upper hull wasn't crumbling like the housings, but it was slick from the greasy harbor water. I'd heard tell of the Boston Harbor Cleanup, but I didn't believe in it.

The wreck had two bridge towers. One of the automobile gates had fallen inward and the other was held up by just one rusty hinge. It was so heavy it didn't move with the wind. But, sometimes, it made these echoing cracks like gunfire a long way off. Let me tell you. I know what guns sound like.

The inside of the ferry was a hollow cave that smelled like the sea at low tide. You know the smell? I didn't, then. It's like something died and was pickled in gasoline. I followed this dark stairway from the auto bay to the passenger deck. You could see Boston from there, the domes looked like the foggy blue crystals Mama had on the shelf at home. I don't know what happened to them. They must have been auctioned off to pay for my ticket here. Anyway, the high buildings were just a bunch of sticks. I could see the boats just outside of Revere. I shaded my eyes but I couldn't pick out Aunt Sara's.

On the inland side of the wreck, I found a narrow little ladder that looked like it went up to the bridge. It shook some when I started to climb it, but I thought it was okay.

Halfway up, the ladder shifted. I stopped.

"Don't do this to me," I said softly. "I got enough problems."

The ladder creaked again.

"I said don't!"

The old rivets popped out of the hull. I grabbed on as hard as I could. Slow as a dream, the ladder pulled away from the hull and I began to fall. I cried out.

The ladder stopped in mid-air. I choked on the yell and looked down.

Gray stood below me, two arms holding the ladder, four arms holding the hull and the remaining two ready to catch me. I grinned and relaxed. "Hey there!" I called down to him.

Gray pushed the ladder back against the hull. "Ira, come down."

"I want to look at the bridge."

"It is not safe."

"You're here now, right? You're not going to let anything happen to me."

Gray considered for a moment. He didn't move at all when he did that, just stood still as a big, gray leather rock. "True. Go to the top of the ladder and stand on the ledge. I will follow."

I climbed to the top and stood away from the edge. Gray ripped the ladder entirely away from the boat and threw it over the side. Then, he leaped the thirty or forty feet to the upper deck and sat down to keep from bumping his head.

When he was alive, Papa described Gray like this:

"Well, he's huge, close to nine feet tall and a quarter ton in weight. You can't think of him as a whole, but only in pieces. Like, he's got the body of a bear but with these overlapping plates of leather of a rhino. His limbs are thick like the legs of an elephant, blunt at the end but with maybe a dozen small fingers, as hard and supple as the legs of a spider. His head is scaled to the rest of him with two wide-set eyes and a little mouth in the center, like the face of a buffalo. There are bumps and protrusions around his face that belong to nothing on earth.

"He's not ugly—in fact, he's kind of beautiful—but he's strange."

I don't know whether he's strange or not—I grew up with him and he always looked normal to me. But that part about the animals is right. I looked them up myself.

"This relic is dangerous," he said. "I wish you had invited me."

I looked away and felt a little guilty. "I wanted to see it for myself."

Gray was silent a moment. "Just so. I had forgotten you are getting older. You must use your own judgment, of course. Should I go?"

I leaned against him. His hard body was cold for a minute, but as I lay there, it grew warmer and softer. Gray was all the home I needed. Which was good, since I didn't have one anymore. "No. It'll be more fun with somebody to talk to." And Aunt Sara wouldn't be able to yell at me. "Let's look at the bridge."

The windows were broken and there were these different-sized holes in the boards where the instruments had been. Gray didn't say anything while I looked but followed me down the other side to the passenger compartments. There, the top had caved in and the open space was sunny. Pieces of metal and wire and chain were all over the floor. Old mattresses and rags were piled up against the walls. "Looks like dynamite in a mattress factory," I said and giggled.

"Adolescents' parties, perhaps." Gray pointed to one wall. "Look at the graffiti."

I nodded but I wasn't much interested. There was a crazy smell here, sour-sharp like ammonia or lemons. I had never smelled anything like it, and it made me curious. Rags were piled against the bundle of chains in the corner and the smell seemed to come from there. I reached toward the pile and Gray stopped me.

"Wait a moment," said Gray.

I held back. He never did anything without a reason. He's funny that way—not like people, you see. He always knows what he's doing.

He delicately pulled apart the rags. In the center was an egg the size of a basketball.

"Huh." I stared at the egg. It was wrinkled gray, with smears of yellow and red on the sides.

"What kind of egg is it?" I leaned over Gray's arm.

"I have no idea."

"It could be anything!"

Gray nodded.

"It could be dragons. Or griffins." Gray just looked at me. I grinned at him. "Well, okay. It *could* be aliens nobody has ever heard of. It could take us somewhere." Somewhere different. Better.

"The universe is a large place. It could be many things."

"Can we hatch it?"

Gray replaced the rags, then turned to me. "If you wish."

The sun was getting low. I could feel the chill in the wind. The cold might be bad for the egg. Dragons. Griffins. Gray never said there weren't any; just that they were hard to find. "Should we take it back to Aunt Sara's boat? It's going to get cold here."

Gray was silent. "It was put here on purpose. Something thinks this is the best place for it."

That made sense. "I'll come back and check it tomorrow."

Gray stood. "It is getting late. We should go back."

"Okay."

Gray helped me down the side of the wreck and walked beside me. "Ira," he said suddenly.

"Yes."

"Let me come with you when you visit the egg."

I shrugged. You could trust Gray. You could trust him with anything. "All right." We walked on a little further. I felt cold and tired. "Carry me?"

Gray did not answer but picked me up and held me close against his belly with a middle set of arms. Gray's belly grew warm and I got sleepy. For a second, I thought I could hear my mother but it was just a night bird.

"Mama was watching me climb the wreck."

"Did she say anything?"

I shrugged. "No. She was just worried." I liked the feel of Gray's arm, the muscles under the thick leather. Like elephants or rhinos. I'd seen pictures, like I said before. "I miss them."

"I do, too."

I could see Papa walking next to Gray. Then it got too dark, but I could still hear him walking. I felt sad and sleepy and about to cry. "Papa?"

I don't think he heard me, but in a minute he began to sing:

> I dreamed I saw Joe Hill last night,
> alive as you and me,
> I said Joe Hill you're ten years dead,
> I never died, said he.

He used to sing that to me at night, when I couldn't sleep.

Gray was quiet. I snuggled deep into his arms. I felt warm and safe and I didn't feel I had to cry for a while. Pretty soon, I fell asleep.

Damn.

Sara Monahan hated boats.

Boats wobbled, wiggled, and writhed to the beating of the sea. Boats were dirty. Boats smelled.

She cut the motor in the dory and let it drift the last five or six meters to the dock. It was time enough for her to light a cigarette and cough, ready the line and toss it over the cleat on the dock and pull the dory in. She didn't think about it. Sara Monahan had been a boat person all her life, first when she was born on the eve of the 2005 stock market crash and her father had spent their last savings on the boat hoping that it would be cheaper to keep up than a house. Then, she had grown into a young girl in the flooded city of Hull, amidst the squalor of *that* place. Sara shuddered at the memory. She'd never blamed the police when they bombed it, just her father when he wouldn't leave and her mother for siding with him.

They'd never made it out of the firestorm.

She'd dragged Roni wailing to the dory and gunned the ancient motor, praying it wouldn't die and gotten out just ahead of the police fighters. Sara and Roni had kept watch at the casualty lists in the refugee camps for nearly a year just in case. Nothing.

Screw Boston. Screw the police.

They'd made their way to Revere. Sara had scraped by studying for the welding certification exams and started work laying steel in the new building boom. Roni had boned up on the merchant marine and had emigrated as soon as she had passed. They'd barely written to each other for fourteen years.

Christ.

She looked up suddenly. It was nearly sunset. Never get anywhere if she kept thinking like this. She smelled her singed hair and the burnt metal on her jacket. A shower. She thought about Roni and Roni's kid: Ira. And Ira's nanny: Gray.

She groaned and got out on the dock. It rocked—Lord how she hated things that rocked. She boarded and clambered inside the *Hercules*. Sara threw her mask into a chair and leaned against the hull, waiting to see in the gloom. Nobody here. You could tell an empty boat. Something in the way it moved.

There was a grubby note from her son Jack that he'd gone to Kendall's for the night. Great. First a long drink, *then* shower. She coughed again. A photograph on the wall attracted her attention. It was Roni and her husband Gilbert on their wedding day. Sara opened the bottle and stared at the picture for a long minute. Gilbert was a little fat and wore glasses.

She upended the bottle and took a long drink, turned back to the photograph.

"I have better taste in men than you do, honey," she said to Roni. "Look at that guy. I've seen better faces on kitchen doors."

But mine stayed, her sister seemed to answer. *He didn't leave me pregnant with a son. Where is Mike now?*

"God knows, Roni." Sara drank some more from the bottle. "But when he touched you, you remembered it. Could you say the same?"

Roni didn't answer.

Just as well. If Roni could still talk, the first thing Sara would have asked was: where did she dig Gray up?

"Sara?"

"I'm not here." She stared at Roni. How come you look so miserably happy? You're dead.

"It's Sam."

Sam?

"Sam!" She capped the bottle and looked out on deck. There he was, little and bald and bearded. "Damn you for a fish. Sam! I haven't seen you all summer."

Sam grinned at her. "Been out to George's Bank, fishing. Just got in this morning. Came over to see how you were."

"We're fine." She grabbed his hand and pulled him inside. "You're just in time to save me from drinking alone."

One eyebrow cocked at her. "A young woman like you drinking alone? Shameful. I'll have to help. I'm civilized. I need a coffee cup to drink from."

"Bless you." She laughed.

They sat at the galley table, the bottle between them.

Sam nodded towards the dock. "Where is everybody? It's all empty slips."

Sara shrugged. "Looking for work, mostly. I was lucky to get a job in town. Most of them took off for Marblehead or Quincy—some new buildings, some dock work." Sara was almost giddy with the drinks she'd had earlier and with seeing Sam. "It's good to see you. I've been here mostly by myself this summer. Me and the kids."

Again, the eyebrow. "Kids? Have you been naughty?"

She grinned at him. "Hardly." Then she remembered and the smile left her. "It's bad news, Sam. It happened while you were away. My sister and her husband—well, they got caught in one of the union riots on Maxwell Station." Sara smiled faintly and shrugged. "Her kid and his—nanny, I guess—came to live with me."

Sam took her hands. "Sara. I am so sorry."

"Yeah." She turned back into the galley. "It happens all the time, right? To other people." Sara shook her head. "I still can't believe it, you know? It's been months but I keep expecting them to show up." She lifted a hand and let it fall, helplessly. She shrugged and looked at him, gripped his hands hard. "But it's good to see you, Sam."

They shared the bottle.

Sam looked around. "Where are they?"

Sara scratched her hair. To hell with a shower. It was worth it to see Sam. She lit a cigarette from her previous one. Sam watched her without comment. "Jack's over to Kendall's staying the night. Ira's out with Gray."

"His nanny?"

She giggled. "Yeah. Nine feet tall and looks like a rhino with eight legs. My sister got Ira an *alien* nanny."

"Jesus."

He looked owl-like with the twilight reflecting off his big eyes.

"Jesus," he said again. "It must have been crazy on Maxwell Station."

"Crazy enough to kill them both."

"Don't talk that way."

She took the bottle and killed the last of the rum. "You don't know what it's like. I—Roni was my sister. She went off and we didn't talk much, but still—now, she's gone off and got herself killed."

Sam shrugged. "It was pretty bad there. I read they had something called rotlung—"

She ignored him. "So I get this stupid telex from the staff at Maxwell Station that Gilbert and Roni had died in the 'disturbances.' I had to claim their bodies. I had to sign for them like a goddamn parcel post. And for Ira. And for Gray. And then, the funeral." Gray hulking over the mourners, always seeming to reproach her. Ira huddled against his legs, taking comfort. The tears started to fall down her face. "I'da sent him packing. But he's in the will. Do you understand that? I have to keep him or I don't get Roni and Gilbert's estate." She shrugged. "Not much, anyway. But it's a little bit."

Sam reached across the table and took her hand. She stopped as if struck.

What am I talking about? She smiled at him, embarrassed, and shook her head. "I'm a little drunk, Sam."

"Hush, Sara. It's all right."

She suddenly realized she was crying and wiped her face in her hands. "Jesus, Sam. I'm sorry."

Sam sat in shadow now. She could only see the faint shine of his eyes. "It's all right."

They were silent a long minute, then Sara withdrew her hand. "Know anything about aliens, Sam?"

"Not a thing."

She stood up and got them both glasses of soda. Enough drinking for a bit. Sam didn't protest.

"Well," she sipped the soda. The bubbles tickled her nose and she had to stop herself from sneezing. "Gray's a spatien. I haven't been able to find out much about them. They're supposed to be great workers, but they don't hang around much in this neck of the woods. Not enough work, I guess. All I know about Gray is that Roni and Gilbert found him somewhere out there, and now he's theirs."

Sam shrugged. "I don't know anything about it. There are lots of aliens in Boston, though. They're all cleared and called safe, anyway. Gray must be cleared, too."

"I suppose. I wish I knew more about him."

Sam smiled at her. "Roni trusted him with her kid. That's something."

Sara nodded.

Sam opened his mouth to speak but they heard a heavy tread on the dock. In a moment, the *Hercules* shuddered as Gray stepped on board. He was carrying Ira, asleep. The cabin was so low he had to shift Ira up two sets of arms and walk in on the lower three sets to fit.

"He's asleep," Gray said quietly.

Sara nodded. The bottle was out and she felt in the wrong, as she always did in front of Gray. When Gray took Ira into the boys' room she opened the port and tossed the bottle out into the water. It was stupid, but it made her feel better.

Gray came back out into the little galley. "Is there anything for me to do?" he said in a low voiced rumble.

"No," she whispered. Why was she always whispering? "No," she said more loudly. "Where you been all day?"

"We investigated a wreck near here."

A wreck. "Christ. You were looking at the *Hesperus*? That thing's twenty years old. It's dangerous. I wouldn't let my own kid go there. Nor Ira. You leave that thing alone. You hear me?"

"I hear you." Gray nodded slowly and went back outside. They heard him make his way to the bow and lie down.

Sam and Sara looked at one another for a minute or more.

"Ah, I see," said Sam. "Well, it's not like it's anything Jack didn't do, too."

"I know. But with the two of them out there—it's scary. It's been like that all summer." Roni, she thought. Poor Roni, though it was obscure to her why she felt sorry for Roni, whether it was because she was dead or because she had lived with Gray.

"Look," began Sam. "My dock's all filled with strangers. People from New York and Jersey. Let me come over here—you wouldn't be so alone and I wouldn't be surrounded by strangers."

She looked at him. It was like the breath of home to her. "Sam, I would like that."

"Good. I'll be here tomorrow." He stood up. "I have to go—got a new job tomorrow."

She nodded sleepily to him, stood and followed him to the dock. She called good-bye to him.

When she turned around, the moon had risen. She saw Gray was dark and motionless against the silvered deck, the shrouds and lines like so much spider webbing. Sara passed by him and he did not stir.

Mama was sitting next to my bed when I woke up. She touched my forehead and that startled me awake. "Hi," she said softly. "How are you feeling?"

"Lonely. I went out to the wreck because of that. Were you very worried?"

"Not too much. Gray was there."

"Yeah." I rubbed my eyes. "Are you coming back soon?"

"I can't come back. You know that."

"You're here, aren't you?"

She smiled at me and didn't answer. I smiled back a little bit. I couldn't help it when she did that.

"I miss you." I felt like I wanted to cry again.

"I miss you, too. Are you being a good boy like I told you? How is Gray?"

I wasn't sure so I just shrugged. "You know how he is. It's hard to tell what he's thinking."

"What do you think he's thinking?"

"I don't know." I shrugged again. "I don't think he likes Aunt Sara. She doesn't like him."

"Oh." She looked thoughtful. "You be sure you take care of Gray."

"Mama." I grinned at her. "Gray takes care of me! You have to come back to take care of him."

"I told you. I can't. Will you take care of him?"

It didn't seem like that was the way it would be, but I was willing. "Okay."

Then, she was gone and Aunt Sara knocked at the door.

"Honey?" Aunt Sara opened the door and looked inside. "Were you talking to somebody?"

She coughed like Mama. For a moment, it was almost as if Mama had come back for good. But I smelled the cigarette smoke instead of the sweet swamp smell and knew it was just Aunt Sara coughing from that and not Mama coughing up like she did just before bed, back home. I didn't want to talk to her right then. So I pretended I was asleep. I could see she watched me for a long time, then closed the door and went off to bed herself.

Jack came back early in the morning before she left. He was a quick boy, slick in his movements, getting by on a wink and a grin. He was easy about most things. Sara watched him as he came on the dock towards the *Hercules*, whistling. She couldn't help grinning. Mike had been exactly the same way: wild Irish good looks, a quick grin. When he had touched her. . . .

She shook her head. Mike had left fourteen years ago.

"Hey, ma."

"Hey, kid. How was Kendall?"

"Okay. Got any food around here?"

She nodded. "Gray still outside?"

"I didn't check." He rummaged around in a cupboard and brought out an apple. "When are we going to get rid of that creep?"

"Don't talk about him that way."

Jack stared at the ceiling and rolled his eyes. Sara laughed, looked at the clock. "Christ. I've got to get to work. You take care, now."

Sara grabbed her welding helmet from the hook on the door and dashed down the dock. As she reached the dory, there was an eruption of water next to it. She stifled a scream and backed away.

Gray held onto the dock and looked up at her. "Sorry."

"Christ on a stick." She stepped into the dory. "What the hell are you doing here?"

"Repairing the dock."

"Christ on a stick!" She gunned the motor and shot away towards Boston.

The Citibank building was not even half done; there were another three hundred stories to go.

The wind howled through the steel I-beams like a wolf. She grinned as she walked over the girders to the corner where she had left her torch. Over them, the crane crouched spider-like. It served as crane, resting space and the building's spine all at once. When the building's frame was finished, the top of the crane—the cab, pulleys, and gears—would be dismantled and shipped to another site. The crane's frame would remain forever part of the building. Her part of the job, welding the I-beams into place, would be finished in a month or so: the steel only went to the hundred and fiftieth floor. After that, it would be composites.

She liked being up here, building the bare bones of the building. People had been building and tearing down in Boston forever. Fitzpatrick, the union boss, was the seventh Fitzpatrick in the steelman's union. Christ, she thought. What must that feel like? Your father, your grandfather, every Fitzpatrick stretching back towards the Civil War. Maybe further. It was like a long chain—God! She'd love that feeling, to be tied to a family like that, to have brothers and uncles and sisters—

"Hey, Sara!"

Sara was so startled she almost lost her balance, something that hadn't happened to her in ten years. She turned and saw Sam walking across the girders towards her. "*This* is your new job?" she cried.

"You bet!"

"Great!"

He winked at her as he looped a safety line over the far corner. Sam held thumb and forefinger together and waved it to her, then pulled himself up over the top support beam.

Maybe her luck was changing. She leaned against a corner and looked down on Boston. It was a bright, sunny day. The light was broken and refracted and reflected by so many glass buildings it was hard to see exactly where the sun was. She liked the crazy quilt mirrors around her. Maybe Sam would like it, too.

Fitzpatrick shouted over to them and pointed down. Below them, the first I-beam of the shift was being brought up from the street. A few men with sledgehammers made ready to pound it in when it reached them. Sam moved away towards the crane team where he was working. She smiled after him and cranked up the torch.

Jack was in the kitchen when I got up. He grunted when I came out. I didn't like him much. I guess he felt the same way. He reminded me of the supervisor's kids back home. They always looked like they could get anything they wanted. They were always clean—or if they got dirty, it was something that washed off. Not like that gray gunk that made up the marsh around the station. It took alcohol to get that stuff off and then the smell made you sick. They stayed on the boardwalk. We stayed in the marsh. That was the way it was.

I only remember the Station. Gray tells me he and Papa and Mama were living on the Platform that orbits Maxwell Station until I was two or three, but we couldn't get enough work. That was where the station crew found Gray. He and Mama hit it off from the first—Papa, too. I wouldn't know: it was before I was born. The work went bust when I was born and a little while later we moved down on the station. My first memories are of the marsh.

Papa always said what a bad place it was. And it was, I guess. It was wet all the time, and there were slugs the size of your head that would take a bite out of you if you weren't careful. The air was different, too. It seemed you could never get quite enough to breathe—though everybody said the air was just fine. One thing you can say about earth: the air is good.

But the place was good, too. You could get away from people in the marsh. You could fish and swim. It was quiet—here there's always this kind of a rumble from the city.

Anyway, Jack didn't say anything to me when I got up. He barely moved out of my way when I went out on deck to look for Gray. I wanted to tell him not to say anything about the wreck. Gray's good, but he won't keep a secret unless you tell him. He's dumb that way.

He wasn't on deck and I didn't see him around the *Hercules* so I went back inside.

"Have you seen Gray anywhere?" I tried to be polite.

Jack didn't say anything. He yanked open the refrigerator and pulled out some milk.

"Did you hear me?"

"I heard you. I'm not deaf."

"Have you seen him?"

He looked at me. "I don't know where the creep is."

At home, I'd have gone for him right then. But, at home, nobody's ever thought to call Gray a creep. I didn't belong here. I never did. I never will.

He looked at me like I was a bug. "You're a creep, too. Why don't you leave? Huh? Asshole. I want my fucking life back. Leave us—we were okay until you got here."

I wanted to cry. "Maybe I will," I shouted and ran out of the boat, across the dock and into the marsh. After a while, I slowed down. Pretty soon, I didn't want to cry so much.

It at least looked more like home here. I remembered the egg and I started to head over towards the wreck.

I was halfway there before I remembered my promise. I mean, I hadn't said "I promise" to Gray, but it was still a promise. That was the thing: Gray knew what he meant when he asked me, and I knew what he meant when I answered.

I stopped in the middle of some soft ground and sat on a rock. I didn't have any place to go. I felt kind of lost and miserable.

Pretty soon, Papa came and sat down beside me. I would have hugged him but I was afraid he'd disappear. He wasn't as solid about being there as Mama.

"I think I'll run off," I said.

He sighed and leaned on his knees, pushed his glasses against his nose like he always did when he was thinking. He did the same thing that night Boss Skaldson said they were going to strike.

"You can't leave your family," he said..

"Family!" I picked up a stick and scratched the ground. "They don't want me. I never saw them before this summer."

"Still, they're your family now. Family's got to take you in when you got nowhere else to go." He coughed and turned away from me to spit something on the ground.

I looked at the ground. "I want you and Mama back." I stood up and walked away from him a little. "Why'd you have to go and get killed?"

"It had to be done, Ira. There were reasons—"

"*Family!* You and Mama ran off and left me with Gray. Family."

"Ira—"

"Gray's all the family I got."

I turned around and he was gone. There was nothing there but wind.

"I'm sorry," I said softly. "I didn't mean it."

I waited there for a long time, but he didn't come back.

Sam was painting the front deck when she drew the dory along the dock. "Hey," she called out to him.

"Yo!" Sam leaned over the railing. "You got a little trouble brewing."

She brought the dory close to him so he could speak softly. "With Gray?"

He shook his head. "Don't think so. Between Jack and Ira. Ira left this morning running like hell was after him—angry, you understand. Came back about an hour ago dragging his tail. Sad little kid. The big guy hasn't been around all day."

"Hm."

"I think," he looked up quickly at her and back at the water, a little embarrassed grimace on his face, "Jack doesn't take too kindly to Ira."

Sara pondered that. "I should get home," she said abruptly.

"Yeah, I've got to finish the forward deck before it gets too cold for the paint to dry." He left the railing and she could hear him whistling a quiet, mournful tune.

She tied up the dory and walked down the dock towards their slip. She was still a good distance away when she heard a slap and Ira crying. Jack was shouting something unintelligible. There was an eruption of water next to the boat and Gray was suddenly standing on the deck. He moved inside faster than she'd ever seen him move. Sara started to run.

From the deck she heard Gray's voice: "Stop talking like that."

"How come, creep? Huh?" Jack shouted.

She stopped outside. There was a short pause.

"Because you are torturing someone you love," said Gray.

There was no sound for perhaps a minute, then Jack began sobbing and she ran inside.

"What's going on?" she cried. Jack ran to her and buried his face against her. "Did he hurt you? Jack! What's going on?"

Gray was motionless. Ira looked at Gray, then back at Sara.

Jack pulled back from her and she could see the mark of a slap on the side of his face. "Did Gray do this to you?" she said quietly.

Jack didn't answer.

"If you hurt my son," she said to Gray. Her voice was low and terrible. "If you ever touch my son . . . I'll hurt you."

"I did it," said Ira. His face was white but calm.

She looked at Jack. "Is that true?"

Jack nodded.

"Why?"

Ira put his hands in his pockets and hunched his shoulders. "He called Gray a creep. It wasn't the first time."

She looked at Ira, then back to Jack, then back to Ira. Finally, she turned to Gray. "I still meant what I said."

"I know," said Gray.

Gray and I were gone the next day before sunup. I was ready to run off right then. I was ready to run off after dinner, but Gray said it wasn't right. I told him about what Papa had said and he said remember the three loves. Hell, I said, he'd been drilling me with that spatien stuff since I could talk. You shouldn't abandon your family, he said.

It was that kind of conversation.

Family.

On the way to the wreck, Gray didn't say anything. I didn't know what he was thinking, but I could tell he was thinking pretty hard about something. I guessed it was about Sara and Jack.

The egg was nearly twice as big as it had been the day before yesterday, and the smears were gone. Whatever it was, it had to have something better inside it than this. I began to think about what it could be. Gray was no help. He wouldn't even guess what it was. It always makes me mad, the way he won't guess anything. He only says things when he knows the answer to them, and what's the fun of that?

The egg was even more pretty now, with speckles of gold and silver, and the gray had begun to turn to a light blue. Whatever was inside of it had to be beautiful, too. I was still thinking of griffins and dragons, but if it wasn't either of them, it was probably something strange and unusual. I began to think about selling it. With the money, maybe we could buy a ticket out of here. Even Maxwell Station was better than this.

I helped Gray replace the rags over the egg, then the two of us sat on the edge of the wreck watching the ocean.

"I still want to run off," I said.

"You want your family back," he said.

It almost made me cry I felt so lonesome. He always did this to me, just when I thought I had things figured out, he'd say something true like that and it'd bust everything up.

"Do you remember the three loves?" he said quietly.

I'd known that since I could talk. "Again? Love of family, love of work, love of duty."

"Just so," he murmured. "And always in that order."

I shrugged, having a feeling I wasn't going to like what followed. But he didn't say anything more, just looked out to sea for a long time.

"I have to go to the Miller's Hall on Friday. Do you want to come?" he said finally.

Go to Alien's Center? Was he serious? "Sure." I was hot to go.

Gray nodded. "Just so. We will leave close to dawn. Can you be up that early?"

You bet I could.

Sam was standing on top of the beam, a safety line leading from him to the crane cable above him. He was so little, Sara thought. But it seemed no hardship for him to use the fourteen pound sledgehammer. He lifted it high in the air and brought it down on the edge of the beam. The beam rang like a great steel bell and edged another quarter inch between the two framing girders.

He was much stronger than he looked.

He suddenly smiled at her and she started, realizing how closely she had been watching him.

"Hey, lady," he called down to her softly. Sam leaned back over the edge of the girder, looking from one end to the other. He pulled himself back on top and walked to the other end and again lifted the hammer. Bells rang among the towers.

She lit a cigarette, watching the gulls fly down below them.

"Okay, check your end."

Sara nodded and pulled herself up to the edge of the framing girder and measured the angle. "Okay here."

"Weld that sucker."

She pulled down the mask and lit her torch. Three spot welds to hold the end, then up with the mask and she walked the beam to the other side. Three more spot welds.

"Come on down so I can get the rest," she grinned up at him, took a drag on the cigarette. He smiled and danced off the beam like a leprechaun.

Later, at noon, he brought his lunchbox over to her and they ate, watching the sunlight reflect between the buildings.

"You know what I like about Fridays," he said finally.

"No. What?"

He rubbed his hands together maniacally. "Payday. I can buy the *world*."

She laughed. "Hardly. Not on these wages."

Sam shrugged. "Well, it's my first payday." He looked away towards the harbor. "Say, how about dinner?"

"Dinner?" It was as if a sudden wind blew through her. The air did not grow colder but it seemed closer to her skin. "What do you mean?"

"I don't know." He poured himself a cup of coffee from the thermos. "It's been a long summer. I've been out on the Bank, you've been here. I could use the company—do you know what it's like to talk about fishing for three months?"

She laughed and felt relieved and a little disappointed. "I have to go home tonight, though. The kids would worry if I didn't show up."

"Gray could take care of them."

"Gray." She started putting the remains of her lunch back into the lunchbox. "I don't want him around my kids when I can help it."

"Hey." He reached out and touched her arm.

Sara looked at him. He was smiling. "That was a joke," he said gently.

"Yeah." She smiled a little. "Not much of a joke."

"So I'm brain damaged. Three months with the fishing fleets'll do that to you."

"Well," she said slowly. "I still can't go out tonight. I got to get home."

He didn't say anything for a long minute and Sara suddenly wanted to stroke his cheek, feel the smooth skin laid over with a light bristle. A man's cheek. It had been a long time since she had touched a man's skin. Or a woman's skin. Just hugs and touching with Jack, or Ira. But not the touching between—

"You could come over to my boat for dinner tonight," he said. His eyes were bright and his munchkin face was crinkled with a silent laughter.

She couldn't help grinning. "Are you going to make me dinner?"

"You bet." He rubbed his hands together. "Got some bluefish I brought back and some snapper. I know a guy on the pier I can trade with for a lobster. If you don't like that, I can get—"

Sara touched his arm and he stopped, looked at her hand, then at her.

"Is that a 'yes'?" he said.

"Christ. You—Christ." She threw up her hands. "Dinner. Now, let's work before Fitzpatrick fires us both."

Miller's Hall is named after this guy that first saw the aliens when they landed at Provincetown. Well, they didn't really land there. Some came out of the ship and asked directions to Boston. That's the way the story goes. Gray said it was a little different. He says they weren't really sure what was going on and whatever they asked those people might have sounded like asking for directions, but it wasn't that at all. Anyway, Miller is the guy's name.

We caught a ride with Kendall to Wellington Station and took the subway into town.

I'd never been downtown before. Miller's Hall sits across the street from the North End—where the Old North Church is. Gray told me about it and this guy named Paul Revere who carried these lights all across the towns, giving people fire. Up the other street from it is the old Customs House. Gray said it was also called the Gateway to the West. I'd never read anything like this, but maybe he'd read something I didn't.

The building itself was designed by the aliens so it doesn't look like people ought to live in it. Some do, though. I met a few. One side looks kind of melted, and the other shoots way up above the other buildings in this sharp pointed tower. It's a big place, most of a city block and maybe thirty or forty stories tall. There's a bigger diplomatic building out past Long Wharf in the harbor. It's huge, maybe two hundred stories or something. But, it's for big meetings and things. Miller's Hall is where the aliens rest.

While we were coming in on the subway, I tried to get Gray to tell me what we were doing here. He wouldn't tell me, just made that buzzing noise he makes when he doesn't want to answer a question.

"Well," I said, exasperated, "is it about the egg? At least tell me that."

He stopped and picked me up so I was looking at him straight in the eye. He didn't say anything for a minute and I began to get scared. Gray'd never acted that way before. He suddenly looked so *different* from me. I began to think maybe I should have stayed on the *Hercules*.

"Ira. Do you trust me?" he said in a very quiet voice.

"Sure." I shrugged.

"This is very important. Do not mention this thing at all today. Not on the street. Not in this building. Not on the train. Not on the boat home. Nowhere. Not until I say you can. Do you understand me?" Papa was behind him nodding.

That made me mad, both of them ganging up on me like that. "Then why didn't you leave me home if things are so secret."

He didn't say anything for a minute. "We are finding out information. Some information may have something to do with the egg. Some may not. It is useless to speculate. But because we, together, are hatching the egg, this concerns you. You have a right to be here."

"Okay, okay." I punched him on the shoulder. "Okay, already. Don't go formal on me."

"You still don't understand." He paused. "It is important you don't speak here. I do not know how to threaten or persuade you. I can only ask. More: do not display any untoward knowledge. You know my language, you know Lingua—this I have taught you. Hide that."

He put me down and we went inside.

The lounge had ten or twenty aliens of weird types. None of them paid much attention to us—I guess we weren't any weirder to them than they were to us. But the place looked strange to me. I mean it was all windows on all four sides, big windows, looking out over the harbor from maybe ten or twenty meters up. I looked back out the door we came in and it was glass and showed the street.

"What are these window things. Holograms?" I asked.

Gray shook his head. "No. They are windows." He looked at them a moment, then turned his head back to me. "N-space was used in the construction of Miller's Hall."

A little alien, shorter than me, came stalking over to me. He stood up at me, all shrunk up and deformed looking, wrinkled brown skin and these *big* blue eyes, swearing a blue streak. Finally, he calmed down enough to stare at me. "What are you staring at?" he said finally.

I started to get mad again, but I remembered what I promised Gray.

"Nothing," I said.

He humphed and hawed a minute. "Nothing. Nothing, he says. Nothing." He put his face almost nose to nose with me and all I could see was those blue eyes.

"Nothing. Tell me, runt, do *you* believe in fairies."

"No," I muttered.

"*Hah!*" he yelled and jumped back, laughing and clapping his hands. "A smart one! Hah!" He walked off clapping his hands.

I looked up at Gray and he looked down at me.

"What is that?" I asked.

"Don't worry. He likes you," Gray said.

"How can you tell?" I reached over and grabbed one of his lower legs and held it. I felt nervous all of a sudden.

"He didn't eat you, did he?"

I looked up at him and he just stared back. I punched him hard on the leg. That was Gray's idea of a joke. Like his name. All spatiens are Gray. No spatien had a human name until Gray. Naming himself something special with a name that all spatiens could use was Gray's idea of a joke. Like this.

It made me mad that he'd make a joke now, when ten minutes before he was warning me to keep quiet. Then, I figured out that Gray was trying to make me feel better, from what he had talked with me about outside. Maybe he'd even set it up. I punched him again on the leg.

We took a long elevator up into the pointed part of the Hall. Up here you could see all the islands, the different buildings out in the harbor, all the hovercraft. I looked down into the city and saw all the Back Bay canals, all with these little boats and canoes going down like people walking down streets. Gray was watching me.

"A hundred years ago, they were streets, not canals."

"Jeez." I shook my head. "What happened?"

"Boston sank. It's still sinking. Before that it was water again. They dumped landfill into the river and made Back Bay. When the Mayflower first came here, Boston was nearly an island." He pointed to the water in Back Bay, and the walls around the inner city ring. "The walls follow the contours of the original Boston." He paused. "The borders are being recycled."

He stared at me and I wrinkled my nose at him. "Ha. Ha. Some joke."

Gray shrugged and led me away from the windows through a long corridor. Again, there were windows on both sides. One side showed the harbor, the other showed the city. It was a different angle now, looking down on the streets with the big buildings, the old Customs House, things like that.

In the next room, there were just two opposite walls made of windows, both looking out on the same section of the harbor. This made me dizzy. I could see the same gulls flying on opposite sides of the room.

"Are *these* holograms?" I asked, not looking at either of them.

"No. Just windows."

The room had high ceilings like an auditorium. On the floor there was a thick carpet and big pillows where there were various kinds of aliens—too many to keep track of. It was like in one of those bird zoos—aviaries, that's the word—where there are forty or fifty kinds of birds and they move around and are these specks of color, some of them standing still and looking around, some of them hiding, a whole bunch of them shooting over you like bullets. But they aren't all that separate. They're all blurred together. The only way you can tell them apart is by staring hard at the ones that stand still, reading the little descriptions, and wait for the ones that are going like fire over you, hoping like hell you've remembered the names right. You just forget the ones that are hiding.

Well, I didn't have any descriptions.

I saw the little guy that had bugged me in the lounge walking around the sides, kind of watching me from the edge of the crowd.

We walked up to this one lounge and sat down. No one paid us much attention and we sat there for maybe ten minutes. I was getting fidgety.

"What do we do now?"

"We wait here."

"For what?" Maybe Gray had something planned.

"I am not sure."

That was all I could get out of him. He wouldn't even guess—spatiens are like that. They never talk about anything unless it's right there. A pain.

A couple of minutes later Gray began to rub my shoulders the way he does and I got relaxed and a little sleepy, so I leaned against him and he was real warm. I fell asleep like somebody clubbed me.

I dreamed about Papa. He was trying to tell me something but I couldn't hear him. It was like he was a long way away. He was all agitated and excited and nervous. He kept calling to me, and even though he was only across the room I couldn't hear him. I woke up and there was a kind of buzzing in the room. I sat up and looked around and saw a lot of the aliens looking towards the other door—the other door from where Gray and I had come in, that is. Through the other door was this centaur—that's what they're called. Not like the Greek myths, you understand. This wasn't half a man, half a horse. This was more like the body of a sow bug and the forward body of a praying mantis—like he was made of sharp points. All but his eyes. His eyes were big, with slit pupils like a cat's.

He came in the room, moving jerky—at first I thought there was something wrong with him. Then, I saw it was like he was in freeze frame motion. He didn't move smoothly, but in little jumps like a snapshot. I looked closer and saw I could just barely see him move between those freeze frames. He'd stop, look down at somebody—he must have been nearly three meters tall —somebody on his other side would speak to him and suddenly, he'd be turned to them. He was so fast it almost made me sick to watch him.

He sidled along the wall, talking to people. The whole room was watching him. It came to me, then, that he was moving towards us, stalking us, almost. With those wicked looking hands. It made me shake. I looked up at Gray. He was watching the centaur. I'd never seen him watch anything so close, even me.

Finally, the centaur came near us, looked up and saw us both, but only acted like he'd seen Gray. He straightened up and came over to us. "Old-one-of-many-names," he said in Lingua. "I did not know you were here."

Gray made kind of a half squat bow, never taking his eyes off the centaur. "Holy one, I, myself, can barely believe my good fortune."

The centaur leaned back against his lower half like an old man sitting down in an armchair. "It has been a long time since I have seen you. I have not seen a member of your family since we destroyed that nest—half a cycle ago? Perhaps a full cycle? Are you the last?"

Again, Gray made the half bow. "I do not think I am the last, Holy One. I estivated for almost two cycles before I was found. This was due to the destruction of my nest."

"Ah." The centaur raised his hand and let it fall like a shrug. "Of course. Is this your pet?" he said, looking at me for the first time.

I was almost crazy with nervousness, trying not to look like I knew anything, crazy to find out this thing had killed Gray's family. I wished I had a rifle, a laser, something. It wouldn't have done any good. You could see up close that he spent most of his time waiting for us to catch up. His attention was wandering all around the room. Sharp, though. Damned sharp. I just did my best to look stupid.

"It is no pet, holy one. It is my nephew."

"Are you certain?" The centaur put one arm on the other like a man folding his arms, but this looked like he was getting ready for something.

"I am certain, holy one. How are your offspring?"

The centaur looked up at him. "Fine. I brought two pupa with me and they will be molting soon. No eggs as yet. Pity, as I have been hungering for a delicacy a great deal. But it would be a shame to return home with no children so I have restrained myself. Soon, though, they will molt and of course become children. Tell me: do you think I would be too shamed by returning with only one child?"

"You have no eggs, holy one?"

"None as yet. I have tried several times but the flesh will not obey me." The centaur turned his head all the way around behind him, watching something for a quick moment and then brought it back again with a snap. I wanted to throw up. "Give me the pupa you have. It would be well cooked. Look," he pointed to me. "It does not even know language."

"I cannot, holy one."

"Come. Give it to me as a present." He stiffened somehow and looked just like a whip in mid-air.

I heard a soft sound from Gray and turned towards him. He'd extended every finger on every arm and each one grew a razor.

"I cannot, holy one," he said softly. "Forgive me."

They stared at each other for some minutes, then the centaur relaxed. "It is a very great sin. But, perhaps the fault is mine. I encourage my appetites as much as I can. Perhaps that is not always a virtue." His head snapped around and back again. "I must go, my friend. Until we meet again."

He turned and moved away as smoothly as if he'd been on wheels.

"What's going on?" I whispered to Gray.

"Hush." He retracted all of his fingers and sat back down.

"I want to go home. Let me out of this place."

He reached for me and held me close to him. "Be patient a while longer. We cannot leave just yet. It wouldn't be polite."

We sat there for maybe half an hour more, then Gray stood up. "We can go now."

Outside a fog had come into the city. I pulled my jacket in close. "Jesus. What was that all about?"

He didn't say anything immediately, just looked around the street and acted like he was listening for something. "It went better than I expected. I think we can talk now. It was about the egg."

"Christ!" Gray can really be a pain in the ass sometimes. "I know that. Who was the centaur? Why did we need to come here? Did he really destroy your nest—home, or whatever? Talk to me!"

Gray seemed to mull over that for a minute or two. "The centaur is— bishop is the best word, I think. I have met him slightly several times. His family and my family disputed over some territory in the Maxwell Station system. My family was destroyed, or if not completely destroyed forced to evacuate the system. I do not know where they are. Your people found me in the asteroid belt about a thousand years later. Before you were born. I thought the egg might be a centaur egg, but I could not find out directly— centaurs do not allow information about them to be published. They will talk about almost anything, but refuse to allow it to be written down. All I was able to find out was that there was only one centaur family on earth, and that it was the bishop's."

I shuddered. "Would he really have eaten me?"

Gray nodded. "They consider pre-sentients a delicacy."

"Pre-sentients?"

"A centaur has odd and rigid rules over what is a person and what is not: communication defines a person in most circumstances."

"Jesus! I could have talked to him!"

"I know that."

I hit him on the leg. "Why did you tell me to keep it a secret? I could have been killed. It just seems stupid."

We kept walking. "If you had spoken, he might have challenged you to an eating duel."

"I can eat with the best of them."

"An eating duel," said Gray carefully, "is a duel in which the loser gets eaten. To the centaurs, losers are not persons by definition."

"Oh," I said, feeling very small. "Why was I here at all, then?" I felt so lost and confused.

"I did not want the bishop to think I had come for revenge. If I brought my family, he would know for certain I had not come for war. I don't want to die either, Ira."

We walked a little further and I reached up and took his hand. "I'm sorry about your family, Gray."

Gray didn't say anything for a block or so. "They are gone."

As evening had fallen, a fog had come into town from the nooks and canals of Back Bay, rolled into the city like a stumbling drunk. As the elevator descended towards it, Sara had the feeling of diving into water or cotton or something else she could drown in. She was to meet Sam on his boat about eight. But right now, she needed a drink. She left the building almost as soon as she hit the ground floor.

Now, she was below the bright sunlight she had left on the ninetieth floor. The fog had given the city a dreamy, half-real quality. The locust trees in front of the old Customs House burned yellow through it, the fall colors pastel and washed out. The upper city was completely lost. Here, there was only this corner, filled with tourist shops, street vendors and a man selling flowers, each close and intimate in the fog.

She bought a pretzel from a cart and waited while the vendor warmed it in one of those battery powered alien ovens. One of those would be good on the *Hercules*, she thought.

Sitting beneath the locust trees and eating slowly, guiltily—Sam would be cooking dinner for her in a couple of hours—she was suddenly struck with the memory of Hull, burning. For a long moment, she could smell the explosions like fireworks mixed with the smell of burning houses and the sea. She remembered hitting a nameless man across the face with a crowbar—dark asian hair, stubble, wild eyes, blood spilling from his forehead as he fell into the water—when he had tried to take the dory away from her. She had tried to get to the house—the only house they had ever had after all that time living on boats, that her father and mother wouldn't leave and would not believe they had to leave until it was too late—when she found Roni, burned, arm broken, half swimming through the hip-deep water. Sara dragged Roni into the dory. She started up the motor again to get to the house when the MDC planes came in low and dropped something—she never knew what—that exploded into a sheet of flame. The firestorm raced towards them in a boiling, guttering wave. She turned the dory and gunned the motors. The flames leaped from house to house, low-pitched explosions following her. Don't foul the prop! Don't foul the prop! The dory burst out into the harbor. Up on Telegraph Hill, the gangs were shooting back. Hog Island was firing anti-aircraft guns at the MDC planes. Two planes banked towards it, fired two missiles—Sara grabbed Roni and dove into the bottom of the boat. There was a blinding flash and the sea roared around them. A hot wind sucked the breath from her lungs. There was a sound too loud to be understood. Then, it passed and utter silence came to her. Am I deaf?

She looked back and Hog Island was flattened. The fires had been blown by the wind into smoke.

Sara sat unseeing on the park bench, holding herself. She could never even identify where her house had been, much less her parents. It had taken hours just to find the *Hercules*. At least, that was intact. There were no looters. Maybe they were dead. Maybe they had been blinded by the flash. Maybe Sara was so deep in shock she couldn't see them. She left Hull, the smoke masking the sun into a deep red disk hanging sickly in the west, a cold south wind blowing them towards Boston. Roni never took her eyes off Sara that whole night. She watched every move Sara made.

Sara looked up at the locust tree and shook herself. Almost seven. Time to go. She stood up slowly, shaking off the memory. Someday, someday, she would bury that memory. Roni getting herself killed only made it worse. "Damn you, Roni," she said under her breath. "I didn't drag you out of there just to die like a dog."

It was that same south wind that blew across her on the way home. She lit a cigarette and rummaged in the dory's small hold. There was a half-empty fifth of rye whisky buried under a tow line. Do we want to begin here? Yes, I think we do. It is always better to begin early. You're in too lousy a mood for dinner with Jesus Christ himself, much less Sam. That's it. Take a good one. Feel that deep, aching warmth burn in your belly.

Jack was waiting for her on the *Hercules*.

"Hey, honey," she said as she tied up. "I'm home."

Jack nodded shortly. He leaned against the hull and stared moodily out the window.

Damn. He's acting like a teenager again. "Something wrong?"

"No."

"Sam asked me over to his boat for dinner." No response. "Your Mama's got a date."

Jack didn't look at her. "That's good," he said distractedly.

Damn. He's getting more like his father every day. Don't think about Mike. Don't. He was slime. He was scum. And didn't I want him back for the longest time?

She sat next to him and watched him in the darkening light. The whisky and the sunset light met and mellowed in her. Ah, Sara. Don't you miss him, though.

"Hey, honey," she said softly.

Jack looked at her and she started to reach out and hold him but she could feel him stiffen. "What's the matter, Jack?"

Jack shrugged again. "I don't know. I'm still thinking about it." He looked up at her searchingly, then seemed to find something that reassured him. He grinned. "I'll be okay. You go have a good time with Sam. Gonna find me a pop?"

It was an old joke, but thin now. She slapped his knee lightly. "Watch your mouth. Christ. I've got to take a shower."

She left Jack on the Hercules some time later, walked nervously over to Sam's *Casey*. She was wearing a dress—she hadn't worn a dress in years. She was even wearing earrings.

Sam was wearing a jacket—from the way he wore it, he hadn't worn a jacket in years, either. That made her feel better.

He didn't say anything as he gestured her inside, then leaned down and whispered conspiratorially: "I've got steak."

"Go on," she laughed.

"No. Honest." He pointed to the galley. "It's in there. You can see it for yourself."

"That's a day's salary."

"Steak," he said. "Meat. Beef. Carne. Le boef. Thick, juicy, broiled, bloody—"

She laughed and touched his mouth to make him stop and he did and her fingertips tingled. Sara pulled them back and folded her arms, embarrassed.

"Anyway," he said suddenly after a silence, "I've got it. And we're gonna eat it. You may as well adjust."

"I'm adjusted. Let's eat it now."

He shook his head and held up his hands palm towards her. "Not so fast. We have to make preparations. We can't insult the cattle gods."

She sat down and began to laugh. It was uncontrollable and she sobbed and held her stomach.

"It wasn't that funny," he said with a shy grin.,

"Damn you," she giggled. "You did this to me in high school, too. I'd forgotten."

"My dear, my dignity is ruined."

"Christ, it's good to see you again."

He didn't reply. "Dinner is served."

Steak was rare—usually meat came like a slab, grown in the huge meat farms in the midwest. Steak came from an animal. A cow? No. Steer. It came from a steer. Steak was expensive.

Sam had broiled it perfectly.

"Do you like it?"

She made an inchoherent noise around a piece of gristle and nodded.

Half an hour later, she leaned back and patted her full stomach. "I am satisfied. Life is good."

Sam leaned towards her. "There's more."

She shrugged. "It could only be a letdown."

He reached above them and out of a cabinet pulled down a bottle. "I don't think so." He handed her the bottle.

Her eyes grew round. "Glenfiddich! Christ on a stick! How long have you had this?"

Sam grinned at her and leaned on the table. "My daddy gave it to me. He brought it back from Scotland a few years ago."

"Christ," she said again. "This is too much. Put it back, Sam."

"Too late." He brought down two glasses. "You don't want me to drink alone."

The scotch made her feel warm and sleepy, like the world had no more sharp edges. Sam turned on the radio and they listened to some fluffy pop station. She didn't like it. "Turn it to something else." She took the bottle and held it lovingly in her arms. "Got a cigarette?" she said.

"Don't smoke."

"He doesn't smoke," she said to the bottle. "He's a wonder, Sam is."

Sam found a jazz station faint but clear. "That's better." He hummed along with a clarinet.

"Yeah," she said and half-filled both their glasses.

"Want to dance?" he said with a faint giggle.

"Sure."

They stood up and swayed together and he felt so right, in her arms, close, moving slowly together to the faint jazz. It had been so long she wanted to cry. Just to be touched. Just to be warm with someone else.

Outside, she heard a cry.

"Jack?" she said and the scotch blew through her mind.

There was somebody shouting and somebody answering.

"Jack!" She was outside. Sam followed her but she didn't notice. Gray was standing outside the cabin holding Jack up in the air, struggling. The cabin inside was a mess, the cushions were slashed. The table was overturned.

"Let him go!" She shrieked, grabbed a crowbar. *"Let him go!"*

Ira launched himself at her and grabbed her arms. The gouge on the bar looped in the air towards his face. Gray's fingers closed on it and held it as if it were stuck in concrete.

There was a long moment where Gray held Jack in one set of arms, the crowbar in another and grasped the railing with a third. "Jack is all right," he said and pulled the crowbar from her.

"Jesus," she heard Sam say behind her.

Jack stood absolutely still.

"What is going on?" she asked him. "What is going on?"

Jack looked at her, then at Ira, Gray, back at her. Back to Gray.

"What happened?" she asked Gray.

Gray did not speak for a long minute watching Jack. "I do not know. I do not know what is happening at all."

"And what the hell happened to the goddamn cabin?" Sara demanded.

"I did it," said Gray slowly. "It was an accident. I did not mean to. I misjudged things. I will fix it. I will fix it sometime tomorrow."

"Tomorrow!" Ira burst out. "We were going. . . ." and his voice trailed off. He looked at Sara and then looked down.

"Go where?" she said, suspicious. Where would Ira be going that he would hide it? "The ferry. You two were going to the *Hesperus* tomorrow?"

Gray nodded. "We were."

She looked at him coldly. "I told you not to take him there."

He did not speak.

"Don't do it again. I won't have you around if you do that. I won't have you anywhere near me." She stood up next to him and stared up into his face. She could feel the nearness of his rhino body, hear the rasp of leather as he breathed. "You hear me? You understand this time?"

He seemed to shrink on himself a little. "I understand."

"Sara," softly from behind her. "It's not that big a thing."

Sara whirled on Sam. "Get off my boat, Sam. Don't tell me how to raise my family. Get out of here."

Sam shook his head as if he'd been slapped. He stiffly turned and walked back towards his own boat.

"Okay," she said. "Okay now." She turned to Jack and Ira. "Get inside and into bed. That's enough. There ain't going to be any more fireworks tonight."

I was laying in the bunk an arm's length from Jack. I could hear him breathing, snuffling sometimes and muttering. Damn. I don't know what he was doing when we came back, but it was him, not Gray, that had ripped up the cabin. Him. And Gray'd lied for him. Gray would never lie for me.

Gray'd never lied before.

Before, that I knew about, I said to myself. How'd I know what was lie and what was truth?

All my life, I'd been with Gray and now it was like something had been pulled out from under me. He wasn't mine any more. I leaned over on my side and shook my head.

"Ira?" said Jack softly.

"What do you want?"

He didn't say anything for a minute. "I'm sorry I called Gray names."

Sorry. Yeah, right. Gray liked the son-of-a-bitch. Gray *protected* him. Christ.

"Ira?"

"I heard you."

There was a rustle in the cabin and I knew he was turned towards me. "I've been pretty mean to you."

I didn't say anything.

He leaned back and made some kind of a sound, like crying maybe. Like coughing. "I'm sorry."

Like that made it better or something.

"You know."

I just wished he'd shut up. I didn't want to hear him.

"You know," he said again. "I never knew my dad. He split before I was born. And with Mama the way she is, we never really had a family. Now, with you and Gray—it's as if I had a real family."

I sat up and looked at him. "I ain't your brother. Gray can be if he wants to. I don't want any part of you." I stood up. He didn't move, just watched me. "I don't want any part of your friggin' mother. Or you. Or Gray. I just want to get shut of the whole friggin' lot of you." I finished getting dressed. "If the whole mess of you died, I'd piss on your grave."

I left, quiet like, so nobody'd be awake. I looked outside, but Gray was gone. Good riddance. I was on my own now. It was just me.

I walked through the marshes toward the egg. Day was just coming around. The light was kind of a pale violet. I stopped in the marsh and watched it. My Mama stood with it and watched it with me.

"You're misjudging Gray," she said.

I looked at her. "I don't want you telling me what to judge and not. You're dead." I turned back towards the wreck and didn't wait to see if she disappeared or not.

The ferry was the same. Sunlight was just pouring over the hull when I got there, golden and rosy. The egg was where we'd left it—where I'd left it. It was bigger yet. The skin seemed swelled almost to bursting.

"You and me," I said to it. And it seemed like it could hear me. "You and me. We'll take a ride around the world. I don't care if you're a griffin or a dragon or anything." Tears started to leak out of my eyes. I shook them away. "I don't care. You and me. We'll get out of this goddamn place."

The egg didn't say anything and the tears started up again.

Sara got up too and sat in the head for a while. It had been a while since she had drunk that much. Her head felt hot and she rested it against the hatch to cool it. After a little while, she felt better. She went out into the main cabin, but didn't want to go back to bed. The cold and lonely bed frightened her for some reason.

Mike. I still want you to come back.

The thought came to her out of the clear darkness in the back of her mind. Fourteen years and she hadn't left it behind.

She sat in one of the chairs in the galley and lit a cigarette. And Sam— did he know what he was getting into? What a snakepit. She wished she hadn't snapped at him. He was only trying to be a good guy.

Yeah. Right. She inhaled the cigarette savagely. Good guys. They're all good guys. Sam was no different.

"Mama?" came from behind her.

She turned. It was Jack, half dressed and looking at her vaguely. Had Mike looked that young when they were in school? "Yeah, honey?"

"It wasn't Gray who ripped up the cushions."

He stood next to her and watched, his eyes dry and calm. As if he'd already cried until he had cried himself out but still had one thing left to do.

"Who did it, honey?"

" 'I did. Gray and Ira came back and I went crazy, ripping the place apart. I just went crazy."

She pulled him to her and held him. He submitted to it, leaning against her. So this is what it's come to, Roni. I got to get rid of them. Gray for sure. Maybe Ira, too. Because, Roni, in the end, at the final curtain, nothing means as much to me as my little boy. Not you. Not Ira—certainly not Gray. Not Sam. Not even Mike, gone for so long. In the end, it's me and him.

"It's all right, honey." She held him tight. I'm sorry, Roni. That's the way it is. "It's all right."

After a while, he pulled away and looked at her sideways, then turned and shuffled back to bed. He closed the door after him.

She stayed up and smoked another cigarette, thinking how to tell Gray. He was first. He would have to leave tomorrow. Then. Then, we would see about Ira.

She must have sat there for at least an hour, thinking, dreaming. The sky began to lighten and the sun rose.

There was an eruption of water outside and the entire boat shook as Gray landed on the deck. Dripping, he stalked into the cabin, ran past Sara and ripped the door open.

"Jack! Where is Ira?"

Sara stood and saw past Gray Ira's empty bed. "Oh, my God."

Jack looked up at Gray. "I don't know. He left a couple of hours ago."

Sara cried out. "Why didn't you tell me, Jack?"

Jack looked at her out of Mike's blue eyes—different now, colder, stronger. "He wanted to go and he didn't want me along. I wanted to protect him. Like Gray protected me."

"Loyal child," said Gray. "But foolish. No. I am the fool." He turned and began to leave the cabin.

"Gray, wait!"

"No time! The boy is in danger. I did not follow him, thinking he was too upset. It was time for him to be by himself. But he disappeared like a ghost to me. He is gone."

"Where are you going?" she wailed after him.

"The wreck. The egg is hatching—I fear it."

"Wait—damn you, wait! We can take the dory. It's got a good motor. It'll get us there quicker than you can go."

He stopped for a moment, absolutely still. Looked down at her. "You are right. I will take it."

"You will not, you son-of-a-bitch! It's mine, like Jack's my kid and Ira's my nephew."

Gray shook his head. "You are right. I will follow."

They climbed into the dory and thank God it started the first time for once. Gray sat in the middle and they left the dock and shot out across harbor at full speed.

"What is this egg, anyway?" she yelled above the wind.

"I don't know. We found it in the wreck and it pleased the boy to hatch it. I thought it no danger—at first I thought it might be a centaur egg."

Sara felt befuddled. Centaurs? "A centaur?"

"A species that would consider Ira a delicacy." He held his hands together and even in that position Sara could sense the anguish in him. "But I asked the centaur bishop and the bishop said there were no eggs here. So I felt safe. No other egg species here is dangerous."

"So there's no danger."

"There is always danger, but I thought I could head it off and still let the boy play for a while. But now the thing hatches and Ira is away from me. I do not know what the thing is." He fell silent. "His mother and father might protect him."

"*What?*"

He turned to her. "He sees his mother and father at times. They speak to him. They may lead him away."

"Are you crazy?"

"No."

"Ira sees ghosts? Christ. The poor kid. Making this up."

The wind cut through them and the spray splattered across them as Sara turned the boat inland. They could already see the *Hesperus* outlined dark against the beach and the rising sun.

"I am not sure he is making them up."

"You've been encouraging this? I don't believe it. They aren't real." She wished she had a cigarette. That's it. Gray had to go.

Gray looked at her out of those huge eyes.

"How do you know they aren't?"

For her life, she could not answer.

The egg was moving a little now. Kind of wobbling side to side.

I looked and found this old metal bar to help break the egg, help the dragon get loose. I stood next to it—it was smelling pretty ripe now—and didn't do anything. I couldn't decide. Even dragons might be fragile when they were still in the egg. I could hurt it. I chewed on my lip and put down the bar, sat back and watched it.

"Ira? Ira!" called my father from the edge of the boat. I wasn't going to go see them. They were just ghosts. They called again. Oh, well. The egg was going to be a little longer, I figured. I went to the edge and looked down. Both of them were there.

"Come down here," called Papa. Mama nodded. "Come down," she said.

I sat on the edge of the hull and shook my head. "I don't want to listen to you any more. You're dead. Gray's gone weird on me. I don't like Aunt Sara and Jack. Leave me alone. I got the egg."

They looked at one another.

"Son?" said my father softly. "Gray and Sara are coming to get you. They'll take you back. You know they will."

I could hear a motor on the other side of the wreck. "Are you trying to fool me?"

Papa shook his head. "Absolutely not. They're almost here."

"What about the egg?"

"The egg can take care of itself. Come on!" yelled my mother.

I jumped the three meters down to the beach and tumbled. It hurt my feet.

Mama and Papa led me into the marsh. Deep into the swamp, hurrying me, urging me to go so fast I couldn't see where I was going. I could barely breathe for running. The tall grass whipped my face and the mud was knee deep. Where the hell was I? Finally, they stopped.

I sat down in the water. I couldn't breathe. It was like nothing in the world was so important as breathing.

"He's safe now," said my Mama.

"What?" I said and looked up. They were gone. They were gone and I didn't know where the hell I was. They'd tricked me. "God damn you!" I yelled after them. "God damn you to hell!"

* * *

Gray moved to the front of the boat, looking for all the world like a hound ready to leap in the water after fallen birds.

"Back a little, for Christ's sake," yelled Sara. "Don't swamp the boat."

"I can't find him."

"Of course you can't find him. We're not there yet."

"You don't understand. Since he was born, I have always known where he is. Now he is gone." Gray turned towards Sara. "He is no longer a child. Perhaps that is why I cannot find him."

Sara shrugged. When this was over, Gray had to leave before he made her crazy. "That egg's in the wreck, right?"

"Yes."

"Then, that's where he'll be."

They beached the dory and moved around the side of the wrecked ferry. "Where is the egg?"

"In the center of the wreck."

Sara looked at the rusty hull. "We're going to have to climb that?"

Gray shook his head. "There is no time," he said. He picked her up and held her in two sets of arms, then leaped to the top of the hull. He released her and moved purposefully inward. She followed.

In the center of the wreck, the sunlight had already made the area warm. The egg was moving.

"Ira?" called Gray. Sara called also.

"That thing's going to hatch soon." The thing was huge now, almost a meter broad and the surface was a writhing pink and green.

"He is not here." Gray turned towards her. "We had best back away from it."

The egg exploded. A shard caught Sara's shoulder and knocked her down. Something brightly colored that seemed to be made chiefly of mouth and teeth and tail shot into the air and hovered over them. It moved jerkily—its huge, outsized mouth opening and closing mechanically. It quivered. Shook itself in the air. Pawed at its teeth, pulling shards of broken eggshell out from between its fangs. Sara watched it, frozen. Unable to move so much as her eyeballs from the thing. It was a dragon. Its feathers were bright orange. Its wings beat too fast to be seen—but she could feel the air from them. It looked around, cocked its head this way and that as if testing the air. Then, it saw her.

It seemed to smile. And Sara wanted to scream but she had no time. As suddenly as it saw her it dove—faster than anything she had ever seen, faster than anything had a right to be. Something huge and massive and equally as fast shot over her and intercepted the dragon.

The dragon screamed and its talons and teeth were a blur. Gray made a noise like a cry and tried to knock it away and it rolled away in the air, tumbling and screaming. It caught itself and shot above them, saw Gray and dove for him. Gray was more ready this time and there was a brief blur of movement, each slashing, the dragon biting, that seemed to take forever. Then, the dragon tumbled across the deck and slammed the hull so hard it rang. It shook its head and moaned. Gray leaped over to it, all over knives now. Each arm sprouted a dozen. He slashed it and the dragon screamed and tore off one of his arms. He picked it up with another arm and slammed it against the hull. The dragon tried to reach the hand holding it, but couldn't. Gray slammed it against the hull again. He slammed it again. It sounded like a pile driver. The dragon clawed at him but had no strength. He slammed it again and again until it no longer moved and then he continued, methodically and mechanically.

Sara approached him. The dragon was a bloody mess. "Gray?"

Gray did not answer but slammed the dragon into the wall.

"Gray? I think it's dead."

Gray looked at her, then at the dragon. "Oh." Then he looked at himself. "Oh." He sat back and stared at the stump of his arm. "I am hurt." There were slashes through the armor in his chest and arms. The hand at the end of one of his other arms was nearly chewed off. All of the wounds oozed something like tar.

"What can I *do*, Gray?"

"Do? Oh. Yes." He looked over to where the egg had been. "One of those old mattresses. And the tarp."

She dragged the mattress to him and he tore out the padding and stuffed it in the slashes and the stump of his arm. The oozing stopped.

He looked at her. "I will live. I have repair cement at home to cover this, then I will be better."

Sara sat back and shook her head, laughed tensely, softly. . . . Of course. "Repair cement."

He looked at her. "Spatiens do not heal. They must be repaired."

"You sound like you think you're a robot."

"No." He appeared thoughtful. "Not exactly. Spatiens were built thousands of years ago. Those that did this are dead or gone now. We are all that's left." He looked at her. "Think of me as an archeological find that has been somewhat damaged."

She laughed again. He moved and she saw the dragon, all needles and teeth. "What was it?"

"An object of my stupidity." He balled one fist and for a moment, Sara thought he was going to hit it again. Instead, he pushed the bedding tighter into his wounds. "Stupid. I thought only the centaurs would be creatures such as this. All things like to share their heritage. This is one of the centaurs' pets."

"A pet. Dear God. A pet." She pulled her knees up to her chin and felt very cold.

Gray looked up. "That tarp. Get me that tarp. He's coming back."

She brought the tarp to him and he wrapped his body into a sort of toga. "What are you doing?"

"It is shameful to show wounds that have not been cared for. At least, it is shameful to show them to your children."

She looked at him. "Children?"

"You did not know? You are all, all of you, my family. Why else would I follow him here? Why would I try so hard to understand you? Why would I spend my life for you? To me, what else could you be?"

I ran back toward the wreck until I couldn't breathe. My side felt like somebody'd taken and shoved a hot poker in it. My face felt hot like I was going to cry. Tricked. By my own folks. By my own parents. I sat down next to a clump of Indian rice and cried and rested until I could breathe again. Christ. *Christ!*

After a minute or two, I could move and walked back to the ferry. It was quiet. I climbed up on the hull and sneaked around to the center to see if the egg was all right.

It was like one of those pictures you see in magazines, distant, not meaning anything until you see one little feature that hits you like a fist.

They were sitting next to the hull, just watching me. The egg was all broken up. Gray was all tangled up in a tarp. The dragon—and it had been a dragon, after all—was all crumpled up next to the wall.

I stepped towards them. They were just watching me. Gray wrapped up like that reminded me of when they brought Papa home, all bandaged up and covered with blood, the miners singing that mournful song. I'd never heard anybody but papa sing that song before, and I couldn't forget it now. It just ran over and over in my head:

> *I dreamed I saw Joe Hill last night,*
> *alive as you and me,*
> *I said Joe Hill you're ten years dead,*
> *I never died, said he.*

And they couldn't find Mama, just pieces of her 'cause the supervisors had thrown a grenade and she'd caught it and it had blown up before she could throw it away. Papa's face was so still. And I knew he was dead, gone, and everything I ever wanted from him seemed small, and I seemed small. Damn you, I wanted to say then. Damn you for leaving me. I never wanted that. Fuck the miners. Fuck the supervisors.

And the dragon was dead. My ticket away. And Gray was standing there, shrouded like he was dead. "Fuck you! Goddamn you, Gray! Goddamn you Sara! Fuck you! Fuck this boat! Fuck the dragon! *Fuck all of you!*"

I just stood there, swearing, and I wanted to pick up things and throw them at them the way I wanted to hurt the miners that brought Papa home, the way I wanted to hurt him for leaving me.

I felt strangled, dying. I stared at them, quiet now. They didn't say anything. I left the ferry and went back into the marsh and collapsed. I beat the ground with my fists and my feet. It wasn't fair. Everybody left me. Everybody ran away and I was just left there, alone.

"Jesus," Sara said at last, and started to follow Ira.

"Wait." Gray touched her gently and his voice sounded more weary and defeated than any voice she had ever heard. "He needs—to be alone, perhaps." Gray pushed himself to his feet and the tarp partially unraveled. The rents in his skin made her feel queasy. He swayed on his feet. "I am no fit member of your family. All things I have tried to do I have failed. I—"

"Hush," she said and tried to steady him. "Let's go home. Ira will come home eventually."

"I do not know what to do," Gray breathed softly. She could smell him this close, and he smelled rich and strong, like sweat or bread. She helped him to the ocean side of the ferry, and he climbed down as slowly and as carefully as an old man.

He did not move in the boat until she got him home. He stumbled as he walked next to her onto the dock and into the boat. Jack was there and helped her put him in her bed.

"Where's the repair cement?" she asked.

Gray looked at her as if from a great distance. "In the equipment locker. Next to the diesel starter fluid."

Sara found a can with various symbols she could not read hidden behind a can of oil. It belonged in the medicine cabinet, she decided. Enough of this separateness.

Jack didn't say a word and the two of them cleaned the tattered tarp and bedclothes out of the wounds and filled them with cement using a putty knife. Gray gave them soft instructions but after a time, his voice fell silent and Sara thought him asleep. She motioned Jack out of the cabin and began to leave herself.

"Thank you," said Gray suddenly.

She turned to him and realized he no longer looked alien to her. Different, yes. But he looked the way she would have expected him to look. Scarred. Tired. He belonged there.

"It's a small thing to do for someone who saved my life." She shrugged and looked out the porthole to the bow. He'd been sleeping there all summer. "We need to build you a real room. There's not enough room for you."

"I do not need much."

She smiled at him. "None of us do. But nobody in my family sleeps in the open like an animal."

Sara thought she heard a second "thank you" behind her, but she wasn't sure. It wouldn't have mattered if she had.

Jack was looking at her anxiously. "Is he going to be all right?"

"I don't know." Sara looked back toward the cabin. "I hope so."

Jack looked at her, then down at the ground, then back at her. "Are you going to send him away?"

Sara sat at the table in the galley. She lit a cigarette and wished she had a drink. "Do you want me to?"

Jack shook his head.

She exhaled smoke. "Okay. How come?"

"'Cause," he stopped, embarrassed. "He deserves to be here."

"I agree. I'm not going to send him away."

Jack looked relieved. "I was scared you would. On account of me." His eyes grew wide. "Where's Ira?"

"Out. He'll be back soon." I hope.

She could tell from Jack's face he didn't believe her. Well, she'd never been able to tell a lie to Mike, either. But, Jack wasn't his father. Christ. It was stupid to even think that way. Mike's been gone fourteen years, for God's sake.

Sara reached over and gripped him by the shoulder for a minute and he came over to her and they sat there holding each other for some minutes.

She heard Ira before she saw him. He came in, sullen, a wildness in his eyes. Christ, he looked like Roni. How come she'd never seen it? And he was such a *little* kid, barely even there.

"Go on, Jack," she said softly. "Go on over to Kendall's. Stay there tonight."

Jack looked first at her, then at Ira, then nodded to himself and left.

The silence lay between Ira and Sara for some minutes.

"I came by to get my things," he said.

"Oh?" She inhaled and tried to think. What could she do? What the hell was going on in that small head?

"Yeah. I'm leaving. I ain't got no place here."

His eyes were just like Roni's. Stubborn, too. Just as stubborn as she was when she left.

She stubbed her cigarette out. "Look. I want you here. You're my nephew. You're my blood. I want Gray here. Christ. But I'm not keeping anybody here who doesn't want to stay." His expression didn't change. I guess I wouldn't be convinced, either, she thought. She tried to be cool. "Your stuff's in your room. Gray's in my room, resting. You ought to say goodbye to him."

Ira snorted. "I don't want to. I'm getting out of here."

Something snapped in Sara. She grabbed Ira and pushed him down in the chair. "You little shit. What the hell do you think you're doing? Gray went out there to save your little ass."

"Gray killed my dragon. I wanted to get out of here."

"That thing was going to have you for lunch! Gray saved me. He saved you. And he was damned near killed doing it. You want to leave? Fine. You do it. You take your things and get the hell out. Somebody saves your life and you don't give a damn? Fine. You take your ungrateful, snotnosed face out of here. But you will thank him before you leave or I'll beat you black and blue. You got that? You hear me?"

He stared at her.

She sat back in the chair, ashamed. Aren't things bad enough without you shouting at a little boy? Tact. That's what you got in spades, Sara. "He's in there."

Ira stood up hesitantly, looked at the door to the cabin, then back at her. He touched the door, looked inside, entered the room.

She heard faint voices, harsh sounds. Suddenly, she felt as if everything would be all right. That, and a warmth and a strength she'd never felt before. It was like a kind of singing inside of her. She stepped outside and smelled the October sea air. It was brisk.

Gray and Ira didn't need her right then.

She walked down to Sam's boat and knocked on the railing. After a few minutes, Sam looked out.

"Hi," he said warily.

"Hello, there," she said cheerfully. "Want to dance?"

"Gray?" I said softly. "Are you here?"

"In front of you," he said. I'd never heard him tired before.

"Are you okay?"

He didn't say anything for a minute. "No."

I turned on the light. His chest was all over covered with that repair gunk, big deep gashes. Oh, God. And he looked so tired and shrunken, like his skin didn't fit him anymore. "Oh, Gray."

He reached out and drew me to his side and I started crying. He held me and I'd never felt so small and helpless, like I was a baby or broken or dead. "I never meant it, Gray. I never meant it. Don't go away." And my Mama was there and my Papa and they'd all gone away and if Gray went away too there'd be nobody.

"Hush," he said in a croon. "Hush, Ira. I'm not going anywhere. I love you. Sara loves you. Nobody's leaving anybody."

I thought I heard Mama and Papa near me but I didn't look for them. I didn't need to.

Gray slowly grew warm and soft and he held me. He almost filled the bed and I had to scrunch up against the hull, but I didn't mind. After a while he looked down at me.

"What are the three loves?"

"Love of family, love of work, and love of duty." I sat up and looked at him right in those big eyes of his. "And always, *always*, in that order."

ROBERT SILVERBERG

Tales from the Venia Woods

Robert Silverberg is one of the most famous SF writers of modern times, with dozens of novels, anthologies, and collections to his credit. Silverberg has won five Nebula Awards and three Hugo Awards. His novels include *Dying Inside, Lord Valentine's Castle, The Book of Skulls, Downward to the Earth, Tower of Glass, The World Inside, Born with the Dead,* and *Shadrach in the Furnace.* His collections include *Unfamiliar Territory, Capricorn Games, Majipoor Chronicles, The Best of Robert Silverberg, At the Conglomeroid Cocktail Party,* and *Beyond the Safe Zone.* His most recent books are the novels *Tom O'Bedlam, Star of Gypsies, At Winter's End* and *The New Springtime.* For many years he edited the prestigious anthology series *New Dimensions,* and has recently, along with his wife, Karen Haber, taken over the editing of the Universe anthology series. His story "Multiples" was in our First Annual Collection, "The Affair" was in our Second Annual Collection, "Sailing to Byzantium"—which won a Nebula Award in 1986 —was in our Third Annual Collection, "Against Babylon" was in our Fourth Annual Collection, "The Pardoner's Tale" was in our Fifth Annual Collection, and "House of Bones" was in our Sixth Annual Collection. He lives in Oakland, California.

Here he takes us to an evocative and vividly drawn Alternate World, one where the Roman Empire never fell, for a deceptively quiet story of childhood dreams, conflicting loyalties, and the futility of good intentions.

▼

Tales from the Venia Woods

ROBERT SILVERBERG

This all happened a long time ago, in the early decades of the Second Republic, when I was a boy growing up in Upper Pannonia. Life was very simple then, at least for us. We lived in a forest village on the right bank of the Danubius, my parents, my grandmother, my sister Friya, and I. My father Tyr, for whom I was named, was a blacksmith, my mother Julia taught school in our house, and my grandmother was the priestess at the little Temple of Juno Teutonica nearby.

It was a very quiet life. The automobile hadn't yet been invented then—all this was around the year 2650, and we still used horsedrawn carriages or wagons—and we hardly ever left the village. Once a year, on Augustus Day—back then we still celebrated Augustus Day—we would all dress in our finest clothes and my father would get our big iron-bound carriage out of the shed, the one he had built with his own hands, and we'd drive to the great municipium of Venia, a two-hour journey away, to hear the imperial band playing waltzes in the Plaza of Vespasian. Afterward there'd be cakes and whipped cream at the big hotel nearby, and tankards of cherry beer for the grownups, and then we'd begin the long trip home. Today, of course the forest is gone and our little village has been swallowed up by the ever-growing municipium, and it's a twenty-minute ride by car to the center of the city from where we used to live. But at that time it was a grand excursion, the event of the year for us.

I know now that Venia is only a minor provincial city, that compared with Londin or Parisi or Roma itself it's nothing at all. But to me it was the capital of the world. Its splendors stunned me and dazed me. We would climb to the top of the great column of Basileus Andronicus, which the Greeks put up eight hundred years ago to commemorate their victory over

Caesar Maximilianus during the Civil War in the days when the Empire was divided, and we'd stare out at the whole city; and my mother, who had grown up in Venia, would point everything out to us, the senate building, the opera house, the aqueduct, the university, the ten bridges, the Temple of Jupiter Teutonicus, the proconsul's palace, the much greater palace that Trajan VII built for himself during that dizzying period when Venia was essentially the second capital of the Empire, and so forth. For days afterward my dreams would glitter with memories of what I had seen in Venia, and my sister and I would hum waltzes as we whirled along the quiet forest paths.

There was one exciting year when we made the Venia trip twice. That was 2647, when I was ten years old, and I can remember it so exactly because that was the year when the First Consul died—C. Junius Scaevola, I mean, the Founder of the Second Republic. My father was very agitated when the news of his death came. "It'll be touch and go now, touch and go, mark my words," he said over and over. I asked my grandmother what he meant by that, and she said, "Your father's afraid that they'll bring back the Empire, now that the old man's dead." I didn't see what was so upsetting about that—it was the same to me, Republic or Empire, Consul or Imperator— but to my father it was a big issue, and when the new First Consul came to Venia later that year, touring the entire vast Imperium province by province for the sake of reassuring everyone that the Republic was stable and intact, my father got out the carriage and we went to attend his Triumph and Processional. So I had a second visit to the capital that year.

Half a million people, so they say, turned out in downtown Venia to applaud the new First Consul. This was N. Marcellus Turritus, of course. You probably think of him as the fat, bald old man on the coinage of the late 27th century that still shows up in pocket change now and then, but the man I saw that day—I had just a glimpse of him, a fraction of a second as the consular chariot rode past, but the memory still blazes in my mind seventy years later—was lean and virile, with a jutting jaw and fiery eyes and dark, thick curling hair. We threw up our arms in the old Roman salute and at the top of our lungs we shouted out to him, "Hail, Marcellus! Long live the Consul!"

(We shouted it, by the way, not in Latin but in Germanisch. I was very surprised at that. My father explained afterward that it was by the First Consul's own orders. He wanted to show his love for the people by encouraging all the regional languages, even at a public celebration like this one. The Gallians had hailed him in Gallian, the Britannians in Britannic, the Japanese in whatever it is they speak there, and as he traveled through the Teutonic provinces he wanted us to yell his praises in Germanisch. I realize that there are some people today, very conservative Republicans, who will tell you that this was a terrible idea, because it has led to the resurgence of all kinds of separatist regional activities in the Imperium. It was the same sort of regionalist fervor, they remind us, that brought about the crumbling of the Empire two hundred years earlier. To men like my father, though, it was a brilliant political stroke, and he cheered the new First Consul with tremendous Germanisch exuberance and vigor. But my father managed to be a staunch regionalist and a stauch Republican at the same time. Bear in mind that over my mother's fierce objections he had insisted on naming his children for ancient Teutonic gods instead of giving them the standard Roman names that everybody else in Pannonia favored then.)

Other than going to Venia once a year, or on this one occasion twice, I never went anywhere. I hunted, I fished, I swam, I helped my father in the smithy, I helped my grandmother in the Temple, I studied reading and writing in my mother's school. Sometimes Friya and I would go wandering in the forest, which in those days was dark and lush and mysterious. And that was how I happened to meet the last of the Caesars.

There was supposed to be a haunted house deep in the woods. Marcus Aurelius Schwarzchild it was who got me interested in it, the tailor's son, a sly and unlikable boy with a cast in one eye. He said it had been a hunting lodge in the time of the Caesars, and that the bloody ghost of an Emperor who had been killed in a hunting accident could be seen at noontime, the hour of his death, pursuing the ghost of a wolf around and around the building. "I've seen it myself," he said. "The ghost, I mean. He had a laurel wreath on, and everything, and his rifle was polished so it shined like gold."

I didn't believe him. I didn't think he'd had the courage to go anywhere near the haunted house and certainly not that he'd seen the ghost. Marcus Aurelius Schwarzchild was the sort of boy you wouldn't believe if he said it was raining, even if you were getting soaked to the skin right as he was saying it. For one thing, I didn't believe in ghosts, not very much. My father had told me it was foolish to think that the dead still lurked around in the world of the living. For another, I asked my grandmother if there had ever been an Emperor killed in a hunting accident in our forest, and she laughed and said no, not ever: the Imperial Guard would have razed the village to the ground and burned down the woods, if that had ever happened.

But nobody doubted that the house itself, haunted or not, was really there. Everyone in the village knew that. It was said to be in a certain dark part of the woods where the trees were so old that their branches were tightly woven together. Hardly anyone ever went there. The house was just a ruin, they said, and haunted besides, definitely haunted, so it was best to leave it alone.

It occurred to me that the place might just actually have been an imperial hunting lodge, and that if it had been abandoned hastily after some unhappy incident and never visited since, it might still have some trinkets of the Caesars in it, little statuettes of the gods, or cameos of the royal family, things like that. My grandmother collected small ancient objects of that sort.

Her birthday was coming, and I wanted a nice gift for her. My fellow villagers might be timid about poking around in the haunted house, but why should I be? I didn't believe in ghosts, after all.

But on second thought I didn't particularly want to go there alone. This wasn't cowardice so much as sheer common sense, which even then I possessed in full measure. The woods were full of exposed roots hidden under fallen leaves; if you tripped on one and hurt your leg, you would lie there a long time before anyone who might help you came by. You were also less likely to lose your way if you had someone else with you who could remember trail marks. And there was some occasional talk of wolves. I figured the probability of my meeting one wasn't much better than the likelihood of ghosts, but all the same it seemed like a sensible idea to have a companion with me in that part of the forest. So I took my sister along.

I have to confess that I didn't tell her that the house was supposed to be haunted. Friya, who was about nine then, was very brave for a girl, but I thought she might find the possibility of ghosts a little discouraging. What I did tell her was that the old house might still have imperial treasures in it, and if it did she could have her pick of any jewelry we found.

Just to be on the safe side we slipped a couple of holy images into our pockets—Apollo for her, to cast light on us as we went through the dark woods, and Woden for me, since he was my father's special god. (My grandmother always wanted him to pray to Jupiter Teutonicus, but he never would, saying Jupiter Teutonicus was a god that the Romans invented to pacify our ancestors. This made my grandmother angry, naturally. "But *we* are Romans," she would say. "Yes, we are," my father would tell her, "but we're Teutons also, or at least I am, and I don't intend to forget it.")

It was a fine Saturday morning in spring when we set out, Friya and I, right after breakfast, saying nothing to anybody about where we were going. The first part of the forest path was a familiar one: we had traveled it often. We went past Agrippina's Spring, which in medieval times was thought to have magical powers, and then the three battered and weather-beaten statues of the pretty young boy who was supposed to be the first Emperor Hadrian's lover two thousand years ago, and after that we came to Baldur's Tree, which my father said was sacred, though he died before I was old enough to attend the midnight rituals that he and some of his friends used to hold there. (I think my father's generation was the last one that took the old Teutonic religion seriously.)

Then we got into deeper, darker territory. The paths were nothing more than sketchy trails here. Marcus Aurelius had told me that we were supposed to turn left at a huge old oak tree with unusual glossy leaves. I was still looking for it when Friya said, "We turn here," and there was the shiny-leaved oak. I hadn't mentioned it to her. So perhaps the girls of our village told each other tales about the haunted house too; but I never found out how she knew which way to go.

Onward and onward we went, until even the trails gave out, and we were wandering through sheer wilderness. The trees were ancient here, all right, and their boughs were interlaced high above us so that almost no sunlight reached the forest floor. But we didn't see any houses, haunted or otherwise, or anything else that indicated human beings had ever been here. We'd been hiking for hours, now. I kept one hand on the idol of Woden in my pocket and I stared hard at every unusual looking tree or rock we saw, trying to engrave it on my brain for use as a trail marker on the way back.

It seemed pointless to continue, and dangerous besides. I would have turned back long before, if Friya hadn't been with me; but I didn't want to look like a coward in front of her. And she was forging on in a tireless way, inflamed, I guess, by the prospect of finding a fine brooch or necklace for herself in the old house, and showing not the slightest trace of fear or uneasiness. But finally I had had enough.

"If we don't come across anything in the next five minutes—" I said.

"There," said Friya. "Look."

I followed her pointing hand. At first all I saw was more forest. But then I noticed, barely visible behind a curtain of leafy branches, what could have been the sloping wooden roof of a rustic hunting lodge. Yes! Yes, it was! I saw the scalloped gables, I saw the boldly carved roof-posts.

So it was really there, the secret forest lodge, the old haunted house. In frantic excitement I began to run toward it, Friya chugging valiantly along behind me, struggling to catch up.

And then I saw the ghost.

He was old—ancient—a frail, gaunt figure, white-bearded, his long white hair a tangle of knots and snarls. His clothing hung in rags. He was walking slowly toward the house, shuffling, really, a bent and stooped and trembling figure clutching a huge stack of kindling to his breast. I was practically on top of him before I knew he was there.

For a long moment we stared at each other, and I can't say which of us was the more terrified. Then he made a little sighing sound and let his bundle of firewood fall to the ground, and fell down beside it, and lay there like one dead.

"Marcus Aurelius was right!" I murmured. "There really is a ghost here!"

Friya shot me a glance that must have been a mixture of scorn and derision and real anger besides, for this was the first she had heard of the ghost story that I had obviously taken pains to conceal from her. But all she said was, "Ghosts don't fall down and faint, silly. He's nothing but a scared old man." And went to him unhesitatingly.

Somehow we got him inside the house, though he tottered and lurched all the way and nearly fell half a dozen times. The place wasn't quite a ruin, but close: dust everywhere, furniture that looked as if it'd collapse into splinters if you touched it, draperies hanging in shreds. Behind all the filth we could see how beautiful it all once had been, though. There were faded paintings on the walls, some sculptures, a collection of arms and armor worth a fortune.

He was terrified of us. "Are you from the quaestors?" he kept asking. Latin was what he spoke. "Are you here to arrest me? I'm only the caretaker, you know. I'm not any kind of a danger. I'm only the caretaker." His lips quavered. "Long live the First Consul!" he cried, in a thin, hoarse, ragged croak of a voice.

"We were just wandering in the woods," I told him. "You don't have to be afraid of us."

"I'm only the caretaker," he said again and again.

We laid him out on a couch. There was a spring just outside the house, and Friya brought water from it and sponged his cheeks and brow. He looked half starved, so we prowled around for something to feed him, but there was hardly anything: some nuts and berries in a bowl, a few scraps of smoked meat that looked like they were a hundred years old, a piece of fish that was in better shape, but not much. We fixed a meal for him, and he ate slowly, very slowly, as if he were unused to food. Then he closed his eyes without a word. I thought for a moment that he had died, but no, no, he had simply dozed off. We stared at each other, not knowing what to do.

"Let him be," Friya whispered, and we wandered around the house while we waited for him to awaken. Cautiously we touched the sculptures, we blew dust away from the paintings. No doubt of it, there had been imperial grandeur here. In one of the upstairs cupboards I found some coins, old ones, the kind with the Emperor's head on them that weren't allowed to be used any more. I saw trinkets, too, a couple of necklaces and a jewel-handled dagger. Friya's eyes gleamed at the sight of the necklaces, and mine at the dagger, but we let everything stay where it was. Stealing from a ghost is one thing, stealing from a live old man is another. And we hadn't been raised to be thieves.

When we went back downstairs to see how he was doing, we found him sitting up, looking weak and dazed, but not quite so frightened. Friya offered him some more smoked meat, but he smiled and shook his head.

"From the village, are you? How old are you? What are your names?"

"This is Friya," I said. "I'm Tyr. She's nine and I'm twelve."

"Friya. Tyr." He laughed. "Time was when such names wouldn't have been permitted, eh? But times have changed." There was a flash of sudden vitality in his eyes, though only for an instant. He gave us a confidential, intimate smile. "Do you know whose place this was, you two? The Emperor Maxentius, that's who! This was his hunting lodge. Caesar himself! He'd stay here when the stags were running, and hunt his fill, and then he'd go on into Venia, to Trajan's palace, and there'd be such feasts as you can't imagine, rivers of wine, and the haunches of venison turning on the spit— ah, what a time that was, what a time!"

He began to cough and sputter. Friya put her arm around his thin shoulders.

"You shouldn't talk so much, sir. You don't have the strength."

"You're right. You're right." He patted her hand. His was like a skeleton's. "How long ago it all was. But here I stay, trying to keep the place up—in case Caesar ever wanted to hunt here again—in case—in case—" A look of torment, of sorrow. "There isn't any Caesar, is there? First Consul! Hail! Hail Junius Scaevola!" His voice cracked as he raised it.

"The Consul Junius is dead, sir," I told him. "Marcus Turritus is First Consul now."

"Dead? Scaevola? Is that so?" He shrugged. "I hear so little news. I'm only the caretaker, you know. I never leave the place. Keeping it up, in case—in case—"

But of course he wasn't the caretaker. Friya never thought he was: she had seen, right away, the resemblance between that shriveled old man and the magnificent figure of Caesar Maxentius in the painting behind him on the wall. You had to ignore the difference in age—the Emperor couldn't have been much more than thirty when his portrait was painted—and the fact that the Emperor was in resplendent bemedalled formal uniform and the old man was wearing rags. But they had the same long chin, the same sharp, hawklike nose, the same penetrating icy-blue eyes. It was the royal face, all right. I hadn't noticed; but girls have a quicker eye for such things. The Emperor Maxentius' younger brother was who this gaunt old man was, Quintus Fabius Caesar, the last survivor of the old imperial house, and therefore, the true Emperor himself. Who had been living in hiding ever since the downfall of the Empire at the end of the Second War of Reunification.

He didn't tell us any of that, though, until our third or fourth visit. He went on pretending he was nothing but a simple old man who had happened to be stranded here when the old regime was overthrown, and was simply trying to do his job, despite the difficulties of age, on the chance that the royal family might some day be restored and would want to use its hunting lodge again.

But he began to give us little gifts, and that eventually led to his admitting his true identity.

For Friya he had a delicate necklace made of long slender bluish beads. "It comes from Aiguptos," he said. "It's thousands of years old. You've studied Aiguptos in school, haven't you? You know that it was a great empire long before Roma ever was?" And with his own trembling hands he put it around her neck.

That same day he gave me a leather pouch in which I found four or five triangular arrowheads made of a pink stone that had been carefully chipped sharp around the edges. I looked at them, mystified. "From Nova Roma," he explained. "Where the redskinned people live. The Emperor Maxentius loved Nova Roma, especially the far west, where the bison herds are. He went there almost every year to hunt. Do you see the trophies?" And, indeed, the dark musty room was lined with animal heads, great massive bison with thick curling brown wool, glowering down out of the gallery high above.

We brought him food, sausages and black bread that we brought from home, and fresh fruit, and beer. He didn't care for the beer, and asked rather timidly if we could bring him wine instead. "I am Roman, you know," he reminded us. Getting wine for him wasn't so easy, since we never used it at home, and a twelve-year-old boy could hardly go around to the wineshop to buy some without starting tongues wagging. In the end I stole some from the Temple while I was helping out my grandmother. It was thick sweet wine, the kind used for offerings, and I don't know how much he liked it. But he was grateful. Apparently an old couple who lived on the far side of the woods had looked after him for some years, bringing him food and wine, but in recent weeks they hadn't been around and he had had to forage for himself, with little luck: that was why he was so gaunt. He was afraid they were ill or dead, but when I asked where they lived, so I could find out whether they were all right, he grew uneasy and refused to tell me. I wondered about that. If I had realized then who he was, and that the old couple must have been Empire loyalists, I'd have understood. But I still hadn't figured out the truth.

Friya broke it to me that afternoon, as we were on our way home. "Do you think he's the Emperor's brother, Tyr? Or the Emperor himself?"

"What?"

"He's got to be one or the other. It's the same face."

"I don't know what you're talking about, sister."

"The big portrait on the wall, silly. Of the Emperor. Haven't you noticed that it looks just like him?"

I thought she was out of her mind. But when we went back the following week, I gave the painting a long close look, and looked at him, and then at the painting again, and I thought, yes, yes, it might just be so.

What clinched it were the coins he gave us that day. "I can't pay you in money of the Republic for all you've brought me," he said. "But you can have these. You can't spend them, but they're still valuable to some people, I understand. As relics of history." His voice was bitter. From a worn old velvet pouch he drew out half a dozen coins, some copper, some silver. "These are coins of Maxentius," he said. They were like the ones we had seen while snooping in the upstairs cupboards on our first visit, showing the same face as on the painting, that of a young, vigorous bearded man. "And these are older ones, coins of Emperor Laureolus, who was Caesar when I was a boy."

"Why, he looks just like you!" I blurted.

Indeed he did. Not nearly so gaunt, and his hair and beard were better trimmed; but otherwise the face of the regal old man on those coins might easily have been that of our friend the caretaker. I stared at him. He began to tremble. I looked at the painting on the wall behind us again. "No," he said faintly. "No, no, you're mistaken—I'm nothing like him, nothing at all—" And his shoulders shook and he began to cry. Friya brought him some wine, which steadied him a little. He took the coins from me and looked at them in silence a long while, shaking his head sadly, and finally handed them back. "Can I trust you with a secret?" he asked. And his tale came pouring out of him.

A glittering boyhood, almost sixty years earlier, in that wondrous time between the two Wars of Reunification: a magical life, endlessly traveling from palace to palace, from Roma to Venia, from Venia to Constantinopolis, from Constantinopolis to Nishapur. He was the youngest and most pampered of five royal princes; his father had died young, drowned in a foolish swimming exploit, and when his grandfather Laureolus Caesar died the imperial throne would go to his brother Maxentius. He himself, Quintus Fabius, would be a provincial governor somewhere when he grew up, perhaps in India or Nova Roma, but for now there was nothing for him to do but enjoy his gilded existence.

Then death came at last to old Emperor Laureolus, and Maxentius succeeded him; and almost at once there began the ten-year horror of the Second War of Reunification, when somber and harsh colonels who despised the lazy old Empire smashed it to pieces, rebuilt it as a Republic, and drove the Caesars from power. We knew the story, of course; but to us it was a tale of triumph of virtue and honor over corruption and tyranny. To Quintus Fabius, weeping as he told it to us from his own point of view, the fall of the Empire had been not only a harrowing personal tragedy but a terrible disaster for the entire world.

Good little Republicans though we were, our hearts were wrung by the things he told us, the scenes of his family's agony: the young Emperor Maxentius trapped in his own palace, gunned down with his wife and children at the entrance of the imperial baths. Camillus, the second brother, who had been Prince of Constantinopolis, pursued through the streets of Roma at dawn and slaughtered by revolutionaries on the steps of the Temple of Castor and Pollux. Prince Flavius, the third brother, escaping the capital in a peasant's wagon, hidden under huge bunches of grapes, setting up a government-in-exile in Neapolis, only to be taken and executed before he had been Emperor a full week. Which brought the succession down to sixteen-year-old Prince Augustus, who had been at the university in Parisi. Well named, he was: for the first of all Emperors was an Augustus, and another one two thousand years later was the last, reigning all of three days before the men of the Second Republic found him and put him before the firing squad.

Of the royal princes, only Quintus Fabius remained. But in the confusion he was overlooked. He was hardly more than a boy; and, although technically he was now Caesar, it never occurred to him to claim the throne. Loyalist supporters dressed him in peasant clothes and smuggled him out of Roma while the capital was still in flames, and he set out on what was to become a lifetime of exile.

"There were always places for me to stay," he told us. "In out-of-the-way towns where the Republic had never really taken hold, in backwater provinces, in places you've never heard of. The Republic searched for me for a time, but never very well, and then the story began to circulate that I was dead. The skeleton of some boy found in the ruins of the palace in Roma was said to be mine. After that I could move around more or less freely, though always in poverty, always in secrecy."

"And when did you come here?" I asked.

"Almost twenty years ago. Friends told me that this hunting lodge was here, still more or less intact as it had been at the time of the Revolution, and that no one ever went near it, that I could live here undisturbed. And so I have. And so I will, for however much time is left." He reached for the wine, but his hands were shaking so badly that Friya took it from him and poured him a glass. He drank it in a single gulp. "Ah, children, children, what a world you've lost! What madness it was, to destroy the Empire! What greatness existed then!"

"Our father says things have never been so good for ordinary folk as they are under the Republic," Friya said.

I kicked her ankle. She gave me a sour look.

Quintus Fabius said sadly, "I mean no disrespect, but your father sees only his own village. We were trained to see the entire world in a glance. The Imperium, the whole globe-spanning Empire. Do you think the gods meant to give the Imperium just to anyone at all? Anyone who could grab power and proclaim himself First Consul? Ah, no, no, the Caesars were uniquely chosen to sustain the Pax Romana, the universal peace that has enfolded this whole planet for so long. Under us there was nothing but peace, peace eternal and unshakable, once the Empire had reached its complete form. But with the Caesars now gone, how much longer do you think the peace will last? If one man can take power, so can another, or another. There will be five First Consuls at once, mark my words. Or fifty. And every province will want to be an Empire in itself. Mark my words, children. Mark my words."

The Pax Romana? *What* Pax Romana? Old Quintus Fabius would have had us believe that the Empire had brought unbroken and unshakeable peace to the entire world, and had kept it that way for twenty centuries. But what about the Civil War, when the Greek half of the Empire fought for fifty years against the Latin half? Or the two Wars of Unification? And hadn't there been minor rebellions constantly, all over the Empire, hardly a century without one, in Persia, in India, in Britannica, in Africa Aethiopica? No, I thought, what he's telling us simply isn't true. The long life of the Empire had been a time of constant brutal oppression, with people's spirits held in check everywhere by military force. The real Pax Romana was something that existed only in modern times, under the Second Republic. So my father had taught me.

But Quintus Fabius was an old man, wrapped in dreams of his own wondrous lost childhood. Far be it from me to argue with him about such matters as these. I simply smiled and nodded, and poured more wine for him when his glass was empty. And Friya and I sat there spellbound as he told us, hour after hour, of what it had been like to be a prince of the royal family in the dying days of the Empire, before true grandeur had departed forever from the world.

When we left him that day, he had still more gifts for us. "My brother was a great collector," he said. "He had whole houses stuffed full of treasure. All gone now, all but what you see here, which no one remembered. When I'm gone, who knows what'll become of them? But I want you to have these. Because you've been so kind to me. To remember me by. And to remind you always of what once was, and now is lost."

For Friya there was a small bronze ring, dented and scratched, with a serpent's head on it, that he said had belonged to the Emperor Claudius of the earliest days of the Empire. For me a dagger, not the jewel-handled one I had seen upstairs, but a fine one all the same, with a strange undulating blade, from a savage kingdom on an island in the Oceanus Magnus. And for us both, a beautiful little figure in smooth white alabaster of Pan playing on his pipes, carved by some master craftsman of the ancient days.

The figurine was the perfect birthday gift for grandmother. We gave it to her the next day. We thought she would pleased, since all of the old gods of Roma are very dear to her; but to our surprise and dismay she seemed startled and upset by it. She stared at it, eyes bright and fierce, as if we had given her a venomous toad.

"Where did you get this thing? Where?"

I looked at Friya, to warn her not to say too much. But as usual she was ahead of me.

"We found it, grandmother. We dug it up."

"You dug it up?"

"In the forest," I put in. "We go there every Saturday, you know, just wandering around. There was this old mound of dirt—we were poking in it, and we saw something gleaming—"

She turned it over and over in her hands. I had never seen her look so troubled. "Swear to me that that's how you found it! Come, now, at the altar of Juno! I want you to swear to me before the Goddess. And then I want you to take me to see this mound of dirt of yours."

Friya gave me a panic-stricken glance.

Hesitantly I said, "We may not be able to find it again, grandmother. I told you, we were just wandering around—we didn't really pay attention to where we were—"

I grew red in the face, and I was stammering, too. It isn't easy to lie convincingly to your own grandmother.

She held the figurine out, its base toward me. "Do you see these marks here? This little crest stamped down here? It's the Imperial crest, Tyr. That's the mark of Caesar. This carving once belonged to the Emperor. Do you expect me to believe that there's Imperial treasure simply lying around in mounds of dirt in the forest? Come, both of you! To the altar, and swear!"

"We only wanted to bring you a pretty birthday gift, grandmother," Friya said softly. "We didn't mean to do any harm."

"Of course not, child. Tell me, now: where'd this thing come from?"

"The haunted house in the woods," she said. And I nodded my confirmation. What could I do? She would have taken us to the altar to swear.

Strictly speaking, Friya and I were traitors to the Republic. We even knew that ourselves, from the moment we realized who the old man really was. The Caesars were proscribed when the Empire fell; everyone within a certain level of blood kinship to the Emperor was condemned to death, so that no one could rise up and claim the throne in years hereafter.

Some minor members of the royal family did manage to escape, so it was said; but giving aid and comfort to them was a serious offense And this was no mere second cousin or great-grandnephew that we had discovered deep in the forest: this was the Emperor's own brother. He was, in fact, the legitimate Emperor himself, in the eyes of those for whom the Empire had never ended. And it was our responsibility to turn him in to the quaestors. But he was so old, so gentle, so feeble. We didn't see how he could be much of a threat to the Republic. Even if he did believe that the Revolution had been an evil thing, and that only under a divinely chosen Caesar could the world enjoy real peace.

We were children. We didn't understand what risks we were taking, or what perils we were exposing our family to.

Things were tense at our house during the next few days: whispered conferences between our grandmother and our mother, out of earshot, and then an evening when the two of them spoke with father while Friya and I were confined to our room, and there were sharp words and even some shouting. Afterward there was a long cold silence, followed by more mysterious discussions. Then things returned to normal. My grandmother never put the figurine of Pan in her collection of little artifacts of the old days, nor did she ever speak of it again.

That it had the imperial crest on it was, we realized, the cause of all the uproar. I had thought all along that grandmother was secretly an Empire loyalist herself. A lot of people her age were; and she was, after all, a traditionalist, a priestess of Juno Teutonica, who disliked the revived worship of the old Germanic gods that had sprung up in recent times—"pagan" gods, she called them—and had argued with father about his insistence on naming us as he had. So she should have been pleased to have something that had belonged to the Caesars. But, as I say, we were children then. We didn't take into account the fact that the Republic dealt harshly with anyone who practiced Caesarism. Or that whatever my grandmother's private political beliefs might have been, father was the unquestioned master of our household, and he was a devout Republican.

"I understand you've been poking around that old ruined house in the woods," my father said, a week or so later. "Stay away from it. Do you hear me? Stay away."

And so we would have, because it was plainly an order. We didn't disobey our father's orders.

But then, a few days afterward, I overheard some of the older boys of the village talking about making a foray out to the haunted house. Evidently Marcus Aurelius Schwarzchild had been talking about the ghost with the polished rifle to others beside me, and they wanted the rifle. "It's five of us against one of him," I heard someone say. "We ought to be able to take care of him, ghost or not."

"What if it's a ghost rifle, though?" one of them asked. "A ghost rifle won't be any good to us."

"There's no such thing as a ghost rifle," the first speaker said. "Rifles don't have ghosts. It's a real rifle. And it won't be hard for us to get it away from a ghost."

I repeated all this to Friya.

"What should we do?" I asked her.

"Go out there and warn him. They'll hurt him, Tyr."

"But father said—"

"Even so. The old man's got to go somewhere and hide. Otherwise his blood will be on our heads."

There was no arguing with her. Either I went with her to the house in the woods that moment, or she'd go by herself. That left me with no choice. I prayed to Woden that my father wouldn't find out, or that he'd forgive me if he did; and off we went into the woods, past Agrippina's Spring, past the statues of the pretty boy, past Baldur's Tree, and down the now-familiar path beyond the glossy-leaved oak.

"Something's wrong," Friya said, as we approached the hunting lodge. "I can tell."

Friya always had a strange way of knowing things. I saw the fear in her eyes and felt frightened myself.

We crept forward warily. There was no sign of Quintus Fabius. And when we came to the door of the lodge we saw that it was a little way ajar, and off its hinges, as if it had been forced. Friya put her hand on my arm and we stared at each other. I took a deep breath.

"You wait here," I said, and went in.

It was frightful in there. The place had been ransacked—the furniture smashed, the cupboards overturned, the sculptures in fragments. Someone had slashed every painting to shreds. The collection of arms and armor was gone.

I went from room to room, looking for Quintus Fabius. He wasn't there. But there were bloodstains on the floor of the main hall, still fresh, still sticky.

Friya was waiting on the porch, trembling, fighting back tears.

"We're too late," I told her.

It hadn't been the boys from the village, of course. They couldn't possibly have done such a thorough job. I realized—and surely so did Friya, though we were both too sickened by the realization to discuss it with each other—that grandmother must have told father we had found a cache of Imperial treasure in the old house, and he, good citizen that he was, had told the quaestors. Who had gone out to investigate, come upon Quintus Fabius, and recognized him for a Caesar, just as Friya had. So my eagerness to bring back a pretty gift for grandmother had been the old man's downfall. I suppose he wouldn't have lived much longer in any case, as frail as he was; but the guilt for what I unknowingly brought upon him is something that I've borne ever since.

Some years later, when the forest was mostly gone, the old house accidentally burned down. I was a young man then, and I helped out on the firefighting line. During a lull in the work I said to the captain of the fire brigade, a retired quaestor named Lucentius, "It was an Imperial hunting lodge once, wasn't it?"

"A long time ago, yes."

I studied him cautiously by the light of the flickering blaze. He was an older man, of my father's generation.

Carefully I said, "When I was a boy, there was a story going around that one of the last Emperor's brothers had hidden himself away in it. And that eventually the quaestors caught him and killed him."

He seemed taken off guard by that. He looked surprised and, for a moment, troubled. "So you heard about that, did you?"

"I wondered if there was any truth to it. That he was a Caesar, I mean."

Lucentius glanced away. "He was only an old tramp, is all," he said, in a muffled tone. "An old lying tramp. Maybe he told fantastic stories to some of the gullible kids, but a tramp is all he was, an old filthy lying tramp." He gave me a peculiar look. And then he stamped away to shout at someone who was uncoiling a hose the wrong way.

A filthy old tramp, yes. But not, I think, a liar.

He remains alive in my mind to this day, that poor old relic of the Empire. And now that I am old myself, as old, perhaps, as he was then, I understand something of what he was saying. Not his belief that there necessarily had to be a Caesar in order for there to be peace, for the Caesars were only men themselves, in no way different from the Consuls who have replaced them. But when he argued that the time of the Empire had been basically a time of peace, he may not have been really wrong, even if war had been far from unknown in Imperial days.

For I see now that war can sometimes be a kind of peace also: that the Civil Wars and the Wars of Reunification were the struggles of a sundered Empire trying to reassemble itself so peace might resume. These matters are not so simple. The Second Republic is not as virtuous as my father thought, nor was the old Empire, apparently, quite as corrupt. The only thing that seems true without dispute is that the worldwide hegemony of Roma these past two thousand years under the Empire and then under the Republic, troubled though it has occasionally been, has kept us from even worse turmoil. What if there had been no Roma? What if every region had been free to make war against its neighbors in the hope of creating the sort of Empire that the Romans were able to build? Imagine the madness of it! But the gods gave us the Romans, and the Romans gave us peace: not a perfect peace, but the best peace, perhaps, that an imperfect world could manage. Or so I think now.

In any case the Caesars are dead, and so is everyone else I have written about here, even my little sister Friya; and here I am, an old man of the Second Republic, thinking back over the past and trying to bring some sense out of it. I still have the strange dagger that Quintus Fabius gave me, the barbaric-looking one with the curious wavy blade, that came from some savage island in the Oceanus Magnus. Now and then I take it out and look at it. It shines with a kind of antique splendor in the lamplight. My eyes are too dim now to see the tiny imperial crest that someone engraved on its haft when the merchant captain who brought it back from the South Seas gave it to the Caesar of his time, four or five hundred years ago. Nor can I see the little letters, S P Q R, that are inscribed on the blade. For all I know, they were put there by the frizzy-haired tribesman who fashioned that odd, fierce weapon: for he, too, was a citizen of the Roman Empire. As in a manner of speaking are we all, even now in the days of the Second Republic. As are we all.

WILLIAM KING

Visiting the Dead

Here's a visit to an unsettling high-tech world of the future where nothing is quite what it seems, by brand-new British author William King. This was King's first sale, and appeared in *Interzone*. King has also published fiction in *Zenith*, and no doubt we'll be hearing a lot more from him in days to come.

▼

Visiting the Dead

WILLIAM KING

The train rattled on through the dark, carrying me towards the funeral. My skull ached with the pressure of unaccustomed gravity, my chest felt as if some small hard thing were trying to burst out of it, and the slightest movement caused a surge of nausea. What, from the comfort of high orbit, had seemed a trip of vital emotional importance was fast becoming a nightmare.

I looked at the vital signs monitor on the wrist of the Frame and, to my surprise, none of the readouts were red. The slight whir of the servo-motors caught the attention of the carriage's only other occupant; a slim dark-haired girl who had been studying me discreetly in the reflection of the blacked-out window. She turned to look at me; our glances met. Embarrassed, she felt compelled to speak.

"Well, Aunt Jane, what do you think of Earth after all this time?"

"It's strange, Deborah. I'm not sure I like all of it." I attempted a gesture meant to emphasize my point but by the time the exo-skeleton shifted my arm, rotated my wrist and amplified my finger movement I had already spoken. The gesture and the heat took a lot out of me. I could feel gravity tug at me like the weight of my ninety-one years. I grimaced more in exasperation than pain.

"Oh, I'm sorry. This must be a hard time for you," she said apologetically.

I looked at her closely. She had long hair, a snub nose, wide blue eyes and rosy cheeks. She leaned back, pushing herself into the hard leather of the coach, studying the ceiling as she adjusted her tee shirt. I tried unsuccessfully to see some trace of my dead brother in her. I nodded, feeling the wide, cushioned neck brace of the Frame biting where it had not been adjusted properly.

"Come far?" I asked, most banal question of many between travellers.

She twisted her head to one side to look at me before she replied. I think she thought I was mocking her.

"Just from Glasgow. Mother asked me to meet you at the airport." That courtesy must have cost her mother an effort. Sheena had never liked me.

"Been doing field study," she continued. "I don't know why they bothered to send me. It was just the same as the simulations."

"Ah, but how would you have known that unless they had sent you? Surely it wasn't the same?"

She gestured emphatically with her left hand. "Oh yes it was, exactly the same. In every detail." I was impressed. Once, simulated experience had possessed a cartoon quality. Of course that was nearly thirty years ago, in the mid-twenties. Simulations were something I had given up when I moved to the Overtowns.

"How about touch and smell?" I asked. She gave me the sort of look you give a slow child.

"Of course," she said. "I forgot. Simulations are illegal in the Overtowns, aren't they? A decadent terrestrial vice."

"We have more important things to do."

"The starships? I saw a documentary on Gupta and Carmichael on the tube last night. Off to Barnards Star. Showed a lot of pictures of the ship. It looked really dull, just a big dumbbell. They set out ten years before I was born."

That would make her twenty-one. It's hard to tell these days; anti-agathics have come so far. Barnard probe left in '26.

"How old are you, if you don't mind me asking? You have the same look as those two, sort of smooth and old."

"Was born last century. 1967."

"You don't look it."

"Thank you. We have a good anti-ageing programme. Gene re-tooling, anti-agathics and so on. We need it for the starships."

She didn't look too interested. I searched for another topic of conversation.

"It used to be so cold here in the winter," I said. "I can remember when it used to snow sometimes."

She ran her hand through her hair and let out a long breath. "No kidding," she said. "Before the greenhouse effect?"

"Before that and the sea rising. Before the Central European desert. Rainfall was different."

The by-products of centuries of industralization had caused the build up of heat. I wondered if those previous generations had considered the consequences. Mine hadn't.

"I've been in the simulations of it," she said. I was going to say that unless you had been there you couldn't know the difference but I remembered what she had said about the simulations. Maybe they really were that accurate.

We sat and talked all the way to the Portryan stop, exchanging information in the way only strangers on a train can. She told me to call her Debbie. At the stop a Grey Man inspected our tickets. I could not look him in the eye. I am not proud of my part in their creation.

The Castle was built by a returned explorer in the 16th century, a sprawling white pile covering many acres. It had a nasty annex built for the homeless in the housing crisis of '97, good air conditioning and, more importantly, facilities for the disabled.

Technically speaking a Frame is capable of taking stairs, but not many people I know would risk it. Ramps and lifts are safer.

My room was standard. If the blankets had not been tartan and the wall-paper had not had a discreet bluebell pattern it could have been anywhere on Earth from Tokyo to Timbuktu.

I debated whether to call my brother's family but put it off. They knew I was in town, Deborah had gone ahead. I made the call I could not put off, the one to my doctor. I plugged the extension cable from the Frame into the phone. As I talked it would broadcast its information to orbit. I dialled the number.

Nancy Chan appeared. She looked pale and tense, not her usual jovial self. "How is the suicide attempt coming along?" she asked.

There would be a three second delay throughout the conversation. It's a long way to the Trojan points. Even light can seem slow.

"Don't start that again, Nancy. I told you Brian was the last surviving member of my original family. I'll be damned if I miss his funeral."

"You could have watched it by remote. Just because he's dead doesn't mean you have to try and join him. You know how bad the political situation is getting down there. Heimdal Station reports massive troop buildups in North Africa, Turkey and what used to be Soviet Georgia. Looks like the big one."

The timelag suddenly seemed very long. My mouth felt dry. I shook my head.

"We've intercepted coded transmissions from Cairo, Tehran, Riyadh. All say the same thing. Troops been moving in from as far as Ethiopia and Pakistan. Looks like the hardliners have finally seized control in the United Islamic Republic."

I remembered a tube broadcast I had watched in the arrival lounge at Heathrow, a satellite propaganda show straight from Tehran. A lean Arab had been explaining in Oxbridge tones why biological research had to stop in Federal Europe. He had shown some horror shots of experimentation on clones, said the creation of soulless automata was the work of the devil. Two Canadian tourists had laughed; a Grey Man had stopped sweeping and smiled, pleased by the laughter.

I shrugged. "Surely it's not that bad."

"It is. It'll be Jihad, holy war. A delegation has just returned to Tehran from the Hague. Euro-parliament refused to sign the Ethical Science Treaty."

"I'm not surprised. Most of the European economy is based on Grey Men and other forms of vat labour. They won't give it up without a fight."

"Well the Council is putting out a warning. Any Overtowner who isn't back up in one week may have to remain on Earth if war comes. Too dangerous to run a shuttle down through the interceptors and antimissile satellites."

"Thanks for telling me. I'll be seeing you, Nancy."

"Yeah. Take care, Councillor."

Nancy broke the connection. I decided to crawl from my Frame into the bed. It took a lot of effort. For a brief second I longed for the clear, soaring freedom of the Overtowns. It was a useless feeling so I pushed it aside.

I drifted off to sleep, feeling as if my chest was about to cave in.

Next morning I was awakened by the sound of a light rain tapping against the window. I lay in the warm bed, savouring my aches and debating my next move. I called the old family home and was greeted by Sheena. She informed me that the funeral would be at one pm, then she cut the connection.

After breakfast I decided to go for a walk along the beach. The chance of seeing a place I had once loved seemed to outweigh the discomfort of travelling by Frame. Anyway I felt I was becoming acclimatized.

I clambered into the Frame and lumbered to the shore. It was not as I remembered it. The old concrete seawall was gone, eaten away by the rising tides; the sea now flowed where the beach once had been. Part of the town was submerged. A bubble harbour nestled between the drowned remains of the two old piers. Warm rain pattered off my face and dripped down the carbon-fibre shell of the Frame. Palms swayed lightly in the breeze. Welcome back to Scotland, I thought. The shower slackened and died.

I studied the new harbour, superimposing my memories of the old. Where small fishing boats had docked, there were now pleasure hovercraft. A new hydrofoil sat where once great ferries had rested. Passengers disembarked while servile Grey Men carried their bags.

I walked along the new shorefront which once had been well above sea level, trying to ignore the tumbled houses and the fusty smell that came from them. Some kids on dwarf pachyderms raced exuberantly past along the remnants of roads where I remembered motorcars.

Nothing of the old days remained except the outline of the land. There were the two arms of the bay, reaching out to frame the distant sky, between them a sea the colour of stormclouds.

The slopes of the hills were bare of conifers, killed by acid rain at the end of last century. Imported palms had replaced them. On the hills were the mirror-bright condominiums where the population dream their lives away in Simulation.

The topography was the same but I knew that if I lived long enough even the shape of the earth would change, eaten by erosion and the hungry centuries.

"Aunt!" I heard a shout. It was Deborah. "Folk at the hotel said they saw you come this way."

She reined her pachyderm to a halt. I noticed the hairs bristling from its grey hide and its ugly stunted trunk. "I wanted to talk to you about something."

I nodded.

"I've never met anyone who has really been in space," she said. "I may never get another chance if the news broadcasts are right."

"War?"

"Might be. Border incident, some combatants opened fire on U.I.R. invaders. Turns out they were fifteen years old and unarmed. Tube just showed pictures."

She seem shocked and disoriented. I spoke as softly as I could.

"Those combatants wouldn't know any better. They would have been told to open fire on anyone crossing the border. They follow orders."

"Tube says that the kids were probably boy soldiers from the Revolutionary Guard, sent to provoke an incident. It would say that, wouldn't it?"

"Might be right. There's been a lot of tension between the United Islamic Republic and Europe recently."

Suddenly she pointed out to sea. I turned swiftly, almost overbalancing the Frame. I don't know what I expected—helicopter gunships maybe.

I saw them out in the deep water. A group of humanoids, leaping from the waves like dolphins, playing and throwing something large backwards and forwards. We watched them in silence until they sank beneath the surface and did not come back up.

"Swimmers," said Deborah softly. "When I was little we used to say that it was good luck to see one."

"When I was little there were no Swimmers, not like those." I looked back at her pachyderm, an efficient pollutionless mode of transport which fed on the palm leaves. The Swimmers were products of the same thing. Genetic engineering. My chosen career.

"Swimmers have a dome-city just outside the mouth of the loch. Its beautiful, but close up Swimmers don't look like us: more like seals."

Another intelligent race, one I hadn't seen before except on the tube. I felt as if the world had grown strange and that I had stayed the same. Once I had designed combatants, combat replicants, for the Pentagon. It was hard to reconcile the image of the frolicing Swimmers with the biological war machines that stand guard along the European border, waiting for the Jihad.

The Swimmers farm the Atlantic algae fields that help counter the ecological imbalance caused by the destruction of the rain forests. Like the Grey Men they are servants of humanity, happy but not free, variations on a prototype I helped create.

We stopped at a café, sat drinking coffee inside a converted farmhouse. Grey Men waited on tables, smiled at customers, prepared food.

"Most of the old town is underwater now," said Deborah. I took a sip of the coffee. It was hot and frothy. It took me back briefly to my teenage days, drinking capucino and discussing all the burning issues.

"Fish probably swim in that old café," I said. Deborah looked lost. "A lot of the landmarks of my youth have gone."

"We sometimes swim there using artificial gills. Its mostly just walls and the outlines of streets."

Deborah was looking down into her cup. Some of the young ones I had seen earlier came in and sat down. They talked softly about the U.I.R. and what war might mean. There was tension in the air.

"What's it like up there in the Overtowns?" Deborah asked.

"Different. People are different. More purposeful. Have to be. Space is an unforgiving environment."

"My mother says that they are all dreamers up there."

I smiled. "No, the dreamers are all down here. Most downsiders are settling into a sort of apathy. Work done by AI, robots, constructs. You name it, anything but humans. Most of the population seem to be hooked into the simulations."

"What's wrong with that?"

"Nothing, just that nothing new is being done by people."

"The big AI's are making far more discoveries than the Overtown scientists."

"Your machines are doing the important stuff."

"We made them. They look after us. Life's good."

This was true. In the secular states wealth was everywhere. Even in the United Islamic Republic the standard of living was high for most of the population.

"Anyway as soon as the machines find anything out they let us know. We can experience anything we want through the simulations. I can visit truly alien worlds, meet truly alien minds created by an AI. It's a lot more interesting than the boring pictures the probeship sends back."

"Yes, that's the problem. Those Downsiders who don't live in religious dictatorships are turning inwards, exploring fantasies instead of the real universe."

"That's your problem if you're not happy with it."

"Doesn't it worry you that your people may end up machine-dependent? That human evolution may have reached a dead end. Mankind needs challenges to grow. That's why we don't allow simulations or very smart AI's in the Overtowns."

"Progress hasn't stopped here. We're just taking a different path. One you don't like. You sound like the Fundamentalists. No offence."

It was an argument not worth continuing. Neither of us really understood the other. Deborah called for our bill. A Grey Man waiter brought it. He had happy, vacant eyes.

The funeral was a lonely affair. The cemetery was high on a hillside. It had escaped the drowning of the town. The church had not been so lucky. I could see its spire rising above the sunken streets.

There were very few at the service. Those who had come were all old. Formal religion wasn't popular among the young here.

The minister was a woman. Without the benefit of anti-agathics she looked all of her seventy years. She conducted the whole service at the graveside. As her voice droned through the clichés of the eulogy my mind drifted to memories of Brian.

I tried to remember happy things but it was the horror of his last two years that haunted me.

The disease had eaten him away from within. It had taken the blurred lines of his face and pulled the thin bone structure out from below. The peculiar thing was that his face had re-acquired the lean angularity of his youth as death approached.

We had talked a lot over the tubelink as he lay in bed, discussed old times. We had gone over our old feud, decided it was silly. He had thought that I should have stayed behind, become a farmer. I had other plans. It had caused friction at the time.

Brian had felt that humankind should sort out its problems here on Earth before leaping into space. I couldn't wait that long. Of course Earth had sorted out its problems without help from either of us.

Cheap fusion, smart computers, genetic screening and the withering of the nation state had seen to that. The transition had not been painless. Food riots, holy wars and partial economic collapse had been landmarks along the way. There were new problems now but the old world was dead, drowned beneath the twin tides of resurgent fundamentalism and advancing technology. The conflict between the two had redrawn the map more than the rising of the sea.

We advanced. I took a cord with five others and we lowered the coffin into the grave. The smell of mud and freshly turned Earth was quite distinct. I dropped the cord. It fell away from my hand like the Earth below a rocketliner.

The minister said her final words. We dispersed from the grave towards the waiting cars. A lot of people with familiar-looking faces and cold expressions stared at me. We all shook hands.

"You'll be coming back to the house," said Sheena.

"Do you think I should?"

"Oh, yes," she replied. "He'll want to see you."

A small electric coach took us back to the farm. For a while the only sound was the keening whine of the motor as it laboured on the steep hill road. The countryside opened up to the wide open moor of the Ganlach. Great white windmills dominated the landscape. Giant propellors that looked as if they could have lifted a passenger airliner aloft quivered in the breeze.

At the close of the twentieth century this area had been a windfarm, selling power back to the national grid. Cheap fusion had done away with that idea. The towers still stood because no-one had bothered to take them down. Polymer plastic has no value as scrap.

At the foot of one tower pink sheep, colour-coded for the insulin their milk carried, were watched by a Grey Man shepherd. I looked away.

"You don't like that do you?" said Sheena.

"No, I don't." I could not keep the edge out of my voice. The vibration of the car was passing through the Frame and making my teeth rattle.

"They love it. It's what they were made for, menial work."

"I know. That doesn't make it right." The sad thing was that the Grey Men really did love it. We had engineered them well. They were perfect slaves.

"There's no need for you to look down your nose at us. It was you and people like you that created those constructs," said Sheena.

"I know." Too late to uncreate them now. The future had rushed at us headlong. We go forward or we go under had been our slogan. Had we been so wrong? Times change. The slaves were happy and would not be so if freed.

My sensibilities were products of the last century and the citizens of the new age did not conform to them. Whose fault was that?

The coach pulled into the farmyard and the natural stench of the place filled my nostrils. Suddenly I wanted to run but it was too late. I was on my way to a meeting with my dead brother.

The birds sang as I walked down to the stream. I knew I would find him there, lying on a rock, watching the fish. The grass crumpled under my feet and the copse of oaks was ahead, casting dappled shadows in the summer sun. I wore my nine-year-old body; my real one was in the Frame back at the farmhouse, wearing an induction helmet.

Deborah had been right. The simulation was perfect; the illusion pumped directly into the brain could not be distinguished from the real world.

He was just as I remembered him at thirteen, lanky and awkward with a thatch of blonde hair and a smiling, rosy-cheeked face. No pain lines now.

"Hello," he said and smiled. I didn't smile back. I kept my distance. The experience was too disturbing. There was an aspect of nightmare about it.

"You're dead," I said. "I thought you said you would never let them record you. What happened, did you get scared at the end?"

He nodded. "Anything seemed better than death. It's for the kids too. They can visit me when they like."

He picked up a stone and lobbed it into the water. I watched the ripples. A dragonfly hovered above them.

"Of course I won't look the same to them. I chose this setting for you. Do you like it?"

I shrugged. "It's exactly as I remember it. So are you."

He smiled slowly. "Aye, it would be the same. The machine provides the big details out of my memory, the rest are filled in by your mind."

"That means it's not accurate. It's blurred. My memories have probably altered details of the original."

"What does it matter? How can you tell?"

I felt trapped. The echo of the question I had asked Deborah on the train rang in my ears.

"You're not Brian. You're just a computer program that thinks its him, a sub-program in whatever is holding this illusion together."

"No. You're wrong. I'm Brian. I remember every little detail of my life. I was recorded. They mapped my brain a bit at a time and transferred the results to a computer. I'm the same. I have the same emotions, the same reactions. I just live here now."

"No you don't. You're just a simulation. You're perfect in every detail but you're no more him than a photograph would be." I felt a coldness in the pit of my stomach, a growing sense of unreality and estrangement.

"I'm me," he said. "You have to believe that. All the emotions, the memories make me what I am. If I chose they could download me into a clone body and I would be back in your world. I would be the same person. The cell structure would be identical, my memories and personality would be the same. If that's not real what is?"

"What about your soul? Did they record that too?"

"Maybe. Anyway, I thought you were an agnostic?"

"I don't know. I'm confused."

He seemed to become desperate. "Souls? They were just the old way of explaining your personalities, our individuality. A superstition. All we ever were was software driving flesh. You know as well as I do that it can all be explained in terms of electrochemical reaction. Hell, you've built people. Biology and artificial intelligence research outdated the old religion."

"Software souls driving meat machines? Maybe science is the new religion."

"Look, we were brought up between two ages, the old explanations and the new. The last generation with a choice. The kids don't have the same problems with these concepts as us. They don't have the same fear of death either."

"That's because they visit simulations where it seems the dead still live. The afterlife has invaded the real world."

"Look, maybe they're right. Perhaps this is the only form of immortality we will ever have. Don't you at least want to consider that?"

"No," I almost screamed. "I want to get out of here. How do I do it?"

"I'll get you out. You are wrong. I am me and I do care about you."

I saw only genuine concern on his face. I nodded, embarrassed. I hugged him and he felt real. Then I was back in my body, tied into the Frame.

"I have to get back," I said.

Deborah accompanied me to the station. All the way it looked as if she were trying to summon up the courage to say something. She carried my bag to the platform and we stood there. The silence grew. I looked at her expectantly. She stared at her feet, confused.

"You think he's gone forever, don't you? That's why you're sad." I could see it came as a revelation to her.

I stared at her, trying to find the words. What could I say? My brother was gone, dead as the hope of heaven. To her it did not matter. She could visit him, visit the dead. Perhaps one day the dead would visit her. A sort of resurrection is possible.

The fundamentalists think it is a mockery of the work of God. I'm not sure I disagree with them. They say that the new science glorifies Satan. If Satan is the absence of God as darkness is the absence of light then they are correct.

The fear of nothingness is a terrible thing. Almost anything is preferable. It is this fear that fuels the Jihad, the fear that we are mortal and the universe doesn't care. God is supposed to care. They hate the Grey Men because the constructs remind them that we are simply machines constructed from protoplasm. Do machines have souls?

I looked at Deborah and tried to find words. They did not come, so I stayed silent.

"You're not coming back, are you? Not ever."

I nodded. "If you ever want to come to the Overtowns, get in touch."

She shook her head. Abruptly she stuck out a hand. I took it gently, afraid that the Frame might crush it. We shook hands. "Saw it in a simulation," she said sadly. "Is that right?"

"Yes, perfect," I said. She smiled. I boarded the train. She waved as it pulled out of the station. I tried to wave back but the clumsiness of the Frame and the smooth acceleration of the mag-lev kept me from doing so until she was out of sight.

Now war has come. The work of Satan is no longer to be tolerated by the believers. The godless and all their works are to be overthrown. This is the word from Tehran.

The armies of the righteous have swept through Spain and Greece but soon they will encounter the main strength of their enemy. Then they will die, finally and forever.

The believers see only the soft decadent face of their foe. They do not know what a terrible power they have roused, one that has sunk the lands and may raise the dead. The vats will spew forth a million combatants and nothing human can stand against them.

This struggle will determine the face of the new millennium. The believers think they shall win because they fight against Satan and for God. I believe the outcome will be different.

BRUCE STERLING
Dori Bangs

One of the major new talents to enter SF in recent years, Bruce Sterling sold his first story in 1976, and has since sold stories to *Universe*, *OMNI*, *The Magazine of Fantasy and Science Fiction*, *The Last Dangerous Visions*, *Lone Star Universe*, and elsewhere. He has attracted special acclaim in the last few years for a series of stories set in his exotic Shaper/Mechanist future, a complex and disturbing future where warring political factions struggle to control the shape of human destiny, and the nature of humanity itself. His story "Cicada Queen" was in our First Annual Collection; his "Sunken Gardens" was in our Second Annual Collection; his "Green Days in Brunei" and "Diner in Audoghast" were in our Third Annual Collection; his "The Beautiful and the Sublime" was in our Fourth Annual Collection; his "Flowers of Edo" was in our Fifth Annual Collection, and his "Our Neural Chernobyl" was in our Sixth Annual Collection. His books include the novels *The Artificial Kid*, *Involution Ocean*, and *Schismatrix*, a novel set in the Shaper/Mechanist future, and, as editor, *Mirrorshades: the Cyberpunk Anthology*. His most recent books were the novel *Islands in the Net* and the collection *Crystal Express*. Upcoming is another novel, *The Difference Engine*, in collaboration with William Gibson.

In the funny, hard-edged, and poignant story that follows, Sterling spins a very odd kind of Alternate Worlds story, unlike any you've ever seen before—we guarantee it.

▼

Dori Bangs

BRUCE STERLING

True facts, mostly: Lester Bangs was born in California in 1948. He published his first article in 1969. It came in over the transom at *Rolling Stone*. It was a frenzied review of the MC5's "Kick Out the Jams."

Without much meaning to, Lester Bangs slowly changed from a Romilar-guzzling college kid into a "professional rock critic." There wasn't much precedent for this job in 1969, so Lester kinda had to make it up as he went along. Kind of *smell* his way into the role, as it were. But Lester had a fine set of cultural antennae. For instance, Lester invented the tag "punk rock." This is posterity's primary debt to the Bangs oeuvre.

Lester's not as famous now as he used to be, because he's been dead for some time, but in the 70s Lester wrote a million record reviews, for *Creem* and the *Village Voice* and *NME* and *Who Put The Bomp*. He liked to crouch over his old manual typewriter, and slam out wild Beat-influenced copy, while the Velvet Underground or Stooges were on the box. This made life a hideous trial for the neighborhood, but in Lester's opinion the neighborhood pretty much had it coming. *Epater les bourgeois*, man!

Lester was a party animal. It was a professional obligation, actually. Lester was great fun to hang with, because he usually had a jagged speed-edge, which made him smart and bold and rude and crazy. Lester was a one-man band, until he got drunk. Nutmeg, Romilar, belladonna, crank, those substances Lester could handle. But booze seemed to crack him open, and an unexpected black dreck of rage and pain would come dripping out, like oil from a broken crankcase.

Toward the end—but Lester had no notion that the end was nigh. He'd given up the booze, more or less. Even a single beer often triggered frenzies of self-contempt. Lester was thirty-three, and sick of being groovy; he was restless, and the stuff he'd been writing lately no longer meshed with the surroundings that had made him what he was. Lester told his friends that he was gonna leave New York and go to Mexico and work on a deep, serious novel, about deep serious issues, man. The real thing, this time. He was really gonna pin it down, get into the guts of Western Culture, what it really was, how it really felt.

But then, in April '82, Lester happened to catch the flu. Lester was living alone at the time, his mom, the Jehovah's Witness, having died recently. He had no one to make him chicken soup, and the flu really took him down. Tricky stuff, flu; it has a way of getting on top of you.

Lester ate some Darvon, but instead of giving him that buzzed-out float it usually did, the pills made him feel foggy and dull and desperate. He was too sick to leave his room, or hassle with doctors or ambulances, so instead he just did more Darvon. And his heart stopped.

There was nobody there to do anything about it, so he lay there for a couple of days, until a friend showed up and found him.

More true fax, pretty much: Dori Seda was born in 1951. She was a cartoonist, of the "underground" variety. Dori wasn't ever famous, certainly not in Lester's league, but then she didn't beat her chest and bend every ear in the effort to make herself a Living Legend, either. She had a lot of friends in San Francisco, anyway.

Dori did a "comic book" once, called *Lonely Nights*. An unusual "comic book" for those who haven't followed the "funnies" trade lately, as *Lonely Nights* was not particularly "funny," unless you really get a hoot from deeply revealing tales of frustrated personal relationships. Dori also did a lot of work for *WEIRDO* magazine, which emanated from the artistic circles of R. Crumb, he of "Keep On Truckin'" and "Fritz the Cat" fame.

R. Crumb once said: "Comics are words and pictures. You can do anything with words and pictures!" As a manifesto, it was a typically American declaration, and it was a truth that Dori held to be self-evident.

Dori wanted to be a True Artist in her own real-gone little 80s-esque medium. Comix, or "graphic narrative" if you want a snazzier cognomen for it, was a breaking thing, and she had to feel her way into it. You can see the struggle in her "comics"—always relentlessly autobiographical—Dori hanging around in the "Café La Boheme" trying to trade food stamps for cigs; Dori living in drafty warehouses in the Shabby Hippie Section of San Francisco, sketching under the skylight and squabbling with her roommate's boyfriend; Dori trying to scrape up money to have her dog treated for mange.

Dori's comics are littered with dead cig-butts and toppled wine-bottles. She was, in a classic nutshell, Wild, Zany, and Self-Destructive. In 1988 Dori was in a car-wreck which cracked her pelvis and collarbone. She was laid up, bored, and in pain. To kill time, she drank and smoked and took painkillers.

She caught the flu. She had friends who loved her, but nobody realized how badly off she was; probably she didn't know it herself. She just went down hard, and couldn't get up alone. On February 26 her heart stopped. She was thirty-six.

So enough "true facts." Now for some comforting lies.

As it happens, even while a malignant cloud of flu virus was lying in wait for the warm hospitable lungs of Lester Bangs, the Fate, Atropos, she who weaves the things that are to be, accidentally dropped a stitch. Knit one? Purl two? What the hell does it matter, anyway? It's just human lives, right?

So Lester, instead of inhaling a cloud of invisible contagion from the exhalations of a passing junkie, is almost hit by a Yellow Cab. This mishap on his way back from the deli shocks Lester out of his dogmatic slumbers. High time, Lester concludes, to get out of this burg and down to sunny old Mexico. He's gonna tackle his great American novel: *All My Friends are Hermits*.

So true. None of Lester's groovy friends go out much any more. Always ahead of their time, Lester's Bohemian cadre are no longer rock and roll animals. They still wear black leather jackets, they still stay up all night, they still hate Ronald Reagan with fantastic virulence; but they never leave home. They pursue an unnamed lifestyle that sociologist Faith Popcorn— (and how can you doubt anyone with a name like *Faith Popcorn*)—will describe years later as "cocooning."

Lester has eight zillion rock, blues, and jazz albums, crammed into his grubby NYC apartment. Books are piled feet deep on every available surface: Wm. Burroughs, Hunter Thompson, Celine, Kerouac, Huysmans, Foucault, and dozens of unsold copies of *Blondie*, Lester's book-length band-bio.

More albums and singles come in the mail every day. People used to send Lester records in the forlorn hope he would review them. But now it's simply a tradition. Lester has transformed himself into a counter-cultural info-sump. People send him vinyl just because he's *Lester Bangs*, man!

Still jittery from his thrilling brush with death, Lester looks over this lifetime of loot with a surge of Sartrean nausea. He resists the urge to raid the fridge for his last desperate can of Blatz Beer. Instead, Lester snorts some speed, and calls an airline to plan his Mexican wanderjahr. After screaming in confusion at the hopeless stupid bitch of a receptionist, he gets a ticket to San Francisco, best he can do on short notice. He packs in a frenzy and splits.

Next morning finds Lester exhausted and wired and on the wrong side of the continent. He's brought nothing with him but an Army duffel-bag with his Olympia portable, some typing paper, shirts, assorted vials of dope, and a paperback copy of *Moby Dick*, which he's always meant to get around to re-reading.

Lester takes a cab out of the airport. He tells the cabbie to drive nowhere, feeling a vague compulsive urge to soak up the local vibe. San Francisco reminds him of his *Rolling Stone* days, back before Wenner fired him for being nasty to rock-stars. Fuck Wenner, he thinks. Fuck this city that was almost Avalon for a few months in '67 and has been on greased skids to Hell ever since.

The hilly half-familiar streets creep and wriggle with memories, avatars, talismans. Decadence, man, a no-kidding *death of affect*. It all ties in for Lester, in a bilious mental stew: snuff movies, discos, the cold-blooded whine of synthesizers, Pet Rocks, S&M, mindfuck self-improvement cults, Winning Through Intimidation, every aspect of the invisible war slowly eating the soul of the world.

After an hour or so he stops the cab at random. He needs coffee, white sugar, human beings, maybe a cheese Danish. Lester glimpses himself in the cab's window as he turns to pay: a chunky jobless thirty-three-year-old in a biker jacket, speed-pale dissipated New York face, Fu Manchu mustache looking pasted on. Running to fat, running for shelter. . . . no excuses, Bangs! Lester hands the driver a big tip. Chew on that, pal—you just drove the next Oswald Spengler.

Lester staggers into the cafe. It's crowded and stinks of patchouli and clove. He sees two chainsmoking punkettes hanging out at a formica table. CBGB's types, but with California suntans. The kind of women, Lester thinks, who sit crosslegged on the floor and won't fuck you but are perfectly willing to describe in detail their highly complex postexistential *weltanschauung*. Tall and skinny and crazy-looking and bad news. Exactly his type, really. Lester sits down at their table and gives them his big rubber grin.

"Been having fun?" Lester says.

They look at him like he's crazy, which he is, but he wangles their names out: "Dori" and "Krystine." Dori's wearing fishnet stockings, cowboy boots, a strapless second-hand bodice-hugger covered with peeling pink feathers. Her long brown hair's streaked blonde. Krystine's got a black knit tank-top and a leather skirt and a skull-tattoo on her stomach.

Dori and Krystine have never heard of "Lester Bangs." They don't read much. They're *artists*. They do cartoons. Underground comix. Lester's mildly interested. Manifestations of the trash aesthetic always strongly appeal to him. It seems so American, the *good* America that is: the righteous wild America of rootless European refuse picking up discarded pop-junk and making it shine like the Koh-i-noor. To make "comic books" into *Art*— what a hopeless fucking effort, worse than rock and roll and you don't even get heavy bread for it. Lester says as much, to see what they'll do.

Krystine wanders off for a refill. Dori, who is mildly weirded-out by this tubby red-eyed stranger with his loud come-on, gives Lester her double-barreled brush-off. Which consists of opening up this Windex-clear vision into the Vent of Hell that is her daily life. Dori lights another Camel from the butt of the last, smiles at Lester with her big gappy front teeth and says brightly:

"You like *dogs*, Lester? I have this dog, and he has eczema and disgusting open sores all over his body, and he smells *really* bad . . . I can't get friends to come over because he likes to shove his nose right into their, you know, *crotch* . . . and go *Snort! Snort!*"

" 'I want to scream with wild dog joy in the smoking pit of a charnel house,' " Lester says.

Dori stares at him. "Did you make that up?"

"Yeah," Lester says. "Where were you when Elvis died?"

"You taking a survey on it?" Dori says.

"No, I just wondered," Lester says, "There was talk of having Elvis's corpse dug up, and the stomach analyzed. For dope, y'know. Can you *imagine* that? I mean, the *thrill* of sticking your hand and forearm into Elvis's rotted guts and slopping around in the stomach lining and liver and kidneys and coming up out of dead Elvis's innards triumphantly clenching some crumbs off a few Percodans and Desoxyns and 'ludes . . . and then this is the *real* kick, Dori: you pop these crumbled-up bits of pills in your *own mouth* and bolt 'em down and get high on drugs that not only has Elvis Presley, the *King*, gotten high on, not the same brand mind you but the same *pills*, all slimy with little bits of his innards, so you've actually gotten to *eat* the King of Rock and Roll!"

"*Who* did you say you were?" Dori says. "A rock journalist? I thought you were putting me on. 'Lester Bangs,' that's a fucking weird name!"

Dori and Krystine have been up all night, dancing to the heroin head banger vibes of Darby Crash and the Germs. Lester watches through hooded eyes: this Dori is a woman over thirty, but she's got this wacky airhead routine down smooth, the Big Shiny Fun of the American Pop Bohemia. "Fuck you for believing I'm this shallow." Beneath the skin of her Attitude he can sense a bracing skeleton of pure desperation. There is hollow fear and sadness in the marrow of her bones. He's been writing about a topic just like this lately.

They talk a while, about the city mostly, about their variant scenes. Sparring, but he's interested. Dori yawns with pretended disinterest and gets up to leave. Lester notes that Dori is taller than he is. It doesn't bother him. He gets her phone number.

Lester crashes in a Holiday Inn. Next day he leaves town. He spends a week in a flophouse in Tijuana with his Great American Novel, which sucks. Despondent and terrified, he writes himself little cheering notes: "Burroughs was almost fifty when he wrote *Nova Express*! Hey boy, you only thirty-three! Burnt-out! Washed-up! Finished! A bit of flotsam! And in that flotsam your salvation! In that one grain of wood. In that one bit of that irrelevance. If you can bring yourself to describe it. . . ."

It's no good. He's fucked. He knows he is, too, he's been reading over his scrapbooks lately, those clippings of yellowing newsprint, thinking: it was all a box, man! *El Cajon!* You'd think: wow, a groovy youth-rebel Rock Writer, he can talk about *anything*, can't he? Sex, dope, violence, Mazola parties with teenage Indonesian groupies, Nancy Reagan publicly fucked by a herd of clapped-out bull walruses . . . but when you actually READ a bunch of Lester Bangs Rock Reviews in a row, the whole shebang has a delicate hermetic whiff, like so many eighteenth-century sonnets. It is to dance in chains; it is to see the whole world through a little chromed window of Silva-Thin 'shades. . . .

Lester Bangs is nothing if not a consummate romantic. He is, after all, a man who *really no kidding believes* that Rock and Roll Could Change the World, and when he writes something which isn't an impromptu free lesson on what's wrong with Western Culture and how it can't survive without grabbing itself by the backbrain and turning itself inside-out, he feels like he's wasted a day. Now Lester, fretfully abandoning his typewriter to stalk and kill flophouse roaches, comes to realize that HE will have to turn himself inside out. Grow, or die. Grow into something but he has no idea what. He feels beaten.

So Lester gets drunk. Starts with Tecate, works his way up to tequila. He wakes up with a savage hangover. Life seems hideous and utterly meaningless. He abandons himself to senseless impulse. Or, in alternate terms, Lester allows himself to follow the numinous artistic promptings of his holy intuition. He returns to San Francisco and calls Dori Seda.

Dori, in the meantime, has learned from friends that there is indeed a rock journalist named "Lester Bangs" who's actually kind of *famous*. He once appeared on stage with the J. Geils Band "playing" his typewriter. He's kind of a big deal, which probably accounts for his being kind of an asshole. On a dare, Dori calls Lester Bangs in New York, gets his answering machine, and recognizes the voice. It was him, all right. Through some cosmic freak, she met Lester Bangs and he tried to pick her up! No dice, though. More Lonely Nights, Dori!

Then Lester calls. He's back in town again. Dori's so flustered she ends up being nicer to him on the phone than she means to be.

She goes out with him. To rock clubs. Lester never has to pay; he just mutters at people, and they let him in and find him a table. Strangers rush up to gladhand Lester and jostle round the table and pay court. Lester finds the music mostly boring, and it's no pretense; he actually *is* bored, he's heard it all. He sits there sipping club sodas and handing out these little chips of witty guru insight to these sleaze-ass Hollywood guys and bighaired coke-whores in black Spandex. Like it was his *job*.

Dori can't believe he's going to all this trouble just to jump her bones. It's not like he can't get women, or like their own relationship is all that tremendously scintillating. Lester's whole set-up is alien. But it *is* kind of interesting, and doesn't demand much. All Dori has to do is dress in her sluttiest Goodwill get-up, and be This Chick With Lester. Dori likes being invisible, and watching people when they don't know she's looking. She can see in their eyes that Lester's people wonder Who The Hell Is She? Dori finds this really funny, and makes sketches of his creepiest acquaintances on cocktail napkins. At night she puts them in her sketch books and writes dialogue balloons. It's all really good material.

Lester's also very funny, in a way. He's smart, not just hustler-clever but scary-crazy smart, like he's sometimes profound without knowing it or even *wanting* it. But when he thinks he's being most amusing, is when he's actually the most incredibly depressing. It bothers her that he doesn't drink around her; it's a bad sign. He knows almost nothing about art or drawing, he dresses like a jerk, he dances like a trained bear. And she's fallen in love with him and she knows he's going to break her goddamn heart.

Lester has put his novel aside for the moment. Nothing new there; he's been working on it, in hopeless spasms, for ten years. But now juggling this affair takes all he's got.

Lester is terrified that this amazing woman is going to go to pieces on him. He's seen enough of her work now to recognize that she's possessed of some kind of genuine demented genius. He can smell it; the vibe pours off her like Everglades swamp-reek. Even in her frowsy houserobe and bunny slippers, hair a mess, no makeup, half-asleep, he can see something there like Dresden china, something fragile and precious. And the world seems like a maelstrom of jungle hate, sinking into entropy or gearing up for Armageddon, and what the hell can anybody do? How can he be happy with her and not be punished for it? How long can they break the rules before the Nova Police show?

But nothing horrible happens to them. They just go on living.

Then Lester blunders into a virulent cloud of Hollywood money. He's written a stupid and utterly commercial screenplay about the laff-a-minute fictional antics of a heavy-metal band, and without warning he gets eighty thousand dollars for it.

He's never had so much money in one piece before. He has, he realizes with dawning horror, sold out.

To mark the occasion Lester buys some freebase, six grams of crystal meth, and rents a big white Cadillac. He fast-talks Dori into joining him for a supernaturally cool Kerouac adventure into the Savage Heart of America, and they get in the car laughing like hyenas and take off for parts unknown.

Four days later they're in Kansas City. Lester's lying in the back seat in a jittery Hank Williams half-doze and Dori is driving. They have nothing left to say, as they've been arguing viciously ever since Albuquerque.

Dori, white-knuckled, sinuses scorched with crank, loses it behind the wheel. Lester's slammed from the back seat and wakes up to find Dori knocked out and drizzling blood from a scalp wound. The Caddy's wrapped messily in the buckled ruins of a sidewalk mailbox..

Lester holds the resultant nightmare together for about two hours, which is long enough to flag down help and get Dori into a Kansas City trauma room.

He sits there, watching over her, convinced he's lost it, blown it; it's over, she'll hate him forever now. My God, she could have died! As soon as she comes to, he'll have to face her. The thought of this makes something buckle inside him. He flees the hospital in headlong panic.

He ends up in a sleazy little rock dive downtown where he jumps onto a table and picks a fight with the bouncer. After he's knocked down for the third time, he gets up screaming for the manager, how he's going to *ruin that motherfucker!* and the club's owner shows up, tired and red-faced and sweating. The owner, whose own tragedy must go mostly unexpressed here, is a fat white-haired cigar-chewing third-rater who attempted, and failed, to model his life on Elvis' Colonel Parker. He hates kids, he hates rock and roll, he hates the aggravation of smart-ass doped-up hippies screaming threats and pimping off the hard work of businessmen just trying to make a living.

He has Lester hauled to his office backstage and tells him all this. Toward the end, the owner's confused, almost plaintive, because he's never seen anyone as utterly, obviously, and desperately fucked-up as Lester Bangs, but who can still be coherent about it and use phrases like "rendered to the factor of machinehood" while mopping blood from his punched nose.

And Lester, trembling and red-eyed, tells him: fuck you Jack, I could run this jerkoff place, I could do everything you do blind drunk, and make this place a fucking *legend in American culture*, you booshwah sonofabitch.

Yeah punk if you had the money, the owner says.

I've *got* the money! Let's see your papers, you evil cracker bastard! In a few minutes Lester is the owner-to-be on a handshake and an earnestcheck.

Next day he brings Dori roses from the hospital shop downstairs. He sits next to the bed; they compare bruises, and Lester explains to her that he has just blown his fortune. They are now tied down and beaten in the corn-shucking heart of America. There is only one possible action left to complete this situation.

Three days later they are married in Kansas City by a justice of the peace.

Needless to say marriage does not solve any of their problems. It's a minor big deal for a while, gets mentioned in rock-mag gossip columns; they get some telegrams from friends, and Dori's mom seems pretty glad about it. They even get a nice note from Julie Burchill, the Marxist Amazon from *New Musical Express* who has quit the game to write for fashion mags, and her husband Tony Parsons the proverbial "hip young gunslinger" who now writes weird potboiler novels about racetrack gangsters. Tony & Julie seem to be making some kind of go of it. Kinda inspirational.

For a while Dori calls herself Dori Seda-Bangs, like her good friend Aline Kominsky-Crumb, but after a while she figures what's the use? and just calls herself Dori Bangs which sounds plenty weird enough on its own.

Lester can't say he's really *happy* or anything, but he's sure *busy*. He re-
names the club "Waxy's Travel Lounge," for some reason known only to
himself. The club loses money quickly and consistently. After the first month
Lester stops playing Lou Reed's *Metal Machine Music* before sets, and that
helps attendance some, but Waxy's is still a club which books a lot of tiny
weird college-circuit acts that Albert Average just doesn't get yet. Pretty soon
they're broke again and living on Lester's reviews.

They'd be even worse off, except Dori does a series of promo posters for
Waxy's that are so amazing that they draw people in, even after they've been
burned again and again on weird-ass bands only Lester can listen to.

After a couple of years they're still together, only they have shrieking
crockery-throwing fights and once, when he's been drinking, Lester wrenches
her arm so badly Dori's truly afraid it's broken. It isn't, luckily, but it's sure
no great kick being Mrs. Lester Bangs. Dori was always afraid of this: that
what he does is *work* and what she does is *cute*. How many Great Women
Artists are there anyway, and what happened to 'em? They went into patching
the wounded ego and picking up the dropped socks of Mr. Wonderful, that's
what. No big mystery about it.

And besides, she's thirty-six and still barely scraping a living. She pedals
her beat-up bike through the awful Kansas weather and sees these yuppies
cruise by with these smarmy grins: hey we don't *have* to invent our lives,
our lives are *invented for us* and boy does that ever save a lot of soul-searching.

But still somehow they blunder along; they have the occasional good break.
Like when Lester turns over the club on Wednesdays to some black kids for
(ecch!) "disco nite" and it turns out to be the beginning of a little Kansas
City rap-scratch scene, which actually makes the club some money. And
"Polyrock," a band Lester hates at first but later champions to global mega-
stardom, cuts a live album in Waxy's.

And Dori gets a contract to do one of those twenty-second animated logos
for MTV, and really gets into it. It's fun, so she starts doing video animation
work for (fairly) big bucks and even gets a Macintosh II from a video-hack
admirer in Silicon Valley. Dori had always loathed feared and despised
computers but this thing is *different*. This is a kind of art that *nobody's ever
done before* and has to be invented from leftovers, sweat, and thin air! It's
wide open and way rad!

Lester's novel doesn't get anywhere, but he does write a book called *A
Reasonable Guide to Horrible Noise* which becomes a hip coffeetable cult
item with an admiring introduction by a trendy French semiotician. Among
other things, this book introduces the term "chipster" which describes a kind
of person who, well, didn't really *exist* before Lester described them but once
he'd pointed 'em out it was *obvious to everybody*.

But they're still not *happy*. They both have a hard time taking the "marital
fidelity" notion with anything like seriousness. They have a vicious fight
once, over who gave who herpes, and Dori splits for six months and goes

back to California. Where she looks up her old girlfriends and finds the survivors married with kids, and her old boyfriends are even seedier and more pathetic than Lester. What the hell, it's not happiness but it's something. She goes back to Lester. He's gratifyingly humble and appreciative for almost six weeks.

Waxy's does in fact become a cultural legend of sorts, but they don't pay you for that; and anyway it's hell to own a bar while attending sessions of Alcoholics Anonymous. So Lester gives in, and sells the club. He and Dori buy a house, which turns out to be far more hassle than it's worth, and then they go to Paris for a while, where they argue bitterly and squander all their remaining money.

When they come back Lester gets, of all the awful things, an academic gig. For a Kansas state college. Lester teaches Rock and Popular Culture. In the '70s there'd have been no room for such a hopeless skidrow weirdo in a, like, Serious Academic Environment, but it's the late '90s by now, and Lester has outlived the era of outlawhood. Because who are we kidding? Rock and Roll is a satellite-driven worldwide information industry which is worth billions and *billions*, and if they don't study *major industries* then what the hell are the taxpayers funding colleges for?

Self-destruction is awfully tiring. After a while, they just give it up. They've lost the energy to flame-out, and it hurts too much; besides it's less trouble just to live. They eat balanced meals, go to bed early, and attend faculty parties where Lester argues violently about the parking privileges.

Just after the turn of the century, Lester finally gets his novel published, but it seems quaint and dated now, and gets panned and quickly remaindered. It would be nice to say that Lester's book was rediscovered years later as a Klassic of Litratchur but the truth is that Lester's no novelist; what he is, is a cultural mutant, and what he has in the way of insight and energy has been eaten up. Subsumed by the Beast, man. What he thought and said made some kind of difference, but nowhere near as big a difference as he'd dreamed.

In the year 2015, Lester dies of a heart attack while shoveling snow off his lawn. Dori has him cremated, in one of those plasma flash-cremators that are all the mode in the 21st-cent. undertaking business. There's a nice respectful retrospective on Lester in the *New York Times Review of Books* but the truth is Lester's pretty much a forgotten man; a colorful footnote for cultural historians who can see the twentieth century with the unflattering advantage of hindsight.

A year after Lester's death they demolish the remnants of Waxy's Travel Lounge to make room for a giant high-rise. Dori goes out to see the ruins. As she wanders among the shockingly staid and unromantic rubble, there's another of those slips in the fabric of Fate, and Dori is approached by a Vision.

Thomas Hardy used to call it the Immanent Will and in China it might have been the Tao, but we late 20th-cent. postmoderns would probably call it something soothingly pseudoscientific like the "genetic imperative." Dori, being Dori, recognizes this glowing androgynous figure as The Child They Never Had.

"Don't worry, Mrs. Bangs," the Child tells her, "I might have died young of some ghastly disease, or grown up to shoot the President and break your heart, and anyhow you two woulda been no prize as parents." Dori can see herself and Lester in this Child, there's a definite nacreous gleam in its right eye that's Lester's, and the sharp quiet left eye is hers; but behind the eyes where there should be a living breathing human being there's *nothing,* just kind of chill galactic twinkling.

"And don't feel guilty for outliving him either," the Child tells her, "because you're going to have what we laughingly call a natural death, which means you're going to die in the company of strangers hooked up to tubes when you're old and helpless."

"But did it *mean* anything?" Dori says.

"If you mean were you Immortal Artists leaving indelible grafitti in the concrete sidewalk of Time, no. You've never walked the earth as Gods, you were just people. But it's better to have a real life than no life." The Child shrugs. "You weren't all that happy together, but you *did* suit each other, and if you'd both married other people instead, there would have been *four* people unhappy. So here's your consolation: you helped each other."

"So?" Dori says.

"So that's enough. Just to shelter each other, and help each other up. Everything else is gravy. Someday, no matter what, you go down forever. Art can't make you immortal. Art can't Change the World. Art can't even heal your soul. All it can do is maybe ease the pain a bit or make you feel more awake. And that's enough. It only matters as much as it matters, which is zilch to an ice-cold interstellar Cosmic Principle like yours truly. But if you try to live by my standards it will only kill you faster. By your own standards, you did pretty good, really."

"Well okay then," Dori says.

After this purportedly earth-shattering mystical encounter, her life simply went right on, day following day, just like always. Dori gave up computer-art; it was too hairy trying to keep up with the hotshot high-tech cutting edge, and kind of undignified, when you came right down to it. Better to leave that to hungry kids. She was idle for a while, feeling quiet inside, but finally she took up watercolors. For a while Dori played the Crazy Old Lady Artist and was kind of a mainstay of the Kansas regionalist art scene. Granted, Dori was no Georgia O'Keeffe, but she was working, and living, and she touched a few people's lives.

Or, at least, Dori surely would have touched those people, if she'd been there to do it. But of course she wasn't, and didn't. Dori Seda never met

Lester Bangs. Two simple real-life acts of human caring, at the proper moment, might have saved them both; but when those moments came, they had no one, not even each other. And so they went down into darkness, like skaters, breaking through the hard bright shiny surface of our true-facts world.

Today I made this white paper dream to cover the holes they left.

LUCIUS SHEPARD

The Ends of the Earth

One of the most popular new writers to enter SF in a decade or more, Lucius Shepard won the John W. Campbell Award in 1985 as the year's Best New Writer, and no year since has gone by without him adorning the final ballot for one major award or another, and often for several. In 1987, he won the Nebula Award for his landmark novella "R & R," and in 1988 he picked up a World Fantasy Award for his monumental short-story collection *The Jaguar Hunter*. His first novel was the acclaimed *Green Eyes*; his second the best-selling *Life During Wartime*; he is at work on several more, including *The Off-Season*. Upcoming is another story collection called *The Ends of the Earth*. His story "Black Coral" was in our Second Annual Collection; his stories "The Jaguar Hunter" and "A Spanish Lesson" were in our Third Annual Colleciton; "R & R" was in our Fourth Annual Collection; "Shades" was in our Fifth Annual Collection; and "The Scalehunter's Beautiful Daughter" was in our Sixth Annual Collection. Born in Lynchburg, Virginia, he now lives somewhere in the wilds of Nantucket.

In the nightmarish, hallucinatorally vivid story that follows, he demonstrates once again the old truth that if you *do* play the game, you should never bet more than you're willing to *lose* . . .

▼

The Ends of the Earth

LUCIUS SHEPARD

Those whose office it is to debunk the supernatural are fond of pointing out that incidences of paranormal activity most often take place in backwaters and rarely in the presence of credible witnesses, claiming that this in itself is evidence of the fraudulent character of the phenomena involved; yet it has occurred to me that the agents of the supernatural, especially those elements whose activities are directed toward evil ends, might well exhibit reticence in appearing before persons capable of verifying their existence and thus their threat to humankind. It seems surprising that such shadowy forces—if, indeed, they do exist—choose to appear before any witnesses at all, and equally surprising—if their powers are as vast as described in popular fiction—that they do not simply have done with us. Perhaps they are prevented from doing so by some restraint, a limit, say, on how many souls they are allowed to bag, and perhaps the fact that they manifest as they do is attributable to a binding regulation similar to the one dictating that corporations (shadowy forces in themselves) must make a public notice of the date and location of their stockholders' meetings. In order to avoid scrutiny of their business practices, a number of corporations publish these notices in shoppers' guides and rural weeklies, organs unlikely to pass before the eyes of government agencies and reporters, and it makes sense that the supernatural might choose this same tactic as a means of compliance with a cosmic rule. That supposition may seem facetious, but my intent is quite serious, for while I cannot say with absolute certainty whether the circumstances that provoked my interest in these matters was in essence supernatural or merely an extraordinary combination of ordinary people and events, I believe that six months ago in Guatemala, a place notable for its inaccessibility and unreliable witnesses, I witnessed something rare and secret, something that may have reflected the exercise of a regulatory truth pertaining to both the visible and invisible worlds.

Prior to leaving for Guatemala, I had been romantically involved for the preceding three years with Karen Maniaci, a married woman who managed a Manhattan art gallery, and it was our breakup, which was marked by bitterness on my part and betrayal on hers, that persuaded me I needed a drastic change in order to get on with living. This process of persuasion lasted several months, months during which I wandered gloomily about New York, stopping in my tracks to stare at dark-haired women of approximately five feet nine in height and 120 pounds; and at length I concluded that I had better get out of town . . . either that or begin to play footsie with mental illness. I was thirty-seven and had grown too cautious to want to risk myself in a dangerous enterprise; yet there is a theatricality inherent in being jilted, a dramatic potential that demands resolution, and to satisfy it, I chose that other option of the heartbroken: a trip to some foreign shore, one isolate from the rest of the world, where there were no newspapers and no reminders of one's affair. Livingston, Guatemala, seemed to qualify as such. It was described in a guidebook that happened upon in The Strand bookstore as ". . . a quiet village at the egress of the Rio Dulce into the Caribbean, hemmed in against the sea by the Petén rain forest. Settled by black Caribes and the descendants of East Indian slaves brought by the British to work the sugar plantations upriver. There are no roads into Livingston. One reaches it either by ferry from Puerto Morales or by powerboat from Reunión at the junction of the Rio Dulce and the Petén highway. The majority of the houses are neat white stucco affairs with red tile roofs. The natives are unspoiled by tourism. In the hills above the village is a lovely tiered waterfall called Siete Altares (Seven Altars), so named because of the seven pools into which the stream whose terminus it forms plunges on its way to the sea. Local delicacies include turtle stew. . . ."

It sounded perfect, a paradise cut off from the grim political realities of the mother country, a place where a man could go to seed in the classic style, by day wandering the beach in a Bogart suit, waking each morning slumped over a table, an empty rum bottle beside his elbow, a stained deck of cards scattered around him with only the queen of hearts showing its face. A few days after reading the guidebook entry, following journeys by plane, train, and an overcrowded ferry, I arrived in Livingston. A few days after that, thanks to a meeting in one of the bars, I took possession of a five-room house of yellow stucco walls and concrete floors belonging to a young Spanish couple, doctors who had been studying with local *curanderos* and wanted someone to look after their pets—a marmalade cat and a caged toucan—while they toured for a year in the United States.

I have traveled widely all my life, and it has been my experience that guidebook descriptions bear little relation to actual places; however, though changes had occurred—most notable the discovery of the village by the singer Jimmy Buffett, whose frequent visits had given a boost to the tourist industry, attracting a smattering of young travelers, mainly French and Scandinavians who lived in huts along the beach—I discovered that the guidebook had not grossly exaggerated Livingston's charms. True, a number of shanty bars had sprung up on the beach, and there was a roach-infested hotel not mentioned in the book: three stories of peeling paint and cell-sized rooms furnished with torn mattresses and broken chairs. But the Caribe houses were in evidence; and the turtle stew was tasty; and the fishing was good; and Siete Altares was something out of a South Seas movie, each pool shaded by ceiba trees, their branches dripping with orchids, hummingbirds flitting everywhere in the thickets. And the natives *were* relatively unspoiled, perhaps because the tourists kept to the beach, which was separated from the village by a steep drop-off, and which—thanks to the bars and a couple of one-room stores—provided them with all the necessities of life.

Early on, I suffered a domestic tragedy. The cat ate the toucan, leaving its beak and feet for me to find on the kitchen floor. But in general, things went well. I began to work, my mind was clearing, and the edge had been taken off my gloom by the growing awareness that other possibilities for happiness existed apart from a neurotic career woman who was afraid to trust her feelings, was prone to anxiety attacks and given to buying bracelets with the pathological avidity that Imelda Marcos once displayed toward the purchase of shoes. I soon fell into a pleasant routine, writing in the mornings, working on a cycle of short stories that—despite my intention of avoiding this pitfall—dealt with an unhappily married woman. Afternoons, I would lie in a hammock struck between two palms that sprouted from the patio of the house, and read. Evenings, I would stroll down to the beach with the idea of connecting with one of the tourist girls. I usually wound up drinking alone and brooding, but I did initiate a flirtation with an Odille LeCleuse, a Frenchwoman in her late twenties, with high cheekbones and milky skin, dark violet eyes and a sexy mouth that always looked as if she were about to purse her lips. She was in thrall—or so I'd heard—to Carl Konwicki, an Englishman of about my own age, who had lived on the beach for two years and supported himself by selling marijuana.

By all reports, Konwicki was a manipulator who traded on his experience to dominate less-seasoned travelers in order to obtain sex and other forms of devotion, and I couldn't understand how Odille, an intelligent woman with a degree in linguistics from the Sorbonne, could have fallen prey to the likes of him. I spotted him every day on the streets of the village: an asthenic, olive-skinned man, with a scraggly fringe of brown beard and a hawkish Semitic face. He commonly wore loose black trousers, an embroidered vest, and a Moroccan skullcap, and there was a deliberate languor to his walk, as if he were conscious of being watched; whenever he would pass by, he would favor me with a bemused smile. I felt challenged by him, both because of Odille and because my morality had been enlisted by what I'd heard of his smarty brand of gamesmanship, and I had the urge to let him know I saw through his pose. But realizing that—if Odille was involved with him —this kind of tactic would only damage my chances with her, I restrained myself and ignored him.

One night about two months after my arrival, I was going through old notebooks, searching for a passage that I wanted to include in a story, when a sheet of paper with handwriting on it slipped from between the pages and fell to the floor. The handwriting was that of my ex-lover, Karen. I let it lie for a moment, but finally, unable to resist, I picked it up and discovered it to be a letter written early in the relationship. A portion read as follows:

> . . . When I went to the therapist today (I know . . . I'll probably tell you all this on the phone later, but what the hell!), I told her about what happened, how I almost lost my job by making love to you those days in the office, and she didn't seem terribly surprised. When I asked her how a responsible adult who cares about her job could possibly jeopardize it in such a way, she simply said that there must have been a great deal of gain in it for me. It seems she's trying to lead me toward you—she's quite negative about Barry. But that's probably just wishful thinking—what she's doing is trying to lead me toward what I want. Of course, what I want is you, so it amounts to the same thing.

It was curious, I thought, scanning the letter, how words that had once seemed precious could now seem so vapid. I noted the overusage of the words "terribly" and "terrible," particularly in conjunction with the words "surprising" and "surprised." That had been her basic reaction to falling in love, I realized. She had been terribly surprised. *My God*, she'd said to herself. *An emotion! Quick, I'll hie me to the head doctor and have it excised*. I read on.

> . . . I can't imagine living without you, Ray. When you said something the other day about the possibility of getting hit by a bus, I suddenly got this awful chill. I had a terrible sense of loss just hearing you say that. This is interesting, in that I used to try to figure out if I loved Barry by imagining something awful happening to him and seeing how I felt. I usually felt bad, but that's about it. . . .

I laughed out loud. The last I'd heard on the subject was that Barry, who bored Karen, whom she did not respect, who had recently gotten into rubber goods, was back in favor. Barry had one virtue that I did not: he was controllable, and in control there was security. She could go on lying to him, having affairs with no fear of being caught—Barry was big into denial. And now she was planning a child in an attempt to pave over the potholes of the relationship, convincing herself that this secure fake was the best she could expect of life. She was due fairly soon, I realized. But it didn't matter. No act of hers could bring conscience and clarity into what had always been a charade. Her lies had condemned the three of us, and most of all, she had condemned herself by engaging in a kind of method living, chirping a litany of affirmation. "I think I can, I think I can," playing The Little Adultress That Could, and thus losing the hope of her heart the strength of her soul. I imagined her at sixty-five, her beauty hardened to a grotesque brittleness, wandering through a mall, shopping for drapes thick enough to blot out the twenty-first century, while Barry shuffled along in her wake, trying to pin down the feeling that something had not been quite right all these years, both of them smiling and nodding, looking forward to a friendly gray fate.

The letter brought back the self-absorbed anguish that I'd been working to put behind me, and I felt—as I had for months prior to leaving New York—on the verge of exploding, as if a pressure were building to a hot critical mass inside me, making my thoughts flurry like excited atoms. My face burned; there were numbing weights in my arms and legs. I paced the room, unable to regain my composure, and after ten minutes or so, I flung open the door, frightening the marmalade cat, and stormed out into the dark.

I did not choose a direction, but soon I found myself on the beach, heading toward one of the shanty bars. The night was perfect for my mood. Winded: a constant crunch of surf and palm fronds tearing; combers rolling in, their plumed sprays as white as flame. A brilliant moon flashed between the fronts, creating shadows from even the smallest of projections, and set back from the shore, half-hidden in deep shadow among palms and sea grape and cashew trees, were huts with glinting windows and tin roofs. The beach was a ragged, narrow strip of tawny sand strewn with coconut litter and overturned cayucos. As I stepped over a cayuco, something croaked and leaped off into the rank weeds bordering the beach. My heart stuttered, and I fell back against the cayuco. It had only been a frog, but its appearance made me aware of my vulnerability. Even a place like Livingston had its dangers. Street criminals from Belize had been known to ride motorboats down from Belize City or Belmopan to rob and beat the tourists, and in my agitated state of mind, I would have made the perfect target.

The bar—Café Pluto—was set in the lee of a rocky point: a thatched hut with a sand floor and picnic-style tables, lit with black lights that emitted an evil purple radiance and made all the gringos glow like sunburned corpses. Reggae from a jukebox at the rear was barely audible above the racket of the generator. I had several drinks in rapid succession, and ended up out front of the bar beside a topple palm trunk, drinking rum straight from the bottle and sharing a joint with Odille and a young blond Australian named Ryan, who was writing a novel, and whose mode of dress—slacks, shirt, and loosened tie—struck an oddly formal note. I was giddy with the dope, with the wildness of the nights, the vast blue-dark sky and its trillion watts of stars, silver glitters that appeared to be slipping around like sequins on a dancer's gown. Behind us the Café Pluto had the look of an eerie cave lit by seams of gleaming purple ore.

I asked Ryan what his novel was about, and, with affected diffidence, he said, "Nothing much. Saturday night in a working-class bar in Sydney." He took a hit of the joint, passed it to Odille. "It wasn't going too well, so I thought I'd set it aside and do something poetic. Run away to the ends of the earth." He had a look around, a look that in its casual sweep included the sea and sky and shore. "This *is* the ends of the earth, isn't it?"

I was caught by the poignancy of the images, thinking that he had inadvertently captured the essence of place and moment. I pictured the globe spinning and spinning, trailing dark frays of its own essential stuff, upon one of which was situated this slice of night and stars and expatriate woe, tatters with no real place in human affairs. . . . Wind veiled Odille's face with a drift of hair. I pushed it back, and she smiled, letting her eyelids droop. I wanted to take her back to the house and fuck her until I forgot all the maudlin bullshit that had been fucking me over the past three years.

"I hear you're doing some writing, too," said Ryan in a tone that managed to be both defiant and disinterested.

"Just some stories," I said, surprised that he would know this.

" 'Just some stories.' " He gave a morose laugh and said to the sky, "He's modest. . . . I love it." Then, turning a blank gaze on me: "No need to hide your light, man. We all know you're famous."

"Famous? Not hardly."

"Sure you are!" In a stentorian voice, he quoted a blurb on my last book. " 'Raymond Kingsley, a mainstay of American fiction.' "

"Uh-huh, right."

"Even the Master of Time and Space thinks you're great," said Ryan. "And believe me, he's sparing with his praise."

"Who're you talking about?"

Ryan pointed behind me. "Him."

Carl Konwicki was coming down the beach. He ambled up, dropped onto the fallen palm trunk, and looked out to sea. Odille and Ryan seemed to be waiting for him to speak. Irritated by this obeisance, I belched. Konwicki let his eyes swing toward me, and I winked.

"How's she going?" I took a man-sized slug of rum, wiped my mouth with the back of my hand, and fixed him with a mean stare. He clucked his tongue against his teeth and said, "I'm fine, thank you."

"Glad to hear it." Drunk. I hated him, my hate fueled by the frustration that had driven me out of the house. Hate was chemical between us, the confrontational lines as sharply etched as the shadows on the sand. I gestured at his skullcap. "You lived in Morocco?"

"Some."

"What part?"

"You know . . . around." The wind bent a palm frond low, and for an instant, Konwicki's swarthy face was edged by a saw-toothed shadow.

"That's not very forthcoming," I said. "Do questions bother you?"

"Not ones that have a purpose."

"How about light conversation . . . that a worthwhile purpose?"

"Is that *your* purpose?"

"What else would it be?"

"Wow!" said Ryan. "This is like intense . . . like a big moment."

Odille giggled.

"I got it," I said. "What would *you* like to talk about? How about the translation you're doing . . . what is it?"

"The *Popol-Vuh*," said Konwicki distractedly.

"Gee," I said. "That's already been translated, hasn't it?"

"Not correctly."

"Oh, I see. And you're going to do it right." I had another pull on the rum bottle. "Hope you're not wasting your time."

"Time." Konwicki smiled, apparently amused by the concept; he refitted his gaze to the toiling sea.

"Yeah," I said, injecting a wealth of sarcasm into my voice. "It's pretty damn mind-bending, isn't it?"

The surf thundered; Konwicki met my eyes, imperturbable. "I've been looking forward to meeting you."

"Me, too," I said. "I hear you sell great dope." I clapped a hand to my brow as if recognizing that I had made a social blunder. "Pardon me. . . . I didn't intend that to sound disparaging."

Konwicki gave me one of his distant smiles. "You're obviously upset about something," he said. "You should try to calm down."

I sat close beside him on the palm trunk, close enough to cause him to shift away, and was about to bait him further; but he stood, said, "Ta ra," and walked into the bar.

"I'd score that round even," said Ryan. "Mr. Kingsley dominating the first half, the Master coming on late."

Odille was gazing after Konwicki, wrapping a curl of hair around one forefinger. She gave me a wave, said, "I'll be back, O.K.?", and headed for the bar. I watched her out of sight, tracking the oiled roll of her hips beneath her cutoffs, and when I turned back to Ryan, he was smiling at me.

"What is it with them?" I asked.

"With Odille and the Master? Just a little now-and-then thing." He gave me a sly look. "Why? You interested?"

I snorted, had a hit of rum.

"You can win the lady," said Ryan. "If you've a stout heart."

I looked at him over the top of the bottle, but offered no encouragement.

"You see, Ray," said Ryan, affecting the manner of a lecturer, "Odille's a wounded bird. The poor thing had a disappointment in love back in Paris.

She sought solace in distant lands and had the misfortune of meeting the Master. It's not much of a misfortune, you understand. The Master's not much of a Master, so he can't offer a great deal in the way of good or ill. But he confused Odille, made her believe he could show her how to escape pain through his brand of enlightenment. And that involved a bit of sack time."

Given this similarity in history between Odille and myself, I imagined fate had taken a hand by bringing us together. "So what can I do?"

"Things a bit hazy, are they, Ray?" Ryan chuckled. "Odille's grown disillusioned with the Master. She's looking for someone to burst his bubble, to free her." He reached for the bottle, had a swig, and gagged. "God, that's awful!" He slumped against the topple palm trunk, screwed the bottle into the sand so that it stood upright. The surf boomed; the wildfire whiteness of the combers imprinted afterimages on my eyes.

"Anyway," Ryan went on, "she's definitely looking for emotional rescue. But you can't go about it with *déclassé* confrontation. You'll have to beat the Master on his own terms, his own ground."

Perhaps it was the rum that let me believe that Ryan had a clear view of our situation. "What *are* his terms?" I asked.

"Games," he said. "Whatever game he chooses." He had another pull off the bottle. "He's afraid of you, you know. He's worried that you're into disciples, and all his children will abandon him for the famous writer. He realized he can't befuddle you with his usual quasi-erudite crap. So he'll come up with something new for you. I have no idea what. But he'll play some game with you. He's got to. . . . It's his nature."

"How's he befuddled you? You seem to have a handle on him."

"He's got no need," said Ryan. "I'm his fool, and a fool can know the king's secrets and make fun of them with impunity."

I started to ask another question, but let it rest. The wind pulled the soft crush of the surf into a breathy vowel; the moon had lowered behind the hills above the village, its afterglow fanning up into the heavens; the top of the sky had deepened to indigo, and the stars blazed, so dense and intricate in their array that I thought I might—if I were to try—be able to read there all scripture and truth in sparkling sentences. And it was not only in the sky that clarity ruled. What Ryan had said made sense. Odille was testing me . . . perhaps unconsciously, but testing me nonetheless, unwilling to abandon Konwicki until she was sure of me. I didn't resent this—it was a tactic often used in establishing relationships. But I was struck by how clear its uses seemed on the beach at Livingston. Not merely the social implications, but its elemental ones: the wounded lovers, the shabby Mephistophelian figure of Konwicki with his sacred books and petty need to exercise power. Man, woman, and Devil entangled in a sexual knot.

"Did I ever tell you my theory of the Visible?" I asked Ryan.

"We only just met," he reminded me.

"God, you're right! I've been under the illusion that we were old pals." I plucked the rum bottle from the sand and drank. "In places like this, I've always thought it was possible to see how things really are between people. To discern relationships that are obscured by the clutter of urban life. The old relationships, the archetypes."

He stared blearily up at me. "Sounds bloody profound, Ray."

"Yeah, I suppose it is," I said, and then added: "Profundity's my business. Or maybe it's bullshit . . . one or the other."

"So," he said, "are you going to play?"

"I think so . . . yeah."

"Beautiful," said Ryan. "That's really beautiful."

A few moments later, Konwicki and Odille came out of the bar and walked toward us, deep in conversation.

Ryan laughed and laughed. "Let the games begin," he said.

We talked on the beach for another hour, smoking Konwicki's dope, which smoothed out the rough edges of my drunk, seeming to isolate me behind a thick transparency. I withdrew from the conversation, watching Konwicki. I wasn't gauging his strengths and weaknesses; despite my exchange with Ryan, I had not formalized the idea that there was to be a contest between us. I was merely observing, intrigued by his conversational strategy. By sidestepping questions, claiming to know nothing about a subject, he managed to intimate that the subject was not worth knowing and that he possessed knowledge in a sphere of far greater relevance to the scheme of things. Odille hung on his every world for a while, but soon began to lose interest, casting glances and smiles at me; it appeared she was trying to maintain a connection with Konwicki, but was losing energy in that regard.

For the most part, Konwicki avoided looking at me; but at one point, he cut his eyes toward me and locked on. We stared at each other for a long moment, then he turned away with acknowledgment. During that moment, however, the skin on my face went cold, my muscles tensed, and a smile stretched my lips. A feral smile funded by a remorseless hatred quite different from the impassioned, drunken loathing I originally had felt. This emotion, like the smile, seemed something visited upon me and not an intensification of my emotions, and along with it came a sudden increase in my body temperature. A sweat broke on my forehead, my chest and arms, and my vision reddened, and I had a peculiar sense of doubled perceptions, as if I were looking through two different pairs of eyes, one of which was capable of seeing a wider spectrum. I decided to slack off on the rum.

At length, Konwicki suggested we get out of the wind, which was blowing stronger, and go over to his place to listen to music. I was of two minds about the proposal; while I wasn't ready to give up on Odille, neither was I eager to mix it with Konwicki, and I was certain that if I went with them, there would be some bad result. The dope had taken the edge off my enthusiasm. But Odille took my hand, nudged the softness of her breast into my arm.

"You *are* coming, aren't you?" she said.

"Sure," I said, as if a thought to the contrary had never occurred.

We walked together along the beach, trailing Konwicki and Ryan, and Odille talked about taking a trip to Escuilpas someday soon to see the Black Virgin in the cathedral there.

"Women come from all over Central America to be blessed," she said. "They stand in line for days. Huge fat women in white turbans from Belize. Crippled old island ladies from Roatán. Beautiful slim girls from Panama. All waiting to spend a few seconds kneeling in the shadow of a black statue. When I first heard about it, I thought it sounded primitive. Now it seems strangely modern. The New Primitivism. I keep imagining all those female shadows in the bright sun, radios playing, vendors selling cold drinks." She gave her hair a toss. "I could use that sort of blessing."

"Is it only for women?"

She let her eyes drift toward me. "Sometimes men wait with them."

I asked if what Ryan had told me about her love affair in Paris was the truth. I had no hesitancy in asking this—intimacies were the flavor of the night. A flicker of displeasure crossed her face. "Ryan's an idiot."

"I doubt he'd argue the point."

Odille went a few steps in silence. "It was nothing. A fling, that's all."

Her glum tone seemed to belie this.

"Yeah, I had a fling myself right before I came down here. Like to have killed me, that fling."

She glanced up at me, still registering displeasure, but then she smiled. "Perhaps with us it's a matter of. . . ." She made a frustrated gesture, unable to find the right words.

"Victims recognizing the symptoms?" I suggested.

"I suppose." She threw back her head and looked up into the sky as if seeking guidance there. "Yes, I had a bad experience, but I'm over it."

"Completely?"

She shook her head. "No . . . never completely. And you?"

"Hey, I'm fine," I said. "It's like it never happened."

She laughed, cast an appraising look my way. "Who was she?"

"This married woman back in New York."

"Oh!" Odille put a hand on my arm in sympathy. "That's the worst, isn't it? Married, I mean."

"The worst? I don't know. It was pretty goddamn bad."

"What was she like?"

"Frightened. She got married because she had a run of back luck. . . . At least, that's what she told me. Things started going bad around her. Her parents got divorced, her dog ran away, and that seemed a sign something worse might happen. I guess she thought marriage would protect her." I walked faster. "She's a fucking mess."

"How so?"

"She doesn't know what the hell she wants. Whenever she doubts something, she'll broadcast an opinion pro or con until the contrary opinion has been shouted down in her own mind." I kicked at the sand. "The last time we talked, she explained how she was happy in her marriage for the same reasons that she'd once claimed to be miserable. The vices of this guy who she'd ridiculed. . . . She told everyone how much he bored her, how childish he was. All those vices had been transformed into solid virtues. She told me she knew that she couldn't have the kind of relationship with Barry—that's her husband—that we'd had, but you had to make trade-offs. Barry at least always wore a neatly pressed suit and could be counted on not to embarrass—though never to scintillate—at business functions." I sniffed. "As a husband, he made the perfect accessory for evening wear."

"You sound bitter."

"I am. She put me through hell. Of course, I bought into it, so I've got no one to blame but myself."

"She was beautiful, of course?"

"She didn't think so." I changed the subject. "Was yours married?"

"No, just a shit." Her expression became distant, and I knew that for a moment she was back in Paris with the Shit. "For a long time afterward, I threw myself into other relationships. I thought that would help, but it was a mistake. . . . I can see that now."

"Everything seems like a mistake afterward," I said.

"Not everything," she said coyly.

I wasn't sure how to take that, and it wasn't just that her meaning was vague; it was also that I was put off by her coyness. Before I could frame a response, she said, "Talking to Carl has helped me a great deal."

"Oh, I see." I tried to disguise my disappointment, believing this to be a sign that her connection with Konwicki was still vital.

"No, you don't. Just having someone to talk to was helpful. Carl's a fraud, of course. Nothing he says is without guile. But he does listen, and it's hard to find a good listener. That's basically all there was between us. I helped him with his work, and . . . there was more. But it wasn't important."

I wondered if she was playing with me, making me guess at her availability, and was briefly angered by the possibility; but then, recalling how uncertain my own motivations and responses had been. I decided that if I couldn't forgive her, I couldn't forgive myself.

"What are you thinking about?" Odille asked.

Her features, refined by the moonlight, looked delicate, etched, as if a kind of lucidity had been revealed in them, and I believed that I could see down beneath the games and the layers of false construction, beneath all those defenses, to who she most was, to the woman, no longer an innocent in the accepted sense of the word, but innocent all the same, still hopeful in spite of pain and disillusionment.

"Konwicki," I lied. "You helped him translate the *Popol-Vuh*?"

"He was being discreet. He's acquired an old Mayan game and some papers that go with it. That's what he's translating."

"What sort of game?"

"From what I've been able to gather, it's a role-playing game. The papers seem to imply that it has to do with spirit travel. The gods. All the old cultures have myths that deal with that. It might be something that the priests used to evoke trances . . . something like that."

For no reason I could determine, this news made me edgy.

"Is that really what you were thinking about?" Odille asked.

"I was being discreet," I said, and she laughed.

Konwicki's place was a thatched hut with one large room and a sand floor over which a carpet of dried palm fronds had been laid, and was a scrupulously neat advertisement for his travels. Wall hangings from Peru, a brass hookah, a Japanese scroll, a bowl holding some Nepalese jewelry—rings of coral and worked silver, pillows embroidered in a pattern of turquoise thread that I recognized as being from Isfahan. Gourd bowls and various cooking implements hung from pegs, and a hurricane lantern provided a flickering orange light. An old Roxy Music album was playing on a cassette recorder, Bryan Ferry's nostalgia seeming more effete than usual in those surroundings. In one corner was an orange crate containing a stack of papers covered with Mayan hieroglyphs. I started to pick up the top paper, and Konwicki, who was sitting against the rear wall, rolling a joint, said, "Don't touch that . . . please!"

"What's the problem? My vibes might unsettle the spiritual fabric?"

"Something like that." He licked the edge of the rolling paper.

Ryan had stretched out on his back between Konwicki and a cardboard box that held some clay figures, a comic book spread open over his eyes; Odille was on her knees facing Konwicki, watching him roll.

"Why don't you tell me what else is off-limits?" I said.

He lit the joint, let smoke trickle from his nostrils. "Did you come here just to be contentious?" he asked.

"I'm not sure why I came," I said. "I figured you'd tell me."

He gave a shrug, blew more smoke. "Why are you so hostile?"

I dropped down cross-legged next to Odille. "You know what's going on here, man. But for one thing. I don't like guys like you . . . guys who want to grow up to be Charles Manson, but don't have the balls, so they hang out and maneuver weaker people into fucking them.'"

I said this mildly, and that was not a pose; I felt calm, without malice, merely making an observation. My dislike of Konwicki—it appeared—had shifted into a philosophical mode.

"And what sort of person are you?" he asked with equal mildness.

"Why don't you tell me?"

He made a show of sizing me up. "How about this? A horny, lonely man who's having trouble adjusting to the onset of middle age."

"Gee, Carl," I said. "I like my kind of guy a lot better than I do yours."

He sniffed, amused. "There's no accounting for taste." He passed me the joint, and in the spirit of the moment, took a hit, let it circulate, then took another, deeper one. Seconds later I realized that Konwicki had exercised the home-field advantage in our little war and pulled out his killer weed. Even though I was already ripped, I could feel its effects moving through me like a cool, soft wind; it was the kind of weed that immobilizes, the kind with which you need to plan where you want your body to fall. My thoughts became muddled; my extremities felt cold. Yet when the joint was passed to me again, I had still another hit, not wanting to seem a wimp.

"Good shit, huh?" said Konwicki, watching Ryan suck on the joint.

"Gawd!" said Ryan, leaking smoke. "What clarity!"

I'm not sure why I reached for the clay figurines in the box next to Ryan—the need to hold on to something, probably. The wind tattering the thatch made a sound like something huge being torn apart. The inconstant wash of orange light along the walls mesmerized me, and the lantern flame itself was too bright to look at directly. In every minute event, I perceived myriad subtleties, and I could have sworn I was floating a couple of inches above the ground. Perhaps I thought the figurine would give me ballast, bring me back down, because I was blitzed, wrecked, fucked-up. My hand moved in slow motion, effecting a lovely arc toward the box that contained the figurines. But the second I picked one up, I was cured of my sensory overload and felt stone-cold sober, in absolute control.

"Christ!" said Konwicki with annoyance. "Put that down!"

The figurine was a pre-Columbian dwarf of yellowish brown clay with stumpy legs, a potbelly, a hooked nose, and thick, brutish lips. The eyes were slitted folds. About the size of a Barbie doll. Ugly as a wart. Holding it gave me focus and made me feel not merely whole, but powerful. The only remnant of my buzz was a sense that the figurine was full of something heavy and shifting, like a dollop of mercury. It seemed to throb in my hand.

"Put it down!" Konwicki's tone had become anxious.

"Why? Is it valuable?" I turned the figure, examining it from every angle. "Don't worry, man! I won't drop it."

"Just put it down, all right?"

Holding the figurine in my left hand, away from Konwicki, I leaned forward and saw that the cardboard box contained five more figurines, all standing. "What are they? They look like a set."

Konwicki held out his hand for the figurine, but I was feeling more and more in control. As if the figurine were a strengthening magic. I wasn't about to let it go. Odille, I saw, was regarding Konwicki with distaste.

"I'm not going to drop it, man. You think I'm too stoned or something? Hey"—I flashed him a cheery grin—"I feel great. Tell me what they are."

Ryan, too, was staring at Konwicki; he laughed soddenly and said in an Actor's Equity German accent, "Tell him, Master."

Konwicki grimaced like a man much put upon. "They're part of a game. An old Mayan game. I bought it off a *chiclero* in Flores."

"Really?" I said. "How do you play?"

"I can set the figures up, but I don't know what happens after that."

"If you know how to set them up, you must know something about it."

An exasperated sigh. "All right . . . I'll set them up, but be careful."

A long piece of plyboard was leaning against the wall to his left; it was stained a rusty orange and marked with a mosaic of triangular zones. He laid the board flat and arranged the five figures, three at the corners, the other two at the center edge opposite one another. The corner nearest me was vacant, and after a brief hesitation, I set the dwarf down upon it.

"What next?" I said.

"I told you. I don't know. Whoever's playing picks one of the figures to be his corner. But after that. . . ." He shrugged.

"How many can play?"

"From two to six people."

"Why don't you and I give it a shot?" I said.

It was curious how I felt as I said that. I was giving him an order, one I knew he'd obey. And I was eager for him to obey. I wanted him on the board, vulnerable to my moves, even though I didn't know what moves existed. That animal grin that had first manifested itself in front of the Café Pluto once again spread across my face.

"Come on, Carl," I said mockingly. "Don't you want to play?"

He pretended to be complying for the sake of harmony, giving Odille a glance that said, *What can I do?*, and stretched out his hand, letting it hover above the figurines as if testing a discharge that issued from the head of each. At last he touched a clay warrior with a feathered headdress and a long spear. I felt less competent, and my thoughts frayed once again; it appeared that my relapse had boosted Konwicki's spirits. His bland smile switched on, and he leaned back against the wall. The noise of wind and sea smoothed out into a slow, oscillating roar, as if something big and winged were making leisurely flights around the outside of the hut.

On impulse, I picked up the dwarf, and, suddenly brimming with gleeful hostility, I set it down beside a figurine at the center of the board, a lumpy female gnome with a prognathous jaw and slack breasts. Konwicki countered by moving a figurine resembling a squat infant to the side of his warrior. Thereafter we made a number of moves in rapid succession using the same four figurines. Complex moves, each consisting of more than one figurine, sometimes in tandem, utilizing every portion of the board. The entire process could not have taken more than a few minutes, but I could have sworn the game lasted for an hour at least. The room had been transformed into a roaring cell that channeled the powers of wind and sea, drew them into a complex circuit. A weight was shifting inside me, shifting just as the interior weights of the figurines seemed to shift, as if some liquid were being tipped this way and that, guiding my hand. Along with the apprehension of strength was the feeling of a separate entity at work, a quick, nasty brute of a being with a potbelly and arms like tree trunks, grunting and scuttling here and there, stinking of clay and blood. And yet I maintained enough sense of myself to be afraid. Things were getting out of hand, I realized, but I had no means of controlling them. As I stared at the board, it began to appear immense, to exhibit an undulating topography, and I could feel myself dwindling, becoming lost among those rust-colored swells and declivities, coming closer to some terrible danger.

And then it was over . . . the game, the feelings of power and possession. Konwicki tried a smile, but it wouldn't stick. He looked wasted, worn-out. Exactly how I felt. Despite the intensity and strangeness of what I had experienced, I blamed it all on substance abuse. And I was sick of games, of repartee. I struggled to my feet, held out a hand to Odille. "You want to take a walk?" I asked.

I'd expected that she would look to Konwicki for approval or for some sort of validation; but without hesitation, she let me help her to stand.

"Carl," I said with my best anchorman sincerity. "It's been fun."

He kept his face deadpan, but in his eyes was a shine that struck me as virulent, venomous. "That's how it is, huh?" he said, directing his words. I thought, to neither me nor Odille, but to the space between us.

"Night, all," I said, and steered Odille toward the door. I kept waiting for Konwicki to make some hostile remark; but he remained silent, and we got through the door without incident. We went along the edge of the shore, and after we had gone about thirty yards, Odille said, "You don't want to walk, do you, Raymond? Tell me what you really want."

"This how it is in Paris?" I said. "Everything made clear beforehand?"

"This isn't Paris."

"How are you with honesty?" I asked.

"Sometimes not so good." She shrugged as if to say that was the best she could offer.

"You're a beautiful woman," I said. "Intelligent, appealing. I'm tired of being in pain. Whatever possibilities exist for us . . . that's what I want."

She made a noncommittal noise.

"What?" I said.

"I thought you'd say you loved me."

"I want to love you, and that's the same thing," I said. "What the depth of my feelings are at this moment doesn't matter. One thing I've learned about love . . . you're a fool if you judge it by how dizzy it makes you feel." To an extent, this was a lie I was telling myself, but it was such a clever lie that it came cloaked in the illuminative suddenness of a truth recognized, allowing me to adopt the role of a sincere man struggling to be honest . . . which was the case. Perhaps we are all such fraudulent creatures at heart that we must find a good script before we can successfully play at being honest.

"But the dizziness," said Odille. "That's important, too."

"I'm starting to get dizzy now. How about you?"

"You're a clever man, Raymond," she said after a pause. "I don't know if I'm a match for you."

"If I'm so damned clever, don't try and baffle me with humility."

She said nothing, but the wind and surf and the thudding of coconuts falling onto the sand seemed an affirmation. At last she stood on tiptoe, and her lips grazed my cheek. "Let's go home," she whispered.

Late that night, Odille came astride me. Her skin gleamed palely in the moonlight shining through the window, her black hair stuck to the sweat on her shoulders in eloquent curls, and each of her rapid exhalations was cored with a frail note as if she were singing under her breath. Her breasts were small and long and slightly pendulous, with puffy dark areolae, reminding me of *National Geographic* breasts, shaped something like the slippers Aladdin wears in illustrations from *The Arabian Nights*; and her features looked so cleanly drawn as to appear stylized. Her delicacy, its exotic particularity, inspired desire, affection, passion. And one thing more, an emotion that underlay the rest: the need to degrade her. Part of my mind rebelled against this urge, but it was huge in me, a brutish drive, and I hooked my fingers into the plump meat of her thighs, gripping hard enough to leave bruises, and began to use her roughly. To my surprise, she responded in kind; her fingernails raked my chest, and soon our lovemaking evolved into a savage contest that lasted nearly until dawn.

I slept no more than a few hours, and even that was troubled by a dream in which I found myself in a dwarfish, heavily muscled body with ocher skin, crouching on the crest of a dune of rust-colored sand, one that overlooked a complex of black pyramids. A hot wind blew fans of grit into the air, stinging my face and chest. The complex appeared to be a mile or so away, but I knew this was an illusion created by the clarity of the air, and that it would take me hours to reach the buildings. I knew many things about the place. I knew, for instance, that the expanse of sand between the dune and the complex was rife with dangers, and I also knew that there was life within the complex . . . a form of life dangerous to me. I understood this was a dream, albeit of an unusual sort, and that awareness was, I thought, a kind of wakefulness, leading me to believe that the dangers involved were threats not only to my dream self but to my physical self as well. Yet despite this knowledge, I was moved to start walking toward the complex.

I walked for about an hour, growing dehydrated and faint from the heat. The buildings seemed no nearer to hand, and the sun was a violet-white monster, seething with prominences, that looked much closer than the sun with which I was familiar, and although great banks of silvery-edged gray clouds were crossing the sky with the slowness of cruising galleons, they never once obscured the sun, breaking apart as they drew near to permit its continued radiance, re-forming once they had passed. It was as if the light were a solid barrier, an invisible cylindrical artifact around which they were forced to detour. Crabs with large pincers, their shells almost the same color as the sand, burrowed in the dunes; they were quite aggressive, occasionally chasing me away from their homes . . . or hunting me.

After another hour, I came to an exceptionally smooth stretch of sand, lying flat as a pond, in this wholly unlike the rest of the desert, which wind had sculpted into an infinite sequence of undulations and rises, and in color a shade more coppery. The world was so quiet that I could hear the whine of my circulatory system, and I was afraid to step forward, certain that the sand hid some peril; I supposed it to be something in the order of quicksand. At last, deciding to give it a test, I unbuckled the belt that held my sheathed knife (I was not in the least surprised to discover that I had a knife), and, removing the weapon, I tossed the belt out onto the sand. For a moment, it lay undisturbed. But then the sand beneath it began to circulate in the manner of a slow whirlpool. I sprang back from the edge of the sand, retreating into the lee of a dune, just as the whirlpool erupted, spraying coppery orange filaments high into the air, filaments that were—I realized as they fell back to earth around me—serpents with flat, questing heads, the largest of them seven or eight feet in length. The pit from which they had been spewed was expanding. I scrambled higher on the dune, clawing at the sand, and gazed down into a vast maw, where thousands of white sticks—human bones, I saw—were being pushed up and then scattered downward as if falling off the shoulders of a huge, dark presence that was forcing its way up through them from some unimaginable depth. . . .

At that moment I waked, blinking against the sunlight, still snared by the tag ends of the dream, still trying to climb out of danger to the top of the dune, and discovered Odille propped on an elbow, looking down at me with a concerned expression. The sight of her seemed to nullify all the fearful logic of the dream, and I felt foolish for having been so caught up in it. The corners of Odille's lips hitched up in a faint smile. "You were tossing about," she said. "So I woke you. I'm sorry if. . . ."

"No," I said, "I'm glad you did. I was having a bad dream." I boosted myself to a sitting position. My muscles ached, and dried blood striped my chest. "Jesus Christ!" I said, staring at the scratches; I remembered how it had been the previous night and was embarrassed.

"Are you all right?" Odille asked.

"I don't know," I said. "You . . . did I . . . ?"

"Hurt me? I have some bruises. But it looks to me"—she pointed at my abrasions—"that you lost the battle."

"I'm sorry," I said, still flustered. "I don't know what got into me. I've never . . . I mean, last night. I've never been like that . . . not so. . . ."

She put a forefinger to my lips. "Nor have I. But apparently, it's what we both wanted. Maybe we needed it, maybe. . . ." She made an angry noise.

"What's wrong?"

"I'm just sick of explaining myself in terms of the past."

I thought I knew her meaning, and I wondered if that was what it had been for both us—a usage of each other's bodies in order to inflict pain on phantom lovers. I pulled her down, let her rest on my shoulder; her hair fanned across my chest, cool and heavy and silky. I wanted to say something, but nothing came to mind. The pressure of her body aroused me, but I felt tender now, empty of that perverse lust that had enlivened me hours before. She shifted her head so she could see my eyes.

"I won't ask what you're thinking," she said.

"Nothing bad."

"Then I will ask."

"I was thinking about making love with you again."

She made a pleased noise. "Why don't you?"

I turned to face her, drawing her against me, but as we began to kiss, to touch, I realized I was afraid of making love, of reinstituting that fierce animalism. That puzzled me. In retrospect, I had been somewhat repelled by my behavior, but in no way frightened. Yet now I had a sense that I might be opening myself to some danger, and I recalled how I'd felt while playing the game with Konwicki—there had been a feeling identical to that I'd had during our lovemaking. One of helplessness, of possession. I forced myself to dismiss all that, and soon my uneasiness passed. The sun melted like butter across the bed, and the sounds of morning, of birds and the sea and a woman vendor crying, "*Coco de aguas*," came through the window like music to flesh out the rhythm that we made.

For a month or thereabouts, I believe that I was happy. Odille and I began to make a life, an easy and indulgent life that seemed in its potentials for pleasure and consolation proof against any outside influence. It was not only our sexuality that was a joy; we were becoming good friends. I came to see that like many attractive women, she had a poor self-image, that she had been socialized to believe that beauty was a kind of cheapness, a reason for shame, and that her disastrous affair might have been a self-destructive act performed to compensate for a sense of worthlessness. Saying it like that is an over-simplification, but it was in essence true, and I thought that she had known her affair would be ill-fated; I wondered if my own affair had been similar, a means of punishment for a shameful quality I perceived in myself, and I wondered further if our budding relationship might not have the same impetus. But I should have had no worries in that regard. Everything—sex, conversation, domestic interaction—was too easy for us; there was no great tension involved, no apprehension of loss. We were healing each other, and although this was a good thing, a healthy thing, I missed that tension and realized that its absence was evidence of our impermanence. I tried to deny this, to convince myself that I was in love with her as deeply as I had been in love with Karen, and to an extent my self-deception was a success. Atop the happiness we brought to one another, I installed a level of passionate intensity that served to confound my understanding of the relationship, to counterfeit the type of happiness that I believe necessary to maintain closeness. Yet even at my happiest, I had the intimation of trouble hovering near, of a menace not yet strong enough to effect its will. And as time wore on, I began to have recurring dreams that centered upon those black pyramids in the rust-colored desert.

At the outset, all the dreams were redolent of the first, dealing with dangers overcome in the desert. But eventually I made my way into the complex. The pyramids were enormous, towering several hundred feet high, and as I've said were reminiscent of old Mayan structures, with fancifully carved roof combs and steep stairways leading up the faces to temples set atop them, all of black stones polished to a mirror brilliance that threw back reflections of my body—no longer that of a dwarf, but my own, as if the dwarf were merely a transitional necessity—and were joined with incredible precision, the seams almost microscopic. The sand had drifted in over the ebony flagstones, lying in thin curves, and torpid serpents were coiled everywhere, some slithering along leisurely, making sinuous tracks in the sand. Here and there I saw human bones half-buried in the sand, most so badly splintered that it was impossible to tell from which part of the body they had come. Many of the buildings had been left unfinished or else had been designed missing one or more outer walls, so that passing beside them, I had views of their labyrinthine interiors: mazes of stairways that led nowhere, ending in midair, and oddly shaped cubicles.

Before entering the complex, I had been visited with certain knowledge that the buildings were not Mayan in origin, that the Mayan pyramids were imperfect copies of them; but had I not intuitively known this, I might have deduced it from the nature of the carvings. They were realistic in style and depicted nightmare creatures—demons with spindly legs, grotesque barbed phalli, and flat, snakelike heads with gaping mouths and needle teeth and fringed with lank hair—who were engaged in dismembering and otherwise violating human victims. In a plaza between two pyramids, I came upon a statue of one of these creatures, wrought of the same black stone, giving its skin a chitinous appearance. It stood thirty feet in height, casting an obscenely distorted shadow; the sun hung behind its head at an oblique angle, creating a blinding corona of violet-white glare that masked its features and appeared to warp the elongated skull. But the remainder of its anatomy was in plain view. I ran my eyes along the statue, taking in clawed feet; knees that looked to be double-jointed; the distended sac of scrotum and the tumescent organ; jutting hipbones; the dangling hooked hands, each finger wickedly curved and tipped with a talon the length of a sword; the belly swollen like that of a wasp. I was mesmerized by the sight, ensnared by a palpable vibration that seemed to emanate from the figure, by an alluring resonance that made me feel sick and dizzy and full of buzzing, incoherent thoughts. From beneath heavy orbital ridges, the eyes glinted as if cored with miniature suns, and my shock at this semblance of life broke the statue's hold on me. I backed away, then turned and sprinted for my life. . . .

I came back to consciousness thrashing around in the dark, hot bedroom. Odille was still asleep, and I slid out from beneath the sheet, being careful not to wake her. I crossed to the door that led to the living room, my heart pounding, skin covered with a sheen of sweat. The room beyond was slashed by a diagonal of moonlight spilling through the window, and the furniture cast knife-edged shadows on the floor. I wiped my forehead with the back of my arm and was startled by the coldness and smoothness of my skin. I looked at my arm, and the feeling of cold ran all through me—the skin on my wrist and hand was black and shining like polished stone, channeling streams of moonlight along it. I let out a gasp, and holding my arm away from me, I staggered into the living room and onward into the kitchen, the arm banging against the door, making a heavy metallic sound. I tripped, spun around, trying to keep my balance, and fetched up against the sink. I didn't want to look at the arm again, but when I did, I was giddy with relief. Nothing was wrong with it; it was pale and articulated with muscle. A normal human arm. I touched it to make sure. Normal. I leaned against the sink, taking deep breaths. I stayed there for another fifteen minutes, trying to counter the dream and its attendant hallucination with rationalizations. I was smoking too much dope, I told myself; I'd lived for too long under emotional pressure. Or else something was very wrong.

Houses and intricate buildings in dreams, says Freud, signify women, and for this reason, I supposed that the pyramids might be related to my experiences with Karen—a notion assisted by the patent sexuality of the serpent imagery. There was no doubt that I had been damaged by the affair. For a year and a half prior to falling in love with her, I had been forced to watch my father die of cancer, and had spent all my time in taking care of him. My resources had been at a low ebb when Karen had come along, and I'd seen her as a salvation. I'd been obsessed with her, and the slow process of rejection—itself as lingering as a cancer—had turned the power of my obsession against me, throwing me into a terrible depression that I had tried to remedy with cocaine, a drug that breeds its own obsessions and eventually twist one's concept of sexuality. I wondered if I was still obsessed, if I was sublimating the associated drives into my dream life. But I rejected that possibility. All that was left of my feelings for Karen was a vengeful reflex that could be triggered against my will, and it occurred to me that this was a matter of injured pride, of anger at myself for having allowed that sad woman to control and torment me. The dreams, I thought, might well be providing a ground for my anger, draining off its vital charge. And yet I couldn't rid myself of the suspicion that the dreams and the game I had played with Konwicki were at the heart of some arcane process, and one morning as I walked along the beach, I turned my steps in the direction of Konwicki's hut, hoping that he might be able to shed some light on the matter.

I hadn't spoken to him since the night of the game, and I had seen him only twice, then at a distance; in the face of that, it was logical to assume that he had come to terms with what had happened. But the instant his hut came into view, I tensed and began to anticipate a confrontation. Ryan was sitting outside, dressed with uncharacteristic informality in cutoffs and a short-sleeved shirt; his head was down, knees drawn up. When he heard my footsteps, he jumped to his feet and stood in front of the door.

"You can't go in," he said as I came up.

I was taken aback by that, and also by his pathetic manner. His eyes darted side to side as if expecting a new threat to materialize; nerves twitched in his jaw, and his hands were in constant motion, plucking at his cutoffs, fingers rubbing together. He looked paler, thinner.

"What's the problem, man?" I asked.

"You can't go in," he said stubbornly.

"I just want to talk to him."

He shook his head.

"What's the hell wrong with you?"

Konwicki's voice floated out from the hut. "It's all right, Ryan."

I brushed past Ryan, saying, "You better get yourself together," and went on in. The light was bad, a brownish gloom, and Konwicki was sitting cross-legged against the rear wall; beside him was something bumpy covered by a white cloth, and noticing a corner of orange wood protruding from the cloth, I realized that he had been fooling around with the game.

"What can I do for you?" he said in a dry tone. "Sell you some drugs?"

I sat down close to him, off to the side, so I could watch the door; the dried palm fronds crunched beneath my weight. "How you been?"

He made a noise of amusement. "I've been fine, Ray. And you?"

I gestured at the covered board. "Playing with yourself?"

A chuckle. "Just studying a bit. Working on my project, you know."

I didn't believe him. There was a new solidity to his assurance, and I suspected it had something to do with the figures and the board. "Are you learning how to play it?" I asked.

After a silence, framing his words with—it seemed—a degree of caution, he said. "It's not something you can learn . . . not like chess, anyway. It's more of a role-playing game. It's essential to develop an affinity with one's counter. Then the rules—or rather, the potentials—become evident."

The light was so dim that the details of his swarthy features were indistinct, making it difficult to detect nuances of expression. But I had the feeling he was laughing at me. I didn't want to let him know that I was leery about the game, and I changed the subject. "Sounds interesting. But that's not why I came here. I wanted to"—I pretended to be searching for the right words—"clear the air. I thought we could. . . ."

"Be friends?" said Konwicki.

"I was hoping we could at least put an end to any lingering animosity. We're all going to be living here for a while, and it's pointless to be carrying on petty warfare . . . even if it's only giving each other the cold shoulder."

"That's very reasonable of you, Ray."

"Are you going to be reasonable? You and Odille were done before I came along. You must be aware of that."

"If you knew me, you wouldn't approach me this way."

"That's why I'm here . . . to get to know you."

"Just like a Yank, to think he can know something through talking." Konwicki's hand strayed toward the board as if by reflex, but he did not complete the movement. "I don't let go of things easily. I hang on to them, even things I don't really want. Unless I'm made to let go."

I ignored the implicit challenge. "Why's that?"

Konwicki leaned back and folded his arms, a shift in posture that conveyed expansiveness. "I've traveled in America," he said. "I've seen slums in Detroit, New York, Los Angeles. Ghastly ruins. Much more terrible in their physical entity than anything in England. But there's still vitality in America, even in the slums. Some of the slums in London, they're absolutely without vitality. Gray places with here and there a petunia in a flowerpot brightening a cracked window, and old toothless women, and children with stick arms and legs, and women whose bodies are too sallow and sickly to sell, and men whose brains have shrunk to the size of their balls. All of them moving about like people in a dream. Bending over to sniff at corpses, poking their fingers in a fire to see how hot it is. So much trash and foulness lying about that the streets stink even when they're frozen. To be born there is like being born on a planet where the gravity is so strong you can't escape it. It's not something you can resist with anger or violence. It's like treacle has been poured over you, and you crawl around in it like a fly with your wings stuck together. I've never escaped. I've run around the world; I've cultivated myself and given myself an education. I've developed refined sensibilities. But everywhere I've gone, I've carried that gravity with me, and I'm the same ignorant, bloody-minded sod I always was. So don't you tell me something's not good for me. I'll want it more than ever. Things that aren't good for me make me happy. And don't say that something's done. I'm too damn stupid to accept it. And too damn greedy."

Despite its passion, there was a hollowness to this statement, and after he had done, I said, "I don't believe you."

He gave a caustic laugh. "That's good, Ray. That's very perceptive. I've other imperatives now. But it used to be true."

I let his words hang in the air for a bit, then said, "Have you been having odd dreams lately?"

"I dream all the time. What sort of dreams are you talking about?"

"About the game we played."

"The game? This game?" He touched the cloth covering the board.

I nodded.

"No . . . why? Are you?"

His mocking voice told me that he was not being direct, and I realized there was no use in continuing the conversation; either he was lying, or else he was running yet another game on me, hoping to make me think he knew something by means of arch denial. I tried to dismiss the importance of what I'd said. "A couple . . . just weird shit. I haven't been sleeping well."

"I'm sorry to hear that."

If Konwicki was dreaming of that strange desert, if there was an occult reality to the game we'd played. I knew—because of my partial admission —I must look like a fool to him; to me, with his arms folded, half-buried in the dimness, he seemed as impenetrable as a Buddha. The thatched roof crackled like a small fire in a gust of wind, and behind Konwicki, mapping the darkness of the wall, were tiny points of lights, uncaulked places between the boards through which the day was showing; they lent the wall the illusion of depth, of being a vast sky mapped with stars, all arranged in a dwindling perspective so as to draw one's eyes toward a greater darkness beyond them. I began to feel daunted, out of my element, and I told myself again that this was the result of manipulation on Konwicki's part, that by intimating through denial some vague expertise, he was playing upon my fears; but this was no comfort. I tried to think of something to say that would pose a counterspell to the silent pall that was settling over me, I had a great faith in words, believing that their formal noise elegantly utilized could have the weight of truth no matter how insincere had been the impulse to speak, and so when words failed me, I felt even more at sea. I looked away from Konwicki, gathering myself. The doorway framed a stretch of pale brown sand and sun-spattered water and curving palm trunks, and the brilliance of the scene was such a contrast to the gloom within, I imagined that these things comprised a single presence that was peering in at us like an eye at a keyhole, and that Konwicki and I were microscopic creatures dwelling inside the mechanism of a lock that separated dark and light.

The weight of the silence forced me to stand and squeezed me toward the door. "We haven't settled anything," I said, brushing off my trousers, making a bustling, casual business of retreat. "But I hope you understand that I don't need any aggravation. Neither does Odille. If you want to make peace, we're open to it." I stepped into the doorway. "See you around."

Once outside under the sun, breathing the salt air, I felt easier, confident. I had, I thought, handled things fairly well. But as I turned to head back to the house, I tripped over Ryan, who had reclaimed his place beside the door, sitting with his knees drawn up. I went sprawling, rolled over, intending to apologize. But Ryan didn't appear to have noticed me. He continued to sit there, staring at a patch of sand, fingers plucking at a fray on his cutoffs, and after getting to my feet, watching him for a second or two, I started walking, maintaining a brisk pace, feeling a cold spot between my shoulder blades that I imagined registered the pressure of a pair of baleful eyes.

That same night, following a bout of paranoid introspection, I dreamed that I went inside one of the pyramids, a structure not far from the statue of the snake-headed creature that I had encountered in earlier dreams. Leery about entering, watching for signs that would warn me off, I passed through a missing wall and climbed a stair that ended several hundred feet above in midair and was connected to a number of windowless cubicles, all of the same black stone. I considered exploring the cubicles, but when I put my hand to the door of one, I heard a woman's muffled voice alternately sobbing and spewing angry curses; I pictured a harpy within, some female monstrosity, and I withdrew my hand. On every side a maze of other stairways lifted around me, rising without apparent support like a monumental fantasy by Escher or Piranesi, reducing perspective to a shadowy puzzle, and I felt diminished in spirit by the enormity of the place. Snakes lay motionless on the stairs, looking at a distance like cracks admitting to a bright coppery void; black spiders, invisible until they moved, scuttled away from my feet, and their filmy webs spanned between each step. From a point three-quarters of the way up, the desert appeared the color of dried blood, and set at regular intervals about the complex were five more colossal statues, each similar to the first in its repulsive anatomy, but sculpted in different poses; one crouching, one with its head thrown back, and so on. I couldn't help wondering if these six figures were related to the counters of Konwicki's game.

I had intended to go all the way to the top, but I grew uncomfortable with the isolation, the silence, and started back down. My progress was slowed by an attack of dizziness. I could still hear the woman crying, and the percussive effect of her sobs made me dizzier. The spaces beneath were swelling upward like black gas, and, afraid that I would fall, overcoming my nervousness concerning the cubicles, I flung open the door to one, thinking I would sit inside until my vertigo had passed. A fecal stink poured from the cubicle, and something moved in the darkness at the rear, startling me.

"Who's there?" called a man's voice.

There was something familiar about the voice, and I peered into the cubicle. A pale shape was slumped against the far wall.

"Come on out," I said.

The man shifted deeper into the corner. "Why are you here?"

"I'm dreaming all this," I said. "I don't have much choice."

A feeble, scratchy laugh. "That's what they all say."

I stepped inside, closing until I had clear sight of the man. For a moment I failed to recognize him, but then I realized it was Ryan—Ryan as he might have looked after a hard twenty years, his blond hair grayed and the youthful lines of his face dissolved into sagging flesh. The creases in his skin had filled in with grime and looked to be deep cuts. His clothes were in tatters. "Jesus, Ryan!" I said. "What happened?"

"I'm in jail." Another cracked laugh. "I have to stay put until. . . ."

"Till what?"

He shook his head.

I knelt beside him. "Where are we, Ryan?"

He giggled. "The endgame."

"What the hell's that mean?"

"The game," he said, "is not a game."

I waited for him to continue, but he had lost his train of thought. I repeated the question.

"The game is just a way of getting here. You've already done playing, and now you have to wait till all the moves have been made."

I asked him to explain why—if I'd done playing—moves were still to be made, and he replied by saying that a move wasn't a move until it had been made everywhere. "It's like this place," he said. "A place isn't really a place. One place leads to another, and that place leads to another yet, and on and on. There's nothing that's only itself." That thought seemed to sadden him, and he said, "Nothing."

The woman let out a piercing scream, and her curses echoed through the pyramid.

I tried to pull Ryan to his feet, thinking that there might be some more pleasant place for him to wait; he struck at my hands, a flurry of weak blows that did no damage, but caused me to release him.

"Leave me alone," he said. "I'm safe here."

"Safe from what?"

"From you," he answered. "The Master thinks he's the dangerous one, but I know it's you. He's made the wrong move. Sooner or later he'll see I'm right, and he'll try and stop it. But you can't stop it. The travelers have to come and go; the transitions have to. . . ." His speech became incoherent for a few seconds; then he snapped out of it. "Of course, there are no right moves. Even the winner pays a price once the game is done. But not to worry, Ray," he said with a flash of his old cockiness. "It'll hurt, but it'll be a much cheaper price than the one the Master has to pay. Or else you can always keep playing if you want to be noble and take the risk."

He lapsed into incoherence once again; I attempted to bring him to his senses, but all he would say was to repeat that "it" couldn't be stopped, "it" had to happen, and to ramble on about "exchanges, necessary transitions." Giving up on him, I left the cubicle and went out onto the sand. The sun was low, its violet-white disk partially down on the horizon, and the shadows had grown indistinct. I strolled about the complex, feeling for the first time at ease among the buildings; I was comfortable even in proximity to the snake-headed statue. I stepped back from it, admiring its needle teeth and flat skull, all its obscene proportions, and although I felt as before a sense of resonant identity with it, on this occasion I was not frightened by the feeling, but rather was pleased. Indeed, I found the entire landscape soothing. The snakes, the crabs scuttling down the sanguine faces of the dunes, the black silence of the complex . . . all this had a bleak majesty and seemed the product of a pure aesthetic.

On waking and remembering the dream, however, I was more disturbed by my acceptance of that bizarre landscape than I had been by my fear of it. It was still dark, and Odille was asleep beside me. I eased out of bed, pulled on jeans and a shirt, and went into the patio. The edges of the tile roof framed a rectangle of stars and dark blue sky, with the crowns of palms showing half in silhouette, the ragged fronds throwing back pale green shines from the lights of the house next door. I dropped onto a lawn chair and lay back, trying to settle my thoughts. After a few minutes I heard the whisper of Odille's sandals on the concrete; she had thrown on a bathrobe, and her hair was in disarray, loose about her shoulders. She sat opposite me, put a hand on my knee, and asked what was wrong.

I had previously told her that I'd been having bad dreams, but had not been specific; now, though, I told her the entire story—the game, the feelings I'd had, the dreams, and my meeting with Konwicki. Once I had done, she lowered her head, fingering the hem of her robe, and after a pause she asked, "What are you worried about? The game . . . that it's real?"

I was ashamed to admit it.

"That's ridiculous!" she said. "You can't believe that."

"It's just the dreams . . . and Ryan. I mean, what's the matter with him?"

She made a noise of disgust. "He's weak. Carl's found a way to undermine him with drugs or something. That's all."

We were silent for several seconds; a palm frond scraped the roof, and the surf was a distant hiss.

"I knew something was bothering you," she said. "But. . . ." She got to her feet, walked a couple of paces off, and stood with her arms folded. "Carl's getting to you. I wouldn't have thought it possible." She sighed, jammed her hands in the pocket of the robe. "I'm going to see him."

"The hell you are!"

"I am! And if *he* believes there's anything to the game, I'll find out about it." I started to object, but she talked over me. "You aren't worried about me, are you? About my going back to him?"

"I guess not."

"That doesn't sound like a vote of confidence." She knelt beside my chair. "Don't you understand how much I hate him?"

"I never understood why you were with him in the first place."

"I was vulnerable. He took advantage of my confusion. He confused me even more. He violated my trust; he weakened me. If I could, I'd. . . ." She drew a deep breath, let it out slowly. "Don't tell me you haven't ever done anything that you knew was bad for you even when you were doing it."

"No," I said, surprised by her vehemence. "I can't tell you that." I stroked her hair. "What did he do to you?"

Her face worked, suppressing emotion. "The same sort of thing he's trying to do to you . . . except, I didn't have anybody to tell me what was going on. Listen! Nothing's going to happen. I'm just going to talk to him. He'll lie, but I know when he's lying. I'll be able to tell whether he's concerned for himself or looking for a way to hurt you. And that'll put your mind at ease."

"It's not necessary."

"Yes, it is!" She put her arms around my neck. "I want you to get past this so I can have your undivided attention."

There was an edge to her intensity, a hectic brightness in her eyes, that quieted my objections, and later that night when she said she loved me, I believed her for the first time.

Two nights later as we sat at dinner in a small restaurant, a one-room place of stucco and thatch lit by candles, Odille told me that she had spoken with Konwicki. "You don't have to be concerned about the game," she said. "Carl's only trying to unnerve you." She had a forkful of rice, chewed. "I told him all about your dreams . . . everything. You should have seen him. He was like a starving man who'd been handed a steak. He said, Yes, yes, it was the same for him. Dreams, odd intuitions. Then I described your last dream, the one with Ryan, and what he'd said about Carl's making the wrong move. He loved that. He said, Yes, that was true. And he didn't know how to stop it from happening. After that, he offered an apology for everything that had happened between us. He said the game had changed him, that he could see now what a reprehensible sort he'd been."

"A reprehensible sort?" I said. "Were those his words?"

"I believe so."

"Reprehensible . . . shit!" I stared at her over the rim of my coffee cup. "It sounds to me like he's corroborating the dreams. Why else would he admit that he'd made a bad move?"

"Because," said Odille, "he knows if he were to deny it, he'd have no way of affecting you. But now, claiming that it's all true, especially the part about him possibly losing, he has an excuse to talk to you, to play with your mind. He can pretend to be your ally. You watch. He'll come to see you. He'll try to align himself with you. He'll have a plan that'll involve the two of you working together to save each other from the game . . . its perils. Then he'll start manipulating." She had another bite, swallowed. "He thought he was fooling me, but he was transparent."

"Are you sure about all this?"

"Of course. Carl's a greedy little man who thinks he's smarter than the rest of the world. He can't imagine that anyone could see through him. If there was anything to the game, he never would have told me." She took my hand. "Just wait. Watch what happens. You'll see I'm right."

Odille's reassurances had not convinced me of the fecklessness of my fears. Recalling Konwicki's statement that familiarity with one's counter was important, I set out to reinhabit the feelings I'd had while playing, to recall the moves that had been made. It was not hard to recapture those feelings; they returned to me every night in dreams. But the moves were a different matter. Other than the first, I could remember only the last two: one in which all four figures had been places in close proximity, and another in which the figure of the infant had been placed in a zone adjoining that of the dwarf. I asked Odille what she could recall about the counters from working on the translation, and she said that all she knew was what Konwicki had told her.

"He used to joke with me about them," she said. "He identified himself with the warrior, and he said my counter was the female . . . the one you moved during the game. He described her to me. A real maniac, a terrible creature. Sluttish, foul-mouthed, vile. She was always throwing tantrums. Physically abusive."

"Maybe he was trying to demean you by describing her that way."

"I'm sure he was. But once he did show me some of the translation he'd done about her, and it looked authentic."

"What were they . . . the counters? Did he ever tell you that?"

"Archetypes," she said. "Mayan archetypes, Spirit forms . . . that was the term he used. I'm not sure what that meant. Whoever made the figures, whoever assigned them their characters, had a warped idea of human potential. All the characters were repellent in some way. . . . I remember that much. But when he told me all that, I was trying to pull away from him, and I didn't pay much attention."

A week went by, and I made no further progress. I was spinning my wheels, wasting myself in futile effort. Then I took stock of the situation, and suddenly all my paranoia seemed ludicrous. That I could have even half-believed I had been possessed by a Mayan spirit in the shape of a dwarf was evidence of severe mental slippage, and it was time to get a grip. The dreams must have some connection to the abuses I had suffered during the past few years, I thought, and to be this much of a fool for love was debasing, particularly in the face of the abuses I met with every day in Livingston. Malnutrition, tyranny, ignorance. I determined that I was going to take a hard line with my psyche. If I had dreams, so what? Sooner or later they would run their course. And I also determined to grant Odille's wish, to give her my undivided attention; I realised that while I hadn't been neglecting her, neither had I been utilizing the resources of the relationship as a lover should. Things were changing between us in a direction that I would never have predicted, and I owed it to her, to myself, to see where that would lead.

Our lives were calm for the next couple of weeks. The dreams continued, but I refused to let them upset me. Odille and I fell into the habit of taking twilight walks along the beach, and one evening after a storm, with dark blue ridges of cloud pressing down upon a smear of buttermilk yellow on the horizon, we walked out to the point beyond the Café Pluto, a hook of land bearing a few palms whose crowns showed against the last of sunset like feathered headdresses. Nearby stretches of cobalt water merged with the purplish slate farther out, and there were so many small waves, it looked as if the sea were moving in every direction at once. We sat on a boulder at the end of the point, watching the light fade in the west, and after a minute, Odille asked if I had ever been to Paris.

"A long time ago," I said.

"What did you think?"

"It was the winter," I said. "I didn't see too much. I had no money, and I was staying in a house that belonged to this old lady named Bunny. She was straight out of a Tennessee Williams play. She'd been Lawrence Durrell's lover . . . or maybe it wasn't Durrell. Somebody famous, anyway. She was an invalid, and the house was a mess. Cat shit everywhere. There was a crazy Romanian who was printing an anarchist newsletter in the basement. And Bunny's kids, they were true degenerates. Her fifteen-year-old raped the maid. The twenty-year-old was dealing smack. Bunny just lay around, and I ended up having to take care of her."

"God, you've lived!" said Odille, and we both laughed.

I put an arm around her. "Are you homesick?"

"Not so much . . . a little." She leaned into me. "I was just wondering how you'd like Paris."

We had talked about the future in only the most general of terms, but I felt comfortable now considering a future with her, and that surprised me, because even though I was happier than I'd been in a very long time, I had also been nervous about formalizing the relationship.

"I suppose we're going to have to leave here eventually," I said.

She looked up at me. "Yes."

"It doesn't matter to me where we go. I don't have to be any particular place to do my work."

"I know," she said. "That's your greatest virtue."

"Is that so?" I kissed her, the kiss grew long, and we lay back on the boulder. I touched her breasts. In the darkness the whites of her eyes were aglow; her breath was sweet and frail. Waves slapped at the rock. Finally I turned onto my back, pillowed my head on my hands. Icy stars made simple patterns in the sky, and it seemed to me at the moment that everything in the world had that same simplicity.

"Someday," Odille said after a long silence, "I'd like to go back to Paris . . . just to see my friends again."

"Want me to go with you?"

She was silent for a bit; then she sat up and stared out to sea. I had asked the question glibly, thinking I knew the answer, yet now I was afraid that I'd misread her. At last she said, "You wouldn't like it. Americans don't like Parisians."

"The way I hear it, it's mutual," I said, relieved. "But there are exceptions."

"I guess so." She glanced down at me and smiled. "Anyway, we don't have to stay in Paris. We could come to the States. I wouldn't mind that." She tipped her head to the side. "You look puzzled."

"I wasn't sure we'd get around to talking about this. And even if we did, I thought it would be awkward."

"So did I for a while. But then I realized we were past awkwardness." With both hands, she lifted the heft of her hair and pushed it back behind her head. "Sometimes I've tried to imagine myself without you. I can do it. I can picture myself living a life, being with someone else. All that. But then I realize how artificial that was . . . that kind of self-examination. It was as if I were wishing for that prospect, because I was afraid of you. To end doubt, or to learn whether my doubts were real, all I had to do was stop thinking about them. Just give in to the moment. That was easier said than done, I thought. But then I tried it, and it *was* easy." She ran a hand along my arm. "You did it, too. I could tell when you stopped."

"Could you, now?"

"Don't you believe me?"

Before I could answer, there was a crunching in the brush behind us, and two figures emerged from shadows about thirty feet away. It took me a second to identify them against the dark backdrop—Konwicki, with Ryan hanging at his shoulder. I stood, wary, and Odille came to her knees. "What the fuck are you doing?" I asked them. "Tracking us?"

"I have to talk with you," said Konwicki. "About the game."

"Some other time, man." I took Odille's arm and began steering her back along the point, giving Konwicki and Ryan a wide berth, but keeping an eye on them.

"Listen," said Konwicki, coming after us. "I'm not after mucking you about. We're in serious trouble." I kept walking, and he grabbed my shoulder, spun me around. "I've been having dreams, too. They're different from yours. But they're indicators all the same."

His face betrayed anxiety, but I wasn't buying the act. I shoved him back. "Keep your hands off me!"

"The game's a conduit," he said as we walked away. "A means of transport to another world, another plane . . . something. And to another form as well." He caught up with me, blocked our path; Ryan scuttled behind him. "I don't know how the Mayans discovered it, but it was a major influence on the architecture, on every facet of their culture. The ritual cruelties of their religion, the—"

"Get out of my way." I was cold inside—a sign that I was preparing for violence. My senses had grown acute. The slop of the waves, Konwicki's breathing, the leaves rustling—all were sharp and distinct. Ryan's pale face, peering from behind Konwicki, seemed as bright as a star.

"You're a fool if you don't listen to me," Konwicki said. "The game we played was real. I admit I wouldn't be here if I didn't think I was in danger, but there's—"

"You made the wrong move, that it?" I said.

"Yes," said Konwicki. "I didn't know it at the time. I didn't know we were actually playing. And later, after I realized something strange was happening, I didn't see the mistake I'd made." He wagged both hands as if dismissing all that. "We've got an option, man . . . I think. The winner can keep the game going for one more move at least. It'll be a risk, but a relatively minor one." He looked as if he were about to grab me in frustration, doing a fine imitation of a desperate man. "That way we have a chance of figuring out what else we can do."

"I'm not one of your goddamn chumps!" I said. "I know Odille told you about my dream. You're trying to use it against me."

"Yes, yes, you're right," he said. "I *was* using it. I wanted to fuck with you. I admit it. But after Odille talked to me, I began thinking about some of the things she'd told me. And some of the things you'd said, too."

I spat on the sand. "Jesus!"

"I'm telling the truth. I promise you!" he said. "After I talked to her. I had another look at the game . . . at the papers. Some of the things she'd told me gave me new insights into the translation." His words came in a rush. "You see, I believed that the figures—the dwarf, the warrior—that they were the entities involved. I thought they were conveyances that carried you to the pyramids. And they are. One of us was going to be transported. That much was certain. I thought it would be me, but it's not. . . . It's you. And I'd overlooked the obvious." A dismayed laugh. "It's a matter of elementary physics. For every action there's a reaction."

He paused for breath, and, having heard enough, I said, "Odille told me you'd come up with something clever. Guess she was wrong about that."

I started to push past him, but he shoved me back. "For God's sake, will you listen?"

"I'm going to tell you once more," I said. "Keep your hands off me."

"That's right, you stupid clot!" he said. "Just go home and bugger you stupid whore and don't worry about a bloody thing!"

"Such talk," I said; my arms had begun to tremble.

"Let's just go!" Odille pulled at me, and I allowed myself to be hauled along; but Konwicki planted a hand on my chest, bringing me up short.

"I'm trying to save your sodding life, you ass!" he said. "Are you going to listen to me, or. . . ." He was, judging from his disdainful expression, about to deliver some further pomposity.

"No," I said, and nailed him in the stomach, not wanting to hurt my hand. He caved in, went to his knees, then rolled up into a fetal position, the wind knocked out of him. Ryan darted toward me, then retreated into the shadows; a second later I heard him running off through the bushes.

It had been years since I'd hit anyone, and I was ashamed of myself; Konwicki had been no threat. I dropped to my knees beside him, counseled him to take shallow breaths, and once he had recovered somewhat, I tried to help him up. He pushed my hands away and fixed me with a hateful stare.

"Right, you bastard!" he said. "I warned you, but that's all right. You'll have to take what comes now."

After that night on the point, I concluded that Livingston had lost its charm; I wanted to avoid further conflicts, and I was certain more would arise. Odille was in accord with this, and we planned to leave as soon as I could find someone responsible to take over the Spanish doctor's house. We decided to settle in Panajachel near Lake Atitlán until I finished my current writing project, and then visit New York city en route to Paris; almost without acknowledging it, we had made an oblique, understated commitment to each other, one that by contrast to our pasts and the instability around us was a model of rigor. Perhaps our relationship had begun as an accommodation, a shelter from the heavy weather of our lives, but against all odds, something more had developed; although I wasn't ready to admit it to her, unwilling to risk a total involvement, I had fallen in love with Odille. It wasn't any one instance or event that had brought this home to me, but rather a slowly growing awareness of my reactions to her. I had begun to focus more and more upon her, to treasure images of her. To savor all the days. And yet I detected in myself a residue of tension, one I also detected in her, and this was evidence that we were afraid of the obsessive bonding that had occurred, and were preparing for disappointment, obeying the conditioning of our pasts.

Ten days passed, and I hadn't found anyone to take the house. I wrote to the Spanish doctors, telling them that an emergency had come up, that I had to leave and wanted to delegate my responsibilities to the local priest, who had become something of a friend, and who—aside from his clerical duties—maintained a small museum that displayed some Mayan artifacts of indifferent value. I began to pack my papers in anticipation of their response. Early one evening I went to the telegraph office to call my agent in the States and tell her about the move, to see if she had money for me. The office was a low building of yellow stucco next to the generator that provided the village's power, and was manned by a harried-looking clerk who was arguing with an Indian family, and was guarded by a soldier wearing camouflage gear and carrying a machine gun. The phones lined the rear wall of the office, and, choosing the one farthest from the argument, I put in the call. Five minutes later I heard my agent's voice through a hiss of static, and after we had taken care of business, I asked what was new in the big city.

"The usual," she said. "Boring parties and editors playing musical chairs. You're better off down there . . . as long as you're working. *Are* you working?"

"Don't worry," I said.

My agent let some dead time accumulate, then said, "I guess I should tell you this, Ray. You're going to find out sooner or later."

"What's that?"

"Karen had her baby."

For an instant I felt strangely light, free of some restraint. "I didn't think she was due this soon."

"There were complications. But she's all right. So's the baby. It's a boy. It's really cute, Ray. A little doll. It just lies there and squeaks."

I let out a nasty laugh. "Just like its mama."

"I thought you went down there to let go of her. You don't sound like you're letting go."

"Must be the connection." I stared at the pocked, grimy wall, seeing nothing.

Another pause. "What're you working on, Ray?"

"You'll see it soon," I said. "Look, I've got to go."

"I didn't mean to upset you."

"I'm not upset. I'll call you in a couple of weeks, O.K.?"

I walked outside, cut down onto the beach. Dusk had given way to darkness, and the jungled shore was picked out by shanty lights; there was also a scattering of lights on the hills lifting behind the village, showing the location of small farms and platanals. The moon, almost full, had risen to shine through a notch between the hills, paving the chop of the water close to shore with silvery glitter, but threatening clouds and dark brooms of rain were visible farther out—a storm would be hitting the coast within a matter of minutes. I was angry as I walked, but my anger was undirected. Karen was no longer an object of hatred, merely a catalyst that opened me to violent emotion, and I realized that part of the reason she had maintained a hold over me for so long was due, not to any real feeling, but to my romantic nature, my stubborn denial that the light in the heart could be snuffed out. I had hung on to the belief that—despite Karen's betrayal—the good, strong core of my feelings would last; now I was forced to face the fact that they were dead, and that made me angry and caused me to doubt everything I felt for Odille.

A voice called to me as I was passing a stand of palmettos. I ignored it, but the voice continued to call, and I whirled around to see Ryan running down the beach, his blond hair flying, dressed in the cutoffs and soiled shirt that had become his uniform. He staggered to a halt a few feet away, gasping.

"What do you want?" I asked.

He held up a hand, trying to catch his breath. "Gotta talk to you," he managed. He looked alien to me, a pale little twist of a creature, and I felt vastly superior. Stronger, more intelligent. The fierceness of the loathing that fueled these feelings didn't strike me as unusual.

"Talk about what?" I said.

"Odille . . . you have to break it off with her."

"You jealous, Ryan?"

"Konwicki . . ."

"Fuck Konwicki!" I gave Ryan a shove that sent him reeling backward, catching at the air with his hands. "If he's got a problem, tell him to come talk to me himself."

"You have to stop seeing her," said Ryan defiantly. He slipped a hand beneath his shirtfront as if soothing a stomachache, and kept his eyes lowered. "I'm warning you. . . . Bad things are going to happen if you don't."

"Goodness me, Ryan," I said, taking a little walk around him, examining him contemptuously, as if he were an unsightly objet d'art. "I wonder what they could be."

Ryan's chin quivered. "He's . . . he's. . . ."

"C'mon, man! Spit it out!" I said. "Has he been doing bad things to *you*? He must have been doing something nasty, mighty bad to turn you into such a twitchy little toad. Is it drugs? Is he feeding you bad drugs, or. . . ."

Anger came boiling out of him. "Don't talk to me like that!"

I knew at that moment that Ryan had a weapon. The way he kept shifting his right hand under his shirt as if adjusting his grip, keeping his weight back on his heels, balanced, ready to strike. And I wanted him to strike.

"I got it," I said. "Konwicki's into boys now. That's it, right? And you're his boy! That explains why I've never seen you with a girl."

"Stop it!" He set himself, the muscles of his right forearm flexing.

"What's it like with him, man? He make your little doggy sit up and beg?"

"You better stop!"

"Does he make a lot of noise, Ryan?" I laughed, and the laugh startled me, sounding too guttural to be my own. "Or is he the strong, silent type?"

With a shout, he pulled a knife from beneath his shirt and slashed at me. I caught his wrist, gave it a sharp twist. He cried out, the knife fell to the sand, and he backed away, cradling his wrist, his expression shifting between panic and anguish. "I'm sorry," he said. "I'm sorry. He told me I had to. . . ." Then he broke into a stumbling run and went crashing through the palmettos. I scooped up the knife and began to hunt him. That was how it seemed. A hunt. One in which I was expert. I've never been much of an athlete, yet that night I ran easily, with short, chopping strides that carried me in a zigzagging path among the palmettos. I kept pace with Ryan, running off to his left and a little behind, intending to harry him until he dropped. He glanced back over his shoulder, saw me, and ran faster, frantically calling out to Konwicki.

On hearing that, I slowed my pursuit. It was Konwicki I really wanted, and since Ryan had been his messenger, it was likely that he was now going to see him. And yet we were heading away from the beach, away from Konwicki's house. I decided to trust my instincts. If Konwicki had somehow convinced Ryan to kill me—and I thought that must be the case, that he'd hoped to evade the judgment of the game by eliminating me—after the deed, he would have wanted Ryan to meet him somewhere out of the way. I dropped back a bit, letting Ryan think he had lost me, keeping track of him by ear, picking out the sound of his passage through the foliage from the noises of insects and frogs and wind. We were moving onto the slope of one of the hills behind the village, and despite the uphill path, I was still running easily, enjoying myself. The musky scents of the vegetation were as cloying as perfume; clouds flowing across the moon, driven by a gusting wind, made the world go alternately dark and bright with an erratic rhythm that added to my excitement. I exulted in the turbulent weather, in my strength, and I threw the knife into the brush, knowing that I wasn't going to need it.

As I passed through a banana grove, a flickering yellow light penetrated the bushes to my left from one of the farmhouses. The wind was rapidly gaining in force, tattering the banana leaves, lifting them high like the feathery legs of giant insects, and something about their articulated shapes fluttering in a sudden wash of moonlight made me uneasy. I began to have an inconstant feeling in my flesh, a dull vibration that nauseated me; I tried to push it aside, to concentrate on the running, but it persisted. I estimated that I must be a quarter of the way up the hill, and I could hear Ryan jogging along almost parallel to me. He had stopped calling out to Konwicki, but now and then he would cry out, perhaps because of the pain in his wrist. I was having some pain myself. Twinges in my joints, in my bones. Growing sharper by the moment. And there was something wrong with my eyes. Every object had a halo, the veins of leaves glowed an iridescent green, and overhead

I could see dozens of filmy layers between the clouds and the earth, drifting, swirling, coalescing. I shook my head, trying to clear my vision, but if anything, it grew worse. The halos had congealed into auras of a dozen different colors; hot spots of molten scarlet and luminous blue were insects crawling in the dirt. The pain kept growing worse, too. The twinges became jolts of agony shooting through my limbs, and with the onset of each, I staggered, unable to stay on course. Then a tremendous pain in my chest sent me to all fours, my eyes squeezed shut; panting. I tried to stand, and in doing so, caught sight of my left hand—gnarled, lumpy fingers thick as sausages, clawing at rusty orange sand, lengthening and blackening. A fresh surge of pain knocked me down, and I twisted about and gouged at the earth for what seemed a very long time. Rain started to fall, and another burst of pain dredged up a bass scream from my chest that merged with the wind, like the massive *Om* of a foghorn wedded to a howl. One instant I felt I was splitting in half, the next that I was growing huge and heavy. I receded from the storm and the world, dwindling to a point within myself, and from that moment on I was incapable of action, only of mute and horrified observation as another "I" took control of my thoughts, one whose judgments were funded by an anger far more potent and implacable than my own.

I lashed out with my left arm, clutched something thin and hard, tore at it; the next second a banana tree fell across my chest. But the pain was diminishing rapidly, and after it had passed, rather than feeling exhausted, I felt renewed. I climbed to my feet and looked out over the treetops. The storm that during transition had seemed so chaotic and powerful now seemed inconsequential, hardly worth my notice. Lightning scratched red forking lines down the sky; inky clouds rushed overhead. A flickering nimbus of bluish white overlaid the jungle, and beneath it, the lights of the houses ranging the hill were almost too dim to make out. I could find no sign of the defeated. Frustrated, I moved toward the nearest house—a structure with board walls and a roof of corrugated metal—knocking away branches, pushing masses of foliage aside, my hair whipped into my eyes by the wind. When I reached the house, I stood gazing down at the roof, trying to sense the occupants. The energy flows binding the metal, stitchings of coruscant lines and dazzles, could not hide the puny lives within: shifting clots of heat and color. My quarry was not there, but in a fury I swung my arm and tore a long rip in the roof, delighted by the shriek of the tortured metal. Dark frightened faces stared at me through the rip, then vanished. A moment later I spotted them running out the door and into the jungle, becoming streaks of red beneath the ghostly luminescence of the leaves. I would have enjoyed pursuing them, but my time was limited, and I was concerned that the completion of my task would be hampered by the victor—lodged like a stone in my brain—whose pitiful morality was a nagging irritant. I wondered at his motives for entering the contest. Surely he must have known what was at stake. There is no morality in this darkness.

I comforted myself with the thought that before too long the victor would have his due, unless—and I thought this unlikely—he chose to renew the challenge; and I pressed on through the jungle. Something ran across my path—an animal of some sort. It swerved aside, but before it could escape, I grazed it with a claw, tearing its belly and flipping it into the air. The kill improved my temper. I had never relished employing my license here. The weak strains of life are barely a music, and the walls that hold back death are tissue-thin. But I was pleased to see the blood jet forth. I watched the animal's essence disperse, misting upward in pale threads to rejoin the Great Cloud of Being, and then continued on my way.

At the crest of the hill, I paused and gazed back down the slope. From this vantage the landscape of that soft female world seemed transformed, infused with new strength. Great smoking clouds streamed from the seas and the jungle pitched and tossed as if troubled by my sight. The souls of trees were thin gold wires stretched to breaking. The thunder was a power, the lightning a name. I stood attuning myself to the night, absorbing its black subtleties and cold meanings, and thus strengthened, restored to the fullness of purpose, I went along the crest, searching the darkness for the defeated, listening among the whispers of the dead for the sound of one soon to die, for that telltale dullness and sonority. At last I heard him venting his rage against one of the alternates in a house a third of the way down the hill. His obvious lack of preparation dismayed me, and once again I felt less than enthusiastic about my duty. It would be a mercy to end these intermittent rituals of violence and let the brood come as an army to urge on this feeble race to the next plane.

The house was a glowing patch in the midst of a toiling darkness, and was made of sapling poles and thatch; orange light striped the gaps between the poles and leaked from beneath the door. I called to the defeated. The angry conversation within was broken off, but no one came out. Perhaps, I thought, he had mistaken my call for an element of the storm. I called again, a demanding scream that outvoiced the thunder. Still he remained within. This was intolerable! Now I would be forced to instruct him. I ripped aside the poles at the front of the house, creating a gaping hole through which I saw two figures shrinking back against the rear wall. I held out my hand in invitation, but as the alternate collapsed to the floor, the defeated went scuttling about like a frightened crab, running into the table, the chairs. Disgusted, I reached in and picked him up. I lifted him high, looked into his terrified face. He struggled, prying at my claws, kicking, squealing his fear.

"Why do you struggle?" I asked. "Your life is an exhausted breath, the failure of an enervated creation. You are food with a flicker of intelligence. True power is beyond you, and the knowledge of pain is your most refined sensibility." Of course, he did not understand; my speech must have seemed to him like a tide roaring out from a cave. But to illustrate the point, I traced a line of blood across his ribs, being careful not to cut too deeply. "Your ideas are all wrong," I told him. "Your concept of beauty, a gross mutation; your insipid notions of good and evil, an insult to their fathering principles." Once again I made him bleed, tracing the second line of instruction, slitting the skin of his stomach with such precision that it parted in neat flaps, yet the sac within was left intact. "Evil is as impersonal as mathematics. That its agencies derive pleasure from carrying out its charge is meaningless. Its trappings, its gauds and hellish forms, are nuance, not essence. Evil is the pure function of the universe, the machine of stars and darkness that carries us everywhere." At the third line, I saw in his face the first lights of under-standing, and in his shrieks I detected a music that reflected the incisiveness of my as yet incomplete design. His eyes were distended, bloody spittle clung to his lips and beard, and there was a new eagerness in his expression; he would—had he been able to muster coherent thought—have interpreted this eagerness as a lust for death, yet I doubted he would be aware that to feel such a lust was the signature of a profound lesson learned. I thought, however, that once we returned to the desert, once I had time to complete the design, our lessons would go more quickly. I traced a fourth line. His body spasmed, flopping bonelessly, but he did not lose consciousness, and I admired his stamina, envied him the small purity of his purpose. The bond that held me in that place was weakening, and I grasped him more tightly, squeezing a trickle of darkness from his mouth. "You and I," I said, slicing the skin over his breastbone, "are gears of the machine. Together we interlock and turn, causing an increment of movement, a miniscule resolution of potential." With the barest flick, I laid open one of his cheeks, and he responded with a high, quavering wail that went on and on as if I had opened a valve inside him, released some pressure that issued forth with a celebratory keening. Beneath the wash of blood, I had a glimpse of white. "I can see to your bone," I said. "The stalk of your being. I am going to pare you down to your essential things, both of flesh and knowledge. And when we return to the temples, you will have clear sight of them, of their meaning. They, too, are part of the machine." His head lolled back; his mouth went slack, and his eyes—they appeared to have gone dark—rolled up to fix on mine. It was as if he had decided to take his ease and bleed and study his tormentor, insulated from pain and fear. Perhaps he thought the worst was over. I laughed at that, and the storm of my laughter merged with the wind and all the tearing night, making him stiffen. I bent my head close to him, breathed a black breath to keep him calm during the transition, and whispered, "Soon you will know everything."

That is a mere approximation of what I remember, an overformal and inadequate rendering of an experience that seems with the passage of time to grow ever more untranslatable. Trapped by the limitations of language, I can only hint at the sense of alienness that had pervaded me, at the compulsions of the thing I believed I had become. I woke on the beach before dawn not far from Konwicki's house, and I thought that after the possession—or the transformation, or whatever it had been—had ended, in the resultant delirium, I must have wandered down from the hillside and passed out. No other possibility offered itself. My muscles still ached from the experience, and my memories were powerful and individual and sickening. I remembered how it felt to have the strength to tear iron like rotten cloth; I remembered a cold disdain for a world I now embraced in gratitude and relief; I remembered the sight of a black hand wicked with curved talons closing around Konwicki and lifting him high; I remembered intelligence without sentiment, hatred without passion; I remembered a thousand wars in the spirit that I had never fought; I remember killing a hundred brothers for the right to survive; I remembered a silence that caused pain; I remembered thoughts like knives, a wind like religion, a brilliance like fear; I remembered things for which I had no words. Things that made me tremble.

But as the sun brought light into the world, light brought doubt into my mind and caused the memories to diminish in importance. Their very sharpness was a reason to doubt them; memories, I believed, should be fragmentary, chaotic, and these—despite their untranslatable essence—were a poignant, almost physical, weight inside my head. Their vividness seemed a stamp of fradulence, of the manufactured, and thus my problems with interpreting what had happened became complex and confusing. How much, for instance, had Odille known? Had she, out of hatred for Konwicki, manipulated me? Had she known more than she had said, trying to encourage a deadly confrontation? And if so, what sort of confrontation was she trying to encourage? And what about coincidence? The coincidence of so many elements of those days and the dreams and the game. Was it really coincidence, or could what seemed coincidence have been a matter of selective memory? And Konwicki . . . had he been honest with me that night on the point, or had he, too, been engaged in manipulation? Could Odille's desertion have left him more bereft than he had allowed, and was that a significant motivation? I wished I had let him finish speaking, that I had learned what he meant by the phrase "for every action there's a reaction." Was that merely another coincidence, or did it refer to an exchange of travelers between this world and that desert hell? And most pertinent, had my deep-seated anger against an old lover been a sufficiently powerful poison to cause me to imagine an unimaginable horror, to erect an insane rationalization for a crime of passion? Or had anger been the key that opened both Konwicki and me to the forces of the game? Each potential answer to any of these questions cast a new light upon the rest, and therefore to determine an ultimate answer became a problem rather like trying to put together a jigsaw puzzle whose pieces were constantly changing shape.

The sun had cleared the horizon, shining palely through thin gray clouds; clumps of seaweed littered the beach, looking at a distance like bodies washed up by the surf, and heaps of foam like dirty soapsuds demarked the tidal margin. My head felt packed with cotton, and I couldn't think. Then I was struck by an illumination, a hope. Maybe none of it had happened. A psychotic episode of some kind. I went stumbling through the mucky sand toward Konwicki's place, growing more and more certain that I would find him there. And when I burst into the darkened shack, I saw someone asleep on an air mattress against the wall, a head with brown hair protruding from beneath a blanket.

"Konwicki!" I said, elated.

The head turned toward me. A tanned teenage girl propped herself on an elbow, the blanket slipping from her breasts; she rubbed her eyes, pouted, and said grouchily, "Who're you?"

The air in the room stank, heavy with the sourness of sexual activity and marijuana. I couldn't tell if the girl was pretty; her environment suppressed even the idea of prettiness. "Where's Konwicki?" I asked.

"You a friend of Carl's?"

"Yeah, we're soul mates." Being a wiseass helped stifle my anxiety.

The girl noticed her exposure, covered herself.

"Where is he?" I asked.

"I dunno." She slumped back down. "He went somewhere with Ryan last night. He'll probably be back soon." She shaded her eyes, peered into the thin light. "What's it like out there? Still drizzling?"

"No," I said dully.

The girl shook her hair back from her eyes. "I think I'll catch a swim."

I stood looking down at the cardboard box that contained the Mayan figurines.

"That means I'd like to put on my suit," said the girl.

"Oh . . . right. Sorry." I started out the door.

"After I'm dressed," said the girl, "you can wait here if you want. Carl's real free with his place."

I stood outside, uncertain what to do. While I was considering my options, the girl came out the door, wearing a red bikini; she waved and walked toward the water's edge. I stared in through the door at the cardboard box. Konwicki would not be returning, I realized, and the answer to all my questions might lie in that box. I checked to make sure that the girl wouldn't be a problem—she was splashing through the shallows—and darted inside. I picked up the box, then remembered the papers; I stuffed as many of them as possible in among the figurines, stuck some more under my arm, and went jogging along the shore toward home.

These were the facts, then. Konwicki was missing. The police were indifferent to the matter. Gringos were prone to make unannounced exits of this sort, they said. Likely he had gotten a girl in trouble. Ryan had been found on the hill, incapable of rational speech, his wrist broken; I saw him once before he was flown home under sedation, and he looked very like the Ryan of my dream. Drugs, said the local doctor. An Indian family with a small farm claimed that a demon had torn a hole in their roof and chased them through the jungle; but the sightings of demons was commonplace among the hill people, and their testimony was disregarded, the hole in the roof chalked up to storm damage—a ceiba tree had fallen onto it. A deer had been found disemboweled in the jungle, but the wound could have been made by a machete. A shack had been destroyed, apparently by the wind. As the days passed and the memories of that night grew faint, I came to see this combination of facts as an indictment against myself. It was conceivable that in chasing Ryan, I had frightened an Indian family who had already been terrified by a tree crashing down upon their roof, and that in my rage, a rage funded by the bizarre materials of Konwicki's game, I had erected a delusionary system to deny my participation in a violent act. Having this conclusion, I became desperate to prove it wrong. I refused to accept that I was a murderer, and I pored over Konwicki's notes, trying to legitimize the game. I discovered what he had meant by saying that the game could be prolongd; according to his notes, the winner could choose to continue alone for one more move, and thereby negate the penalties that accrued to both winner and loser . . . though why anyone would choose this option was beyond me. Perhaps the Mayans ranked their priorities differently from those of our culture, and personal survival was not high among them. The fact that Konwicki had not told me that I, the winner, would save him and risk myself by continuing seemed to testify that he was been trying to trick me into going on. However, that wasn't sufficient proof. Even if he had not given the game any credence, he might—as Odille had suggested—have said the exact same thing in order to gain a hold on me. The events of that night lay on an edge between the rational and the irrational, and the problem of which interpretation to place upon them was in the end a matter of personal choice.

Yet I was obsessed with finding a solution, and for the next month I pursued the question. I no longer had dreams of the pyramids and the desert, but I had other dreams in which I saw Konwicki's tormented face. From these dreams I would wake covered with sweat, and I would go into my study and spend the remaining hours of the night staring at the four counters that had been employed in the game: the dwarf, the warrior, the woman, the infant. I grew distracted. My thoughts would for a time be gleefully manic, sharp, and then would become muzzy and vague. I was afflicted by the smell of blood; I had fevers, aural hallucinations of roaring and screams. And I fell into a deep depression, as deep as the one that had owned me in New York, unable to disprove to my own satisfaction the notion that I had killed a man.

Throughout this period, Odille was loving and supportive, exhausting herself on my behalf, and during moments of clarity, I realized how fortunate

I was to have her, how much I had come to love her. It was this realization that began to pull me out of my depression . . . that, and the further realization that she was beginning to fray under the pressures of dealing with my breakdown. Over the span of a week, she grew sullen and short-tempered. I would find her pacing, agitated, and when I would try to console her, she would often as not react with hostility. Usually I was able to break through to her, to bring her back to normalcy. Then one night, returning from the corner store, where I had gone to buy olive oil, matches, some other things for the kitchen, as I came into the living room, I heard Odille out on the patio, sobbing, cursing, her voice thickened like a drunkard's. It was the voice I'd heard in my dream, coming from one of the cubicles in the pyramid. I stopped in my tracks, and as I listened, a dissolute feeling spread through my guts. There was no doubt about it. Not only were the timbre and rhythms identical, but also the words.

"Bastard," she was saying. "Oh, you bastard. God, I hate you, I hate you! You. . . ." A wail. "Dead man, that's what I'll call you. I'll say, 'How are you, dead man?' And when you ask what I mean by that, I'll say that I'm just anticipating . . . you fucking bastard!"

I went out onto the patio, walking softly. It was hot, and a few drops of rain were falling, speckling the concrete. Sweat poured off my neck and chest and back; my shirt was plastered to my skin. The lights were off, the moon high, printing a filigree of leaf shadow on the concrete, and Odille was perched on the edge of a chair in the shadows, her head down and hands clasped together—a tense, prayerful attitude. It seemed hotter the nearer I came to her. "Odille," I said.

She threw back her head, her strained face visible through strands of hair; she looked like a madwoman caught at some secretive act.

I started toward her, but she jumped up and backed away. "Don't touch me, you bastard!"

"Jesus, Odille!"

I moved forward a step or two, and she screamed. "You lied to me! Always lies! Even in Irún . . . even then you were lying!"

She had told me enough about her affair in Paris to make me think it was her old lover—and not me—that she was addressing. "Odille," I said. "It's me . . . Ray!" She blinked, appeared to recognize me; but when I came forward again, she said, "I won't listen to you anymore, Carl. Everything you say is self-serving. It has nothing to do with what I'm feeling, what I'm thinking."

I took her by the shoulders. "Look at me, Odille. It's Ray."

"Oh God . . . Ray!" The tension drained from her face. "I'm sorry, I'm so sorry!" Her mouth twisted into an expression of revulsion, and she pushed me back. "Sitting there mooning about that bitch in New York. You think I don't know? I do . . . I know! Every time you touch me, I know!"

"Odille!"

Again her face grew calm, or rather, registered an ordinary level of distress. "Oh God!" she said. "I feel out of control, I feel . . . !"

I tried to embrace her, and she slapped me hard, knocking me off-balance. She came at me, shouting, slapping, and clawing, and I went backward over the arm of a chair. My head struck the concrete, sending spears of white light shooting back into my eyes; I grabbed at her leg as she stepped over me, but I was stunned, my coordination impaired, and I only grazed her calf with my fingernail. By the time I managed to stand, Odille was long gone.

I went into the living room and stood by a table that I had marked into zones like the game board; the four counters were set upon it, and on the floor was the box containing the remaining two counters. In the pool of lamplight, the rough brownish orange finish of the clay had the look of pocked skin; shadows had collected in their eye sockets, making them appear ghoulish. I would have liked to break them, to scatter them with a sweep of my hand and dash them to the floor; but I was frightened of them. I recalled now what Ryan had said in my dream about the victor paying a price, and I also recalled Konwicki's description of the female counter. A maniac, Odille had said. Foulmouthed and physically abusive. It was possible to dismiss the evidence of dreams, to blame Odille's emotional state on stress, on the turbulent emotional climate of her past, to dissect experience and devise a logical system that would explain away everything inexplicable. But there had been one too many coincidences, and I knew now that the game and all its hallucinatory consequences had been real, that the potency of the game was in part due to the fact that this world and the one from which the game derived were ultimately coincidental, lying side by side, matching one another event for event; the game was a bridge between those worlds, allowing the evil character of one to tap into and transform the weak principles of the other. Maybe the Mayans had played the game too often; maybe it had infected them, and they had fled their cities, looking for someplace untainted by that other world. Maybe that ominous vibration of the old ruins, of Tikal and Palenque and Cobán, was a remnant of the power of evil, a lingering pulse of the ancient machinery. The theory was impossible to prove or disprove, but I had the feeling that I was not far from right. And what was to happen now? Was I to lose Odille, watch her decline into a madness that accorded with the character assigned her counter by some impersonal agency, some functionary of a universal plan?

So it appeared.

It was curious, my calmness at that moment. I had no idea whether or not there was a remedy to the situation. I thought about Konwicki's notes, his declaration that the game could be prolonged if the winner chose to put himself at risk for one more move, and I remembered, too, how Ryan had hinted at much the same thing in the dream; but there was nothing in Konwicki's notes that explained how one should initiate the tactic. Still, I acted as if there was remedy, as if I had a decision to make. I sat down in a straight-backed chair, staring at the counters, and thought about what we make when we make love, the weave of dependencies and pleasures and habituations that arise from the simple act of bestowing love, which is an act of utter honesty, of revelation and admission, of being innocent enough to open oneself completely to another human being and take a step forward into the dangerous precinct of their wills, hoping that they have taken the same immeasurable step, hoping they will not backtrack and second-guess what they know absolutely—that here is a rare chance to deny the conventional wisdom, to attempt an escape from the logics that supposedly define us. Karen Maniaci had taken that step and then had become afraid. It was not blameful, what she had done; it was only sad. And perhaps her rejection of love, her sublimation of desire, and her decision to view the life of her heart in terms of an emotional IRA, a long-term yuppie investment, choosing the security of what she could endure over the potentials of hope—maybe that was all of which she was capable. But that was the imperfect past. I thought of Odille then—her childhood of white lace and Catholic virtue, her intelligence and her ordinary passage through schools and men and days to this beach at the ends of the earth, this place where one thing more than the expected had happened—and I thought of the risk we had taken with one another without knowing it . . . to begin with, anyway. At some point we must have known, and still we had taken it. As it had been with Karen, it was now—I did not understand how to step back from that commitment, even though it was clear that the prospect of yet another risk lay before me.

Perhaps the game was—as Konwicki had suggested—merely a matter of attunement, not of rules; and perhaps once I'd entered the game's sphere of influence, I had only to acknowledge it, to make a choice, and then that choice would be actualized within its boundaries. Whatever the case, I must have reached a decision that bore upon the game, because I realized that the table and the counters had undergone a transformation. The surface of the table had become an undulating surface of rusty orange upon which the counters stood like colossi, and in the distance, apparently miles and miles away, was a complex of black pyramids. It was as if I were a giant peering in from the edge of the world, looking out over a miniature landscape . . . miniature, but nonetheless real. The wind was blowing the sand into tiny scarves that attenuated and sparkled as they vanished, and hanging above the pyramids was a fuming violet-white sun. Acting without thought, feeling again that sense of power and possession, I removed three of the counters, leaving the dwarf to stand facing the black buildings alone. After a moment I took one of the two remaining counters from the cardboard box and set it close to the gnome. The figure depicted a youth, its proportions less distorted than those of the dwarf, yet with muscles not so developed as those of the warrior. I leaned back in my chair, feeling drained, wasted. The table had returned to normal, a flat surface marked with lines of chalk.

I was more than a little afraid. I wasn't sure what exactly I had done, but now I wanted to retreat from it, deny it. I pushed back my chair, becoming panicked, darting glances to the side, expecting to see an immense black talon poking toward me from window or door. The house seemed a trap— I remembered Konwicki and Ryan in the hut on the hill—and I scurried out into the night. It was spitting rain, and the wind was driving in steadily off the sea, shredding the palms, breaking the music from a radio in the house next door into shrads of brght noise. I felt disoriented, needing—as I had that first night at Konwicki's—something to hold, something that would give me weight and balance, and I sprinted down onto the beach, thinking that Odille would be there. At the Café Pluto or one of the other bars. Maybe now that the game had been joined once again, she would have grown calm, regained her center. The moon flashed between banks of running clouds, and chutes of flickering lantern lights spilled from shanty windows, illuminating patches of weeds, strips of mucky sand littered with fish corpses and offal and coconut tops. In the darkness above the tossing palms, I glimpsed a phantom shape, immense and snake-headed, visible for a fraction of a second, and I picked up my pace, running now out of fear, the salt air sharp in my lungs, expecting a great claw to lay open my backbone. Then I spotted Odille—a shadow at the margin of the sea, facing toward the reef. The tide was going out, leaving an expanse of dark sand studded with driftwood and shells. I ran faster yet, and as I came near, she turned to me, backed away, saying something lost in the noise of the wind and surf. I caught her by her shoulders, and she tried to twist free.

"Let me go!" she said, pushing at my chest.

I glanced behind me. "Come on! We've got to get out of here!"

"No!" She broke loose from my grasp. "I can't!"

Again I caught hold of her.

"Leave me alone!" she said. "I'm. . . ." She brushed strands of wet hair away from her face. "I don't know what's wrong with me. I must be crazy, acting like that."

"You'll be all right."

"You can't know that!"

I pulled her close, pressed her head onto my shoulder. She was shaking. "Calm down, just calm down. You're all right. Don't you feel all right? Don't you feel better?" I stroked her hair, my words coming in a torrent. "It's just the pressure, all the pressure. We've both been acting crazy. But it's over now. We have to leave; we have to find a new place." I searched the sky for signs of the monster I'd seen earlier, but there was only the darkness, the rushing moon, the lashing fronds. "Are you O.K.? Are you feeling O.K.?"

"Yes, but—"

"Don't worry. It's just the pressure. I'm surprised we both haven't gone nuts."

"You're not going to leave me?" Her tone was similar to that of a child who'd been expecting a beating and had been granted a reprieve.

"Of course not. I love you. I'm not going to leave you . . . ever."

Her arms tightened around my neck, and she said that she couldn't stand the idea of losing me; that was why, she thought, she'd lost control. She just couldn't bear going through the same heartbreak again. I reassured her as best I could, my mouth dry with fear, continuing to look in every direction for signs of danger. The sea rolled in, smooth swells of ebony that detonated into white flashes on the reef.

"Come on," I said, taking her hand, pulling her along. "Let's go back to the house. We have to get out. This place, it's no good anyway. Too much bad shit has happened. Maybe we can find a boat to take us upriver tonight. Or tomorrow morning. O.K.?"

"O.K." she forced a smile, squeezed my hand.

We went stumbling along the shore, beating our way against the wind. As we were passing close to a clump of palms, their trunks curved toward the sea, a figure stepped from behind them, blocking our path, and said, "Dass far as you go, mon!"

He was standing barely a dozen feet away, yet I had to peer in order to make him out: a cocoa-skinned boy in his teens, about my height and weight, wearing jeans and a shirt with the silk-screened image of a blonde woman on the front. In his hand was a snub-nosed pistol. His eyes looked sleepy, heavy-lidded—Chinese eyes—and he was swaying, unsteady on his feet. His expression changed moment to moment, smiling one second and the next growing tight, anxious, registering the shifts in chemical valence of whatever drug he was behind.

"Gimme what you got, mon!" He waggled the pistol. "Quickly, now!"

I fumbled out my wallet, tossed it to him; he let it slip through his fingers and fall to the sand. Keeping his eyes on me, the gun trained, he knelt and groped for the wallet. Then stood, pried it open with the fingers of his left hand, and removed the contents. My vision was acting up; superimposed on the boy's face was another face, one with coarse features and pocked ocher skin—the image of the counter depicting the youth.

"Shit . . . boog muthafucka! Dis all you got? Quetzales all you got? I want gold, mon. Ain't you got no gold?"

"Gold!" I said, easing Odille behind me. To the surprise of half my mind, I felt in control of the situation. The bastard planned to kill me, but he was in for a fight. I was in the game again, flooded with unnatural strength and cold determination, my fear dimmed by my partnered consciousness with a muscular little freak who thrived on bloodlust.

"Ras clot!" said the boy, his face hardening with rage, jabbing the gun toward me, coming a few steps closer. "Gold! American dollars! You t'ink I goin' to settle fah dis?" He waved the fistful of Guatemalan currency at me.

The rain had let up, but the wind was increasing steadily; all along the beach the bushes and palms were seething. The sky above the hills had cleared, and the moon was riding just high enough so that the tip of the highest hill put a black notch in its lowest quarter. With ragged blue clouds sailing close above, their edges catching silver fire as they passed, it was a wild and lovely sight, and my heart stalled on seeing it. I felt calm, alert, as if attentive to some call, and I watched the tops of some silhouetted acacias inland swaying and straightening with a slow, ungainly rhythm, bending low all to one side and lurching heavily back to upright again, like the shadows of dancing bears. At the center of the wind, I heard a silence, a vast pool of dead air, and I knew that other world, that place half my home, was whirling close, ready to loose its monsters upon whoever failed this test. I was not unnerved; I was empowered by that silence, unafraid of losing.

"Didn't you hear me, mon?" said the boy. "T'ink I foolin' wit' you? I ast if you got gold."

"Yeah, I got gold," I said coolly. "I got more gold than you can handle. Look in the secret compartment."

"What you mean?"

"There's a seam inside the billfold," I said, gloating over what was to come. "An inner flap. You have to look real close. Slit it open with your fingernail."

The boy stared into the wallet, and I flew at him, driving my shoulder into his abdomen, my arms wrapping around his legs, bringing him down beneath me. I clawed for his gun hand, caught the wrist as we went rolling in the wet sand left by the receding tide. I butted him under the jaw and smashed his hand against the sand again and again, butting him once more, and at last he let the gun fall. I had a glimpse of a dagger falling onto the rust-colored sand, and as we grappled together, face-to-face, in his eyes I saw the shadowy, depthless eyes of the counter, the coarse slitted folds, the hollowed pupils. I smelled cheap cologne, sweat, but I also smelled a hot desert wind. The boy spat out words in a language that I didn't recognize, tearing at my hair, gouging at my eyes; he was stonger than he had appeared. He freed one hand, punched at the back of my neck, brought his knee up into my chest, sending me onto my back. Then he straddled me, twisting my head, forcing my face into the sand and flailing away with his fist, punching at my liver and kidneys. There was sand in my nose and mouth, and the pain in my side was enormous. I couldn't breathe. Black lights were dancing behind my eyes, swelling to blot out everything, and in desperation I heaved up, unseating the boy, grabbing at his legs; I saw leaden clouds, a boiling sun, and then darkness filmed across the sky once again. The boy broke free, coming to his knees. But in doing so, he turned away from me, and that was his undoing. I knocked him flat on his stomach, crawled atop him, and barred my forearm under his neck, locking him in a choke hold by clutching my wrist. We went rolling across the sand and into the water. A wave lifted us; black water coursed over my face; the moon blurred into a silver stream like the flashing of a luminous eel. I surfaced, sputtering. I was on my back, the boy atop me, humping, straining, his fingers clawing. His Adam's apple worked against my arm, and I tightened the hold, digging into his flesh with a twisting motion. He made a cawing noise, half gurgle, half scream. I think I laughed. Another wave swept over us, but we were anchored, heels dug into the sand. I heard Odille crying out above the tumult of wind and waves, and suddenly my glee and delight in the contest, the sense of possession, of abnormal strength . . . all that was gone.

The boy spasmed; his back arched like a wrestler bridging, trying to prevent a pin; and he went stiff, his muscles cabled. But I could feel the life inside him flopping about like a fish out of water, feel the frail tremor of his held breath. I didn't know what to do. I could release him. . . . I doubted he would have any fight left, but what if he did? And if he lived, wouldn't he continue to be a menace, wouldn't the game be unresolved, and—if not the boy—would not some new menace arise to terrorize me? I didn't so much think these things as I experienced a black rush of thought of which they were a part, one that ripped through me with the force of the tide that was sucking us farther from the shore, and once this rush had passed, I knew that the choice had already been made, that I was riding out the final, feeble processes of a death. Even this realization came too late, for at the moment the boy went limp, and his body floated up from mine in the drag of the tide.

Horrified, I pushed him away, scrambled to my feet, and stood in the knee-deep water, fighting for balance. For the briefest of instants, I spotted something huge, something with needle teeth and a flat skull, bending to the boy. The Odille was clinging to me, dragging me away from the shore, saying things I barely heard. I turned back to the boy, saw his body lifting, sliding down the face of a swell, almost lost in the darkness. I searched the sky and trees for signs of that other world. But there was nothing. The game was over. Whatever had come for the boy already had him, already was tormenting the last of him in that place of snakes and deserts and black silences. That place forever inside me now. I looked for the boy again. He had drifted out of sight, but I knew he was there, and I would always know how his body went sliding into the troughs, rising up, growing heavier and heavier, but not heavy enough to prevent him from nudging against the reef, his skin tearing on the sharp rocks, then lifting in the race of the outgoing tide and passing over the barrier, dropping down and down through schools of mindless fish and fleshy flowers and basking sharks and things stranger and more terrifying yet into the cold and final depths that lay beyond.

When I returned to the house, I discovered that the figurines depicting the youth and the warrior had been shattered. The marmalade cat fled from our footsteps and peered out from beneath a chair with a guilty look. I didn't puzzle over this; I was for the moment unconcerned with validation and coincidence . . . except for my comprehension that the life of one world was the shade of another, that the best and brightest instances of our lives were merely functions of dark design. That and the memory of the boy dying in the shallows colored everything I did, and for a very long time, although I went about the days and work with my accustomed verve, I perceived a hollowness in every incidence of fullness and was hesitant about expressing my emotions, having come to doubt their rationality. Odille, while she had not been aware of the undercurrents of the fight on the beach, seemed to have undergone a similar evolution. We began to drift apart, and neither of us had the energy or will to pull things back together.

On the day she left for Paris, I walked her to the dock and waited with her as the ferry from Puerto Morales unloaded its cargo of fat black women and scrawny black men and chickens and fruit and flour. She leaned against a piling, holding down the brim of a straw hat to shield her eyes from the sun, looking very French, very beautiful. However, I was no longer moved by beauty. Some small part of me regretted her leaving, but mostly I was eager to have her gone, to pare life down to its essentials once again in hopes that I might find some untainted possibility in which to place my faith.

"Are you all right?" she asked. "You look . . . peculiar."

"I'm fine," I said, and then, to be polite, I added, "I'm sorry to see you go."

She tipped back her head so as to better see my face. "I'm sorry, too. I'll never understand what went wrong. I thought. . . ."

"Yeah, so did I." I shrugged. *"C'est la vie."*

She laughed palely, turned to the ferry, obviously nervous, wanting to end an awkward moment. "Will you be all right?" she asked suddenly, as if for an instant she were reinhabiting the depth of her old concern and caring. "I'll worry about you here."

"I'm not going to stay much longer . . . a couple of weeks. The doctors will be back by then."

"I don't know how you can stay a minute longer. Aren't you worried about the police?"

"They're tired of hassling me," I said. "Hell, one of the lieutenants . . . you remember the one with the waxed mustache? He actually told me the other day that I was a hero." I gave a sarcastic laugh. "Like Bernhard Goetz, I'm keeping the city clean."

Odille started to say something, but kept it to herself. Instead, she let her fingers trail across my hand.

At last the ferry was empty, ready for boarding. She stood on tiptoe, kissed me lightly, and then was gone, merging with the crowd of blacks that poured up the gangplank.

The ferry veered away from the dock, venting black smoke, and I watched until it had rounded a spit of land, thinking that the saddest thing about Odille and me was that we had parted without tears. After a minute or so,

I headed back to the house. I had planned to work, but I was unable to concentrate. The inside of my head felt like glass, too fragile to support the weighty process of thought. I fed the cat, paced awhile; eventually I went into the living room and gazed down at the cardboard box that contained the four remaining figurines. I had been intending to destroy them, but each time I had made to do so, I'd been restrained by a fear of some bad result. It occurred to me that I enjoyed this irresolute state of affairs, that I found it romantic to cling to the belief that—mad from unrequited love—I had done terrible violence, and that I'd been shying away from anything that might prove the contrary. I became enraged at my self-indulgence and lack of fortitude; without thinking, I picked up a figurine and hurled it at the wall. It shattered into a hundred pieces, and to my astonishment, a stain began to spread where it had struck. A spatter of thick crimson very like a smear of fresh blood. I tried to blink the sight away, but there it was, slowly washing down the wall. I was less afraid than numb. I looked into the box and saw that the figurine I'd broken was the infant. Ryan. I glanced again at the wall. The stain had vanished.

I started laughing, infinitely amused, wondering if I should call New Zealand and check on the particulars of Ryan's health; but then I realized that I would never pin down the truth, that his health or illness or death could be explained in a dozen ways, and I was afraid that I might not stop laughing, that I would continue until laughter blocked out everything else. Everything was true. Insanity and the supernatural were in league. Finally I managed to get myself under control. I packed my papers, a few clothes, and after wrapping the three remaining figurines in crumpled newspaper, I carried them to the house of the local priest and donated them to his museum. He was delighted by the gift, though puzzled at my insistence that he not allow them to be handled, that they be treated with the utmost care. Nor did he understand my hilarity on telling him that I was placing my fate in God's hands.

At the jetty, I found a swarthy, white-haired East Indian man with a powerboat who said he would transport me up the Río Dulce to the town of Reunión for an exorbitant fee. I did not attempt to haggle. Minutes later we were speeding north through the jungle along the green river, and as the miles slipped past, I began to relax, to hope that I was putting the past behind me once and for all. The wind streamed into my face, and I closed my eyes, smiling at the freshness of the air, the sweetness of escape.

"You look happy," the old man called out above the roar of the engine. "Are you going to meet your sweetheart?"

I told him, no, I was going home to New York.

"Why do you want to do that? All those gangsters and slums! Don't tell me New York is as beautiful as this!" He waved at the jungle. "The Dulce, Livingston . . . nowhere is there a more lovely place!"

With a sudden jerk of the wheel, he swerved the boat toward the middle of the river, sending me toppling sideways, balanced for an instant on the edge of the stern, my face a foot above the water. Something big and dark was passing just beneath the surface. The old man clutched at my arm, hauling me back as I was about to overbalance and go into the water. "Did you see?" he said excitedly. "A manatee! We nearly struck it!"

"Uh-huh," I said, shaken, my heart racing, wondering if the priest had mishandled one of the figurines back in Livingston.

"I would wager," said the old man, unmindful of my close call, "that there are no manatees in New York. None of the marvelous creatures we have here."

No manatees, I thought; but dark things passing beneath the surface—we had plenty of those. They came in every form. Male, female, shadows in doorways, rooms in abandoned buildings with occult designs chalked on the walls. Everywhere the interface with an uncharted reality, everywhere the familiar world fraying into the unknown.

Escape was impossible, I realized. I had always been in danger, and I always would be, and it occurred to me that the supernatural and the ordinary were likely a unified whole, elements of a spectrum of reality whose range outstripped the human senses. Perhaps strong emotion was the catalyst that opened one to the extremes of that spectrum; perhaps desire and rage and ritual in alignment allowed one to slide from light to light, barely noticing the dark interval that had been bridged. There was a comforting symmetry between these thoughts and what I had experienced, and that symmetry, along with my brush with drowning, seemed to have settled things in my mind, to have satisfied—if not resolved—my doubts. This was not so simple an accommodation as my statement implies. I am still prone to analyze these events, and often I am frustrated by my lack of comprehension. But in some small yet consequential way, I had made peace with myself. I had achieved some inner balance, and as a result I felt capable of accepting my share of guilt for what had happened. I had, after all, been playing head games with Konwicki before taking up the counters, and I had to shoulder responsibility for that . . . if for nothing else.

"Well, what do you say?" The old man asked. "Have you anything in New York to rival this?"

"I suppose not," I said, and he beamed, pleased by my admission of the essential superiority of the Guatemalan littoral.

We continued along the peaceful river, passing through forbidding gulfs bordered by cliffs of gray stone, passing villages and reed beds and oil barges, and came at last to Reunión, where I parted company with the old man and caught the bus north, sadder and wiser, free both of hate and love, though not of trouble, returning home to the ends of the earth.

NANCY KRESS
The Price of Oranges

Here's a funny, bittersweet, and deeply moving study of friendship, faith, love . . . and some very hard choices.

Born in Buffalo, New York, Nancy Kress now lives with her family in Brockport, New York. She began selling her elegant and incisive stories in the mid-seventies, and has since become a frequent contributor to *IAsfm*, *F & SF*, *OMNI*, and elsewhere. Her books include the novels *The Prince of Morning Bells*, *The Golden Grove*, *The White Pipes*, and *An Alien Light*, and the collection *Trinity and Other Stories*. Her most recent book is the novel *Brain Rose*. Her story "Trinity" was in our Second Annual Collection; her "Out of All Them Bright Stars"—a Nebula winner—was in our Third Annual Collection, and her "In Memoriam" was in our Sixth Annual Collection.

▼

The Price of Oranges

NANCY KRESS

"I'm worried about my granddaughter," Harry Kramer said, passing half of his sandwich to Manny Feldman. Manny took it eagerly. The sandwich was huge, thick slices of beef and horseradish between fresh slabs of crusty bread. Pigeons watched the park bench hopefully.

"Jackie. The granddaughter who writes books," Manny said. Harry watched to see that Manny ate. You couldn't trust Manny to eat enough; he stayed too skinny. At least in Harry's opinion. Manny, Jackie—the world, Harry sometimes thought, had all grown too skinny when he somehow hadn't been looking. Skimpy. Stretch-feeling. Harry nodded to see horseradish spurt in a satisfying stream down Manny's scraggly beard.

"Jackie. Yes," Harry said.

"So what's wrong with her? She's sick?" Manny eyed Harry's strudel, cherry with real yeast bread. Harry passed it to him. "Harry, the whole thing? I couldn't."

"Take it, take it, I don't want it. You should eat. No, she's not sick. She's miserable." When Manny, his mouth full of strudel, didn't answer, Harry put a hand on Manny's arm. "*Miserable.*"

Manny swallowed hastily. "How do you know? You saw her this week?"

"No. Next Tuesday. She's bringing me a book by a friend of hers. I know from this." He drew a magazine from an inner pocket of his coat. The coat was thick tweed, almost new, with wooden buttons. On the cover of the glossy magazine a woman smiled contemptuously. A woman with hollow, starved-looking cheeks who obviously didn't get enough to eat either.

"That's not a book," Manny pointed out.

"So she writes stories, too. Listen to this. Just listen. 'I stood in my backyard, surrounded by the false bright toxin-fed green, and realized that

268

the earth was dead. What else could it be, since we humans swarmed upon it like maggots on carrion, growing our hectic gleaming molds, leaving our slime trails across the senseless surface?' Does that sound like a happy woman?"

"Hoo boy," Manny said.

"It's all like that. 'Don't read my things, Popsy,' she says. 'You're not in the audience for my things.' Then she smiles without ever once showing her teeth." Harry flung both arms wide. "Who else should be in the audience but her own grandfather?"

Manny swallowed the last of the strudel. Pigeons fluttered angrily. "She never shows her teeth when she smiles? Never?"

"Never."

"Hoo boy," Manny said. Did you want all of that orange?"

"No, I brought it for you, to take home. But did you finish that whole half a sandwich already?"

"I thought I'd take it home," Manny said humbly. He showed Harry the tip of the sandwich, wrapped in the thick brown butcher paper, protruding from the pocket of his old coat.

Harry nodded approvingly. "Good, good. Take the orange, too. I brought it for you."

Manny took the orange. Three teenagers carrying huge shrieking radios sauntered past. Manny started to put his hands over his ears, received a look of dangerous contempt from the teenager with green hair, and put his hands on his lap. The kid tossed an empty beer bottle onto the pavement before their feet. It shattered. Harry scowled fiercely but Manny stared straight ahead. When the cacophony had passed, Manny said, "Thank you for the orange. Fruit, it costs so much this time of year."

Harry still scowled. "Not in 1937."

"Don't start that again, Harry."

Harry said sadly, "Why won't you ever believe me? Could I afford to bring all this food if I got it at 1988 prices? Could I afford this coat? Have you seen buttons like this in 1988, on a new coat? Have you seen sandwiches wrapped in that kind of paper since we were young? Have you? Why won't you believe me?"

Manny slowly peeled his orange. The rind was pale, and the orange had seeds. "Harry. Don't start."

"But why won't you just come to my room and *see*?"

Manny sectioned the orange. "Your room. A cheap furnished room in a Social Security hotel. Why should I go? I know what will be there. What will be there is the same thing in my room. A bed, a chair, a table, a hot plate, some cans of food. Better I should meet you here in the park, get at least a little fresh air." He looked at Harry meekly, the orange clutched in one hand. "Don't misunderstand. It's not from a lack of friendship I say this. You're good to me, you're the best friend I have. You bring me things from a great deli, you talk to me, you share with me the family I don't have. It's enough, Harry. It's *more* than enough. I don't need to see where you live like I live."

Harry gave it up. There were moods, times, when it was just impossible to budge Manny. He dug in, and in he stayed. "Eat your orange."

"It's a good orange. So tell me more about Jackie."

"Jackie." Harry shook his head. Two kids on bikes tore along the path. One of them swerved towards Manny and snatched the orange from his hand. "Aw riggghhhtttt!"

Harry scowled after the child. It had been a girl. Manny just wiped the orange juice off his fingers onto the knee of his pants. "Is everything she writes so depressing?"

"Everything," Harry said. "Listen to this one." He drew out another magazine, smaller, bound in rough paper with a stylized linen drawing of a woman's private parts on the cover. On the cover! Harry held the magazine with one palm spread wide over the drawing, which made it difficult to keep the pages open while he read. " 'She looked at her mother in the only way possible: with contempt, contempt for all the betrayals and compromises that had been her mother's life, for the sad soft lines of defeat around her mother's mouth, for the bright artificial dress too young for her wasted years, for even the leather handbag, Gucci of course, filled with blood money for having sold her life to a man who had long since ceased to want it.' "

"Hoo boy," Manny said. "About a *mother* she wrote that?"

"About everybody. All the time."

"And where *is* Barbara?"

"Reno again. Another divorce." How many had that been? After two, did anybody count? Harry didn't count. He imagined Barbara's life as a large roulette wheel like the ones on TV, little silver men bouncing in and out of red and black pockets. Why didn't she get dizzy?

Manny said slowly, "I always thought there was a lot of love in her."

"A lot of that she's got," Harry said dryly.

"Not Barbara—Jackie. A lot of . . . I don't know. Sweetness. Under the way she is."

"The way she is," Harry said gloomily. "Prickly. A cactus. But you're right, Manny, I know what you mean. She just needs someone to soften her up. Love her back, maybe. Although *I* love her."

The two old men looked at each other. Manny said, "Harry. . . ."

"I know, I know. I'm only a grandfather, my love doesn't count, I'm just there. Like air. 'You're wonderful, Popsy,' she says, and still no teeth when she smiles. But you know, Manny—you are right!" Harry jumped up from the bench. "You are! What she needs is a young man to love her!"

Manny looked alarmed. "I didn't say—"

"I don't know why I didn't think of it before!"

"Harry—"

"And her stories, too! Full of ugly murders, ugly places, unhappy endings. What she needs is something to show her that writing could be about sweetness, too."

Manny was staring at him hard. Harry felt a rush of affection. That Manny should have the answer! Skinny wonderful Manny!

Manny said slowly, "Jackie said to me, 'I write about reality.' That's what she said, Harry."

"So there's no sweetness in reality? Put sweetness in her life, her writing will go sweet. She *needs* this, Manny. A really nice fellow!"

Two men in jogging suits ran past. One of their Reeboks came down on a shard of beer bottle. "Every fucking time!" he screamed, bending over to inspect his shoe. "Fucking park!"

"Well, what do you expect?" the other drawled, looking at Manny and Harry. "Although you'd think that if we could clean up Lake Erie. . . ."

"Fucking derelicts!" the other snarled. They jogged away.

"Of course," Harry said, "it might not be easy to find the sort of guy to convince Jackie."

"Harry, I think you should maybe think—"

"Not here," Harry said suddenly. "Not here. *There.* In 1937."

"*Harry*. . . ."

"Yeah," Harry said, nodding several times. Excitement filled him like light, like electricity. What an idea! "It was different then."

Manny said nothing. When he stood up, the sleeve of his coat exposed the number tattooed on his wrist. He said quietly, "It was no paradise in 1937 either, Harry."

Harry seized Manny's hand. "I'm going to do it, Manny. Find someone for her there. Bring him here."

Manny sighed. "Tomorrow at the chess club, Harry? At one o'clock? It's Tuesday."

"I'll tell you then how I'm coming with this."

"Fine, Harry. Fine. All my wishes go with you. You know that."

Harry stood up too, still holding Manny's hand. A middle-aged man staggered to the bench and slumped onto it. The smell of whiskey rose from him in waves. He eyed Manny and Harry with scorn. "Fucking fags."

"Good night, Harry."

"Manny—if you'd only come . . . money goes so much farther there. . . ."

"Tomorrow at one. At the chess club."

Harry watched his friend walk away. Manny's foot dragged a little; the knee must be bothering him again. Harry wished Manny would see a doctor. Maybe a doctor would know why Manny stayed so skinny.

Harry walked back to his hotel. In the lobby, old men slumped in upholstery thin from wear, burned from cigarettes, shiny in the seat from long sitting. Sitting and sitting, Harry thought—life measured by the seat of the pants. And now it was getting dark. No one would go out from here until the next daylight. Harry shook his head.

The elevator wasn't working again. He climbed the stairs to the third floor. Halfway there, he stopped, felt in his pocket, counted five quarters, six dimes, two nickels, and eight pennies. He returned to the lobby. "Could I have two dollar bills for this change, please? Maybe old bills?"

The clerk looked at him suspiciously. "Your rent paid up?"

"Certainly," Harry said. The woman grudgingly gave him the money.

"Thank you. You look very lovely today, Mrs. Raduski." Mrs. Raduski snorted.

In his room, Harry looked for his hat. He finally found it under his bed —how had it gotten under his bed? He dusted it off and put it on. It had cost him $3.25. He opened the closet door, parted the clothes hanging from their metal pole—like Moses parting the sea, he always thought, a Moses come again—and stepped to the back of the closet, remembering with his body rather than his mind the sharp little twist to the right just past the far gray sleeve of his good wool suit.

He stepped out into the bare corner of a warehouse. Cobwebs brushed his hat; he had stepped a little too far right. Harry crossed the empty concrete space to where the lumber stacks started, and threaded his way through them. The lumber, too, was covered with cobwebs; not much building going on. On his way out the warehouse door, Harry passed the night watchman coming on duty.

"Quiet all day, Harry?"

"As a church, Rudy," Harry said. Rudy laughed. He laughed a lot. He was also indisposed to question very much. The first time he had seen Harry coming out of the warehouse in a bemused daze, he must have assumed that Harry had been hired to work there. Peering at Rudy's round, vacant face, Harry realized that he must hold this job because he was someone's uncle, someone's cousin, someone's something. Harry had felt a small glow of approval; families should take care of their own. He had told Rudy that he had lost his key and asked him for another.

Outside it was late afternoon. Harry began walking. Eventually there were people walking past him, beside him, across the street from him. Everybody wore hats. The women wore bits of velvet or wool with dotted veils across their noses and long, graceful dresses in small prints. The men wore fedoras with suits as baggy as Harry's. When he reached the park there were children, girls in long black tights and hard shoes, boys in buttoned shirts. Everyone looked like it was Sunday morning.

Pushcarts and shops lined the sidewalks. Harry bought a pair of socks, thick gray wool, for 89 cents. When the man took his dollar, Harry held his breath: each first time made a little pip in his stomach. But no one ever looked at the dates of old bills. He bought two oranges for five cents each, and then, thinking of Manny, bought a third. At a candystore he bought *G-8 And His Battle Aces* for fifteen cents. At The Collector's Cozy in the other time they would gladly give him thirty dollars for it. Finally, he bought a cherry Coke for a nickel and headed towards the park.

"Oh, excuse me," said a young man who bumped into Harry on the sidewalk. "I'm so sorry!" Harry looked at him hard: but, no. Too young. Jackie was twenty-eight.

Some children ran past, making for the movie theater. Spencer Tracy in *Captains Courageous*. Harry sat down on a green-painted wooden bench under a pair of magnificent Dutch elms. On the bench lay a news-magazine. Harry glanced at it to see when in September this was: the 28th. The cover pictured a young blond Nazi soldier standing at stiff salute. Harry thought again of Manny, frowned, and turned the magazine cover down.

For the next hour, people walked past. Harry studied them carefully. When it got too dark to see, he walked back to the warehouse, on the way buying an apple kuchen at a bakery with a curtain behind the counter looped back to reveal a man in his shirt sleeves eating a plate of stew at a table bathed in soft yellow lamplight. The kuchen cost thirty-two cents.

At the warehouse, Harry let himself in with his key, slipped past Rudy nodding over *Paris Nights*, and walked to his cobwebby corner. He emerged from his third-floor closet into his room. Beyond the window, sirens wailed and would not stop.

"So how's it going?" Manny asked. He dripped kuchen crumbs on the chessboard; Harry brushed them away. Manny had him down a knight.

"It's going to take time to find somebody that's right," Harry said. "I'd like to have someone by next Tuesday when I meet Jackie for dinner, but I don't know. It's not easy. There are requirements. He has to be young enough to be attractive, but old enough to understand Jackie. He has to be sweet-natured enough to do her some good, but strong enough not to panic at jumping over fifty-two years. Somebody educated. An educated man—he might be more curious than upset by my closet. Don't you think?"

"Better watch your queen," Manny said, moving his rook. "So how are you going to find him?"

"It takes time," Harry said. "I'm working on it."

Manny shook his head. "You have to get somebody here, you have to convince him he *is* here, you have to keep him from turning right around and running back in time through your shirts. . . . I don't know, Harry. I don't know. I've been thinking. This thing is not simple. What if you did something wrong? Took somebody important out of 1937?"

"I won't pick anybody important."

"What if you made a mistake and brought your own grandfather? And something happened to him here?"

"My grandfather was already dead in 1937."

"What if you brought me? I'm already here."

"You didn't live here in 1937."

"What if you brought *you?*"

"I didn't live here either."

"What if you. . . ."

"Manny," Harry said, "I'm not bringing somebody important. I'm not bringing somebody we know. I'm not bringing somebody for permanent. I'm just bringing a nice guy for Jackie to meet, go dancing, see a different kind of nature. A different view of what's possible. An innocence. I'm sure there are fellows here that would do it, but I don't know any, and I don't know how to bring any to her. From there I know. Is this so complicated? Is this so unpredictable?"

"Yes," Manny said. He had on his stubborn look again. How could somebody so skimpy look so stubborn? Harry sighed and moved his lone knight.

"I brought you some whole socks."

"Thank you. That knight, it's not going to help you much."

"Lectures. That's what there was there that there isn't here. Everybody went to lectures. No TV, movies cost money, they went to free lectures."

"I remember," Manny said. "I was a young man myself. Harry, this thing is not simple."

"Yes, it is," Harry said stubbornly.

"1937 was not simple."

"It will work, Manny."

"Check," Manny said.

That evening, Harry went back. This time it was the afternoon of September 16. On newsstands the New York *Times* announced that President Roosevelt and John L. Lewis had talked pleasantly at the White House. Cigarettes cost thirteen cents a pack. Women wore cotton stockings and clunky, high-heeled shoes. Schrafft's best chocolates were sixty cents a pound. Small boys addressed Harry as "sir."

He attended six lectures in two days. A Madame Trefania lectured on theosophy to a hall full of badly-dressed women with thin, pursed lips. A union organizer roused an audience to a pitch that made Harry leave after the first thirty minutes. A skinny, nervous missionary showed slides of religious outposts in China. An archeologist back from a Mexican dig gave a dry, impatient talk about temples to an audience of three people. A New Deal Democrat spoke passionately about aiding the poor, but afterwards addressed all the women present as "Sister." Finally, just when Harry was starting to feel discouraged, he found it.

A museum offered a series of lectures on "Science of Today—and Tomorrow." Harry heard a slim young man with a reddish beard speak with idealistic passion about travel to the moon, the planets, the stars. It seemed to Harry that compared to stars, 1989 might seem reasonably close. The young man had warm hazel eyes and a sense of humor. When he spoke about life in a space ship, he mentioned in passing that women would be freed from much domestic drudgery they now endured. Throughout the lecture, he smoked, lighting cigarettes with a masculine squinting of eyes and cupping of hands. He said that imagination was the human quality that would most help people adjust to the future. His shoes were polished.

But most of all, Harry thought, he had a *glow*. A fine golden Boy Scout glow that made Harry think of old covers for the *Saturday Evening Post*. Which here cost five cents.

After the lecture, Harry stayed in his chair in the front row, outwaiting even the girl with bright red lipstick who lingered around the lecturer, this Robert Gernshon. From time to time, Gernshon glanced over at Harry with quizzical interest. Finally the girl, red lips pouting, sashayed out of the hall.

"Hello," Harry said. "I'm Harry Kramer. I enjoyed your talk. I have something to show you that you would be very interested in."

The hazel eyes turned wary. "Oh, no, no," Harry said. "Something *scientific*. Here, look at this." He handed Gernshon a filtered Vantage Light.

"How long it is," Gernshon said. "What's this made of?"

"The filter? It's made of . . . a new filter material. Tastes milder and cuts down on the nicotine. Much better for you. Look at this." He gave Gernshon a styrofoam cup from MacDonald's. "It's made of a new material, too. Very cheap. Disposable."

Gernshon fingered the cup. "Who are you?" he said quietly.

"A scientist. I'm interested in the science of tomorrow, too. Like you. I'd like to invite you to see my laboratory, which is in my home."

"In your home?"

"Yes. In a small way. Just dabbling, you know." Harry could feel himself getting rattled; the young hazel eyes stared at him so steadily. *Jackie*, he thought. Dead earths. Maggots and carrion. Contempt for mothers. What would Gernshon say? When would Gernshon say *anything*?

"Thank you," Gernshon finally said. "When would be convenient?"

"Now?" Harry said. He tried to remember what time of day it was now. All he could picture was lecture halls.

Gernshon came. It was nine-thirty in the evening of Friday, September 17. Harry walked Gernshon through the streets, trying to talk animatedly, trying to distract. He said that he himself was very interested in travel to the stars. He said it had always been his dream to stand on another planet and take in great gulps of completely unpolluted air. He said his great heroes were those biologists who made that twisty model of DNA. He said science had been his life. Gernshon walked more and more silently.

"Of course," Harry said hastily, "like most scientists, I'm mostly familiar with my own field. You know how it is."

"What is your field, Dr. Kramer?" Gernshon asked quietly.

"Electricity," Harry said, and hit him on the back of the head with a solid brass candlestick from the pocket of his coat. The candlestick had cost him three dollars at a pawn shop.

They had walked past the stores and pushcarts to a point where the locked business offices and warehouses began. There were no passers-by, no muggers, no street dealers, no Guardian Angels, no punk gangs. Only him, hitting an unarmed man with a candlestick. He was no better than the punks. But what else could he do? What else could he *do*? Nothing but hit him softly, so softly that Gernshon was struggling again almost before Harry got his hands and feet tied, well before he got on the blindfold and gag. "I'm sorry, I'm sorry," he kept saying to Gernshon. Gernshon did not look as if the apology made any difference. Harry dragged him into the warehouse.

Rudy was asleep over *Spicy Stories*. Breathing very hard, Harry pulled the young man—not more than 150 pounds, it was good Harry had looked for slim—to the far corner, through the gate, and into his closet.

"Listen," he said urgently to Gernshon after removing the gag. "Listen. I can call the Medicare Emergency Hotline. If your head feels broken. Are you feeling faint? Do you think you maybe might go into shock?"

Gernshon lay on Harry's rug, glaring at him, saying nothing.

"Listen, I know this is maybe a little startling to you. But I'm not a pervert, not a cop, not anything but a grandfather with a problem. My granddaughter. I need your help to solve it, but I won't take much of your time. You're now somewhere besides where you gave your lecture. A pretty long ways away. But you don't have to stay here long, I promise. Just two weeks, tops, and I'll send you back. I promise, on my mother's grave. And I'll make it worth your while. I promise."

"Untie me."

"Yes. Of course. Right away. Only you have to not attack me, because I'm the only one who can get you back from here." He had a sudden inspiration. "I'm like a foreign consul. You've maybe traveled abroad?"

Gernshon looked around the dingy room. "Untie me."

"I will. In two minutes. Five, tops. I just want to explain a little first."

"Where am I?"

"1989."

Gernshon said nothing. Harry explained brokenly, talking as fast as he could, saying he could move from 1989 to September, 1937 when he wanted to, but he could take Gernshon back too, no problem. He said he made the trip often, it was perfectly safe. He pointed out how much farther a small Social Security check, no pension, could go at 1937 prices. He mentioned Manny's strudel. Only lightly did he touch on the problem of Jackie, figuring there would be a better time to share domestic difficulties, and his closet he didn't mention at all. It was hard to keep his eyes averted from the closet door. He did mention how bitter people could be in 1989, how lost, how weary from expecting so much that nothing was a delight, nothing a sweet surprise. He was just working up to a tirade on innocence when Gernshon said again, in a different tone, "Untie me."

"Of course," Harry said quickly, "I don't expect you to believe me. Why should you think you're in 1989? Go, see for yourself. Look at that light, it's still early morning. Just be careful out there, is all." He untied Gernshon and stood with his eyes squeezed shut, waiting.

When nothing hit him, Harry opened his eyes. Gernshon was at the door. "Wait!" Harry cried. "You'll need more money!" He dug into his pocket and pulled out a twenty-dollar bill, carefully saved for this, and all the change he had.

Gernshon examined the coins carefully, then looked up at Harry. He said nothing. He opened the door and Harry, still trembling, sat down in his chair to wait.

Gernshon came back three hours later, pale and sweating. "My God!"

"I know just what you mean," Harry said. "A zoo out there. Have a drink."

Gernshon took the mixture Harry had ready in his toothbrush glass and gulped it down. He caught sight of the bottle, which Harry had left on the dresser: Seagram's V.O., with the cluttered, tiny-print label. He threw the glass across the room and covered his face with his hands.

"I'm sorry," Harry said apologetically. "But then it cost only $3.37 the fifth."

Gernshon didn't move.

"I'm really sorry," Harry said. He raised both hands, palms up, and dropped them helplessly. "Would you . . . would you maybe like an orange?"

Gernshon recovered faster than Harry had dared hope. Within an hour he was sitting in Harry's worn chair, asking questions about the space shuttle; within two hours taking notes; within three become again the intelligent and captivating young man of the lecture hall. Harry, answering as much as he could as patiently as he could, was impressed by the boy's resilience. It couldn't have been easy. What if he, harry, suddenly had to skip fifty-two more years? What if he found himself in 2041? Harry shuddered.

"Do you know that a movie now costs six dollars?"

Gernshon blinked. "We were talking about the moon landing."

"Not any more, we're not. I want to ask *you* some questions, Robert. Do you think the earth is dead, with people sliming all over it like on carrion? Is this a thought that crosses your mind?"

"I . . . no."

Harry nodded. "Good, good. Do you look at your mother with contempt?"

"Of course not. Harry—"

"No, it's my turn. Do you think a woman who marries a man, and maybe the marriage doesn't work out perfect, whose does, but they raise at least one healthy child—say a daughter—that that woman's life has been a defeat and a failure?"

"No. I—"

"What would you think if you saw a drawing of a woman's private parts on the cover of a magazine?"

Gernshon blushed. He looked as if the blush annoyed him, but also as if he couldn't help it.

"Better and better," Harry said. "Now, think carefully on this next one —take your time—no hurry. Does reality seem to you to have sweetness in it as well as ugliness? Take your time."

Gernshon peered at him. Harry realized they had talked right through lunch. "But not all the time in the world, Robert."

"Yes," Gernshon said. "I think reality has more sweetness than ugliness. And more strangeness than anything else. Very much more." He looked suddenly dazed. "I'm sorry, I just—all this has happened so—"

"Put your head between your knees," Harry suggested. "There—better now? Good. There's someone I want you to meet."

Manny sat in the park, on their late-afternoon bench. When he saw them coming, his face settled into long sorrowful ridges. "Harry. Where have you been for two days? I was worried, I went to your hotel—"

"Manny," Harry said, "this is Robert."

"So I see," Manny said. He didn't hold out his hand.

"*Him,*" Harry said.

"Harry. Oh, Harry."

"How do you do, sir," Gernshon said. He held out his hand. "I'm afraid I didn't get your full name. I'm Robert Gernshon."

Manny looked at him—at the outstretched hand, the baggy suit with wide tie, the deferential smile, the golden Baden-Powell glow. Manny's lips mouthed a silent word: *sir?*

"I have a lot to tell you," Harry said.

"You can tell all of us, then," Manny said. "Here comes Jackie now."

Harry looked up. Across the park a woman in jeans strode purposefully towards them. "Manny! It's only Monday!"

"I called her to come," Manny said. "You've been gone from your room two days, Harry, nobody at your hotel could say where—"

"But *Manny,*" Harry said, while Gernshon looked, frowning, from one to the other and Jackie spotted them and waved.

She had lost more weight, Harry saw. Only two weeks, yet her cheeks had hollowed out and new, tiny lines touched her eyes. Skinny lines. They filled him with sadness. Jackie wore a blue tee-shirt that said LIFE IS A BITCH—THEN YOU DIE. She carried a magazine and a small can of mace disguised as hair spray.

"Popsy! You're here! Manny said—"

"Manny was wrong," Harry said. "Jackie, sweetheart, you look—it's good to see you. Jackie, I'd like you to meet somebody, darling. This is Robert. My friend. My friend Robert. Jackie Snyder."

"Hi," Jackie said. She gave Harry a hug, and then Manny one. Harry saw Gernshon gazing at her very tight jeans.

"Robert's a . . . a scientist," Harry said.

It was the wrong thing to say; Harry knew the moment he said it that it was the wrong thing. Science—all science—was, for some reason not completely clear to him, a touchy subject with Jackie. She tossed her long hair back from her eyes. "Oh, yeah? Not *chemical*, I hope?"

"I'm not actually a scientist," Gernshon said winningly. "Just a dabbler. I popularize new scientific concepts, write about them to make them intelligible."

"Like what?" Jackie said.

Gernshon opened his mouth, closed it again. A boy suddenly flashed past on a skateboard, holding a boom box. Metallica blasted the air. Overhead, a jet droned. Gernshon smiled weakly. "It's hard to explain."

"I'm capable of understanding," Jackie said coldly. "Women *can* understand science, you know."

"Jackie, sweetheart," Harry said, "what have you got there? Is that your new book?"

"No," Jackie said, "this is the one I said I'd bring you, by my friend. It's brilliant. It's about a man whose business partner betrays him by selling out to organized crime and framing the man. In jail he meets a guy who has founded his own religion, the House of Divine Despair, and when they both get out they start a new business, Suicide Incorporated, that helps people kill themselves for a fee. The whole thing is just a brilliant denunciation of contemporary America."

Gernshon made a small sound.

"It's a comedy," Jackie added.

"It sounds . . . it sounds a little depressing," Gernshon said.

Jackie looked at him. Very distinctly, she said, "It's reality."

Harry saw Gernshon glance around the park. A man nodded on a bench, his hands slack on his knees. Newspapers and MacDonald's wrappers stirred fitfully in the dirt. A trash container had been knocked over. From beside a scrawny tree enclosed shoulder-height by black wrought iron, a child watched them with old eyes.

"I brought you something else, too, Popsy," Jackie said. Harry hoped that Gernshon noticed how much gentler her voice was when she spoke to her grandfather. "A scarf. See, it's llama wool. Very warm."

Gernshon said, "My mother has a scarf like that. No, I guess hers is some kind of fur."

Jackie's face changed. "What kind?"

"I—I'm not sure."

"Not an endangered species, I hope."

"No. Not that. I'm sure not . . . that."

Jackie stared at him a moment longer. The child who had been watching strolled towards them. Harry saw Gernshon look at the boy with relief. About eleven years old, he wore a perfectly tailored suit and Italian shoes. Manny shifted to put himself between the boy and Gernshon. "Jackie, darling, it's so good to see you. . . ."

The boy brushed by Gernshon on the other side. He never looked up, and his voice stayed boyish and low, almost a whisper. "Crack. . . ."

"Step on one and you break your mother's back," Gernshon said brightly. He smiled at Harry, a special conspiratorial smile to suggest that children, at least, didn't change in fifty years. The boy's head jerked up to look at Gernshon.

"You talking about my mama?"

Jackie groaned. "No," she said to the kid. "He doesn't mean anything. Beat it."

"I don't forget," the boy said. He backed away slowly.

Gernshon said, frowning, "I'm sorry. I'm not sure exactly what all that was, but I'm sorry."

"Are you for real?" Jackie said angrily. "What the fucking hell *was* all that? Don't you realize this park is the only place Manny and my grandfather can get some fresh air?"

"I didn't—"

"That punk runner meant it when he said he won't forget!"

"I don't like your tone," Gernshon said. "Or your language."

"My language!" The corners of Jackie's mouth tightened. Manny looked at Harry and put his hands over his face. The boy, twenty feet away, suddenly let out a noise like a strangled animal, so piercing all four of them spun around. Two burly teenagers were running towards him. The child's face crumpled; he looked suddenly much younger. He sprang away, stumbled, made the noise again, and hurled himself, all animal terror, towards the street behind the park bench.

"No!" Gernshon shouted. Harry turned towards the shout but Gernshon already wasn't there. Harry saw the twelve-wheeler bearing down, heard Jackie's scream, saw Gernshon's wiry body barrel into the boy's. The truck shrieked past, its air brakes deafening.

Gernshon and the boy rose in the street on the other side.

Car horns blared. The boy bawled, "Leggo my suit! You tore my suit!" A red light flashed and a squad car pulled up. The two burly teenagers melted away, and then the boy somehow vanished as well.

"Never find him," the disgruntled cop told them over the clipboard on which he had written nothing. "Probably just as well." He went away.

"Are you hurt?" Manny said. It was the first time he had spoken. His face was ashen. Harry put a hand across his shoulders.

"No," Gernshon said. He gave Manny his sweet smile. "Just a little dirty."

"That took *guts*," Jackie said. She was staring at Gernshon with a frown between her eyebrows. "Why did you do it?"

"Pardon?"

"Why? I mean, given what that kid is, given—oh, all of it—" she gestured around the park, a helpless little wave of her strong young hands that tore at Harry's heart. "Why bother?"

Gernshon said gently, "What that kid is, is a kid."

Manny looked skeptical. Harry moved to stand in front of Manny's expression before anyone wanted to discuss it. "Listen, I've got a wonderful idea, you two seem to have so much to talk about, about . . . bothering, and . . . everything. Why don't you have dinner together, on me? My treat." He pulled another twenty dollar bill from his pocket. Behind him he could feel Manny start.

"Oh, I couldn't," Gernshon said, at the same moment that Jackie said warningly, "Popsy. . . ."

Harry put his palms on both sides of her face. "Please. Do this for me, Jackie. Without the questions, without the female protests. Just this once. For me."

Jackie was silent a long moment before she grimaced, nodded, and turned with half-humorous appeal to Gernshon.

Gernshon cleared his throat. "Well, actually, it would probably be better if all four of us came. I'm embarrassed to say that prices are higher in this city than in . . . that is, I'm not able to . . . but if we went somewhere less expensive, the Automat maybe, I'm sure all four of us could eat together."

"No, no," Harry said. "We already ate." Manny looked at him.

Jackie began, offended, "I certainly don't want—just what do you think is going on here, buddy? This is just to please my grandfather. Are you afraid I might try to jump your bones?"

Harry saw Gernshon's quick, involuntary glance at Jackie's tight jeans. He saw, too, that Gernshon fiercely regretted the glance the instant he had made it. He saw that Manny saw, and that Jackie saw, and that Gernshon saw that they saw. Manny made a small noise. Jackie's face began to turn so black that Harry was astounded when Gernshon cut her off with a dignity no one had expected.

"No, of course not," he said quietly. "But *I* would prefer all of us to have dinner together for quite another reason. My wife is very dear to me, Miss Snyder, and I wouldn't do anything that might make her feel uncomfortable. That's probably irrational, but that's the way it is."

Harry stood arrested, his mouth open. Manny started to shake with what Harry thought savagely had better not be laughter. And Jackie, after staring at Gernshon a long while, broke into the most spontaneous smile Harry had seen from her in months.

"Hey," she said softly. "That's nice. That's really, genuinely, fucking nice."

*　*　*

The weather turned abruptly colder. Snow threatened but didn't fall. Each afternoon Harry and Manny took a quick walk in the park and then went inside, to the chess club or a coffee shop or the bus station or the library, where there was a table deep in the stacks on which they could eat lunch without detection. Harry brought Manny a poor boy with mayo, sixty-three cents, and a pair of imported wool gloves, one dollar on pre-season sale.

"So where are they today?" Manny asked on Saturday, removing the gloves to peek at the inside of the poor boy. He sniffed appreciatively. "Horseradish. You remembered, Harry."

"The museum, I think," Harry said miserably.

"What museum?"

"How should I know? He says, 'The museum today, Harry,' and he's gone by eight o'clock in the morning, no more details than that."

Manny stopped chewing. "What museum opens at eight o'clock in the morning?"

Harry put down his sandwich, pastrami on rye, thirty-nine cents. He had lost weight the past week.

"Probably," Manny said hastily, "they just talk. You know, like young people do, just talk. . . ."

Harry eyed him balefully. "You mean like you and Leah did when you were young and left completely alone."

"You better talk to him soon, Harry. No, to her." He seemed to reconsider Jackie. "No, to *him.*"

"Talk isn't going to do it," Harry said. He looked pale and determined. "Gernshon has to be sent back."

"Be sent?"

"He's *married*, Manny! I wanted to help Jackie, show her life can hold some sweetness, not be all struggle. What kind of sweetness is she going to find if she falls in love with a married man? You know how that goes! Jackie—" Harry groaned. How had all this happened? He had intended only the best for Jackie. Why didn't that count more? "He has to go back, Manny."

"How?" Manny said practically. "You can't hit him again, Harry. You were just lucky last time that you didn't hurt him. You don't want that on your conscience. And if you show him your, uh . . . your—"

"My closet. Manny, if you'd only come see, for a dollar you could get—"

"—then he could just come back any time he wants. So how?"

A sudden noise startled them both. Someone was coming through the stacks. "Librarians!" Manny hissed. Both of them frantically swept the sandwiches, beer (fifteen cents), and strudel into shopping bags. Manny, panicking, threw in the wool gloves. Harry swept the table free of crumbs. When the intruder rounded the nearest bookshelf, Harry was bent over *Making Paper Flowers* and Manny over *Porcelain of the Yung Cheng Dynasty*. It was Robert Gernshon.

The young man dropped into a chair. His face was ashen. In one hand he clutched a sheaf of paper, the handwriting on the last one trailing off into shaky squiggles.

After a moment of silence, Manny said diplomatically, "So where are you coming from, Robert?"

"Where's Jackie?" Harry demanded.

"Jackie?" Gernshon said. His voice was thick; Harry realized with a sudden shock that he had been crying. "I haven't seen her for a few days."

"A few *days*?" Harry said.

"No. I've been . . . I've been. . . ."

Manny sat up straighter. He looked intently at Gernshon over *Porcelain of the Yung Cheng Dynasty* and then put the book down. He moved to the chair next to Gershon's and gently took the papers from his hand. Gernshon leaned over the table and buried his head in his arms.

"I'm so awfully sorry, I'm being such a baby. . . ." His shoulders trembled. Manny separated the papers and spread them out on the library table. Among the hand-copied notes were two slim books, one bound between black covers and the other a pamphlet. *A Memoir of Auschwitz. Countdown to Hiroshima.*

For a long moment nobody spoke. Then Harry said, to no one in particular, "I thought he was going to science museums."

Manny laid his arm, almost casually, across Gernshon's shoulders. "So now you'll know not to be at either place. More people should have only known." Harry didn't recognize the expression on his friend's face, nor the voice with which Manny said to Harry, "You're right. He has to go back."

"But Jackie. . . ."

"Can do without this 'sweetness,' " Manny said harshly. "So what's so terrible in her life anyway that she needs so much help? Is she dying? Is she poor? Is she ugly? Is anyone knocking on her door in the middle of the night? Let Jackie find her own sweetness. She'll survive."

Harry made a helpless gesture. Manny's stubborn face, carved wood under the harsh fluorescent light, did not change. "Even *him* . . . Manny, the things he knows now—"

"You should have thought of that earlier."

Gernshon looked up. "Don't, I—I'm sorry. It's just coming across it, I never thought human beings—"

"No," Manny said. "But they can. You been here, every day, at the library, reading it all?"

"Yes. That and museums. I saw you two come in earlier. I've been reading, I wanted to *know*—"

"So now you know," Manny said in that same surprisingly casual, tough voice. "You'll survive, too."

Harry said, "Does Jackie know what's going on? Why you've been doing all this . . . learning?"

"No."

"And you—what will you do with what you now know?"

Harry held his breath. What if Gernshon just refused to go back? Gernshon said slowly, "At first, I wanted to not return. At all. How can I watch it, World War II and the camps—I have *relatives* in Poland. And then later the bomb and Korea and the gulags and Vietnam and Cambodia and the terrorists and AIDS—"

"Didn't miss anything," Harry muttered.

"—and not be able to *do* anything, not be able to even hope, knowing that everything to come is already set into history—how could I watch all that without any hope that it isn't really as bad as it seems to be at the moment?"

"It all depends what you look at," Manny said, but Gernshon didn't seem to hear him.

"But neither can I stay, there's Susan and we're hoping for a baby . . . I need to think."

"No, you don't," Harry said. "You need to go *back*. This is all my mistake. I'm sorry. You need to go back, Gernshon."

"Lebanon," Gernshon said. "D.D.T. The Cultural Revolution. Nicaragua. Deforestation. Iran—"

"Penicillin," Manny said suddenly. His beard quivered. "Civil rights. Mahatma Gandhi. Polio vaccines. Washing machines." Harry stared at him, shocked. Could Manny once have worked in a hand laundry?

"Or," Manny said, more quietly, "Hitler. Auschwitz. Hoovervilles. The Dust Bowl. What you *look* at, Robert."

"I don't know," Gernshon said. "I need to think. There's so much . . . and then there's that girl."

Harry stiffened. "Jackie?"

"No, no. Someone she and I met a few days ago, at a coffee shop. She just walked in. I couldn't believe it. I looked at her and just went into shock—and maybe she did too, for all I know. The girl looked exactly like me. And she *felt* like—I don't know. It's hard to explain. She felt like *me*. I said hello but I didn't tell her my name; I didn't dare." His voice fell to a whisper. "I think she's my granddaughter."

"Hoo boy," Manny said.

Gernshon stood. He made a move to gather up his papers and booklets, stopped, left them there. Harry stood, too, so abruptly that Gernshon shot him a sudden, hard look across the library table. "Going to hit me again, Harry? Going to kill me?"

"Us?" Manny said. "Us, Robert?" His tone was gentle.

"In a way, you already have. I'm not who I was, certainly."

Manny shrugged. "So be somebody better."

"Damn it, I don't think you understand—"

"I don't think *you* do, Reuven, boychik. This is the way it *is*. That's all. Whatever you had back there, you have still. Tell me, in all that reading, did you find anything about yourself, anything personal? Are you in the history books, in the library papers?"

"The Office of Public Documents takes two weeks to do a search for birth and death certificates," Gernshon said, a little sulkily.

"So you lost nothing, because you really *know* nothing," Manny said. "Only history. History is cheap. Everybody gets some. You can have all the history you want. It's what you make of it that costs."

Gernshon didn't nod agreement. He looked a long time at Manny, and something moved behind the unhappy hazel eyes, something that made Harry finally let out a breath he didn't know he'd been holding. It suddenly seemed that Gernshon was the one that was old. And he *was*—with the fifty-two years he'd gained since last week, he was older than Harry had been in the 1937 of *Captains Courageous* and wide-brimmed fedoras and clean city parks. But that was the good time, the one that Gernshon was going back to, the one Harry himself would choose, if it weren't for Jackie and Manny . . . still, he couldn't watch as Gernshon walked out of the book stacks, parting the musty air as heavily as if it were water.

Gernshon paused. Over his shoulder he said, "I'll go back. Tonight. I will."

After he had left, Harry said, "This is my fault."

"Yes," Manny agreed.

"Will you come to my room when he goes? To . . . to help?"

"Yes, Harry."

Somehow, that only made it worse.

Gernshon agreed to a blindfold. Harry led him through the closet, the warehouse, the street. Neither of them seemed very good at this; they stumbled into each other, hesitated, tripped over nothing. In the warehouse Gernshon nearly walked into a pile of lumber, and in the sharp jerk Harry gave Gernshon's arm to deflect him, something twisted and gave way in Harry's back. He waited, bent over, behind a corner of a building while Gernshon removed his blindfold, blinked in the morning light, and walked slowly away.

Despite his back, Harry found that he couldn't return right away. Why not? He just couldn't. He waited until Gernshon had a large head start and then hobbled towards the park. A carousel turned, playing bright organ music: September 24. Two children he had never noticed before stood just beyond the carousel, watching it with hungry, hopeless eyes. Flowers grew in immaculate flower beds. A black man walked by, his eyes fixed on the sidewalk, his head bent. Two small girls jumping rope were watched by a smiling woman in a blue-and-white uniform. On the sidewalk, just beyond the carousel, someone had chalked a swastika. The black man shuffled over it. A Lincoln Zephyr V-12 drove by, $1090. There was no way it would fit through a closet.

When Harry returned, Manny was curled up on the white chenille bed-spread that Harry had bought for $3.28, fast asleep.

"What did I accomplish, Manny? What?" Harry said bitterly. The day had dawned glorious and warm, unexpected Indian summer. Trees in the park showed bare branches against a bright blue sky. Manny wore an old red sweater, Harry a flannel workshirt. Harry shifted gingerly, grimacing, on his bench. Sunday strollers dropped ice cream wrappers, cigarettes, newspapers, Diet Pepsi cans, used tissues, popcorn. Pigeons quarreled and children shrieked.

"Jackie's going to be just as hard as ever—and why not?" Harry continued. "She finally meets a nice fellow, he never calls her again. Me, I leave a young man miserable on a sidewalk. Before I leave him, I ruin his life. While I leave him, I ruin my back. *After* I leave him, I sit here guilty. There's no answer, Manny."

Manny didn't answer. He squinted down the curving path.

"I don't know, Manny. I just don't know."

Manny said suddenly, "Here comes Jackie."

Harry looked up. He squinted, blinked, tried to jump up. His back made sharp protest. He stayed where he was, and his eyes grew wide.

"Popsy!" Jackie cried. "I've been looking for you!"

She looked radiant. All the lines were gone from around her eyes, all the sharpness from her face. Her very collar bones, Harry thought dazedly, looked softer. Happiness haloed her like light. She held the hand of a slim, red-haired woman with strong features and direct hazel eyes.

"This is Ann," Jackie said. "I've been looking for you, Popsy, because . . . well, because I need to tell you something." She slid onto the bench next to Harry, on the other side from Manny, and put one arm around Harry's shoulders. The other hand kept a close grip on Ann, who smiled encouragement. Manny stared at Ann as at a ghost.

"You see, Popsy, for a while now I've been struggling with something, something really important. I know I've been snappy and difficult, but it hasn't been—everybody needs somebody to love, you've often told me that, and I know how happy you and Grammy were all those years. And I thought there would never be anything like that for me, and certain people were making everything all so hard. But now . . . well, now there's Ann. And I wanted you to know that."

Jackie's arm tightened. Her eyes pleaded. Ann watched Harry closely. He felt as if he were drowning.

"I know this must come as a shock to you," Jackie went on, "but I also know you've always wanted me to be happy. So I hope you'll come to love her the way I do."

Harry stared at the red-haired woman. He knew what was being asked of him, but he didn't believe in it, it wasn't real, in the same way weather going on in other countries wasn't really real. Hurricanes. Drought. Sunshine. When what you were looking at was a cold drizzle.

"I think that of all the people I've ever known, Ann is the most together. The most compassionate. And the most moral."

"Ummm," Harry said.

"Popsy?"

Jackie was looking right at him. The longer he was silent, the more her smile faded. It occurred to him that the smile had showed her teeth. They were very white, very even. Also very sharp.

"I . . . I . . . hello, Ann."

"Hello," Ann said.

"See, I told you he'd be great!" Jackie said to Ann. She let go of Harry and jumped up from the bench, all energy and lightness. "You're wonderful, Popsy! You, too, Manny! Oh, Ann, this is Popsy's best friend, Manny Feldman. Manny, Ann Davies."

"Happy to meet you," Ann said. She had a low, rough voice and a sweet smile. Harry felt hurricanes, drought, sunshine.

Jackie said, "I know this is probably a little unexpected—"

Unexpected. "Well—" Harry said, and could say no more.

"It's just that it was time for me to come out of the closet."

Harry made a small noise. Manny managed to say, "So you live here, Ann?"

"Oh, yes. All my life. And my family, too, since forever."

"Has Jackie . . . has Jackie met any of them yet?"

"Not yet," Jackie said. "It might be a little . . . tricky, in the case of her parents." She smiled at Ann. "But we'll manage."

"I wish," Ann said to her, "that you could have met *my* grandfather. He would have been just as great as your Popsy here. He always was."

"Was?" Harry said faintly.

"He died a year ago. But he was just a wonderful man. Compassionate *and* intelligent."

"What . . . what did he do?"

"He taught history at the university. He was also active in lots of organizations—Amnesty International, the ACLU, things like that. During World War II he worked for the Jewish rescue leagues, getting people out of Germany."

Manny nodded. Harry watched Jackie's teeth.

"We'd like you both to come to dinner soon," Ann said. She smiled. "I'm a good cook."

Manny's eyes gleamed.

Jackie said, "I know this must be hard for you—" but Harry saw that she didn't really mean it. She didn't think it was hard. For her it was so real that it was natural weather, unexpected maybe, but not strange, not out of place, not out of time. In front of the bench, sunlight striped the pavement like bars.

Suddenly Jackie said, "Oh, Popsy, did I tell you that it was your friend Robert who introduced us? Did I tell you that already?"

"Yes, sweetheart," Harry said. "You did."

"He's kind of a nerd, but actually all right."

After Jackie and Ann left, the two old men sat silent a long time. Finally Manny said diplomatically, "You want to get a snack, Harry?"

"She's happy, Manny."

"Yes. You want to get a snack, Harry?"

"She didn't even recognize him."

"No. You want to get a snack?"

"Here, have this. I got it for you this morning." Harry held out an orange, a deep-colored navel with flawless rind: seedless, huge, guaranteed juicy, nurtured for flavor, perfect.

"Enjoy," Harry said. "It cost me ninety-two cents."

S.P. SOMTOW
Lottery Night

Born in Bangkok, Thailand, S.P. Somtow (also known to some as Somtow
Sucharitkul) has lived in six countries and was educated at Eton and Cambridge. Multitalented as well as multilingual, he has an international reputation as an avant-garde composer, and his works have been performed in
more than a dozen countries on four continents. Among his compositions
are "Gongula 3 for Thai and Western Instruments" and "The Cosmic Tril-
ogy." His book publications include the novels *Starship and Haiku*, *Mall-
world*, *Light on the Sound*, *The Darkling Wind*, and *The Fallen Country*.
His most recent books are the novels *The Shattered Horse*, *Vampire Junction*,
and, just released, a new novel, *Moon Dance*. In 1986, he received the
Daedalus Award for *The Shattered Horse*. His story "Fiddling for Water-
buffaloes" was in our Fourth Annual Collection. A resident of the United
States for many years, he now makes his home in California.

In the fast, funny, and gonzo story that follows, he takes us to one of the
strangest and most evocative worlds you're ever likely to experience—mod-
ern-day Bangkok.

Warning: this story is not for the squeamish!

▼
Lottery Night

S. P. SOMTOW

"You've got everything you need now." My grandmother was even more fidgety than usual; she didn't quite look me in the eye as she fanned herself continually with a folded-over fashion magazine. "Your sleeping bag . . . don't forget that. And insect repellent."

"We've been through it a thousand times," I said, trying to conceal my trepidation at the adventure to come.

"Food—"

"A Snickers and a Big Mac," I said. "It's all here." I tapped the brown paper bag. I hoped it wouldn't rain. The air was humid; on the balcony of our high-rise, my little sister Kaew was glued to a soap opera on the portable television—a courtroom scene—and my mother was pounding coconuts.

"I almost forgot . . . the amulets! You mustn't forget the amulets!" My *khun yaai* scrambled up off the floor and hobbled into her room, muttering darkly to herself, just as my father let himself in, took off his shoes and began unbuttoning his khaki police uniform. He glanced at me, squatting in the middle of the room, wishing I could eat the Big Mac now—that was a special treat my Aunt Joom bought for me down at the mall, you could have bought three bowls of noodles for the same price—and immediately began hectoring my mother.

"I really don't understand why we have to send the boy," he said. "Looks like another monsoon shower tonight. I could go myself."

"There's no need to baby him," my little sister piped up. "He's fourteen years old and he polishes his rocket every night."

"I do *not!*" I said. "Well, not every night."

"Where ever did you learn such filthy language, little girl?" my grandmother screeched from the inner room. My father couldn't stop himself from laughing.

My mother patiently pounded coconuts. On television, in the soap opera, the judge was declaring that the two-headed daughter of the peasant woman was the rightful heir to the Petchari millions, and the lawyer had just revealed that he was actually the god Indra in disguise.

"I mean, honored mother of my wife," my father went on, after he had recovered from laughing. "I *am* the patriarch of this family, and it's only proper if there's any favor to be sought from the venerable ancestors, *I* should be the one to—"

"Don't be silly," my grandmother said, coming back in with a tray of amulets. My father quickly ducked so that his head would not be higher than hers. "In the first place, it's your doing that we're reduced to these present straits; in the second, he was her favorite great-great-nephew; in the third, you know very well that your Great-Aunt Snit hated your guts. She couldn't even stand to be in the same room as you when she was alive. Why on earth would she want to tell you a winning lottery number?"

"Even so," my father said, "the dead can be propitiated with the right gifts . . . and . . . and that was *years* ago, and it was because she was senile and kept mistaking me for the man who jilted her for an Indian woman."

My mother strained the pulped coconut through a cheesecloth and poured some of the juice into a *Batman* glass for my sister to drink. "We can't take any chances," she said. There was a sad finality to her voice, and my father sat down sulkily on a floor cushion.

"It's all superstition anyway," he said. "If everyone could win the lottery by sleeping in a cemetery and having some charitable ghost whisper the winning number in a dream . . . why, everybody'd be a millionaire! Some of those grave-yards get more crowded than the kick-boxing stadium on Wednesday nights . . . and speaking of *chok muai* . . ." He stalked out to the balcony and started to twiddle the channel. The shrill snarl of the war oboe filled the air, punctuated by the pounding of drums. He turned the volume up so high it even drowned out the traffic.

"Oh, please, *khun poh*! I wanna see what happens to the two-headed—" my sister started whining.

"Shut up. I've got a lot of money riding on the red tonight."

My mother and grandmother looked at each other and rolled their eyes. To me, it was just one more indication of our desperate plight. My father had faithfully gambled on the blue for ten years.

"The amulets," my grandmother said. She lifted each one in turn, held it in between her palms in an attitude of reverence. As my father farted and belched in the background, she enumerated their virtues. "Here's an old and very powerful *luangpoh* I acquired from a Chinaman who makes his living gambling on cockfights . . . here's an amethyst *pohng ham* that was dug up in Chiang Rai . . ." She put each one around my neck and ran through a couple of mantras appropriate to each. "Are you sure you'll be all right with all this American food?" she said. "I don't want you getting diarrhea in a graveyard in the middle of the night. You might attract a *phii krasue*."

I shuddered. For the first time it occurred to me that tonight's outing wasn't just another boyish lark—it was to be an encounter with the super-natural world that surrounds us all. No one wants to attract a *phii krasue*. Many *phii krasue* are seductively beautiful at first—until they lose their heads. We'd had one in the family once, my great-great-great-uncle Noi, whose bad karma had caused him to be reincarnated as one of these vile creatures. I had been raised on tales of how his head used to detach itself from his body, and, dragging the slimy guts behind it, would slither around the family compound using its tongue as a pseudopod. *Phii krasue* live entirely on shit, of course, and there was a practical side to having a malevolent spirit around in those olden days without indoor plumbing, but as soon as my family had been able to afford a toilet, back in the late 1950s, my grandmother had an exorcist brought in to propel my multi-uncle on to the next world.

This was long before I was born. I had never seen the much-vaunted village home, never even so much as set foot beyond the city limits of Bangkok except when we went to the beach; then again, everyone knows there is nothing worthwhile outside the City-of-Angels-the-Divine-and-Great-Me-tropolis-Etc.-Etc.

My grandmother finished bedecking me with amulets and was now blessing me. My father was still absorbed in his boxing match. My mother was in the kitchen, praying to a plaster reproduction of the Emerald Buddha that sat in a niche above the refrigerator, next to the photographs of Their Divine Majesties. The smell of burning joss-sticks wafted through the living room. I closed my eyes, trying to achieve a state of *samadhi* before setting out on this pilgrimage that might mean the difference between the family retreating to the boondocks or moving to a more upscale condominium on Sukhumvit.

In the midst of my rêverie I heard my grandmother singing. It was an old lullaby from the village in a hick dialect, but it was strangely soothing. A mood of profound inner *shanti* swept over me, but it was soon disrupted by the sound of my elders arguing.

"I really should drive him down to the cemetery myself," my father was saying.

"Don't be a fool," said my grandmother. "That old Datsun pickup of yours won't make it past the edge of the *soi*."

"Yes, but I could take him in my police car," said my father, "and maybe get a couple of hundred baht in traffic bribes on my way home."

"How crass," said the *khun yaai*.

"I'll take the bus," I said. "The *soi* is flooded anyway."

*   *   *

I didn't want a ride from my father because I had a secret errand or two to do on the way to the cemetery where *Khun Chuad* Snit's remains had lain since the time of the Divine King Chulalongkorn. I needed time to get in the right state of mind; I wanted to eat the Big Mac; and I had a mind to see if my American friend, Joey Friedberg, wanted to come along.

The *soi* was completely flooded from yesterday's monsoon outburst and I had to take a boat to the main road at a cost of two baht. I was dressed in my best—I didn't want to feel ashamed in front of my ancestors—a Ralph Lauren shirt from the best counterfeiter in town, a gold Rolex that would have fooled Mr. Rolex himself. I didn't want to ruin my clothes, so instead of climbing up the drainage pipe to get into Joey's apartment, I actually rang at the front gate. My Aunt Joom, who worked for the Friedbergs as a maid or something, buzzed me in.

The first thing I heard was the television. Traditional *ranaat* music filmed the living room. It was one of those cultural programs that are only watched by old people and American anthropologists. You see, the Friedbergs were a very unusual species of American. Like real people, they didn't wear shoes in the house, and instead of going to isb, Joey actually went to a Thai school. Joey's mother made a living entirely by writing scholarly papers about our national peculiarities, for which the Ford Foundation supplied everything: the apartment, the servants, the chauffeur. (She had even done a fifty-page monograph analyzing all the Sanskrit components of the true name the City-of-Angels-the-Divine-and-Great-Metropolis-Etc.-Etc., which is, of course, the only city whose name is so long it is always written with two "Etc.".s.) She didn't appear to have a husband. At the moment, Mrs. Friedberg was having Aunt Joom walk back and forth across the living room striking various statuesque poses, and taking endless snapshots.

"Oh, Samraan," she called out to me, confusing me a bit, because I wasn't used to being called by my True Name, "Joey'll be right out . . . Joom, *undulate* a bit more, will ya? . . . beautiful, beautiful."

Joey came out of his bedroom. He was loaded down with gear: compasses, Swiss army knives, canteens, dangling all over his gangly frame. We stood for a while, transfixed by Aunt Joom's virtuoso performance. She was wiggling her hips, fluttering her eyelids, and slithering sinuously across the room as the lanky Mrs. Friedberg snapped furiously away, leaping over sofas and climbing onto credenzas, to get the best possible angles.

"Rad!" said Joey.

"Totally," I said in English, impressed in spite of myself.

"The illusion is complete," Joey said, switching to Thai.

"I've known her all my life, and I *still* can hardly tell she isn't a woman," I said.

Aunt Joom paused for a breath. "Let me get you a Coke," she said to me.

"You really don't have to, Joom dear," said Mrs. Friedberg. "You're not a servant, you know." Nonetheless, Joom minced off to the kitchen, every inch the proper serving maid, though the nuances of her servility were doubtless lost on her mistress. Mrs. Friedberg sighed. "I can't wait to get these pictures developed."

"What're they for, Mom?"

"Oh, it's a paper called '*Katoey*: transvestitism in the resonating contexts of contemporary Thai society." She shook her long red hair into place and noticed me at last. Joey and I stood side by side. My friend was, of course, much taller than me, and his height was further accentuated by his im-maculately spiked blond hair. He limped a bit, and one arm was longer than the other; it was from an auto accident he'd been in when he was five that had put him in a coma for a year. He wore a neon pink teeshirt that depicted a surfing triceratops. "Going camping, dears?" Mrs. Friedberg said to us.

"Aw c'mon, Mom," said Joey. "I told you all about it, didn't I? Like, it's lottery night—tomorrow's the last day to buy lottery tickets—and we're spend-ing the night at the tomb of Samraan's *Khun Chuad* Snit!"

"Oh, ah . . . right! The business about sleeping in a graveyard and getting winning lottery numbers from ghosts, right? Interesting example of cultural syncretism . . . gotta do a paper on it sometime . . . well, be careful, dears," she said, "and Joey, maybe you can do some field notes or something." Absently, she handed him a five hundred baht note. White people never know the value of money.

I closed my eyes and thought of the ordeal to come. It was a bad idea to bring Joey, I thought. Even though I'd promised, even though he and his mother were almost like Thai people. I was going to end up as a footnote in Mrs. Friedberg's dissertation and even Joey wasn't going to take the spirits seriously. Maybe they'd be so angry at my bringing a *farang* that they wouldn't materialize at all. I found myself attempting to put myself back into a state of *samadhi*. Without thinking, I began to hum the lullaby my grandmother had sung to me earlier that day.

When I opened my eyes again, Mrs. Friedberg was staring at me, wide-eyed. "Why Samraan, that was such a curious, *wonderful* song. What was it?"

"Just . . . a song, Mrs. Friedberg. My grandmother's . . ."

"From the provinces?"

I was suddenly embarrassed at having betrayed the hick origins of my family. I don't know why I was so sensitive about losing face; they wouldn't have understood anyway. I didn't know what to say, so I just stared at the floor.

"Does your grandmother know any more of those songs? Ya know, the Ford Foundation's shelling out mega-shekels for ethnomusicology these days—"

"Right, Mom, later," Joey said, rolling his eyes. He just couldn't wait to be out of there.

As we reached the door, we heard Mrs. Friedberg's final admonishment. "And don't get stoned!"

"Who's she fucking kidding?" Joey said to me, pulling a reefer out of his pocket just as we reached the corner of Soi Jintana and the main road. We were on higher ground and the water was only ankle deep. Banana trees lined the walls of the apartment complex. The sun was setting behind veils of smog; the odors of gasoline and night-blooming jasmine wafted across the skyline of high-rises and silhouetted pagodas. Traffic screeched endlessly by and we had to wait ten minutes before we could safely jaywalk the intersection. At the corner, a withered Indian hawked lottery tickets.

"Not yet," I said. "Not until tomorrow."

"I can't wait," Joey said. A pretty young prostitute of indeterminate gender accosted him, and he yelled back. *"Hii men meuan turian kuan!!"*

"Ai haa! You can't say things like that!" The irate whore was coming after us, swinging her purse. She was making straight for me—of course, it hadn't occurred to her that it was the *farang* boy calling her names.

"Duck!" I grabbed Joey's arm and pushed him into an alley.

'Didn't I get it right?" he said as he lit up.

"Of course you got it right," I said, "but you can't just be going around telling someone her pussy smells like a puréed durian fruit and hope to get away with—"

"Shit!" he said, laughing too loud. "She's fucking gaining on us!" Wielding the purse with deadly accuracy, the woman fetched me a hefty clout on the side of the head. Joey yanked me into the back doorway of a crowded noodle shop, and we dived under a table and scrambled through the forest of diners' legs to reach the front door.

A bus appeared and we ran wildly after it. About a dozen people were hanging on the door and the bus careened at a forty-five degree angle as it rounded a corner. As we hopped on board, the prostitute tripped over a stray dog and sprawled into a sidewalk noodle vendor. We hung out of the side of the bus, clutching the door-pole with one hand, our legs trailing the traffic as we wove lurching through the ooze of jam-packed cars, glinting in the sunset like the scales of a giant serpent.

"Why do I always have to rescue you, little brother?" Joey said.

"Fuck off," I said in English, "and don't call me 'little brother.' " Joey might be my best friend, but that didn't give him the right to count me as his relative. Foreigners never know their place.

My great-great-aunt's tomb was in a pretty out-of-the-way *tambol* of the City of Etc. Etc. In the days when Great-great-aunt Snit had been cremated and her ashes interred there, there was this temple in the middle of nowhere, surrounded by paddy fields. Now there were a few signs of development; beside the temple was the skeleton of a shopping mall-in-progress, and there was a half-built overpass that hulked over the cemetery. There was a palatial movie theatre across the street from the cemetery. It was showing *Aliens*; a thirty-foot-tall statue of the H.R. Giger monster welcomed the patrons, its mechanized jaws opening and closing to the strains of a Michael Jackson song. At its entrance, a bunch of kids hawked boxes of incense sticks and candles in case someone might want to make a quick offering at the shrine across the street.

"Hey, maybe we can go to the movie first," Joey said. "We've got all night."

"I don't know why I ever brought you along." He just wasn't taking this seriously enough. And my whole family's fate at stake! "You're only going to embarrass me."

"Embarrass you? How come you're so sure *you're* going to get a revelation from the spirits? How do you know they won't come to *me*?"

"They don't speak English."

"But they're supernatural beings, right? They probably all know English. They probably don't even speak real languages—they're probably all telepaths."

"They won't come to you, Joey, because . . . because . . . they don't have spirits in America. They don't have reincarnation and stuff. In America, people just die and turn to dust."

"The Friedbergs aren't like other Americans. We're liberals."

"And how, pray, are the supernatural beings to know that? You all look alike to them."

"Fuckin' bigot," he said in English, and slapped a mosquito.

By now we had crossed the street and reached the gate of the cemetery, and I was experiencing real dread. It was all very well hearing all one's life that I was the favorite great-nephew of this long-dead woman, but my only memory of her was that of a white-haired, cadaverous figure with a face like a skeleton and teeth blackened from betel nut, sitting cross-legged in the shadows, screeching abuse at any family member who passed by without showing appropriate obeisance. I had been ushered into her presence perhaps three or four times; each time it was either my birthday or New Year's Day. I would prostrate myself at her feet, as was proper for such a momentous occasion, with such a venerable ancestor, and look up into her fierce sunken eyes, and she would hand me a little velvet bag containing a little spending money.

"Getting big," she would say. "Getting big, aren't you, tadpole! Can you talk yet?"

I could, of course, but she was too senile to realize it, and besides, I was too scared to utter a word in her exalted presence. Her house smelled of sandalwood and of the scented paste old women put on their faces to soften their skin.

She died before my fifth birthday; the funeral was a lot of fun, with all my favorite foods, including Mr. Donut, which had just opened in Siam Square and was the biggest craze of 1979 among the young.

It was a wrought-iron gate in a design of angelic *thephanoms* with folded palms. Joey vaulted up; much to my annoyance, I had to have help from him to get over. It seemed to get dark the minute our feet touched the ground. The walls of the cemetery cut off the brash neon lights of the movie theaters and the noodle shops. The air was thick with mosquitoes. "Here," I said, breaking out the insect repellent, "use this." We stood in the shadow of the wall for a while, rubbing our arms and legs with the nasty-smelling liquid from the British Dispensary. The last of the sunlight died.

Joey turned on his flashlight. "Well, we'd better find the tomb," he said. I started to walk toward where I thought the path was. I bumped into a gravestone. A temple dog howled in the distance, and I smelled incense. Joey found me, led me toward the gravel pathway. As our eyes got more used to the darkness, three low pagodas were visible in the middle distance, bathed in moonlight and faint reflected neon. "C'mon, little brother," said Joey.

I started to cuss him out, but I remembered in time that I was in a sacred place. I murmured a quick prayer to the Lord Buddha, hoping it would compensate for my impiety. We walked on. The pagodas never seemed to get any nearer. The insects twittered and keened and made it hard to think. We walked on. Out of the insect voices came a persistent rhythmic buzzing, and I suddenly realized that it came from Joey. He was listening to his Walkman. "Dépêche Mode!" He was shouting, as those with earphones are wont to do. His voice echoed. I saw rows and rows of white marble tombs and I realized that I had become very frightened.

"Respect the dead," I said, yanking away his headphones.

We walked on.

The path turned. There was another kind of music now, high-pitched, tinkly. We must be getting close to our goal. I heard footsteps. Froze in my tracks. Soft, padding footsteps on gravel. Something was approaching. Someone . . . in a long, white robe, with long white hair . . . moving ineluctably in our direction . . . humming weirdly . . .

"C'mon," Joey said. "Maybe he knows the way."

"He's p-p-probably a—"

The figure stopped. "Please excuse me," he said in a thick Indian accent, "I am having lost my way. Are you not the two gentlemen who ordered an exorcism?"

"Awesome!" said Joey.

"No . . . we're here for the lottery."

"Oh . . . second fork on the left is where most of the lottery dream-seekers are, isn't it?" he said. "But where, oh where are those customers of mine?"

"What kind of exorcism are you doing?" Joey said.

"Oh . . . no major thing," said the Brahmin priest, ". . . just a little matter of a *phii krasue* that has gotten out of hand. My client's sister-in-law, Khun Mayurii, was doomed to wander the earth in this hideous shape because of some unflattering remarks she once made concerning a minor functionary of His Divine Majesty's Ministry of the Interior."

"What terrible karma," I said, shaking my head in rueful sympathy.

"Well, sirs, if you should ever need any help along those lines . . ." he solemnly removed a card from his robes and handed it to me. I read: "Shri Narayan Dass: houses blessed, exorcisms, scrying, love potions, and general astrology, reasonable rates."

"Quite a racket," Joey said.

"Don't be disrespectful!" I said. "Don't you see he's a spirit doctor, a *mo phii*?"

"No, the young *farang* boy is being quite correct," said Shri Narayan Dass. "It is something of a racket, but it beats selling polyester in Pahurat to the *nouveau riche*." He fished something else out of his capacious robes —it was a length of cotton rope. "Take this *saisin*," he said. "That should stave off the more egregious evil spirits."

I thanked him humbly and watched him leave the path and shamble, muttering incantations, into the darkness.

"Jesus," Joey said, "that dude could really clean up on the Beverly Hills guru circuit. Why are exorcists always Indians, anyways?"

"They must have ancient secrets which the Thais, people of a modern kingdom, have lost," I said, wondering about this for the first time.

We followed the exorcist's instructions, and presently we reached the oldest part of the cemetery, where my great-great-aunt's ashes were. As my father had predicted, it was a madhouse. There was a Porsche parked on the grass beside one ostentatious monument, and a woman in black was praying hysterically beside it, weeping and shrieking imprecations in Chinese. There was hardly a tomb without a straw mat laid out next to it and someone desperately trying to sleep or slapping mosquitoes. There was a woman hawking meatballs on skewers with chili sauce as well as lottery tickets. A man in a pair of silk pajamas was watching a *Twilight Zone* episode on a portable television set. The fragrance of incense melded with the stagnant odor of a nearby canal.

Where was my great-great-aunt's tomb? Every New Year I had paid my respects there with the rest of my family. In daylight I could have found it in my sleep, but now everything looked different. I wandered around in circles while Joey went off to buy food.

It was maddening. The place was getting more and more crowded by the minute. Suddenly I heard Joey cry out, "This way!"

"You've never been here before." Angrily, I stalked toward him.

His eyes were glazed over. "Something awesome's happening . . . like, déjà vu, dude! I've been here before! I remember . . . Jesus, I remember—"

"Control yourself!" He must have smoked that entire joint while I was looking the other way.

"I know the way, I'm telling you!" he said, jumping up and down. He dragged me past the food vendor toward—

"Tadpole!" A familiar voice. It was Aunt Joom. "How nice to see you!"

She was wearing an embroidered silk sarong, gold bracelets, necklaces and earrings, and pancake makeup an inch thick. She had been praying at a tomb. As Aunt Joom got up from her prostrate position with a chillingly feminine wiggle of the hips, I could see Khun Chuad Snit's photograph, a frayed black-and-white thing in a gold-bordered frame, in the light of Aunt Joom's votive candles. I was infuriated to learn that Joey had been right about the location of the monument.

"Oh, don't worry, darling," said Aunt Joom, as she applied another layer of lipstick, "I'm not here to steal your lottery dream. Your great-great-aunt never liked me anyway. It's the exorcism, you know, across the way. Khun Phairoj, who's hired the priciest Brahmin to help rid his sister-in-law of the curse of—"

"We met him," Joey interjected.

"Well, he made a pledge to the Four-Faced-Brahma shrine next to the Erawan hotel that, if the exorcism worked, he'd have a troupe of dancers immediately perform 'The Dance of the Celestial Chickens' . . . well, a group of us girls is standing by in case everything works out as planned."

"I see." I wasn't surprised; transvestites are always in demand as dancers, as they can switch roles with ease.

"Just don't sleep next to me," Joey jested.

Aunt Joom laughed. "We *katoeys* always make white people queasy, I don't know why. But while I'm here . . . why don't I buy you some meatballs? You look like you're starving."

"I've got a Big Mac," I said.

"Bah. That stuff'll give you Reagan's revenge every time."

"I'd love some meatballs," said Joey, and the two of them went off, hand in hand, cracking obscene jokes about meatballs, leaving me alone with my Big Mac, my Snickers bar, and the spirits of my ancestors.

First I took out the *saisin* the exorcist had given me—better safe than sorry. I looped it around some bushes so that the cord made a sacred circle around my great-great-aunt's memorial. It was past midnight. The carnival atmosphere had subsided. It was time for serious business, communion with the supernatural. The moon had disappeared behind a high-rise that towered over the temple wall. In the distance, the exorcism was going on; most of the crowd, including my aunt, had gone to watch, leaving only the dedicated lottery-dreamers. Joey, stuffed with *luk chin* in chili sauce, had gone to sleep with his Walkman, and there was a buzz of Metallica coming from around his head.

Carefully I lit seven joss-sticks and seven candles. I arranged the candles beneath my great-great-aunt's photograph. I lifted my folded palms to my lips and murmured a prayer to the Lord Buddha, then hung a *puangmalai* wreath of jasmine petals across the tombstone. Soft sound in the night: the stridulant crickets and the snoring dreamers, the far-off music of the exorcism and the farther-off traffic along the overpass. As far as I could see, I was the only one awake. I was alone, the still center of the crowded city.

What was I to say to my great-great-aunt?

I gazed at the photograph in its brass frame. I had seen the picture before—we had one like it in a family album at home—but it was nothing like the withered betel-nut-chewing crone of my childhood memories. This was a young woman. Her hair was like a woman on a videotape box I'd once seen at Joey's house—Claudette Colbert in *Cleopatra*. She wore Western-style clothes—the height of 1920s fashion—and I remembered that she had once been the third minor wife of a provincial functionary of the government of His Divine Majesty the Sixth Rama. We'd been somebody back in those days! Our karma had certainly taken a sad turn for the worse, with my father forced to eke out a living collecting bribes from traffic violators, unable to afford the down payment even on a one-room condominium.

I put my hands together in the *phnom mue* gesture and addressed the photograph in tones of deepest humility: "Great-great-aunt," I said, "things really aren't going too well for your descendants at the moment."

Light flickered. Had the photograph been smiling a moment before? Somehow the monument seemed taller, the fragrance of incense more pungent. I felt a chill. There were spirits present. Somewhere. The cold tickled the base of my spine. Even though it was a hot tropical night, the dark air pregnant with impending rain. The cold moved up the small of my back.

"Great-great-aunt!" I said. "You're frightening me! Don't you remember me, the one you used to give the little bags of money to twice a year?" The photograph wavered . . . or was it the candlelight, the wisps of incense? "Listen, we really have to win the lottery," I said urgently. "We're getting farther and farther behind on the rent. My father drinks too much and he spends the rest of the money gambling on boxers. I know you don't like my grandmother because she accused you of being a whore for agreeing to be the mistress of a government official but it was just your ticket out of the village and into the provincial capitol—and it wasn't her fault your husband died of syphilis! I know you always thought my father was a layabout, and I know how disappointed you were that my mother married him . . . but it's all karma anyway. So show compassion to me, honored great-great-aunt, and even if you don't tell me the number for the jackpot, at least give us one of the lesser prizes, enough to scrape by for a month or two while my father gets his life back together again."

A peal of thunder made me jump. I looked around, panicking. Joey was still asleep. A slithering sound in the grass nearby. A snake? I listened. Only the crickets. I made sure that the protective *saisin* was securely fastened. No evil spirit would dare profane such a barrier. I listened carefully again. No snakes . . . only the moist wind rifling the leaves of the mango trees next to the cemetery wall.

"*Khun Chuad*?" I said. "Are you listening to me?"

There was thunder, more distant. My heart was thumping. The grass was whispering. I unrolled the sleeping bag and lay on it with my head propped up against the stone. My stomach growled. I was getting nervous. I wolfed down the candy bar and the Big Mac. I could hear the chanting of the exorcist, somewhere far away. I burped. "Excuse me," I whispered, hoping that my venerable ancestor would not take offense. "I shouldn't have eaten my food so fast. Grandmother is always telling me to chew slowly—"

I stopped.

There was someone standing just beyond the *saisin* . . . a woman. She was young. A strange perfume emanated from her. She wore a traditional *phasin* of black silk. Her lips were red and glossy, her hair done in that 1920s flapper style . . . she was a living, breathing incarnation of the photograph of my great-great-aunt Snit. And yet . . .

"My favorite grand-nephew," she said. Very softly. Shook her head. The moonlight danced in her soft dark hair. "Come to me . . . I always loved you best."

There was something not quite right about her.

My heartbeat quickened. I felt hot and cold all over and suddenly I realized I was beginning to get an erection. I breathed in perfume mingled with incense and it intoxicated me. How could this be? I got up . . . took a tentative step toward her . . .

Something grabbed my foot.

"Joey! Let go!"

"Stay inside the sacred circle, you idiot!"

"But it's my great-great-"

He leaped off his sleeping bag, tried to restrain me. I freed myself. The vision of my ancestor shimmered in the humid air. He lurched after me but his limp made him trip over a stone. Just as I reached the *saisin*, he managed to get hold of my ankles. I reached out my arms to the woman as she floated toward me in a cloud of mist. Her eyes glittered. She grasped my hands. She was cold, colder than ice. I screamed.

At that moment, with my friend trying to pull me back into the circle and the spirit trying to pull me out, I felt the first pangs of Reagan's revenge. A moist, noisy fart tore through my sphincter. I could have died of embarrassment. I looked up into eyes that were glowing like charcoal embers. The hands gripped tighter, burning my wrists. Joey tugged with all his might, his back against the tomb.

"Let go, one of you," I gasped. "Or I'll crap in my pants!"

"Don't do that!" Joey shouted. "Can't you see, that's exactly what it wants you to do!"

I didn't think I could hold it for another second. I was going to defile my great-great-aunt's tomb and I was never going to receive her blessing now. I had to get away . . . find a good spot, maybe among the mango trees . . .

I wriggled free of Joey and was pulled across the sacred cord. No sooner was I clear of its protection than I saw that the hands that gripped me were no hands . . . they were the slimy, prehensile tongue of a *phii krasue*! "The Lord Buddha protect me!" I said. The tongue tightened its hold, squeezing my arms like a hungry python. I could see the face. Bits of skull showed through the torn flesh. Yellow goo spewed from pustulant sores. The *phii krasue's* oesophagus and intestines flailed about on the grass like a mass of serpents.

"Get back inside the circle!" Joey screamed. I turned around. Rising from the tomb in a miasma of candlelit incense fumes was the skeletal form of Great-great-aunt Snit! The ghost looked at me, its finger pointing straight at me, and I felt all the terror I'd felt when I was three years old and being ushered into her presence, and I knew I was going to shit myself but I didn't dare do so because I knew that the *phii krasue* wanted to feast upon my excrement . . .

Where was Joey? He was nowhere to be seen. His voice had been coming from the place where my great-great-aunt's ghost now stood, her shroud flapping in the wind. The *phii krasue's* intestines were inching up my leg. I couldn't move my hands. I struggled. Sweat was pouring down my neck and mingling with the creature's slime. My wrists were getting so slick that the demon's tongue was losing its purchase. I managed to ease my hand toward my chest, reached into my shirt, pulled out one of my grandmother's amulets.

The *phii krasue* screamed! The tongue slithered away and on the creature's forehead was a fuming burning mark in the shape of the Lord Buddha! I got up as the evil spirit tumbled onto the grass. The scream was waking up all the lottery dreamers. Flashlights were coming on all around me. The pain was pounding at my abdomen. I was flushed with embarrassment. The *phii krasue* circled me warily, now and then trying to lasso my ankles with its tongue.

"The Lord Buddha preserve us! It's a *phii krasue*!" someone shouted. My writhing assailant and I stood in a pool of flashlight beams.

"How dare you wake me up!" came another voice from behind another tombstone. "I've two more digits to go!"

"Joey!" I screamed. But Joey was not there. In his place loomed the specter of my great-great-aunt, impassively watching me in my shame.

I had to find a bush, a tree, some secluded spot—

I started to run.

"It's after the boy!" someone shouted.

"It must be that spirit they've been exorcizing down at the other end of the cemetery."

"After it!"

I ran, tripping over gravestones, stopping now and then to brandish an amulet behind me. Others were right behind me; some waving their own amulets, some there just to enjoy the spectacle. The meatball vendor was back too, cheerfully hawking as we ran. I sprinted, clutching my stomach.

Voices in the distance . . . there was the exorcism in full swing, by the side of the canal! There was Shri Narayan Dass on a dais above the throng, sitting in the lotus position in his white exorcizing robes, chanting up a storm, with clouds of incense whirling about his face. Statues of Hindu gods glared down from a plinth behind him. Sacred exorcising music, tinkling xylophones and wailing oboes, poured out of a portable CD player. I saw Aunt Joom, in her dancing costume, ready to go on. Khun Phairoj, the sponsor of the exorcism, sat in a big rattan chair, a fat man looking even fatter in his white Yves St. Laurent suit. A length of *saisin* cord wound round and round the nearby trees and through the folded palms of all the celebrants in the ritual. The exorcist was in the throes of a *khao* song, foaming at the mouth and spewing forth sublimely incomprehensible utterances as the spirits of celestial beings held his *vinyaan* in thrall.

In the throes of a somewhat more earthly need, I hardly had time to take in the splendor of the situation—although I did notice Mrs. Friedberg in the audience, holding the *saisin* in one hand while feverishly taking notes with the other.

It was Aunt Joom who saw me first. "It's Samraan! And the *phii krasue* is after him!" she shrieked.

The screaming became contagious. Panicking, people were crawling over each other in their haste to reach the gate. Aunt Joom, wringing her hands, stood looking this way and that. "Aunt Joom, I've got Reagan's revenge!" I screamed. "That's why it's after me!"

Suddenly there came an eerie voice from high above, from the platform on which the spirit doctor had been meditating. "Don't hold it anymore, boy! We can assuage the creature's hideous hunger and trap it at the same time!"

"Yes, sir," I shouted. "I'll try." There was no need to try. I had begun to *khii laad* the moment I heard the voice of Shri Narayan Dass.

"You must now be running toward me!" came the spirit doctor's voice, high-pitched, ethereal, plaintive. "Come to me. Try to let it out just a bit at a time . . ."

I stumbled forward with the *phii krasue* hobbling my left leg. The creature's clammy tongue slid up and down my calf. It fed frenziedly, propelled by the filthy obsession that was the sole purpose of its existence. The exorcist came stomping down the steps, holding aloft an image of a many-headed Hindu deity. With his other hand he twirled a length of *saisin*, like a bullroper in a western. An acolyte struggled to keep up, carrying a huge silver bowl of lustral water. Behind him came the crowd. The creature fed. I could hardly breathe as the wet guts twined around my stomach, pumping me for more.

They were all around me now—how could Joey be sleeping through all this?—cheering on the exorcist as he bore down on the monster and me. Dipping a sheaf of twigs into the lustral water, intoning a sacred prayer to Yama, the god of the underworld, Shri Narayan Dass began asperging us both. The chanting crescendoed.

"Be at peace now, evil spirit! Go and be reborn in a decent human shape!"

With each shower, I felt the creature shudder, its grip tightening. I tried to scream but only a squawk came out. Finally the exorcist, standing over us as we thrashed, began flagellating us with the sacred twigs, chanting wildly, foaming at the mouth, his eyes completely white.

The crowd gasped. The *phii krasue* began to scream; a heartrending cry, the cry of a woman in pain. I felt the intestines relax their hold on me. I turned. Smoke billowed upward toward the moon. The sacred waters struck me; I felt all my uncleanness melt from me. I slid into the grass. I saw the monster slowly begin to transform into the corpse of a beautiful woman; Khun Mayuril, the unfortunate woman whose karma had caused her to walk the earth as the lowliest of demons . . .

I heard Aunt Joom's voice from somewhere in the throng. "For the sake of mercy, give the boy something to eat!" That was the last thing I wanted. I lay on my back, against the soft earth, watching the clouds stream across the face of the moon. A few more drops fell on my face . . . surely not the lustral waters. No. The monsoon was about to break. We were all going to be drenched. A few more drops. People were murmuring, looking hastily around for shelter, and I could see Khun Phairoj, kneeling, weeping beside the body of his late sister-in-law.

It was at that moment that I saw Joey Friedberg. He was walking slowly toward me out of the darkness. He walked strangely, with the grace of a woman. He wasn't walking at all. He was gliding. Floating toward me on a carpet of mist.

"Joey," I said softly, "how could you have slept through all that? The exorcism—the *phii krasue*—"

"Samraan," Joey said. It was a haunting voice, a voice out of some past life. . . . the voice of a beautiful woman, rich against the patter of impending rain.

"Joey—you didn't turn into a *katoey*, did you?" It had never occurred to me that the Americans had any people like my aunt Joom.

"No, my child . . ."

"You're possessed!"

"You're dreaming," Joey said, and enveloped me in incense fumes. The corpse of Khun Mayurii was melting and the people around about us were draining into the dark sky. He took me by the hand—his hand was soft and caked with perfume powder—and led me out of my body. We climbed up the tombstones and climbed to the clouds on a staircase of heavenly rain. The gates of the sky swung open and I saw winged *apsaras* on lotus pads, singing in endless praise of Phra Indra, King of Heaven, each one with breasts glistening like ripe mangoes after rainfall. Music of celestial xylophones mingled with Metallica from Joey's Walkman.

"I am not what I seem to be," Joey said, looking into my eyes.

Suddenly I realized that he had become imbued with the *vinyaan* of my great-great-aunt. Appalled at my previous rudeness, I fell down prostrate at the nearest cloudbank and placed my palms between his feet. "*Sadhu, Sadhu,* honored ancestor," I said piteously, "don't be mad at me because I didn't recognize you straight away. Please look with favor upon our family's distress . . ."

Joey Friedberg looked off into the distance. Far away, silhouetted against the moon, was a pavilion. I could see gods and angels moving against the moonlight as in a shadow play. I could see the cemetery below us. Dozens of people had sought shelter under the mango trees. The exorcist stood, waving his arms, intoning over the place where the *phii krasue* had fallen. Khun Phairoj was summoning the dancers; he had pledged a dance of thanksgiving, and rain or no rain the dance would now have to occur. Aunt Joom and the other transvestites, in their soggy finery, were coming out into the rain. There was some kind of altercation, but presently the music started up, and the *katoeys* danced—though the grace of their movements was somewhat hampered by their umbrellas. In heaven, too, there was dancing; *asparas* flitted by, strewing us with jasmine petals, and we were bathed in sourceless light.

"I could give you the winning lottery number if I really wanted to," said *Khun Chuad* Snit, "but the wheel of karma moves in mysterious ways, and even if I told you, it wouldn't make any difference."

The ways of dead people are not our ways. They have a very oblique way of expressing themselves, and often they'll tell you something that can be interpreted many ways; it gives them a way out while preserving their reputation for infallibility. Nevertheless, I asked her what she meant.

"Joey Friedberg will take care of you," she said. My American friend twitched, as though he were trying to dodge my great-great-aunt's *vinyaan*.

"Why Joey?" I said. I didn't want him taking care of me. It was an annoying habit of his that I'd been trying to wean him of since knowing him.

"Well you may ask," she said. "But you see, I *am* Joey Friedberg."

"You *are*—"

"He is my reincarnation."

"Oh, come on! That's the dumbest thing I ever heard. They don't even *have* reincarnation in America!"

"Now, now," she said, and smiled through Joey's lips, the smile of an indulgent old woman. "All living things are part of the eternal cycle of karma . . . I must admit that I was a little nonplussed to find myself being reborn in the body of a *farang*, but then I'm afraid I did a terrible thing in my last life . . ."

I listened in horrified fascination, eager to learn what monstrous crime she had committed to be reincarnated so far from the City-of-Angels-the-Divine-Metropolis-Etc.-Etc. "I killed a cockroach," she said ruefully.

"But everyone kills cockroaches!"

"Ah, but this particular cockroach happened to be a reincarnation of my grandfather, you see. One must always be very careful about the wanton destruction of life; one never knows who it might be. Think about it next time you step on an ant."

"But . . . Great-great-aunt Snit . . . Joey's older than me! How could he possibly be you? You died after he was born . . ." I had her there, I thought. She'll never talk her way out of that one.

"The fact of the matter is, I spent quite a while in the underworld, going through the usual tortures, being punished for the usual minor offenses like adultery and so on. There is in the underworld an enormous chamber, something like a border immigration center, where the new souls come in. I happened to be in charge of the—as it were—immigrant register one day, when they brought in the soul of a young American boy who was in a car accident. He had been in a coma for a year, and his soul had been flitting back and forth at the border of the kingdom of death. He was crying and carrying on so, but I couldn't send him back; the dictates of Yama, the Death Lord are irreversible. I prostrated myself before His Dread Majesty and said, 'But my Lord, there *is* a loophole. The boy's brain is dead, and the *farang*, in their mechanistic way, consider him gone for good; but we Thais know that it is the heart that is the seat of life, and the boy's heart is still beating.' Which was *almost* true—there was a machine that was beating in place of his heart. The Death Lord, who has a macabre sense of humor, began laughing uproariously; then he said to me, 'Your compassion for this child is commendable, and goes a long way toward mitigating the evil for which you were cast into the underworld. I can't send him back, but maybe I could commute your sentence. If, as you say, the *farang* soul is dead but the Thai is not, I suppose I could simply send a Thai *vinyaan* to occupy the child's body, and no one will be the wiser. For I am a servant of the teaching of the Lord Buddha, and it is my duty to reward compassion by hastening your soul in its trillion-year journey back towards enlightenment." Then Lord Yama waved his hands, and— poof!—I was reborn."

"That is the weirdest thing I have ever heard," I said.

"It is all part of the great chain of being," my great-great-aunt said, shrugging. "Take it or leave it."

"But the lottery tickets—"

"It's out of my hands."

"But you *know* the winning number! You as much as said so! Wait . . . does that mean Joey knows?"

"Hard to say. The conscious mind has little knowledge of past lives." Her voice was getting fainter. To my dismay, we were plummeting back to earth. I could see the whole of the city whirling beneath me: the great palace of the Chakri Kings, the glittering shopping malls and freeways, the great river choked with houseboats in the shadow of the Temple of Dawn . . .

"Joey . . ." Desperation flooded me. I had failed! How could I face my parents, knowing they would have to give up their apartment? "Joey!" I was shaking him now, gripping his shoulders as he convulsed under the spell of possession . . .

I was still shaking him as the dream faded away.

They canal was still swollen from the torrent, but the rain had ended as abruptly as it had started; that is how the monsoon rains are. I came to, still shaking Joey, who was rubbing his eyes. "Did I miss something?" he said. It was still dark . . . not even midnight yet.

"We can go home now," I said. "It's useless. You're my great-great-aunt, and we're not going to win the lottery anyway."

"Why not?" Joey said. "ʜᴋ 2516635—that's the wining number, isn't it? I assume you got it too."

I gaped at him.

"It's early yet," he said. "Maybe we can catch the midnight showing of *Aliens* before we go home." He looked at me. "How'd you manage to stay so dry, little brother?"

ʜᴋ 2516635. By an amazing stroke of karma, we found that lottery ticket the next morning at the stationary store at the head of the *soi*. Joey and I bought the whole ticket and split it in half.

A day later, a group of us gathered to watch the drawing on television. We were at the Friedberg's house: my grandmother, my parents, my little sister, and some raucous friends of the Friedbergs from the American embassy. We sat around the television set while Aunt Joom served us elegant hors d'oeuvres and Coke. A revolution was going on that day; the embassy people were sitting around pontificating about it, quite oblivious to the antics of the announcer. They were playing a music video in between each drawing, and the suspense was mounting . . . mounting . . . mounting . . .

The Friedbergs' friends droned on: "Who's going to get into power this time?" . . . "I got interviewed by ᴄɴɴ this afternoon." . . . "That new field marshall, what's his name, really seems to have the support of the ᴄɪᴀ . . ."

"Shut up, you guys!" Joey said. "Anyone who's lived here can tell you that this revolution's gonna fizzle out before dawn."

"Yeah, revolutions only work in October," I said. After all, I distinctly remembered the last five. "Coups in other months are always abortive."

"Army's got to have something to do," my father said, guzzling a Singha beer.

"How anyone can be interested in such things is beyond me," my mother said, as she vigorously pounded shrimp paste in a mortar and pestle, stinking up the entire living room. "What possible difference can it make when Their Divine Majesties are the true heart of the Siamese people?" Meanwhile, my grandmother, serenely confident of victory, was ignoring the entire thing, merely humming away to herself, one of those peasant melodies.

Everyone started arguing, and it was a moment before Aunt Joom noticed our winning number pop up on the screen. "Merciful Buddha!" she shrieked. "Be quiet everyone! Look! It's come! It's the number!"

"We're rich," my father said softly.

I didn't even mind that it was Joey who had come up with the winning number. We were going to have our new condominium after all, my father was going to have our new car—everything was going to be all right after all!

At that moment, the army took over the television station and announced that there would be a few changes.

We watched in horror as a general in a shiny uniform came on the air and informed us that, because of tampering by certain high officials, it had become necessary to declare the lottery void. The abovementioned high officials would all be resigning in the morning, and his humble self the general had been asked to form a new government to preside over the aftermath of the scandal. He apologized for the revolution, but things would be back to normal in the morning.

"I know that general!" I said. "That's Khun Phairoj, the man whose sister-in-law I . . ."

My father shook his head. "It's not even October."

"Does that mean we're not going to be rich?" said my little sister Kaew.

"On the contrary," said Mrs. Friedberg. "I may as well tell you now. I've obtained a big grant from the Ford Foundation to study your grandmother's peasant songs. It's not much by Ford Foundation standards, but your share of it could come to . . . say, a million baht." General excitement all around.

"Besides, honored father," I said, "I rescued the prime minister's sister-in-law from wandering the earth as a *phii krasue*. Surely you can get a promotion out of that."

I heard Joey calling from the balcony. "Awesome, Samraan! There are tanks rolling up the main road."

"Here we go again," my father said.

I went to join my friend. Two tanks were proceeding up the street on their way to seize the government. It was another humdrum evening in the Divine Metropolis. The street was crowded with food vendors, shoppers, laughing students; no one but Joey seemed to notice the revolution. The monsoon rain was about to come again. The air was heavy with moisture and gasoline fumes and the fragrance of ripening bananas.

Joey watched the tanks starry-eyed, transfixed. It's a quality I had grudgingly come to admire in the Americans: their ability to feel as though everything around them, no matter how many times the world has seen it, is happening for the first time. They have a spanking-newness about them, a sense of wonder. Perhaps it is simply that in their country they rarely have revolutions, exorcisms, or lotteries. I don't know.

I do know, however, that the spirit of my great-great-aunt had come to rest in the body of my friend. That she had shown that I was still her favorite descendant by arranging for the money we had prayed for to come to us— in spite of the lottery being rigged. The heart of the Lord of Death had been moved, the Ford Foundation mobilized, continents and oceans traversed: all this so my family's karma could be fulfilled.

So awed was I by the cosmic grandeur of our personal lives, and so overcome with gratitude, that I fell on my knees in front of my great-great-aunt's latest incarnation and place my folded palms between Joey Friedberg's feet. Thank you for protecting me, honored great-great-aunt, I thought, thank you in the name of the Lord Buddha.

"Why the fuck are you doing *that*?" Joey said, bemused and confused.

"You really don't know, do you?" I studied his face for any trace of remembrance of that night's vision. There was nothing, as is proper. The conscious mind cannot suffer the burden of so many past lives, or it would go mad.

"Well, at least my little brother's treating me with proper respect at last."

"He sure is." For once I didn't mind being called the little brother of a *farang*. "He sure is."

ALEXANDER JABLOKOV

A Deeper Sea

With only a handful of elegant, coolly pyrotechnic stories, like the one that follows, Alexander Jablokov has established himself as one of the most highly regarded and promising new writers in SF. He is a frequent contributor to *Isaac Asimov's Science Fiction Magazine, Amazing,* and other markets. He lives in Somerville, Massachusetts, where he is involved in working on a projected anthology of "Future Boston" stories being put together by the Cambridge Writer's Workshop; he himself has written several stories set in the "Future Boston" milieu. He has just completed work on his first novel.

Here he unravels an age-old chain of consequences that takes us from the ancient Cretan island of Thera to the chill depths of Jupiter space, and in so doing spins a taut, hard-edged, fast-paced tale of war, intrigue, adventure, betrayal, transformation, atrocity—and the search for absolution.

▼

A Deeper Sea

ALEXANDER JABLOKOV

JUPITER ORBIT, JANUARY 2033

The whale screamed in fear, the complex harmonics of its terror rumbling in the warm water around Ilya Stasov. He hung tensely in the null-g hub of the research space station Jupiter Forward. Stasov had concealed himself in an aquarium with the ecology of a Caribbean coral reef. He hung there, pulling water through his artificial gills, and listened to the whale as it screamed from the cold wastes of interplanetary space. The multicolored fish surrounding Stasov had adapted to the lack of gravitational orientation, and floated with their dorsal fins in all directions, oblivious to the whale's cry.

The sperm whale screamed again. Stasov tightened himself into a ball, as if to escape the sound, then straightened and twitched a finger, calling on the imaging capabilities of Jupiter Forward's computer system. The space station orbited in Ganymede's trailing trojan point, and the whale floated near it. Instead of leaving the tank and going into space to confront the whale, Stasov brought the Jovian system into the water.

Banded Jupiter appeared in the aquarium like a sunken fishing float. A moray eel in a crevice watched it carefully, judging its edibility. Stasov imagined the chill of interplanetary space penetrating the tropical water. Ganymede rolled among the sea anemones like a jetting snail. He sucked hyperoxygenated water through his carotid gill attachments and looked for the cyborg sperm whale.

"Calm," he murmured through his throat mike, "Calm." He was linked directly to the whale's auditory centers.

The whale's image was still invisible in his view. Another finger twitch, and Jupiter shrank while Ganymede swelled. The water darkened in the tank and the stars peeked through above the coral. The fish ignored these astronomical manifestations and went calmly about their business. The image of Ganymede grew to the point that Stasov felt himself flying over its rough surface. He no longer saw the tank in which he floated.

The sperm whale suddenly breached the surface of darkness and rose up out of Ganymede's invisible shadow. Fusion rockets burned blue along his length. Sunlight gleamed along the whale's great ridged bulk and glittered on the tessellations of the phased microwave array on his back.

But where was the goddam dolphin? "Weissmuller," Stasov said. "Speak to Clarence." Silence. "The whale needs your words." A longer silence. "Damn it, Weissmuller, where are you?" His left hand throbbed and he clenched it into a fist, as well as he could.

His only answer was the roaring hiss of Jupiter's magnetic field and the low murmur of the engineers as they checked the function of the whale's engines. Stasov keyed in more astronomical data. Ganymede shrank to a marble. The entire Jovian system now floated in the tank, satellite orbits marked, the computer giving him direct perception of their gravity wells sinking like holes in deep perspective. The space station of Jupiter Forward appeared in Ganymede's trojan point, a bright dot. The computer located the transponder on the dolphin's space suit and displayed it as a spark. Stasov looked at Weissmuller's current location and swore.

The dolphin had dived into Io's gravity well and been slingshot out towards Europa. Jupiter's plunging gravity well gaped before Stasov's eyes and he felt as if he were being sucked down into a whirlpool. He fought down a moment of terror. The dolphin's spark climbed slowly up towards him. Weissmuller always played things close to the edge. It would be hours before the dolphin could get back to Jupiter Forward.

Stasov examined Clarence's image, wanting to stroke the whale's back to comfort him. A trigger fish examined the hologram, seemingly surprised to see a sperm whale its own size, then darted away with a contemptuous flick of its fins. The real Clarence, desperately alone in space, of course perceived nothing of this.

Despite the immense modifications to his body, Clarence was still vaguely cetacean, though he now had vast, complex control planes to guide him through the Jovian atmosphere, making him look like a whale decorated with streamers as a float in a parade. Stasov spoke calming words, but he wasn't an expert in sperm whale dialect. That wasn't why he was there. The whale continued to send out echo-location clicks in the microwave band, unable to understand how he had lost consciousness on an island in the Maldives, in the Indian Ocean, and awoken here, in a mysterious place he had never heard of, a place of no water, no fish, and a dozen featureless spheres.

Irregular bursts of rocket appeared along Clarence's sides, spinning him.

Data streamed into the tank, crowding the fish: fuel use, accelerations, circuit status. Voices muttered technical jargon. Stasov felt as he had when as a child, put to bed early, listening to the intent, incomprehensible adult conversation of his parents' friends through the closed bedroom door.

"Erika," Stasov said, keying another comm line.

"Director Morgenstern's line," a heavy male voice answered.

"Miller." Stasov hadn't expected the Security Chief's voice. But if he had him . . . "Why is the dolphin running loose around Io?"

"There's something wrong with your comm, Colonel. You sound like you're underwater. You'd better check it."

Stasov kept one eye on the increasingly agitated whale. "I'm not a colonel," he snapped. "I hold no such rank. Please give me Director Morgenstern. We can deal with your dereliction of duty later."

"Dereliction, Colonel?" Paul Miller's voice had the lazy drawl that Stasov associated with thuggish political policemen and prison camp guards, whether they were American, Russian, or Japanese. "The dolphin wanted to go. My men aren't KGB officers." He chuckled. Stasov knew that sound well: the laugh of an interrogator putting a subject at ease before hitting him again. He'd heard it over and over during his months at Camp Homma. It had begun to seem an essential part of torture. "Should we have held him under physical restraint? That would be a treaty violation. Do you want me to order my men to commit a—"

"Damn it, Miller, quit babbling and get me the Director!" Stasov tried to conceal his sudden fear under anger.

"You just watch yourself, Colonel." Miller's voice was suddenly cold. "None of us are under your orders. It's a long way from Uglegorsk. The Director's busy. I don't have to—"

"Ilya," Erika Morgenstern's voice broke in. "What's the problem?"

"Cut all of the whale's systems immediately," Stasov said tensely. "None of the problems are on the engineering side. He's not responsible. Weissmuller's off somewhere around Io and I can't handle the whale alone. I know it throws the schedule off. And the budget. But do it."

Morgenstern didn't hesitate. The hectic flaring lights along the whale's sides died and it floated, quiescent. "Done," she said. Subliminally Stasov heard cries of surprise and frustration from the engineers testing the vehicle. The vehicle. Clarence the cyborg sperm whale, hanging in orbit around Jupiter. He was there. Stasov could see him, but still wasn't sure he believed it. Test levels dropped to zero.

Stasov swam slowly to the tank's surface and edged out through the enhanced-surface-tension barrier that held the liquid sphere together, feeling the boundary as a line of almost painful pressure on his skin. He floated into the air, globules of water drifting off his body and reuniting with the large, quivering sphere of the fish tank. Once he had detached the carotid oxygenation connections he drew a deep, painful breath of the unfriendly air, re-establishing his ventilation reflexes. His diaphragm contracted painfully, having relaxed during his conditioned apnea.

A tiny fish flopped in the air, pulled out of the water along with him. Stasov shepherded it back to the tank. The cold air gave him goose bumps, and he shivered. He pulled himself over to an actual porthole and peered out at space. Clarence floated, surrounded by vehicles and swarming human beings, afflicting him as had the parasites that had clung to him in the seas of Earth. It would be hours before Weissmuller returned. Something had to be done. Stasov felt a twisting in his belly. It had been a long time since he'd tortured a dolphin. He knew that if he did it again, it would be his last act. But he could see no other way.

"Ilya," Erika Morgenstern said in exasperation. "You have to realize what these people think you are. What they call you—"

"The Shark of Uglegorsk," he finished. "You and I have been through all that. They don't understand anything."

Morgenstern stared at him with those efficient brown-green eyes that seemed able to see through both glare and darkness with equal ease. The first time he had seen those eyes they had spelled his salvation. He tried never to forget that. "You're the one who's not aware of anything. I have to balance two hundred fifty people from twenty countries aboard this space station, and turn in a job of research to boot. Hatred and fear aren't imaginary."

Stasov rubbed his maimed left hand and looked back at her. The room was in half darkness, as she preferred, giving her head, with its flat face and short, graying coppery hair, the look of an astronomical object. She held court in an imperial style which would have dismayed her superiors at the UN Planetary Exploration Directorate—had they been permitted to know about it—guarded by acolytes like Miller, aloof, inaccessible, but aware of everything that went on aboard Jupiter Forward. Stasov was sometimes startled by what had become of her.

"They should still be able to do their jobs," he said. "Or is your authority over them insufficient?"

She didn't flush—she had more control than that—but she narrowed her eyes in an expression of authority, to let him know that he'd gone too far. He stared back at her with the pale-blue-eyed absence of expression that let her know that he'd been through worse than she could ever throw at him.

A hologram of Jupiter gave the room what light it had. The planet was sliced apart to show magnetic fields and convection cells, as if Morgenstern could as easily order a modification in the circulation of the Great Red Spot as she could in the air pressure of the storage lockers or the menu in the dining hall.

"We've come this far together," she said. "Since Homma. Now we're about to drop a cyborg sperm whale into the Jovian atmosphere." She shook her head. "I'm still not sure I believe it. But I can't risk the anger of the Delphine Delegation. They provide most of our financing. You know that. Miller's an idiot, but he's right. We cannot physically restrain an intelligent cetacean. It violates the Treaty of Santa Barbara." Her voice still had a trace of an accent from her native New Zealand.

"Articles 12 and 13," Stasov muttered. "Open Seas and Freedom of Entities. Damn right I know it. Better than anyone else. And dolphins love the letter of the law. They think it's the stupidest thing they ever heard, but they use it whenever it's convenient. They can afford good lawyers."

"Exactly. I can't jeopardize the project. Not now. Not ever. The Delphine Delegation keeps us on a short enough financial tether as it is."

"Miller didn't oppose me because of the Treaty," Stasov spat. "He did it because he thinks dolphins are wonderful innocent creatures, and because he hates me for what he imagines I did to them. There's nothing more terrifying than a sentimental thug. By letting him oppose me, *you* are jeopardizing the project. That's not just a machine out there. It's a perceptive being, trapped in a metal shell and hauled to a world he doesn't understand. He's going mad. Weissmuller's *already* crazy. Even for a dolphin. Look clearly, Erika. The project could end here."

She looked at him. He didn't have to say any more. Looking clearly was what she did best. It had taken her from an after-college job as a junior observer on a UN War Crimes commission to one of the most powerful jobs in the UN Planetary Exploration Directorate. And it had been the look behind Stasov's eyes, in the gardens of Camp Homma, that had given her the first glimpse of the direction to move in.

"All right," she said, finally. "Do what you have to."

"Do you mean that?"

"Of course I do!" she blazed. "I said it, didn't I? I'm giving you full authority, answerable only to me. Do what you want to your dolphin Messiah and his acolyte. Just get the project moving."

"Don't mock me, Erika," Stasov said heavily. "Don't ever mock me." He stood, raising himself up slowly in the low gravity. Director Morgenstern's comm terminal had been flickering constantly, and there were undoubtedly a dozen crises already piled up while she had chatted with her unpopular and essential Cetacean Liaison. "The project will move."

She eyed him, suddenly the more uncertain, younger woman he remembered. "Ilya. What do you mean to do?"

"Don't ask me," he said, his voice dead. "I'll only do what's necessary."

UGLEGORSK, OCTOBER 2019

"You don't seem like a man who would be interested in stories, Colonel," Georgios Theodoros said as he stumbled up the wet stone steps, his long coat inadequate protection against the wind blowing off the Tatar Strait.

Colonel Stasov smiled, the third large star on his officer's shoulder boards new enough that he still enjoyed the novelty of the salutation, even from a foreign civilian. "It's not just a story, is it? It's evidence that what we are doing has been done before."

"I'm not sure that's true. It's all allegorical, allusive." Theodoros, a dreamy-eyed Greek with an ecclesiastical beard, stopped on one of the landings, affecting to examine the view, but actually to rest. There was little enough to look at. The sea before him was gray, with sharp-toothed waves. The thick clouds lowering over it obscured the boundary between sea and sky. This was nothing like the warm, dark Aegean where he did his delphine research. The island Sakhalin was a rough, hard place. That was why this Russian Colonel with his pale blue eyes was so intense in his work. Though those eyes sometimes shone with the joy of a true discoverer, a look that had automatically led Theodoros to accept the other as a friend.

"No," Stasov stated decisively. "What humans and dolphins did during the reign of the Cretan Thalassocracy is significant to us here. That's why we brought you. Not just to hear stories. Thirty-five hundred years ago they developed the mental technology to deal with the problem. I believe you have brought the vestiges of that technology with you to Uglegorsk." He tugged at the binoculars he wore around his neck.

"They claimed to speak to dolphins," Theodoros murmured. "Perhaps they did." For years, no one had listened to his theories, and now that someone was willing to, he found himself somehow reluctant, uncertain of the consequences. The Soviets weren't interested in mere theories. They meant to act.

The research station at Uglegorsk sprawled out beneath them. Beauty being pointless against the cold rocks of Sakhalin, the station had seemingly striven for extreme ugliness, and succeeded in the Soviet manner. The metal huts, some of WWII Lend-Lease vintage, were rusted and patched. Holding pens crowded the shoreline, their captive dolphins splashing and leaping. The base was dominated by the concrete vault of the dolphin laboratory, built with more recent American aid.

Theodoros's specialty was human-dolphin interactions during the second millennium BCE, a research topic too vague for delphine researchers and too practical for classicists and mythologists. So he had been surprised when he received an official invitation from the Vladivostok Oceanographic Institute to fly out to Uglegorsk to talk with Ilya Stasov. It hadn't been simply a polite facility tour followed by an hour talk, either. He'd been questioned intently for three days. A map of the Aegean Sea now hung in the main seminar room, the sites of Cretan cities marked on it, with a big star on Thera, the island that was the remnants of the great volcano whose eruption had brought an end to Cretan civilization. The Soviet researchers gathered in front of it to argue, arms waving, in their loud Russian. He and Stasov spoke English with each other.

The burly Colonel sat down on a rock wall and stared off to sea. "Could you tell me the story, Georgios? Never mind how insignificant it seems."

Had the man really climbed up all this way for a view of various shades of gray? Through binoculars yet? Theodoros shivered and sat down next to Stasov.

"It took place on Delos, long enough ago that the Egyptians had no Pharaoh, and built with reeds. A singer lived on this island, a lyre player who had dedicated his life to Apollo and played to the sky and the sea. After a storm, the singer went down to the sandy shore to see what the sea had tossed up. On the beach lay a whale, sighing at the knowledge of his certain death. He cried thick, bitter tears.

" 'Why are you here, brother?' the lyre player called. 'Why are you not off tossing the sea over your back, as is the natural duty of whales?'

" 'I have come to hear your songs,' the whale replied. 'Sing to me, while I die.'

"The singer sang to the whale for three days, while the birds wheeled and cried overhead and the sun rose and set and the whale's flesh began to stink. At the end of the third day the whale died. The man wept and sprinkled water on the whale's head, since dust seemed improper, and wished him good hunting in the world to which whales go, for he did not think that Hades had a place for him.

"He looked out into the sea and saw a dolphin dancing. The dolphin leaped and gamboled, but said nothing. When he saw the man on the shore he first ignored him, then slid up onto the shore.

" 'Do you wish to sing to your dead brother?' the lyre player asked. The dolphin said nothing. 'His soul needs your songs to speed him to the dark sea where he now swims.' Still the dolphin said nothing. 'He cries for the sound of your voice.' The dolphin remained silent. In a rage, the singer raised up his lyre and broke it over the dolphin's head. 'Speak not then, dumb beast, and go to your death unknown.'

"Blood came from the dolphin's blowhole and he cried out. 'Why do you torment me so?'

" 'To teach you the responsibilities of death and the songs that it calls for,' the singer said.

" 'I will hear you then,' the dolphin said. 'Teach me the songs, if you will not let me be silent.'

"And so the man taught the dolphin to sing the rhythmic songs of the ancients, those sung by shepherds at first light, by fishermen pulling in full nets, by priests to the brow of the impending storm. The dolphin took the songs and made them his own, adding the sounds of the sea.

"Apollo, hearing the songs, came down laughing, though his hands smelled of blood and corruption. He was an Asian god then, from Lycia, but was on his way to lead the Greeks.

" 'I have slain the monster, Typhaon, at Crisa beneath snowy Parnassus,' he told them. 'My Temple and wooded grove are to be there. Now that you are able to sing, friend dolphin, you will aid me. Find me my priests.'

" 'The sea moves,' the dolphin said. 'The land is solid. I will search.'

"The dolphin swam the seas until he saw a ship of Cretan priests bound for Pylos. He sang to them from the sea and they followed him, to that place beneath Parnassus that was, forever afterward, to be called Delphi, after the dolphin who had led them. Men and dolphins spoke from that time afterward."

Theodoros felt the warm light of the Aegean island die, and found himself again sitting on a cold stone wall above the Tatar Strait.

"It's there," Stasov said, pacing back and forth in front of Theodoros. "I know it is. But why did they stop talking?" His pale eyes stared at Theodoros as if suspecting the Greek of concealing something.

"The story doesn't say. My guess would be that it had something to do with the eruption of Strogyle, the great volcano on Thera. Whether it was the cause or not, that seems to mark the end of Cretan civilization. Once the men stopped talking, perhaps the dolphins did also."

"And have refused ever since out of sheer spite? Perhaps, perhaps. But I think there's more. The volcano . . . interesting . . ." Stasov continued to pace, then froze, staring out over the water. He put his binoculars to his eyes.

"What do you see?" asked Theodoros.

"I see a need for our work," Stasov said. He pointed. In the haze at the horizon Theodoros could barely discern a dark ship. "That's a Japanese vessel. The Americans have been allowing them to build armed cruisers. A mistake. The Japanese claim the southern half of Sakhalin, you know."

Theodoros had no idea why anyone would be interested in the place, but decided not to say so. "I don't think the Americans can do too much to stop them, Colonel Stasov."

"True enough. Though the Americans may soon find themselves in a war they don't want." Stasov paused. "Do the dolphins have a religion, do you suppose?"

"Colonel Stasov, I suggest that we should first learn how to talk with them, and only then worry about their religion."

"True, perhaps," Stasov replied, staring thoughtfully out to sea. "Though that may be the wrong way round." He roused himself. "Come down then.

You can drink with us one last time before you leave. You have given me much to think about."

Theodoros, his stomach churning at the thought of another of the massive drinking bouts which, besides arguing, seemed to be the only form of entertainment at Uglegorsk, followed Stasov back down the stairs.

The vaulted dolphin research center was as huge inside as an aircraft hangar. The floor was always wet, and the air smelled of seaweed and iodine. Cables snaked across the floor with no attention to safety. Theodoros tripped over them constantly, even sober, while the Russians had no trouble even when roaring drunk.

The farewell party had spread among the tanks, as such events always did, as if the researchers wanted to include the dolphins in their festivities. Stasov and Theodoros found a quiet corner to finish their discussion. Stasov balanced a bottle of vodka on a signal processing box and handed the other a pickle out of an unlabeled jar. It seemed to the Greek that everything was pickled here: the cucumbers, the cabbage, the peppers, the fish, and the researchers. He tossed back a shot of vodka, took a bite of pickle, and grimaced.

Stasov chuckled. "You've learned to do it like a real Russian. The trick is to never look as though you enjoy it."

"I *don't* enjoy it."

"Ha. You are a real Russian."

The huge form of General Anatoly Ogurtsov loomed over them. "More of these damn foreign computers for you, Ilya?" He waved a stack of requisition sheets at him. "How can our budget support this?"

Stasov shrugged. "Sit down, Antosha." He poured the General a glass of vodka. "I need sophisticated array processors. Who else makes them but the Japanese?"

"Damn their yellow souls," Ogurtsov said, in ceremonial anathema. "They do make good gadgets. I hope we can buy enough to defeat them when we go to war." He sighed hugely. "That's all image processing gear. Why do you need it?"

"I think I know how to reach the dolphins," Stasov said. "Aural images."

"An interesting thought," Theodoros said. "What sort of images?"

"That's where I'll need your help. I'll need good sonic maps of the Aegean, and best guesses from oceanographic archaeologists on the conformation of the sea bottom at about 1500 BCE. Can you do it?"

"I think so." Theodoros was startled once again. When he had come here, to find the crude pens of inferior concrete already cracking, the drunken technicians, the obsolete foreign electronic equipment cadged or stolen from other research projects, he had been sure that he was wasting his time. Compared to the clean redwood boards and earnest college students of Santa Barbara or the elegant institutes at Monaco, this place was a hell hole. But somehow . . .

"We'll do it, you know," Ogurtsov rumbled. "Ilya will make sure that we do."

"General," Theodoros said. "I have no doubt that you're right."

THE ALEUTIANS, SEPTEMBER 2022

The Americans had found it surprisingly difficult to defend their Alaskan frontier, but they fought viciously every step of the way. The assault of Kagalaska Island, supposedly a surprise attack, faced brutal resistance from its first moment. Such *desant* operations were new to the Soviet Navy, and they were only gradually learning how to handle landing assaults. The price of the lessons was high.

Long before his own ship came into range, Colonel Ilya Stasov was listening to the first casualty reports.

"Death, death, death," the dolphin keened. "The fuckers left me behind. Their lives have found completion. They're dead." Her voice came over a background roar, leaving it almost incomprehensible.

"Calm down, Harmonia," Stasov said, realizing that it was an easy instruction to give if you were out of the battle area. "What happened?"

". . . exploding eggs. They don't listen to us anymore. You shark spawn, Stasov, you said they would listen!"

"It must be a new type of mine, Harmonia," Stasov yelled in reply, as the noise in his headphones increased. "Some new magnetic detector. We'll get the data—"

"Fish, fish. I won't go back until you give me a fish."

"You don't have to go back. Pull out now. We'll do a magnetic field analysis—"

"I want a belly full of fish for this, turd swallower!" With that, the line went dead. As it did, the landing ship itself thrummed, and the thunder of an explosion roared down the hatch from outside. He waited for the sound to die away, but instead it grew insanely louder, reverberating. It was the roar of the attack, and was not about to end. He raced up the companionway.

"Priblyudov!" he yelled at the comm officer over the noise. "The Americans have sowed the shore with a new type of mine. I've lost most of my first wave of dolphins. Send this info back to the *Novgorod*." He waved a sheet of notes. The comm officer stared at him dully. "Hurry up!"

While Priblyudov stumbled to obey, Stasov plugged his earphones into the console and linked back up with his microphones. He stepped out onto the deck in the cold northern sunlight. Stasov stared in horror at the bare rock of Kagalaska, which loomed ahead of the long deck of the landing ship, wreathed in smoke. Rockets flared over his head and the 76 mm bow guns thundered at the shore. Below decks, he knew, a battalion of troops was gathered, with battle tanks and assault vehicles. Two landing ships had already hit the island. Stasov listened to his earphones.

The gray waters were covered with flaming oil. The dolphins, *his* dolphins, were strangling in it, their death cries cutting high above the rumbling of the engines and the crunching of propellers. The hazy arctic air was full of the sharp stink of oil and burning flesh. The other two landing ships had spilled their loads and the rocky shore ahead was covered with assault troops, swarming like isopods. Stasov closed his eyes, listening to the screams of death in his earphones. The thud of the American torpedo as it found the landing ship's unarmored side was impossibly loud, agony in his ears.

The ship slowed as if hitting a sandbar, and listed. Stasov slid down to the railing, vaulted over it, and hit the water. He felt freezing water on his face, but his assault uniform instantly compensated, keeping his body warm. Another explosion, which he felt with his body, and the landing ship sank as if pulled under by a giant hand. Stasov stroked away to keep from being sucked down with it.

He pulled off his now-useless headphones and activated his throat mike. He called to those of his dolphins that had survived that far. Pitifully few.

Suddenly Stasov heard the call of a hunting orca, a killer whale which sped through the struggling forms of the drowning assault troops who had escaped the landing ship, calling "Speak, food!" and devouring them when they did not reply. He came to Stasov. "Speak, food!" "I am Ilya Sergeiivich Stasov," he replied, insulting the orca by speaking in dolphin dialect. "Go fuck a walrus." It was amazing how quickly the ancient prohibition on conversation with humans vanished once it had been violated at Uglegorsk. The orca nudged him once, breaking several ribs, snorted "Spoiled food," and vanished into the polluted darkness.

The thunder of the assault lessened as the American troops were pushed back from the beachhead. The bodies of men and dolphins littered the shore, flopped on the rocks by the receding tide. A black line of oil and blood marked the highest rise of the water. Stasov climbed through the bodies. A rough road had been laid out and tanks ground up it. Bulldozers were already cutting out a landing strip. A few pockets of resistance were still being mopped up inland, but otherwise the island was in Soviet hands. Stasov made his way to the *desant* commander's temporary HQ.

"The American *Aegis* cruiser *Wainwright* is approaching in convoy from Kodiak," General Lefortov said. The whites of his eyes had turned yellow and he looked like a dead man. The assault force had suffered numbingly high casualties. They were far from land-based aircraft and the air cover provided by the carrier *Nizhni Novgorod* was insufficient to defend against an *Aegis* task force. "What can your dolphins do?"

"What's left of them?"

General Lefortov pointed his dead eyes at Stasov. He'd lost enough of his own men to be indifferent to the fate of Stasov's precious dolphins. "We lost two attack submarines in the Bering Sea. The enemy advance is unopposed. What can you do?"

"Do?" Stasov said wearily. He thought about the dolphins and equipment he had left. "We can sink it. It'll cost—"

"It might cost the war if we don't. Prepare your troops. I'll print up your orders."

"Yes sir."

BATAAN, THE PHILIPPINES, MAY 2024

Stasov slipped gently across the smooth wood of the porch into the hot butter of the Philippine sunlight. He moved slowly, his joints rough and unlubricated, as if he were a child's bicycle left long out in the rain. The Japanese guards at the door of the barracks smiled at him as he passed, an expression he had long since ceased to try to interpret. Cracking dolphin communications had been easier. He had adopted a purely behavioral operant conditioning model, letting blows, punishment cells, and food full of vermin modify his actions without the intervention of his conscious mind. He no longer tried to reason with the outside world, he simply responded to it. That let him keep his soul to himself.

They'd started feeding him well several weeks before, a signal of his imminent release. He had refused to feel hope. It was not beyond them to use the illusion of freedom to get him to betray himself. Yesterday they had allowed him an hour in a hot Japanese bath, and this morning they had dressed him in a rather elegant suit of blue silk. It was much too large, made, perhaps, to the measurements in his records, from the start of his incarceration. His fingers had had trouble tying the knot on the tie, so one of the guards had delicately done it for him. It was not the regulation military knot he had been trying for, at least not of his army, but it would do. The high collar hid the scars on his neck where his carotid oxygenator had once attached. It wasn't until he actually walked out into the sun that Stasov began to think that he might be free.

Outside the barracks was a tiled patio where the camp's officers had often had parties at night with the local women. A woman waited for him there now. Not one of those dark-haired beauties that had been one of Luzon's main exports for centuries, but a fair-skinned woman with coppery hair, the New Zealand member of the UN delegation to Camp Homma. She held a notebook.

"Colonel Stasov?" she said, standing. She was a plain-faced woman, strong. "My name is Erika Morgenstern."

They shook hands. "Not Colonel," he murmured. "Not any more." The hot sun made him dizzy, and the smell of the exuberant bougainvillaea that bloomed all around them seemed to clog his nostrils. His knees buckled and he sat down.

She watched him narrowly. "Are you in need of medical assistance?"

He shook his head. "No, certainly not. I have been . . . cared for."

"The Americans are unhappy about Camp Homma," she said, scribbling in her notebook. "Any information you can give the UN will be useful. Any violations of humane conditions."

He looked at her. "If I am being released, the time for Camp Homma must be almost over. The Japanese have a new empire to contend with. Including Sakhalin, I understand. American concerns are a minor problem." Stasov had been captured at Uglegorsk with the collapse of the last Soviet naval effort in the Sea of Okhotsk, by Japanese troops bent on avenging the atrocities of the Soviet occupation of Hokkaido.

The Japanese had chosen Bataan for their war crimes detention camp, for they were displaying as much their victory over their American allies in the Pacific War as over their Soviet enemy. They named the camp Homma, after the Japanese general who had commanded the invasion of the Philippines in 1942, a deliberate insult to which the Americans were powerless to reply.

"Nevertheless," she said. "If you have been mistreated—"

"If I have been mistreated it is only just," he replied. "Americans make poor victors. They are too forgiving. The Japanese are more like Russians. They demand justice, and perhaps a bit more. Or have you forgotten that you are talking to the Shark of Uglegorsk?"

She looked startled. "Having a nickname is not a crime. The Japanese have charged you with genocide and slavery, crimes you committed against the very species whose intelligence was demonstrated by your researches. These charges, however, are *ex post facto*—are you familiar with the term?"

"Soviet law is not very sophisticated, I'm afraid."

A Japanese guard brought them tea in graceful earthenware cups. With calm deliberation, Stasov poured the tea on the ground and let the cup fall on the pavement, where it cracked into pieces. The guard bowed expressionlessly, cleaned up the shards, and walked slowly away.

"What did they want from you?" Morgenstern asked. "What did they want to know?"

"They were curious about my work, my methods. My secrets."

"What did they learn?"

Stasov grimaced. "I learned more from them than they did from me. The Japanese have little sympathy for cetaceans. They murder them with less concern than even Russians. Their curiosity was purely practical. I told them little, and that little took them a long time to discover. I know what that's like. I've been on the other side of it. But they showed me that my life is not yet closed. I will continue living. That's no small thing to learn, and I should be grateful." The rustle of a rat in a palm tree made him jump. It took a moment for his heart to slow. "Are you a dolphin researcher, Ms. Morgenstern?"

"No. My interest is planetary exploration. Little enough use for that now, I'm afraid. After the Pacific War, the world's too poor to afford it."

He stared at her for a long time, long enough for her to worry that he was having some sort of traumatic stress attack. "That's an interesting point," he said, finally, his voice betraying no particular emotion. "Interesting indeed. No, we can't afford it. But others might be able to."

Two days later they crossed Manila Bay to Cavite, where the Soviet delegation waited. Sea gulls spun in the hot, wet air. The water was glass smooth, with a long, sickening swell. Suddenly, all around them, the water was filled with the flashing forms of dolphins. They leaped out of the water, occasionally clearing the boat itself. Stasov sat at the stern underneath the flapping Rising Sun and looked out at them.

The white-jacketed Japanese pilot accelerated and began to slew back and forth, though whether to avoid the dolphins or to hit them was not clear.

"Are they glad to see you alive?" Morgenstern shouted over the roar of the motor.

Stasov looked thoughtful. "Glad isn't the word. They know that something has been left undone. They will see me do it."

"Isn't something always left undone, Ilya? I don't understand."

"If something is always left undone, then no one would ever be allowed to die."

Morgenstern turned away from her incomprehensible charge and looked back out at the dolphins. Most of them were dark blue-gray, their smooth skins gleaming in the sun, but some of them had rough attachments on their sides, the cyborg modifications that made them machines of war.

"Those are Soviet military dolphins," Morgenstern said. "What are they doing in Manila Bay?"

Stasov shook his head. "None of my concern, now. Something for the Japanese and Americans to worry about."

"Why? Soviet forces have demobilized."

"They have. The Pacific Fleet is gone, the Japanese occupy Vladivostok, and there isn't a Red Army unit existing east of the Lena. But the dolphins aren't Soviet citizens, are they? And they have not signed any instrument of surrender." He sat back in his seat and straightened the knot on his tie.

They had talked little about dolphins over the past two days. They had, instead, spoken mostly of space exploration, of Morgenstern's hopes and dreams, as if Stasov had come into her life to rescue her. As if he and his dolphins could somehow get her into space.

She looked out at the dolphins sliding in and out of the water and remembered the images from the TV: the flat burning shape of the Japanese aircraft carrier *Hiryu* at the Battle of La Perouse Strait and the vanishing prow of the *Aegis* cruiser *Jonathan Wainwright* as it failed to defend Kaga-laska, both ships sunk by dolphins. The Soviets had been defeated, but the dolphins were still out there, and no one knew what they would do.

She looked at Colonel Ilya Sergeiivich Stasov, the Shark of Uglegorsk, and noticed that, for the first time since she had met him at Homma, he was smiling.

THE MALDIVES, JUNE 2029

Stasov clambered down over the slippery, seaweed-covered rocks to take a look at the octopus trapped in the tide pool. It had come too high up near shore at high tide, probably in pursuit of crabs to eat, and been imprisoned when the water receded. Snails and sea urchins tumbled helplessly as the octopus whirled its tentacles. The red starfish and the sea anemones clinging to the rocks on the side of the pool went calmly about their business, ignoring the frantic interloper. Stasov reached in and prodded the octopus with his finger. It flushed dark with fear and irritation and huddled down between two rocks. The overturned sea urchins waggled their spines and slowly began to right themselves.

The waves slapped louder as the tide rose over the rocks, gleaming eye-hurtingly in the glaring sunlight. Here and there the water met momentary resistance from a ridge or a seaweed pile, but it rose inexorably over all obstacles, finally pouring into the tide pool and reuniting it with the sea. The octopus jetted and vanished in the direction of deeper, safer waters.

Stasov climbed back up from the water, away from the heavy iodine smell of the dark seaweed. Isopods, those marine pill bugs, scuttled madly under his feet amid the barnacles and black lichens at the upper reach of the tidal zone. Above was the rough, bare rock where the sperm whale lay baking in the morning sun.

Its smooth black bulk loomed above the rough rock like a dream of a living mountain, sharply outlined against the cloudless sky. It had leaped from the sea sometime during the night and smashed itself on the land. Without help it would be dead by noon. Staring up at it, mesmerized, Stasov tripped over a stretch of the limp tubing that now crisscrossed the island. A firm hand grabbed his elbow and held him.

"We're ready to pump," Habib Williams's wheezy voice said. "Tubes are soft now, but under pressure they're like tree trunks. Get one of them wrapped around your leg and you got some trouble. Not to mention one leg fewer." Williams was a short, skinny man with a bald, brown head. His white suit was cut with precise jauntiness and he carried a flowered Japanese parasol. He peered at Stasov with narrow, obvious suspicion. "Now tell me. Why are we here?" He reached down with the parasol's crook and flipped the switch that was the only external feature of a satiny ovoid the size of a desk.

It hummed, and seawater filled the tubing. Water sprayed out of hundreds of nozzles, played rainbows in the sun, and ran down the whale's sides.

Stasov gazed at him, pale blue eyes as featureless as robin's eggs. "We're saving a whale," he said. "That's your job, isn't it?"

Williams scowled. "It is. Cetacean rescue for the Indian Ocean. Fine, a respectable occupation, pleases my mother, though it means I can't get home much. I know my profession. What I don't know is why I, and Marta and Jolie and Ahmed, are *here*, on this tiny rock in the Maldives. The water is as clear and calm as I've ever seen it. There hasn't been even the hint of a storm in a month. Halcyon weather. This time of year we sit in a garden in Colombo and play cards. Marta usually wins. She claims it's skill."

He walked around the perimeter of the spray, stepping over the streams which now flowed in the cracks down to the sea. Stasov followed. On the other side of the whale were the two heavy-lift helicopters that had brought the rescue team from Sri Lanka. Next to them was Stasov's own aircraft, a tiny military surplus helicopter, its red star dimmed by sun and salt. Stasov thought of the red starfish in the tide pool. That helicopter had fought in the Aleutians, but its star now seemed to have an aquatic rather than a military character. Things did manage to change, sometimes. Ahmed and Jolie had set up a crane which curled over the sperm whale like a scorpion's tail.

"Then, this morning, the sun comes up, and the Indian Ocean seasearch satellite tells me there's a giant parmacety lying on the rocks in the middle of the ocean like a toy some god's child forgot. It happens. I've seen gams of whales beach themselves and pods of dolphins bash themselves against cliffs until the water is red. Sperm whales do reverse brodies and drop themselves on islands to die. I don't know why they do it, but I'm used to it. What I'm not used to is getting to the scene at top speed and finding Colonel Ilya Sergeiivich Stasov lying next to the whale, wrapped in a blanket, listening to the whale die."

"I hold no such rank," Stasov said sharply. His large hands tightened on each other. "The research vessel *Andrei Sakharov* has been in the Maldives for the past two weeks, not half an hour's flight from here, at Ihavandiffulu Atoll." Stasov had trouble pronouncing the outlandish word. "And she has been my station for two years."

"Oh, has she?" Williams said with heavy sarcasm. "And aren't you afraid you'll be sunk if you venture into the open sea? The sea has become a dangerous place, these days. I would assume for Soviet ships more than anyone."

"We've had no trouble." Stasov took a breath. "I heard a call on one of our hydrophone buoys. Two weeks ago. A deep call, out in the Arabian Basin. If you play back your recordings, you'll hear it. Three humpbacks, in close chorus. A simple call. It said 'The Bubble Is Rising.' It was a call to prayer. So I am here."

Williams stared at him, incredulous. "Are you serious?"

"Absolutely." Stasov lifted his suntanned high-cheekboned face to the sky. "The Bubble Has Risen."

"Bullshit." Williams restrained his temper with a visible effort and turned away.

Stasov shook his head, knelt, and folded up his blanket. "The whale is dying. You want to play militia officer, interrogate me and throw me off your island. Understandable. But while we argue theology, the whale's mass is slowly crushing its lungs. Don't your people have the respirator ready yet?"

The cetacean rescuer jerked his parasol shut, snapping several of its delicate wooden ribs. Stasov followed him to the crane. Williams carefully removed his white suit and finally stood, in paunchy dignity, wearing only a pair of red bikini shorts. Stasov also stripped.

The two men stepped onto the crane and were lifted up to the whale's back, which was warm and smooth under their bare feet. They were immediately soaked by the spray that played over the whale.

Williams pulled the crane's respirator nozzle over to the whale's blowhole, located asymmetrically on the top left side of the snout. He stimulated the proper acupressure points with an ultrasonic probe, anaesthetizing the sensitive blowhole. He then inserted the nozzle and adjusted the suction cups that held it firm. A signal to Ahmed, and a rush of air inflated the whale's lungs.

"We can give him a breath of air, but we're going to lose him," Williams said. "A lot of damage down below where you can't see it. He must have done a world record jump, from the looks of it. Cracked ribs, organ ruptures, internal hemorrhaging. A mess. Is this poor dying thing your Bubble, Stasov?" He snorted in disgust. "Dolphin superstition. Another of their mass of stupid lies."

From the whale's back the two men could see the whole stretch of sea surrounding the island. Countless white splashes broke the otherwise calm water. Dolphins, hundreds of dolphins, were dancing in the sea. They surrounded the island out to the horizon. Williams stared out at them, his face twisted with disgust.

"We've heard many lies over the past few years," Stasov said, sweeping his arms at the dolphins. "The nature of dolphin Revelation isn't one of them."

"Are you asking me to accept the religion of those thugs?" Williams said. "Are they here to kill us? You." A sudden look of realization swept across his face. "They want to kill you. For what you did to them at Uglegorsk, and after."

Stasov shook his head slowly. "They know that I'm to live, for now. And when it is time for me to die, they'll let me handle it myself. Dolphins are capable of an elementary politeness. No, Mr. Williams, they are here to witness the rising of the Bubble. The Great Whale swims beneath the surface of reality, and the buffetings of Her flukes are the swirls and eddies of our lives. A sweep of Her fluke has thrown this sperm whale out of the sea. God rises to breathe. When She does, all will change."

"No, Stasov, I don't buy it." Williams looked as if he wanted to pace, but there wasn't room enough on the whale's slick back. "You pretend not to believe it, officially, but you know that the dolphins have been at war with the human race since the end of the Pacific War. They sank the cruise ship *Sagittarius* off Martinique. They've cut through the hulls of fishing vessels. They've killed swimmers in the open water. It's been random murder."

"Murder?" Stasov asked. "War? The actions of insane beasts? Which is it?"

"You've played your legal games all the way along. That's how you escaped punishment, and the way they will, too."

"The evidence that they've actually killed anyone is ambiguous."

"Ambiguous!" Williams's face turned red. "Colonel Stasov, pain and death are not ambiguous."

"That's quite true," Stasov said seriously. "I know. But whatever has happened, the Americans and the Japanese have been forced to negotiate at Santa Barbara, recognizing dolphin rights. As they should have done years ago, at the end of the Pacific War."

"This is your doing, damn you! You tortured them. Your cetacean research station at Uglegorsk ranks with Dachau and Auschwitz. I watched them die at Kagalaska. I was there."

Stasov breathed slowly. "It was a war. A war for survival." His voice was calm, almost dreamy. "But next time you give your diatribe, use some of our own Soviet concentration camps, such as Vorkuta and Kolyma, instead of those German ones. My grandfather died at Vorkuta. It lends a nice symmetry." So Williams had been at Kagalaska. Had he watched his comrades' blood crystallize on the blue rime ice and felt despair when the *Wainwright* sank?

"You tortured them and now you accept their faith?" Williams asked.

"I didn't know I was torturing them," Stasov said softly. "I didn't know. But without understanding their faith, we would never have been able to communicate with them at all."

"We'll talk with them at Santa Barbara. But you, thank God, won't be there."

"No. I am forbidden. I am a war criminal." Stasov shaded his eyes. Was she finally there, at the northern horizon? He watched as the huge white shape of the *Andrei Sakharov* pulled itself over the edge of the water. From this distance she looked pure, almost Japanese. Her rough welding and patched cables didn't show. "We want the whale, Mr. Williams." His voice was distant. "We intend to take it over from you."

"What?" Williams followed Stasov's gaze. His face hardened when he saw the ship with the red star on its prow. "Damn you, you can't have it."

"Is that your choice, Mr. Williams? The *Sakharov* is equipped with the full complement of systems for keeping the whale alive. It will die otherwise, within hours. You know that."

The *Sakharov* had once been an Aleksandr Brykin class nuclear-submarine tender with another name, and had loaded sea launched ballistic missiles into their launch tubes, missiles which, fortunately for the human race's survival, had never been fired.

"Better dead than in your hands," Williams shouted.

Stasov gestured, taking in the dolphin-filled sea visible from the whale's back. "The dolphins don't seem to agree with you."

"Fuck the dolphins! They probably want to haul the whale into the ocean so they can rape it." He ran a hand over his scalp, gaining control of himself. "No. I can't do it. It will imperil the treaty negotiations at Santa Barbara." He smiled, pleased at this legalistic solution. "If we turned a whale over to Colonel Ilya Sergei—"

"I'm glad you take so much trouble to pronounce my entire name," Stasov said icily. "But who is being legalistic now? Unless we intervene, the whale will die." He paused, in wonder at the threat he was about to utter. He had long ago resolved to put the military behind himself. "The *Sakharov* took on a platoon of Russian troops when we resupplied at Karachi a week ago. We are taking them to Oman. I think they would be willing to assist us in saving this whale's life."

Williams stared out at the approaching ship. "You don't give me any choice," he said stonily.

"Choice is usually an illusion."

OFF HOKKAIDO, SEPTEMBER 2030

The aerobody had developed a noticeable list to starboard and vibrated vigorously, as if drilling through air suddenly solid. The airship's pilot, Benjamin Fliegle, took a slow sip of the steaming green tea in his stoneware cup and set it back in its heated, gimbaled holder on the control board. The sleet was heavy outside, and the windshield wiper, inadequately heated, stuttered under a thick layer of ice. Fliegle, his small shaven head perched on top of his orange saffron robe like a potato on a pumpkin, leaned forward and pounded on the windshield with his fist. The wiper tossed a chunk of wet ice and moved more smoothly. The aerobody tilted perilously and he grabbed the wheel. "Pesky thing," he muttered.

The rear hatch opened and admitted a figure in heavy insulation, as well as a blast of wet, freezing air.

"How does it look?" Fliegle said.

"Not bad," Olivia Knester said as she stripped her suit off. "Just noisy. I'll overhaul it in the shop when we get back to Kushiro, but it won't give us any trouble now." Now naked, Knester also pulled on an orange saffron robe. She was a chunky, middle-aged woman with extravagant curled eyebrows which tried to compensate for the shaved skull above them. "However, Benjamin . . ."

"Yes, Olivia?"

"The engine isn't buying your theories about the virtual identities of reciprocating parts. It will not 'wear into perfection,' it will wear into junk. Keep the crankcase oil full. Until we achieve satori and leave the Wheel, we must keep it lubricated." She turned to Stasov. "Put on your suit. We should find the proper pod of orcas soon. Benjamin, it's time to start listening."

Fliegle dropped the aerobody's altitude to fifty feet and cut back the engines until they moved at twenty miles an hour. A lever on the panel released the hydrophone. As Stasov pulled on his wetsuit, Fliegle put in his earphones and leaned back in his seat with his eyes closed. The altitude continued to drop.

"Benjamin!" Knester said sharply.

The nose went back up. "Sorry."

Stasov put on his fins, fitted underwater lenses into his eyes, and snugged the oxygenator onto the valves on his neck. Then he attached the microphone to his throat, strapped the transducer and signal processor to his chest, and activated the bone conduction speakers behind his jaw hinge. Orca speech included frequencies from 5 Hz to 80 kHz, far beyond the range of human hearing. His equipment compressed and processed the information so that he could communicate.

Sitting on the rocky peninsula of Shiretoko Hanto, communicating with the notoriously touchy orcas, had left the esoteric Buddhist monks of Yumeji Monastery unconcerned with human things. Fortunately this attitude encompassed Stasov's own past, so he had received even-handed treatment. The monks reassured him. Everyone wanted to escape the Wheel, but everyone was bound to it. Death, in the dolphin view, was the only possible escape, an escape the Buddhists did not permit themselves. Stasov found himself more dolphin than Buddhist.

"I hear him," Fliegle said. Knester nodded at Stasov, and the double bay doors swung open.

He stepped out, tucked, and fell through the gray and vaporous air, then smacked painfully into a cresting wave. As the water closed over his face, reflexes drilled into his autonomic nervous system took over. His diaphragm ceased to inflate his lungs, in a conditioned apnea, and he began to derive oxygen from his carotid gill connections.

He listened to the chatter in his earphones, sorting signals from noise. A long descending note rumbled, found the resonant frequencies of his joints, and intensified until his entire body was in pain. An orca's shout could break bones, rupture internal organs, and fill the lungs with blood. The orca's voice died away, then sounded deeper, and he was suddenly filled with unreasoning terror. Orcas' voices could kill, or they could stimulate a fear response, pump adrenalin into the human bloodstream, and race the human heart. Cetacean tricks were old to Stasov. Somewhere inside his mind a stopcock opened, the dark waters of fear drained, and he was calm again.

"Greetings, Stasov," a cool voice said. It used the sliding tones of the simple orca dialect used for speaking to children, or humans. The voice was familiar. Where had he heard it before? "Thou hast words to speak. Speak them then, for thoughts must be herded and swallowed, lest they escape to the open sea." Of course.

"It is a long way from Kagalaska, Bottom-Thumper," Stasov said, using the slightly contemptuous nickname this orca had earned for his childhood habit of bumping the hulls of Japanese fishing boats. "I trust your hunger has been stayed?"

"My hunger is infinite. But thou art still spoiled food. I must content myself with swallowing the minds of men, leaving their bodies to the sharks and fishes."

"Are you still chasing prime numbers?" Stasov asked.

"I am. I taste the fins of the Goldbach Conjecture. Soon I will sink my teeth into it. It shall not escape."

Bottom-Thumper was a highly respected mathematician, both among humans and orcas. Dolphins, on the other hand, had no interest whatsoever in mathematics. "Your prey weakens," Stasov said politely.

"Do not seek to distract me with minnows. Let loose thy desires and get thee from my sea!" The thunder of Bottom-Thumper's voice buzzed in Stasov's ribs. He hung alone in darkness, only the speed of Bottom-Thumper's replies indicating the orca's proximity.

"The Bubble Has Risen," Stasov said. "We have the Foreswimmer, the whale that signals the coming of God's Echo. We want to take him out of this sea, and let him swim in the deeper waters of the planet Jupiter. I ask you to allow this and to make the proposal in your negotiations at Santa Barbara."

Absurd and makeshift, it somehow all fit together, the only way Stasov had found out of the trap he had placed himself in. Unfortunately, it involved putting himself here in the black water, making a request which could cost him his life. Cost him his life much too soon.

"Do I hear the echo of thy guilt, Stasov?" the orca asked. "I detect its ancient fleeting shape in thy voice. Thou are foolish, as men are wont to be. Thy crimes were necessary and thus were not crimes at all. Thou may live or die, as thou thyself choose. Does an orca need to tell that to a human?"

"Is this prey then released to our jaws?" Stasov asked formally, ignoring the orca's reasoning.

"It is," Bottom-Thumper replied. "But ye humans know not the swift current that has seized you. We shall provide a guard to windward: who will be the Echo of God."

"The Messiah," Stasov said in shock.

"Thy term, inadequate and misleading, but it will do."

He had expected the orca to insist on providing an intelligent cetacean as escort to the sperm whale, whose intelligence was about that of a great ape, but had not expected the Messiah himself. It all made sense, though. It all fit together. "We will make the proper arrangements. It will not be easy. We have never taken a cetacean into space before. For an orca—"

"Not an orca! The voice of God echoes without speaking and the Echo is not an orca!" Bottom-Thumper was suddenly in a high rage, his syllables ragged like fish with their heads bitten off. The orca spoke in an odd grammatical tense, that was used either to describe dreams, or make statements so true they were apodictic, such as 'all things die' or 'before my conception I did not exist.' Stasov could barely follow the grammar.

"Watch your rectum," Stasov said in dolphin, recalling the insult he had made to Bottom-Thumper when they first met in the bloody waters off Kagalaska. "The walrus is still awaiting your pleasure."

The orca went silent for a long moment. "I should have eaten thee then, Stasov, in that swarming, evil-tasting sea. But my belly was full of men. For the last time, I fear. Thou hast the Foreswimmer, a wounded sperm whale ye wish to lift to Jupiter, a planet none of us sea dwellers has ever seen. God's Remora must accompany the whale, for the Time of the Breath is near. Go now to the Aegean Dolphin Sanctuary. There is thy goal. And much good luck may thou and all thy fellow humans have with whom thee will find there."

And then he laughed. And laughed. And *laughed*, a sound like an immense train at a grade crossing. Razor-edged, their thoughts suffused with blood even as they reasoned their way through the most subtle philosophies, bitter thinkers on the end of all, dispensers of justice and death, orcas laughed long, hard, and often. Bottom-Thumper's laughter stopped.

"Art thou willing to pay the price?"

"I am, whatever it is." Stasov could not slow the pounding of his heart.

"Float out thy limbs and remain still. Well met then, Ilya Sergeiivich Stasov."

Stasov relaxed his arms and legs and floated spread-eagled. Suddenly, silently, the smooth shape of the orca sped by, thirty feet long, black, powerful, and vanished again.

The pain was as sudden as the smash of an ax. Stasov twisted his body in agony and managed to activate the buoyancy harness. It righted him and carried him to the surface. He spit water, gasped in the cold air, and was finally able to scream.

The aerobody floated overhead in the pewter sky, a blunt-nosed wedge with two propellers flickering aft. It turned lazily around and drifted over him, buzzing like an immense insect. A harness lowered and scooped him up delicately. The sea opened around him. He looked down. Scarlet drops of blood fell past his dangling feet, the only flecks of color against the gray of the sea and sky. A six-foot-long hooked dorsal fin cut the surface of the water. The orca's head was just visible, water flowing over it in a smooth layer. Bottom-Thumper spouted once and vanished.

Knester was ready with salve and bandages. "Such accuracy," she said admiringly. "He charged a price only a human could pay."

"Damn him," Stasov said through clenched teeth.

"Don't be such a baby. A wound like this is a compliment. Usually an orca will smash you with a fluke, toss you in the air, or puncture your eardrum by shouting when making an exchange, to show his contempt. A blood price is a genuine honor, but usually involves death or maiming for life. The spinning of the Wheel is beyond our knowledge, so I can't guess why he thought you deserved such delicacy."

"We're old friends," Stasov said. She was right. It wasn't every man who was charged a blood price by an orca and ended up losing only the last two fingers on his left hand.

LENINGRAD, FEBRUARY 2031

Erika Morgenstern forged grimly up the street into the teeth of the wind. Huge rafts of dirty ice thrust up out of the Neva River, revealing black water beneath a quickly freezing scum.

The dark granite blocks of the embankment held the elegant Baroque city out of the greedy water. Despite the cold, she paused, to marvel at the golden spire of the Cathedral of Sts. Peter and Paul as it rose above the frozen city.

Ilya Stasov was housed in an eerily beautiful eighteenth-century red-stucco building with white pilasters, vivid against the snow. Two guards in bulky greatcoats, rifles slung across their shoulders, checked her papers before unlocking the door.

"You have been meeting at the Institute for Space Research?" one of them asked, a friendly youngster with straight flaxen hair sticking out from under his fur cap. "That is good. We have long waited for the Americans to ask for our help. We are smart, but poor."

That wasn't quite it, of course, and she was from New Zealand, not America, but Morgenstern wasn't about to argue with him. Instead, she smiled back. "Yes. We're going to Jupiter." She wasn't sure she believed it herself, but the agreement had been signed just that morning.

"Together, ah? That's the only way to go so far." He opened the door for her and saluted.

The hall was dark, and like all Russian hallways smelled of cabbage, this time with an overtone of frankincense from the icon lamp that glowed in the corner.

Typewriters clacked somewhere in the rear. She only belatedly identified a low moaning as a recording of a humpbacked whale call. A silent, suspicious woman, her hair tied severely back, led Morgenstern up the stairs to the front of the house.

Stasov greeted her with a formal triple cheek kiss. She held on to him for a moment longer. He had put on weight since Homma, but was still thin. "It is good to see you," he said. "Have you succeeded?" His hair was shaved close, like a swimmer's. He looked tired, and had circles under his eyes.

"Yes," she said. She thought about the years of effort that had finally brought her here to Leningrad. "We're going. In principle. As to your idea about our funding . . ."

The silent woman brought two glasses of strong tea. Stasov sweetened his with a teaspoon of blackberry jam. His left hand was no longer bandaged, and he held his glass with his thumb and first two fingers. "It is not a joke. The Delphine Delegation will provide the funding, as they have agreed at Santa Barbara."

"But why? To haul a maimed sperm whale off to Jupiter? It doesn't make any sense!"

"I have told you, though you choose not to accept it. It marks the arrival of their God. If you don't understand that, of course it doesn't make any sense."

"God save us from religion." She felt a deep sense of frustration. "I feel like I'm being financed by some dotty maiden aunt who wants her Pekinese to see Jupiter."

He tapped the rim of his glass with his spoon. "This maiden aunt will have billions of dollars in reparation money from the Santa Barbara agreement. That money is as good as any other. It is the only way you will succeed."

"I understand that. But I don't have to like it."

"None of us have to like what we have to do." A bell rang in the next room. "Excuse me," he said. "That's Vladivostok." He walked out, slumped, his limbs heavy. He looked infinitely tired.

She looked around as she listened to his low voice on the phone. The room was packed with papers. Diagrams and maps covered the elaborately figured wallpaper. The lion-footed desk was covered with strip charts and sonograms. A small bed, severely made in a military manner, was the only clear area. A heavy red folder lay on the desk. In a mood of idle curiosity, Morgenstern flipped it open. 'Minutes—Santa Barbara negotiations,' it said. The date was yesterday's. She flipped through. Every day of the negotiations, supposedly kept under rigid security, was there, extensively marked and annotated in Stasov's angular hand. She closed the notebook and sat back down in her chair.

Stasov's voice continued. She listened to it, but couldn't make out the words. After a moment, she realized that he wasn't speaking English or Russian. He was speaking a dolphin dialect. The . . . person on the other end of the line was not a human being.

"Did the dolphins fight a war with us?" she asked when he returned.

"With whom?"

"Don't be coy with me, Ilya!" she said heatedly. "Did they sink ships, those veterans of yours?"

"Until the Treaty of Santa Barbara is signed, the war between human and cetacean will continue, as it always has. It's simply that recently the struggle has been a trifle more even. That's all I will say."

"What do you have to do with Santa Barbara?"

He glanced at the red folder. "I'm not permitted to have anything to do with Santa Barbara. But I like to stay informed."

"How do you hold all this in your head? The whale . . . you might have started another war when you took it from the Indian Ocean people by force."

"I had to do it," Stasov said. "There was no other way. It's a step on the way out."

"Did you see all this, when we met at Homma?"

"I saw the sun. I saw freedom. I saw that I still had to live. I felt my redemption, but did not yet see its shape. There are still a number of things I have to do. Some of them frighten me."

"Did you see me, Ilya?" she asked, with a feeling of constriction in her throat. "Have you ever seen me? Or just what I can do?"

"I saw you, Erika. But I saw myself as well. Don't try to force me into a position I do not hold. You understand better than anyone what it is that I'm after."

She sighed. "You don't look well, Ilya. Do you sleep?"

"Poorly. Nightmares."

"Of course," she said. "Homma."

"No," he answered. "Uglegorsk."

THE AEGEAN SEA, APRIL 2031

The cliffs rose up a thousand feet above the water, encircling the twenty-mile-wide harbor like protective arms. Whitewashed villages clung to the cliff tops, glinting in the morning sunlight. The sky was a vivid, cloudless blue. Stasov leaned back against the mast, feeling it warm on his back. The *St. John Chrysostom* creaked serenely across the still water in the harbor.

His guide, Georgios Theodoros, silently trimmed the boat's bright sail. It billowed out in the breeze and they began to flop over the water. Soon they had emerged from the bay of Thera onto the open waters of the Aegean Sea.

"They call it the Temple of Poseidon Pankrator," Theodoros said. He rested easily at the stern of the boat, bearded face turned to the sun like a cat's, eyes half closed while he kept one arm over the tiller. "Poseidon, Ruler of All. Wishful thinking, attributing ancient supremacy to the Sea God. He ruled the sea, and horses. Not much else. But the Temple *is* the only structure this near which survived the eruption of the volcano Strogyle, that black day four thousand years ago, so perhaps Poseidon took it back to his bosom." That eruption had left behind the harbor of Thera, which was the immense caldera of the collapsed volcano.

It had been years since Stasov had seen Theodoros. The Greek had aged gracefully, gray appearing in his beard. He had gained a certain unpleasant notoriety due to the association of his theories with Stasov's infamous work at Uglegorsk, but he showed no hurt or anger. In his home waters he was quite an eccentric. Though the regulations governing the Aegean dolphin territories prohibited the use of noisy motor-driven vessels, they certainly did not require the hand-built wood hull blackened with pitch, the dyed woven linen sail, and the watchful painted eyes on the *St. John Chrysostom*'s prow.

"I never guessed what it would take," Theodoros said. "All my studies, and I never understood."

"I never guessed how much it would cost," Stasov replied. "But without you I would never have figured anything out."

Theodoros looked out over the sea. "It may have been a mistake, Ilya. But of course that's absurd. We had to discover their intelligence. If only . . ."

"If only they weren't a contemptible, corrupt, sexually perverse bunch of braggarts, cowards, and fools?" Stasov snorted. It was now proverbial that the more one studied dolphins, the more one disliked them. "Why didn't your ancient sources mention that?"

"They mention it, but obliquely. The humans of that era were perhaps not much different, and didn't see that it deserved much comment."

"But how did *they* figure it out?" Stasov asked in wonder. "That was four thousand years ago! They had no sound generators, no signal processing laboratories. How did the men of the Cretan Thalassocracy learn to speak to dolphins?"

"You've got it backwards. I think dolphins learned to talk from humans, being too pigheaded to think of something like that on their own, just like the unlettered Greeks learned civilization from the Cretans."

"Learned?" Stasov said. "Or were compelled to learn?"

"Did the ancient Cretans enslave dolphins to guide their ships into dangerous harbors, assist in salvage operations, and scout out enemy defenses? Most likely. I doubt, however, that they felt any great guilt at having done so."

"But still." Stasov hit the wooden gunwale with his fist. "To sail out in a ship like this, dive into the water, and learn to speak to an animal. It's incredible. The equipment we used, the time . . ."

"Don't underestimate your own achievement, Ilya. In ancient days, remember, the dolphins had not resolved to be silent. Breaking that resolution was the difficult thing."

"Difficult," Stasov said, eyes downcast. "That's one word for it."

Theodoros ignored his companion's sudden gloom. "And we were all closer to nature then, and the gods. Remember that story about the lyre player, the whale, and the dolphin that I told you back at Uglegorsk? A whale was more than a whale. He was the Foreswimmer, he who comes before, the First Bubble that rises from the spout of God to foretell the coming Breath, the new incarnation. The dolphin over whose dim head our singer broke his lyre is the Echo of God, or as others have termed him, God's Remora, Her humble, material associate, the Messiah. And that brings us here."

"Whatever happened to that dolphin?" Stasov asked. "After he guided the priests to Delphi."

"Did he die, his task finished?" Theodoros shrugged, looking closely at Stasov. "The story doesn't say. Dolphins perceive the universe by sensing sounds they generate themselves. This makes them arrogant, as if they define the universe, and their final arrogance is their belief that they can finish what they have to do, find closure, and die, achieving completion. Fortunately humans, dependent on the world outside themselves, are incapable of such a self-satisfied attitude."

Stasov turned away. "After four thousand years, they tell me, the Messiah has been born. The orcas are angry that he is not of their number but otherwise don't seem to find it much of a matter for comment."

"Why should they? He is a material Messiah, immanent, not transcendent. A money changer. A Pharisee. Even dolphin theology is crude and stupid."

That made Stasov smile. "At last we've found your pet peeve, Georgios. Lack of theological rigor."

"Don't laugh, you're the one who has to deal with it. So you want to push these lazy, incompetent creatures to the Time of the Breath. Why?"

"I shattered their silence, and now I forever hear their voices. If I bring on the Breath, and they reach their new incarnation, perhaps I can find peace."

Theodoros looked sorrowful. "You won't, Ilya. You never will. Peace is only within. But here we are." He dropped sail and the boat stilled. No land was visible. A buoy marked the shallows where the Temple lay. "Into the sea with you. Seek the Messiah. I will await your return here." He smiled sunnily at Stasov, who sat, motionless, staring at the smoothly shining water.

"You have to face them," Theodoros said. "You have madly driven this far. How can you stop?"

"I can't. I always want to, but I can't." Stasov put on his fins and slipped

337

into the water. Dolphins commented to each other somewhere in the distance, but the water around him was empty. He swam towards the voices, recognizing them. Bottom-Thumper at Hokkaido, and these three here. Who else?

In a few moments he came into sight of the Temple of Poseidon Pankrator. Buried by volcanic ash and millennia of bottom sediment, the Temple had been lost until a sounding survey detected a density anomaly. After negotiation with the Delphine Delegation it had been cleaned and restored. A forest of the distinctive Cretan columns, wider at the top than at the bottom, held up a roof edged with stylized bull's horns. Everything had been repainted its original bright polychrome, the columns red with green capitals, the bull's horns gleaming with gold. The Temple was used as a symbolic site for formal human-dolphin negotiations, since it had been from the men of the Cretan Thalassocracy that dolphins had first learned the habits of speech.

Stasov swam slowly over the old sacred precincts, tracing out the lines of the religious complex of which the Temple of Poseidon Pankrator had once been the center. The rest of the ruins had been cleared of debris and left just as they were. In front of the Temple was a large open area. This had once been the Sacred Pool, where dolphins had swum to pay homage, with the sullen sarcasm that must even then have been part of their personalities, to the humans' anthropomorphic version of the Sea God.

Three dolphins swam fitfully around the Temple. The sun probed through the water and gleamed on the ultrasonic cutting blades that made up the front edges of their flippers and dorsal fins. Their sides were armored and their bellies packed with superconducting circuitry. They turned and swam towards him in attack formation. Phobos, Deimos, and Harmonia. A coincidence, that those three had survived. The children of Aphrodite, wife of the cuckolded artificer Hephaestos, and Ares the War God. Fear, Panic, and Harmony, the contradictory emotions of Love and War, with a healthy assist from sullenly impartial technology.

"Colonel!" Deimos said, and the dolphins stopped, awaiting orders. They would still obey him, he knew. If he commanded them to cut Theodoros's boat apart, they would do it without a moment's hesitation, despite the treaty violation it would entail. His authority over them would always exist, for they knew he had the power to change the shape of the world, a power that caused them agony and terror.

Stasov ran his maimed left hand down Deimos's side, feeling the scars and machinery. In the war's second year Deimos and a dozen of his fellows had preceded a run of Soviet attack submarines from Murmansk through the perilous sea gap between Greenland and Iceland, where the enemy had placed his most sensitive submarine detection technology. Packed with equipment which made them appear to all sensors as Alfa class submarines, the dolphins had drawn ASW forces away from the real Soviet attack. Five of the nine submarines had gotten through, to provide a useful diversion of enemy forces from the main theater of war in the North Pacific. Deimos alone of his comrades had survived, and been decorated with an Order of Lenin.

"I am not a Colonel," Stasov said. He was tired of saying it.

"What are you then?" Harmonia said. Her artificial left eye glittered at him, its delicate Japanese optics covered with seaweed and algae. "An orca that walks?"

"An orca with hands," Phobos agreed. "A good definition of a human." He was the largest of the three and had gotten through the war miraculously unscathed. "We know what you want. You want God. That's why you're still alive."

"Why the hell do you care?" Harmonia made a thrumming noise indicative of disgust. "Why should we?" Her eye kept twisting and focusing at nothing. She had lost the left side of her skull during the landings at Kagalaska. Her job had been cutting free mines with her ultrasonic fin blades while suppressing their magnetic detection circuitry. At Kagalaska the dolphins had encountered a new model. Stasov had never figured out how Harmonia had managed to survive. "Why have you dragged us here to do this? I'm bored."

"He wants to hurt us more," Deimos said. "This way he can drive *all* of us. He will use the Remora like a narwhal's tusk. He will pierce us. Isn't that true, Colonel?"

"It's true," Stasov said. "But it doesn't matter. It had no effect on the validity of my request."

"Stop knocking a dead body around with your snout," the massive Phobos said. "Save logical games for the orcas, who like them. They bore us."

The three dolphins' voices sank through the water like lumps of lead. Each phrase seemed a deliberate effort, but that did not silence them.

"I'm not playing games," Stasov said. "I am serious."

"But why do you care?" cried Harmonia.

"I do. I always have."

Phobos swam up and knocked Stasov aside as if he were a vagrant piece of seaweed. Three chevrons, now dark and tarnished, marked his dorsal fin, one for each of the American submarines whose destruction had been attributable to his skillful use of his sonic and magnetic detectors. He had also helped sink the American *Aegis* cruiser *Wainwright*, saving the landings on Kagalaska.

Even now, his side bruised, Stasov felt that same surge of gratitude that had overcome him when he watched the cruiser sink into the North Pacific. "Answer her question," Phobos said. "Why do you care?"

Harmonia did not allow Stasov to answer. "*We* certainly don't. God talk is stupid."

"God will rise when She wants to," Deimos said. "We can't push Her flippers with our snouts."

They circled Stasov like mechanical, murderous sharks.

"Tell us why this matters to you," Phobos roared.

Would they slice him apart with their ultrasonic blades, these decorated veterans of that heroic, futile war, and stain the clear water with his blood? He felt like a man returned to the grave of his comrades, only to have their bony hands reach out from death to pull him beneath the surface. He would welcome their cold touch, because he knew they had the right.

"It matters because it has to happen," Stasov said. "It is necessary."

The dolphins hooted contempt. "You always do what is necessary, Colonel," Deimos said. "You tortured us until you ripped the voice from our throats—because it was necessary. You took away our bodies and turned us into mechanical sharks—because it was necessary. You killed us in your incomprehensible human war—because it was necessary. Now you come to tear us from the womb of our sea and throw us into the cold deeps of space *because it is necessary?*"

"Eating is necessary," Harmonia said. "Fucking is necessary. Breathing is necessary. Death is necessary. You're as stupid as a sea turtle that fucks in the sea and then climbs out into the air to lay its eggs where the land dwellers can steal them. I'm sure the turtle thinks it's necessary."

"You're like a shark maddened by the smell of blood," Phobos said, suddenly quiet, "who eats and eats and can't stop until its belly bursts. Won't you ever have your fill of us, Ilya Stasov?"

Crying under water seemed so maddeningly futile. He reached his arms out to them, a meaningless gesture. But what could he give them? An apology? A confession?

"You are right," he said. "I need to do it so that at last I can rest. I can try to forget what I have done to you."

"Rest," Deimos said. "A human word." Dolphins slept with only one hemisphere of their brains at a time so that they could always keep swimming. They could never stop, because they had to breathe. "Why should we grant it to you? The Treaty does not require it."

"And if the Treaty does not require it," Phobos added, "we will not do it. Name us the proper articles or leave."

"Brothers," Harmonia said, suddenly quiet. "Stasov wishes to die. He cannot until he is finished."

"Yes," Stasov said. "Give me your Messiah. And let me die."

UGLEGORSK, JUNE 2031

It was the scene of his nightmares. The tanks were now empty, the floor dry, the electronics long since packed up and discarded, but the high vault of the laboratory still contained all of the pain and terror that Stasov could imagine. From the platform where he stood the pattern of tanks on the floor looked like an ice cube tray in an abandoned refrigerator. The vault's concrete was cracked and aging, the color of long-buried bone.

Stasov held tightly to the thin metal railing though there was no danger of falling. Even empty the building whispered. The Japanese had long ago given up on the idea of turning the Uglegorsk station into an atrocity museum. It was too far from anywhere, and the torment there had not involved blood or physical torture but pain too subtle for a human to see. They concluded that the museum would have been utterly unvisited. So it had lain empty, until Stasov's irregular request for a last look at it.

The Japanese had been extraordinarily polite and cooperative, and had left Stasov to wander on his own through the ruins. Perhaps, Stasov thought, it was because they knew he could punish himself more effectively than they had ever been able to.

Suddenly something thunked on the metal stairs. Stasov shivered. Was the place really haunted? The thunk became regular, and Stasov heard the heavy breathing of someone pulling himself up the stairs.

A large figure loomed out of the darkness. "Ilya," he said. "It's been a long time."

"Antosha!" Stasov embraced the massive Anatoly Ogurtsov and kissed him. He hadn't seen the General since the middle of the war. Veterans of Uglegorsk never spoke to each other, even if they lived in the same town. The slightest word would have shattered the icy barriers they had set up around that time. Stasov suspected he knew why the other was there. Ogurtsov would ask a question, eventually. Stasov only hoped that he would be able to answer it.

Ogurtsov stepped back. His right foot was a prosthetic. When he noticed Stasov's attention, he slapped it with his cane. "Not an orca, unfortunately," he rumbled. "Nothing appropriate like that. A single bullet through the knee at Unimak. An ordinary soldier's wound." He reached into his jacket and pulled out a vodka bottle. He pulled the stopper out with his teeth and offered it to Stasov. "To old times."

"To old times," Stasov responded, and took a swallow. He almost choked.

Ogurtsov chuckled. "Now don't insult me, Ilya. I make that stuff myself. An old man's hobby. Flavored with buffalo grass."

"It's excellent," Stasov managed to choke, tears in his eyes.

"Have you lost your taste for vodka?" Ogurtsov laughed. "I remember," he gestured with his cane at the tanks below, "how we sat, you, me, and that Greek philosopher, Theodoros, and unriddled the ways of the dolphins. The drunker we got, the more sense we made of their myths and their gods. And we figured it out."

"And we did it. We tortured them until they spoke."

Ogurtsov regarded him warily. "How were we to know? How should we have realized the incredibly strong response of the cetacean brain to the sense of sound? The aural illusions we generated for them tormented them, drove them mad. It's as if those optical illusions you find in children's books drove humans to extremes of agony."

"We didn't know," Stasov whispered. "For months, years, we tortured them with illusions of moving seabeds, of impossible echoes. Their absolute faith in their senses broke them like dry sticks in our hands."

"It was a long time ago," Ogurtsov said. He put his arm around Stasov's shoulders. "Let's get out of here."

They climbed down the stairs and walked among the crumbling tanks. "Remember the first time one of them spoke?" Stasov said.

"Ilya, please—"

"Do you remember?"

Ogurtsov shook himself. "Of course I remember." He paused by a tank and looked in at its cracked and stained bottom. "There were four of us. You, me, Sadnikova, and Mikulin. Mikulin died last year, did you know? He tripped and fell down in the snow. He was drunk. He froze to death.

"I can see it. Sadnikova stood over there, her hands on the signal generator. I stood here, you next to me. Mikulin on the other side. It was our final, most sophisticated sonic pattern. The eruption of Strogyle and the sinking of the sea bottom. We'd spent months on it. We played it for that one we called Kestrel, because he swam so fast. I don't know what—"

"He died in the Battle of La Perouse Strait."

"So he got his wish at last." Ogurtsov grabbed onto the edge of the tank. "We played the illusion. And he cried out—"

" 'Let—me—die'," Stasov said through clenched teeth. "That's what he finally screamed. 'Let me die!' " He shivered. "That's how we began to talk."

"We never listened to what they said, you know. We made them talk, but we never listened. We've never understood why they want to die."

They walked through the rest of the building silently. At the back door they stopped. The sky had its usual high overcast. The *Sterlet*, the boat from the Vladivostok Oceanographic Institute, floated just off shore, its gaily fluttering red flag the only spot of color against the sea and sky. It was the vessel that would take Stasov to Vladivostok, finally back in Russian hands. From there he would go to Tyuratam, and from the spaceport there to Jupiter.

"They fought a war against us, didn't they?" Ogurtsov said. "And most of the human race never really believed it. The slimy aquatic bastards."

"Yes," Stasov answered. "They did. They sank ferry boats, pleasure craft, fishing boats. Whenever they knew they wouldn't get caught, whenever events would be confused. Terrorism, plain and simple."

Ogurtsov shook his head. "We trained them well. Phobos probably sank more than his share. He was a mean one."

"I don't doubt it."

They went down to the water and strolled along the rocky shore, letting the waves lap against their feet. Ogurtsov maneuvered easily over the rocks, occasionally kicking a loose one with his prosthetic foot. He looked at Stasov.

342

"I've talked to people in Leningrad. You've gotten everything. Everything we hid. Why do you want it?"

Stasov did not return his glance. The question had finally come. "I don't know what you're talking about."

"Ilya!" Ogurtsov took his shoulder, his hand massive. Stasov stopped. "You've cleaned out the black files, the ones the War Crimes Commission was always after. Circuit diagrams, sonic structures, echo formats. All the ways we generated those sonic images, and the effects that they had. The recordings of dolphins in pain. All of our results." He shook Stasov's shoulder. "I thought most of it had been destroyed."

"No," Stasov said. "We never throw anything away. You know that, Antosha."

"No one knows that stuff exists. The Japanese suspected, the yellow bastards, but they couldn't get their hands on it. They tried hard enough to open you up."

"They tried. I learned more from them than they did from me."

"Why do you want that stuff? After what we've been through? We never wanted to have anything to do with it ever again."

"I don't *want* it," Stasov said. "I've never wanted it. But I need it."

Ogurtsov stopped, as immovable as a mountain, holding Stasov in his grip. "Ilya, I feel guilty. We all do, each in our own way, some, I grant you, more than others. But we try to forgive ourselves, because we didn't know what we were doing. What gives you the right to think that your guilt is more important than anyone else's?"

"I know what I have to do, Antosha. That's all. I'm not trying to compete with you."

Ogurtsov dropped his hand, letting him go. "Do it then," he said, his voice tired. "Do it and be damned."

JUPITER ORBIT, JANUARY 2033

Weissmuller pumped his way towards Jupiter Forward. His entire body ached with fatigue. He'd never swum so far before, and he couldn't stop to take a rest. That was all right. The universe was really not such a big place after all. Surgically implanted physiological indicators buzzed into his bones, frantically warning him that Jupiter's magnetic field was about to give him a radiation overdose. The medical personnel at Jupiter Forward had warned him strictly. He belched in contempt. What was the problem? Humans were always afraid of all sorts of things they couldn't see or hear. The problem of ionizing radiation was too bizarre and subtle to interest Weissmuller. It could be taken care of. Humans liked solving things like that. That was what humans were for.

Though he accepted it as his due, Weissmuller's spacesuit was a marvel.

343

It followed his contours closely. Since dolphins cannot see upwards, the head dome was clear on the underside of the head only, revealing the slyly grinning jaws. The suit circulated water around the dolphin's body while hugging it closely to prevent bruising his tender dolphin skin. The microwave array thrust up between the oxygen tanks on either side of his dorsal fin.

Myoelectric connections to Weissmuller's swimming muscles operated his suit rockets, so that his motions in space were the same as they were in the water. The powerful movements of his tail operated thrust rockets; his fins fired steering rockets. A velocity dependent retro-rocket simulated the resistance of water, slowing him if he ceased to thrust with his tail. He was kept stable by automatic sightings on the fixed stars which washed around him like sea foam.

Weissmuller felt a resonant self-satisfaction. All the way down to Io and back! Jupiter and its satellites floated around him like diatoms. His echo-location signals told him that Ganymede and Jupiter were each about five kilometers away, since the microwave signals took seven seconds to get to them and back. He knew that the distance was actually much greater, but the illusion was powerful, giving him the feeling that the Jovian system could have been dropped into the Aegean Sea and lost. Even the most distant satellite, Sinope, seemed a mere hundred twenty kilometers from Jupiter.

"I fuck you, Jove!" he shouted, and shrieked in delight. He felt an erection and cursed the human engineers who had not designed the suit to provide him a release for it. He hunched, trying to rub it against something. No good. The suit fit too well. Humans had hands, so they could masturbate. Their one evolutionary advantage. He wanted a female to assault, but there wasn't one for millions of kilometers.

He thought of a shark he and the rest of his pod had killed. The dolphins had violated it repeatedly, contemptuously, then sent its body spinning into the depths, cursing it as it sank. The thought gave him a warm glow. And that sailor, who had fallen off his fishing boat near Malta! Humans were poorly built, and Weissmuller still fondly remembered the way the man's ribs had cracked like brittle coral against his snout. Had there been witnesses, of course, the dolphins would have ignored him, or even saved his life by pushing him to shore, the sort of grandstand behavior that so impressed humans. But it had been night and the man alone in the sea. How he had struggled! One of Weissmuller's brothers still bore scars from the man's scaling knife, making him a target for mockery.

Weissmuller's lust was now an agony. Could he ever violate Jupiter the same way? Could even the humans, through one of their massive, incomprehensible devices? Damn them for this insulating suit!

He distracted himself by thinking of international securities markets. The flows appeared as clearly in his mind as the currents in the Cyclades, which he had maneuvered since youth. What a roiled and complex sea the humans had invented! Capital flowed from Japan the way fresh water pours from an iceberg. The money fluid washed back and forth, rising here because of the hectic warmth of success, roiled and turbulent there because of an opposing flow. His investments, concealed under a variety of front organizations like clever hermit crabs, were doing well. It was another sea where Weissmuller could swim. No other dolphin could. But then, no other dolphin was God's Remora. He could eat the morsels from Her jaws.

Ahead, finally, was Jupiter Forward. Exuberantly, Weissmuller did a poly-octave Tarzan yell which stretched up into the ultrasonic. He arched grace-fully around the space station—and whipped his tail to brake. The vast bulk of Clarence, the cyborg whale, floated beyond it, a tiny human figure just above the whale's head. Ilya Stasov. Weissmuller fought down the urge to turn and flee. He was bone-tired, and the radiation alarms were becoming actively painful. Besides, what could Stasov do to him? After all, he was the Messiah.

"Ah, Weissmuller," Stasov said. "Thanks for coming back. Find anything interesting?" Aided by computer voice synthesis, he could speak almost as well as a dolphin. Weissmuller found his speech slightly menacing, as if the dolphin words concealed orca teeth.

"None of your business," he said sullenly. "Bugger off."

"I'm afraid it is my business." The tone was mild. "You must talk to Clarence."

Weissmuller approached the whale. Microwave echo-location was useless at this range, since the click and its return overlapped, but the clever humans had installed a processor which gave the dolphin a calculated synthetic echo. The human-modified sperm whale was now huge, much larger than even blue whales had ever been. Weissmuller had never heard a blue whale. They had vanished long before he was born.

"Don't threaten me! You can't. Article 15 of the Treaty of Santa Barbara. I'll tell the Delphine Delegation and they'll replace you. See if they won't."

"Don't be an idiot, Weissmuller. They won't replace me."

Weissmuller twitched irritably, setting off random bursts of fire from his rockets. He knew they would never replace Stasov, no matter what the human did. Stasov had continued to live when he should have been dead, because his tasks were unfinished. The thought of what completion would mean frightened the dolphin. "I won't do what you say, I don't care what—"

"You must talk to Clarence now, Weissmuller. He's in terror. He doesn't know where he is. He needs your help."

"Fuck you!" Weissmuller shrieked, and buffeted Stasov with his powerful tail. The man sailed off helplessly, tumbling until he managed to regain control with his own clumsy maneuver rockets.

"You float like a jellyfish," Weissmuller called. "A sea urchin!"

When Weissmuller had been young, he'd heard a story about ghost voices, about long-dead whales whose last calls had echoed around the seas for decades, refracting through thermoclines, sucked into the depths by cold subsurface cataracts, resonating through abyssal trenches, to finally rise up and moan their long-sunken words to the hearing of a terrified dolphin. When Stasov finally spoke, he spoke with the voice of a ghost.

"When I first did this, I had no idea of what I had done. Now I understand. It is . . . necessary. Forgive me."

"Forgive you? Feed me, and I'll forgive you. Ha ha." While orcas and humans laughed, dolphins expressed their pleasure more in the way an elderly pervert snorts at short-skirted schoolgirls.

Suddenly, Weissmuller heard the wide sounds of the sea—the clicks, groans, wails, chitters, and thumps of the aquatic obbligato. Ranging far away were the overlapping calls of a gam of humpback whales and the sharp slap as one of them breached and fell back in the water. Nearer were the loud thumps of a school of the tiny fish humans called sea drums. He was afraid. This sea was far away. The dolphin pinged out a tentative echo-location signal.

The echo returned. Bottom was a mile down, past an ill-defined thermocline. There was a set of three submerged volcanic peaks, one with a coral atoll around it, some twenty kilometers away. Nearer was a seamount that made it to the surface, creating a tiny island. Weissmuller knew the place, though he had never been there. The dolphin language had a word for every place in the sea, a word that is a schematic of the echo that the place returned, a sort of physical pun. An intelligent dolphin could carry a map of all the world's seas in his head like an epic poem.

Weissmuller was near the Maldives, in the Indian Ocean. He could hear the shapes of the distant whales as well as those of the fish that swirled around him. He pinged out a stream of signals. They returned, bearing their load of information, the details of the terrain, the sizes of the schools of fish.

With that, the pain began. His mind knew that what he heard was not real, but the part of his brain that processed the information was beyond conscious control. He felt a growing panic.

He heard the terrified call of a sperm whale. It was alone and had lost track of its gam in a storm. Weissmuller ignored it. The fears of the huge foolish whales were none of his concern. It called for help. He yelled at it to shut up so that he could hear that marvelous, all-encompassing sea.

Suddenly, the bottom moved. The dolphin felt a primal terror. The sea and its creatures moved eternally, but the land always remained steady. When the bottom of the sea became unstable, everything ended.

He was no longer in the Maldives. He swam the Aegean, and could sense the landmarks of the Sea of Crete as they had been four thousand years before. This was where it had started and where it had ended. The water roared and the bottom shook, marking the destruction of the only universe intelligent dolphins had ever known. Panic pierced through him. The bottom of the sea rippled like the body of a skate, and his mind dissolved in agony.

As the sea bottom rippled it lost its contours, becoming as smooth as the back of a whale. And indeed that was what it was. The floor of the sea had become a whale which thrust powerfully beneath him. Her spout could blow him to the stars.

"Ah, my remora," a giant voice spoke, using the dolphin language but not sounding like a dolphin or an orca. "The parasite on God. I should rub you off on the barnacled hull of a human ship and leave you to sink to the bottom of the sea."

"No!" Weissmuller screamed. "You can't! I am your Echo. I know it all. All! I have done my duty. I know how humans work. I know their money, their markets. I can defeat them. I can achieve our destiny. You know me!"

God's back rose up towards him and the edges of the sea closed in. The surface of the water above him became solid. Weissmuller heard his own echoes returning faster and faster, with improbable clarity. And he would be unable to breathe! He was trapped. He was going to die.

"I know you," God's voice said. "You are a coward and a fool."

"No! Forgive me! Forgive—"

The walls closed in around him, and then vanished, leaving the vasts of space. Weissmuller keened desperately and flailed around in terror. "Stasov!" he shrieked. "Where are you? Let me die!"

"You know me," Stasov said quietly.

"I know you! You changed the world so we would speak. You tore the voice from our throats! Your teeth gave us birth. Oh, it hurts. Life hurts!"

"It always hurts. You are the Echo of God. The thinking races of the sea have raised you up here so that you may pull them after you. You will hurt most of all. Or so you will believe." Stasov paused. "I'll never forgive you for having forced me to do this. Instead of completion I end with the knowledge that pain is never finished."

"A human problem, not mine," Weissmuller said. "I will talk to the whale." Then, plaintively: "I'm sorry I went to Io. I feel sick. Ilya?"

Stasov silently activated the whale's voice. Clarence promptly sounded an elaborate and specific call.

Weissmuller shook, panicked. "It's a death call, Stasov. A death call!"

"What else do you expect?" Stasov said coldly. "Do you think that you're the only one who wants to die? I've heard that call before."

Stasov had once watched a gam of seven fin whales get chased for three days across the South Atlantic by two cooperating pods of orcas. It was a vicious, hard pursuit. Finally the fins, tired and spent, sent a call to the orcas, who stopped pursuing immediately and waited. The fins gathered close together and talked to each other while the orcas swept around them. Finally, one fin whale emerged from the gam and swam out to the orcas. The whales had decided among themselves which was going to be eaten. The orcas tore that one to pieces and let the others swim away unharmed.

"Clarence wants to negotiate his death with you."

"What do I say to him? I don't know what to say!"

"Tell him he has to live. To live and suffer. Just like the rest of us."

One of Jupiter Forward's spinning rings was filled with water, providing Weissmuller with a place to live. He could swim around and around it, leaping into the air at those place that engineers had raised the ceiling, and feel almost at home. No solid place intruded. There was nowhere for a human being to stand, so Erika Morgenstern and Ilya Stasov floated in the water. Morgenstern hated this, as an affront to her dignity, but there was no way to compel the dolphin to visit her office.

"What did he do to you, Ilya?" she whispered. "I haven't seen you look like this since . . . since we met."

"It's what I did to him that matters," he answered, his voice flat.

"But what—"

"I had to do it *again*. What I once did all unknowing, I just did with full understanding of what it meant."

The dolphin appeared around the curve of the ring, skimming the water towards them. He had learned to use the low gravity and the Coriolis force of the spinning ring to extend his leaps. He hit the water with his belly, splashing them, and vanished. A moment later he nuzzled the Director's crotch. She gasped, then, having been briefed by Stasov, reacted by driving her heel into the dolphin's sensitive blowhole. Weissmuller surfaced and keened in pain.

"Stop it," Stasov said. "It's what you deserve."

"Screw you, Madame Director," Weissmuller said. In air his breath was foul with old fish. He moved his head towards her and, despite herself, she ran her hands down his smooth sides. He wriggled. "Did you buy Vortek like I told you?"

Her hands stopped. "Yes."

"And?"

"It's up seventeen in the past month, damn you! How did you know? How could a dolphin possibly know anything about the technical knowledge market? And more importantly, why did you tell me?" She pushed him away.

"I wanted you to understand that I'm not just kidding around. I know where the tuna school. Believe it."

"What are you talking about?"

The dolphin was silent for a long moment. "About one kilometer south-southwest of Portland Point, in the sea off the island of Jamaica, is the wreckage of the *Constantino de Braganza*, a Spanish treasure ship out of Cartagena, sunk in 1637 by a Dutch privateer as she tried to flee to the safety of Port Royal. We heard it happen but we didn't know what humans were fighting for. It carried three tons of gold bullion, another ton and a half of specie, and an equal amount of silver, all of which now lies on the bottom, along with the bones of men." He spoke almost tonelessly, as if reciting a long-ago lesson. "Given the rights of the Delphine Delegation in such matters, I think it might be possible for us to assist you directly, Madame Director Morgenstern. If you agree to assist us. We know where the ships lie. We remember."

"You mean the goddam Treaty of Santa Barbara gives the dolphins—"

"Full salvage rights," Weissmuller interrupted gleefully. "Anything that went down more than fifty years ago. Article 77, and sections 1 and 2 of Article 78. You thought your technology gave you the advantage. Ha. You forgot about our memory. It's long. Longer than you ever dreamed. Humans think they're so smart. Big joke."

She turned to Stasov. "You must have known. How did you allow them to swindle us like this?"

He stared back at her and did not reply.

"All that money," she murmured. "All that money . . ."

"We want to make a deal," Weissmuller prompted.

"What are you offering me?" she asked.

Weissmuller twitched and wailed suddenly, as if he were a mystic in a trance. "Full control of the next project! Not subject to restrictions, regulations, and the need to resolve conflicts between various entities. I'm the first dolphin in space. I won't be the last. Not by a long shot. We want to escape, and we need the hands of humans to do it. Humans must carry us to the stars. I hate it! Our destiny, in the hands of *humans*. All I can do is pay you. There's a Venetian galley off the coast of Dalmatia, full of gold. It sank in 1204. I hope you rot in hell." He twisted and disappeared into the water.

"*They* aren't the ones who want it, Ilya," she whispered. "I don't know why, but *you* want them to go to the stars. That's why you helped them with the Treaty of Santa Barbara."

"That's true," he answered simply.

"I've known it since I visited you in Leningrad and saw that folder, as I suppose you meant me to. It was just part of your expiation." She swallowed. "Just as I was another. You tried to show me, but I never listened. I had no idea how little I meant to you."

"Erika, I had no choice. I had to make up for the evil I had done. I've explained it to you before."

"Is your guilt the most important thing in the universe? Is everything you've done since I found you at Camp Homma justified by it?"

They drifted apart in the water as if physically pushed by her intensity.

"I needed to reach an ending," Stasov said. "I needed to find completion."

She stared at him, suddenly frightened. "And have you?"

He shook his head slowly. "Nothing is ever complete. But I reached my ending before I left Homma. I realized that when I tortured Weissmuller, with the full knowledge of what I was doing. I'd always had that knowledge.

I'd always known. I ripped their minds apart so that we could conquer some rocks in the North Pacific. I tormented them to satisfy my curiosity."

"No," she breathed. "No. You never knew."

"Perhaps I didn't know they could speak. But I always knew they could suffer. And as long as I live, they *will* suffer."

"They'll suffer even if you don't live."

He looked at her for a long moment. "True. But that will be none of my concern."

Stasov floated in space, the great form of the whale in front of him.

"Ilya," Weissmuller said, his voice large and hollow. "I have done all that I had to. We can float now, humans, dolphins, and orcas, on a great sea of cash. With that money we can swim to the stars. It's hateful! I feel more disgusted that I ever thought I'd be."

"Yes," Stasov said. "The Time of the Breath is upon us." Jupiter loomed above him, through some odd error of perception, like a heavy fruit ready to fall. Clarence drifted quiescent, singing a simple song to himself, almost a lullaby. His physical systems had been checked, and Weissmuller had managed to calm him down, finally doing the job that most humans believed he had been brought to do. Stasov alone knew that he had been brought to lead his people forth from the sea.

Looking at the dolphin and his massive companion, Stasov had a sudden image of dolphins, grinning faces at the front of the bodies that were their ships, slipping through the spaces between the stars, gamboling amid the debris of the cometary Oort cloud that surrounded each star, whipping, in tight formation, over the frozen surface of a neutron star, and finally plunging through a planet's warm, blue atmosphere to fall hissing, red-hot, into the alien sea, there to swim and play as they always had. When the time came to move on, they would blast with a roar back into the infinite spaces that had become their second home. Humans, more sedate and deliberate, would follow after in their own ships, dolphins leaping in their bow waves and guiding them to a safe port.

Morgenstern would, he knew, continue the task that had driven her since youth, even though she had discovered that her passion had been used by another for his own purposes. Neither she nor the dolphins had seen any reason to pull cetaceans into space, but Stasov had decided.

"What happens to the Remora once his God breathes?" Weissmuller said. "What happens to the Echo once God has located what She is after? What am I now?"

"Nothing," Stasov said. "And less than nothing."

The countdown was reaching its conclusion and Clarence's rockets prepared themselves to blast.

"Then let me die! I can go with Clarence and sink into the endless seas of Jupiter. I've done what I had to."

"No," Stasov said. "You're still necessary to others. It's my turn to die."

"You selfish shark spawn!" Weissmuller shrieked. "You've played with us, ripped us apart, driven us to our destiny, and called up *our* God to help you create the echo that *you* want to hear. You always get your way! I say I will die and there isn't anything you can do about it!" He thrust his tail and his rockets flared. "I won't stop at Io this time!"

Stasov had expected this, and was already straddling the dolphin, as if riding him through the sea. He manually stopped down the oxygen flow until Weissmuller was suffocating. The rockets died, and the dolphin shuddered beneath him.

"Ilya," Weissmuller said forlornly. "I fear the net. Humans caught us when we followed the tuna, suffocated and killed us, thoughtlessly. They didn't realize that when we listen we do not think, and are thus easily captured. You tortured us with false echoes and woke us up. Are you going to haul us to the stars in your nets? Won't you ever leave us alone? Won't you ever stop tormenting us?"

"There's only one way to stop. I see that. You don't have to tell me."

"Do you think death will stop you? The pain is always there. Damn you!"

Stasov drifted near Clarence, until the surface of the whale suddenly changed from something next to him to something beneath him. He found the point of attachment and tied himself to it.

With smooth thrust, fusion flames blossomed around Clarence's midsection. Clarence sang a journey song, one full of landmarks in a sea that he would never hear again. Could he invent new ones for the deeper sea of Jupiter?

Stasov rested against the gravity created by Clarence's acceleration.

He would never hear Clarence's new songs.

Soon he would sink into the deepest sea of all.

MICHAEL SWANWICK
The Edge of the World

One of the most popular and respected of all the decade's new writers, Michael Swanwick made his debut in 1980 with two strong and compelling stories, "The Feast of St. Janis" and "Ginungagap," both of which were Nebula award finalists that year. Since then, he has gone on to become a frequent contributor to *OMNI*, *Isaac Asimov's Science Fiction Magazine*, and *Amazing*; his stories have also appeared in *Penthouse*, *Universe*, *High Times*, *Triquarterly*, and *New Dimensions*, among other places. His powerful story "Mummer Kiss" was a Nebula Award finalist in 1981, and his story "The Man Who Met Picasso" was a finalist for the 1982 World Fantasy Award. He has also been a finalist for the John W. Campbell Award. His fast-paced and evocative first novel, *In the Drift*, was published in 1985 as part of the resurrected Ace Specials line. His most recent book is the critically acclaimed novel *Vacuum Flowers*, and he has just finished work on a third novel, *The Drowning Lands*. Upcoming is a collection of his short fiction, titled *Gravity's Angels*, and a collection of his collaborative work, *Slow Dancing Through Time*. His story "Trojan Horse" was in our Second Annual Collection, his story "Dogfight," written with William Gibson, was in our Third Annual Collection; his story "Covenant of Souls" was in our Fourth Annual Collection, and his "The Dragon Line" was in our Sixth Annual Collection. Swanwick lives in Philadelphia with his wife Marianne Porter and their young son Sean.

In the intense, scary, evocative, and mystical story that follows, he takes us to the edge of the world—and beyond.

▼

The Edge of the World

MICHAEL SWANWICK

The day that Donna and Piggy and Russ went to see the Edge of the World was a hot one. They were sitting on the curb by the gas station that noontime, sharing a Coke and watching the big Starlifters lumber up into the air, one by one, out of Toldenarba AFB. The sky rumbled with their passing. There'd been an incident in the Persian Gulf, and half the American forces in the Twilight Emirates were on alert.

"My old man says when the Big One goes up, the base will be the first to go," Piggy said speculatively. "Treaties won't allow us to defend it. One bomber comes in high and *whaboom*"—he made soft nuclear explosion noises—"it's all gone." He was wearing camouflage pants and a khaki T-shirt with an iron-on reading: KILL 'EM ALL AND LET GOD SORT 'EM OUT. Donna watched as he took off his glasses to polish them on his shirt. His face went slack and vacant, then livened as he put them back on again, as if he were playing with a mask.

"You should be so lucky," Donna said. "Mrs. Khashoggi is still going to want that paper done on Monday morning, Armageddon or not."

"Yeah, can you believe her?" Piggy said. "That weird accent! And all that memorization! Cut me some slack. I mean, who cares whether Ackronnion was part of the Mezentian Dynasty?"

"You ought to care, dipshit," Russ said. "Local history's the only decent class the school's got." Russ was the smartest boy Donna had ever met, never mind the fact that he was flunking out. He had soulful eyes and a radical haircut, short on the sides with a dyed-blond punklock down the back of his neck. "Man, I opened the *Excerpts from Epics* text that first night, thinking it was going to be the same old bullshit, and I stayed up 'til dawn. Got to school without a wink of sleep, but I'd managed to read every last word.

This is one weird part of the world; its history is full of dragons and magic and all kinds of weird monsters. Do you realize that in the eighteenth century three members of the British legation were eaten by demons? That's in the historical record!"

Russ was an enigma to Donna. The first time they'd met, hanging with the misfits at an American School dance, he'd tried to put a hand down her pants, and she'd slugged him good, almost breaking his nose. She could still hear his surprised laughter as blood ran down his chin. They'd been friends ever since. Only there were limits to friendship, and now she was waiting for him to make his move and hoping he'd get down to it before her father was rotated out.

In Japan she'd known a girl who had taken a razor blade and carved her boyfriend's name in the palm of her hand. How could she do that, Donna had wanted to know? Her friend had shrugged, said, "As long as it gets me noticed." It wasn't until Russ that Donna understood.

"Strange country," Russ said dreamily. "The sky beyond the Edge is supposed to be full of demons and serpents and shit. They say that if you stare into it long enough, you'll go mad."

They all three looked at one another.

"Well, hell," Piggy said. "What are we waiting for?"

The Edge of the World lay beyond the railroad tracks. They bicycled through the American enclave into the old native quarter. The streets were narrow here, the sideyards crammed with broken trucks, rusted-out buses, even yachts up in cradles with staved-in sides. Garage doors were black mouths hissing and spitting welding sparks, throbbing to the hammered sound of worked metal. They hid their bikes in a patch of scrub apricot trees where the railroad crossed the industrial canal and hiked across.

Time had altered the character of the city where it bordered the Edge. Gone were the archers in their towers, vigilant against a threat that never came. Gone were the rose quartz palaces with their thousand windows, not a one of which overlooked the Edge. The battlements where blind musicians once piped up the dawn now survived only in Mrs. Khashoggi's texts. Where they had been was now a drear line of weary factory buildings, their lower windows cinderblocked or bricked up and those beyond reach of vandals' stones painted over in patchwork squares of gray and faded blue.

A steam whistle sounded and lines of factory workers shambled back inside, brown men in chinos and white shirts, Syrian and Lebanese laborers imported to do work no native Toldenarban would touch. A shredded net waved forlornly from a basketball hoop set up by the loading dock.

There was a section of hurricane fence down. They scrambled through.

As they cut across the grounds, a loud whine arose from within the factory building. Down the way another plant lifted its voice in a solid wham-wham-wham as rhythmic and unrelenting as a headache. One by one the factories shook themselves from their midday drowse and went back to work. "Why do they locate these things along the Edge?" Donna asked.

"It's so they can dump their chemical waste over the Edge," Russ explained. "These were all erected before the Emir nationalized the culverts that the Russian Protectorate built."

Behind the factory was a chest-high concrete wall, rough-edged and pebbly with the slow erosion of cement. Weeds grew in clumps at its foot. Beyond was nothing but sky.

Piggy ran ahead and spat over the Edge. "Hey, remember what Nixon said when he came here? *It is indeed a long way down.* What a guy!"

Donna leaned against the wall. A film of haze tinted the sky gray, intensifying at the focal point to dirty brown, as if a dead spot were burned into the center of her vision. When she looked down, her eyes kept grabbing for ground and finding more sky. There were a few wispy clouds in the distance and nothing more. No serpents coiled in the air. She should have felt disappointed but, really, she hadn't expected better. This was of a piece with all the natural wonders she had ever seen, the waterfalls, geysers and scenic vistas that inevitably included power lines, railings and parking lots absent from the postcards. Russ was staring intently ahead, hawklike, frowning. His jaw worked slightly, and she wondered what he saw.

"Hey, look what I found!" Piggy whooped. "It's a stairway!"

They joined him at the top of an institutional-looking concrete and iron stairway. It zigzagged down the cliff toward an infinitely distant and nonexistent Below, dwindling into hazy blue. Quietly, as if he'd impressed himself, Piggy said, "What do you suppose is down there?"

"Only one way to find out, isn't there?" Russ said.

Russ went first, then Piggy, then Donna, the steps ringing dully under their feet. Graffiti covered the rocks, worn spraypaint letters in yellow and black and red scrawled one over the other and faded by time and weather into mutual unreadability, and on the iron railings, words and arrows and triangles had been markered onto or dug into the paint with knife or nail: JURGEN BIN SCHEISSKOPF. MOTLEY CRUE. DEATH TO SATAN AMERICA IMPERI-ALIST. Seventeen steps down, the first landing was filthy with broken brown glass, bits of crumbled concrete, cigarette butts, soggy, half-melted cardboard. The stairway folded back on itself and they followed it down.

"You ever had *fugu*?" Piggy asked. Without waiting for an answer, he said, "It's Japanese poisonous blowfish. It has to be prepared very carefully —they license the chefs—and even so, several people die every year. It's considered a great delicacy.'

"Nothing tastes that good," Russ said.

"It's not the flavor," Piggy said enthusiastically. "It's the poison. Properly prepared, see, there's a very small amount left in the sashimi and you get a threshold dose. Your lips and the tips of your fingers turn cold. Numb.

That's how you know you're having the real thing. That's how you know you're living right on the edge."

"I'm already living on the edge," Russ said. He looked startled when Piggy laughed.

A fat moon floated in the sky, pale as a disk of ice melting in blue water. It bounced after them as they descended, kicking aside loose soda bottles in styrofoam sleeves, crushed Marlboro boxes, a scattering of carbonized spark plugs. On one landing they found a crumpled shopping cart, and Piggy had to muscle it over the railing and watch it fall. "Sure is a lot of crap here," he observed. The landing smelled faintly of urine.

"It'll get better farther down," Russ said. "We're still near the top, where people can come to get drunk after work." He pushed on down. Far to one side they could see the brown flow from the industrial canal where it spilled into space, widening and then slowly dispersing into rainbowed mist, distance glamoring it beauty.

"How far are we planning to go?" Donna asked apprehensively.

"Don't be a weak sister," Piggy sneered. Russ said nothing.

The deeper they went, the shabbier the stairway grew, and the spottier its maintenance. Pipes were missing from the railing. Where patches of paint had fallen away the bolts anchoring the stair to the rock were walnut-sized lumps of rust.

Needle-clawed marsupials chittered warningly from niches in the rock as they passed. Tufts of grass and moth-white gentians grew in the loess-filled cracks.

Hours passed. Donna's feet and calves and the small of her back grew increasingly sore, but she refused to be the one to complain. By degrees she stopped looking over the side and out into the sky, and stared instead at her feet flashing in and out of sight while one hand went slap-grab-tug on the rail. She felt sweaty and miserable.

Back home she had a half-finished paper on the Three Days Incident of March, 1810, when the French Occupation, by order of Napoleon himself, had fired cannonade after cannonade over the Edge into nothingness. They had hoped to make rainstorms of devastating force that would lash and destroy their enemies, and created instead only a gunpowder haze, history's first great failure in weather control. This descent was equally futile, Donna thought, an endless and wearying exercise in nothing. Just the same as the rest of her life. Every time her father was reposted, she had resolved to change, to be somebody different this time around, whatever the price, even if—no, especially if—it meant playacting something she was not. Last year in Germany when she'd gone out with that local boy with the Alfa Romeo and instead of jerking him off had used her mouth, she had thought: Everything's going to be different now. But no.

Nothing ever changed.

"Heads up!" Russ said. "There's some steps missing here!" He leaped, and the landing gonged hollowly under his sneakers. Then again as Piggy jumped after.

Donna hesitated. There were five steps gone and a drop of twenty feet before the stairway cut back beneath itself. The cliff bulged outward here, and if she slipped she'd probably miss the stairs altogether.

She felt the rock draw away from her to either side, and was suddenly aware that she was connected to the world by the merest speck of matter, barely enough to anchor her feet. The sky wrapped itself about her, extending to infinity, depthless and absolute. She could extend her arms and fall into it forever. What would happen to her then, she wondered. Would she die of thirst and starvation, or would the speed of her fall grow so great that the oxygen would be sucked from her lungs, leaving her to strangle in a sea of air? "Come on Donna!" Piggy shouted up at her. "Don't be a pussy!"

"Russ—" she said quaveringly.

But Russ wasn't looking her way. He was frowning downward, anxious to be going. "Don't push the lady," he said. "We can go on by ourselves."

Donna choked with anger and hurt and desperation all at once. She took a deep breath and, heart scudding, leaped. Sky and rock wheeled over her head. For an instant she was floating, falling, totally lost and filled with a panicky awareness that she was about to die. Then she crashed onto the landing. It hurt like hell, and at first she feared she'd pulled an ankle. Piggy grabbed her shoulders and rubbed the side of her head with his knuckles. "I knew you could do it, you wimp."

Donna knocked away his arm. "Okay, wise-ass. How are you expecting to get us back up?"

The smile disappeared from Piggy's face. His mouth opened, closed. His head jerked fearfully upward. An acrobat could leap across, grab the step and flip up without any trouble at all. "I—I mean, I—"

"Don't worry about it," Russ said impatiently. "We'll think of something." He started down again.

It wasn't natural, Donna realized, his attitude. There was something obsessive about his desire to descend the stairway. It was like the time he'd brought his father's revolver to school along with a story about playing Russian roulette that morning before breakfast. "Three times!" he'd said proudly.

He'd had that same crazy look on him, and she hadn't the slightest notion then or now how she could help him.

Russ walked like an automaton, wordlessly, tirelessly, never hurrying up or slowing down. Donna followed in concerned silence, while Piggy scurried between them, chattering like somebody's pet Pekingese. This struck Donna as so apt as to be almost allegorical: the two of them together yet alone, the distance between filled with noise. She thought of this distance, this silence, as the sun passed behind the cliff and the afternoon heat lost its edge.

The stairs changed to cement-jacketed brick with small buttresses cut into the rock. There was a pile of stems and cherry pits on one landing, and the railing above them was white with bird droppings. Piggy leaned over the rail and said, "Hey, I can see seagulls down there. Flying around."

"Where?" Russ leaned over the railing, then said scornfully, "Those are pigeons. The Ghazoddis used to release them for rifle practice."

As Piggy turned to follow Russ down again, Donna caught a glimpse into his eyes, liquid and trembling with helplessness and despair. She'd seen that fear in him only once before, months ago when she'd stopped by his house on the way to school, just after the Emir's assassination.

The living room windows were draped and the room seemed unnaturally gloomy after being out in the morning sun. Blue television light flickered over shelves of shadowy ceramic figurines: Dresden milkmaids, Chantilly Chinamen, Meissen pug-dogs connected by a gold chain held in their champed jaws, naked Delft nymphs dancing.

Piggy's mother sat in a limp dressing gown, hair unbrushed, watching the funeral. She held a cup of oily-looking coffee in one hand. Donna was surprised to see her up so early. Everyone said that she had a bad problem with alcohol, that even by service wife standards she was out of control.

"Look at them," Piggy's mother said. On the screen were solemn processions of camels and Cadillacs, sheikhs in jellaba, keffigeh and mirrorshades, European dignitaries with wives in tasteful gray Parisian fashions. "They've got their nerve."

"Where did you put my lunch?" Piggy said loudly from the kitchen.

"Making fun of the Kennedys like that!" The Emir's youngest son, no more than four years old, salaamed his father's casket as it passed before him. "That kid's bad enough, but you should see the mother, crying as if her heart were broken. It's enough to turn your stomach. If I were Jackie, I'd—"

Donna and Piggy and Russ had gone bowling the night Emir was shot. This was out in the ruck of cheap joints that surrounded the base, catering almost exclusively to servicemen. When the Muzak piped through overhead speakers was interrupted for the news bulletin, everyone had stood up and cheered. *Up we go*, someone had begun singing, and the rest had joined in, *into the wild blue yonder.* . . . Donna had felt so sick with fear and disgust she had thrown up in the parking lot. "I don't think they're making fun of anyone," Donna said. "They're just—"

"Don't talk to her!" The refrigerator door slammed shut. A cupboard door slammed open.

Piggy's mother smiled bitterly. "This is exactly what you'd expect from these ragheads. Pretending they're white people, deliberately mocking their betters. Filthy brown animals."

"*Mother!* Where is my fucking lunch?"

She looked at him then, jaw tightening. "Don't you use that kind of language on me, young man."

"All right!" Piggy shouted. "All right, I'm going to school without lunch! Shows how much you care!"

He turned to Donna and in the instant before he grabbed her wrist and dragged her out of the house, Donna could no longer hear the words, could only see that universe of baffled futility haunting Piggy's eyes. That same look she glimpsed today.

The railings were wooden now, half the posts rotting at their bases, with an occasional plank missing, wrenched off and thrown over the side by previous visitors. Donna's knees buckled and she stumbled, almost lurching into the rock. "I have to stop," she said, hating herself for it. "I cannot go one more step."

Piggy immediately collapsed on the landing. Russ hesitated, then climbed up to join them. They three sat staring out into nothing, legs over the Edge, arms clutching the rail.

Piggy found a Pepsi can, logo in flowing Arabic, among the rubble. He held it in his left hand and began sticking holes in it with his butterfly knife, again and again, cackling like a demented sex criminal. "Exterminate the brutes!" he said happily. Then, with absolutely no transition he asked, "How are we ever going to get back up?" so dolorously Donna had to bite back her laughter.

"Look, I just want to go on down a little bit more," Russ said.

"Why?" Piggy sounded petulant.

"So I can get down enough to get away from this garbage." He gestured at the cigarette butts, the broken brown glass, sparser than above but still there. "Just a little further, okay guys?" There was an edge to his voice, and under that the faintest hint of a plea. Donna felt helpless before those eyes. She wished they were alone, so she could ask him what was wrong.

Donna doubted that Russ himself knew what he expected to find down below. Did he think that if he went down far enough, he'd never have to climb back? She remembered the time in Mr. Herriman's algebra class when a sudden tension in the air had made her glance across the room at Russ, and he was, with great concentration, tearing the pages out of his math text and dropping them one by one on the floor. He'd taken a five-day suspension for that, and Donna had never found out what it was all about. But there was a kind of glorious arrogance to the act; Russ had been born out of time. He really should have been a medieval prince, a Medici or one of the Sabakan pretenders.

"Okay," Donna said, and Piggy of course had to go along.

Seven flights farther down the modern stairs came to an end. The wooden railing of the last short, septambic flight had been torn off entire, and laid across the steps. They had to step carefully between the uprights and the rails. But when they stood at the absolute bottom, they saw that there were stairs beyond the final landing, steps that had been cut into the stone itself. They were curving swaybacked things that millennia of rain and foot traffic had worn so uneven they were almost unpassable.

Piggy groaned. "Man, you *can't* expect us to go down that thing."

"Nobody's asking you," Russ said.

They descended the old stairway backwards and on all fours. The wind breezed up, hitting them with the force of an expected shove first to one side and then the other. There were times when Donna was so frightened she thought she was going to freeze up and never move again. But at last the stone broadened and became a wide, even ledge, with caves leading back into the rock.

The cliff face here was green-white with lichen, and had in ancient times been laboriously smoothed and carved. Between each cave (their mouths alone left in a natural state, unaltered) were heavy-thighed women—goddesses, perhaps, or demons or sacred dancers—their breasts and faces chipped away by the image-hating followers of the Prophet at a time when Mohammed yet lived. Their hands held loops of vines in which were entangled moons, cycling from new through waxing quarter and gibbous to full and then back through gibbous and waning quarter to dark. Piggy was gasping, his face bright with sweat, but he kept up his blustery front. "What the fuck is all this shit, man?"

"It was a monastery," Russ said. He walked along the ledge dazedly, a wondering half smile on his lips. "I read about this." He stopped at a turquoise automobile door someone had flung over the Edge to be caught and tossed by fluke winds, the only piece of trash that had made it down this far. "Give me a hand."

He and Piggy lifted the door, swung it back and forth three times to build up momentum, then lofted it over the lip of the rock. They all three lay down on their stomachs to watch it fall away, turning end over end and seeming finally to flicker as it dwindled smaller and smaller, still falling. At last it shrank below the threshold of visibility and became one of a number of shifting motes in the downbelow, part of the slow, mazy movement of dead blood cells in the eyes' vitreous humors. Donna turned over on her back, drew her head back from the rim, stared upward. The cliff seemed to be slowly tumbling forward, all the world inexorably, dizzyingly leaning down to crush her.

"Let's go explore the caves," Piggy suggested.

They were empty. The interiors of the caves extended no more than thirty feet into the rock, but they had all been elaborately worked, arched ceilings carved with thousands of *faux tesserae*, walls adorned with bas-relief pillars.

Between the pillars the walls were taken up with long shelves carved into the stone. No artifacts remained, not so much as a potsherd or a splinter of bone. Piggy shone his pocket flash into every shadowy niche. "Somebody's been here before us and taken everything," he said.

"The Historic Registry people, probably." Russ ran a hand over one shelf. It was the perfect depth and height for a line of three-pound coffee cans. "This is where they stowed the skulls. When a monk grew so spiritually developed he no longer needed the crutch of physical existence, his fellows would render the flesh from his bones and enshrine his skull. They poured wax in the sockets, then pushed in opals while it was still warm. They slept beneath the faintly gleaming eyes of their superiors."

When they emerged it was twilight, the first stars appearing from behind a sky fading from blue to purple. Donna looked down on the moon. It was as big as a plate, full and bright. The rilles, dry seas and mountain chains were preternaturally distinct. Somewhere in the middle was Tranquility Base, where Neil Armstrong had planted the American flag.

"Jeez, it's late," Donna said. "If we don't start home soon, my mom is going to have a cow."

"We still haven't figured a way to get back up," Piggy reminded her. Then, "We'll probably have to stay here. Learn to eat owls and grow crops sideways on the cliff face. Start our own civilization. Our only serious problem is the imbalance of sexes, but even that's not insurmountable." He put an arm around Donna's shoulders, grabbed at her breast. "You'd pull the train for us, wouldn't you, Donna?"

Angrily she pushed him away and said, "You keep a clean mouth! I'm so tired of your juvenile talk and behavior."

"Hey, calm down, it's cool." That panicky look was back in his eyes, the forced knowledge that he was not in control, could never be in control, that there was no such thing as control. He smiled weakly, placatingly.

"No, it is not. It is most emphatically not 'cool.' " Suddenly she was white and shaking with fury. Piggy was a spoiler. His simple presence ruined any chance she might have had to talk with Russ, find out just what was bugging him, get him to finally, really notice her. "I am sick of having to deal with your immaturity, your filthy language and your crude behavior."

Piggy turned pink and began stuttering.

Russ reached a hand into his pocket, pulled out a chunk of foil-wrapped hash, and a native tin pipe with a carved coral bowl. The kind of thing the local beggar kids sold for twenty-nine cents. "Anybody want to get stoned?" he asked suavely.

"You bastard!" Piggy laughed. "You told me you were out!"

Russ shrugged. "I lied." He lit the pipe carefully, drew in, passed it to Donna. She took it from his fingers, felt how cold they were to her touch, looked up over the pipe and saw his face, thin and ascetic, eyelids closed, pale and Christlike through the blue smoke. She loved him intensely in that instant and wished she could sacrifice herself for his happiness. The pipe's stem was overwarm, almost hot, between her lips. She drew in deep.

The smoke was raspy in her throat, then tight and swirling in her lungs. It shot up into her head, filled it with buzzing harmonics: the air, the sky, the rock behind her back all buzzing, ballooning her skull outward in a visionary rush that forced wide-open first her eyes and then her mouth. She choked and spasmodically coughed. More smoke than she could imagine possibly holding in her lungs gushed out into the universe.

"Hey, watch that pipe!" Piggy snatched it from her distant fingers. They tingled with pinpricks of pain like tiny stars in the darkness of her flesh. "You were spilling the hash!" The evening light was abuzz with energy, the sky swarming up into her eyes. Staring out into the darkening air, the moon rising below her and the stars as close and friendly as those in a children's book illustration, she felt at peace, detached from worldly cares. "Tell us about the monastery, Russ," she said, in the same voice she might have used a decade before to ask her father for a story.

"Yeah, tell us about the monastery, Unca Russ," Piggy said, but with jeering undertones. Piggy was always sucking up to Russ, but there was tension there too, and his sarcastic little challenges were far from rare. It was classic beta male jealousy, straight out of Primate Psychology 101.

"It's very old," Russ said. "Before the Sufis, before Mohammed, even before the Zoroastrians crossed the gulf, the native mystics would renounce the world and go to live in cliffs on the Edge of the World. They cut the steps down, and once down, they never went back up again."

"How did they eat then?" Piggy asked skeptically.

"They wished their food into existence. No, really! It was all in their creation myth: In the beginning all was Chaos and Desire. The world was brought out of Chaos—by which they meant unformed matter—by Desire, or Will. It gets a little inconsistent after that, because it wasn't really a religion, but more like a system of magic. They believed that the world wasn't complete yet, that for some complicated reason it could never be complete. So there's still traces of the old Chaos lingering just beyond the Edge, and it can be tapped by those who desire it strongly enough, if they have distanced themselves from the things of the world. These mystics used to come down here to meditate against the moon and work miracles.

"This wasn't sophisticated stuff like the Tantric monks in Tibet or anything, remember. It was like a primitive form of animism, a way to force the universe to give you what you wanted. So the holy men would come down here and they'd wish for . . . like riches, you know? Filigreed silver goblets with rubies, mounds of moonstones, elfinbone daggers sharper than Damascene steel. Only once they got them they weren't supposed to want them. They'd just throw them over the Edge. There were these monasteries all along the cliffs. The farther from the world they were, the more spiritually advanced."

"So what happened to the monks?"

"There was a king—Althazar? I forget his name. He was this real greed-head, started sending his tax collectors down to gather up everything the monks brought into existence. Must've figured, hey, the monks weren't using them. Which as it turned out was like a real major blasphemy, and the monks got pissed. The boss mystics, all the real spiritual heavies, got together for this big confab. Nobody knows how. There's one of the classics claims they could run sideways on the cliff just like it was the ground, but I don't know. Doesn't matter. So one night they all of them, every monk in the world, meditated at the same time. They chanted together, saying, It is not enough that Althazar should die, for he has blasphemed. He must suffer a doom such as has been visited on no man before. He must be unmade, uncreated, reduced to less than has ever been. And they prayed that there be no such king as Althazar, that his life and history be unmade, so that there never had been such king as Althazar.

"And he was no more.

"But so great was their yearning for oblivion that when Althazar ceased to be, his history and family as well, they were left feeling embittered and did not know why. And not knowing why, their hatred turned upon themselves, and their wish for destruction, and they too all of a single night, ceased to be." He fell silent.

At last Piggy said, "You believe that crap?" Then, when there was no answer, "It's none of it true, man! Got that? There's no magic, and there never was." Donna could see that he was really angry, threatened on some primal level by the possibility that someone he respected could even begin to believe in magic. His face got pink, the way it always did when he lost control.

"No, it's all bullshit," Russ said bitterly. "Like everything else."

They passed the pipe around again. Then Donna leaned back, stared straight out, and said, "If I could wish for anything, you know what I'd wish for?"

"Bigger tits?"

She was so weary now, so pleasantly washed out, that it was easy to ignore Piggy. "I'd wish I knew what the situation was."

"What situation?" Piggy asked. Donna was feeling langorous, not at all eager to explain herself, and she waved away the question. But he persisted. "What situation?"

"Any situation. I mean, all the time, I find myself talking with people and I don't know what's really going on. What games they're playing. Why they're acting the way they are. I wish I knew what the situation was."

The moon floated before her, big and fat and round as a griffin's egg, shining with power. She could feel that power washing through her, the background radiation of decayed chaos spread across the sky at a uniform three degrees Kelvin. Even now, spent and respent, a coin fingered and thinned to the worn edge of nonexistence, there was power out there, enough to flatten planets.

Staring out at that great fat boojum snark of a moon, she felt the flow of potential worlds, and within the cold silver disk of that jester's skull, rank with magic, sensed the invisible presence of Russ's primitive monks, men whose minds were nowhere near comprehensible to her, yet vibrated with power, existing as matrices of patterned stress, no more actual than Donald Duck, but no less powerful either. She was caught in a waking fantasy, in which the sky was full of power and all of it accessible to her. Monks sat empty-handed over their wishing bowls, separated from her by the least fictions of time and reality. For an eternal instant all possibilities fanned out to either side, equally valid, no one more real than any other. Then the world turned under her, and her brain shifted back to realtime.

"Me," Piggy said, "I just wish I knew how to get back up the stairs."

They were silent for a moment. Then it occurred to Donna that here was the perfect opportunity to find out what was bugging Russ. If she asked cautiously enough, if the question hit him just right, if she were just plain lucky, he might tell her everything. She cleared her throat. "Russ? What do you wish?"

In the bleakest voice imaginable, Russ said, "I wish I'd never been born."

She turned to ask him why, and he wasn't there.

"Hey," Donna said. "Where'd Russ go?"

Piggy looked at her oddly. "Who's Russ?"

It was a long trip back up. They carried the length of wooden railing between them, and every now and then Piggy said, "Hey, wasn't this a great idea of mine? This'll make a swell ladder."

"Yeah, great," Donna would say, because he got mad when she didn't respond. He got mad, too, whenever she started to cry, but there wasn't anything she could do about that. She couldn't even explain why she was crying, because in all the world—of all his friends, acquaintances, teachers, even his parents—she was the only one who remembered that Russ had ever existed.

The horrible thing was that she had no specific memories of him, only a vague feeling of what his presence had been like, and a lingering sense of longing and frustration.

She no longer even remembered his face.

"Do you want to go first or last?" Piggy had asked her.

When she'd replied, "Last. If I go first, you'll stare at my ass all the way up," he'd actually blushed. Without Russ to show off in front of, Piggy was a completely different person, quiet and not at all abusive. He even kept his language clean. But that didn't help, for just being in his presence was enough to force understanding on her: that his bravado was fueled by his insecurities and aspirations, that he masturbated nightly and with self-loathing, that he despised his parents and longed in vain for the least sign of love from them. That the way he treated her was the sum and total of all of this and more.

She knew exactly what the situation was.

Dear God, she prayed, let it be that I won't have this kind of understanding when I reach the top. Or else make it so that situations won't be so painful up there, that knowledge won't hurt like this, that horrible secrets won't lie under the most innocent word.

They carried their wooden burden upward, back toward the world.

MEGAN LINDHOLM

Silver Lady and the Fortyish Man

Here's a sly and sprightly story that examines the kind of magic that can survive in even that most prosaic of locales—the neighborhood shopping mall.

Megan Lindholm is a popular young fantasy writer who gained wide critical recognition with her first novel, *The Wizard of the Pigeons*. Her other novels include *The Reindeer People*, *Wolf's Brother*, and *Luck of the Wheels* and she is at work on another novel called *Cloven Hooves*. She lives in Roy, Washington.

▼

Silver Lady and the Fortyish Man

MEGAN LINDHOLM

It was about 8:15 P.M. and I was standing near the register in a Sears in a sub-standard suburban mall the first time the fortyish man came in. There were forty-five more minutes to endure before the store would close and I could go home. The Muzak was playing and a Ronald McDonald display was waving at me cheerily from the children's department. I was thinking about how animals in traps chew their legs off. There was a time when I couldn't understand that type of survival mechanism. Now I could. I was wishing for longer, sharper teeth when the fortyish man came in.

For the last hour or so, salespeople had outnumbered customers in the store. A dead night. I was the only salesperson in Ladies' Fashions and Lingerie and I had spent the last two hours straightening dresses on hangers, zipping coats, putting T-shirts in order by size and color, clipping bras on hangers, and making sure all the jeans faced the same way on the racks. Now I was tidying up all the bags and papers under the register counter. Boredom, not dedication. Only boredom can drive someone to be that meticulous, especially for four dollars an hour. One part boredom to two parts despair.

So a customer, *any* kind of a customer, was a welcome distraction. Even a very ordinary fortyish man. He came straight up to my counter, threading his way through the racks without even a glance at the dresses or sweaters or jeans. He walked straight up to me and said, "I need a silk scarf."

Believe me, the last thing this man needed was a silk scarf. He was tall, at least six foot, and had reached that stage in his life where he buckled his belt under his belly. His dark hair was thinning, and the way he combed it did nothing to hide the fact. He wore fortyish-man clothing, and I won't describe it, because if I did you might think there was something about the way he dressed that made me notice him. There wasn't. He was ordinary in the most common sense of the word, and if it had been a busy night in the store, I'd never even have seen him. So ordinary he'd be invisible. The only remarkable thing about him was that he was a fortyish man in a Sears store on a night when we had stayed open longer than our customers had stayed awake. And that he'd said he needed a silk scarf. Men like him *never* buy silk scarves, not for any reason.

But he'd said he needed a silk scarf. And that was a double miracle of sorts, the customer knowing what he wanted, and I actually having it. So I put on my sales smile and asked, "Did you have any particular color in mind, sir?"

"Anything," he said, an edge of impatience in his voice. "As long as it's silk."

The scarf rack was right by the register, arranged with compulsive tidiness by me earlier in the shift. Long scarves on the bottom rack, short scarves on the top rack, silk to the left, acrylics to the right, solid colors together in a rainbow spectrum on that row, patterns rioting on that hook, all edges gracefully fluted. Scarves were impulse sales, second sales, "wouldn't you like a lovely blue scarf to go with that sweater, miss?" sales. No one marched into a Sears store at 8:15 at night and demanded a silk scarf. People who needed silk scarves at 8:15 at night went to boutiques for them, little shops that smelled like perfumes or spices and had no Hamburglars lurking in the aisles. But this fortyish man wouldn't know that.

So I leaned across the counter and snagged a handful, let my fingers find the silk ones and pull them gently from their hooks. Silk like woven moonlight in my hands, airy scarves in elusive colors. I spread them out like a rainbow on the counter. "One of these, perhaps?" I smiled persuasively.

"Any of them, it doesn't matter, I just need a piece of silk." He scarcely glanced at them.

And then I said one of those things I sometimes do, the words falling from my lips with sureness, coming from god knows where, meant to put the customer at ease but always getting me into trouble. "To wrap your Tarot cards, undoubtedly."

Bingo, I'd hit it. He lifted his eyes and stared at me, as if suddenly seeing me as a person and not just a saleswoman in a Sears at night. He didn't say anything, just looked at me. It was like having cross-hairs tattooed on my forehead. In exposing him, I had exposed myself. Something like that. I cleared my throat and decided to back off and get a little more formal.

"Cash or charge?" I asked, twitching a blue one from the slithering heap on the counter, and he handed me a ten, and dug for the odd change. I stuffed the scarf in a bag and clipped his receipt on it and that was it. He left, and I spent the rest of my shift making sure that all the coat hangers on the racks were exactly one finger space apart.

* * *

I had taken the job in November, hired on in preparation for the Christmas rush, suckered in by the hope that after the new year began I would become full time and get better wages. It was February, and I was still getting less than thirty hours a week and only four dollars an hour. Every time I thought about it, I could feel rodents gnawing at the bottom of my heart. There is a sick despair to needing money so desperately that you can't quit the job that doesn't pay you enough to live on, the job that gives you just enough irregular hours to make job hunting for something better next to impossible. Worst of all was the thought that I'd fashioned and devised this trap myself. I'd leaped into it, in the name of common sense and practicality.

Two years ago I'd quit a job very similar to this one, to live on my hoarded savings and dreams of being a free-lance writer. I'd become a full-time writer, and I loved it. And I'd almost made it. For two years I skimped along, never much above poverty level, but writing and taking photographs, doing a little free-lance journalism to back up the fiction, writing a story here, a story there, and selling them almost often enough to make ends meet.

Almost.

How the hell long can anyone live on *almost*? Buying almost new clothes at the second-hand store, almost fresh bread at the thrift store, almost stylish shoes at the end-of-season sales. Keeping the apartment almost warm, the dripping, rumbling refrigerator keeping food almost cold, telling my friends I was almost there. Almost writing the one really good story that would establish me as a writer to be reckoned with. I still loved it, but I started to notice little things. How my friends always brought food when they came to visit, and my parents sent money on my birthday, and my sister gave me "hand-me-downs" that fit me perfectly, and, once, still had the tags on. This is fine, when you are twenty or so, and just striking out on your own. It is not so good when you are thirty-five and following your chosen career.

One day I woke up and knew that the dream wasn't going to come true. My Muse was a faithless slut who drank all my wine and gave me half a page a day. I demanded more from her. She refused. We quarreled. I begged, I pleaded, I showed her the mounting stacks of bills, but she refused to produce. I gave her an ultimatum, and she ignored me. Left me wordless, facing empty white pages and a stack of bills on the corner of my desk. One of two things happened to me then. I've never decided which it was. Some of my friends told me I'd lost faith. Others said I'd become more practical. I went job-hunting.

In November, I re-entered the wonderful world of retail merchandising, to work a regular nine-to-five job and make an ordinary living, with clockwork paychecks and accounts paid the first time they billed me. I'd leaped back into salesmanship with energy and enthusiasm, pushing for that second sale, persuading women to buy outfits that looked dreadful on them, always asking if they wanted to apply for our charge card. I'd been a credit to the department. All management praised me. But no one gave me a raise, and full time hours were a mirage on the horizon. I limped along, making *almost* enough money to make ends meet. It felt very familiar. Except that I didn't love what I did. I was stuck with it. I wasn't any better off than I had been.

And I wasn't writing anymore, either.

My Muse had always been a fickle bitch, and the moment I pulled on panty-hose and clipped on an "I AM SEARS" tag, she moved out, lock, stock, and inspiration. If I had no faith in her power to feed me, then to hell with me, was the sentiment as she expressed it. All or nothing, that was her, like my refrigerator, either freezing it all or dripping the vegetable bin full of water. All or nothing, no half-way meetings. So it was nothing, and my days off were spent, not pounding the keys, but going to the laundromat, where one can choose between watching one's underwear cavort gaily in the dryer window, or watching gaunt women in mis-matched outfits abuse their children. ("That's *it*, Bobby! That's it, I absolutely mean it, you little shit! Now you go stand by that basket and you hold onto it with both hands, and don't you *move* until I tell you you can. You move one step away from that basket and I'm going to whack you. You hear me, Bobby? YOU (Whack!) GET YOUR (Whack!) HANDS ON THAT (Whack!) BASKET! Now shut up or I'll *really* give you something to cry about!") I usually watched my underwear cavorting through the fluff-dry cycle.

And so I worked at Sears, from nine to one, or from five to nine, occasionally getting an eight hour day, but seldom more than a twenty-four hour week, watching income not quite equal out-go, paying bills with a few dollars and many promises, spacing it out with plastic, and wondering, occasionally, what the hell I was going to do when it all caught up with me and fell apart.

Days passed. Not an elegant way to express it, but accurate. So there I was again, one weekday night, after eight, dusting the display fixtures and waiting for closing time, wondering why we stayed open when the rest of the mall closed at seven. And the fortyish man came in again. I remembered him right away. He didn't look any different from the first time, except that this time he was a little more real to me because I had seen him before. I stood by my counter, feather duster in hand, and watched him come on, wondering what he wanted this time.

He had a little plastic container of jasmine potpourri, from the bath and bedding department. He set it on the counter and asked, "Can I pay for this here?"

I was absolutely correct as a salesperson. "Certainly, sir. At Sears, we can ring up purchases from any department at any register. We do our best to make things convenient for our customers. Cash or charge?"

"Cash," he said, and as I asked, "Would you like to fill out an application for our Sears or Discover Charge Card? It makes shopping at Sears even more convenient, and in addition to charging, either card can be used as a check cashing card," he set three Liberty Walking silver dollars, circa 1923, on the plastic countertop between us. Then he stood and looked down at me, like I was a rat and he'd just dropped a pre-fab maze into place around me.

"Sure you want to use those?" I asked him, and he nodded without speaking.

So I rang up the jasmine potpourri and dropped the three silver dollars into the till, wishing I could keep them for myself, but we weren't allowed to have our purses or any personal cash out on the selling floor, so there was no way I could redeem them and take them home. I knew someone would nab them before they ever got to the bank, but it wasn't going to be me, and wasn't that just the way my whole life had been going lately? The fortyish man took his jasmine potpourri in his plastic Sears bag with the receipt stapled on the outside of it and left. As he left, I said, "Have a nice evening, sir, and thank you for shopping at our Sears store." To which he replied solemnly, "Silver Lady, this job is going to kill you." Just like that, with the capital letters in the way he said it, and then he left.

Now I've been called a lot of things by a lot of men, but Silver Lady isn't one of them. Mud duck. More of a mud duck, that's me, protective coloring, not too much makeup, muted colors in my clothes, unobtrusive jewelry if any at all. Camouflage. Dress just enough like anyone else so that no one notices you, that's the safest way. In high school, I believed I was invisible. If anyone looked at me, I would pick my nose and examine it until they looked away. They hardly ever looked back. I'd outgrown those tricks a long time ago, of course, but *Silver Lady*? That was a ridiculous thing to call me, unless he was mocking me, and I didn't think he had been. But somehow it seemed *worse* that he had been serious, and it stung worse than an insult, because he had seemed to see in me something that I couldn't imagine in myself. Stung all the sharper because he was an ordinary fortyish man, run of the mill, staid and regular, pot-belly and thinning hair, and it wasn't *fair* that he could imagine more about me than I could about myself. I mean, hell, I'm the writer, the one with the wild imagination, the vivid dreams, the razor-edged visions, right?

So. I worked out my shift, chewing on my tongue until closing time, and it wasn't until I had closed my till, stapled my receipts together, and chained off the dressing room that I noticed the little box on the corner of my counter. Little cardboard jewelry box, silver tone paper on the outside, no bag, no label, no nothing, just the silver stripes and Nordstrom in elegant lettering on the outside. A customer had forgotten it there, and I shoved it into my skirt pocket to turn it in at Customer Convenience on my way out.

I went home, climbed the stairs to my apartment, stepping in the neighbor's cat turd on the way up, got inside, cleaned off my shoe, washed my hands five or six times, and put the kettle on for a cup of tea. I dropped into a chair and got jabbed by the box in my pocket. And the "oh, shit, here's trouble come knocking" feeling washed over me in a deep brown wave.

I knew what would happen. Some customer would come looking for it, and no one would know anything about it, but security would have picked me up on their closed circuit camera inside their little plastic bubbles on the ceiling. This was going to be it, the end of my rotten, low-paying little job, and my rent was due in two weeks, and this time the landlord wanted all of it at once. So I sat, holding the little silver box, and cursing my fate.

I opened it. I mean, what the hell, when there's no place left but down, one might as well indulge one's curiosity, so I opened it. Inside were two large earrings, each as long as my thumb. Silver ladies. They wore long gowns and their hair and gowns were swept back from their bodies by an invisible wind that pressed the metallic fabric of their bodices close against their high breasts and whipped their hair into frothy silver curls. They didn't match, not quite, and they weren't intended to be identical. I knew I could go to Nordstrom's and search for a hundred years and I'd never find anything like them. Their faces were filled with serenity and invitation, and they weighed heavy in my hand. I didn't doubt they were real silver, and that someone had fashioned them, one at a time, to be the only ones of their kinds. And I *knew*, like *knowing* about the Tarot cards, that the fortyish man had made them and brought them and left them, and they were for me.

Only I don't have pierced ears.

So I put them back on the cotton in their little box and set them on my table, but I didn't put the lid back on. I looked at them, now and then, as I fixed myself a nutritious and totally adequate Western Family chicken pot pie for dinner and ate it out of the little aluminum pan and followed it with celery with peanut butter on it and raisins on top of the peanut butter.

That evening I did a number of useful and necessary things, like defrosting the refrigerator, washing out my panty-hose, spraying my shoes with Lysol spray, and dribbling bleach on the landing outside my apartment in the hopes it would keep the neighbor's cat away. I also put my bills in order by due date, and watered the stump of the houseplant I'd forgotten to water last week. And then, because I wasn't writing, and the evening can get very long when you're not writing, I did something I had once seen my sister and two of her girlfriends do when I was thirteen and they were seventeen and rather drunk. I took four ice cubes and a sewing needle and went into the bathroom and unwrapped a bar of soap. The idea is, you sandwich your earlobes between the ice cubes and hold them there until they're numb. Then you put the bar of soap behind your earlobe to hold it steady, and you push the sewing needle through. Your earlobes are numb, so it doesn't hurt, but it is weird because you hear the sound the needle makes going through your earlobe. On the first ear. On the second ear, it hurt like hell, and a big drop of blood welled out and dripped down the side of my neck, and I screamed

"Oh, SHIT!" and banged my fist on the bathroom counter and broke a blood vessel in my hand, which hurt worse than my ears.

But it was done, and when my ears quit bleeding, I went and got the earrings and stood before the mirror and threaded their wires through my raw flesh. The wires were thin, and they pulled at the new holes in my ears, and it couldn't have hurt more if I'd hung a couple of anvils from my bleeding earlobes. But they looked beautiful. I stood looking at what they did to my neck and the angle of my jaw and the way they made the stray twining of my hair seem artful and deliberate. I smiled, serene and inviting, and almost I could see his Silver Lady in my own mirror.

But like I say, they hurt like hell, and tiny drips of my blood were sliding down the silver wires, and I couldn't imagine sleeping with those things swinging from my ears all night. So I lifted them out and put them back in their box and the wires tinged the cotton pink. Then I wiped my earlobes with hydrogen peroxide, shivering at the sting. And I went to bed wondering if my ears would get infected.

They didn't, they healed, and the holes didn't grow shut, even though I didn't keep anything in them to hold them open. A Friday came when there was a breath of spring in the air, and I put on a pale blue blouse that I hadn't worn in so long that it felt like new again. Just before I left my apartment, I went back, and got the box and went to the bathroom and hung the silver ladies from my ears. I went to work.

Felicia, my department head, complimented me on them, but said they didn't look, quite, well, professional, to wear to work. I agreed she was probably right, and when I nodded, I felt their pleasant weight swinging on my ears. I didn't take them off. I collected my cash bag and went to open up my till.

I worked until six that day, and I smiled at people and they smiled back, and I didn't really give a damn how much I sold, but I sold probably twice as much as I'd ever sold before, maybe because I didn't give a damn. At the end of my shift, I got my coat and purse and collected my week's paycheck and decided to walk out through the mall instead of through the back door. The mall was having 4-H week, and I got a kick out of seeing the kids with their animals, bored cats sitting in cages stuffed full of kitty toys, little signs that say things like, "Hi, my name is Peter Pan, and I'm a registered Lop Rabbit," an incubator full of peeping chicks, and, right in the middle of the mall, someone had spread black plastic and scattered straw on top of it, and a pudgy girl with dark pigtails was demonstrating how to groom a unicorn.

I looked again, and it was a white billy goat, and one that was none too happy about being groomed. I shook my head, and felt the silver ladies swing, and as I turned away, the fortyish man stepped out of the Herb and Tea Emporium with an armful of little brown bags. He swung into pace beside me, smelling like cinnamon, oranges and cloves, and said, "You've just got to see this chicken. It plays tic-tac-toe."

Sure enough, some enterprising 4-H'er had rigged up a board with red and blue lights for the x's and o's, and for a quarter donation, the chicken would play tic-tac-toe with you. It was the fattest old rooster I'd ever seen, its comb hanging rakishly over one eye, and it beat me three times running. Which was about half my coffee money for the week, but what the hell, how often do you get the chance to play tic-tac-toe with a chicken?

The fortyish man played him and won, which brought the rooster up to the bars of the cage, flapping its wings and striking out, and I found myself dragging the fortyish man back out of beak range while the young owner of the rooster tried to calm his bird. We just laughed, and he took my elbow and guided me into a little Mexican restaurant that opens off the mall, and we found a table and sat down. The first thing I said was, "This is ridiculous. I don't even know you, and here I find myself defending you from irate roosters and having dinner with you."

And he said, "Permit me to introduce myself, then. I am Merlin."

I nearly walked out right then.

It's like this. I'm a skeptic. I have this one friend, a very nice woman. But she's always saying things like, "I can tell by your aura that you are troubled today," or talking about how I stunt my spiritual growth by ignoring my latent psychic powers. Once she phoned me up at eleven at night, long distance, *collect*, to tell me she'd just had a psychic experience. She was house-sitting for a friend in a big old house on Whidby Island. She was sitting watching television, when she clearly heard the sound of footsteps going up the stairs. Only from where she was sitting, she could (she says) see the stairs quite clearly and there was no one there. So she froze, and she heard footsteps going along the upstairs hallway and then she heard the bathroom door shut. Then, she said, she heard the unmistakable and noisy splashing of a man urinating. The toilet flushed, and then all was silence. When she got up the nerve to go check the upstairs bathroom, there was no one there. But—THE SEAT WAS UP! So she had phoned me right away to jar me from my skepticism. Every time she comes over, she always has to throw her rune chips for me, and for some reason, they always spell out death and disaster and horrendous bad fortune just around the bend for me. Which may actually prove that she's truly psychic, because that fortune had never been far wrong for me. But it doesn't keep me from kidding her about her ghostly urinator. She's a friend, and she puts up with it, and I put up with psychic-magic-spiritualism jazz.

But the fortyish man I didn't know at all—well, at least not much, and I wasn't going to put up with it from him. That was pushing it too far. There he was, fortyish and balding and getting a gut, and expecting me to listen to him talk weird as well. I mean, okay, I'm thirty-five, but everyone says I look a lot younger, and while only *one* man had ever called me Silver Lady, the rest haven't exactly called me Dog Meat. Maybe I'm not attractive in the standard, popular sense, but people who see me don't shudder and look away. Mostly they just tend not to see me. But at any rate, I *did* know that I wasn't so desperate that I had to latch onto a fortyish man with wing-nut ideas for company. Except that just then the waitress walked past on her way to the next table, laden with two combination plates, heavy white china loaded to the gunnels with enchiladas and tacos and burritos, garnished with dollops of white sour cream and pale green guacamole, with black olives frisking dangerously close to the lip of the plate, and I suddenly knew I could listen to anyone talk about anything a lot more easily than I could go home and face Banquet Fried Chicken, its flaking brown crust covered with thick hoarfrost from my faulty refrigerator. So I did.

We ordered and we ate and he talked and I listened. He told me things. He was not *the* Merlin, but he did know he was descended from him. Magic was not what it had been at one time, but he got by. One quote I remember exactly. "The only magic that's left in the world right now is the magic that we make ourselves, deliberately. You're not going to stumble over enchantment by chance. You have to be open to it, looking for it, and when you first think you might have glimpsed it, you have to *will* it into your life with every machination available to you." He paused. He leaned forward to whisper, "But the magic is never quite what you expect it to be. Almost, but never exactly." And then he leaned back and smiled at me, and I knew what he was going to say next.

He went on about the magic he sensed inside me, and how he could help me open myself up to it. He could feel that I was suppressing a talent. It was smooth, the way he did it. I think that if I had been ten or fifteen years younger, I could have relaxed and gone alone with it, maybe even been flattered by it. Maybe if *he* had been five or ten years younger, I would have chosen to be gullible, just for the company. But dinner was drawing to a close, and I had a hunch what was going to come after dinner, so I just sort of shook my head and said that nothing in my life had ever made me anything but a skeptic about magic and ESP and psychic phenomena and all the rest of that stuff. And then he said what I knew he would, that if I'd care to come by his place he could show me a few things that would change my mind in a hurry. I said that I'd really enjoyed talking to him and dinner had been fun, but I didn't think I knew him well enough to go to his apartment. Besides, I was afraid I had to get home and wash my hair because I had the early shift again tomorrow morning. He shrugged and sat back in his chair and said he understood completely and I was wise to be cautious, that women weren't the only ones distressed by so-called "date-rapes." He said that in time I would learn that I could trust him, and someday we'd probably laugh about my first impression of him.

I agreed, and we chuckled a little, and the waitress brought more coffee and he excused himself to use the men's room. I sat, stirring sugar and creamer into my coffee, and wondering if it wouldn't be wiser to skip out now, just leave a little note that I had discovered it was later than I thought and I had to hurry home but that I'd had a lovely time and thank-you. But that seemed like a pretty snakey thing to do to him. It wasn't like he was repulsive or anything, actually he was pretty nice and had very good eyes, dark brown, and a shy way of looking aside when he smiled and a wonderful voice that reminded me of cello strings. I suppose it was that he was fortyish and balding and had a pot-belly. If that makes me sound shallow, well, I'm sorry. If he'd been a little younger, I could probably have warmed up to him. If *I'd* been a little younger, too, maybe I would even have gone to his apartment to be deskepticised. But he wasn't and I wasn't and I wouldn't. But I wasn't going to be rude to him, either. He didn't deserve that. So I sat, toughing it out.

He'd left his packages of tea on the table and I picked one up and read it. I had to smile. Magic Carpet Tea. It smelled like orange spice to me. Earl Grey tea had been re-named Misplaced Dreams Tea. The scent of the third was unfamiliar to me, maybe one of those pale green ones, but it was labeled Dragon's Breath Tea. The fortyish man was really into this psychic-magic thing, I could tell, and in a way I felt a little sorry for him. A grown man, on the slippery-slide down side of his fortieth birthday, clinging to fairy-tales and magic, still hoping something would *happen* in his life, some miracle more wondrous than financing a new car or finding out the leaky hot-water heater is still under warranty. It wasn't going to happen, not to him, not to me, and I felt a little more gentle toward him as I leaned back in my chair and waited for him to return.

He didn't. You found that out a lot faster than I did. I sat and waited and drank coffee, and it was only when the waitress re-filled my cup that I realized how long it had been. His coffee was cold by then, and so was my stomach. I knew he'd stuck me with the check and why. I could almost hear him telling one of his buddies, "Hey, if the chick's not going to come across, why waste the bread, man?" Body slammed by humiliation that I'd been so gullible, I wondered if the whole magic thing was something he just used as a lure for women. Probably. And here I'd been preening myself, just a little, all through dinner, thinking that he was still seeing in me the possibility of magic and enchantment, that for him I had some special fey glow.

Well, my credit cards were bottomed out, I had less than two bucks in cash, and my check book was at home. In the end, the restaurant manager reluctantly cashed my paycheck for me, probably only because he knew Sears wouldn't write a rubber check and I could show him my employee badge. Towards the end he was even sympathetic about the fortyish man treating me so badly, which was even worse, because he acted like my poor little heart was broken instead of me just being damn mad and embarrassed. As I was leaving, finally, let me get *out* of here, the waitress handed me the three little paper bags of tea with such a condescending "poor baby" look that I wanted to spit at her. And I went home.

The strange part is that I actually cried after I got home, more out of frustration and anger than any hurt, though. I wished that I knew his real name, so I could call him up and let him know what I thought of such a cheap trick. I stood in front of the bathroom mirror, looking at my red eyes and swollen runny nose, and I suddenly knew that the restaurant people had been seeing me more clearly than I or the fortyish man did. Not Silver Lady or even mud duck, but plain middle-aged woman in a blue-collar job with no prospects at all. For a moment it got to me, but then I stood up straight and glared at the mirror. I felt the silver ladies swinging from my ears, and as I looked at them, it occurred to me that they were probably worth a lot more than the meal I had just paid for, and that I had his tea, to boot. So, maybe he hadn't come out of it any better than I had, these earrings hadn't gotten him laid, and if he had skipped out without paying for the meal, he'd left his tea as well, and those specialty shop teas don't come cheap. For the first time, it occurred to me that things didn't add up, quite. But I put it out of my mind, fixed myself a cup of Misplaced Dreams Tea, read for a little while, and then went to bed.

I dreamed about him. Not surprising, considering what he'd put me through. I was in a garden, standing by a silver bench shaded by an arching trellis heavy with a dark green vine full of fragrant pink flowers. The fortyish man was standing before me, and I could see him, but I had the sense that he was disembodied, not really there at all. "I want to apologize," he said, quite seriously. "I never would have left you that way voluntarily. I'm afraid I was magicked away by one of my archrivals. The same one who has created the evil spell that distresses you. He's imprisoned me in a crystal, so I'm afraid I won't be seeing you for a while."

In this dream, I was clad in a gown made of peacock feathers, and I had silver rings on all my fingers. Little silver bells were on fine chains around my ankles. They tinkled as I stepped closer to him. "Isn't there anything I can do to help you?" my dream-self asked.

"Oh, I think not," he replied. "I just didn't want you to think badly of me." Then he smiled. "Silver Lady, you are one of the few who would worry first about breaking the enchantment that binds me, rather than plotting how to break your own curse. I cannot help but believe that the forces that balance all magic will find a way to free us both."

"May you be right, my friend," I replied.

And that was the end of the dream, or the end of as much as I can remember. I awoke in the morning with vague memories of a cat batting at tinkling silver chimes swinging in a perfumed wind. I had a splitting headache. I got out of bed, got dressed, and went to work at Sears.

For a couple of days, I kept expecting him to turn up again, but he didn't.

I just kept going along. I told Felicia that I couldn't live on the hours and pay I was getting, and she told me that she was very disappointed with the number of credit applications I was turning in, and that full-time people were only chosen from the most dedicated and enthusiastic part-timers. I said I'd have to start looking for work elsewhere, and she said she understood. We both knew there wasn't much work of any kind to be had, and that I could be replaced with a bored house-wife or a desperate community college student at a moment's notice. It was not reassuring.

In the next three weeks, I passed out twenty-seven copies of my resume to various bored people at desks. I interviewed for two jobs that were just as low-paying as the one I already had. I found a fantastic job that would have loved to hire me, but its funding called for it to be given to a displaced homemaker or a disadvantaged worker. Then I called on a telephone interviewing position ad in the paper. They liked my voice and asked me to come in. After a lot of pussyfooting, it turned out to be a job where you answered toll calls from heavy breathers and conversed animatedly about their sexual fantasies. "Sort of an improvisational theater of the erotic," said my interviewer. She had some tapes of some sample calls, and I found myself listening to them and admitting, yes, it sounded easy. Best of all, the interviewer told me, I could work from my own home, doing the dishes or sorting laundry while telling some man how much I'd like to run a warm sponge over his body, slathering every nook and cranny of his flesh with soapsuds until he gleamed, and then, when he was hard and warm and wet, I'd take him and . . . for six to seven dollars an hour. They even had pamphlets that explained sexual practices I might not be familiar with and gave the correct jargon to use when chatting about them. Six to seven dollars an hour. I told the interviewer I'd have to think about it, and went home.

And got up the next day and defrosted the refrigerator again and swept the carpet in the living room because I was out of vacuum bags. Then I did all the mending that I had been putting off for weeks, scrubbed the landing outside my apartment door and sprayed it with Cat-B-Gon, and thought about talking on the telephone to men about sex, and how I could do it while I was ironing a shirt or arranging flowers in a vase or wiping cat-turds off my shoe. Then I took a shower and changed and went in to work at Sears for the five to nine evening shift. I told myself that the work wasn't dirty or difficult, that my co-workers were pleasant people and that there was no reason why this job should make me so depressed.

It didn't help.

The mall was having Craft Week, and to get to Sears I had to pass all the tables and people. I wondered why I didn't get busy and make things in the evenings and sell them on the weekends and make ends meet that way. I passed Barbie dolls whose pink crocheted skirts concealed spare rolls of toilet paper, and I saw wooden key-chains that spelled out names, and ceramic butterfly windchimes, and a booth of rubber-stamps, and a booth with clusters of little pewter and crystal sculptures displayed on tables made of old doors set across saw-horses. I slowed a little as I passed that one, for I've always had a weakness for pewter. There were the standard dragons and wizards, and some thunder-eggs cut in half with wizard figures standing inside them. There were birds, too, eagles and falcons and owls of pewter, and one really nice stag almost as big as my hand. For fifty-two dollars. I was looking at it when I heard a woman standing behind me say, "I'd like the crystal holding the wizard, please."

And the owner of the stall smiled at her and said, "You mean the wizard holding the crystal, right?" and the woman said, in this really snotty voice, "Quite."

So the owner wrapped up the little figurine of a wizard holding a crystal ball in several layers of tissue paper, and held it out to the woman and said, "Seventeen-seventy-eight, please," and the woman was digging in her purse and I swear, all I did was try to step out of their way.

I guess my coat caught on a corner of the door or something, for in the next instant everything was tilting and sliding. I tried to catch the edge of the door-table, but it landed on the woman's foot, really hard, as all the crystal and pewter crashed to the floor and scattered across the linoleum like a shattered whitecap. The woman screamed and threw up her hands and the little wrapped wizard went flying.

I'm not sure if I really saw this.

The crystal ball flew out of the package and landed separately on the floor. It didn't shatter or tinkle or crash. It went Poof! with a minute puff of smoke. And the crumple of tissue paper floated down emptily.

"You stupid bitch!" the woman yelled at me, and the owner of the booth glared at me and said, "I hope to hell you have insurance, klutz!"

Which is a dumb thing to say, really, and I couldn't think of any answer. People were turning to stare, and moving toward us to see what the excitement was, and the woman had sort of collapsed and was holding onto her foot, saying, "My god, it's broken, it's broken."

I knew, quite abruptly and coldly, that she wasn't talking about her foot.

Then the fortyish man grabbed me by the elbow and said, "We've got to get out of here!" I let him pull me away, and the funny thing is no one tried to stop us or chase us or anything. The crowd closed up around the woman on the floor like an amoeba engulfing a tidbit.

Then we were in a pickup truck that smelled like a wet dog, and the floor was cluttered with muddy newspapers and styrofoam coffee cups and wrappers from Hostess Fruit Pies and paper boats from the textured vegetable protein burritos they sell in the Seven-Eleven stores.

Part of me was saying that I was crazy to be driving off with this guy I hardly knew who had stuck me with the bill for dinner, and part of me was saying that I had better get back to Sears, maybe I could explain being this late for work. And part of me just didn't give a shit anymore, it just wanted to flee. And that part felt better than it had in ages.

We pulled up outside a little white house and he turned to me gravely and said, "Thank you for rescuing me."

"This is really dumb," I said, and he said, "Maybe so, but it's all we've got. I told you, magic isn't what it used to be."

So we went inside the little house and he put the tea kettle on. It was a beautiful kettle, shining copper with a white and blue ceramic handle, and the cups and saucers he took down matched it. I said, "You stuck me with the bill at the restaurant."

He said, "My enemies fell upon me in the restroom and magicked me away. I told you. I never would have chosen to leave you that way, Silver Lady. But for your intervention today, I would still be in their powers." Then he turned, holding a little tin cannister in each hand and asked, "Which will you have: Misplaced Dreams or Forgotten Sweetness?"

"Forgotten Sweetness," I said, and he put down both cannisters of tea and took me in his arms and kissed me. And yes, I could feel his stomach sticking out a little against mine, and when I put my hand to the back of his head to hold his mouth against mine, I could tell his hair was thinning. But I also thought I could hear windchimes and scent an elusive perfume on a warm breeze. I don't believe in magic. The idea of willing enchantment into my life is dumb. Dumb. But as the fortyish man had said, it was all we had. A dumb hope for a small slice of magic, no matter how thin. The fortyish man didn't waste his energy carrying me to the bedroom.

I never met a man under twenty-five who was worth the powder to blow him to hell. They're all stuck in third gear.

It takes a man until he's thirty to understand what gentleness is about, and a few years past that to realize that a woman touches a man as she would like him to touch her.

By thirty-five, they start to grasp how a woman's body is wired. They quit trying to kick-start us, and learn to make sure the battery is charged before turning the key. A few, I've heard, learn how to let a woman make love to them.

Fortyish men understand pacing. They know it doesn't have to all happen at once, that separating each stimulus can intensify each touch. They know when pausing is more poignant than continuing, and they know when continuing is more important than a ceramic kettle whistling itself dry on an electric burner.

And afterwards I said to him, "Have you ever heard of 'Lindholm's Rule of Ten'?"

He frowned an instant. "Isn't that the theory that the first ten times two people make love, one will do something that isn't in sync with the other?"

"That's the one," I said.

"It's been disproved," he said solemnly. And he got up and went to the bathroom while I rescued the smoking kettle from the burner.

I stood in the kitchen, and after a while I started shivering, because the place wasn't all that well heated. Putting my clothes back on didn't seem polite somehow, so I called through the bathroom door, "Shall I put on more water for tea?"

He didn't answer, and I didn't want to yell through the door again, so I picked up my blouse and slung it around my shoulders and shivered for a while. I sort of paced through his kitchen and living room. I found myself reading the titles of his books, one of the best ways to politely spy on someone. *Theories of Thermodynamics* was right next to *The Silmarillion*. All the books by Carlos Castenada were set apart on a shelf by themselves. His set of Kipling was bound in red leather. My ass was freezing, and I suspected I had a rug burn on my back. To hell with being polite. I went and got my underwear and skirt and stood in the kitchen, putting them on.

"Merlin?" I called questioningly as I picked up my pantyhose. They were shot, a huge laddered run up the back of one leg. I bunched them up and shoved them into my purse. I went and knocked on the bathroom door, saying, "I'm coming in, okay?" And when he didn't answer, I opened the door.

There was no one in there. But I was sure that was where he had gone, and the only other exit from the bathroom was a small window with three pots of impatiens blooming on the sill. The only clue that he had been there was the used rubber floating pathetically in the toilet. There is nothing less romantic than a used rubber.

I went and opened the bedroom door and looked in there. He hadn't made his bed this morning. I backed out.

I actually waited around for a while, pretending he would come back. I mean, his clothes were still in a heap on the floor. How he could have gotten re-dressed and left the house without my noticing it, I didn't try to figure out. But after an hour or so, it didn't matter how he had done anything. He was *gone*.

I didn't cry. I had been too stupid to allow myself to cry. None of this made sense, but my behavior made the least sense of all. I finished getting dressed and looked at myself in the bathroom mirror. Great. Smeared makeup and nothing to repair it with, so I washed it all off. Let the lines at the corners of my mouth and the circles under my eyes show. Who cared. My hair had gone wild. My legs were white-fleshed and goosebumpy without the pantyhose. The cute little ankle-strap heels on my bare feet looked grotesque. All of me looked rumpled and used. It matched how I felt, an outfit that perfectly complemented my mood, so I got my purse and left.

The old pickup was still outside. That didn't make sense either, but I didn't really give a damn.

I walked home. That sounds simpler than it was. The weather was raw,

I was barelegged and in heels, it was getting dark and people stared at me. It took me about an hour, and by the time I got there I had rubbed a huge blister on the back of one of my feet, so I was limping as well. I went up the stairs, narrowly missing the moist brown pile the neighbor's cat had left for me, unlocked my apartment door and went in.

And I still didn't cry. I kicked off my shoes and got into my old baggy sweatsuit and went to the kitchen. I made myself hot chocolate in a little china pot with forget-me-nots on it, and opened the eight ounce canned genuine all-the-way-from-England Cross and Blackwell plum pudding that my sister had given me last Christmas and I had saved in case of disasters like this. I cut the whole thing up and arranged it on a bone china plate on a little tray with my pot of hot chocolate and a cup and saucer. I set it on a little table by my battered easy chair, put a quilt on the chair and got down my old leather copy of Dumas' *The Three Musketeers*. Then I headed for the bathroom, intending to take a quick hot shower and dab on some rose oil before settling down for the evening. It was my way of apologizing to myself for hurting myself this badly.

I opened the bathroom door, and a stenchful cloud of sulphurous green smoke wafted out. Choking and gasping, I peered in, and there was the fortyish man, clad only in a towel, smiling at me apologetically. He looked apprehensive. he had a big raw scrape on one knee, and a swollen lump on his forehead. He said, "Silver Lady, I never would have left you like that, but. . . ."

"You were teleported away by your arch rival," I finished.

He said, "No, not teleported, exactly, this involved a spell requiring a monkey's paw and a dozen nightshade berries. But they were *last* year's berries, and not potent enough to hold me. I had a spell of my own up my sleeve and. . . ."

"You blasted him to kingdom come," I guessed.

"No." He looked a little abashed. "Actually, it was the 'Incessant Rectal Itch' spell, a little crude, but always effective and simple to use. I doubt that he'll be bothering us again soon." He paused, then added, "As I've told you, magic isn't what it used to be." Then he sniffed a few times and said, "Actually, I've found that Pinesol is the best stuff for getting rid of spell residues. . . ."

So we cleaned up the bathroom. I poured hydrogen peroxide over his scraped knee and he made gasping noises and cursed in a language I'd never heard before. I left him doing that and went into the kitchen and began re-heating the hot chocolate. A few moments later he came out dressed in a sort of sarong he'd made from one of my bed sheets. It looked strangely elegant on him, and the funny thing was, neither of us seemed to feel awkward as we sat down and drank the hot chocolate and shared the plum pudding. The last piece of plum pudding he took, and borrowing some cream cheese from my refrigerator, he buttered a cabalistic sign onto it. Then he went to the door and called, "Here, kitty, kitty, kitty."

The neighbor's cat came at once, and the ratty old thing let the fortyish man scoop him up and bring him into my living room, where he removed two ticks from behind its ears and then fed it the plum pudding in small bites. When he had done that, he picked it up and stared long into its yellowish eyes before he intoned, "By bread and cream I bind you. Nevermore shalt thou shit upon the threshold of this abode." Then he put the cat gently out the door, observing aloud, "Well, that takes care of the curse you were under."

I stared at him. "I thought my curse had something to do with me working at Sears."

"No. That was just a viciously cruel thing you were doing to yourself, for reasons I will never understand." He must have seen the look on my face, because after a while he said, "I told you, the magic is never quite what you think it to be."

Then he came to sit on the floor beside my easy chair. He put his elbow on my knee and leaned his chin in his hand. "What if I were to tell you, Silver Lady, that I myself have no real magic at all? That, actually, I climbed out my bathroom window and sneaked through the streets in my towel to meet you here? Because I wanted you to see me as special."

I didn't say anything.

"What if I told you I really work for Boeing, in Personnel?"

I just looked at him, and he lifted his elbow from my knee and turned aside a little. He glanced at his own bare feet, and then over at my machine. He licked his lips and spoke softly. "I could get you a job there. As a word processor, at about eleven dollars an hour."

"Merlin," I said warningly.

"Well, maybe not eleven dollars an hour to start. . . ."

I reached out and brushed what hair he had back from his receding hairline. He looked up at me and then smiled the smile where he always looked aside from me. We didn't say anything at all. I took his hand and led him to my room, where we once more disproved Lindholm's Rule of Ten. I fell asleep curled around him, my hand resting comfortably on the curve of his belly. He was incredibly warm, and smelled of oranges, cloves, and cinnamon. Misplaced Dreams Tea, that's what he smelled like. And that night I dreamed I wore a peacock feather gown and strolled through a misty garden. I had found something I had lost, and I carried it in my hand, but every time I tried to look at it to see what it was, the mist swirled up and hid my hand from me.

In the morning when I woke up, the fortyish man was gone.

It didn't really bother me. I knew that either he would be back, or he wouldn't, but either way no one could take from me what I already had, and what I already had was a lot more magic than most people get in their lives. I put on my ratty old bathrobe and my silver ladies and went out into the livingroom. His sarong sheet was folded up on the easy chair in the livingroom, and the neighbor's cat was asleep on it, his paws tucked under his chin.

And my Muse was there, too, perched on the corner of my desk, one knee under her chin as she painted her toenails. She looked up when I came in and said, "If you're quite finished having a temper tantrum, we'll get on with your career now." So I sat down at my machine and flicked the switch on and put my fingers on the home row.

Funny thing. The keys weren't even dusty.

ALAN BRENNERT
The Third Sex

Alan Brennert was beginning to make a reputation for himself in the genre in the 1970s as a writer of finely crafted short stories, but then he was lured away by Hollywood. Since then, he has served as executive story consultant on *The Twilight Zone* during its recent television revival, written teleplays for *China Beach*, *The Mississippi*, and *Darkroom*, and has twice been nominated for the Writers Guild Award. His first novel was *Kindred Spirits*; another, *Time and Chance*, was just published by Tor and a story collection titled *Her Pilgrim Soul and Other Stories* is coming soon.

In spite of all this, he still finds time for the occasional short story, which show up from time to time in *The Magazine of Fantasy and Science Fiction*, *Pulphouse*, and elsewhere. He's lost none of his touch—as demonstrated by the brilliant story that follows, from *Pulphouse*, about someone who is caught, quite literally, between two worlds.

▼
The Third Sex

ALAN BRENNERT

I couldn't have been more than three years old, that night I wandered into my parents' bedroom; I'd had the dream again, the one where I was being crushed between floor and ceiling, unable to breathe or break free. Shaken, I raced down the hall, pushed upon my parents' door—then stopped as I saw what they were doing.

Locked in a sweaty tangle of sheets, they were jerking back and forth, making short, breathless sounds; for a minute I thought maybe they were having the same bad dream I'd just had. Their arms were wrapped around one another, the two of them lying face-to-face, so close I couldn't tell where one began and the other left off. When they saw me, my mother called out my name, my father swore, they pulled apart with a wet, sucking sound . . . and as the sheets fell away I saw a thick, curved finger between my father's legs, and between my mother's, another pair of lips. I rushed up, fascinated, asking a million questions at once; my father just looked at my mother, sighed, and tried to answer my questions—what is that called? what is that *for?*—as completely and honestly as you can, to a three-year-old; and when I went to bed that night, I reached down under my pajamas and touched the smooth, unbroken skin between my thighs, and dreamed of the day— Daddy never mentioned it, but I knew it had to come—when my own penis or vagina would start to grow. But somehow, it never did.

I'd been a perfectly normal newborn infant in all other respects, though not the first of my kind to appear. At first no one had a clue what to put on the birth certificate, much less what to name me, so they equivocated and the name on the county records is Pat; Pat Jacquith. Later, of course, they realized I had to have some identity, and since they were hoping for a daughter, that's what I became . . . at least until that night in their bedroom.

"You're Daddy's little girl," my father had always told me, but if I *was* a girl, why didn't I have what Mommy had, that second pair of lips, that bristly hair? All I had was a pee-hole; it hardly seemed fair. And in years to come, when Mommy would take me out, shopping for skirts, or dolls, or frilly bedclothes, I knew I wasn't *really* like Mommy, would never *be* like Mommy . . . and I felt ashamed. Ashamed to be seen in clothes I didn't belong in, pretending to be something I wasn't.

So I started picking fights, at school . . . jumping hedges, shinnying up hills, sliding down cliffs . . . anything to get my pretty dresses torn, or dirty. We lived in a woodsy suburb called Redmond, and between the ages of six and thirteen I could usually be found in t-shirt and jeans, hiking, bicycling, or swimming in Lake Washington. I was a bit taller than the average girl, a bit shorter than the average boy; my voice was pitched a little lower than most girls, a little higher than most boys, but with a scratchy quality that somehow made it acceptable for either sex. I had no curves to speak of, and as the girls had begun to blossom with puberty, I stayed pretty much the same, going on hikes or playing shortstop in sandlot baseball games; but even this new, tomboy role would start to feel wrong, in its own way, soon enough.

I was fourteen; it was summer; a dozen of us, guys and girls, were camping at Lake Sammamish. I was wearing a one-piece bathing suit, my only concession to femininity, and when I dressed in the bushes I was careful, as always, to keep my distance from the others. To my left, Melissa Camry was suiting up behind a stand of bushes; to my right, my friend Davy Foster—a tall, loping blond who'd been my best pal for years—was stripping off his clothes in back of a tall tree. I caught a glimpse of Davy's genitals, and a peek at Melissa's impressively large breasts, and I felt an erotic tingle, but for which one, I didn't know; and then they were dressed and into the water, and swimming between them I continued to feel excited, but confused, as well.

Afterward, Davy and I went hiking, our trail coming to an end at the crest of a low, but steep, cliff. The rockface was intimidating; neither of us could resist the challenge. We descended carefully, finding ample foot- and hand-holds for the first ten feet; then, midway down the bluff, Davy flailed about, looking for a foothold, not finding any: the cliff was sheer granite for the next ten feet. Davy called up to me, "Hard way down," and, propelling himself away from the cliff, plummeted into the bushes below. In moments I was faced with the same choice, and so, feeling almost like a parachutist, I followed his lead. We found ourselves lying tangled, ass-over-teakettle, in shrubbery. We looked at one another, splayed at weird angles, our legs looped through each other's, and started giggling. And couldn't stop. The harder we tried to untangle ourselves, the harder we giggled; we'd grab at a branch, trying to haul ourselves up, only to have the branch snap off as we fell deeper into the bramble. Davy leaned down to help me, his cheek grazing mine—

And then, somehow, we were kissing. I wasn't feeling the same kind of tingle I had earlier, but it still felt nice; the wonderful pressure of lips against mine, our tongues meeting, licking . . . Before I knew it Davy had his hand under my shirt (withdrawing it when he found that my tits were no larger than his); I slid my panties down around my thighs, part of me knowing I shouldn't knowing there was nothing down there for him to enter, but not caring. Davy's penis was stiff, the tip of it was flushed red; he guided it awkwardly toward my crotch—

And then he saw.

He stopped and drew back, eyes wide with shock and disbelief. "What—" he started to say, and by then I knew I'd made a mistake, a bad one; but some part of me tried to pretend it would all be all right, and I reached out to him, imploring, "Please . . . Davy, please—" There was fear, now, in his eyes, but I didn't want to see it. "We don't have to. We can just keep on touching, can't we, we can keep on kissing—"

I tried to draw him closer to me, but he jerked back, jumping to his feet, swaying as he sought to keep his balance amid the thick bramble. Wordlessly he pulled up his pants, and despite my pleas, staggered out of the underbrush and ran like hell out of sight.

I cried for half an hour before getting up the courage to head back to camp, certain that I'd return to have them all staring at me, whispering about me behind my back; but Davy not only never told anyone else, he never said another word about it to me, either . . . because when we all graduated to high school the next year, Davy somehow managed to transfer to a different school . . .

I never wanted to see again what I saw in his eyes, that afternoon; never wanted to feel so *different*, ever again. And so, two months before my fifteenth birthday, I simply decided to deny it. All of it.

Overnight, I was no longer Pat, but Patty. Out went the jeans and sneakers; now, to my parents' shock, I wanted dresses, and nylons, and makeup—I became obsessed with learning everything there was to learn about putting on foundation, blusher, and eyeshadow. Mother was eager and willing to teach me, and my first hour in front of her dressing mirror I was amazed and delighted as my boyish features were transformed, through the miracle of Helena Rubenstein, into a soft, feminine face. My eyes, which had always seemed a bland brown, now looked almost exotic—hooded and sophisticated—with a touch of mascara and Lancôme; and as I carefully applied a coat of coral lip gloss, the image was complete. I stared at the girl in the mirror, so feminine, so pretty . . . and cried with joy and relief as I realized that the girl was *me*. Mother held me, relieved herself that she finally had a daughter again; that perhaps things might work out, after all.

Once I'd had a taste of what I could become, there was no stopping me: I had my ears pierced, and came to love the feeling when I shook my hair out and felt my hoop earrings jiggling to and fro; I even loved the sound my porcelain nails made when I drummed them impatiently on my desk in class. By the end of my freshman summer I convinced my parents to let me color my hair, and so I began the new year as a blonde, flirtatious sophomore, thrilled that boys would open doors for me, or light my cigarettes for me— each ritual confirming my own femininity.

I dated around, saw lots of boys, but knew I could take the role only so far. The dates would often end up in a boy's car, parked at a romantic lookout, with the two of us necking hot and heavily, his hands roaming my body; my breasts were still nonexistent, but now, taken in the context of my new look, the boys didn't seem to mind. But the petting always stopped short of one point: when the boy's hand reached for my panties. I'd let him masturbate against them, or bring him off myself, but that was all. They couldn't know it was as frustrating for me as for them. They at least could masturbate, but all I knew was the pleasure of touching, of caressing, of kissing. I read about orgasms, listened to my girlfriends talk endlessly about them; the more I listened, the more envious I became. And so I kept search- ing, hoping that someday, the right boy, the right touch, might bring me that release, that . . . fulfillment . . . everyone else seemed capable of. Most of the boys I dated didn't see me more than once or twice before dismissing me as a tease; but that reputation worked to my advantage, too, because there was always a ready supply of boys who saw me as a challenge, a prize to be won, and I was more than willing to let them try.

It was in my last semester of high school that my parents unexpectedly whisked me away for a rare day trip into Seattle. At first they tried to pass it off as a whim, but as the white brick buildings of the university medical center swung into view, they dropped the pretense; they seemed excited and enthused, and I became more than a little afraid at the whisper of jealousness in their tones. I could tell the extent of their preoccupation because when, nervously, I lit up a cigarette, neither of them gave me any grief about my smoking. Whatever this was about, it was important.

They wanted to be with me when I saw the doctor—a surgeon named Salzman, a balding, gentle man in his early fifties—but Dr. Salzman insisted on seeing me alone. My heart pounding for no reason that I knew, I sat in his comfortable office, in front of his expansive desk; I took a pack of Virginia Slims from my purse, then hesitated, but Dr. Salzman just pushed a heavy crystal ashtray toward me and I lit up, feeling a bit more relaxed, but certain that this amiable man was going to tell me I had three days to live.

"You've grown up to be quite a lovely young lady," he said approvingly. "I imagine you don't remember the last time I saw you?"

I smiled, shook my head. "I'm afraid not. Was I very small?"

He nodded. "Seven months." He leaned forward a bit in his chair, saw my nervousness, then laughed, putting me immediately at ease. "Don't look so worried. There's nothing wrong with you, at least nothing you don't already know about." He paused a moment, then, in a slightly more sober tone: "When did your parents tell you? About your—condition?"

It felt so strange, talking about this with someone other than my parents, but there was nothing threatening about this man. "They said it was a . . . birth defect."

Salzman nodded to himself. "Yes, that about covers it as well as a child could understand. But you're no longer a child, are you?"

Suddenly it was a welcome relief just to have someone to talk to, someone who wouldn't cringe in fear. "It's called—androgyny, isn't it? I looked it up. But that's just something out of mythology, isn't it? How can I be—I mean, why—?"

Salzman stood, paced a little behind his desk. "It *used* to be something out of mythology. Your case, eighteen years ago, was the first on the West Coast, but before that there was one in Denver, two in New York, a few in the Midwest . . . the incidences are still rare, less than one hundredth of one percent, but . . ." He circled round and sat on the edge of his desk. "You were lucky; the first few cases attracted the most attention. Lived most of their youth under a microscope, and for all that we still don't know anything about the causes. Your parents wanted you to have as normal a life as possible, so we restricted ourselves to periodic exams. There was nothing we could do until you reached maturity, anyway."

I sat up, snubbing out the cigarette in the crystal ashtray. "Do? You mean there's something—"

"Slow down, now," Salzman cautioned. "What you are, you are; you have a . . . different chromosome, not X, not Y, something entirely new . . . and no one can change your genetic makeup. But we *can* give you a closer cosmetic resemblance to a normal female. We can start you on a course of hormone therapy to facilitate breast and hip development, augmented with silicone implants . . ."

I was leaning forward in my seat, my heart racing, barely able to contain my excitement. Dr. Salzman went on, "Now, as to sex organs, we can make a surgical incision in your—please tell me if this is getting too clinical—in your groin; then place a sort of plastic sac just inside the skin, and fashion a vagina and clitoris out of skin taken from elsewhere on your body. This is similar to what we do for male-to-female transsexuals, and it may require a follow-up operation to make sure the vagina remains open, but—"

"Oh, Doctor, *thank* you," I said, tears starting to well up in my eyes; "You don't know how often I've dreamed about—"

He held up a hand. "Don't thank me yet. There *are* limits. Like a transsexual, you won't, of course, be able to conceive children; but unlike a transsexual, whose vaginal lining is made of penile tissue, yours will be relatively insensate . . . no more sensitive to pleasure than any other part of your body. Do you understand?"

My hopes plummeted. "Why not?" I asked, voice low.

He looked at me with sadness and sympathy. "Because, child, you don't have any sex organs, and no tissue of the same sensitivity as a penis, or a clitoris. Perhaps the estrogen will give you some sensitivity in your breasts;

perhaps not. This will be *cosmetic* change only . . . but won't that still go a long ways to relieving your gender discomfort?"

I thought about it a moment, my reservations melting away. I could go to bed with a man . . . get married . . . live something approaching a normal life. What did the rest matter, really? "Yes. Of course," I said. I stood, and couldn't help but hug him in gratitude. "When can I have the surgery?"

"We'll want to do a routine exam on you now, and if everything's satisfactory, we can do it whenever I can schedule an OR. Within the week, if you like."

When I left the office my parents saw at once the happiness in my eyes, and the three of us embraced, and laughed, and cried. All the way back they talked about how long they had been waiting for this day; how happy they were that their daughter was going to have a normal, healthy life. That night, there was laughter from their bedroom for the first time in years. The week until surgery passed quickly. And then, the night before I was to go to the medical center, I told my parents I was going out to meet friends, got into the flame-red Datsun my father had bought me for my seventeenth birthday, and I ran away from home.

I left a note, saying how sorry I was, explaining why I had to leave, and how I knew I couldn't live with their disappointment and betrayal. But I simply couldn't go through with it.

Oh, at first I was thrilled; I lay awake in bed, that first night, dreaming about being a girl, a real girl, for the first time. I had a date the next night, a new boy named Charles: good-looking, studious, and a little nervous. We ended up at the lookout outside town, but as we sat there, necking and petting, I realized nothing was happening—not even the whisper of anticipation I usually felt with a new boy, wondering if this, maybe, were the one who would be *different*—and as his hand reached under my blouse, I pushed him away with a little shove. "Charles, please *don't*. Let's go back to town." To prevent any further moves, I lit a cigarette and used it as a subtle shield between us. Charles turned slowly away, started the car, and headed back.

I caught a glimpse of myself in the rearview mirror and, reflexively, began to primp, more concerned with my own appearance than Charles, beside me. It wasn't until he dropped me off that I saw the hurt and anger in his eyes, and by then it was too late; he was gone before I could apologize. He hadn't even been in danger of discovering my secret; I'd just become bored, and used the same coquettish tone I always did to end the scene, without any thought to him. My God, I thought; what kind of selfish, manipulative little bitch am I turning into?

That night, I undressed in front of the full-length mirror on the inside of my closet door, and stood staring at my reflection, taken aback at what I saw. I saw a girl's face, immaculately made up—pink lipstick, blue eyeshadow, a hint of blusher along the cheekbones—framed by strawberry-blonde hair. A girl's face, sitting atop a boyish body . . . not muscular enough to *be* a boy's, but too contourless to be a girl's, either. The juxtaposition seemed suddenly, and painfully, ridiculous. Looking at the head of a *Cosmo* girl sitting atop a neutered body, I *knew* for the first time that I was neither boy nor girl, but—something else.

I slept badly that night, and the next morning could barely bring myself to apply my makeup. As the days wore on, as the date of surgery approached, the operation seemed less like a deliverance than a . . . a mutilation. A plastic sac inside my groin? The thought made me shiver. And if I did go through with it, then what? I'd still have no sex organs, no orgasms; would I make the best of it, get a job, fall in love and marry? Or would I continue to search, irrationally, for that one man who *might* bring me complete satisfaction, in the process hurting how many others who failed to make the grade?

I looked at the fickle blonde in my makeup mirror, and knew which path *she* would take. I left her behind in Redmond that night I drove away; I stopped at a mini-mall on Route 22 and picked up a suitcase full of unisex clothing—jeans, shirts, sweaters. At the nearest salon I had my blonde mane trimmed short, in a style of indeterminate sex; when the blonde grew out, I returned to my natural brown. I drove as far from Redmond as I could manage, with no particular destination, no purpose beyond discovering just who, and what, I really was.

A stranger, looking at me, had little clue to whether I was a man or a woman; depending on the pitch of my voice at any given time, I could be either one. It wasn't unusual for me to sit at the counter of a roadside diner, and for the waitress to ask, "What can I get you, sir?"; only to have the person at the cash register hand me my change with a friendly, "Have a nice day, ma'am." I became a chameleon, my gender determined as much by the observer's biases as by anything physical; and the further I drove, the freer I felt, a living Rorschach test with no demands put upon me to be one sex or the other.

I worked my way cross-country, waiting on tables, clerking in stores, delivering packages. I gave my name as Pat, which was both true and ambiguous. I'd never overtly state my sex unless it was absolutely necessary—on a job application, or if I was pulled over for a traffic ticket—and then only check "female" out of expediency, since that's what all my IDs read. But such instances were rare. It's amazing how much gender identification is really just in the eye of the beholder; I gave no cues, but each person I met brought his or her own lens to the focus of my identity. If I was driving fast, or aggressively, other drivers treated me like a man; if I was looking in a shop window displaying women's fashions, passersby would assume I was a woman. I could, with impunity, enter either a men's or a ladies' room; context, I discovered, was everything.

For the first time, too, I was free to follow my sexual feelings without playing a role. Working in a record store in Wyoming, I let myself experience, finally, the attraction I felt for women as well as men; I slept with a female co-worker, keeping the lights dim, and in lieu of intercourse I spent hours caressing her, holding her, massaging her clitoris with my tongue and fingers. She told me later she'd never really liked sex all that much, but this time was different; this time she was starting to see what it was all about. When a lonely, middle-aged man in a diner made a pass at me, I assumed he thought me a woman; but as we talked, it became apparent he took me for a young gay male. In his hotel room, I performed fellatio on him, and then—careful to roll my underwear down only as far as necessary, explaining it was a minor fetish—let him have anal sex with me; then we just held one another for a long while. And as I lay there, both times, feeling warm and happy, I realized with a start I had given no thought to that all-important "culmination" I had been in search of, so desperately, for so long.

Kansas City, Boston, Fayetteville, New York . . . my odyssey took me across the country and halfway back again. Sometimes I settled in various cities for months at a time, taking college-credit courses in psychology and sociology; but it was impossible to maintain gender ambiguity when you settled in one place for long, and eventually I'd get restless with being either man or woman, anxious to be perceived simply as *me*, and I'd be on the road again, searching.

One thing became clear: with more and more of these cases cropping up, the medical establishment could no longer dismiss them as genetic quirks. And a few times I even got to meet my kindred. In Fayetteville I met a 22-year-old living as a male, his full beard and hairy arms a testament to testosterone; an Army brat, he'd spent a good deal of time under the eye of military doctors, and it seemed to me his macho, swaggering pose was just that—a pose to satisfy his family and government, forcing them to leave him in peace. In New York I was shocked to find another androgyne who'd set up shop as a hooker, catering to any and all sexual persuasions, willing to be either man or woman, stud or harlot; he/she had a collection of wigs, toupees, strap-on dildoes and sponge rubber vaginas, and his/her arms were riddled with track marks. I got out of there, fast, feeling sick and sad. And in Miami I met a young "woman" with long auburn hair, dazzling eyes made up exactly right, full breasts peeping out of a low-cut dress, long red fingernails; the surgeons had done an amazing job on her. We sat in an open-air café as she flirted with every man who passed, preening in her compact mirror, yet if I asked her about her past, what it was like growing up, she found a way to change the subject, a dweller in an eternal, and ephemeral, present.

In Tennessee I finally met someone who'd taken the same path as I: Alex, slender, sandy-haired, living neither as a male nor a female, shunned by family, working as a teller in an S&L. We were astonishingly similar in our outlooks, in the decision we'd both come to, and both of us longed for that same unimaginably distant thing: a sense of belonging, of being loved and needed and necessary. We came together, in desperation more than want, and made love—as best as two neuters, two neither-nors, could make love. There were no sex organs to stimulate, but in our travels we each had learned much about touching, and caressing, and the sensitivities of the flesh; we could appreciate, as well as anybody, the gentle brush of lips along the nape of a neck, the sensuous massage of fingers kneading buttocks, the lick of a tongue inside the rim of an ear. It was very tender, and very loving, but when it was over . . .

When it was over, Alex stroked my cheek and said, almost sadly, "We're much alike. Aren't we?"

I nodded, wordlessly.

"I always thought when I found someone like myself, I'd be truly happy," Alex said, in a soft Tennessee drawl.

"So did I," I said, quietly.

Alex held me, then gave an affectionate peck on my cheek. "I'm sorry, Pat."

We were alike; too alike. Even our sexual responses were nearly identical. It wasn't just the lack of orgasm, it was . . . like making love to yourself; narcissistic, somehow. Patty, the strawberry blonde, would probably have liked it, but I felt only vaguely depressed by it. Both of us knew, instinctively, that the answer to our problem—if there was an answer—lay not in each other, but somewhere else.

My search, my quest for identity and purpose, was unraveling before my eyes. There *was* no purpose. There *was* no identity. I was neither man nor woman, yin nor yang; I was the line, the invisible, impossible-to-measure demarcation *between* yin and yang, as impossible to define as the smallest possible fraction, as elusive as the value of *pi*. I was neither, I was no one, I was nothing.

Not knowing what else to do . . . I went home.

I'd kept in touch with my parents, over the years; letters, postcards, a phone call on Christmas or Thanksgiving. At first they were furious, even hung up the first time I called; eventually though they forgave me, and lately they'd written of how much they wanted to see me again. They were growing old, and I was afraid that if I didn't go now, I might never get the chance; so I headed west, to Washington, to Redmond, and home.

But the closer home I got, the faster my heart raced, the weaker my grip on the steering wheel; finally, somewhere between Bellevue and Kirkland, I lost my nerve and pulled into a motel off 405. It was well past eleven, and after checking in I headed down to the all-night coffee shop in the lobby. Exhausted, hungry, and nervous, I sat at a corner table, ordered a sandwich, and began chatting with a man at an adjoining table; he had the smooth, charming sheen of a salesman, and as he flirted with me, I found myself unconsciously changing the way I sat, the way I crossed my legs, even the way I held my glass of iced tea. I leaned forward, my now very feminine body language belying my androgynous appearance. It all came back so quickly, so easily. Before he could make a proposition, I realized what was happening and hurried off, feigning a stomachache; I hadn't come this far to lapse back into old patterns.

I slept badly, and wasted most of the next day window-shopping in a Kirkland mall, putting off the inevitable as long as I could. I was eating lunch when I looked up to find a man staring at me from a table across the room; this time I fought off the reflex that had overtaken me last night and simply glanced away, but when I looked up again the man was standing in front of me, a quizzical look on his face . . . a face I suddenly recognized.

"Pat?"

It was Davy. For a moment I was stunned that anyone here would recognize me, looking as I now did, but of course Davy had always known Pat, not Patty. The embarrassment of that day in the woods came rushing back; I must have looked terrified as I jumped to my feet, spilling coffee all over the table, and started to hurry away, but Davy rushed after. "Pat—wait—"

Outside he took me by the arm, but it was the gentle look on his face, and the softness of his voice, that brought me to a stop. "It's okay," he said quietly. "I'm not going to . . . I mean, that was a long time ago, right?"

He was only in his twenties, and already his blond hair was thinning, but his eyes were still a bright blue, and now they seemed to be looking straight through me. Part of me wanted to run; thank God, I didn't. He let go of my arm, smiling apologetically. "Been a while," he said.

It took me a moment to collect my thoughts.

"I've been—away," I said. "Traveling."

"Back for a visit, or to stay?"

I wished I knew. "A visit. I was going to head over to Redmond later and see my parents."

We stood there, awkwardly, for several moments, before he said, haltingly, "Look. If you've . . . got an hour to spare, I'd . . . like to talk with you. Let me call my office, okay?"

"I really should be getting—"

"Please?" What was that intensity, that desperation, I read in his eyes? "Just an hour?"

We skirted the edge of Lake Washington in his Jeep, a gray mist obscuring the few sailboats out on this drizzly day. We chatted innocuously for the first half hour, pointing out familiar sights, the snowy caps of nearby mountains, but finally, as we stood at a deserted lookout over the lake, Davy worked up the nerve to say what had been on his mind all afternoon.

"I'm sorry, Pat," he said, quietly.

I looked up at him. "Sorry for what?"

"For running," he said, glancing away uneasily. "For cutting you off like that. But I couldn't handle it. You were the first girl—" He stopped, momentarily panicked that he'd used the wrong word, but when I didn't react negatively he went on, hesitantly, "—that I was ever really . . . attracted to. I mean, you have no idea how many times I thought about it, about you, and me . . . when we were out hiking, or swimming, or in school—"

I couldn't help smiling. "Really?" I said. "I thought you just thought I was just, you know, one of the guys."

"Yeah, well, that's the hell of it. Even though I knew—thought—you were a girl, I couldn't shake this weird feeling that you *were* a guy . . . that being attracted to you was wrong, somehow. So there we are, the perfect situation, and I figure, okay, I'll prove to myself she's just like any other girl, that it's okay for me to want her—"

"Oh, God," I said, realizing. "And instead you found—"

"Yeah," he said. "Talk about gender confusion. I freaked. And for a while, I wasn't even sure what *I* was, much less you." He looked away. "Later, I did a lot of reading, found out about . . . people like you . . . and when I was in college, I saw a therapist who helped me out. Then I met Lyn. But all during high school. . . ."

I put a hand on his; now it was my turn to feel guilty. "Oh, God, Davy, I'm so sorry. I was so shaken up by it myself, I guess I never gave a thought to what it must've been like for you—your first sexual experience and it's so . . . so *bizarre*. . . ."

He put his other hand on top of mine, and the warmth of it was familiar and comforting. "It's okay. I came out of it okay. But I wanted to apologize. For not—" His voice caught. "For not being a friend."

I couldn't think of anything to say, so I hugged him, trying to release some of that guilt which had been dogging him all these years; as we stood there the light drizzle became heavier, and when we separated the sky was darker, the ground turning muddy as a gray slanting rain pebbled the surface of the lake. "I'd better get a move on," I said, glancing at the thunderheads on the horizon.

"Rotten weather to be driving in. Why don't you come home and have dinner with Lyn and me?"

The idea frightened me, I'm not sure why; perhaps it was the warmth of Davy's body, still with me after our embrace. "No, I better not," I said, and in my haste to get back to the car I took the muddy embankment a bit too quickly, my foot sliced sideways, I felt a *pop* in my ankle as I tumbled down the small incline. I yelled, swore, but Davy was right behind me, pulling me up with a strong arm; though the damage, damn it, had already been done. "Take it easy," he said, helping me hobble up the embankment to the road. The pain in my foot was overshadowed, briefly, by the feel of his arm around my waist, but I thought of the last time something like this had happened, the blind alleys it had led us both to for so many years, and I resolved it would not happen again. "I'm all right," I protested, his grip loosening as I moved away—but the moment I took a step without his help all my weight fell on my twisted ankle and a stabbing pain shot up through my knee and into my thigh. I buckled, and Davy was there again to catch me.

"Come on. We'll fix you up back at my place."

I was hardly in a position to argue. We climbed into his Jeep, the rain drumming on its canvas roof as we headed down the road, and I cursed myself, wondering if I hadn't done this on purpose . . .

We were dripping wet, our shoes muddied, when we entered Davy's tract home in Kirkland, but Davy led me unhesitatingly to a dining room chair, carefully propped my ankle up on a second chair, and headed for the kitchen. "I'll get some ice," he said, and as the kitchen door swung shut behind him I saw the flash of headlights outside the dining room window, then heard the hurried slap of footsteps on the wet sidewalk leading to the house. Oh, great, I thought. I looked around for Davy, thinking that this was going to be an awkward introduction at best, but without him here—

The door opened and, along with a spray of rain, a petite blonde in a damp gray suit entered, at first so intent on closing her umbrella she didn't notice me. Then she looked up, stopped in mid-stride, and stared at me, her face contorting into an almost comical look of apprehension.

"Oh, God," she said, in a fast Eastern cadence. "You're not a burglar, are you? I left Chicago after the third burglary. Please tell me you're not a burglar."

I had to smile, but before I could say anything Davy entered with the ice pack, introducing me as an old schoolmate; I couldn't tell from the look on Lyn's face whether Davy had told her anything more about me, but as soon as she saw my ankle she came over, wincing as she touched my foot, lightly. "Ouch. Hold on, I think we've got an Ace bandage in the bathroom." Within minutes she was wrapping a long, slightly ragged bandage around my ankle, as Davy took off the icepack. "Mud," she said with a sardonic grin. "There should be mud miners up here, you know, providing the rest of the country with our unending supply. Mud and rain, rain and mud—"

She finished wrapping, secured the bandage with a butterfly clip, then let Davy wrap the icepack around the ankle again. "There. That should keep the swelling down." She stood, and for the first time I noticed the disparity in height between her and Davy; she stood on tiptoe, kissed him affectionately on the lips. "Guess what, dear heart," she said.

Davy looked apprehensive. "My turn to cook?"

She nodded. Davy sighed, picked up his raincoat from the chair he'd draped it over, looked at me. "You like Chinese?"

"Sure."

"Back in a flash." He was out the door and gone in a shot. Lyn turned, grinned. "Never fails. My turn to cook, I feel this obligation to make veal scallopini; his turn to cook, he goes out for Szechwan. Would you like some Tylenol for that foot?"

"Thanks."

With the Tylenol came hot coffee and a dry sweater; we shifted my ankle to the coffee table in front of the sectional sofa, and Lyn and I dried out in front of the gas logs, as we waited for the mu shu pork and kung pao chicken. I asked her what kind of work she did.

"Loan manager. B of A. You?"

"Retail sales," I hedged. "I've been on the road for quite a while."

"Back to visit your family?"

"Yes. Right."

She took out a pack of Salems, offered me one; and as she lit it for me, over the flame of the lighter I thought I could see her staring at me, oddly, trying to figure me out—not muscular enough for a man, not round enough for a woman. Was I live, or was I Memorex? Or was it just my own paranoia?

"I actually quit," she said, taking a deep drag on the cigarette, "back when I thought I was pregnant." At my puzzled look she explained, "False alarm. Or 'hysterical pregnancy,' as they put it. If it happened to men, you *know* they'd call it something like 'stress-induced symptomatic replication,' but women, we're *hysterical*, right? Like, 'Oh, my God, I burned the roast, and—' " She looked down at her stomach in mock-surprise. " 'Whoops! Honey, do I look *pregnant* to you?' " We laughed, and that led to a general discussion of the peculiarities of men in general . . . and as I listened to Lyn's good-natured but very funny catalog of male excesses, not so different from the catalog of female excesses I'd listened to from men, something occurred to me, something crystallized after all these years.

All my life I'd felt like a member of a different race, human but not-human; similar but separate. And now I realized that this was, to some degree, how men and women viewed each other, at times—like members of a different species entirely. I saw it even more clearly over dinner, because even though Davy and Lyn had a good, loving relationship, there were the inevitable rough edges. Toward the end of the evening they got into a heated argument, as they were showing me around the soon-to-be-renovated basement, over what color tile would be used; Davy kept insisting it would be red, while Lyn said that wasn't it at all, more like terracotta, and they went on like that for almost a minute before I stepped into the breach with:

"Uh . . . Davy? When you say *red*, you mean like a fire-engine?"

"No, no, darker than that, more like—like—"

"Brick?"

"Yeah! Yeah, like brick."

"That's terra-cotta," Lyn said, exasperated.

"Well how the hell am I supposed to know that?"

After a moment, both Davy and Lyn loosened up and Lyn even suggested

I should stick around and interpret while they were redecorating the house. We went upstairs, had some wine, watched a little cable . . . me stealing glances at Davy and Lyn, snuggled up together . . . and slowly my mood darkened. I liked them, liked them both; Davy's steady presence, Lyn's manic energy. I could fantasize myself falling in love with or marrying either one. Everyone in the world, it seemed, could look forward to that—male, female, gay, lesbian, they could all find a partner. Everyone except me. I was grateful when the movie ended and I could retire, alone, to the sofabed in the living room.

Lying there under a thick, warm quilt, listening to the tattoo of raindrops on the roof, I drifted asleep . . . and had a nightmare I hadn't had in years, the one that had plagued me so often as a child, the one that drove me to my parents' bedroom years before.

I looked up to see the ceiling was dropping toward me, as, beneath me, the floor was rushing up. It happened too fast to do anything but shut my eyes against the coming collision; but when I hit, I didn't hit hard but *soft*, as though both floor and ceiling had turned to feather-down and were now smothering me between them. Out of the corner of my eyes I could see a thin wedge of light on either side, kept there only by the obstruction of my own body between floor and ceiling; then the wedge shrank to a slit, then a line, then a series of small pinpoints. I fought against the pressure but it was useless, the pinpoints of light vanishing one after another; I tried to take a breathe but couldn't, my chest in a vise, unable to expand or contract; I was dying, I was defeated, I was—

"Pat! Pat, *wake up!*"

I was in the vise, and I was being held by my shoulders by Davy; my eyes were open, but I was in both places. He shook me, and the vise opened a crack; shook me again, and it fell away. I was in the living room, and I was awake; but I was still terrified. I broke down, as I hadn't in years—not since that day in the woods—but instead of shame and humiliation I felt pain, and loneliness; only the sense of apartness was the same. I held desperately onto Davy, tears running down my cheeks, trying to hold sleep at bay. Davy held me, and stroked my back, and after I'd finished he looked at me, put a hand to my cheek, and said in a soft, sad voice: "I think it's time I made it up to you," and then he was kissing me, tenderly. Part of me wanted to stay like that for the rest of my life, pretending to be what he wanted and needed, suspended forever in illusion; but I drew back, shook my head, tried to pull away. "Davy, *no*—your wife, I can't—"

And then there was a hand on my shoulder; a small hand, not very heavy, and I could feel the tips of her fingers on my skin. I turned. Lyn sat in her nightgown on the edge of the bed, looking not at all angry or disturbed; I started to say something, but she just shook her head, said, "Sshh, sshh," and leaned in, her lips brushing the nape of my neck, her breath moving slowly along the curve of my neck to my face, my mouth . . .

She knew. All along, she *must* have known . . .

Lyn gently pushed me back onto the bed, just as I became aware of a pleasant tickle on my legs; I looked down to see Davy, his hands stroking the knotted muscles of my calves, his lips moving slowly up my legs, covering them with tiny kisses.

Lyn took my face in her hands, put her mouth to mine, and our tongues met and danced round one another in greeting . . .

And then I felt something I had never felt before—a mounting pressure, a thrilling tension, as though every nerve ending in my body were about to burst, but didn't, just kept building and building in intensity—a pleasure I had never known, never imagined I *could* know. And it was then that I realized: the doctors had been wrong; all of them. Very wrong. I wasn't lacking in erogenous tissue. My whole *body* was erogenous tissue.

All it needed was the proper stimulation.

I finally worked up the nerve to see my parents; when Mother opened the door there was a moment's shock at my appearance—so different from the flirty blonde teenager who'd run away years before—but then she reached out and embraced me, holding me as though I might blow away on the wind. Then Daddy stepped up out of the shadows of the living room and did something odd and touching: he reached out and shook my hand, the way he might greet a son coming home from college; and then kissed me on the cheek, as he might a daughter. It was his way, I think, of acknowledging I was both, and neither; his way of telling me that they didn't love a daughter, they didn't love a son . . . they loved a child.

Funny; for years I thought of myself as a freak, a useless throwback to another time—but despite all the psych courses I'd taken, all the books I'd read, I never really thought about that time, eons before recorded history, when my kind shared the earth with men and women. Why we vanished, or died out, may never be known; but the real question is, why were we there in the first place? It wasn't until Lyn, and Davy, that I began wondering . . . thinking about how, in the millennia since, men and women had had such difficulty understanding one another, seeing the other's side . . . as though something were—missing, somehow. A balance; a harmonizing element; the third side of a triangle. Maybe *that* was the natural order of things, and what's come since is the deviation. All along I'd been thinking of my kind as throwbacks, when perhaps we're just the opposite; perhaps we're more like . . . precursors.

The basement's been converted, not into a recreation room as once planned, but into extra living quarters; I have a bedroom, for when Davy and Lyn want to be alone, and a small library/den where I can study. So far, no one's been scandalized by the arrangement; lots of people room together to save rent or mortgage payments, after all. I've enrolled at the University of Washington, aiming first for my Master's, then my Ph.D., in psychology . . . because now, finally, I think I know what that purpose is I was seeking for so many years. If the statistics are right, our numbers will be doubling every ten months; thousands more like me, going through the same identity crises, the same doubt and fear and loneliness . . . and who better to help them than a psychologist who truly understands their problems?

Lyn's quit smoking again, but this time, happily, the pregnancy isn't a—what did she call it?—'stress-induced symptomatic replication.' And I can't help but feel that after so many false starts, maybe, somehow, it was me who tipped the scales—gave them that extra little push they needed. After all, who's to say life can't be transmitted just as easily in saliva or sweat as it is in semen or ova? We only have one problem now: the nagging suspicion that when it comes time to buy baby clothes, neither pink nor blue may be appropriate. Green? Yellow? Violet? Take my word for it: there's big money to be made here for some enterprising manufacturer, one ready to tap an expanding market. Wait and see; wait and see.

NEAL BARRETT, JR.

Winter on the Belle Fourche

Born in San Antonio, Texas, Neal Barrett, Jr. grew up in Oklahoma City, Oklahoma, spent several years in Austin, hobnobbing with the likes of Lewis Shiner and Howard Waldrop, and now makes his home with his family in Fort Worth, Texas. His short fiction has appeared in *The Magazine of Fantasy and Science Fiction*, *Galaxy*, *Isaac Asimov's Science Fiction Magazine*, *Amazing*, *OMNI*, *Fantastic*, *If*, and elsewhere. He made his first sale in 1959, and has been full-time freelancer for the past twelve years. His books include *Stress Pattern*, *Karma Corps*, and the four-volume Aldair series. His story "Sallie C" was in our Fourth Annual Collection, and his very funny "Perpetuity Blues" was in our Fifth Annual Collection. His most recent books are the critically acclaimed novel *Through Darkest America* and its sequel *Dawn's Uncertain Light*; coming up is *The Hereafter Gang*, and a short story collection.

In the bittersweet and darkly lyrical tale that follows, Barrett shows us a strange and momentous meeting, among the silent snows of deep winter, between two of the most oddly mismatched characters ever to share the pages of the same story . . .

▼

Winter on the Belle Fourche

NEAL BARRETT, JR.

He had come down in the cold from the Big Horn Mountains and crossed the Powder River moving east toward the Belle Fourche, all this time without finding any sign and leaving little of his own. There were wolf tracks next to the river and he saw where they had gone across the ice, which told him they were desperate and hungry, that they would turn on each other before long. An hour before dark he pulled the mount up sharp and let his senses search the land, knowing clearly something had been there before. Finally he eased to the ground and took the Hawken rifle with him, stood still in the naked grove of trees, stopped and listened to the quiet in the death-cold air, heard the frozen river crack, heard the wind bite the world. He looked south and saw the Black Hills veiled in every fold, followed them with his eyes until the land disappeared in the same soot color as the sky. He stood a long time and sniffed the air and the water moving slow beneath the ice. He let it all come together then and simmer in his head, and when it worked itself out he walked down in the draw and started scooping off the snow.

A few inches down he found the ashes from the fire. They had camped right here the night before, made a small supper fire and another in the morning. He ran the ashes through his fingers then brought them to his nose. They were real smart Injuns. They hadn't broken dead sticks off the trees but had walked downstream to get their wood. Cupping more snow aside, he bent to smell the earth. Six, he decided. If he dug a little more he'd find they all had mounts, but he didn't need to bother doing that. They wouldn't be on foot out here.

This close to the Powder and the Belle Fourche they could be any kind of red nigger and not any of them friends. He knew, though, this bunch wasn't Sioux or Cheyenne, but Absaroka. He'd smelled them right off. Crow warriors certain, and likely from Big Robert's camp.

He straightened and looked east, absently touching the bowie at his belt, the scalp ring next to that. That's where they'd gone, east and a little north, the way he was headed too. They weren't after him, didn't know that he was there. And that was something to chew on for a while.

The snow came heavy in the night, slacking off around the dawn. He was up before light and keeping to the river. Soon he'd have to figure what to do. It was two hundred miles to Fort Pierre on the Missouri, a lot more than that if he kept to every bend in the river. Del Gue would be waiting at the fort; he didn't need to be chasing after Crow, there were plenty out sniffing after him. Still, it wouldn't take much time to see what kind of mischief they were up to over here. The Absaroka were a little far east from where they rightly ought to be. He didn't think they'd want to keep on riding and maybe tangle with the Sioux, who would go without breakfast any day to skin a Crow.

At noon he found the answer. The snow had lightened up enough for tracks and he saw where the Crow had taken off, digging up dirt in the snow and hightailing it across the frozen river, heading back northwest into Absaroka country. Now he went slowly, keeping his eyes open for whatever had spooked the Crow. Sioux, most likely, though the Cheyenne could be around too. Hard winter and empty bellies made everybody brave, and a man might go where he hadn't ought to be.

He smelled the death before it saw it. The cold tried to hide it but it came through clear and he was off his horse fast, leading it down to cover in the draw. The dead were in the trees just ahead and though he knew there was no one there alive he circled wide to make sure, then walking into the clearing, the Hawken crooked loose against his chest.

Three men, mostly covered by the snow. He brushed them off enough to see they were soldiers, a white lieutenant and two buffalo troopers. Each had been shot and soundly scalped, then cut up some in the playful manner of the Sioux. The soldier's clothes and boots were gone; the Sioux had taken everything but long-handle underwear and socks.

A quick look around showed the Sioux hadn't taken them by surprise. They'd stood their ground and gotten off a few shots, and that was of some interest in itself. North, he found high ground and lighter snow and saw where the Sioux had walked Army-shod mounts northwest among their own. Ten or twelve riders. They'd gone back to the river with their trophies; the Crow had seen them then and turned for home. About this time the day before, the massacre a little before that.

He stopped and tried to work the thing out. What had the three troopers been doing up here? And why only three? It was maybe a hundred and fifty miles to Fort Laramie, a powerful lot to go in heavy snow and the cold maybe thirty-five below. Troopers didn't have a lot of smarts, but anyone'd know more than that.

He mounted up and crossed the river, circled and crossed again. Two miles down he found the trail. Something about the tracks caught his eye and he eased out of the saddle and squatted down. Now there was puzzle for sure. One of the horses had ridden double—*before* those boys had been hit by the Sioux. But there were only three bodies in the snow. Which meant the red coons had likely taken one alive, carried him back home for Injun fun. Nothing you could do for that chile, except hope he got to die, which wasn't real likely for a while. Del Gue had been taken by the Sioux the year before, and barely got out with his topknot intact. A trooper would get an extra measure sure, a skinning and worse than that.

He had the whole story now. There was no use following tracks back to the clearing but he did. He'd kept his scalp for twelve years in the wilds, and part of that from being thorough, taking two stitches in a moccasin when one might do as well, winding up a story like this to see how it came about.

He came upon the cabin without knowing it at all, reined the horse in and just sat there a minute and let the sign all around him sink in. The cabin was built low against the side of a ravine, nearly covered by a drift, and he'd damn near ridden up on the roof. He cursed himself for that. It was the kind of aggravation he didn't like, coming on something like this after he'd gotten the whole story put away. He could see it clear now, like he'd been right there when it happened. The troopers had ridden past this place into the trees, sensed trouble up ahead and the man riding double had ridden back, stopped at the cabin then turned and joined his comrades again. Which meant he'd left someone behind. There were no more tracks in the snow, so whoever that'd be was still there, unless they'd sprouted wings and flown to Independence like a bird.

Snow was nearly three feet high against the door and he carefully dug it clear. Jamming the stock of his Hawken in the snow, he pulled the Colt Walker and the bowie from his belt and stepped back.

"You inside there," he called out. "I'm white an' I don't mean ye any harm, so don't go a-shootin' whatever it is you got."

There was nothing but silence from inside. Edging up close, he bent his head to listen. There was someone in there, all right. He couldn't hear them but he knew.

"Mister," he said, "this chile's no Injun, you oughter have the sense to know that." He waited, cussed again, then raised his foot and kicked solidly at the door. It was old and split and snapped like a bone. Before it hit the floor he was in, moving fast and low, sideways like a bear, coming in with the Colt and the knife and sweeping every corner of the room. Kindling and dead leaves. The musty smell of mice. A fireplace nearly caved-in. Half a chair and a broken whiskey crock. An Army blanket in the corner, and something under that. He walked over and pulled the blanket aside with his foot.

"Great Jehoshaphat," he said aloud, and went quickly to the still and fragile form, touched the cold throat and felt for signs of life he was sure he wouldn't find.

She woke to the memory of cold, the ghost of this sensation close to death, a specter that consumed her, left her hollow, left her numb with the certainty there was no heat great enough to drive the terrible emptiness away. She woke and saw the fire and tried to draw its warmth to her with her eyes. The walls and the ceiling danced with shadow. The shadows made odd and fearsome shapes. She tried to pull her eyes away but could find neither the strength nor the will for such an effort. The shadows made awful, deathly sounds, sounds she could scarcely imagine. And then with a start that clutched her heart she remembered the sounds were real; she had heard them all too clearly through the walls from the trees across the snow.

"Oh Lord Jesus they are dying," she cried aloud, "they are murdered every one!"

Darkness rose from the floor and blocked the fire. It seemed to flow and expand to fill the room, take form as a broad-shouldered demon cloaked in fur; it grew arms and a dark and grizzled beard, a wicked eye.

She screamed and tried to push herself away.

"Ain't any need for that," the demon said. "Don't mean ye any harm."

She stared in alarm. His words brought her no relief at all. "Who—who are you?" she managed to say. "What do you want with me?"

"My name's John Johnston," the figure said. "Folks has mostly took out the *t* but that ain't no fault of mine. Just lie right still. You oughter take in some soup if ye can."

He didn't wait for an answer, but moved across the room. Her heart pounded rapidly against her breast. She watched him carefully, followed his every move. He would likely attack her quite soon. This business of the soup was just a ruse. Well, he would not catch her totally unaware. She searched for some weapon of defense, pulled herself up on one arm, the effort draining all her strength. She was under some heavy animal skin. It held her to the floor like lead. She saw a broken chair, just beyond her reach. With the help of Lord Jesus it would serve her quite well. David had very little more and brought another fearsome giant to his knees.

As she reached for the chair, stretched her arm as far as it would go, the heavy skin slipped past her shoulders to her waist. She felt the sudden cold, stopped, and caught sight of herself. For an instant, she was too paralyzed to move. Frozen with terror and disbelief. She was unclothed, bare beneath the cover! Her head began to swim. She fought against the dizziness and shame. *Oh Lord don't let me faint,* she prayed. *Let me die, but don't let me faint in the presence of the beast!*

Using every ounce of will she could find, she lay back and pulled the cover to her chin. With one hand, she searched herself for signs of violation, careful not to touch any place where carnal sin resides. Surely he had done it in her sleep. Whatever it was they did. Would you know, could you tell? Defilement came with marriage, and she had no experience in that.

The man returned from the fire. She mustered all her courage.

"Stay away from me," she warned. "Don't take another step."

He seemed puzzled. "You don't want no soup?"

"You—you had no right," she said. "You have invaded my privacy. You have looked upon me. You have sinned in God's eyes and broken several commandments. I demand the return of my clothing."

He squatted down and set the soup on the floor. "Ma'am, I didn't do no sinnin' I recall. You was near froze stiff in them clothes."

"Oh, of course. That is just what you would say to excuse your lust. I would expect no less than that."

"Yes, ma'am."

"I cannot find it in my heart to forgive you. That is my failing. I will pray that our Blessed Savior will give me the strength to see you as His child."

"You feel a need fer this soup," Johnston said, "it's on the fire." With that he rose and left her, moved across the room and curled up in a buffalo robe.

He woke at once and grabbed his heavy coat and picked up the Hawken rifle, all this in a single motion out of sleep. The woman hadn't moved. He had propped the broken door back up as best he could, and now he moved it carefully aside and slipped out into the night. The world seemed frozen in sleep, silent and hard as iron, yet brittle enough to shatter into powder at a touch. He couldn't put his finger on the sound that had broken through his sleep. The horse was all right, safely out of the wind by the cabin's far wall. The ground was undisturbed. He circled around and watched, stopped to sniff the air. Nothing was there now, but something had left its ghost behind.

Inside he warmed his hands by the fire. The woman was still asleep. It wasn't fair to say that she hadn't roused him some, that the touch of her flesh as he rubbed life back into her limbs hadn't started up some fires. Not like an Injun girl now, but some. He'd seen maybe two white women stark naked in his life. They seemed to lack definition. Like a broad field of snow without a track or a rock to give it tone. An Injun girl went from one shade to another, depending where you looked. John Hatcher had kept two fat Cheyenne squaws all the time. He kept them in his cabin in the Little Snake Valley and offered Johnston the use of one or both. He had politely declined, preferring to find his own. Hatcher's squaws giggled all the time. An Injun woman tended to act white after a spell and start to giggle and talk back. His wife hadn't done that at all. She'd been pure Injun to the end but there weren't very many like that.

* * *

When she woke once again she felt sick, drained and brittle as a stick. The man was well across the room, squatting silently by the wall.

"I would like that soup now if you please," she said as firmly as she could. She would show him no weakness at all. A man preyed upon that.

He rose and went to the fire, filled a tin cup and set it by her side.

"Take a care," he said, "it's right hot." He returned to the fire and came back and dropped a bundle on the floor. "Your clothes is all dry," he said.

She didn't answer or meet his eyes. She knew any reference to her garments would encourage wicked thoughts in his head. The soup tasted vaguely of corn, meat a little past its prime. It was filling and soothed the hurt away.

"Thank you," she said, "that was quite good."

"There's more if you want."

"I would like you to leave the cabin for a while. I should think half an hour will do fine."

Johnston didn't blink. "What fer?"

"That is no concern of yours."

"You want to get dressed, why you got that buffler robe. Ain't no reason you can't do it under there."

"Why, I certainly will not!" The suggestion brought color to her cheeks.

"Up to you," he said.

"I shall *not* move until you comply."

"Suit yerself."

Oh Lord, she prayed, *deliver me from this brute. Banish transgression from his mind*. Reaching out beneath the robe, she found her clothing and burrowed as far beneath the cover as she could, certain all the while he could see, or surely imagine, every private move she made.

"Certain rules will apply," she said. "I suppose we are confined here for the moment, though I trust the Lord will release us from adversity in good time."

She sat very close to the fire. The warmth never seemed enough. The cold came in and sought her out. The man continued to squat against the wall. It didn't seem possible that he could sit in this manner for long hours at a time. Only the blue eyes flecked with gray assured her he had not turned to stone. He was younger than she'd imagined, perhaps only a few years older than herself. His shocking red hair and thick unkempt beard masked his face; hard and weathered features helped little in determining his age.

"You will respect my privacy," she said, "and I shall certainly respect yours. There will be specific places in this room where you are not to venture. Now. I wish to say in all fairness that I believe you very likely saved my life. I am not ungrateful for that."

"Yes'm," Johnston said.

"My name is Mistress Dickinson. Mistress Emily Elizabeth Dickinson to be complete, though I caution you very strongly, Mr. Johnston, that while circumstances have thrown us together, you will *not* take the liberty of using my Christian name."

"Already knew who you was," Johnston said.

Emily was startled, struck with sudden fear. "Why, that is not possible. How could you know that?"

"Saw yer name when I went through yer belongin's," Johnston said.

"How dare you, sir!"

"Didn't mean to pry. Thought you was goin' to pass on 'fore the morning. Figured I ought git yer buryin' name."

"Oh." Emily was taken aback. Her hand came up to touch her heart. "I . . . see. Yes. Well then . . ."

Johnston seemed to squint his eyes in thought. For the first time, she detected some expression in his face.

"Ma'am, there's somethin' I got to say," Johnston said. "Them soldiers you was with. I reckon you know they're all three of 'em dead."

"I . . . guessed as much." Emily trembled at the thought. "I have prayed for their souls. Our Lord will treat them kindly."

"Some better'n them Sioux did, I reckon."

"Do not take light of the Lord, Mr. Johnston. He does not take light of you."

Johnston studied her closely again. "Jes' what was you an' them fellers doin' up here, you don't mind me askin'."

Emily paused. She had kept this horror repressed; now, she found herself eager to bring it out. Even telling it to Johnston might help it go away.

"Captain William A. Ramsey of Vermont was kind enough to ask me to accompany him and his troopers on a ride," Emily said. "There were twelve men in all when we started. The day was quite nice, not overly cold at all. We left Fort Laramie with the intention of riding along the North Platte River a few miles. A storm arose quite quickly. I believe there was some confusion about direction. When the storm passed by, we found ourselves under attack, much to everyone's alarm. Several men were killed outright. It was . . . quite terrifying."

"Cheyenne, most likely," Johnston said, as if the rest was quite clear. "They kept drivin' you away from the fort. Gittin' between you an' any help."

"Yes. That is what occurred."

"Pocahontas an' John Smith!" Johnston shook his head. "Yer lucky to be alive whether you know that or not."

"The men were very brave," Emily said. "We lost the Indians the third day out, I believe. By then there were only three men left and myself. Whether the others were cruelly slain or simply lost in the cold I cannot say. We could not turn back. I think we rode for six days. There was almost nothing to eat. One of the colored troopers killed a hare but that was all."

"You got rid of the Cheyenne an' run smack into the Sioux," Johnston finished.

"Yes. That is correct."

Johnston ran a hand through his beard. "You don't mind me sayin', this end of the country ain't a fit sort of place fer a woman like yerself."

Emily met his eyes. "I don't see that is any concern of yours."

Johnston didn't answer. She found the silence uncomfortable between them. Perhaps he didn't really mean to pry.

"Mr. Johnston," she said, "I have lived all my life in Amherst, Massachusetts. I am twenty-five years old and my whole life to now has passed in virtually one place. I have been as far as Washington and Philadelphia. I had no idea what the rest of God's world was like. I decided to go and see for myself."

"Well, I reckon that's what ye did."

"And yes. I confess that you are right. It was a foolish thing to do. I had no idea it would be like this. In my innocence, the Oregon Trail seemed a chance to view wildlife and other natural sights. Soon after departing Independence, I sensed that I was wrong. Now I am paying for my sins."

"I'd guess yer folks ain't got a idea where you are," Johnston said, thinking rightly this was so.

"No, they do not. I am certain they believe I am dead. I only pray they think I perished somewhere in the New England states."

"You ain't perished yet," Johnston said.

"I fear that is only a question of time," Emily sighed.

This time he was waiting, fully awake and outside, hunched silently in a dark grove of trees. It was well after midnight, maybe one or two. There was no wind at all and the clouds moved swiftly across the land. He thought about the woman. Damned if she wasn't just like he figured, white in near every way there was, stubborn and full of her own will. It irked him to think she was stuck right to him and no blamed way to shake her loose. There wasn't any place to take her except back to Fort Laramie or on to Fort Pierre, and either way with one horse. He thought about White Eye Anderson and Del Gue and Chris Lapp, and old John Hatcher himself, seeing him drag in with this woman on a string. Why, they'd ride him for the rest of his life.

The shadow moved and when it did Johnston spotted it at once. He waited. In a moment, a second shadow appeared, directly behind the first. He knew he'd been right the night before. How many, he wondered. All six or just two? What most likely happened was the Crow ran back toward the Powder, then got their courage up when the Sioux were out of mind. One was maybe smarter than the rest and found his trail. Which meant there was one red coon somewhere with a nose near as good as his own. Now that was a chile he'd like to meet. Johnston sniffed the world once more and started wide around the trees.

*　*　*

Now, there was only one shadow. The other had disappeared while he circled past the grove. He didn't like that, but there was not much for it. He sat and waited. Part of the dark and the windblown striations of the snow. Part of the patch of gray light that swept the earth. He knew what the Crow was doing now. He was waiting to get brave. Waiting to get his juices ready for a fight.

When it happened, the Indian moved so quickly even Johnston was surprised. The Crow stood and made for the cabin door, a blur against the white and frozen ground. Johnston rose up out of nowhere at all, one single motion taking him where he had to be. He lifted the Crow clearly off the ground, the bowie cutting cold as ice. It was over fast and done and he knew in that instant, knew before the Crow went limp and fell away, where the other one had gone. Saw him from the corner of his eye as he came off the roof straight for him, and knew the man had buried himself clean beneath the snow, burrowed like a mole and simply waited out his time. Johnston took the burden on his shoulder, bent his legs and shook the Indian to the ground. The Crow came up fighting, brought his hatchet up fast and felt Johnston's big foot glance off his chest. He staggered back, looked fearfully at Johnston as if he knew a solid blow would have stopped his heart at once, as if he saw in that moment the widows in the Absaroka camp whose men had met this terrible sight before. Turning on his heels he ran fast across the snow, plowing through drifts for the safety of the trees. Johnston tugged the Walker Colt from his belt, took his aim and fired. The Crow yelled but didn't stop.

Johnston cussed aloud; the red coon was bloodied but still alive. He didn't miss much, and this sure was a poor time to do it. He'd counted on horses. Now the Crow would take them off. He maybe should have gotten the horses first. The Crow would go and lick his wound and come back and that was pure aggravation.

He dragged the dead body well back behind the cabin. He sat beside the corpse, cut the heavy robes away. He saw a picture in his head. He saw his woman. He saw his unborn child within her womb. The child sprang to life. It played among the aspens on the Little Snake River and came to him when he called. The picture went away. He drew the knife cleanly and swiftly across the Indian's flesh below the ribs and thrust his hand inside the warmth.

With no windows at all, with the cold outside and no difference she could see between dismal day and night, the hours seemed confused. She was often too weak to stay awake. When she slept, the rest seemed to do her little good.

She felt relieved to wake and find him gone. Relief and some alarm. His size, his presence overwhelmed her. Yet, those very qualities, the nature of the man, were all that stood between her and some greater menace still. He cannot help being what he is, she told herself. God surely made him this way for some reason, for some purpose, though she could scarcely imagine what that purpose might be.

The soup tasted good. That morning he had made some kind of bread out of corn and there was still a little left. The fire was getting low and she added a little wood. The wood caught and snapped, for an instant lighting every dark corner of the room. He had set his belongings along the wall. A buffalo robe and a saddle. Leather satchels and a pack. His things seemed a part of the man. Fur and hide greased and worn, heavy with the raw and sour smells of the wild.

She had never ventured quite this close to his things. It seemed like a miniature camp, everything set the way he liked. Her eyes fell upon a thick leather packet. She looked away and then quickly looked back. The corner of a paper peeked out, and there was writing on the edge. How very strange, she thought. Literacy was wholly unexpected. She knew this wasn't fair, and chastised herself at once.

Certainly, she did not intend to pry. She would never touch Mr. Johnston's things. Still, what one could plainly see was surely no intrusion. I should not be here at all, she decided. I must turn away at once. Should dizziness occur, I might very well collapse, and this is not the place for that. Indeed, as she turned, this very thing happened. Her foot brushed against the leather packet, and slipped the paper free.

"Now look what I have done," she said, and bent to retrieve the paper at once. In spite of her good intention, the words leaped up to meet her eyes:

> *It makes no difference abroad,*
> *The season fit the same,*
> *The mornings blossom into noons,*
> *And split their pods of flame.*

And then, from the packet, another scrap of paper after that:

> *The sky is low, the clouds are mean,*
> *A traveling flake of snow*
> *Across a barn or through a rut*
> *Debates if it will go.*

"Oh. Oh dear," Emily said aloud. "That last one's quite nice. Or at least I *think* it is." She read the lines again, frowning over this and that, and decided it was slightly overdone.

Still, she wondered, what was verse doing here? Where had this unlettered man of the wilds come across a poem? Perhaps he found it, she reasoned.

Came across it in a cabin such as this where some poor traveler had met his fate.

The sound of the shot nearly paralyzed her with fear. "Oh Blessed Jesus!" she cried. The papers fluttered from her hand. She fled to a corner of the cabin, crouched there and stared at the door. An Indian would enter quite soon. Possibly more than one. They would not slay her, though, they would take her to their camp. She would tell them about Christ. They would renounce their savage ways. They would certainly not touch her in any way.

It seemed forever before the door opened again and Johnston appeared. "Oh, thank the Lord you're all right," Emily sighed. "That shot. I thought—I thought you had surely been killed!"

"Took a shot at a deer," Johnston said. "Wasn't nothin' more'n that." He shook his coat. His beard seemed thick with ice.

"God be praised," Emily said.

Johnston set his Hawken aside. Stomped his feet and ran his hand through a bushy nest of hair. He looked down then and saw the papers on the floor and picked them up. He looked right at Emily and didn't say a thing.

Emily's heart began to pound. "I . . . I'm very sorry," she said. "I certainly had no right."

"Don't matter none," Johnston said. He stood with his backside to the fire.

"Yes, now yes it does," Emily said firmly. "It is I who have transgressed. I am clearly in the wrong. I do not deny my sin."

"I ain't never hear'd so much about sin," Johnston said.

Emily felt her face color. "Well, there is certainly sin abroad, Mr. Johnston. Satan has his eye upon us all."

"I reckon," Johnston said. He scratched and set down. Leaned against the wall in his customary manner.

Emily wondered if she dare break the silence. He didn't seem angry at all, but how on earth would one know? And they could not simply sit there and look at one another.

"Mr. Johnston, I do not excuse my actions," she said, "but perhaps you'll understand when I say I have an interest in poetry myself. As a fact, one small effort has seen the light of publication. Three years ago. February 20, 1852, to be exact. In the *Springfield Daily Republican*." She smiled and touched her hair. "I recall the date clearly, of course, There are dates in one's life one remembers very well. One's birthday, certainly—" Emily blushed, aware she was chattering away. "Well, yes, at any rate . . ."

Johnston said nothing at all.

"You must be quite chilled," Emily said. "There is still a little soup."

"I ain't real hungry," Johnston said.

This time would have to be different; the Crow was wary now and hurt, and an Injun like that was the same as any other creature in the wild in such condition, the same as he'd be himself, Johnston knew, as deadly as a stirred-up snake. The Crow would be in place early this night, out there in spite of the cold, because the first man out could watch and see what the other man would do. It was a deadly advantage, and Johnston was determined to let the Absaroka have it.

The Indian was cautious and he was good. Johnston could scarcely hear him, scarcely smell his fear. He seemed to take forever, moving when the wind rose some, stopping when it died.

Tarnation, Johnston thought, *come on and git it done, chile, 'fore I freeze these bones to the ground*.

At last the Crow struck, coming in swiftly without a sound. The hatchet fell once, slicing the heavy furs, withdrew and hacked again, and Johnston, even in the dark, saw emotion of every sort cross the Absaroka's face, saw surprise and alarm and then final understanding that the furs crouched there against the tree didn't have a man inside, that it was simply too late to remedy that.

Johnston shook the snow aside. "That war your trick, son, not mine," he said aloud. "Ye got no one to blame but yourself . . ."

She hated the boredom most of all. It overpowered fear and apprehension. Now she sorely missed being scared. Now there was nothing at all to do. Was it day outside or was it night? Sometimes Johnston would tell her. For the most part he sat like a stone or wandered out in the night. Worse than sitting in the cabin were the times when she had to go out to attend to bodily needs. It was horrid, a humiliation she could scarcely bear. She had to *ask*. He would not let her venture out alone. He would stand by the door with his weapon while she struggled as far as she dared through the snow. And the cold! That fierce, and unimaginable cold. Winter, she saw now, gave New England a fleeting glance. This terrible empty land was where it was born.

She heard him at the door and then he stepped inside, letting in the cold. "Found us a couple of horses," Johnston said, and dropped his heavy coat on the floor.

"You did?" Emily was surprised. "Why, isn't that odd."

"Ain't nothin' odd to it," Johnston said.

"Yes, well . . ." He seemed very pleased with himself. It dawned on her then that horses had meaning in her life. "Heavens," she said, "that means we can leave this place, does it not?"

"First thing in the mornin'," Johnston said. He didn't even glance her way. He simply wrapped up in his robes and turned his face against the wall.

Emily felt the heat rise to her cheeks, and this brought further irritation. Anger at Johnston, but mostly at herself. What did *she* care what he did?

They certainly had nothing to talk about. No topic that would interest her in the least. Still, the man's rudeness had no bounds at all. He had no concept of social intercourse.

"You are just going to—sleep?" she said. "Right now?"

"I was plannin' on it," Johnston said.

"Well you could at least impart information. There are things one needs to know."

"'Bout what?"

"About the trip." Emily waited. Johnston didn't answer. "What I mean, is how long will it take? I have no idea of the distance to Fort Laramie. As you know, I left under unusual circumstances."

"Ain't goin' to Fort Laramie. Goin' to Fort Pierre."

Emily sat up. "Mr. Johnston, I demand to be returned to Fort *Laramie*. I have no intention of going anywhere else."

"Fort Pierre's whar I'm headed," Johnston said.

"Whatever for?"

"Meetin' someone."

"Well who?"

"Like you're fonda sayin', Miz Dickinson, that ain't no concern of yours."

Emily tried to contain herself. To show Christian restraint. A sudden thought occurred. A woman, that was it. He was going to see a woman. Possibly a wife. The thought defied imagination. What sort of woman would this backwoods ruffian attract?

"Are you married, Mr. Johnston?" Emily asked. "I don't believe you've ever said. But of course you're quite correct. That is no concern of mine."

Johnston kept his silence. He had likely gone to sleep and hadn't heard a word she said. The man had no consideration.

"My wife's dead," Johnston said. The tone of his words brought a chill. "Her an' the chile too. Crows killed 'em both."

Emily felt ashamed. "I'm . . . terribly sorry, Mr. Johnston. Really."

"Reckon I am too."

"You are angry with me I know."

"Ma'am, I ain't angry at all."

"Yes now, you are. I do not fault you for it, Mr. Johnston. I have intruded upon your life. I am guilty of certain violations. And you are still upset about the poems."

"No I ain't."

"Yes you are. That is quite clear to me. I want you to know that I have since shown respect for your possessions. I was tempted, yes. We are all weak vessels, and there is nothing at all to do in this place. Still, I did not succumb. Lord Jesus gave me strength."

"Git some sleep," Johnston said, and pulled the buffalo robe about his head.

* * *

He awoke in fury and disbelief, clutched the Hawken and came to his feet, saw the dull press of dawn around the door, heard the faint sound of horses outside, hardly there at all, as if they'd come up with him out of sleep.

Great God A'Mighty, they'd played him for a fool, him sleeping like a chile and sure he'd got the only two. Maybe it wasn't Crow, he decided. Maybe it was Sioux coming back. And what in tarnation did it matter which brand of red coon it might be—they flat had him cold like a rabbit in a log.

The woman came awake, a question on her face. "Jes' get back in yer corner and keep quiet," Johnston said harshly. He turned to face the door, made sure the Walker Colt was in his belt. How many, he wondered. The horses were silent now.

"Come an' git your medicine," he said softly, "I'm a-waitin' right here."

"Inside the cabin," a man shouted. "This is Lieutenant Joshua Dean. We are here in force, and I must ask you to come out at once unarmed."

Johnston laughed aloud. He decided he was plain going slack. A man who couldn't tell shod horses in his sleep was a man who maybe ought to pack it in.

"I am grateful for what you have done," Emily said. "I owe you my thanks, Mr. Johnston."

"Nothin' to thank me for," Johnston said. The troopers had stopped fiddling about and seemed ready to depart. He wondered why a soldier took an hour to turn around. The lieutenant had eyed the Indian ponies but didn't ask where their riders might be. If he recognized Johnston or knew his name he didn't say.

"We have had our differences, I suppose," Emily said.

"I reckon so."

"God has a reason for what he does, Mr. Johnston. I am sure this adventure serves a purpose in His plan."

Johnston couldn't figure just what it might be. "You have a safe trip, Miz Dickinson," he said.

"I will do just that," Emily said. "I expect Massachusetts will seem dear to me now. I doubt I'll stray again."

She walked away through the snow and the lieutenant helped her mount. Johnston watched till they were well out of sight then went inside to get his things.

As he rode through the flat white world with the slate-dark sky overhead, he thought about the Bitter Root Mountains and the Musselshell River. He thought about the Platte and the Knife and the Bearpaw Range, every peak and river he'd ever crossed clear as glass in his head. He thought about

Swan, eight years dead in the spring and it didn't seem that long at all, and in a way a lot more. Dead all this time and he still saw her face every day.

Before dark he found a spot near the Belle Fourche and staked the horses out safe. One Crow pony had a blaze between its eyes. He favored an Injun horse with good marks. He wondered if Del Gue was still waiting at Fort Pierre. They'd have to get moving out soon to get some hides. He thought again how he'd waited too long to get in the trapping trade, the beaver near gone when he'd come to the mountains and hooked up with old Hatcher. Just bear and mink now and whatever a man could find.

Scooping out a hole in the snow, he snapped a few sticks and stacked them ready for the fire, then walked back and got his leather satchel and dipped his hand inside. Johnston stopped, puzzled at an unfamiliar touch. He squatted on the ground and started pulling things out. There was nothing but an old Army blanket. His paper was all gone.

"Well cuss me fer a Kiowa," he said aloud. That damn woman had filched the whole lot. He was plain irritated. It wasn't like he couldn't spark a fire, but a man fell into easy habits. A little paper saved time, especially if your wood was all wet. Came in handy too if you had to do your business and there wasn't no good leaves about.

She'd gotten every piece there was. He hadn't ever counted, but there were likely near a thousand bits and scraps, rhymes he'd thought up and set down, then saved for the fire. This was by God pure aggravation. He grumbled to himself and found his flint. A man sure couldn't figure what was stewing in a white woman's head. An Injun wasn't like that at all.

ROBERT SILVERBERG

Enter a Soldier. Later: Enter Another

Here's another powerful story by Robert Silverberg. In this one, Silverberg examines a fascinating new technology that enables a group of scientists to pit two very different kinds of soldiers against each other in a tense and absorbing contest of brains and heart and spirit . . . one with some very unexpected results.

▼
Enter a Soldier.
Later: Enter Another

ROBERT SILVERBERG

It might be heaven. Certainly it wasn't Spain and he doubted it could be Peru. He seemed to be floating, suspended midway between nothing and nothing. There was a shimmering golden sky far above him and a misty, turbulent sea of white clouds boiling far below. When he looked down he saw his legs and his feet dangling like child's toys above an unfathomable abyss, and the sight of it made him want to puke, but there was nothing in him for the puking. He was hollow. He was made of air. Even the old ache in his knee was gone, and so was the everlasting dull burning in the fleshy part of his arm where the Indian's little arrow had taken him, long ago on the shore of that island of pearls, up by Panama.

It was as if he had been born again, sixty years old but freed of all the harm that his body had experienced and all its myriad accumulated injuries: freed, one might almost say, of his body itself.

"Gonzalo?" he called. "Hernando?"

Blurred dreamy echoes answered him. And then silence.

"Mother of God, am I dead?"

No. No. He had never been able to imagine death. An end to all striving? A place where nothing moved? A great emptiness, a pit without a bottom? Was this place the place of death, then? He had no way of knowing. He needed to ask the holy fathers about this.

"Boy, where are my priests? Boy?"

He looked about for his page. But all he saw was blinding whorls of light coiling off to infinity on all sides. The sight was beautiful but troublesome. It was hard for him to deny that he had died, seeing himself afloat like this in a realm of air and light. Died and gone to heaven. This is heaven, yes, surely, surely. What else could it be?

So it was true, that if you took the Mass and took the Christ faithfully into yourself and served Him well you would be saved from your sins, you would be forgiven, you would be cleansed. He had wondered about that. But he wasn't ready yet to be dead, all the same. The thought of it was sickening and infuriating. There was so much yet to be done. And he had no memory even of being ill. He searched his body for wounds. No, no wounds. Not anywhere. Strange. Again he looked around. He was alone here. No one to be seen, not his page, nor his brother, nor De Soto, nor the priests, nor anyone. "Fray Marcos! Fray Vicente! Can't you hear me? Damn you, where are you? Mother of God! Holy Mother, blessed among women! Damn you, Fray Vicente, tell me—tell me—"

His voice sounded all wrong: too thick, too deep, a stranger's voice. The words fought with his tongue and came from his lips malformed and lame, not the good crisp Spanish of Estremadura but something shameful and odd. What he heard was like the spluttering foppishness of Madrid or even the furry babble that they spoke in Barcelona; why, he might almost be a Portuguese, so coarse and clownish was his way of shaping his speech.

He said carefully and slowly, "I am the Governor and Captain-General of New Castile."

That came out no better, a laughable noise.

"Adelantado—Alguacil Mayor—Marques de la Conquista—"

The strangeness of his new way of speech made insults of his own titles. It was like being tongue-tied. He felt streams of hot sweat breaking out on his skin from the effort of trying to frame his words properly; but when he put his hand to his forehead to brush the sweat away before it could run into his eyes he seemed dry to the touch, and he was not entirely sure he could feel himself at all.

He took a deep breath. "I am Francisco Pizarro!" he roared, letting the name burst desperately from him like water breaching a rotten dam.

The echo came back, deep, rumbling, mocking. *Frantheethco. Peetharro.*

That too. Even his own name, idiotically garbled.

"O great God!" he cried. "Saints and angels!"

More garbled noises. Nothing would come out as it should. He had never known the arts of reading or writing; now it seemed that true speech itself was being taken from him. He began to wonder whether he had been right about this being heaven, supernal radiance or no. There was a curse on his tongue; a demon, perhaps, held it pinched in his claws. Was this hell, then? A very beautiful place, but hell nevertheless?

He shrugged. Heaven or hell, it made no difference. He was beginning to grow more calm, beginning to accept and take stock. He knew—had learned, long ago—that there was nothing to gain from raging against that which could not be helped, even less from panic in the face of the unknown. He was here, that was all there was to it—wherever *here* was—and he must find a place for himself, and not this place, floating here between nothing and nothing. He had been in hells before, small hells, hells on Earth. That barren isle called Gallo, where the sun cooked you in your own skin and there was nothing to eat but crabs that had the taste of dog-dung. And that dismal swamp at the mouth of the Rio Biru, where the rain fell in rivers and the trees reached down to cut you like swords. And the mountains he had crossed with his army, where the snow was so cold that it burned, and the air went into your throat like a dagger at every breath. He had come forth from those, and they had been worse than this. Here there was no pain and no danger; here there was only soothing light and a strange absence of all discomfort. He began to move forward. He was walking on air. Look, look, he thought, I am walking on air! Then he said it out loud. "I am walking on air," he announced, and laughed at the way the words emerged from him. "Santiago! Walking on air! But why not? I am Pizarro!" He shouted it with all his might, "Pizarro! Pizarro!" and waited for it to come back to him.

Peetharro. Peetharro.

He laughed. He kept on walking.

Tanner sat hunched forward in the vast sparkling sphere that was the ninth-floor imaging lab, watching the little figure at the distant center of the holotank strut and preen. Lew Richardson, crouching beside him with both hands thrust into the data gloves so that he could feed instructions to the permutation network, seemed almost not to be breathing—seemed to be just one more part of the network, in fact.

But that was Richardson's way, Tanner thought: total absorption in the task at hand. Tanner envied him that. They were very different sorts of men. Richardson lived for his programming and nothing but his programming. It was his grand passion. Tanner had never quite been able to understand people who were driven by grand passions. Richardson was like some throwback to an earlier age, an age when things had really mattered, an age when you were able to have some faith in the significance of your own endeavors.

"How do you like the armor?" Richardson asked. "The armor's very fine, I think. We got it from old engravings. It has real flair."

"Just the thing for tropical climates," said Tanner. "A nice tin suit with matching helmet."

He coughed and shifted about irritably in his seat. The demonstration had been going on for half an hour without anything that seemed to be of any importance happening—just the minuscule image of the bearded man in Spanish armor tramping back and forth across the glowing field—and he was beginning to get impatient.

Richardson didn't seem to notice the harshness in Tanner's voice or the restlessness of his movements. He went on making small adjustments. He was a small man himself, neat and precise in dress and appearance, with faded blond hair and pale blue eyes and a thin, straight mouth. Tanner felt huge and shambling beside him. In theory Tanner had authority over Richardson's research projects, but in fact he always had simply permitted Richardson to do as he pleased. This time, though, it might be necessary finally to rein him in a little.

This was the twelfth or thirteenth demonstration that Richardson had subjected him to since he had begun fooling around with this historical-simulation business. The others all had been disasters of one kind or another, and Tanner expected that this one would finish the same way. And basically Tanner was growing uneasy about the project that he once had given his stamp of approval to, so long ago. It was getting harder and harder to go on believing that all this work served any useful purpose. Why had it been allowed to absorb so much of Richardson's group's time and so much of the lab's research budget for so many months? What possible value was it going to have for anybody? What possible use?

It's just a game, Tanner thought. One more desperate meaningless technological stunt, one more pointless pirouette in a meaningless ballet. The expenditure of vast resources on a display of ingenuity for ingenuity's sake and nothing else: now *there's* decadence for you.

The tiny image in the holotank suddenly began to lose color and definition.

"Uh-oh," Tanner said. "There it goes. Like all the others."

But Richardson shook his head. "This time it's different, Harry."

"You think?"

"We aren't losing him. He's simply moving around in there of his own volition, getting beyond our tracking parameters. Which means that we've achieved the high level of autonomy that we were shooting for."

"Volition, Lew? Autonomy?"

"You know that those are our goals."

"Yes, I know what our goals are supposed to be," said Tanner, with some annoyance. "I'm simply not convinced that a loss of focus is a proof that you've got volition."

"Here," Richardson said. "I'll cut in the stochastic tracking program. He moves freely, we freely follow him." Into the computer ear in his lapel he said, "Give me a gain boost, will you?" He made a quick flicking gesture with his left middle finger to indicate the quantitative level.

The little figure in ornate armor and pointed boots grew sharp again. Tanner could see fine details on the armor, the plumed helmet, the tapering shoulder-pieces, the joints at the elbows, the intricate pommel of his sword. He was marching from left to right in a steady hip-rolling way, like a man who was climbing the tallest mountain in the world and didn't mean to break his stride until he was across the summit. The fact that he was walking in what appeared to be mid-air seemed not to trouble him at all.

"There he is," Richardson said grandly. "We've got him back, all right? The conqueror of Peru, before your very eyes, in the flesh. So to speak."

Tanner nodded. Pizarro, yes, before his very eyes. And he had to admit that what he saw was impressive and even, somehow, moving. Something about the dogged way with which that small armored figure was moving across the gleaming pearly field of the holotank aroused a kind of sympathy in him. That little man was entirely imaginary, but *he* didn't seem to know that, or if he did he wasn't letting it stop him for a moment: he went plugging on, and on and on, as if he intended actually to get somewhere. Watching that, Tanner was oddly captivated by it, and found himself surprised suddenly to discover that his interest in the entire project was beginning to rekindle.

"Can you make him any bigger?" he asked. "I want to see his face."

"I can make him big as life," Richardson said. "Bigger. Any size you like. Here."

He flicked a finger and the hologram of Pizarro expanded instantaneously to a height of about two meters. The Spaniard halted in midstride as though he might actually be aware of the imaging change.

That can't be possible, Tanner thought. That isn't a living consciousness out there. Or is it?

Pizarro stood poised easily in mid-air, glowering, shading his eyes as if staring into a dazzling glow. There were brilliant streaks of color in the air all around him, like an aurora. He was a tall, lean man in late middle age with a grizzled beard and a hard, angular face. His lips were thin, his nose was sharp, his eyes were cold, shrewd, keen. It seemed to Tanner that those eyes had come to rest on him, and he felt a chill.

My God, Tanner thought, he's *real*.

It had been a French program to begin with, something developed at the Centre Mundial de la Computation in Lyons about the year 2119. The French had some truly splendid minds working in software in those days. They worked up astounding programs, and then nobody did anything with them. That was *their* version of Century Twenty-Two Malaise.

The French programmers' idea was to use holograms of actual historical personages to dress up the *son et lumiere* tourist events at the great monuments of their national history. Not just preprogrammed robot mockups of the old Disneyland kind, which would stand around in front of Notre Dame or the Arc de Triomphe or the Eiffel Tower and deliver canned spiels, but apparent reincarnations of the genuine great ones, who could freely walk and talk and answer questions and make little quips. Imagine Louis XIV demonstrating the fountains of Versailles, they said, or Picasso leading a tour of Paris museums, or Sartre sitting in his Left Bank cafe exchanging existential *bons mots* with passersby! Napoleon! Joan of Arc! Alexandre Dumas! Perhaps the simulations could do even more than that: perhaps they could be designed so well that they would be able to extend and embellish the achievements of their original lifetimes with new accomplishments, a fresh spate of paintings and novels and works of philosophy and great architectural visions by vanished masters.

423

The concept was simple enough in essence. Write an intelligencing program that could absorb data, digest it, correlate it, and generate further programs based on what you had given it. No real difficulty there. Then start feeding your program with the collected written works—if any—of the person to be simulated; that would provide not only a general sense of his ideas and positions but also of his underlying pattern of approach to situations, his style of thinking—for *le style*, after all, *est l'homme meme*. If no collected works happened to be available, why, find works *about* the subject by his contemporaries, and use those. Next, toss in the totality of the historical record of the subject's deeds, including all significant subsequent scholarly analyses, making appropriate allowances for conflicts in interpretation— indeed, taking advantage of such conflicts to generate a richer portrait, full of the ambiguities and contradictions that are the inescapable hallmarks of any human being. Now build in substrata of general cultural data of the proper period so that the subject has a loam of references and vocabulary out of which to create thoughts that are appropriate to his place in time and space. Stir. *Et voila!* Apply a little sophisticated imaging technology and you had a simulation capable of thinking and conversing and behaving as though it is the actual self after which it was patterned.

Of course, this would require a significant chunk of computer power. But that was no problem, in a world where 150-gigaflops networks were standard laboratory items and ten-year-olds carried pencil-sized computers with capacities far beyond the ponderous mainframes of their great-great-grandparents' day. No, there was no theoretical reason why the French project could not have succeeded. Once the Lyons programmers had worked out the basic intelligencing scheme that was needed to write the rest of the programs, it all should have followed smoothly enough.

Two things went wrong: one rooted in an excess of ambition that may have been a product of the peculiarly French personalities of the original programmers, and the other having to do with an abhorrence of failure typical of the major nations of the mid-twenty-second century, of which France was one.

The first was a fatal change of direction that the project underwent in its early phases. The King of Spain was coming to Paris on a visit of state; and the programmers decided that in his honor they would synthesize Don Quixote for him as their initial project. Though the intelligencing program had been designed to simulate only individuals who had actually existed, there seemed no inherent reason why a fictional character as well documented as Don Quixote could not be produced instead. There was Cervantes' lengthy novel; there was ample background data available on the milieu in which Don Quixote supposedly had lived; there was a vast library of critical analysis of the book and of the Don's distinctive and flamboyant personality. Why should bringing Don Quixote to life out of a computer be any different from simulating Louis XIV, say, or Moliere, or Cardinal Richelieu? True, they had all existed once, and the knight of La Mancha was a mere figment; but had Cervantes not provided far more detail about Don Quixote's mind and soul than was known of Richelieu, or Moliere, or Louis XIV?

Indeed he had. The Don—like Oedipus, like Odysseus, like Othello, like David Copperfield—had come to have a reality far more profound and tangible than that of most people who had indeed actually lived. Such characters as those had transcended their fictional origins. But not so far as the computer was concerned. It was able to produce a convincing fabrication of Don Quixote, all right—a gaunt bizarre holographic figure that had all the right mannerisms, that ranted and raved in the expectable way, that referred knowledgeably to Dulcinea and Rosinante and Mambrino's helmet. The Spanish king was amused and impressed. But to the French the experiment was a failure. They had produced a Don Quixote who was hopelessly locked to the Spain of the late sixteenth century and to the book from which he had sprung. He had no capacity for independent life and thought—no way to perceive the world that had brought him into being, or to comment on it, or to interact with it. There was nothing new or interesting about that. Any actor could dress up in armor and put on a scraggly beard and recite snatches of Cervantes. What had come forth from the computer, after three years of work, was no more than a predictable reprocessing of what had gone into it, sterile, stale.

Which led the Centre Mundial de la Computation to its next fatal step: abandoning the whole thing. *Zut!* and the project was cancelled without any further attempts. No simulated Picassos, no simulated Napoleons, no Joans of Arc. The Quixote event had soured everyone and no one had the heart to proceed with the work from there. Suddenly it had the taint of failure about it, and France—like Germany, like Australia, like the Han Commercial Sphere, like Brazil, like any of the dynamic centers of the modern world, had a horror of failure. Failure was something to be left to the backward nations or the decadent ones—to the Islamic Socialist Union, say, or the Soviet People's Republic, or to that slumbering giant, the United States of America. So the historic-personage simulation scheme was put aside.

The French thought so little of it, as a matter of fact, that after letting it lie fallow for a few years they licensed it to a bunch of Americans, who had heard about it somehow and felt it might be amusing to play with.

"You may really have done it this time," Tanner said.

"Yes. I think we have. After all those false starts."

Tanner nodded. How often had he come into this room with hopes high, only to see some botch, some inanity, some depressing bungle? Richardson had always had an explanation. Sherlock Holmes hadn't worked because he was fictional: that was a necessary recheck of the French Quixote project, demonstrating that fictional characters didn't have the right sort of reality texture to take proper advantage of the program, not enough ambiguity, not enough contradiction. King Arthur had failed for the same reason. Julius Caesar? Too far in the past, maybe: unreliable data, bordering on fiction. Moses? Ditto. Einstein? Too complex, perhaps, for the project in its present level of development: they needed more experience first. Queen Elizabeth I? George Washington? Mozart? We're learning more each time, Richardson insisted after each failure. This isn't black magic we're doing, you know. We aren't necromancers, we're programmers, and we have to figure out how to give the program what it needs.

And now Pizarro.

"Why do you want to work with *him*?" Tanner had asked, five or six months earlier. "A ruthless medieval Spanish imperialist, is what I remember from school. A bloodthirsty despoiler of a great culture. A man without morals, honor, faith—"

"You may be doing him an injustice," said Richardson. "He's had a bad press for centuries. And there are things about him that fascinate me."

"Such as?"

"His drive. His courage. His absolute confidence. The other side of ruthlessness, the good side of it, is a total concentration on your task, an utter unwillingness to be stopped by any obstacle. Whether or not you approve of the things he accomplished, you have to admire a man who—"

"All right," Tanner said, abruptly growing weary of the whole enterprise. "Do Pizarro. Whatever you want."

The months had passed. Richardson gave him vague progress reports, nothing to arouse much hope. But now Tanner stared at the tiny strutting figure in the holotank and the conviction began to grow in him that Richardson finally had figured out how to use the simulation program as it was meant to be used.

"So you've actually recreated him, you think? Someone who lived—what, five hundred years ago?"

"He died in 1541," said Richardson.

"Almost six hundred, then."

"And he's not like the others—not simply a recreation of a great figure out of the past who can run through a set of pre-programmed speeches. What we've got here, if I'm right, is an artificially generated intelligence which can think for itself in modes other than the ones its programmers think in. Which has more information available to itself, in other words, than we've provided it with. That would be the real accomplishment. That's the fundamental philosophical leap that we were going for when we first got involved with this project. To use the program to give us new programs that are capable of true autonomous thought—a program that can think like Pizarro, instead of like Lew Richardson's idea of some historian's idea of how Pizarro might have thought."

"Yes," Tanner said.

"Which means we won't just get back the expectable, the predictable.

There'll be surprises. There's no way to learn anything, you know, except through surprises. The sudden combination of known components into something brand new. And that's what I think we've managed to bring off here, at long last. Harry, it may be the biggest artificial-intelligence breakthrough ever achieved."

Tanner pondered that. Was it so? Had they truly done it?

And if they had—

Something new and troubling was beginning to occur to him, much later in the game than it should have. Tanner stared at the holographic figure floating in the center of the tank, that fierce old man with the harsh face and the cold, cruel eyes. He thought about what sort of man he must have been—the man after whom this image had been modeled. A man who was willing to land in South America at age fifty or sixty or whatever he had been, an ignorant illiterate Spanish peasant wearing a suit of ill-fitting armor and waving a rusty sword, and set out to conquer a great empire of millions of people spreading over thousands of miles. Tanner wondered what sort of man would be capable of carrying out a thing like that. Now that man's eyes were staring into his own and it was a struggle to meet so implacable a gaze.

After a moment he looked away. His left leg began to quiver. He glanced uneasily at Richardson.

"Look at those eyes, Lew. Christ, they're scary!"

"I know. I designed them myself, from the old prints."

"Do you think he's seeing us right now? Can he do that?"

"All he is is software, Harry."

"He seemed to know it when you expanded the image."

Richardson shrugged. "He's very good software. I tell you, he's got autonomy, he's got volition. He's got an electronic *mind*, is what I'm saying. He may have perceived a transient voltage kick. But there are limits to his perceptions, all the same. I don't think there's any way that he can see anything that's outside the holotank unless it's fed to him in the form of data he can process, which hasn't been done."

"You don't *think*? You aren't sure?"

"Harry. Please."

"This man conquered the entire enormous Incan empire with fifty soldiers, didn't he?"

"In fact I believe it was more like a hundred and fifty."

"Fifty, a hundred fifty, what's the difference? Who knows what you've actually got here? What if you did an even better job than you suspect?"

"What are you saying?"

"What I'm saying is, I'm uneasy all of a sudden. For a long time I didn't think this project was going to produce anything at all. Suddenly I'm starting to think that maybe it's going to produce more than we can handle. I don't want any of your goddamned simulations walking out of the tank and conquering *us*."

Richardson turned to him. His face was flushed, but he was grinning. "Harry, Harry! For God's sake! Five minutes ago you didn't think we had anything at all here except a tiny picture that wasn't even in focus. Now you've gone so far the other way that you're imagining the worst kind of—"

"I see his eyes, Lew. I'm worried that his eyes see me."

"Those aren't real eyes you're looking at. What you see is nothing but a graphics program projected into a holotank. There's no visual capacity there as you understand the concept. His eyes will see you only if I want them to. Right now they don't."

"But you can make them see me?"

"I can make them see anything I want them to see. I created him, Harry."

"With volition. With autonomy."

"After all this time you start worrying *now* about these things?"

"It's my neck on the line if something that you guys on the technical side make runs amok. This autonomy thing suddenly troubles me."

"I'm still the one with the data gloves," Richardson said. "I twitch my fingers and he dances. That's not really Pizarro down there, remember. And that's no Frankenstein monster either. It's just a simulation. It's just so much data, just a bunch of electromagnetic impulses that I can shut off with one movement of my pinkie."

"Do it, then."

"Shut him off? But I haven't begun to show you—"

"Shut him off, and then turn him on," Tanner said.

Richardson looked bothered. "If you say so, Harry."

He moved a finger. The image of Pizarro vanished from the holotank. Swirling gray mists moved in it for a moment, and then all was white wool. Tanner felt a quick jolt of guilt, as though he had just ordered the execution of the man in the medieval armor. Richardson gestured again, and color flashed across the tank, and then Pizarro reappeared.

"I just wanted to see how much autonomy your little guy really has," said Tanner. "Whether he was quick enough to head you off and escape into some other channel before you could cut his power."

"You really don't understand how this works at all, do you, Harry?"

"I just wanted to see," said Tanner again, sullenly. After a moment's silence he said, "Do you ever feel like God?"

"Like God?"

"You breathed life in. Life of a sort, anyway. But you breathed free will in, too. That's what this experiment is all about, isn't it? All your talk about volition and autonomy? You're trying to recreate a human mind—which means to create it all over again—a mind that can think in its own special way, and come up with its own unique responses to situations, which will not necessarily be the responses that its programmers might anticipate, in fact almost certainly will not be, and which might not be all that desirable or beneficial, either, and you simply have to allow for that risk, just as God,

428

once he gave free will to mankind, knew that He was likely to see all manner of evil deeds being performed by His creations as they exercised that free will—"

"Please, Harry—"

"Listen, is it possible for me to talk with your Pizarro?"

"Why?"

"By way of finding out what you've got there. To get some first-hand knowledge of what the project has accomplished. Or you could say I just want to test the quality of the simulation. Whatever. I'd feel more a part of this thing, more aware of what it's all about in here, if I could have some direct contact with him. Would it be all right if I did that?"

"Yes. Of course."

"Do I have to talk to him in Spanish?"

"In any language you like. There's an interface, after all. He'll think it's his own language coming in, no matter what, sixteenth-century Spanish. And he'll answer you in what seems like Spanish to him, but you'll hear it in English."

"Are you sure?"

"Of course."

"And you don't mind if I make contact with him?"

"Whatever you like."

"It won't upset his calibration, or anything?"

"It won't do any harm at all, Harry."

"Fine. Let me talk to him, then."

There was a disturbance in the air ahead, a shifting, a swirling, like a little whirlwind. Pizarro halted and watched it for a moment, wondering what was coming next. A demon arriving to torment him, maybe. Or an angel. Whatever it was, he was ready for it.

Then a voice out of the whirlwind said, in that same comically exaggerated Castilian Spanish that Pizarro himself had found himself speaking a little while before, "Can you hear me?"

"I hear you, yes. I don't see you. Where are you?"

"Right in front of you. Wait a second. I'll show you." Out of the whirlwind came a strange face that hovered in the middle of nowhere, a face without a body, a lean face, close-shaven, no beard at all, no mustache, the hair cut very short, dark eyes set close together. He had never seen a face like that before.

"What are you?" Pizarro asked. "A demon or an angel?"

"Neither one." Indeed he didn't sound very demonic. "A man, just like you."

"Not much like me, I think. Is a face all there is to you, or do you have a body, too?"

"All you see of me is a face?"

"Yes."

"Wait a second."

"I will wait as long as I have to. I have plenty of time."

The face disappeared. Then it returned, attached to the body of a big, wide-shouldered man who was wearing a long loose gray robe, something like a priest's cassock, but much more ornate, with points of glowing light gleaming on it everywhere. Then the body vanished and Pizarro could see only the face again. He could make no sense out of any of this. He began to understand how the Indians must have felt when the first Spaniards came over the horizon, riding horses, carrying guns, wearing armor.

"You are very strange. Are you an Englishman, maybe?"

"American."

"Ah," Pizarro said, as though that made things better. "An American. And what is that?"

The face wavered and blurred for a moment. There was mysterious new agitation in the thick white clouds surrounding it. Then the face grew steady and said, "America is a country north of Peru. A very large country, where many people live."

"You mean New Spain, which was Mexico, where my kinsman Cortes is Captain-General?"

"North of Mexico. Far to the north of it."

Pizarro shrugged. "I know nothing of those places. Or not very much. There is an island called Florida, yes? And stories of cities of gold, but I think they are only stories. I found the gold, in Peru. Enough to choke on, I found. Tell me this, am I in heaven now?"

"No."

"Then this is hell?"

"Not that, either. Where you are—it's very difficult to explain, actually—"

"I am in America."

"Yes. In America, yes."

"And am I dead?"

There was silence for a moment.

"No, not dead," the voice said uneasily.

"You are lying to me, I think."

"How could we be speaking with each other, if you were dead?"

Pizarro laughed hoarsely. "Are you asking *me*? I understand nothing of what is happening to me in this place. Where are my priests? Where is my page? Send me my brother!" He glared. "Well? Why don't you get them for me?"

"They aren't here. You're here all by yourself, Don Francisco."

"In America. All by myself in your America. Show me your America, then. Is there such a place? Is America all clouds and whorls of light? Where is America? Let me see America. Prove to me that I am in America."

There was another silence, longer than the last. Then the face disappeared and the wall of white cloud began to boil and churn more fiercely than before. Pizarro stared into the midst of it, feeling a mingled sense of curiosity and annoyance. The face did not reappear. He saw nothing at all. He was being toyed with. He was a prisoner in some strange place and they were treating him like a child, like a dog, like—like an Indian. Perhaps this was the retribution for what he had done to King Atahuallpa, then, that fine noble foolish man who had given himself up to him in all innocence, and whom he had put to death so that he might have the gold of Atahuallpa's kingdom.

Well, so be it, Pizarro thought. Atahuallpa accepted all that befell him without complaint and without fear, and so will I. Christ will be my guardian, and if there is no Christ, well, then I will have no guardian, and so be it. So be it.

The voice out of the whirlwind said suddenly, "Look, Don Francisco. This is America."

A picture appeared on the wall of cloud. It was a kind of picture Pizarro had never before encountered or even imagined, one that seemed to open before him like a gate and sweep him in and carry him along through a vista of changing scenes depicted in brilliant, vivid bursts of color. It was like flying high above the land, looking down on an infinite scroll of miracles. He saw vast cities without walls, roadways that unrolled like endless skeins of white ribbon, huge lakes, mighty rivers, gigantic mountains, everything speeding past him so swiftly that he could scarcely absorb any of it. In moments it all became chaotic in his mind: the buildings taller than the highest cathedral spire, the swarming masses of people, the shining metal chariots without beasts to draw them, the stupendous landscapes, the close-packed complexity of it all. Watching all this, he felt the fine old hunger taking possession of him again: he wanted to grasp this strange vast place, and seize it, and clutch it close, and ransack it for all it was worth. But the thought of that was overwhelming. His eyes grew glassy and his heart began to pound so terrifyingly that he supposed he would be able to feel it thumping if he put his hand to the front of his armor. He turned away, muttering, "Enough. Enough."

The terrifying picture vanished. Gradually the clamor of his heart subsided.

Then he began to laugh.

"Peru!" he cried. "Peru was nothing, next to your America! Peru was a hole! Peru was mud! How ignorant I was! I went to Peru, when there was America, ten thousand times as grand! I wonder what I could find, in America." He smacked his lips and winked. Then, chuckling, he said, "But don't be afraid. I won't try to conquer your America. I'm too old for that now. And perhaps America would have been too much for me, even before. Perhaps." He grinned savagely at the troubled staring face of the short-haired beardless man, the American. "I really am dead, is this not so? I feel no hunger, I feel no pain, no thirst, when I put my hand to my body I do not feel even my body. I am like one who lies dreaming. But this is no dream. Am I a ghost?"

"Not—exactly."

"Not exactly a ghost! Not exactly! No one with half the brains of a pig would talk like that. What is that supposed to mean?"

"It's not easy explaining it in words you would understand, Don Francisco."

"No, of course not. I am very stupid, as everyone knows, and that is why I conquered Peru, because I was so very stupid. But let it pass. I am not exactly a ghost, but I am dead all the same, right?"

"Well—"

"I am dead, yes. But somehow I have not gone to hell or even to purgatory but I am still in the world, only it is much later now. I have slept as the dead sleep, and now I have awakened in some year that is far beyond my time, and it is the time of America. Is this not so? Who is king now? Who is pope? What year is this? 1750? 1800?"

"The year 2130," the face said, after some hesitation.

"Ah." Pizarro tugged thoughtfully at his lower lip. "And the king? Who is king?"

A long pause. "Alfonso is his name," said the face.

"Alfonso? The kings of Aragon were called Alfonso. The father of Ferdinand, he was Alfonso. Alfonso V, he was."

"Alfonso XIX is King of Spain now."

"Ah. Ah. And the pope? Who is pope?"

A pause again. Not to know the name of the pope, immediately upon being asked? How strange. Demon or no, this was a fool.

"Pius," said the voice, when some time had passed. "Pius XVI."

"The sixteenth Pius," said Pizarro somberly. "Jesus and Mary, the sixteenth Pius! What has become of me? Long dead, is what I am. Still unwashed of all my sins. I can feel them clinging to my skin like mud, still. And you are a sorcerer, you American, and you have brought me to life again. Eh? Eh? Is that not so?"

"It is something like that, Don Francisco," the face admitted.

"So you speak your Spanish strangely because you no longer understand the right way of speaking it. Eh? Even I speak Spanish in a strange way, and I speak it in a voice that does not sound like my own. No one speaks Spanish any more, eh? Eh? Only American, they speak. Eh? But you try to speak Spanish, only it comes out stupidly. And you have caused me to speak the same way, thinking it is the way I spoke, though you are wrong. Well, you can do miracles, but I suppose you can't do everything perfectly, even in this land of miracles of the year 2130. Eh? Eh?" Pizarro leaned forward intently. "What do you say? You thought I was a fool, because I don't have reading and writing? I am not so ignorant, eh? I understand things quickly."

"You understand very quickly indeed."

"But you have knowledge of many things that are unknown to me. You must know the manner of my death, for example. How strange that is, talking to you of the manner of my death, but you must know it, eh? When did it come to me? And how? Did it come in my sleep? No, no, how could that be? They die in their sleep in Spain, but not in Peru. How was it, then? I was set upon by cowards, was I? Some brother of Atahuallpa, falling upon me as I stepped out of my house? A slave sent by the Inca Manco, or one of those others? No. No. The Indians would not harm me, for all that I did to them. It was the young Almagro who took me down, was it not, in vengeance for his father, or Juan de Herrada, eh? or perhaps even Picado, my own secretary—no, not Picado, he was my man, always—but maybe Alvarado, the young one, Diego—well, one of those, and it would have been sudden, very sudden or I would have been able to stop them—am I right, am I speaking the truth? Tell me. You know these things. Tell me of the manner of my dying." There was no answer. Pizarro shaded his eyes and peered into the dazzling pearly whiteness. He was no longer able to see the face of the American. "Are you there?" Pizarro said. "Where have you gone? Were you only a dream? American! American! Where have you gone?"

The break in contact was jolting. Tanner sat rigid, hands trembling, lips tightly clamped. Pizarro, in the holotank, was no more than a distant little streak of color now, no larger than his thumb, gesticulating amid the swirling clouds. The vitality of him, the arrogance, the fierce probing curiosity, the powerful hatreds and jealousies, the strength that had come from vast ventures recklessly conceived and desperately seen through to triumph, all the things that were Francisco Pizarro, all that Tanner had felt an instant before—all that had vanished at the flick of a finger.

After a moment or two Tanner felt the shock beginning to ease. He turned toward Richardson.

"What happened?"

"I had to pull you out of there. I didn't want you telling him anything about how he died."

"I don't know how he died."

"Well, neither does he, and I didn't want to chance it that you did. There's no predicting what sort of psychological impact that kind of knowledge might have on him."

"You talk about him as though he's alive."

"Isn't he?" Richardson said.

"If I said a thing like that, you'd tell me that I was being ignorant and unscientific."

Richardson smiled faintly. "You're right. But somehow I trust myself to know what I'm saying when I say that he's alive. I know I don't mean it literally and I'm not sure about you. What did you think of him, anyway?"

"He's amazing," Tanner said. "Really amazing. The strength of him—I could feel it pouring out at me in waves. And his mind! So quick, the way he picked up on everything. Guessing that he must be in the future. Wanting to know what number pope was in office. Wanting to see what America looked like. And the cockiness of him! Telling me that he's not up to the conquest of America, that he might have tried for it instead of Peru a few years earlier, but not now, now he's a little too old for that. Incredible! Nothing could faze him for long, even when he realized that he must have been dead for a long time. Wanting to know how he died, even!" Tanner frowned. "What age did you make him, anyway, when you put this program together?"

"About sixty. Five or six years after the conquest, and a year or two before he died. At the height of his power, that is."

"I suppose you couldn't have let him have any knowledge of his actual death. That way he'd be too much like some kind of a ghost."

"That's what we thought. We set the cutoff at a time when he had done everything that he had set out to do, when he was the complete Pizarro. But before the end. He didn't need to know about that. Nobody does. That's why I had to yank you, you see? In case you knew. And started to tell him."

Tanner shook his head. "If I ever knew, I've forgotten it. How did it happen?"

"Exactly as he guessed: at the hands of his own comrades."

"So he saw it coming."

"At the age we made him, he already knew that a civil war had started in South America, that the conquistadores were quarreling over the division of the spoils. We built that much into him. He knows that his partner Almagro has turned against him and been beaten in battle, and that they've executed him. What he doesn't know, but obviously can expect, is that Almagro's friends are going to break into his house and try to kill him. He's got it all figured out pretty much as it's going to happen. As it *did* happen, I should say."

"Incredible. To be that shrewd."

"He was a son of a bitch, yes. But he was a genius, too."

"Was he, really? Or is it that you made him one when you set up the program for him?"

"All we put in were the objective details of his life, patterns of event and response. Plus an overlay of commentary by others, his contemporaries and later historians familiar with the record, providing an extra dimension of character density. Put in enough of that kind of stuff and apparently they add up to the whole personality. It isn't *my* personality or that of anybody else who worked on this project, Harry. When you put in Pizarro's set of events and responses you wind up getting Pizarro. You get the ruthlessness and you get the brilliance. Put in a different set, you get someone else. And what we've finally seen, this time, is that when we do our work right we get something out of the computer that's bigger than the sum of what we put in."

"Are you sure?"

Richardson said, "Did you notice that he complained about the Spanish that he thought you were speaking?"

"Yes. He said that it sounded strange, that nobody seemed to know how to speak proper Spanish any more. I didn't quite follow that. Does the interface you built speak lousy Spanish?"

"Evidently it speaks lousy sixteenth-century Spanish," Richardson said. "Nobody knows what sixteenth-century Spanish actually sounded like. We can only guess. Apparently we didn't guess very well."

"But how would *he* know? You synthesized him in the first place! If you don't know how Spanish sounded in his time, how would he? All he should know about Spanish, or about anything, is what you put into him."

"Exactly," Richardson said.

"But that doesn't make any sense, Lew!"

"He also said that the Spanish he heard himself speaking was no good, and that his own voice didn't sound right to him either. That we had *caused* him to speak this way, thinking that was how he actually spoke, but we were wrong."

"How could he possibly know what his voice really sounded like, if all he is is a simulation put together by people who don't have the slightest notion of what his voice really—"

"I don't have any idea," said Richardson quietly. "But he *does* know."

"Does he? Or is this just some diabolical Pizarro-like game that he's playing to unsettle us, because *that's* in his character as you devised it?"

"I think he does know," Richardson said.

"Where's he finding it out, then?"

"It's there. We don't know where, but he does. It's somewhere in the data that we put through the permutation network, even if we don't know it and even though we couldn't find it now if we set out to look for it. *He* can find it. He can't manufacture that kind of knowledge by magic, but he can assemble what look to us like seemingly irrelevant bits and come up with new information leading to a conclusion which is meaningful to him. That's what we mean by artificial intelligence, Harry. We've finally got a program that works something like the human brain: by leaps of intuition so sudden and broad that they seem inexplicable and non-quantifiable, even if they really aren't. We've fed in enough stuff so that he can assimilate a whole stew of ostensibly unrelated data and come up with new information. We don't just have a ventriloquist's dummy in that tank. We've got something that thinks it's Pizarro and thinks like Pizarro and knows things that Pizarro knew and we don't. Which means we've accomplished the qualitative jump in artificial intelligence capacity that we set out to achieve with this project. It's awesome. I get shivers down my back when I think about it."

"I do too," Tanner said. "But not so much from awe as fear."

"Fear?"

"Knowing now that he has capabilities beyond those he was programmed for, how can you be so absolutely certain that he can't comandeer your network somehow and get himself loose?"

"It's technically impossible. All he is is electromagnetic impulses. I can pull the plug on him any time I like. There's nothing to panic over here. Believe me, Harry."

"I'm trying to."

"I can show you the schematics. We've got a phenomenal simulation in that computer, yes. But it's still only a simulation. It isn't a vampire, it isn't a werewolf, it isn't anything supernatural. It's just the best damned computer simulation anyone's ever made."

"It makes me uneasy. *He* makes me uneasy."

"He should. The power of the man, the indomitable nature of him—why do you think I summoned him up, Harry? He's got something that we don't understand in this country any more. I want us to study him. I want us to try to learn what that kind of drive and determination is really like. Now that you've talked to him, now that you've touched his spirit, of course you're shaken up by him. He radiates tremendous confidence. He radiates fantastic faith in himself. That kind of man can achieve anything he wants—even conquer the whole Inca empire with a hundred fifty men, or however many it was. But I'm not frightened of what we've put together here. And you shouldn't be either. We should all be damned proud of it. You as well as the people on the technical side. And you will be, too."

"I hope you're right," Tanner said.

"You'll see."

For a long moment Tanner stared in silence at the holotank, where the image of Pizarro had been.

"Okay," said Tanner finally. "Maybe I'm overreacting. Maybe I'm sounding like the ignoramus layman that I am. I'll take it on faith that you'll be able to keep your phantoms in their boxes."

"We will," Richardson said.

"Let's hope so. All right," said Tanner. "So what's your next move?"

Richardson looked puzzled. "My next move?"

"With this project. Where does it go from here?"

Hesitantly Richardson said, "There's no formal proposal yet. We thought we'd wait until we had approval from you on the initial phase of the work, and then—"

"How does this sound?" Tanner asked. "I'd like to see you start in on another simulation right away."

"Well—yes, yes, of course—"

"And when you've got him worked up, Lew, would it be feasible for you to put him right there in the tank with Pizarro?"

Richardson looked startled. "To have a sort of dialog with him, you mean?"

"Yes."

"I suppose we could do that," Richardson said cautiously. "*Should* do that. Yes. Yes. A very interesting suggestion, as a matter of fact." He ventured an uneasy smile. Up till now Tanner had kept in the background of this project, a mere management functionary, an observer, virtually an outsider. This was something new, his interjecting himself into the planning process, and plainly Richardson didn't know what to make of it. Tanner watched him fidget. After a little pause Richardson said, "Was there anyone particular you had in mind for us to try next?"

"Is that new parallax thing of yours ready to try?" Tanner asked. "The one that's supposed to compensate for time distortion and myth contamination?"

"Just about. But we haven't tested—"

"Good," Tanner said. "Here's your chance. What about trying for Socrates?"

There was billowing whiteness below him, and on every side, as though all the world were made of fleece. He wondered if it might be snow. That was not something he was really familiar with. It snowed once in a great while in Athens, yes, but usually only a light dusting that melted in the morning sun. Of course he had seen snow aplenty when he had been up north in the war, at Potidaea, in the time of Pericles. But that had been long ago; and that stuff, as best he remembered it, had not been much like this. There was no quality of coldness about the whiteness that surrounded him now. It could just as readily be great banks of clouds.

But what would clouds be doing *below* him? Clouds, he thought, are mere vapor, air and water, no substance to them at all. Their natural place was overhead. Clouds that gathered at one's feet had no true quality of cloudness about them.

Snow that had no coldness? Clouds that had no buoyancy? Nothing in this place seemed to possess any quality that was proper to itself in this place, including himself. He seemed to be walking, but his feet touched nothing at all. It was more like moving through air. But how could one move in the air? Aristophanes, in that mercilessly mocking play of his, had sent him floating through the clouds suspended in a basket, and made him say things like, "I am traversing the air and contemplating the sun." That was Aristophanes' way of playing with him, and he had not been seriously upset, though his friends had been very hurt on his behalf. Still, that was only a play.

This felt real, insofar as it felt like anything at all.

Perhaps he was dreaming, and the nature of his dream was that he thought he was really doing the things he had done in Aristophanes' play. What was that lovely line? "I have to suspend my brain and mingle the subtle essence of my mind with this air, which is of the same nature, in order clearly to penetrate the things of heaven." Good old Aristophanes! Nothing was sacred to him! Except, of course, those things that were truly sacred, such as wisdom, truth, virtue. "I would have discovered nothing if I had remained on the ground and pondered from below the things that are above: for the earth by its force attracts the sap of the mind to itself. It's the same way with water-cress." And Socrates began to laugh.

He held his hands before him and studied them, the short sturdy fingers, the thick powerful wrists. His hands, yes. His old plain hands that had stood him in good stead all his life, when he had worked as a stonemason as his father had, when he had fought in his city's wars, when he had trained at the gymnasium. But now when he touched them to his face he felt nothing. There should be a chin here, a forehead, yes, a blunt stubby nose, thick lips; but there was nothing. He was touching air. He could put his hand right through the place where his face should be. He could put one hand against the other, and press with all his might, and feel nothing.

This is a very strange place indeed, he thought.

Perhaps it is that place of pure forms that young Plato liked to speculate about, where everything is perfect and nothing is quite real. Those are ideal clouds all around me, not real ones. This is ideal air upon which I walk. I myself am the ideal Socrates, liberated from my coarse ordinary body. Could it be? Well, maybe so. He stood for a while, considering that possibility. The thought came to him that this might be the life after life, in which case he might meet some of the gods, if there were any gods in the first place, and if he could manage to find them. I would like that, he thought. Perhaps they would be willing to speak with me. Athena would discourse with me on wisdom, or Hermes on speed, or Ares on the nature of courage, or Zeus on—well, whatever Zeus cared to speak on. Of course I would seem to be the merest fool to them, but that would be all right: anyone who expects to hold discourse with the gods as though he were their equal *is* a fool. I have no such illusion. If there are gods at all, surely they are far superior to me in all respects, for otherwise why would men regard them as gods?

Of course he had serious doubts that the gods existed at all. But if they did, it was reasonable to think that they might be found in a place such as this.

He looked up. The sky was radiant with brilliant golden light. He took a deep breath and smiled and set out across the fleecy nothingness of this airy world to see if he could find the gods.

Tanner said, "What do you think now? Still so pessimistic?"

"It's too early to say," said Richardson, looking glum.

"He *looks* like Socrates, doesn't he?"

"That was the easy part. We've got plenty of descriptions of Socrates that came down from people who knew him, the flat wide nose, the bald head, the thick lips, the short neck. A standard Socrates face that everybody recognizes, just as they do Sherlock Holmes, or Don Quixote. So that's how we made him look. It doesn't signify anything important. It's what's going on inside his head that'll determine whether we really have Socrates."

"He seems calm and good-humored as he wanders around in there. The way a philosopher should."

"Pizarro seemed just as much of a philosopher when we turned him loose in the tank."

"Pizarro may *be* just as much of a philosopher," Tanner said. "Neither man's the sort who'd be likely to panic if he found himself in some mysterious place." Richardson's negativism was beginning to bother him. It was as if the two men had exchanged places: Richardson now uncertain of the range and power of his own program, Tanner pushing the way on and on toward bigger and better things.

Bleakly Richardson said, "I'm still pretty skeptical. We've tried the new parallax filters, yes. But I'm afraid we're going to run into the same problem the French did with Don Quixote, and that we did with Holmes and Moses and Caesar. There's too much contamination of the data by myth and fantasy. The Socrates who has come down to us is as much fictional as real, or maybe *all* fictional. For all we know, Plato made up everything we think we know about him, the same way Conan Doyle made up Holmes. And what we're going to get, I'm afraid, will be something second-hand, something lifeless, something lacking in the spark of self-directed intelligence that we're after."

"But the new filters—"

"Perhaps. Perhaps."

Tanner shook his head stubbornly. "Holmes and Don Quixote are fiction through and through. They exist in only one dimension, constructed for us by their authors. You cut through the distortions and fantasies of later readers and commentators and all you find underneath is a made-up character. A lot of Socrates may have been invented by Plato for his own purposes, but a lot wasn't. He really existed. He took an actual part in civic activities in fifth-century Athens. He figures in books by a lot of other contemporaries of his besides Plato's dialogues. That gives us the parallax you're looking for, doesn't it—the view of him from more than one viewpoint?"

"Maybe it does. Maybe not. We got nowhere with Moses. Was *he* fictional?"

"Who can say? All you had to go by was the Bible. And a ton of Biblical commentary, for whatever that was worth. Not much, apparently."

"And Caesar? You're not going to tell me that Caesar wasn't real," said Richardson. "But what we have of him is evidently contaminated with myth.

When we synthesized him we got nothing but a caricature, and I don't have to remind you how fast even that broke down into sheer gibberish."

"Not relevant," Tanner said. "Caesar was early in the project. You know much more about what you're doing now. I think this is going to work."

Richardson's dogged pessimism, Tanner decided, must be a defense mechanism, designed to insulate himself against the possibility of a new failure. Socrates, after all, hadn't been Richardson's own choice. And this was the first time he had used these new enhancement methods, the parallax program that was the latest refinement of the process.

Tanner looked at him. Richardson remained silent.

"Go on," Tanner said. "Bring up Pizarro and let the two of them talk to each other. Then we'll find out what sort of Socrates you've conjured up here."

Once again there was a disturbance in the distance, a little dark blur on the pearly horizon, a blotch, a flaw in the gleaming whiteness. Another demon is arriving, Pizarro thought. Or perhaps it is the same one as before, the American, the one who liked to show himself only as a face, with short hair and no beard.

But as this one drew closer Pizarro saw that he was different from the last, short and stocky, with broad shoulders and a deep chest. He was nearly bald and his thick beard was coarse and unkempt. He looked old, at least sixty, maybe sixty-five. He looked very ugly, too, with bulging eyes and a flat nose that had wide, flaring nostrils, and a neck so short that his oversized head seemed to sprout straight from his trunk. All he wore was a thin, ragged brown robe. His feet were bare.

"You, there," Pizarro called out. "You! Demon! Are you also an American, demon?"

"Your pardon. An Athenian, did you say?"

"*American* is what I said. That's what the last one was. Is that where you come from too, demon? America?"

A shrug. "No, I think not. I am of Athens." There was a curious mocking twinkle in the demon's eyes.

"A Greek? This demon is a Greek?"

"I am of Athens," the ugly one said again. "My name is Socrates, the son of Sophroniscus. I could not tell you what a Greek is, so perhaps I may be one, but I think not, unless a Greek is what you call a man of Athens." He spoke in a slow, plodding way, like one who was exceedingly stupid. Pizarro had sometimes met men like this before, and in his experience they were generally not as stupid as they wanted to be taken for. He felt caution rising in him. "And I am no demon, but just a plain man: very plain, as you can easily see."

Pizarro snorted. "You like to chop words, do you?"

"It is not the worst of amusements, my friend," said the other, and put his hands together behind his back in the most casual way, and stood there calmly, smiling, looking off into the distance, rocking back and forth on the balls of his feet.

"Well?" Tanner said. "Do we have Socrates or not? I say that's the genuine article there."

Richardson looked up and nodded. He seemed relieved and quizzical both at once. "So far so good, I have to say. He's coming through real and true."

"Yes."

"We may actually have worked past the problem of information contamination that ruined some of the earlier simulations. We're not getting any of the signal degradation we encountered then."

"He's some character, isn't he?" Tanner said. "I liked the way he just walked right up to Pizarro without the slightest sign of uneasiness. He's not at all afraid of him."

"Why should he be?" Richardson asked.

"Wouldn't you? If you were walking along through God knows what kind of unearthly place, not knowing where you were or how you got there, and suddenly you saw a ferocious-looking bastard like Pizarro standing in front of you wearing full armor and carrying a sword—" Tanner shook his head. "Well, maybe not. He's Socrates, after all, and Socrates wasn't afraid of anything except boredom."

"And Pizarro's just a simulation. Nothing but software."

"So you've been telling me all along. But Socrates doesn't know that."

"True," Richardson said. He seemed lost in thought a moment. "Perhaps there *is* some risk."

"Huh?"

"If our Socrates is anything like the one in Plato, and he surely ought to be, then he's capable of making a considerable pest of himself. Pizarro may not care for Socrates' little verbal games. If he doesn't feel like playing, I suppose there's a theoretical possibility that he'll engage in some sort of aggressive response."

That took Tanner by surprise. He swung around and said, "Are you telling me that there's some way he can *harm* Socrates?"

"Who knows?" said Richardson. "In the real world one program can certainly crash another one. Maybe one simulation can be dangerous to another one. This is all new territory for all of us, Harry. Including the people in the tank."

The tall grizzled-looking man said, scowling, "You tell me you're an Athenian, but not a Greek. What sense am I supposed to make of that? I could ask Pedro de Candia, I guess, who is a Greek but not an Athenian. But he's not here. Perhaps you're just a fool, eh? Or you think I am."

"I have no idea what you are. Could it be that you are a god?"

"A *god?*"

"Yes," Socrates said. He studied the other impassively. His face was harsh, his gaze was cold. "Perhaps you are Ares. You have a fierce warlike look about you, and you wear armor, but not such armor as I have ever seen. This place is so strange that it might well be the abode of the gods, and that could be a god's armor you wear, I suppose. If you are Ares, then I salute you with the respect that is due you. I am Socrates of Athens, the stone-mason's son."

"You talk a lot of nonsense. I don't know your Ares."

"Why, the god of war, of course! Everyone knows that. Except barbarians, that is. Are you a barbarian, then? You sound like one, I must say—but then, I seem to sound like a barbarian myself, and I've spoken the tongue of Hellas all my life. There are many mysteries here, indeed."

"Your language problem again," Tanner said. "Couldn't you even get classical Greek to come out right? Or are they both speaking Spanish to each other?"

"Pizarro thinks they're speaking Spanish. Socrates thinks they're speaking Greek. And of course the Greek is off. We don't know how *anything* that was spoken before the age of recordings sounded. All we can do is guess."

"But can't you—"

"Shhh," Richardson said.

Pizarro said, "I may be a bastard, but I'm no barbarian, fellow, so curb your tongue. And let's have no more blasphemy out of you either."

"If I blaspheme, forgive me. It is in innocence. Tell me where I trespass, and I will not do it again."

"This crazy talk of gods. Of my being a god. I'd expect a heathen to talk like that, but not a Greek. But maybe you're a heathen kind of Greek, and not to be blamed. It's heathens who see gods everywhere. Do I look like a god to you? I am Francisco Pizarro, of Trujillo in Estremadura, the son of the famous soldier Gonzalo Pizarro, colonel of infantry, who served in the wars of Gonzalo de Cordova whom men call the Great Captain. I have fought some wars myself."

"Then you are not a god but simply a soldier? Good. I too have been a soldier. I am more at ease with soldiers than with gods, as most people are, I would think."

"A soldier? You?" Pizarro smiled. This shabby ordinary little man, more bedraggled-looking than any self-respecting groom would be, a soldier? "In which wars?"

"The wars of Athens. I fought at Potidaea, where the Corinthians were making trouble, and withholding the tribute that was due us. It was very cold there, and the siege was long and bleak, but we did our duty. I fought again some years later at Delium against the Boeotians. Laches was our general then, but it went badly for us, and we did our best fighting in retreat. And then," Socrates said, "when Brasidas was in Amphipolis, and they sent Cleon to drive him out, I—"

"Enough," said Pizarro with an impatient wave of his hand. "These wars are unknown to me." A private soldier, a man of the ranks, no doubt. "Well, then this is the place where they send dead soldiers, I suppose."

"Are we dead, then?"

"Long ago. There's an Alfonso who's king, and a Pius who's pope, and you wouldn't believe their numbers. Pius the Sixteenth, I think the demon said. And the American said also that it is the year 2130. The last year that I can remember was 1539. What about you?"

The one who called himself Socrates shrugged again. "In Athens we use a different reckoning. But let us say, for argument's sake, that we are dead. I think that is very likely, considering what sort of place this seems to be, and how airy I find my body to be. So we have died, and this is the life after life. I wonder: is this a place where virtuous men are sent, or those who were not virtuous? Or do all men go to the same place after death, whether they were virtuous or not? What would you say?"

"I haven't figured that out yet," said Pizarro.

"Well, were you virtuous in your life, or not?"

"Did I sin, you mean?"

"Yes, we could use that word."

"Did I sin, he wants to know," said Pizarro, amazed. "He asks, Was I a sinner? Did I live a virtuous life? What business is that of his?"

"Humor me," said Socrates. "For the sake of the argument, if you will, allow me a few small questions—"

"So it's starting," Tanner said. "You see? You really *did* do it! Socrates is drawing him into a dialog!"

Richardson's eyes were glowing. "He is, yes. How marvelous this is, Harry!"

"Socrates is going to talk rings around him."

"I'm not so sure of that," Richardson said.

"I gave as good as I got," said Pizarro. "If I was injured, I gave injury back. There's no sin in that. It's only common sense. A man does what is necessary to survive and to protect his place in the world. Sometimes I might forget a fast-day, yes, or use the Lord's name in vain—those are sins, I suppose, Fray Vicente was always after me for things like that—but does that make me a sinner? I did my penances as soon as I could find time for them. It's a sinful world and I'm no different from anyone else, so why be harsh on me? Eh? God made me as I am. I'm done in His image. And I have faith in His Son."

"So you are a virtuous man, then?"

"I'm not a sinner, at any rate. As I told you, if ever I sinned I did my contrition, which made it the same as if the sin hadn't ever happened."

"Indeed," said Socrates. "Then you are a virtuous man and I have come to a good place. But I want to be absolutely sure. Tell me again: is your conscience completely clear?"

"What are you, a confessor?"

"Only an ignorant man seeking understanding. Which you can provide, by taking part with me in the exploration. If I have come to the place of virtuous men, then I must have been virtuous myself when I lived. Ease my mind, therefore, and let me know whether there is anything on your soul that you regret having done."

Pizarro stirred uneasily. "Well," he said, "I killed a king."

"A wicked one? An enemy of your city?"

"No. He was wise and kind."

"Then you have reason for regret indeed. For surely that is a sin, to kill a wise king."

"But he was a heathen."

"A what?"

"He denied God."

"He denied his own god?" said Socrates. "Then perhaps it was not so wrong to kill him."

"No. He denied mine. He *preferred* his own. And so he was a heathen. And all his people were heathens, since they followed his way. That could not be. They were at risk of eternal damnation because they followed him. I killed him for the sake of his people's souls. I killed him out of the love of God."

"But would you not say that all gods are the reflection of the one God?"

Pizarro considered that. "In a way, that's true, I suppose."

"And is the service of God not itself godly?"

"How could it be anything but godly, Socrates?"

"And you would say that one who serves his god faithfully according to the teachings of his god is behaving in a godly way?"

Frowning, Pizarro said, "Well—if you look at at that way, yes—"

"Then I think the king you killed was a godly man, and by killing him you sinned against God."

"Wait a minute!"

"But think of it: by serving his god he must also have served yours, for any servant of a god is a servant of the true God who encompasses all our imagined gods."

"No," said Pizarro sullenly. "How could he have been a servant of God? He knew nothing of Jesus. He had no understanding of the Trinity. When the priest offered him the Bible, he threw it to the ground in scorn. He was a heathen, Socrates. And so are you. You don't know anything of these matters at all, if you think that Atahuallpa was godly. Or if you think you're going to get me to think so."

"Indeed I have very little knowledge of anything. But you say he was a wise man, and kind?"

"In his heathen way."

"And a good king to his people?"

"So it seemed. They were a thriving people when I found them."

"Yet he was not godly."

"I told you. He had never had the sacraments, and in fact he spurned them right up until the moment of his death, when he accepted baptism. *Then* he came to be godly. But by then the sentence of death was upon him and it was too late for anything to save him."

"Baptism? Tell me what that is, Pizarro."

"A sacrament."

"And that is?"

"A holy rite. Done with holy water, by a priest. It admits one to Holy Mother Church, and brings forgiveness from sin both original and actual, and gives the gift of the Holy Spirit."

"You must tell me more about these things another time. So you made this good king godly by this baptism? And then you killed him?"

"Yes."

"But he was godly when you killed him. Surely, then, to kill him was a sin."

"He had to die, Socrates!"

"And why was that?" asked the Athenian.

"Socrates is closing in for the kill," Tanner said. "Watch this!"

"I'm watching. But there isn't going to be any kill," said Richardson. "Their basic assumptions are too far apart."

"You'll see."

"Will I?"

Pizarro said, "I've already told you why he had to die. It was because his people followed him in all things. And so they worshipped the sun, because he said the sun was God. Their souls would have gone to hell if we had allowed them to continue that way."

"But if they followed him in all things," said Socrates, "then surely they would have followed him into baptism, and become godly, and thus done that which was pleasing to you and to your god! Is that not so?"

"No," said Pizarro, twisting his fingers in his beard.

"Why do you think that?"

"Because the king agreed to be baptized only after we had sentenced him to death. He was in the way, don't you see? He was an obstacle to our power!

445

So we had to get rid of him. He would never have led his people to the truth of his own free will. That was why we had to kill him. But we didn't want to kill his soul as well as his body, so we said to him, Look, Atahuallpa, we're going to put you to death, but if you let us baptize you we'll strangle you quickly, and if you don't we'll burn you alive and it'll be very slow. So of course he agreed to be baptized, and we strangled him. What choice was there for anybody? He had to die. He still didn't believe the true faith, as we all well knew. Inside his head he was as big a heathen as ever. But he died a Christian all the same."

"A what?"

"A Christian! A Christian! One who believes in Jesus Christ the Son of God!"

"The *son* of God," Socrates said, sounding puzzled. "And do Christians believe in God too, or only his son?"

"What a fool you are!"

"I would not deny that."

"There is God the Father, and God the Son, and then there is the Holy Spirit."

"Ah," said Socrates. "And which one did your Atahuallpa believe in, then, when the strangler came for him?"

"None of them."

"And yet he died a Christian? Without believing in any of your three gods? How is that?"

"Because of the baptism," said Pizarro in rising annoyance. "What does it matter what he believed? The priest sprinkled the water on him! The priest said the words! If the rite is properly performed, the soul is saved regardless of what the man understands or believes! How else could you baptize an infant? An infant understands nothing and believes nothing—but he becomes a Christian when the water touches him!"

"Much of this is mysterious to me," said Socrates. "But I see that you regard the king you killed as godly as well as wise, because he was washed by the water your gods require, and so you killed a good king who now lived in the embrace of your gods because of the baptism. Which seems wicked to me; and so this cannot be the place where the virtuous are sent after death, so it must be that I too was not virtuous, or else that I have misunderstood everything about this place and why we are in it."

"Damn you, are you trying to drive me crazy?" Pizarro roared, fumbling at the hilt of his sword. He drew it and waved it around in fury. "If you don't shut your mouth I'll cut you in thirds!"

"Uh-oh," Tanner said. "So much for the dialectical method."

Socrates said mildly, "It isn't my intention to cause you any annoyance, my friend. I'm only trying to learn a few things."

"You are a fool!"

"That is certainly true, as I have already acknowledged several times. Well, if you mean to strike me with your sword, go ahead. But I don't think it'll accomplish very much."

"Damn you," Pizarro muttered. He stared at his sword and shook his head. "No. No, it won't do any good, will it? It would go through you like air. But you'd just stand there and let me try to cut you down, and not even blink, right? Right?" He shook his head. "And yet you aren't stupid. You argue like the shrewdest priest I've ever known."

"In truth I am stupid," said Socrates. "I know very little at all. But I strive constantly to attain some understanding of the world, or at least to understand something of myself."

Pizarro glared at him. "No," he said. "I won't buy this false pride of yours. I have a little understanding of people myself, old man. I'm on to your game."

"What game is that, Pizarro?"

"I can see your arrogance. I see that you believe you're the wisest man in the world, and that it's your mission to go around educating poor sword-waving fools like me. And you pose as a fool to disarm your adversaries before you humiliate them."

"Score one for Pizarro," Richardson said. "He's wise to Socrates' little tricks, all right."

"Maybe he's read some Plato," Tanner suggested.

"He was illiterate."

"That was then. This is now."

"Not guilty," said Richardson. "He's operating on peasant shrewdness alone, and you damned well know it."

"I wasn't being serious," Tanner said. He leaned forward, peering toward the holotank. "God, what an astonishing thing this is, listening to them going at it. They seem absolutely real."

"They are," said Richardson.

"No, Pizarro, I am not wise at all," Socrates said. "But, stupid as I am, it may be that I am not the least wise man who ever lived."

"You think you're wiser than I am, don't you?"

"How can I say? First tell me how wise you are."

"Wise enough to begin my life as a bastard tending pigs and finish it as Captain-General of Peru."

"Ah, then you must be very wise."

"I think so, yes."

"Yet you killed a wise king because he wasn't wise enough to worship God the way you wished him to. Was that so wise of you, Pizarro? How did his people take it, when they found out that their king had been killed?"

"They rose in rebellion against us. They destroyed their own temples and palaces, and hid their gold and silver from us, and burned their bridges, and fought us bitterly."

"Perhaps you could have made some better use of him by *not* killing him, do you think?"

"In the long run we conquered them and made them Christians. It was what we intended to accomplish."

"But the same thing might have been accomplished in a wiser way?"

"Perhaps," said Pizarro grudgingly. "Still, we accomplished it. That's the main thing, isn't it? We did what we set out to do. If there was a better way, so be it. Angels do things perfectly. We were no angels, but we achieved what we came for, and so be it, Socrates. So be it."

"I'd call that one a draw," said Tanner.

"Agreed."

"It's a terrific game they're playing."

"I wonder who we can use to play it next," said Richardson.

"I wonder what we can do with this besides using it to play games," said Tanner.

"Let me tell you a story," said Socrates. "The oracle at Delphi once said to a friend of mine, 'There is no man wiser than Socrates,' but I doubted that very much, and it troubled me to hear the oracle saying something that I knew was so far from the truth. So I decided to look for a man who was obviously wiser than I was. There was a politician in Athens who was famous for his wisdom, and I went to him and questioned him about many things. After I had listened to him for a time, I came to see that though many people, and most of all he himself, thought that he was wise, yet he was not wise. He only imagined that he was wise. So I realized that I must be wiser than he. Neither of us knew anything that was really worthwhile, but he knew nothing and thought that he knew, whereas I neither knew anything nor thought that I did. At least on one point, then, I was wiser than he: I didn't think that I knew what I didn't know."

"Is this intended to mock me, Socrates?"

"I feel only the deepest respect for you, friend Pizarro. But let me continue. I went to other wise men, and they too, though sure of their wisdom, could never give me a clear answer to anything. Those whose reputations for wisdom were the highest seemed to have the least of it. I went to the great poets and playwrights. There was wisdom in their works, for the gods had inspired them, but that did not make *them* wise, though they thought that it had. I went to the stonemasons and potters and other craftsmen. They were wise in their own skills, but most of them seemed to think that that made them wise in everything, which did not appear to be the case. And so it went. I was unable to find anyone who showed true wisdom. So perhaps the oracle was right: that although I am an ignorant man, there is no man wiser than I am. But oracles often are right without there being much value in it, for I think that all she was saying was that no man is wise at all, that wisdom is reserved for the gods. What do you say, Pizarro?"

"I say that you are a great fool, and very ugly besides."

"You speak the truth. So, then, you are wise after all. And honest."

"Honest, you say? I won't lay claim to that. Honesty's a game for fools. I lied whenever I needed to. I cheated. I went back on my word. I'm not proud of that, mind you. It's simply what you have to do to get on in the world. You think I wanted to tend pigs all my life? I wanted gold, Socrates! I wanted power over men! I wanted fame!"

"And did you get those things?"

"I got them all."

"And were they gratifying, Pizarro?"

Pizarro gave Socrates a long look. Then he pursed his lips and spat.

"They were worthless."

"Were they, do you think?"

"Worthless, yes. I have no illusions about that. But still it was better to have had them than not. In the long run nothing has any meaning, old man. In the long run we're all dead, the honest man and the villain, the king and the fool. Life's a cheat. They tell us to strive, to conquer, to gain—and for what? What? For a few years of strutting around. Then it's taken away, as if it had never been. A cheat, I say." Pizarro paused. He stared at his hands as though he had never seen them before. "Did I say all that just now? Did I mean it?" He laughed. "Well, I suppose I did. Still, life is all there is, so you want as much of it as you can. Which means getting gold, and power, and fame."

"Which you had. And apparently have no longer. Friend Pizarro, where are we now?"

"I wish I knew."

"So do I," said Socrates soberly.

"He's real," Richardson said. "They both are. The bugs are out of the system and we've got something spectacular here. Not only is this going to be of value to scholars, I think it's also going to be a tremendous entertainment gimmick, Harry."

"It's going to be much more than that," said Tanner in a strange voice.

"What do you mean by that?"

"I'm not sure yet," Tanner said. "But I'm definitely on to something big. It just began to hit me a couple of minutes ago, and it hasn't really taken shape yet. But it's something that might change the whole goddamned world."

Richardson looked amazed and bewildered.

"What the hell are you talking about, Harry?"

Tanner said, "A new way of settling political disputes, maybe. What would you say to a kind of combat-at-arms between one nation and another? Like a medieval tournament, so to speak. With each side using champions that we simulate for them—the greatest minds of all the past, brought back and placed in competition—" He shook his head. "Something like that. It needs a lot of working out, I know. But it's got possibilities."

"A medieval tournament—combat-at-arms, using simulations? Is that what you're saying?"

"Verbal combat. Not actual jousts, for Christ's sake."

"I don't see how—" Richardson began.

"Neither do I, not yet. I wish I hadn't even spoken of it."

"But—"

"Later, Lew. Later. Let me think about it a little while more."

"You don't have any idea what this place is?" Pizarro said.

"Not at all. But I certainly think this is no longer the world where we once dwelled. Are we dead, then? How can we say? You look alive to me."

"And you to me."

"Yet I think we are living some other kind of life. Here, give me your hand. Can you feel mine against yours?"

"No. I can't feel anything."

"Nor I. Yet I see two hands clasping. Two old men standing on a cloud, clasping hands." Socrates laughed. "What a great rogue you are, Pizarro!"

"Yes, of course. But do you know something, Socrates? You are too. A windy old rogue. I like you. There were moments when you were driving me crazy with all your chatter, but you amused me too. Were you really a soldier?"

"When my city asked me, yes."

"For a soldier, you're damned innocent about the way the world works, I have to say. But I guess I can teach you a thing or two."

"Will you?"

"Gladly," said Pizarro.

"I would be in your debt," Socrates said.

"Take Atahuallpa," Pizarro said. "How can I make you understand why I had to kill him? There weren't even two hundred of us, and twenty-four million of them, and his word was law, and once he was gone they'd have no one to command them. So of *course* we had to get rid of him if we wanted to conquer them. And so we did, and then they fell."

"How simple you make it seem."

"Simple is what it was. Listen, old man, he would have died sooner or later anyway, wouldn't he? This way I made his death useful: to God, to the Church, to Spain. And to Francisco Pizarro. Can you understand that?"

"I think so," said Socrates. "But do you think King Atahuallpa did?"

"Any king would understand such things."

"Then he should have killed you the moment you set foot in his land."

"Unless God meant us to conquer him, and allowed him to understand that. Yes. Yes, that must have been what happened."

"Perhaps he is in this place, too, and we could ask him," said Socrates.

Pizarro's eyes brightened. "Mother of God, yes! A good idea! And if he didn't understand, why, I'll try to explain it to him. Maybe you'll help me. You know how to talk, how to move words around and around. What do you say? Would you help me?"

"If we meet him, I would like to talk with him," Socrates said. "I would indeed like to know if he agrees with you on the subject of the usefulness of his being killed by you."

Grinning, Pizarro said, "Slippery, you are! But I like you. I like you very much. Come. Let's go look for Atahuallpa."

ROBERT SAMPSON

Relationships

Here's a mysterious and evocative story about the persistence of love . . .

Robert Sampson won the Edgar Award for the best mystery story of 1986. His work has appeared in *The New Black Mask Quarterly*, *Espionage Magazine*, *A Matter of Crime*, and elsewhere, and he has published seven books about pulp magazines and pulp series heroes, including *The Night Master* and *Deadly Excitements*. In the science fiction genre, his stories have appeared in *Planet Stories*, *Science-Fiction Adventures*, *Full Spectrum*, and elsewhere.

▼

Relationships

ROBERT SAMPSON

A few days after his forty-eighth birthday, Hadley Jackson learned that he could materialize the women from his past. Only think a little at an angle and there they sat, sassy as life, talking as if time were nothing. As if their lives had continued to touch his. The ability to call them upset him considerably. Not fearfully though; he never felt fear.

To that time, he had been spending ever larger chunks of the evening burrowed in his apartment. He lived with two cats, Gloria and Bill. He had developed the habit of reading aloud to them: selections from news magazines, the poems of Emily Dickinson. The cats were unconcerned by his choices. Reading aloud gave him the feeling that his life still retained both direction and a trace of high white fire.

One Monday he thought of Mildred Campbell. At one time he had cared a good deal for her. They had never reached what, in the contemporary tongue, was called a relationship. Between them, something essential had been omitted. She didn't, or couldn't, return his feelings. Eventually they allowed each other to drift away amid a sort of wan regret.

All of a sudden, there she sat in a chair by his table. She wore a blue dress of some slinky material and dark hose and dark blue heels. The tip of her left shoe vibrated against the carpet, as it did when she wanted to go home and was about to tell him so.

He knew at once that she was not real. Apparently she did, too. It did not seem to bother her.

"This won't do you any good," she said. Her voice, quick and pleasant as ever, was tinted with dark impatience. Sooner or later that emotion marred all their meetings.

"I was just thinking about you."

"Well, I'm far away. To tell the truth, I haven't thought about you for years."

"You never did. Not much," he said.

She laughed at that, and a cat stuck its head through her left shoulder and looked out at him. It made him feel a little sick, then irritated, since it established so clearly that Mildred was some kind of cloud.

"Let's not bother with this," she said. "I liked you for about ten minutes once. But, Lord God, you can't stretch ten minutes forever."

"I liked you longer than that."

"Don't kid yourself," she said. And was gone. The cat still looked at him. It jumped down and slipped under the table.

He touched the chair she had sat in and sniffed the air. No trace of her fragrance remained. It occurred to him that if Mildred came, others might follow. So he sat down again and thought of Ruth. He couldn't angle his thoughts properly; the correct mind set eluded him. Later he wandered slowly around the block, smelling night leaves, wondering if it were possible to leave Creative Chemicals and set up a consulting business.

The following night, he thought of Ruth again. This time she appeared promptly. She wore a long white formal-looking dress with gold at ears and neck. Her hair was paler blond than he had remembered. She was a little tight; that, too, was familiar. Sprawling back on the davenport, she grinned at him and crossed her ankles.

"Old friends meet again." Her lips were bright red. Only something was wrong with her eyes. A whitish film covered them.

"Twenty-odd years," he said. "Pretty long between visits. Where you living now?"

"I'm dead," she replied. "Years and years ago."

"I'm sorry. I thought about you a lot. But I didn't know where you'd moved to."

"That's the way of it," she said. "You get separated and the space between just keeps getting bigger. You never knows where a person gets to or what they do when they get there."

He was shocked at her eyes and could think of nothing to say. Her voice was low and amused. As she turned her head, gold flashed.

"Just because I'm dead, there's nothing wrong with me. I mean, I'm not about to tear out your throat or any dumb thing like that."

"What's it like being dead?"

"I don't know. It isn't anything you can describe. You hear all this foolishness . . ."

Her fingers minutely adjusted her skirt. "I guess I better go," she said. "The damn whiskey's dying in me."

As she rose, he said with sudden regret: "I'm sorry you died."

"It was quick. I remember that."

After she was gone, he sat silently, thinking. A cat nudged his dangling hand. Her eyes had been very terrible. He realized that he had forgotten to ask where she had lived or how her life had been. Shame leaped in him. Or perhaps guilt. The emotion tasted metallic, gray, the taste of nails.

She had recognized him, he thought. After all these years.

He slept in his chair. When he woke, it was still dark outside but the light was on and the cats had crowded between his leg and the chair arm.

The following evening, his daughter, Janet, called from Phoenix. Her voice was enthusiastic, warm, and slipped over certain subjects quickly, as if a question from him would drop them both through a fragile crust. The combination of effusiveness and reticence annoyed him.

"I'm fine," she told him. "Everybody's fine."

"I mean, how are you, really?"

"Just fine, Dad." Her voice took on a note of remote querulousness. His ex-wife, Helen, Janet's mother, another man's wife, had banged up her car on the way to a class in stained glass. Helen wanted to know, Janet said, if he'd like a suncatcher for his window—a glass cactus or sleeping Mexican. He refused. Helen constantly offered him small gifts through his daughter, never directly talking with him. The effect was of receiving messages relayed from another planet. Perhaps, he thought, it's Janet trying to keep us in touch. A cat rubbed its neck against his calf.

"Goodbye," she said. The telephone droned hollowly against his ear.

Later he drove slowly across town to the theater at the Mall. Bright clouds streaked the sky like strips of stained glass, rose and green, whitish-gray.

In the theater, the lights faded down, and an endless succession of commercial messages shouted across the screen. No one in them was older than twenty-five.

As the sales messages jittered past, Hadley thought suddenly of Rosemary Chalson. Years ago, they had met accidentally at a showing of "South Pacific." For nearly the entire picture, he agonized whether to take her hand. As he finally decided to reach out, laughter stirred through the audience. Rosemary clapped both hands under her chin and leaned back, laughing, exposing her gums. This he found disagreeable. Before he decided what to do about her hand, the film ended.

Thinking of her now, and the long tortures of adolescence, he glanced right. Rosemary sat in the next seat, a tub of popcorn in her lap. As ferocious youth bounced across the screen, she lifted a single kernel to her lips.

He blurted: "It's been years . . ."

He saw the startled white flicker in her eyes. Her body angled infinitesimally from him.

Immediately he saw that she was not Rosemary. Dull horror ran through him. He blurted: "Excuse me. Excuse me."

Rising, he struggled past a succession of knees to the aisle. People stared irritably past him, intent on the yelling screen.

Outside the theater, he felt the icy crawl of his back. She looked exactly like Rosemary, he thought. The error frightened him. His mind felt full of dangerous potential, like a cocked gun.

He drove from the Mall, passing beneath apricot lights mounted on high silver poles. The street angled through rows of beige apartments. Nothing moved. The smooth dark sky was unmarred by star or moon. In the hollow street, in the dull light, the apartments seemed images painted on air. Behind them hung featureless nothing, waiting to be shaped.

Some basic similarity existed, he thought, between the street and his laboratory where, for the past week, the complex process of installing a computer system was underway. Behind ranks of cabinets and boxes dangled a wilderness of black cords. The tips of each glittered silver, waiting for connection.

In his life, he thought, there had been too much disconnection. Too many dangling cords. Only past connections remained. He seemed hardly linked to the present.

The woman beside him bent to adjust her seat. When she straightened, he recognized Helen Wycott—Wrycott. He was sharply disturbed. He had not seen her since college. Nor had he thought of her since.

Now they come without being called, he thought.

She eyed him disdainfully. "You always acted too good for everybody."

"I didn't feel that way," he said.

"That's not what it looked like."

They turned into a dark street with dark houses behind strips of yard. Mailboxes shone dully along the curb. He could think of no reason why she came. Over the years, she had put on much weight, and her remembered features floated within a cruel expanse of cheek.

He said: "You always were so clever and quick. I never knew what to say to you."

"You spent too much time thinking about yourself."

"That isn't true," he said, trying to remember.

"It's true, all right. You do it now."

They rode in silence for several blocks. She looked steadily at him, shaking her head.

"You better give this up," she told him. "There's more to life than people you used to know."

"Listen," he said, "I didn't call you here."

"I want off here," she said.

He stopped the car. When he opened her door, she was gone. Night air smelled moistly cool and his hands trembled faintly. Aggravation, he thought.

On going back over their conversation, it struck him that he had, however slightly, won an advantage over her. He drove home briskly, humming to himself and tapping time to himself on the steering wheel. Objectively, of course, he was showing all the signs of dementia. He considered the possible collapse of his mind cheerfully. Perhaps he had now entered a mania phase. How interesting that the symptoms of his detachment from reality expressed themselves as women. That seemed distantly amusing.

When he opened the door of the apartment, the cats ran toward him uttering sharp cries of greeting. Above their noise he heard the light flutter of feminine voices.

In the living room, two women smiled at him. One was Ruth, this evening wearing neatly tailored black with pearls. She lulled effusively on the davenport, clearly having had a great deal to drink. The other woman, wearing a ragged blue cardigan and jeans, sat primly in a straight chair, knees together. He did not recognize her.

Ruth waved breezily at him. "You come sit right down here. We've been deciding what to do with you."

The other woman said: "I bet you don't remember me."

When she smiled, sweetness suffused her bony face. A former friend of his ex-wife. He recalled the smile. Nothing else.

"I remember," he said tentatively.

"Virginia Cox," she said. "Virginia Ames now. I have four grandchildren now."

"That's nice," he said. Ruth tittered. Her fingers floated over his hand, and she leaned toward him.

"It's just been ages," Virginia said. "I thought you were so handsome. Of course, you were married, so I didn't tell you that."

"It's different now," Ruth said.

"Same as it always was," Virginia said. "Just more open."

Ruth slumped back, laughing loudly. "She's right, Hadley. More open."

"I suppose so," he said, still unable to look at her eyes.

"We're shocking him," Virginia said.

"That's a man," Ruth said. She patted his knee, her bright-tipped fingers vanishing and reappearing in the material of his trousers. "Weren't you in love with me once, Hadley?"

He looked from the floor to the amused faces of the women. "I guess once I was."

"He guesses," Ruth purred. "He doesn't know. He guesses."

"Well, the point is, you can't hang in the past forever," Virginia said. The quick smile illuminated her face.

"The past was fun," Ruth added.

"But it's gone now, you know," Virginia said. "You can't keep raking it up. So Ruth and I, we've decided to help you out."

She stood up, not looking at all like a grandmother. "What a pretty cat. What's his name?"

"Bill," he said.

As he glanced toward the cat, Virginia was gone.

"Wait a minute," he cried, turning quickly to Ruth.

"That's all we wanted to tell you," she said.

Her figure wavered and her arms and body slipped sideways, separating from her shoulders and head. She said, "Don't think for a minute we weren't here. Mania, my foot."

"I wanted to say . . ."

"You're sweet," she said. "Can you be home at five tomorrow night?"

Her figures came to pieces, flowing across the room in translucent strands. It was after ten o'clock. Dropping onto the davenport, he ground his face against the flowered cushions.

At five the following evening, the door bell rang once, briefly. As if it had been touched in embarrassment, as a duty, and once was going to be all. When he opened the door, Bill attempted to dart out and had to be captured and held. Facing him in the doorway was a tall, lean-faced woman with heavy dark hair. She smiled tentatively at him and dropped her eyes, which were dark gray. Embarrassment rose in waves from her. In a low voice, she asked:

"Are you Mr. Jackson? Hadley Jackson?"

"Yes, m'am."

"Did you know Ruth Payne once?"

"Ruth? Oh, yes."

Her lips thinned and she looked so uneasy, he felt a pulse of sympathy.

"This probably sounds awful funny," she said, not looking at him. "She wanted me—she kept telling me to see you."

"I see," he said.

She looked directly at him then and their eyes touched. As she examined him some of the tension left her. She seemed intelligent and wary.

"You know about Ruth?" she asked.

"She died."

"Yes, she died."

He thought that she would say more but she did not.

After a moment, he said, "Reconnection," not loudly.

Faint color touched her face; she looked away.

He said swiftly before she could recover herself and flee: "I was just going down the street for a cup of coffee. Would you like one?"

She regarded the air between them as if it were imprinted with complex instructions. "Yes. I think so. That would be nice."

"I'll just get my coat. Come in."

Still holding the cat, he stepped aside. Head lifted, smiling faintly, she entered his apartment for the first time.

JOHN VARLEY

Just Another Perfect Day

John Varley appeared on the SF scene in 1975, and by the end of 1976—in what was a meteoric rise to prominence even for a field known for meteoric rises—he was already being recognized as one of the hottest new writers of the seventies. His books include the novels *Ophiuchi Hotline, Millenium Titan, Wizard,* and *Demon,* and the collections *The Persistence of Vision, The Barbie Murders,* and *Picnic on Nearside.* His most recent book is the collection *Blue Champagne.* He has won two Nebulas and two Hugos for his short fiction. His extremely popular story "Press Enter ■" was in our Second Annual Collection.

Here he shows us a man living through a nearly perfect day—and it had goddamned well *better* be!

▼

Just Another Perfect Day

JOHN VARLEY

Don't Worry.

Everything is under control.

I know how you're feeling. You wake up alone in a strange room, you get up, you look around, you soon discover that both doors are locked from the outside. It's enough to unsettle anybody, especially when you try and try and try to recall how you got here and you just can't do it.

But beyond that . . . there's this feeling. I know you're feeling it right now. I know a lot of things—and I'll reveal them all as we go along.

One of the things I know is this:

If you will sit down, put this message back on the table where you found it, and take slow, deep breaths while counting to one hundred, you'll feel a lot better.

I promise you will.

Do that now.

See what I mean? You do feel a lot better.

That feeling won't last for long, I'm sorry to say.

I wish there was an easier way to do this, but there isn't, and believe me, many ways have been tried. So here we go:

> This is not 1986.
> You are not twenty-five years old.
> The date is

~~January February March April May~~ June
1 2 3 4 5 6 7 8 9 10 11 12
~~2006 2007~~ 2008

A lot of things have happened in

~~twenty twenty-one~~ twenty-two

years, and I'll tell you all you need to know about that in good time.
For now . . . Don't Worry.
Slow, deep breaths. Close your eyes. Count to a hundred.
You'll feel better.
I promise.

If you'll get up now, you'll find that the bathroom door will open. There's a mirror in there. Take a look in it, get to know the

~~forty-five forty-six~~ forty-seven

-year-old who will be in there, looking back at you . . .
And Don't Worry.
Take deep breaths, and so forth.
I'll tell you more when you get back.

Well.
I know how rough that was. I know you're trembling. I know you're feeling confusion, fear, anger . . . a thousand emotions.
And I know you have a thousand questions. They will all be answered, every one of them, at the proper time.
Here are some ground rules.
I will never lie to you. You can't imagine how much care and anguish has gone into the composition of this letter. For now, you must take my word that things will be revealed to you in the most useful order, and in the easiest way that can be devised. You must appreciate that not all your questions can be answered at once. It may be harder for you to accept that some questions cannot be answered at all until a proper background has been prepared. These answers would mean nothing to you at this point.
You would like someone—*anyone*—to be with you right now, so you could *ask* these questions. That has been tried, and the results were needlessly chaotic and confusing. Trust me; this is the best way.
And why should you trust me? For a very good reason.
I am you. You wrote—in a manner of speaking—every word in this letter, to help yourself through this agonizing moment.

Deep breaths, please.
Stay seated; it helps a little.
And Don't Worry.

So now we're past bombshell #2. There are more to come, but they will be easier to take, simply because your capacity to be surprised is just about at its peak right now. A certain numbness will set in. You should be thankful for that.

And now, back to your questions.

Top of the list: What happened?

Briefly (and it must be brief—more on that later):

In 1989 you had an accident. It involved a motorcycle which you don't remember owning because you didn't buy it until 1988, and a city bus. You had a difference of opinion concerning the right of way, and the bus won.

Feel your scalp with your fingertips. Don't be queasy; it healed long ago—as much as it's going to. Under those great knots of scar tissue are the useless results of the labors of the best neurosurgeons in the country. In the end, they just had to scoop out a lot of gray matter and close you back up, shaking their heads sagely and opining that you would probably feel right at home under glass on a salad bar.

But you fooled them. You woke up, and there was much rejoicing, even though you couldn't remember anything after the summer of '86. You were conscious a few hours, long enough for the doctors to determine that your intelligence didn't seem to be impaired. You could talk, read, speak, see, hear. Then you went back to sleep.

The next day you woke up, and couldn't remember anything after the summer of '86. No one was too worried. They told you again what had happened. You were awake most of the day, and again you fell asleep.

The next day you woke up, and couldn't remember anything after the summer of '86. Some consternation was expressed.

The next day you woke up, and couldn't remember anything after the summer of '86. Professorial heads were scratched, seven-syllable Latin words intoned, and deep mumbles were mumbled.

The next day you woke up, and couldn't remember anything after the summer of '86.

And the next day
And the next day
And the day after that.

This morning you woke up and couldn't remember anything after the summer of '86, and I know this is getting old, but I had to make the point in this way, because it is and we've begun to think a pattern is established.

No, no, *don't* breathe deeply, *don't* count to one hundred, face this one head on. It'll be good for you.

Back under control?

I knew you could do it.

What you have is called Progressive Narco-Catalepti-Amnesiac Syndrome (PNCAS, or "Pinkus" in conversation), and you should be proud of yourself, because they made up the term to describe your condition and at least a half-dozen papers have been written proving it can't happen. What seems to happen, in spite of the papers, is that you store and retrieve memories just fine as long as you have a continuous thread of consciousness. But the sleep center somehow activates an erase mechanism in your head, so that all you experienced during the day is lost to you when you wake up again. The old memories are intact and vivid; the new ones are ephemeral, like they were recorded on a continuous tape loop.

Most amnesias of this type behave rather differently. Retrograde amnesia is seen fairly frequently, whereby you gradually lose even the old memories and become as an infant. And progressive amnesias are not unknown, but those poor people can't remember what happened to them as little as five minutes ago. Try to imagine what life would be like in those circumstances before you start crying in your beer.

Yeah, great, I hear you whine. And what's so great about *this*?

Well, nothing, at first glance. I'll certainly be the last one to argue about that. My own re-awakening is too fresh in my mind, having happened only fifteen hours ago. And, in a sense, I will soon be dead, snatched back from this mayfly existence by the greedy arms of Morpheus. When I sleep tonight, most of what I feel to be *me* will vanish. I will awake, an older and less wise man, to confusion, will read this letter, will breathe deeply, count to one hundred, stare into the mirror at a stranger. I will be you.

And yet, now, as I scan rapidly through this letter for the second time today (I said I wrote it, but only in a sense; it was written by a thousand mayflies), they are asking me if there is anything I wish to change. If I want a change, Marian will see that it is made. Is there anything I would like to do differently tomorrow? Is there something I want to tell you, my successor in this body, to beware of, to disbelieve? Are there any warnings I would issue?

The answer is no.

I will let this letter stand, in its entirety.

There are things still for you to learn that will convince you, against all common sense, that you have a wonderful life/day ahead of you.

But you need a rest. You need time to think.

Do this for me. Go back to the date. Mark out the last number and write in the next. If it's a new month, change that, too.

Now you will find the other door will open. Please go into the next room, where you will find breakfast, and an envelope containing the next part of this letter.

Don't open it yet. Eat your breakfast.

Think it over.

But don't take too long. Your time is short, and you won't want to waste it.

That was refreshing, wasn't it?

It shouldn't surprise you that all your favorite breakfast foods were on the table. You eat the same meal every morning, and never get tired of it.

And I'm sorry if that statement took some of the pleasure out of the meal, but it is necessary for me to keep reminding you of your circumstances, to prevent a cycle of denial getting started.

Here is the thing you must bear in mind.

Today is the rest of your life.

Because that life will be so short, it is essential that you waste none of it. In this letter I have sometimes stated the obvious, written out conclusions you have already reached—in a sense, wasted your time. Each time it was done—and each time it will yet be done in the rest of this letter—was for a purpose. Points must be driven home, sometimes brutally, sometimes repetitiously. I promise you this sort of thing will be kept to an absolute minimum.

So here comes a few paragraphs that might be a waste of time, but really aren't, as they dispose neatly of several thousand of the most burning questions in your mind. The questions can be summed up as "What has happened in twenty years?"

The answer is: You don't care.

You can't afford to care. Even a brief synopsis of recent events would take hours to read, and would be the sheerest foolishness. You don't care who the President is. The price of gasoline doesn't concern you, nor does the victor in the '98 World Series. Why learn this trivia when you would only have to re-learn it tomorrow?

You don't care which books and movies are currently popular. You have read your last book, seen your last movie.

Luckily, you are an orphan with no siblings or other close relatives. (It *is* lucky; think about it.) The girl you were going with at the time of your accident has forgotten all about you—and you don't care, because you didn't love her.

There *are* things that have happened which you *need* to know about; I'll speak of them very soon.

In the meantime. . . .

How do you like the room? Not at all like a hospital, is it? Comfortable and pleasant—yet it has no windows, and the only other door was locked when you tried it.

Try it again. It will open now.

And remember . . .

Don't Worry.

Don't Worry. Don't Worry. Don't Worry.

You will have stopped crying by now. I *know* you desperately need someone to talk to, a human face to look into. You will have that very soon now, but for another few minutes I still must reach out to you from your recent past.

Incidentally, the reason the breathing exercises and the counting are so effective is a post-hypnotic suggestion left in your mind. When you see the words Don't Worry, it relaxes you. It seems that some part of your mind retains shadows of memory that you can't reach—which may also account for why you *believe* all this apparent rubbish.

Are the tears dry? It did the same thing to me. Even seeing my own face aged in the mirror didn't affect me like seeing the view from my windows. Then it became *real*.

You are on one of the top floors of the Chrysler Building. Your view to the north included many, many buildings that were not there in 1986, and jumbled among them were many familiar buildings, distinctive as finger-prints. This *is* New York, and it *is* a new century, and that view is impossible to deny and as real as a fist. That's why you wept.

Not too many more bombshells to go now. But the next one is a doozy. Let's creep up on it, shall we?

You've already looked at the three photographs on the table beside your breakfast. Consider them now, in order.

The big, bluff, hearty-looking fellow is Ian MacIntyre, whom you'll meet in a few minutes. He will be your counselor/companion today, and he is the head of a very important project in which you are involved. It's impossible not to like him, though you, like me, will try to resist at first. But he is too wise to push it, and you've always liked people, anyway. Besides, he has a lot of experience in winning your friendship, having done so every day for eight years.

On to the second picture.

Looks almost human, doesn't he? If the offspring of Gumby and E.T. could be considered human. He *is* humanoid: two eyes, nose, mouth, two arms and two legs, and that goofy grin. The green skin you'll get used to quickly enough.

What he is, is a Martian.

See, fifteen years ago the Martians landed and took over the planet Earth.

We still don't know what they plan to do with it, but some of the theories are not good news for *Homo sapiens*.

Don't Worry.

Take a few deep breaths. I'll wait.

That last thought is unworthy of you and unjust. I would *not* waste your time with a practical joke. You must realize I can back up what I say.

To illustrate, I want you to go to the *south* windows of your apartment. Go through the billiard room into the spa, turn left at the gym, and open the door beside the Picasso, the one that didn't open before. You'll find yourself in an area with a view of the Narrows, and I'm sure I won't need to direct you beyond that.

Take a look, and come right back.

All right, you just had to prove you could do things your own way, didn't you? I don't *care* that you brought the letter with you, but your having done so provides one last bit of proof that I know you pretty well, doesn't it?

Now, back to the bloody Martians.

It's amazing how on-target Steve Spielberg was, isn't it? The way that ship *floats* out there . . . and it's *bigger* than the mother ship in *Close Encounters*. That sucker is over thirty miles across. At its lowest point it is two miles in the air. The upper parts reach into space. It has floated out there for fifteen years and not budged *one inch*. People call it The Saucer. There are fifteen others just like it, hovering near other major cities.

And you think you have detected a flaw, don't you? How would you have seen it, you ask, if it had been a cloudy day? If it had been just a normal New York *smoggy* day, for that matter. Then you'd be reading this, scratching your head, wondering what the hell I'm talking about.

The answer will illustrate everyone's concern. There *are* no more cloudy days in New York. The Martians don't seem to like rain, so they don't let it happen here. As for the smog . . . they told us to stop it, and we did. Wouldn't you, with that thing floating out there?

About the name, Martians . . .

We first detected their ships in the neighborhood of Mars. I know you'd have found it easier to swallow, in a perverse way, had I told you they came from Alpha Centauri or the Andromeda Galaxy or the planet Tralfamadore. But people got to calling them Martians because that's what they were called on television.

We don't think they're really from Mars.

We don't know *where* they're from, but it's probably not from around here. And, by that, I mean not just another galaxy, but another universe. We think our own universe exists sort of as a shadow of them.

This will be hard to explain. Take it slowly.

Do you remember *Flatland*, and Mr. A Square? He lived in a two-dimensional universe. There was no up or down, just right and left, forward and backward. He could not *conceive* the notion of up or down. Mr. Square was visited by a three-dimensional being, a sphere, who drifted down through the world of Flatland. Square perceived the sphere as a circle that gradually grew, and then shrank. All he could see at any one moment was a cross-section of the sphere, while the sphere, god-like, could look down into Mr. Square's world, even touch inside Square's body without going through the skin.

It was all just an interesting intellectual exercise, until the Martians arrived. Now we think they're like the sphere, and we are Mr. Square. They live in another dimension, and they don't perceive time and space like we do.

An example:

You saw they appeared humanoid. We don't think they really are.

We think they simply allow us to see a portion of their bodies which they project into our three-dimensional world and cause to *appear* humanoid. Their real shape must be vastly complex.

Consider your hand. If you thrust your fingers into Flatland, Mr. Square would see four circles and not imagine them to be connected. Putting your hand in further, he would see the circles merge into an oblong. Or an even better analogy is the shadow-play. By suitably entwining your two hands in front of a light, you can cast a shadow on a wall that resembles a bird, or a bull, or an elephant, or even a man. What we see of the Martians is no more real than a Kermit the Frog hand puppet.

The ship is the same way. We see merely a three-dimensional cross-section of a much larger and more complex structure.

At least we think so.

Communication with the Martians is very frustrating, nearly impossible. They are so foreign to us. They never tell us anything that makes sense, never say the same thing twice. We assume it would make sense if we could think the way they do.

And it is important.

They are very powerful. Weather control is just a parlor trick. When they invaded, they invaded *all at once*—and I hope I can explain this to you, as I'm far from sure I understand it myself, after a full day with Martians.

They invaded fifteen years ago . . . but they also invaded in 1854, and in 1520, and several other times in the "past." The past seems to be merely another direction to them, like up or down. You'll be shown books, old books, with woodcuts and drawings and contemporary accounts of how the Martians arrived, what they did, when they left . . . and don't be concerned that you don't remember these momentous events from your high school history class, *because no one else does, either.*

Do you begin to understand? It seems that, from the moment they arrived here, in the late part of the twentieth century, they changed the past so that they had already arrived several times before. We have the history books to prove that they did. The fact that no one remembers these stories *being* in the history books before they arrived *this* time must be seen as an object lesson. One assumes they could have changed our memories of events as easily as the events themselves. That they did not do so means they *meant* us to be impressed. Had they changed both the events *and* our memories of them, no one would be the wiser; we would all assume history had *always* been that way because that's the way we remembered it.

The whole idea of history books must be a tremendous joke to them, since they don't experience time consecutively.

Had enough? There's more.

They can do more than add things to our history. They can take things away. Things like the World Trade Center. That's right, go look for it. It's not out there, and we didn't tear it down. It never existed in this world, except in our memories. It's like a big, shared illusion.

Other things have turned up missing as well. Things such as Knoxville, Tennessee; Lake Huron; the Presidency of William McKinley; the Presbyterian Church; the rhinoceros (including the fossil record of its ancestors); Jack the Ripper (and all the literary works written about him); the letter Q; and Ecuador.

Presbyterians still remember their faith and have built new churches to replace the ones that were never built. Who needed the goddamn rhino, anyway? Another man served McKinley's term (and was also assassinated). Seeing book after book where "kw" replaces "q" is only amusing—and very kweer. But the people of Knoxville—and a dozen other towns around the world—*never existed*. They are still trying to sort out the real estate around where Lake Huron used to be. And you can search the world's atlases in vain for any sight of Ecuador.

The best wisdom is that the Martians could do even more, if they wanted to. Such as wiping out the element oxygen, the charge on the electron, or, of course, the planet Earth.

They invaded, and they won quite easily.

And their weapon is very much like an editor's blue pencil. Rather than *destroy* our world, they *re-write* it.

So what does all this have to do with me, I hear you cry.

Why couldn't I have lived out my one day on Earth without worrying about this?

Well . . . who do you think is paying for this fabulous apartment?

The grateful taxpayers, that's who. You didn't think you'd get original Picassos on the walls if you were nothing more than a brain-damaged geek, did you?

And why are the taxpayers grateful?

Because anything that keeps the Martians happy, keeps the taxpayers happy. The Martians scare hell out of *everyone* . . . and you are their fairhaired boy.

Why?

Because you don't experience time like the rest of humanity does.

You start fresh every day. You haven't had fifteen years to think about the Martians, you haven't developed any prejudice toward them or their way of thinking.

Maybe.

Most of that could be bullshit. We don't know if prejudice has anything to do with it . . . but you *do* see time differently. The fact is, the best mathematicians and physicists in the world have tried to deal with the Martians, and the Martians aren't interested. Every day they come to talk to *you*.

Most days, nothing is accomplished. They spend an hour, then go wherever it is they go, in whatever manner they do it. One day out of a hundred, you get an insight. Everything I've told you so far is the result of those insights being compiled—

—along with the work of others. There are a few hundred of you, around the world. No other man or woman has your peculiar affliction; all are what most people would call mentally limited. There are the progressive amnesiacs I mentioned earlier. There are people with split-brain disorders, people with almost unbelievable perceptual aberrations, such as the woman who has lost the concept of "right." Left is the only direction that exists in her brain.

The Martians spend time with these people, people like you.

So we tentatively conclude this about the Martians:

They want to teach us something.

It is painfully obvious they could have destroyed us any time they wished to do so. They *have* enslaved us, in the sense that we are pathetically eager to do anything we even *suspect* they might want us to do. But they don't seem to want to *do* anything with us. They've made no move to breed us for meat animals, conscript us into slave labor camps, or rape women. They have simply arrived, demonstrated their powers, and started talking to people like you.

No one knows if we can learn what they are trying to teach us. But it behooves us to try, wouldn't you think?

Again, you say: Why me?

Or even more to the point: Why should I care?

I know your bitterness, and I understand it. Why should you spend even an hour of your precious time on problems you don't really care about, when it would be much easier and more satisfying spending your sixteen hours of awareness gnawing on yourself, wallowing in self-pity, and in general being a one-man soap opera.

There are two reasons.

One: You were never that kind of person. You've just about exhausted your store of self-pity during the process of reading this letter. If you have only one day—though it hurts like hell . . . so be it! You will spend that day doing something useful.

Reason number two . . .

You've been looking at the third picture off and on since you first picked it up, haven't you? (Come on, you can't lie to me.)

She's very pretty, isn't she?

And that thought is unworthy of you, since you *know* where this letter is coming from. She would not be offered to you as a bribe. The project managers know you well enough to avoid offering you a piece of ass to get your cooperation.

Her name is Marian.

Let us speak of love for a moment.

You were in love once before. You remember how it was, if you'll allow yourself. You remember the pain . . . but that came later, didn't it? When she rejected you. Do you remember what it felt like *the day you fell in love*? Think back, you can get it.

The simple fact is, it's why the world spins. Just the *possibility* of love has kept you going in the three years since Karen.

Well, let me tell you. Marian is in love with you, and before the day is over, you will be in love with her. You can believe that or not, as you choose, but I, at the end of my life here this day, can take as one of my few consolations that I/you will have, tomorrow/ today, the exquisite pleasure of falling in love with Marian.

I envy you, you skeptical bastard.

And since it's just you and me, I'll add this. Even with a girl you *don't* love, "the first time" is always pretty damn interesting, isn't it?

For you, it's always the first time . . . except when it's the second time, just before you sleep . . . which Marian seems to be suggesting this very moment.

As usual, I have anticipated all your objections.

You think it might be tough for her? You think she's suffering?

Okay. Admitted, the first few hours are what you might call repetitive for her. You gotta figure she's bored, by now, at your invariant behavior when you first wake up. But it is a cross she bears willingly for the pleasure of your company during the rest of the day.

She is a healthy, energetic girl, one who is aware that no woman ever had such an attentive, energetic lover. She loves a man who is endlessly fascinated by her, body and soul, who sees her with new eyes each and every day.

She loves your perpetual enthusiasm, your renewable infatuation.

There isn't *time* to fall out of love.

Anything more I could say would be wasting your time, and believe me, when you see what today is going to be like, you'd hate me for it.

We could wish things were different. It is *not* fair that we have only one day. I, who am at the end of it, can feel the pain you only sense. I have my wonderful memories . . . which will soon be gone. And I have Marian, for a few more minutes.

But I swear to you, I feel like an old, old man who has lived a full life, who has no regrets for anything he ever did, who accomplished something in his life, who loved, and was loved in return.

Can many "normal" people die saying that?

In just a few seconds that one, last locked door will open, and your new life and future love will come through it. I guarantee it will be interesting.

I love you, and I now leave you . . .

Have a nice day.

JANET KAGAN
The Loch Moose Monster

Although she has only been selling for a few years, Janet Kagan is rapidly building a large and enthusiastic audience for her work, and may well become a figure of note in the 1990s. Her first novel, a Star Trek novel called *Uhura's Song*, was a nationwide best-seller, and her second novel *Hellspark* (*not* a Star Trek novel) was greeted with similar warmth and enthusiasm. She is a frequent contributor to *Isaac Asimov's Science Fiction Magazine*, and has also sold to *Pulphouse* and *Analog*. Her linked series of stories about Mama Jason has proved to be one of the most popular series to run in *IAsfm* in recent years, with the initial story, "The Loch Moose Monster," winning this year's *IAsfm* Reader's Award Poll by a large margin; the series will be issued in book form by Tor in the near future. She lives in Lincoln Park, New Jersey, with her husband Ricky, several computers, and *lots* of cats.

In the wry and suspenseful story that follows, she takes us along to the frontier planet Mirabile to meet a woman whose job it is to cope with some very dangerous and very odd creatures, and follows her as she unravels a compelling biological mystery.

▼

The Loch Moose Monster

JANET KAGAN

This year the Ribeiros' daffodils seeded early and they seeded cockroaches. Now ecologically speaking, even a cockroach has its place—but these suckers *bit*. That didn't sound Earth authentic to me. Not that I care, mind you, all I ask is useful. I wasn't betting on that either.

As usual, we were short-handed—most of the team was up-country trying to stabilize a herd of Guernseys—which left me and Mike to throw a containment tent around the Ribeiro place while we did the gene-reads on the roaches and the daffodils that spawned 'em. Dragon's Teeth, sure enough, and worse than useless. I grabbed my gear and went in to clean them out, daffodils and all.

By the time I crawled back out of the containment tent, exhausted, cranky, and thoroughly bitten, there wasn't a daffodil left in town. Damn fools. If I'd told 'em the roaches were Earth authentic they'd have cheered 'em, no matter how obnoxious they were.

I didn't even have the good grace to say hi to Mike when I slammed into the lab. The first thing out of my mouth was, "The red daffodils—in front of Sagdeev's."

"I got 'em," he said. "Nick of time, but I got 'em. They're in the greenhouse—"

We'd done a gene-read on that particular patch of daffodils the first year they'd flowered red: they promised to produce a good strain of preying mantises, probably Earth authentic. We both knew how badly Mirabile needed insectivores. The other possibility was something harmless but pretty that ship's records called "fireflies." Either would have been welcome, and those idiots had been ready to consign both to a fire.

"I used the same soil, Annie, so don't give me that look."

"Town's full of fools," I growled, to let him know that look wasn't aimed at him. "Same soil, fine, but can we match the rest of the environmental conditions those preying mantises need in the goddamn greenhouse?"

"It's the best we've got," he said. He shrugged and his right hand came up bandaged. I glared at it.

He dropped the bandaged hand behind the lab bench. "They were gonna burn 'em. I couldn't—" He looked away, looked back. "Annie, it's nothing to worry about—"

I'd have done the same myself, true, but that was no reason to let *him* get into the habit of taking fool risks.

I started across to check out his hand and give him pure hell from close up. Halfway there the com blatted for attention. Yellow light on the console, meaning it was no emergency, but I snatched it up to deal with the interruption before I dealt with Mike. I snapped a "Yeah?" at the screen.

"Mama Jason?"

Nobody calls me that but Elly's kids. I glowered at the face on screen: my age, third-generation Mirabilan, and not so privileged. "Annie Jason Masmajean," I corrected, "Who wants to know?"

"Leonov Bellmaker Denness at this end," he said. "I apologize for my improper use of your nickname." Ship's manners—he ignored my rudeness completely.

The name struck me as vaguely familiar but I was in no mood to search my memory; I'd lost my ship's manners about three hours into the cockroach clean-out. "State your business," I said.

To his credit, he did: "Two of Elly's lodgers claim there's a monster in Loch Moose. By their description, it's a humdinger."

I was all ears now. Elly runs the lodge at Loch Moose for fun—her profession's raising kids. (Elly Raiser Roget, like her father before her. Our population is still so small we can't afford to lose genes just because somebody's not suited, one way or another, for parenting.) A chimera anywhere near Loch Moose was a potential disaster. Thing of it was, Denness didn't sound right for that. "Then why aren't *they* making this call?"

He gave a deep-throated chuckle. "They're in the dining room gorging themselves on Chris's shrimp. I doubt they'll make you a formal call when they're done. Their names are Emile Pilot Stirzaker and Francois Cobbler Pastides and, right now, they can't spell either without dropping letters."

So he thought they'd both been smoking dumbweed. Fair enough. I simmered down and reconsidered him. I'd've bet money he was the one who side-tracked Pastides and Stirzaker into the eating binge.

Recognition struck at last: this was the guy Elly's kids called "Noisy." The first thing he'd done on moving into the neighborhood was outshout every one of 'em in one helluva contest. He was equally legendary for his stories, his bells, and his ability to keep secrets. I hadn't met him, but I'd sure as hell heard tell.

I must have said the nickname aloud, because Denness said, "Yes, 'Noisy.' Is that enough to get me a hearing?"

"It is." It was my turn to apologize. "Sorry. What more do you want me to hear?"

"You should, I think, hear Stirzaker imitate his monster's bellow of rage."

It took me a long moment to get his drift, but get it I did. "I'm on my way," I said. I snapped off and started repacking my gear.

Mike stared at me. "Annie? What did I miss?"

"*You* ever know anybody who got auditory hallucinations on dumbweed?"

"Shit," he said, "No." He scrambled for his own pack.

"Not you," I said. "I need you here to coddle those daffodils, check the environmental conditions that produced 'em, and call me if Dragon's Teeth pop up anywhere else." I shouldered my pack and finished with a glare and a growl: "That should be enough to keep you out of bonfires while I'm gone, shouldn't it?"

By the time I grounded in the clearing next to Elly's lodge, I'd decided I was on a wild moose chase. Yeah, I know the Earth authentic is wild *goose*, but "wild moose" was Granddaddy Jason's phrase. He'd known Jason—the original first generation Jason—well before the Dragon's Teeth had started popping up.

One look at the wilderness where Elly's lodge is now and Jason knew she had the perfect EC for moose. She hauled the embryos out of ship's storage and set them thawing. Built up a nice little herd of the things and turned 'em loose. Not a one of them survived—damn foolish creatures died of a taste for a Mirabilan plant they couldn't metabolize.

Trying to establish a viable herd got to be an obsession with Jason. She must've spent years at it, off and on. She never succeeded but somebody with a warped sense of humor named the lake Loch Moose and it stuck, moose or no moose.

Loch Moose looked as serene as it always did this time of year. The waterlilies were in full bloom—patches of velvety red and green against the sparkles of sunlight off the water. Here and there I saw a ripple of real trout, Earth authentic.

On the bank to the far right, Susan's troop of otters played tag, skidding down the incline and hitting the water with a splash. They whistled encouragement to each other like a pack of fans at a ballgame. Never saw a creature have more pure *fun* than an otter—unless it was a dozen otters, like now.

The pines were that dusty gold that meant I'd timed it just right to see Loch Moose smoke. There's nothing quite so beautiful as that drift of pollen fog across the loch. It would gild rocks and trees alike until the next rainfall.

Monster, my ass—but where better for a wild moose chase?

I clambered down the steps to Elly's lodge, still gawking at the scenery, so I was totally unprepared for the EC in the lobby. If that bright-eyed geneticist back on Earth put the double-whammy on any of the human genes in the cold banks they sent along (*swore* they hadn't, but after the kangaroo rex, damnify believe anything the old records tell me), the pandemonium I found would have been enough to kick off Dragon's Teeth by the dozens.

Amid the chaos, Ilanith, Elly's next-to-oldest, was handling the oversized gilt ledger with great dignity. She lit up when she saw me and waved. Then she bent down for whispered conversation. A second later Jen, the nine-year-old, exploded from behind the desk, bellowing, "Elleeeeee! Nois-eeeee! Come quick! Mama Jason's here!" The kid's lungpower cut right through the chaos and startled the room into a momentary hush. She charged through the door to the dining room, still trying to shout the house down.

I took advantage of the distraction to elbow my way to the desk and Ilanith.

She squinted a little at me, purely Elly in manner, and said, "Bet you got hopped on by a kangaroo rex this week. You're *real* snarly."

"Can't do anything about my face," I told her. "And it was biting cockroaches." I pushed up a sleeve to show her the bites.

"Bleeeeeh," she said, with an inch or two of tongue for emphasis. "I hope they weren't keepers."

"Just the six I saved to put in your bed. Wouldn't want you to think I'd forgotten you."

She wrinkled her nose at me and flung herself across the desk to plant a big sloppy kiss on my cheek. "Mama Jason, you are the world's biggest tease. But I'm gonna give you your favorite room anyhow—" she wrinkled her nose in a very different fashion at the couple to my right "—since *those two* just checked out of it."

One of the *those two* peered at me like a myopic crane. I saw recognition strike, then he said, "We've changed our minds. We'll keep the room."

"Too late," said Ilanith—and she was smug about it. "But, if you want to stay, I can give you one on the other side of the lodge. No view." Score one for the good guys, I thought.

"See, Elly?" It was Jen, back at a trot beside Elly and dragging Noisy behind her. "See?" Jen said again. "If Mama Jason's here, I won't have to go away, right?"

"Right," I said.

"Oh, Jen!" Elly dropped to one knee to pull Jen into one of her full-body-check hugs. "Is *that* what's been worrying you? Leo already explained to your mom. There's no monster—nobody's going to send you away from Loch Moose!"

Jen, who'd been looking relieved, suddenly looked suspicious. "If there's no monster, why's Mama Jason here?"

"Need a break," I said, realizing I meant it. Seeing Elly and the kids was break enough all by itself. "Stomped enough Dragon's Teeth this week. I'm not about to go running after monsters that vanish at the first breath of fresh air."

Elly gave me a smile that would have thawed a glacier and my shoulders relaxed for the first time in what seemed like months.

I grinned back. "Have your two monster-sighters sobered up yet?"

"Sobered up," reported Ilanith, "and checked out." She giggled. "You should have seen how red-faced they were, Mama Jason."

I glowered at no one in particular. "Just as well. After the day I had, they'd have been twice as red if I'd had to deal with 'em."

Elly rose to her feet, bringing Jen with her. The two of them looked me over, Jen imitating Elly's keen-eyed inspection. "We'd better get Mama Jason to her room. She needs a shower and a nap worse than any kid in the household."

Ilanith shook her head. "Let her eat first, Elly. By the time she's done, we'll have her room ready."

"Sounds good to me," I said, "if the kids waiting tables can take it."

"We raise a sturdy bunch around here. Go eat, Annie." She gave me a kiss on the cheek—I got a bonus kiss from Jen—and the two of them bustled off to get my room ready. I frowned after them: Jen still seemed worried and I wondered why.

Ilanith rounded the desk to grab my pack. Standing between me and Leo, she suddenly jammed her fists into her hips. "Oh, nuts. Ship's manners. Honestly, Mama Jason—how did people *ever* get acquainted in the old days?" With an expression of tried patience, she formally introduced the two of us.

I looked him over, this time giving him a fair shake. The face was as good as the reputation, all laugh lines etched deep. In return, I got inspected just as hard.

When nobody said anything for a full half second, Ilanith said, "More? You need more? Didn't I get it right?"

Leo gave a smile that was a match for Elly's. Definitely the EC, I thought. Then he thrust out a huge welcoming hand and said, "That's Leo to you, as I don't imagine I could outshout you."

That assessment visibly impressed Ilanith.

"Annie," I said. I took the hand. Not many people have hands the size of mine. In Denness I'd met my match for once. Surprised me how good that felt. He didn't let go immediately and I wasn't all that anxious for him to do so.

Ilanith eyed him severely. "Leo, there's no need to be grabby!" She tapped his hand, trying to make him let go.

"Shows how much you know about ship's manners," Leo said. "I was about to offer the lady my arm, to escort her into the dining room."

"Perfectly good old-time ritual," I said. "I can stand it if he can."

Leo held out his arm, ship's formal; I took it. We went off rather grandly, leaving Ilanith all the more suspicious that we'd made it up for her benefit.

Leo chuckled as we passed beyond her earshot. "She won't believe that until she double-checks with Elly."

"I know. Good for 'em—check it out for yourself, I always say. Have *you* heard any bellowing off the loch?"

"Yes," he said, "I have heard a couple of unusual sounds off the loch lately. I've no way of knowing if they're all made by the same creature. But I've lived here long enough to know that these are new. One is a kind of sucking gurgle. Then there's something related to a cow's lowing—" he held up a hand "—*not* cow and *not* red deer either. I know both. And there's a bellow that'll bring you out of a sound sleep faster than a shotgun blast."

His lips flattened a bit. "I can't vouch for that one. I've *only* heard it awakening from sleep. It might have been a dream but it never *feels* like dream—and the bellow Stirzaker gave was a fair approximation of it."

The lines across his forehead deepened. "There's something else you should know, Annie. Jen's been acting spooked, and neither Elly nor I can make any sense of it."

"I saw. I thought she was still keyed up over the monster business."

He shook his head. "This started weeks ago, long before Stirzaker and Pastides got everybody stirred up."

"I'll see what I can find out."

"Anything I can do to help," he said. He swung his free hand to tell me how extensive that "anything" actually was. "On either count."

"Right now, you watch me eat a big plate of *my* shrimp with Chris's barbeque sauce on 'em."

Loch Moose was the only source of freshwater shrimp on Mirabile and they were one of my triumphs. Not just the way they tasted when Chris got done with them, but because I'd brought the waterlilies they came from myself and planted them down in Loch Moose on the chance they'd throw off something good. Spent three years making sure they stabilized. Got some pretty dragonflies out of that redundancy, too. Elly's kids use 'em for catching rock lobsters, which is another thing Chris cooks to perfection.

By the time I'd finished my shrimp, the dining room was empty except for a couple of people I knew to be locals like Leo. I blinked my surprise, I guess.

Leo said, Most of the guests checked out this morning. Let's take advantage of it." He picked up my glass and his own and bowed me toward one of the empty booths.

I followed and sank, sighing, into overstuffed comfort. "Now," I said, "tell me what you heard from Stirzaker and Pastides."

He obliged in detail, playing both roles. When he was done, I appreciated his reputation for story-telling, but I knew as well he'd given me an accurate account, right down to the two of them tripping over each other's words in their excitement.

Their description of the chimera would have scared the daylights out of me—if they'd been able to agree on any given part of it aside from the size. Stirzaker had seen the thing reach for him with two great clawlike hands. Pastides had seen the loops of a water snake, grown to unbelievable lengths, undulate past him. They agreed again only when it came to the creature's bellow.

When all was said, I had to laugh. "I bet *their* granddaddy told *them* scary bedtime stories, too!"

"Good God," said Leo, grinning suddenly. "The Loch Ness Monster! I should have recognized it!"

"From which description?" I grinned back. Luckily the question didn't require an answer.

"Mama Jason!"

That was all the warning I got. Susan—all hundred pounds of her—pounced into my lap.

"They were *dumbstruck*, both of them," she said, her manner making it clear that this was the most important news of the century. "You should have seen them eat! Tell her, Noisy—you saw!"

"Hello to you too," I said, "and I just got the full story, complete with sound effects."

That settled her down a bit, but not much. At sixteen, nothing settles them *down*. Sliding into the seat beside me, she said, "Now you tell—about the biting cockroaches."

Well, I'd have had to tell that one sooner or later, so I told it for two, ending with Mike's heroic attempt to rescue the red daffodils.

Susan's eyes went dreamy. "Fireflies," she said. "Think how pretty they'd be around the lake at night!"

"I was," I said, all too curtly. "Sorry," I amended, "I'm still pissed off about them."

"I've got another one for you," Susan said, matching my scowl. "Rowena who lives about twenty miles that way—" she pointed, glanced at Leo (who nudged her finger about 5 degrees left), then went on "—*that* way, claims that the only way to keep from raising Dragon's Teeth is to spit tobacco on your plants whenever you go past them." She gave another glance at Leo, this one a different sort of query. "I think she *believes* that. I know she *does* it!"

"'Fraid so," Leo said.

"Well, we'll know just what EC to check when something unusual pops out of Rowena's plants, won't we?" I sighed. The superstitions really were adding to our problems.

"Mama Jason," said Susan—with a look that accused me of making a joke much too low for her age level—"How many authentics need tobacco spit ECs to pop up?"

"No joke, honey. It's not authentic species I'd expect under conditions like that. It'd be Dragon's Teeth plain and probably not so simple." I looked from one to the other. "Keep an eye on those plants for me. Anything suddenly flowers in a different color or a slightly different form, snag a sample and send it to me fast!"

They nodded, Susan looking pleased with the assignment, Leo slightly puzzled. At last Leo said, "I'm afraid I've never understood this business of Dragon's Teeth. . . ." He broke off, suddenly embarrassed.

"Fine," I said, "as long as you don't spit tobacco on the ragweed or piss on the petunias or toss the soapy washwater on the lettuce patch."

Susan eyed me askance. I said, "Last year the whole town of Misty Valley decided that pissing on the petunias was the only way to stabilize them." I threw up my hands to stave off the question that was already on the tip of Susan's tongue. "*I* don't know how that got started, so don't ask me. I'm not even sure I *want* to know!—The end result, of course, was that the petunias seeded ladybugs."

"Authentic?" Susan asked.

"No, but close enough to be valuable. Nice little insectivores and surprisingly well-suited for doing in ragmites." The ragmites are native and a bloody nuisance. "And before you ask," I added, "the things they *might* have gotten in the same EC included a very nasty species of poisonous ant and two different grain-eaters, one of which would chain up to a salamander with a taste for quail eggs."

"Oh, my!" said Susan, "Misty Valley's where we get our quail eggs!"

"So does everybody on Mirabile," I said. "Nobody's gotten the quail to thrive anywhere else yet." For Leo's benefit, I added, "So many of our Earth authentic species are on rocky ground, we can't afford to lose a lot of individuals to a Dragon's Tooth."

Leo still looked puzzled. After a moment, he shook his head. "I've never understood this business. Maybe for once I could get a simple explanation, suitable for a bellmaker . . . ?"

I gestured to Susan. "My assistant will be glad to give you the short course."

Susan gave one of those award-winning grins. "It goes all the way back to before we left Earth, Leo." Leo arched an eyebrow: " 'We'?" Susan punched him—lightly—on the arm and said, "You know what I mean! Humans!"

She heaved a dramatic sigh and went on in spite of it all. "They wanted to make sure we'd have everything we might possibly need."

"I thought that's why they sent along the embryo and gene banks," Leo said.

Susan nodded. "It was. But at the time there was a fad for redundancy— every system doubled, tripled, even quadrupled—so just to make *sure* we couldn't lose a species we might need, they built all that redundancy into the gene pool, too."

She glanced at me. She was doing fine, so I nodded for her to go on.

"Look, Noisy. They took the genes for, say, sunflowers and they tucked 'em into a twist in wheat helices. Purely recessive, but when the environmental conditions are right, maybe one one-hundredth of your wheat seeds will turn out to sprout sunflowers."

She leaned closer, all earnestness. "And one one-hundredth of the sunflowers, given the right EC, will seed bumblebees, and so on and so forth. That's what Mama Jason calls 'chaining up.' Eventually you might get red deer."

Leo frowned. "I don't see how you can go from plant to animal. . . ."

"There's usually an intermediate stage—a plant that comes out all wrong for that plant but perfect for an incubator for whatever's in the next twist." She paused dramatically, then finished, "As you can see, it was a perfectly *dumb* idea."

I decided to add my two bits here. "The *idea* wasn't as dumb as you make out, kiddo. They just hadn't worked the bugs out before they stuck us with it."

"When she says *bugs*," Susan confided grimly to Leo, "she *means* Dragon's Teeth."

I stepped in again. "Two things went wrong, Leo. First, there was supposed to be an easy way to turn anything other than the primary helix off and on at will. The problem is, that information was in the chunk of ship's records we lost and it was such new knowledge at the time that it didn't get passed to anyone on the ship.

"The second problem was the result of pure goof. They forgot that, in the long run, all plants and animals change to suit their environment. A new mutation may be just the thing for our wheat, but who knows what it's done to those hidden sunflowers? Those—and the chimerae—are the real Dragon's Teeth."

Leo turned to Susan. "Want to explain the chimerae as long as you're at it?"

"A chimera is something that's, well, sort of patched together from two, maybe three, different genetic sources. Ordinarily it's nothing striking—you'd probably only notice if you did a full gene-read. But with all those hidden sets of genes, just about anything can happen."

"Kangaroo rex, for example," I said. "That one was a true chimera: a wolf in kangaroo's clothing."

"I remember the news films," Leo said. "Nasty."

"Viable, too," I said. "That was a tough fight. I'm still sorry I lost." It still rankled, I discovered.

Leo looked startled.

"I wanted to save 'em, Leo, but I got voted down. We really couldn't afford a new predator in that area."

"Don't look so shocked, Noisy," Susan said. "You never know what might be useful some day. Just suppose we get an overpopulation of rabbits or something and we need a predator to balance them out before they eat all *our* crops. That's why Mama Jason wanted to keep them."

Leo looked unconvinced, Susan looked hurt suddenly. "Just because it's ugly, Leo," she said, "doesn't mean you wipe it out. There's nothing pretty about a rock lobster but it sure as hell tastes good."

"I grant you that. I'm just not as sure about things that think *I* taste good."

Susan folded her arms across her chest and heaved another of those dramatic sighs. "Now I know what you're up against, Mama Jason," she said. "Pure ignorance."

That surprised me. I held my tongue for once, waiting to see how Leo would take that.

"Nothing pure about it," he said. "Don't insult a man who's trying to enlighten himself. That never furthered a cause." He paused, then added, "You sound like you take it very personally."

Susan dropped her eyes. There was something in that evasion that wasn't simple embarrassment at overstepping good manners. When she looked up again, she said, "I'm sorry, Leo. I just get so *mad* sometimes. Mama Jason—"

This time I had to come to her rescue. "Mama Jason sets a bad example, Leo. I come up here and rave about the rampant stupidity everywhere else. Susan, better to educate people than insult them. If I say insulting things about them when I'm in family that's one thing. But I would never say to somebody who was concerned about his kids or his crops what you just said to Leo."

"Yeah. I know. I'm sorry again."

"Forgiven," said Leo. "Better you make your mistakes on me and learn from them than make 'em on somebody else who might wallop you and turn you stubborn."

Susan brightened. "Oh, but I *am* stubborn, Leo! You always say so!"

"Stubborn, yes. *Stupid* stubborn—not that I've seen."

Again there was something other than embarrassment in her dropped eyes. I tried to puzzle it out, but I was distracted by a noise in the distance.

It came from the direction of the loch—something faint and unfamiliar. I cocked my head to listen harder and got an earful of sneezes instead.

"S-sorry!" Susan gasped, through a second series of sneezes. "P-pollen!" Then she was off again, her face buried in a napkin.

Leo caught my eye. He thought the sneezing fit was as phony as I did.

"Well," I said, "you may be allergic to the pollen—" she wasn't, I knew very well "—but I came hoping I'd timed it right to see Loch Moose smoke. And to get in some contemplative fishing—" meaning I didn't intend to bait my hook "—before it gets too dark."

Susan held up her hand, finished off one last sequence of sneezes, then said, "What about your nap?"

"What do you think contemplative fishing *is*?"

"Oh. Right. Get Leo to take you, then. He knows all the best places."

"I'd be honored," Leo said.

We left Susan scrubbing her face. Pausing only to pick up poles in the hallway, we set off in silence along the footpath down to Loch Moose. When we got to the first parting of the path, I broke the silence. "Which way to your favorite spot?"

He pointed to the right fork. I'd figured as much. "Mine's to the left," I said and headed out that way. If Susan didn't want me in my usual haunts, I wanted to know why. Leo followed without comment, so I knew he was thinking the same thing.

"Keep your ears open. I heard something before Susan started her 'sneezing fit' to cover it."

We came to another parting in the path. I angled right and again he followed. Pretty soon we were skidding and picking our way down the incline that led to the otters' playground.

When we got to surer footing, Leo paused. "Annie—now that I've got somebody to ask: will you satisfy my curiosity?"

That piqued mine. "About what?"

"*Was* there such a thing as the Loch Ness Monster? I always thought my mother had made it up."

I laughed. "And I thought my granddaddy had, especially since he claimed that people came to Loch Ness from all over the Earth hoping to catch a glimpse of the monster! I looked it up once in ship's records. There really *was* such a place and people really did come from everywhere for a look!"

He was as taken aback about that as I'd been, then he heard what I hadn't said. "And the monster—was *it* real? Did it look like any of the stories?"

"I never found out."

"Pre-photograph?"

"No," I said, "that was the odd thing about it. There were some fuzzy photos—old flat ones, from a period when *everybody* had photographic equipment—that might have been photos of anything. The story was that Nessie was very shy and the loch was too full of peat to get sonograms. Lots of excuses, no results."

"Smoking too much weed, eh?"

"Lot of that going around," I said. "But no, I suspect Nessie was exactly what granddad used her for—a story. What's always fascinated me is that people went to *look*!"

Quite unexpectedly, Leo chuckled. "You underestimate the average curiosity. I don't think you appreciate how many people stayed glued to their TVs while you folks rounded up those kangaroos rexes. A little thrill is high entertainment."

"The hell it is," I said indignantly. "I oughta know: I do it for a living. *They* didn't get their boots chewed off by the damn things.'"

"Exactly my point," said Leo. "Scary but safe. Elly's kids would be the first to tell you what a good combination that is. They watch their kangaroo rex tape about twice a week, and cheer for you every time."

Some things I was better off not knowing, I thought. I sighed. Turning away from Leo, I got the full view of Loch Moose and its surroundings, which drew a second sigh—this time pure content.

The secret of its appeal was that despite the vast sparkle of sunlight that glittered off it, Loch Moose always felt hidden away—a place you and you alone were aware of.

It took me a while to remember that Leo was beside me. No, I take that back. I was aware that he was there all along, but he was as content as I to simply drink it all in without a word.

Sometime—when we were both done admiring the scene—we headed for the boats, by some sort of mutual agreement. I was liking Leo more and more. For another thing, the whistling of the otters made him smile.

The slope down to the boats was dotted with violets. Most of them were that almost fiery shade of blue that practically defines the species, but once in a while they came out white just for the surprise of it. Some were more surprising than white, though. Almost hidden in the deep shade was a small isolated patch of scarlet.

For the life of me, I couldn't remember seeing any material on scarlet violets. I stooped for a closer look. Damned odd texture to the petals, too, like velvet.

"Pretty, aren't they?" Leo said. "Stop by my place while you're here, and I'll show you half an acre of them."

I stood up to look him in the eye. "Popped up all at once? First time, this year?"

"No. I've been putting them in when I found them for, oh, three years now."

"Oh, Leo. Half of Mirabile thinks everything's going to sprout fangs and bite them and the other half doesn't even take elementary precautions. Never *ever* transplant something red unless somebody's done a work-up on it first!"

He looked startled. "Are they dangerous?"

"Don't *you* start!" Dammit, I'd done it—jumped on him with both feet. "Sorry. I'm still fuming over those red daffodils, I guess."

"Annie, I'm too damned old to worry about everything that flowers red. I took them for what my grandmother called 'pansies.' Much to her disappointment, she never could get any started on Mirabile. Maybe they aren't, but that's how I think of them. I'm going to hate it if you tell me I have to pull 'em out because they're about to seed mosquitoes."

And he'd never forgive me either, I could tell.

"We'll get a sample on the way back, Leo. If there's a problem, I'll see if I can stabilize them for you." He looked so surprised, I had to add,

"Practical is not my only consideration. Never has been. 'Pretty' is just fine, provided I've got the time to spare."

That satisfied him. He smiled all the way down to the edge of the water.

Two hands made light work of launching a boat and we paddled across to a sheltered cove I had always favored. I tied the boat to a low branch that overhung the water, dropped a naked hook into the loch, and leaned back. Leo did the same.

What I liked best about this spot, I think, was that it was the perfect view of the otters' playground—without disturbing the play. It also meant I didn't have to bring along treats for the little beggars. Susan had been feeding them since she was—oh—Jen's age. They'd grown so used to it that they hustled the tourists now.

I didn't believe in it myself, but as long as she didn't overdo it to the point they couldn't fend for themselves I wasn't about to make a fuss. I think Susan knew that too. She had a better grasp of the principles than most adults I knew, aside from those on the team, of course.

The hillside and water were alive with the antics of the otters. Some rippled snake-like through the water. One chased one of those king-sized dragonflies. Two others tussled on the ridge and eventually threw themselves down the incline, tumbling over and over each other, to hit the water with a splash.

Leo touched my arm and pointed a little to the side. He was frowning. I turned to take it in and discovered there was an altercation going on, just below the surface of the water. This one was of a more serious nature.

"Odd," I said, speaking aloud for the first time since we'd settled in. He nodded, and we both kept watching, but there wasn't anything to see except the occasional flick of a long muscular tail, the wild splash of water. A squeal of anger was followed by a squeal of distress and the combatants broke off, one of them high-tailing it towards us.

I got only a glimpse as it passed us by but it seemed to me it was considerably bigger than its opponent. Biggest otter I'd seen, in fact. I wondered why it had run instead of the smaller one.

The smaller one was already back at play. Leo shrugged and grinned. "I thought mating season was over," he said. "So did she, considering how she treated him."

"Ah," I said, "I missed the opening moves."

We settled back again, nothing to perturb us but the otter follies, which brought us to laughter over and over again. We trusted nothing would interrupt that by tugging at our lines.

Shadow was beginning to lengthen across us. I knew we had another half hour before it would be too dark for us to make our way easily back up to the lodge. "Leo," I said, "want me to head in? Your way will be in shadows long before mine."

"Staying the night at the lodge. I promised Elly I'd do some handiwork for her. Besides, I could do with another of Chris's meals."

There was a stir and a series of splashes to our right, deep in the cove. That large otter, back with friends. There were two troops of them in the loch now. I made a mental note to make sure they weren't overfishing the shrimp or the trout, then I made a second note to see if we couldn't spread the otters to another lake as well. The otters were pretty firmly established on Mirabile but it never hurt to start up another colony elsewhere.

I turned to get a better look, maybe count noses to get a rough estimate of numbers. I counted six, eight, nine separate ripples in the water. Something seemed a little off about them. I got a firm clamp on my suspicious mind and on the stories I'd heard all day and tried to take an unbiased look. They weren't about to hold still long enough for me to get a fix on them through the branches and the shadows that were deepening by the moment.

One twined around an overhang. I could see the characteristic tail but its head was lost in a stand of waterlilies. Good fishing there, I knew. The trout always thought they could hide in the waterlilies and the otters always knew just where to find them. Then I realized with a start that the waterlilies were disappearing.

I frowned. I untied the boat and gestured for Leo to help me get closer. We grabbed at branches to pull the boat along as silently as possible. To no avail: with a sudden flurry of splashes all around, the otters were gone.

"Hell," I said. I unshipped the oars and we continued on over. I was losing too much of the light. I thrust down into the icy water and felt around the stand of lilies, then I grabbed and yanked, splattering water all over Leo. He made not a word of complaint. Instead, he stuck a damp match into his shirt pocket and tried a second one. This one lit.

It told my eyes what my fingers had already learned: the water lily had been neatly chewed. Several other leaves had been nipped off the stems as well—but at an earlier time, to judge from the way the stem had sealed itself. I dropped the plant back in the water and wiped my hands dry on my slacks.

Leo drowned the match and stuck it in his pocket with the first. It got suddenly very dark and very quiet on the loch.

I decided I didn't want either of us out here without some kind of protective gear. I reached for the overhang and shoved us back toward the sunlit side of the loch. It wasn't until I'd unshipped my oar again that I got my second shock of the day.

That branch was the one I'd seen the otter twined around. That gave me a belated sense of scale. The "otter" had been a good eight feet long!

I chewed on the thought all the way back to the lodge. Would have forgotten the violets altogether but for Leo's refusal to let that happen. I put my pole back in its place and took the scarlet violet and its clump of earth from him. Spotted Susan and said, "Leo wants to see a gene-read. Can you have Chris send rock lobster for two up to my room?"

"It's on its way, Mama." She paused to glance at the violets. "Pretty," she said, "I hope—"

"Yeah, me too."

"Hey!" she said suddenly, "I thought you were here for a break?"

"How else can I lure Leo up to my room?"

"You could just invite him, Mama Jason. That's what you're always telling us: Keep it simple and straightforward. . . ."

"I should keep my mouth shut."

"Then you wouldn't be able to eat your lobster." With that as her parting shot, Susan vanished back into the dining room. I paused to poke my head around the corner—empty, just as before.

We climbed the stairs. I motioned Leo in, laid down the clump of violets and opened my gear. "Violets first," I said, "as long as we're about to be interrupted."

I took my sample and cued up the room computer, linked it to the one back at the lab. There was a message from Mike waiting. "The daffodils have perked up, so they look good," it said, "and the troops have returned from the Guernsey wars triumphant. We'll call if we need you. You do the same."

"You forgot to say how your hand is, dummy," I growled at the screen —then typed the same in, for him to find in the morning.

The first level gene-read on the violets went fast. All it takes is a decent microscope—that I carry—and the computer. The hard part was running it through ship's records looking for a match or a near match. I could let that run all night while I slept through it.

Susan brought the rock lobster and peered over my shoulder as she set it down. "Mama Jason, I can keep an eye on that while you eat if you like."

"Sure," I said, getting up to give her the chair. Leo and I dug into our lobster, with an occasional glance at the monitor. "Watch this part, Leo," I said. Susan had already finished the preliminary and was looking for any tacked on genes that might be readable.

Susan's fingers danced, then she peered at the screen like she was trying to see through it. Mike gets that same look. I suppose I do, too. The screen looks right through the "whatsis"—as Susan would say—and into its genetic makeup. "Mama Jason, I can't see anything but the primary helix."

"Okay." Neither did I. "Try a match with violets." To Leo, I added, "We might as well try the easy stuff first. Why run the all-night program if you don't have to?" I ducked into the bathroom to wash rock lobster and butter off my fingers.

"No luck," Susan called to me.

When I came out, Leo had disappointment written all over his face. "Buck up," I said. "We're not giving up that easily. Susan, ask the computer if it's got a pattern for something called a 'pansy' or a 'pansies.' "

" 'Pansy,' " said Leo and he spelled it for her.

It did. Luckily, that wasn't one of the areas we'd lost data in. "Oh, Mama Jason!" said Susan. "Will you look at *that*?"

We had a match.

"Leo, you lucky dog!" I said. "Your grandma would be proud of you!"

His jaw dropped. "You mean—they really *are* pansies?"

"Dead on," I told him, while Susan grinned like crazy. I patted her on the shoulder—and gave her a bit of a nudge toward the door at the same time. "You bring Susan a sample of the ones you planted around your place, just so she can double-check for stability. But I think you've got exactly what you hoped you had."

I pointed to the left side of the screen. "According to this, they should come in just about every color of the rainbow. We may have to goose them a bit for that—unless you prefer them all red?"

"Authentic," said Leo, "I want them Earth authentic, as long as you're asking *me*."

"Okay. Tomorrow then," I told Susan. She grinned once more and left.

I sat down at the computer again. Wrote the stuff on the pansy to local memory—then I cleared the screen and called up everything ship's records had on otters.

They didn't eat waterlilies and they didn't come eight feet long. Pointing to the genes in question, I told Leo this.

"Does that mean there *is* a monster in the lake?"

"I can't tell you that. I'm not terribly concerned about something that eats waterlilies, Leo, but I do want to know if it's chaining up to something else."

"How do we find out?"

"*I* snag a cell sample from the beasties."

Again his lips pressed together in that wry way. "May I offer you what assistance I can?" A sweeping spread of the hands. "I'm very good at keeping out of the way and at following orders. I'm also a first-rate shot with a rifle and I can tell the difference between a monstrosity and a monster. I promise no shooting unless it's absolutely necessary."

"Let me think on it, Leo." Mostly I wanted to ask Elly if what he said was true.

He must have read my mind, because he smiled and said, "Elly will vouch for me. I'll see you in the morning."

That was all. Except maybe I should mention he kissed my hand on his way out. I was beginning to like Leo more and more.

After he left, I did some thinking on it, then I trotted downstairs to talk to Elly. I leaned against the countertop, careful not to get in the way of her cleaning, and said, "Tell me about Leo."

Elly stopped scrubbing for a moment, looked up, and smiled. "Like you," she said.

"That good or bad?"

The smile broadened into a grin. "Both. That means he's stubborn, loyal, keeps a secret *secret*, plays gruff with the kids but adores them just the same."

"Any permanent attachments?" It popped out before I knew it was coming. I tried to shove it back in, but Elly only laughed harder at my attempt.

"Why, Annie! I believe you've got a crush on Leo!" Still laughing, she pulled out a chair and sat beside me, cupping her chin in her hand. "I shouldn't be surprised. All the kids do."

I gave one of Susan's patented sighs.

"Okay, okay," she said, "I'll leave off. I like it, though. I like Leo and I like you and I think you'd get along together just fine."

"Is he as good a shot as he claims to be? And as judicious about it?"

That sat her upright and looking wary.

"No panic," I said firmly. "You *have* got something in the loch that I want a look at—but it's an herbivore and I doubt it's dangerous. It's big enough to overturn a boat maybe, but—"

"Are you calling in the team?"

"I don't think that's necessary. They could all do with a break—"

"That's what *you* came for. That's hardly fair."

I waved that aside. "Elly, you should know me better by now. I wouldn't have taken this up as a profession if I weren't a born meddler. And I asked about Leo because he offered to give me a hand." I know I scowled. "Money and equipment I can always get—it's the hands we're short."

"You're going to make off with half my kids one of these days."

I couldn't help it. I jerked around to stare at her. She was smiling—and that laugh was threatening to break out all over again. "Annie, surely it's occurred to you that half those kids want to be just like you when they grow up!"

"But—!"

"Oh, dear. Poor Mama Jason. You thought I was raising a whole passel of little Ellies here, didn't you?"

The thing was, I'd never given it any thought at all. More than likely I just assumed Susan and Chris and Ilanith would take over the lodge and . . .

Elly patted my hand. "Don't you worry. Chris will run the lodge and you and the rest can still drop by for vacations."

I felt guilty as hell somehow, as if I'd subverted the whole family.

Elly gave me a big hug. "Wipe that look off your face. You'd think I got chimerae instead of proper kids! The only thing I ask is that you don't cart them off until you're sure they're ready."

"You'll worry yourself sick!"

"No. I'll worry the same way I worry about *you*. Do I look sick?"

She stood off and let me look. She looked about as good as anybody could. She knew it, too. Just grinned again and said, "Take Leo with you. Susan, too, if you think she's ready. I warn you, *she* thinks she is, but she'll listen to you on the subject."

And that was the end of it as far as Elly was concerned. I walked back to my room, thoughtful all the way.

Damnify knew how I could have missed it. And there I'd been aggravating the situation as well, calling Susan "my assistant," letting her do the gene-read on Leo's pansies. Then I thought about it some more.

She'd done a damn fine gene-read. If she'd heard Leo talk about the pansies, she'd have no doubt thought to try that second as well.

The more I thought, the more I saw Elly was right. It was just so unexpected that I'd never really looked at it.

I crawled into that comfortable bed and lay there listening to the night sounds off the loch and all the while I was wondering how soon I could put Susan to work. I drifted off into sleep and my dreams were more pleased by it all than I would have admitted to Elly.

I woke, not rested enough, to an insistent shaking of my shoulder and opened my eyes to see a goggle-eyed something inches from my face. Thinking the dream had turned bad, I mumbled at it to go away and rolled over.

"Please, Mama Jason," the bad dream said. "Please, I *gotta* talk to you. I can't tell Elly, and I'm afraid it's gonna hurt her."

Well, when a bad dream starts threatening Elly, I listen. I sat up and discovered that the bad dream was only Jen, the nine-year-old. "Gimme half a chance, Jen," I said, holding up one hand while I smeared my face around with the other, trying to stretch my eyes into focus so I could see my watch. My watch told me I'd had enough sleep to function rationally, so I levered myself up.

Jen's eyes unpopped, squinched up, and started leaking enormous teardrops. She made a dash for the door, but by then I was awake and I caught her before she made her exit. "Hold on," I said. "You don't just tell me something's out to hurt Elly and then disappear. Ain't done."

Still leaking tears, she wailed, "It's supposed to be a *secret*. . . ."

Which she wanted somebody to force out of her. Okay, I could oblige, and she could tell the rest Mama Jason *made* her tell. I plopped her firmly on the edge of the bed. "Now wipe your nose and tell me what this is about. You'd think *I* was the chimera the way you're acting."

"You gotta promise not to hurt Monster. He's Susan's."

I did nothing of the sort. I waited and she went on, "I didn't know he was so *big*, Mama Jason!" She threw out those two skinny arms to show me just *how* big, which actually made it about three feet long tops, but I knew from the fingertip to fingertip glance that went with the arm fling that she meant *much* bigger. "Now I'm scared for Susan!"

"What do you mean, he's *Susan's?*"

"Susan sneaks out at night to feed him. I never saw him, but he must be *awful*. She calls him Monster and he gurgles." She shivered.

I gathered her up and held her until the shivering stopped. Obviously all this had been going on for some time. She'd only broken silence because of Stirzaker's panicky report. "Okay," I said, still patting her, "I want you to let me know the next time Susan sneaks out to feed this Monster of hers—"

She blinked at me solemnly. "She's out there now, Mama Jason."

"Okay," I said. "Out there *where?*"

The bellow off the loch cut me short and brought me to my feet. Unlike Leo, I knew that hadn't been part of a dream. I was already headed for the window when the sound came again. I peered into the night.

Mirabile doesn't have a moon, but for the moment we've got a decent nova. Not enough radiation to worry about, just enough to see glimmers in the dark.

Something huge rippled through the waters of the loch. I stared harder, trying to make it come clear, but it wouldn't. It bellowed again, and an answering bellow came from the distant shore.

Whatever it was, it was *huge*, even bigger than the drifted otters I'd seen earlier. Had they chained up to something already? There was a splash and another bellow. I remember thinking Elly wouldn't hear it from her room; she was on the downside of the slope, cushioned from the loch noises by the earth of the slope itself.

Then I got a second glimpse of it, a huge head, a long body. With a shock, I realized that it looked like nothing so much as those blurry flat photos of "Nessie."

I turned to throw on some clothes and ran right into Jen, scaring her half to death. "Easy, easy. It's just me," I said, holding her by the shoulders. "Run get Leo—and tell him to bring his rifle." I gave her a push for the door and that kid moved like a house-afire.

So did Leo. By the time I'd got my gear together, double-checking the flare gun to make sure it had a healthy charge left, he was on my doorstep, rifle in hand.

We ran down the steps together, pausing only once—to ask Jen which way Susan had gone. Jen said, "Down to the loch, she calls it your favorite place! I thought you'd *know!*" She was on the verge of another wail.

"I know," I said. "Now you wait here. If we're not back in two hours, you wake Elly and tell her to get on the phone to Mike."

"Mike," she repeated, "Mike. Two hours." She plopped herself down on the floor directly opposite the clock. I knew I could count on her.

Leo and I switched on flashlights and started into the woods. I let him lead for the time being—he knew the paths better than I did and I wanted to move as fast as possible. We made no attempt to be quiet at it, either. In the dark and short-handed, I've always preferred scaring the creature off to facing it down.

We got to the boats in record time. Sure enough, one of them was gone. Leo and I pushed off and splashed across the loch, Leo rowing, me with the rifle in one hand and the flare gun in the other.

Nine times out of ten, the flare gun is enough to turn a Dragon's Tooth around and head it away from you. The rifle's there for that tenth time. Or in case it was threatening Susan.

A couple of large things rushed noisily through the woods to our far right. They might have been stag. They might not have been. Neither Leo nor I got a look at them.

"Duck," said Leo and I did and missed being clobbered by one of those overhanging branches by about a quarter of an inch. Turning, I made out the boat Susan had used. There was just enough proper shore there that we could beach ours beside it.

"All right, Susan," I said into the shadows. "Enough is enough. Come on out. At *my* age, I *need* my beauty sleep."

Leo snorted.

There was a quiet crackle behind him and Susan crawled out from the undergrowth looking sheepish. "I only wanted it to be a surprise," she said. She looked all around her and brightened. "It still is—you've scared them off!"

"When you're as old and cranky as I am, there's nothing you like *less* than a surprise," I said.

"Oh." She raked twigs out of her hair. "Then if I can get them to come out again, would you take your birthday present a month early?"

Leo and I glanced at each other. I knew we were both thinking about Jen, sitting in the hallway, worrying. "Two hours and not a minute more," Leo said.

"Okay, Susan. See if you can get 'em out. I'll want a cell sample, too." I rummaged through my gear for the snagger. Nice little gadget, that. Like an arrow on a string. Fire it off without a sound, it snaps at the critter with less than a fly sting (I know, I had Mike try it on me when he jury-rigged the first one), and you pull back the string with a sample on the end of it.

"Sit down then and be quiet."

We did. Susan ducked into the undergrowth a second time and came out with half a loaf of Chris's bread. She made the same chucking noise I'd heard her use to call her otters. She was expecting something low to the ground, I realized. Not the enormous thing I'd seen swimming in the loch.

I heard no more sounds from that direction, to my relief. I wish I could have thought I'd dreamed the entire thing but I knew I hadn't. What's worse, I picked that time to remember that one of the Nessie theories had made her out a displaced plesiosaur.

I was about to call a halt and get us all the hell out of there till daylight and a full team, when something stirred in the bushes. Susan chucked at it and held out a bit of bread.

It poked its nose into the circle of light from our flashes and blinked at us. It was the saddest-looking excuse for a creature I'd ever seen—the head was the shape of an old boot with jackass ears stuck on it.

"C'mon, Monster," Susan coaxed. "You know how much you love Chris's bread. Don't worry about them. They're noisy but they won't hurt you."

Sure enough, it humped its way out. It looked even worse when you saw the whole of it. What I'd thought was an otter wasn't. Oh, the body was otter, all six feet of it, but the head didn't go with the rest. After a moment's hesitation, it made an uncertain lowing noise, then snuffled at Susan, and took the piece of bread in its otter paws and crammed it down its mouth.

Then it bellowed, startling all three of us.

"He just learned how to do that this year," Susan said, a pleased sort of admiration in her voice. The undergrowth around us stirred.

Out of the corner of my eye, I saw Leo level his rifle. Susan looked at him, worried. "He won't shoot unless something goes wrong, kiddo," I said as softly as I could and still be heard. "He promised me."

Susan nodded. "Okay, Monster. You can call them out then."

She needn't have said it. That bellow already had. There were maybe a dozen of them, all alike, all of them painfully ugly. No, that's the wrong way to put it—they were all *laughably* ugly.

The one she'd dubbed "Monster" edged closer to me. Nosy like the otters, too. It whuffled at my hand. Damn if that head wasn't purely herbivore. The teeth could give you a nasty nip from the looks of them, but it was deer family. The ugly branch of it anyhow.

A second one crawled into Leo's lap. It was trying to make off with his belt buckle. Susan chucked at it and bribed it away with bread. "She's such a thief. If you're not careful, she'll take anything that's shiny. Like the otters, really."

Yes, they were. The behavior was the same I'd seen from Susan's otters —but now I understood why the otters had chased one of these away this afternoon. They were recognizably *not* otters, even if they thought they *were*. Like humans, otters are very conservative about what they consider one of them.

Pretty soon the bread was gone. Monster hustled up the troops and headed them out, with one last look over his shoulder at us.

I popped him neatly with the snagger before Susan could raise a protest. He grunted and gnawed for a moment at his hip, the way a dog would for a flea, then he spotted the snagger moving away from him and pounced.

I had a tug of war on my hands. Susan got into the act and so did a handful of Monster's fellow monsters.

Leo laughed. It was enough to startle them away. I fell over and Susan landed on top of me. She was giggling, too, but she crawled over and got up, triumphant, with the sample in her hands.

"You didn't need it, Mama Jason," Susan said, "but I've decided to forgive you. Monster thought it was a good game." She giggled again and added impishly, "So did I."

"Fine," I said. "I hate to spoil the party, but it's time we got back to the lodge. We're all going to feel like hell in the morning."

Susan yawned. "I spose so. They lose interest pretty fast once I run out of bread."

"Susan, you row Leo back."

"You're not coming?" she said.

"Two boats," I pointed out Susan was sleepy enough that she didn't ask why I wanted Leo in her boat. Leo blinked at me once, caught on, and climbed into the boat with his rifle across his knees.

By the time we reached the lodge, we were all pretty well knocked out. Jen gave us a big grin of relief to welcome us in. But two steps later we ran hard into Elly's scowl, not to mention Chris's, Ilanith's, and a half dozen others.

"I found Jen sitting in the hall watching the clock," Elly said. "She wouldn't go to bed and she wouldn't say why. Once I counted noses, I discovered the three of you were missing. So *you*—" that was me, of course "—owe me the explanation you wouldn't let her give me."

"There's something in the loch," I said. "We got a sample and I'll check it out tomorrow. Right now, we all need some sleep."

"Liar," said Chris. "Who's hungry? Midnight snacks—" she glanced at the clock and corrected "—whatever, food's waiting."

Everybody obligingly trooped into the kitchen, lured by the smell of chowder. I followed, knowing this meant I wasn't going to get off the hook without a full explanation. That meant no way of covering Susan's tracks.

We settled down and dived ravenously into the chowder. Chris poured a box of crackers into a serving tray. "There's no bread," she said with finality, eying Susan to let us all know who was responsible for this woeful state of affairs.

Susan squirmed. "Next time I'll take them crackers. They like your bread better, though."

"If you'd *asked*," Chris said, "I'd have made a couple of extra loaves."

"I wanted it to be a surprise for Mama Jason." She looked around the table. "You *know* how hard it is to think up a birthday present for her!" She pushed away from the table. "Wait! I'll be right back. I'll show you!"

I concentrated on the chowder. Birthday present, indeed! As if I needed some present other than the fact of those kids themselves. If Susan hadn't opened her mouth, Elly would've assumed I'd taken her along with us, as Elly'd suggested earlier. Glancing up, I saw Elly rest a sympathetic eye on me.

Well, I was off the hook, but Susan sure as hell wasn't.

There was a clamor of footsteps on the stairs and Susan was back with a huge box, full to over-spilling with papers and computer tapes. Chris shoved aside the pot of chowder to make space for them.

Susan pulled out her pocket computer and plugged it into the wall modem. "I did it right, Mama Jason. See if I didn't."

The photo album wasn't regulation but as the first page was a very pretty hologram (I recognized Ilanith's work) that spelled out "Happy Birthday, Mama Jason!" in imitation fireworks I could hardly complain. The second page was a holo of a mother otter and her pups. The pup in the foreground was deformed—the same way the creatures Susan had fed Chris's bread to were.

"That's Monster," Susan said, thrusting a finger at the holo. She peeled a strip of tape from beneath the holo and fed it to the computer. "That's his gene-read." She glanced at Chris. "I lured his mother away with bread to get the cell sample. The otters love your bread, too. I never used the fresh bread, Chris, only the stale stuff."

Chris nodded. "I know. I thought it was all going to the otters, though."

"More like 'odders,' " Leo put in, grinning. "Two *dees*."

Susan giggled. "I like that. Let's call 'em Odders, Mama Jason."

"Your critters," I said. "Naming it's your privilege."

"Odders is right." Chris peered over my shoulder and said to Susan, "Why were you feeding Dragon's Teeth?"

"He's so ugly, he's cute. The first ones got abandoned by their mothers. She—" Susan tapped the holo again "—decided to keep hers. Got ostracized for it, too, Mama Jason."

I nodded absently. That happened often enough. I was well into the gene-read Susan had done on her Monster. It was a good, thorough piece of work. I couldn't have done better myself.

Purely herbivorous—and among the things you could guarantee it'd eat were waterlilies and clogweed. That stopped me dead in my tracks. I looked up. "It eats clogweed!"

Susan dimpled. "It loves it! That's why it likes Chris's bread better than crackers."

"Why you—" Chris, utterly outraged, stood up so suddenly Elly had to catch at her bowl to keep from slopping chowder on everything.

I laughed. "Down, Chris! She's not insulting your bread! You use brandy-flour in it—and brandyflour has almost the identical nutrients in it that clogweed has."

"You mean I could use clogweed to make my bread?" The idea appealed to Chris. She sat down again and looked at Susan with full attention.

"No, you can't," Susan said. "It's got a lot of things in it humans can't eat."

Leo said, "I'm not following again. Susan—?"

"Simple, Noisy. Clogweed's a major nuisance. Mostly it's taken care of by sheer heavy labor. Around Torville, everybody goes down to the canals and the irrigation ditches once a month or so and pulls the clogweed out by hand. When I saw Monster would eat clogweed, I figured he'd be worth keeping—if we could, that is."

"Not bad," said Ilanith. "I wondered why the intake valves had been so easy to clean lately." She leaned over to look at Monster's holo. "Two years old now, right?"

"Four," said Susan. "Only one wouldn't have made much difference. Mama Jason, I did a gene-read every year on them. Those're on the next pages. In case I missed something the first time."

I saw that. The whole EC was there, too, along with more holos and her search for matches with ship's records. There were no matches, so the thing was either a Dragon's Tooth or an intermediate. Just this year, she'd started a careful check for secondary and tertiary helices.

She saw how far I'd gotten in her records and said apologetically, "There's a secondary helix, but I didn't have a clue where to look for a match in ship's records, so I had to do it by brute force."

I handed her the sample I'd gotten from Monster little over a half hour ago. "Here, a fresh sample is always helpful."

She took it, then looked up at me wildly. "You mean me? You want me to keep working on it?"

"You want *me* to work on *my* birthday present?" I might just as well have given *her* a present, the way she lit up.

I yawned—it was that or laugh. "I'm going to bed. But nobody's to go down to the loch until Susan's done with her gene-read."

Elly frowned. "Annie? We've got to net tomorrow or Chris won't have anything to cook."

So there was no escaping it after all. "Take a holiday, Elly. There's something in the loch that isn't Susan's clogweed eaters. Leo and I will do a little looking around tomorrow—armed."

"Oh, Mama Jason!" Susan looked distraught. "You don't think Monster chained up to a *real* monster, do you?" Her eyes squinched up; she was close to tears.

"Hey!" I pulled her into a hug. For a moment I didn't know what else to say, then I remembered the first time Mike had gotten a nasty alternative instead of what he wanted. "I'll tell you just what I've said to Mike: sometimes you have to risk the bad to get the good."

I pushed her a bit away to see if that had worked. Not really. "Listen, honey, do you know how Mike and I planned to spend our winter vacation this year?"

When she shook her head I knew I had her attention, no matter how distressed. I told her: "Cobbling together something that would eat clogweed. If all we have to do is stabilize your monsters, you've saved us years of work!"

I pulled her to for another hug. "Best birthday present I've had in years!"

That, finally, brought a smile from her. It was a little wan, but it was there.

"So here's the game plan. You load the sample tonight while it's fresh, then get a good night's sleep and do the gene-read tomorrow while *you're* fresh. Leo and I will do a little tracking as soon as it's light enough. Everybody else gets to sleep late."

That did nothing to take the worry out of Elly's or Chris's eyes but I could see they'd both go along with it, though they were still concerned somebody might decide the kids should be evacuated. "Elly," I said, "we'll work something out, I promise."

That eased the tension in her eyes somewhat, even though I hadn't the vaguest idea *what* we'd work out. Still, a good night's sleep—even a short one—was always guaranteed to help. With a few more hugs, I stumbled off to bed.

Morning came the way it usually did for me this time of year—much too early. Leo, bless him, was up but quiet. The first thing I wanted was a good look at the otters' playground. That was near enough to where I'd seen the creature that maybe we could find some tracks. This side of Loch Moose got its sunlight early, if at all. Luckily, the day was a good one and the scenery was enough to make you glad you had eyes and ears and a nose.

I stood for a moment trying to orient myself, then pointed. "Somewhere around here. I'm pretty sure that's where I heard it." We separated.

Something that big should have left visible evidence of its passing. The popcorn tree was my first break. Something had eaten all the lower leaves from it and done some desultory gnawing at its bark into the bargain. That was several days earlier, from the look of the wood, so I didn't find any tracks to go with it.

Now, the popcorn tree's native to Mirabile, so we were dealing with a creature that either didn't have long to live or was a Dragon's Tooth suited to the EC. Still, it was an herbivore, unless it was one of those exceptions that nibbled trees for some reason other than nourishment.

But it was *big*! I might have discounted the height it could reach as something that stood on its hind feet and stretched, but this matched the glimpse I'd gotten by novalight.

Leo called and I went to see what he'd found. When I caught up with him, he was staring at the ground. "Annie, this thing weighs a ton!" He pointed.

Hoofprints sunk deep into the damp ground. He meant "ton" in the literal sense. I stooped for a closer look, then unshipped my backpack and got out my gear. "Get me a little water, will you, Leo?" I handed him a folded container. "I want to make a plaster cast. Hey!" I added as an afterthought. "Keep your eyes open!"

He grinned. "Hard to miss something that size."

"You have up to now," I pointed out. I wasn't being snide, just realistic. I'm happy to say he understood me.

I went back to examining the print. It was definitely not deer, though it looked related. The red deer survived by sticking to a strict diet of Earth authentic, which meant I couldn't draw any real conclusions from the similarities. I was still betting herbivore, though maybe it was just because I was hoping.

I was purely tired of things that bit or mangled or otherwise made my life miserable. Seemed to me it was about time the Dragon's Teeth started to balance out and produce something useful.

By the time we mixed the plaster and slopped it into the print, I'd decided that I should be grateful for Susan's clogweed-eaters and Leo's pansies and not expect too much of our huge surprise package.

"Leo, I think it's an herbivore. That doesn't mean it isn't dangerous—you know what a bull can do—but it means I don't want it shot on sight."

"You wouldn't want it shot on sight if it *were* a carnivore," he said. "If I didn't shoot the first beastly on sight, I'm not likely to shoot *this* without good reason."

I fixed him with a look of pure disgust. The disgust was aimed at me, though. I knew the name Leonov Denness should have rung bells but I'd gotten distracted by the nickname.

Back when he was Leonov *Opener* Denness, he'd been the scout that opened and mapped all the new territory from Ranomafana to Goddamn! He brought back cell samples of everything he found, that being part of the job; but he'd also brought back a live specimen of the beastly, which was at least as nasty as the average kangaroo rex and could fly to boot. When Granddaddy Jason asked him why he'd gone to the trouble, he'd only shrugged and said, "Best you observe its habits as well as its genes."

The decision on the beastly had been to push it back from the inhabited areas rather than to shoot on sight. Nasty as it was, it could be driven off by loud sounds (bronze bells, now that I thought of it!) and it made a specialty of hunting what passed for rats on Mirabile. Those rats were considerably worse than having to yell yourself hoarse when you traveled through the plains farmlands.

"If you'd jogged my memory earlier," I said, "I wouldn't have bothered to check your credentials with Elly."

"Annie, I didn't think bragging was in order."

"Facts are a little different than brags. Now I can stop worrying about your health and get down to serious business."

Leaving the plaster to harden, I headed him down to the boats. "Two boats today, Leonov Opener Denness. You stake out that side of the loch, I'll stake out this. Much as I'd enjoy your company, this gives us two chances to spot something and the sooner we get this sorted out, the better it'll be for Elly. Whistle if you spot anything. Otherwise, I'll meet you back here an hour after dusk."

We'd probably have to do a nighttime wait, too, but I was hoping the thing wasn't strictly nocturnal. If it was, I'd need more equipment, which meant calling Mike, which meant making it formal and public.

There's nothing more irritating than waiting for a Dragon's Tooth to rear its ugly head, even if you're sure the head's herbivorous. After all these years, I'm pretty good at it. Besides, there were otters and odders to watch and it was one of those perfect days on Loch Moose. I'd have been out contemplative fishing anyhow. This just took its toll of watching and waiting, which is not nearly as restful. Somewhere in the back of my mind, the plesiosaur still swam sinisterly in Loch Ness.

Susan's odders, as ugly as they were, proved in action almost as much fun as the otters, though considerably sillier-looking. And observation proved her right—several times I saw them dive down and come up with a mouthful of lilies or clogweed.

A breeze came up—one of those lovely ones that Loch Moose is justly famous for—soft and sweet and smelling of lilies and pine and popcorn tree.

The pines began to smoke. I found myself grateful to the Dragon's Tooth for putting me on the loch at the right time to see it.

The whole loch misted over with drifting golden clouds of pollen. I could scarcely see my hand in front of my face. That, of course, was when I heard it. First a soft thud of hooves, then something easing into the water. Something big. I strained to see, but the golden mist made it impossible.

I was damned glad Leo had told me his past history, otherwise I'd have worried. I knew he was doing exactly what I was doing at that moment— keeping dead silent and listening. I brought up my flare gun in one hand and my snagger in the other. Even if it was a plesiosaur, a flare right in the face should drive it off. I couldn't bring myself to raise the rifle. Must be I'm mellowing in my old age.

I could still hear the splash and play of the otters and the odders on either side of me. That was a good sign as well. They'd decided it wasn't a hazard to them.

My nerves were singing, though, as I heard the soft splashing coming toward me. I turned toward the sound, but still couldn't see a thing. There was a gurgle, like water being sucked down a drain, and suddenly I couldn't locate it by ear anymore. I guessed it had submerged, but that didn't do a thing for my nerves. . . .

The best I could do was keep an eye on the surface of the water where it should have been heading if it had followed a straight line—and that was directly under my boat. Looking straight down, I could barely make out a dark bulk. I could believe the ton estimate.

It reached the other side. I lost sight of it momentarily. Then, with a surge that brought up an entire float of lilies and splattered water all over me, it surfaced not ten feet from my boat, to eye me with a glare.

I'd thought Susan's odders were as ugly as things came, but this topped them without even trying. Even through the mist, I could see it now.

Like Susan's Monster, it had that same old-boot-shaped head, the same flopping mule ears, streaming water now. What I'd taken for its head in the glimpse I'd gotten the previous night was actually the most unbelievable set of antlers I'd ever seen in my life, like huge gnarled up-raised palms. What Stirzaker had taken for grasping hands, I realized—only at the moment they were filled to the brim with a tangle of scarlet waterlilies. From its throat, a flap of flesh dangled dripping like a wet beard. It stared at me with solemn black eyes and munched thoughtfully on the nearest of the dangling lilies. The drifting pollen was slowly turning it to gold.

I swear I didn't know whether to laugh or to cry.

For a moment, I just stared, and it stared back, looking away only long enough to tilt another lily into its mouth. Then I remembered what I was there for and raised the snagger. I got it first try, snapped the snagger to retrieve.

The thing jerked back, glared, then let out a bellow that Mike must have heard back in the lab. It started to swim closer.

"BACK OFF!" I bellowed. Truthfully, I didn't think it was angered, just nosy, but I didn't want to find out the hard way. I raised the flare gun.

From the distance came the sound of splashing oars. "Annie!" Leo yelled, "I'm coming. Hang on!"

The creature backpedaled in the water and cocked its head, lilies and all, toward the sound of Leo's boat. Interested all over again, it started that way at a very efficient paddle. I got a glimpse of a hump just at the shoulders, followed by the curve of a rump, followed by a tiny flop of tail like a deer's. The same view Pastides had gotten, no doubt.

Suddenly, from the direction of Leo's boat there came the clamor of a bell. The creature back-pedaled again, ears twitching.

With a splash of utter panic, the creature turned around in the water, dived for cover, and swam for shore. I could hear it crash into the undergrowth even over the clanging of the bell.

"Enough, Leo, enough! It's gone!" He shut up with the bell and we called to each other until he found me through the mist. I'm sorry to say by the time he pulled alongside, I was laughing so hard there were tears streaming down my cheeks.

Leo's face—what I could see of it—went through about three changes of expression in as many seconds. He laid aside his bell—it was a big bronze beastly-scarebell—and sighed with relief. He too was gold from all the pollen.

I wiped my eyes and grinned at him. "I wish I could say, 'Saved by the bell,' but the thing wasn't really a danger. Clumsy maybe. Possibly aggressive if annoyed, but—" I burst into laughter again.

Leo said amiably, "I'm sure you'll tell me about it when you get your breath back."

I nodded. Pulling in the sample the snagger had caught, I waved him toward the shore. When we were halfway up the hill to the lodge, I said, "Please, Leo, don't ask until I can check my sample."

He spread his hands. "At least I know it's not a plesiosaur."

I had the urge again—and found the laughter had worn down to hiccupping giggles.

When we got to the lodge, I didn't have to yell for them—we got surrounded the moment we hit the porch. Elly did a full-body check on both of us, which meant she wound up as pollen-covered as we were.

"Susan," I said through the chaos of a dozen questions at once, "run that for me. Let's see what we've got." I held out the sample.

"Me?" Susan squeaked.

"You," I said. I took Leo's arm, well above the rifle, and said, "We want some eats, and then I want to see Susan's results from this morning."

I cued the computer over a bowl of steaming chowder, calling up the odder sample Susan had been working on. She'd found some stuff in the twists all right.

All the possibilities were herbivorous though—and I was betting that one of them would match my silly-looking friend in the loch. I giggled again, I'm afraid. I had a pretty good idea what we were dealing with, but I had to be *sure* before I let those kids back out on the loch.

By the time we'd finished our chowder, Susan had come charging down the stairs. She punched up the results on my monitor—she was not just fast, she was *good*.

I called up ship's records and went straight to my best guess. At a glance, we had a match but I went through gene by gene and found the one drift.

"It's a match!" Ilanith crowed from behind me. "First try, too, Mama Jason!"

Everybody focused on the monitor. "Look again, kiddo. Only ninety-nine percent match." I pointed out the drifted genes. "Those mean it can eat your popcorn trees without so much as a stomach upset."

Ilanith said, "That's okay with me. Elly? Do you mind?"

"I don't know," Elly said. "What *is* it, Annie? Can we live with it?"

I called up ship's records on the behavior patterns of the authentic creature and moved aside to let Elly have a look. "I suspect you'll all have to carry Leo's secret weapon when you go down to the loch to fish or swim, but other than that I don't see much of a problem."

Leo thumped me on the back. "Damn you, woman, what *is* it?"

Elly'd gotten a film that might have been my creature's twin. She looked taken aback at first, then she too giggled. "That's the silliest thing I've seen in years! Come on, Annie, *what is it?*"

"Honey, Loch Moose has got its first moose."

"No!" Leo shouted—but he followed it with a laugh as he crowded in with the rest to look at the screen.

Only Susan wasn't laughing. She caught my hand and pulled me down to whisper, "Will they let us keep it if it's only ninety-nine percent? It's not *good* for anything, like the odders are."

I patted her hand. "It's good for a laugh. I say it's a keeper." I was not about to let this go the way of the kangaroo rex.

"Now I understand why I found her in that state," Leo was saying. He pointed accusingly at me. "This woman was laughing so hard she could scarcely catch her breath."

"You didn't see the damn thing crowned with waterlilies and chewing on them while it contemplated the oddity in the boat. You'd have been as helpless as I was."

"Unbelievable," he said.

"Worse," I told him, "in this case, seeing isn't believing. I still can't believe in something like *that*. The mind won't encompass it."

He laughed at the screen, then again at me. "Maybe that accounts for your granddaddy's monster. It was so silly-looking anybody who saw it wouldn't believe his own eyes."

I couldn't help it—I kissed him on the cheek. "Leo, you're a genius!"

He squeaked like Susan. "Me? What did *I* do?"

"Elly," I said, "congratulations! You now have the only lodge on Mirabile with an *Earth authentic* Loch Ness monster." I grinned at Susan, who caught on immediately. I swear her smile started at the mouth and ran all the way down to her toes.

Feeling rather smug, I went on, "Leo will make bells so your lodgers can scare it away if it gets too close to them, won't you, Leo?"

"Oh!" said Leo. He considered the idea. "You know, Annie, it might just work. If everybody went to Loch Ness to try to get a glimpse of the monster, maybe they'll come *here*, too. Scary but safe."

"Exactly." I fixed him with a look. "Now how do we go about it?"

He grinned. "We follow our family traditions: we tell stories."

"You think if I hang around for a week or so that'll make it a safe monster?"

"Yeah, I think so."

"Good," I said. "Susan? What's the verdict? Are you going off to the lab? If I'm going to stay here, *somebody*'ll have to help Mike coddle those red daffodils."

No squeak this time. Her mouth dropped open but what came out was, "Uh, yes. Uh, Elly?"

Elly nodded with a smile, sad but proud all in one.

So while they bustled about packing, I had a chance to read through all the material in ship's records on both moose and Nessie. By the time they were ready to leave for town, I had a pretty good idea of our game plan. I sent Susan off with instructions to run a full gene-read on both creatures.

Brute force on the moose, to make sure it wouldn't chain up to something bigger and nastier.

Then we co-opted the rest of Elly's kids. Leo gave each of them a different version of our monster tale to tell.

Jen, I thought, did it best. She got so excited when she told it that her eyes popped and she got incoherent, greatly enhancing the tale of how Leonov Opener Denness had saved Annie Jason Masmajean from the monster in Loch Moose.

Leo brought bells from his workshop. They'd been intended to keep beast-lies away in the northern territory but there was no reason they wouldn't do just as good a job against a monster that was Earth authentic.

Two days later, the inn was full of over-nighters—much to Elly's surprise and delight—all hoping for a glimpse of the Loch Moose monster.

In my room, late night and by novalight, Leo got his first peek at the creature. Once again it was swimming in the loch. He stared long and hard out the window. After a long moment, he remembered the task we'd set ourselves. "Should I wake the rest of the lodgers, do you think?"

"No," I said, "you just tell them about it at breakfast. Anybody who doesn't see it tonight will stay another night, hoping."

"You're a wicked old lady."

I raised Ilanith's camera to the window. "Yup," I said, and, twisting the lens deliberately out of focus, I snapped a picture.

"Hope that didn't come out well," I said.

—for Chip and Beth

BRIAN STABLEFORD

The Magic Bullet

Here's an intense and frightening look at a chilling—and chillingly possible—escalation in the age-old War of the Sexes, one that may be just around the corner . . .

One of the most respected as well as one of the most prolific British SF writers, Brian Stableford is the author of more than thirty books, including *Cradle of the Sun, The Blind Worm, Days of Glory, In the Kingdom of the Beasts, Day of Wrath, The Halcyon Drift, The Paradox of the Sets,* and *The Realms of Tartarus.* His nonfiction books include *The Sociology of Science Fiction* and, with David Langford, *The Third Millennium: A History of the World A.D. 2000–3000.* His most recent book is the acclaimed novel *The Empire of Fear.* His stories "The Man Who Loved the Vampire Lady" and "The Growth of the House of Usher" were both in our Sixth Annual Collection. A biologist and sociologist by training, Stableford lives in Reading, England.

▼

The Magic Bullet

BRIAN STABLEFORD

Lisa had never before had such a strange feeling when going out on a case. She hadn't expected to be called out on any more cases. She was due for retirement in a matter of weeks, having nearly reached her sixtieth birthday, and had been desk-anchored for the best part of two years.

This wasn't exactly a case, though. The call she'd received hadn't made her position entirely clear, but she was not to be part of the forensic team examining the scene. She would be, in essence, an advisor—perhaps best described as an expert witness. She had special knowledge of both the place and the victim. She had been a student in the Applied Genetics Department herself, nearly forty years before, and she'd visited it many times since for purely social reasons. She knew Morgan Miller as well as anyone did, though that wasn't saying a great deal.

Had it just been a police matter the invitation would have been couched in more respectful terms, but it wasn't. Although Miller hadn't been working directly for the Ministry of Defence, any attempt to sabotage research in genetic engineering was construed as a hazard to National Security. Men from the Ministry would be in control, and they would want to question her.

She wasn't looking forward to discussing her relationship with Morgan Miller—it had been part of her private life for far too long, and had never before touched her work as a police scientist.

They hadn't told her over the phone whether anything had happened to Miller—they'd said that they were still trying to make contact with him. She inferred, though, that something had. Whatever the true extent of this affair turned out to be, it surely wouldn't stop with arsonous assault on Morgan Miller's mice.

When she thought of it like that, it seemed simply absurd; firebombing a thousand mice was one of the most ridiculous crimes imaginable. The apparent stupidity of it, though, was sinister. Miller's mice had been breeding away, generation after generation, for nearly four decades, undisturbed and unconsidered by anyone else except Miller himself. Now, it seemed, they had become important enough to be worth destroying. Lisa found that thought profoundly disturbing. It suggested that Morgan Miller had been keeping secrets from her.

One secret, anyhow.

She didn't like that idea. It hurt her pride. It might also make her look stupid to the Men from the Ministry, which was bad from a personal point of view, and bad because of her position in the police force. It was little consolation to know that Morgan Miller had always been, by nature, a very secretive man—a man who liked to be a law unto himself.

The scene, when she got there, was chaotic. The fire was out, but the firemen were still wandering around, and the mess they had made was awful. There was wreckage everywhere, and stinking foam soaked the walls and the floor. The forensic team had already moved in, and they acknowledged her arrival with embarrassed nods of recognition. The only other familiar face was the caretaker, Tommy, who had been in the job for twenty years, and knew her as an occasional caller. Now, she obviously seemed to him a sympathetic figure—a possible ally against the uniformed officers and the slings and arrows of outrageous fortune. The mournful look he gave her was a faint but heart-rending echo of her own feelings.

"Hell, Miss Friemann," he said, desolately. "That's his whole damn *life*. What in the world is he going to *do*?"

He always called her "Miss," never "Doctor" (let alone "Superintendent," which was her theoretical rank as a senior police scientist). She didn't mind in the least—she felt that she was a partner in the tragedy, not just a part of the bureaucracy of investigation.

Lisa looked around at the blasted cages: the smashed glass, the twisted wire, the shards of plastic: everything blackened, the odour of a thousand roasted mice mingling with the last traces of the acrid smoke and the vapour from the slimy foam.

"Did you try to call him?" asked Lisa. It was four in the morning, and Professor Miller ought to be tucked up safely in his lonely bed, though she was rather afraid that he wasn't.

"He doesn't answer his phone," said Tommy, sadly.

"Is he away?"

"Not that I know of," the old man replied, still shaking his head in disbelief. "Why, Miss. . . ?"

"Who else did you try? Did you manage to contact Stella?" Stella Filisetti was Miller's latest research fellow. Lisa presumed that Miller had been conducting a desultory affair with her, in parallel with the desultory affair which he had been conducting with Lisa. It tended to be his habit. Lisa didn't mind—not in a strictly jealous fashion—but she couldn't help wondering whether Stella was in on the secret that had made Morgan Miller a target.

"I phoned her right after I called the fire brigade, but she didn't answer. I'm sorry, Miss—maybe I should've called you, too, but I don't have your number. I didn't know at first it was a police matter. All I saw was the smoke. I phoned the brigade right away, then the Professor and Dr. Filisetti. Then I came to see if there was anythin' to be done. Not a damn thing, Miss. Couldn't get past the door. Saw no one. Sorry."

The fire chief, who recognized Lisa from way back, came over to tell her that it had been a well-made bomb, with explosives as well as the incendiary material. Someone had certainly intended to make a mess. Lisa let him finish before telling him that she wasn't officially in charge. She would have liked to put some questions to the uniformed men, and to her own team, but had to be careful of protocol, and decided to wait for a more convenient moment.

The heavy mob arrived, in dark raincoats that were meant to be unobtrusive, but seemed as distinctive as any uniform. Lisa had some contact with the Ministry on a regular basis, but she didn't know these men, and didn't even know what cryptic initials would be used to identify their Department.

It was easy enough to work out why they'd involved themselves so quickly. When someone tried to destroy the work of an experimental scientist, the most likely reason was that he'd discovered something which it was to someone's advantage to know. Commercial advantage might be the relevant issue—commercial concerns had motivated many a firebomb in the past—but where genetic engineers were concerned, the Ministry was always anxious, always sensitive.

One man—a tall, dapper individual in his fifties—introduced himself to Lisa as Peter Smith. It had to be true; no one used Smith as a *nom de guerre* any more. It was utterly *passé*.

"We may have to warn your people off this one, Dr. Friemann," said Smith. He was trying, but not too hard, to sound apologetic. "It could be our baby."

"Have you found Miller?" asked Lisa, not wanting to get involved in a discussion about jurisdiction.

"Not yet. Your people and mine have already gone to his home. I'm on the way there myself—I came here to collect you. We understand that you knew Professor Miller well and could tell us something about his work."

"Stella Filisetti could tell you more."

"We haven't been able to locate her yet."

Lisa took this to imply that Stella Filisetti was suspect number one, but she didn't pursue the point.

* * *

Lisa let Smith guide her out of the lab, and back down to the car park, where a black Renault was waiting for them. The Ministry didn't like to use Japanese cars.

It wasn't far to Morgan Miller's house—the Professor liked to be able to walk to work. Lisa had been there many times before; Miller had lived in the same place throughout the years that she'd known him. It was a big house, with a small but lushly overgrown garden, and ivy crawling all over the walls. It looked horribly decrepit in the cold grey light of dawn, but it always had. It had been built at the very end of the nineteenth century, more than a hundred and fifty years ago, and no amount of regular patching-up could conceal the fact that it was ancient. Miller must have bought it soon after the turn of the Millennium.

As Lisa got out of the car and walked to the door she tried to remember how old Morgan Miller was. She added it up, and made it seventy-seven, give or take a year. It was a wonder he was still working, but the University wouldn't force him to retire. He'd been trained during the golden age of genetic engineering, before the greenhouse crisis and the energy drought and the Great Economic Collapse. His skills were worth retaining, even though he'd never really fulfilled his early potential as a researcher. He'd won no prizes, had made no breakthrough to fame. He was just the eccentric man with the mice: an institution; a legend in his own lifetime.

There was a uniformed inspector waiting on the threshold—waiting, obviously, for Peter Smith. Lisa's heart sank as the inspector caught her eye and looked up, indicating that she should follow his gaze. One of the first-floor windows was doubly spider-webbed with cracks where two bullets had gone through it. Smith nodded to the waiting policeman, and the door was opened for him. Lisa followed him in, knowing what they were going to find.

It wasn't as bad as she expected. He wasn't dead. Both bullets had hit, but neither wound was fatal. He had bled all over the bed, but he was still breathing. It wasn't difficult to work out where the bullets had come from: a roof over the road. The mobile hospital arrived less than a minute after the Renault, and the duty surgeon moved past them, clearing the room while the support staff erected a sterile tent.

Lisa, with an entire career of examining corpses behind her, was by no means squeamish. To see someone you've known all your life go under the knife is hard for anybody, though. She felt frozen up inside, too stunned to begin thinking seriously about the questions that came into her mind. She knew, though, that Peter Smith would soon be directing those questions at her. The fact that she didn't have the ghost of an answer was unexpectedly distressing. Morgan Miller had been shot, and she—his friend, lover and supposed confidante—couldn't begin to guess why.

She sat down in an armchair that she remembered only too well, in the room he used as a study, and stared at the mute screen of the word-processor on the desk. Smith was still talking to the men outside, in the hallway, and she relaxed into the moment's respite, letting her eyes roam over the disc library that filled two walls of the study. Thirty thousand discs, Miller had boasted to her. His own notes and records filled several hundred; the rest was all published stuff—journals, textbooks, reports, theses. There was no fiction, no light relief. For that, he watched broadcast TV or bought video-tapes. He had once told her, unashamedly, that he had never read a novel since leaving school.

It didn't take long for the Men from the Ministry to catch up with the state of play. They had no real witnesses to question, but they had Lisa. From their point of view, *she* was their only lead, until they could find Stella Filisetti—which might well take some time, if she really was involved. If she was, she was obviously not alone. The firebomb and the shooting presumably had different perpetrators. Lisa knew that one plus one added up to a conspiracy, and that Mr. Smith from the Ministry was going to be worried about it.

Amazingly, Smith—who was still being scrupulously polite—made her a cup of tea.

"While we wait," he said evenly, "I'd be obliged if you could tell me all that you can about Professor Miller's work. We have no file, you see, and I understand that you . . . ?" He left the sentence dangling, with polished discretion.

"I knew him socially," said Lisa. "We did talk about his work—but all his records are here. They could tell you far more than I."

Smith let his own gaze travel over the serried ranks of discs. "In time," he said, "we can have a team go through them. But we need to act in the meantime, and we need everything you can give us, as I'm sure you understand. Had he any enemies?"

"He had one," replied Lisa, levelly. "But I haven't the slightest idea who or why. I assure you that I'm not being uncooperative. I really don't know."

Smith smiled, weakly. "You know more than we do," he pointed out. "Suppose you tell me just what kind of man he was?"

Lisa sipped tea, and wondered what the answer to that question really was.

"I'll tell you what I can," she promised. "I want to work it out in my own mind, too. He was a friend of mine. A very good friend."

Smith smiled at her—not knowingly, but smoothly, and she realized that she wasn't *just* a witness. Until they had checked her file very carefully, she was suspect number two.

Clearly, even the Men from the Ministry always began their investigations with *cherchez la femme*.

Brian Stableford

* * *

"I suppose it was unusual in those days," said Lisa, "for a student of
biology to get a police scholarship. But police work and forensic science were
becoming ever more intricately involved with one another, and identification
by gene-typing was on its way to becoming standard. Most of the police
scholarships were going to computer scientists, because computer-related
crime was seen as the boom area. I suppose I was interested in Applied
Genetics first and police work second, and it was really a way of financing
my studies that made me take up the police scholarship.

"Before the Crash there was a flood of research money for all aspects of
applied genetics. Genetic engineering of bacteria and plants was already
making an economic impact on food-production, and there was intense
interest in the possibility of engineering animals for meat production. We
could see the energy crisis coming, of course, and the rise in sea level due
to the greenhouse effect had already begun. Everyone knew that the entire
world agricultural system was on the brink, and the developed nations all
wanted to make progress in factory farming, to take food production out of
the fields. So the Department, in the days when I was a student here, was
heavily committed to the development of techniques for animal engineering.

"Morgan Miller, in those days, was in the very forefront of his profession.
His mice have become a bit of a joke over the years, but at that time animal
engineering was all the rage. What the engineers were learning to do to mice
was just the first step toward engineering pigs, cattle—and it was all the more
exciting because of the difficulties."

"Don't get too technical," Smith warned. "I'm no expert."

"Bacteria and plants are easy to engineer," Lisa explained, "because they
can reproduce asexually. You can only introduce new genes into a very small
number of bacterial cells in a culture, but if you introduce a gene conferring
immunity to a particular antibiotic you can easily isolate the transformed
cells and obtain a pure culture which multiplies very rapidly. Plants produce
vast quantities of seed, and it's not difficult to inject new genetic material
into the seeds—when they develop you only need one usefully transformed
plant, because you can then clone it easily.

"Transforming mammals is a very different mater: mammals produce
relatively few egg-cells, which are fairly delicate. If you extract them from
an ovary, fertilize them in *vitro*, and then pump new DNA into them you
spoil nine hundred and ninety-nine out of a thousand, and even the odd
one that begins to develop usually aborts very quickly. Producing a transformed organism is extremely difficult.

"Several people in the Department, including Miller, were trying to solve
this problem. They were trying to find a way of getting new DNA into a
mammalian egg-cell *without* having to remove it from its ovary. They were
trying to create artificial viruses which would seek out and invade egg-cells,
while leaving ordinary cells alone, integrating their DNA with the chro-

510

mosomes of the eggs. They called these artificial viruses MB viruses—MB stands for "magic bullet." They hoped that once the basic techniques were proven, they could rapidly move on from experimental animals to real practical applications.

"The MB viruses weren't too difficult to develop, though it wasn't easy equipping them to infect egg-cells alone. But egg-cells *are* differentiated within the body by biochemical markers, which can be used to trigger the viruses. I don't know the very intimate details, because it wasn't specifically my field. Professor Miller wasn't my teacher, once I got beyond the elementary stages—he was a friend.

"I know that Morgan's research ran into problems, though, after the development of the MB viruses. It's all very well to transform the egg-cells inside a female mouse; you still have to turn those egg-cells into new mice, and you still have a dreadful wastage rate. The vast majority of the female mice that Morgan shot with his magic bullets simply turned up sterile, because the transformed ova weren't compatible with ordinary sperm. On the very rare occasions when a transformed mouse *was* born, it was no use—you can't take cuttings from a live mouse the way you can from a plant. In order to breed you need two mice of opposite sexes with identical transformations—a real billion-to-one shot.

"So the research became blocked. Gradually, over the years, a lot of workers abandoned the whole line as a blind alley, but Morgan wouldn't give up. By degrees, he lost his place in the forefront, and I suppose he eventually got left in a backwater. He wasn't bitter about it, though—he really wasn't interested in fame or fortune. His pride wasn't invested in his reputation, it was all tied up in his work. He persisted with his magic bullets: experiment after experiment, generation after generation. Everyone respected him for it, I think, even though they did make sarcastic jokes about it.

"I remember that Miller was always impressed by one strange fact about mammal egg-cells, and that was the way that *nature* wasted them. Male mammals produce sperm throughout their lives, as long as testes are capable of it. By the time a female mammal is born, though, she has all the egg-cells she's ever going to have, and she loses most of them long before she reaches puberty and becomes fertile.

"The peak number of egg-cells is actually reached—oddly enough—in the early embryo, and millions of them die before the female is even born. I can't remember the exact figures for mice, but I do recall that the human female starts off with about seven million egg-cells, in the fifth month of gestation. By the time she's born, she has only two million, and by the time she reaches puberty, she's lost the vast majority of those. She runs out altogether long before the end of her life-span—that's when she reaches the menopause.

"What kind of evolutionary sense that makes, I don't know, but I do know that it was something that fascinated Morgan Miller. He told me once that if only he could transform those millions of cells in such a way as to protect them from degeneration, then he could take the ovaries from a new-born mouse and have a vast population to aim his magic bullets at—and then, if he only had some way of making those embryos develop outside the body, in artificial wombs, he would have the odds on his side instead of against him. That was the idea which seemed to dominate his research during the last twenty or twenty-five years. That was the key, he believed, to developing efficient techniques for the genetic engineering of mammals.

"I can't tell you how far Miller got with his work, but I know he didn't reach the end. He never did produce a pair of true-breeding engineered mice. He didn't even manage to develop the artificial wombs necessary to his grand plan. As far as I know, all he ever managed to do was produce generation after generation of sterile mice, shot so effectively by his magic bullets that they might just as well have been dead.

"He managed, I suppose, half a dozen live births of transformed mice every year, but never a pair. He induced giantism, contrived some interesting alterations of fundamental biochemistry—produced, in fact, some fascinating freaks. But without a way of establishing a breeding population, it all came to seem rather futile."

"But somehow," said Smith, "he discovered something that made him worth killing."

"It looks that way *now*," said Lisa, "but your guess is as good as mine as to what it might have been. The mice are all dead, Miller may not pull through. And his lab assistant . . . ?"

"Think she's the one?"

Lisa shrugged. "Never really knew her. Didn't look to me like a dab hand with a high-powered rifle. Have your people come up with anything in her background?"

He shook his head. "Nothing obvious. Thirty-two years old. Unmarried. Good degree in Applied Genetics, doctorate from Oxford. Came here eight years ago. Politically active, but only with radical feminist groups. Votes Green. No relatives outside the country, in spite of her name. Clean credit record. No significant ties with industry."

"In that case," said Lisa, "it looks as if we'll just have to wait for Miller. If the surgeon can save him, he can give us the whole story. "If not . . ."

Smith didn't look particularly optimistic about that. He obviously didn't expect a man in his seventies to survive two bullets in the torso. His thoughts were already dwelling on other lines of inquiry.

"He never married, did he?" asked the tall man, trying to sound as if he were merely making conversation.

"No," said Lisa. "He was wedded to his work. An essentially solitary man. He liked his relationships casual and occasional. It suited him."

"And you never married either?"

"No," she said, levelly. "Two of a kind. Three, if you count Stella."

"You could say that he used you both," he suggested, calmly.

"Or that we used him. Nobody shot him out of jealously, Mr. Smith. And I doubt if Stella shot him because she was a radfem—even though he *was* a trifle Victorian in his attitude to women. Did you find the weapon?"

He shook his head.

"If he does die," said Lisa, grimly, "I don't think you'll find out why until you've searched those discs with a fine-toothed comb. Time seems to be against you."

"Against *us*, Dr. Friemann. This is a police matter too. And for you, a personal matter. We've checked your record too, as you knew we must. I'm satisfied that you're in the clear, and I know that we can rely on your cooperation. I hope you won't take it amiss when I say that I'd rather it *was* a personal matter."

Lisa stared at him, feeling that she was on the brink of exhaustion. She had become unused to missing her sleep. "It wasn't personal," she said, confidently. "No one had anything personal against the mice."

For once, Smith couldn't contrive a smile. Behind him, the door opened and the surgeon came in. Bluntly, he told them both that Miller would be lucky to last two days—and might only last a matter of hours if he were hyped up with sufficient drugs to make him available for questioning, instead of being allowed to rest.

The Man from the Ministry didn't even glance at Lisa.

"Do what you need to do to wake him up," he said. "We have to have the answers, and we can't wait."

Miller was still inside the sterile tent which the medical team had erected by his bed. A senior paramedic remained when the mobile hospital took off; she was the official death watch. Smith told her to leave the room, and she obeyed without question. He let Lisa stay, though—probably not because he trusted her, but because he thought her presence might help to rally the patient's ailing spirits.

As far as Lisa could judge, the professor's ailing spirits would need all the help they could get. He was very weak. If there'd been any real chance of his making a recovery, the surgeon would never have allowed him to be pumped full of drugs to bring him back to consciousness.

Smith didn't waste any time. "Professor Miller," he said, "we need to know who shot you, and why. They bombed your laboratory too. It's all destroyed."

Morgan Miller stared at his interlocutor, but didn't seem to understand. Smith frowned, and looked across at Lisa, appealing for help. She took a gentler line.

"Morgan," she said, softly, sitting down on the edge of the bed. "It's Lisa. Lisa Friemann."

He shifted his gaze to meet hers, and blinked in recognition. "Lisa," he said, faintly. He seemed surprised by the fact that he was able to talk. He paused for a moment, obviously preparing to say something more. Smith tensed, waiting eagerly, but all Miller said was: "It doesn't hurt."

"No," said Lisa, "it won't hurt."

"Bad, though," croaked Miller, "isn't it?"

"Pretty bad," admitted Lisa. "I don't suppose you remember being hit—you must have been asleep."

"Bad dream," he murmured. "Very bad dream."

"You were shot, Morgan. Someone fired from across the street. You were hit twice."

The man on the bed managed a very weak smile. "Magic bullets," he said.

"That's what we want to know," Smith intervened. "Tell us why."

Lisa looked up at the Ministry Man. "Unfortunately," she said, dryly, "I think he was only making a joke."

"Then you'd better tell him," said the tight-lipped Smith, "that we don't have time for jokes."

Lisa returned her attention to Morgan Miller. "Morgan," she said, "who would want to burn the mice? They're all dead, Morgan. All the mice. Who would want to do that?"

A few seconds went by while Miller struggled to digest this information. Then tears came into his eyes, and Lisa knew that she was getting through.

"All dead?" he queried, his voice trembling.

"Burned to death," she said. "All burned. Who would do a thing like that?"

Miller opened his mouth to speak, but no words came out. He had been looking at Lisa, but now he looked beyond her, at Peter Smith.

"Who's he?" he asked. There was a slight catch in his voice because of the tears.

"My name is Peter Smith. I'm from the Ministry of Defence. We need to know why someone might want to steal the results of your work—or to put a stop to it. We need to know what you found out."

"Defence?" repeated Miller, dazedly. At first, Lisa thought that he was simply unable to understand. But then he added: "There isn't any defence."

Lisa imagined the effect that words such as those must have on a man like Smith. All kinds of memories must be coming back to him, of the so-called Plague Wars, which might not have been wars at all, but which wiped out a third of the human race in the early part of the century.

"What . . . ?" Smith began, but Lisa silenced him with an irritated gesture.

"Tell us where to look, Morgan," she said. "Give us the reference. It must be in your files somewhere. You needn't try to tell us. Just tell us where to look."

But Miller turned his head away, and refused to look at either of them. His brow was furrowed, as if he was as deep in thought as the drugs would let him be. Smith opened his mouth again, but caught Lisa's eye and shut it. They waited. Finally, Miller said: "It's hidden. *Nobody* knows."

"Somebody burned the mice," said Lisa, patiently. "Whatever you had hidden, somebody knows *now*. You have to tell us what it is."

Miller moved his head from side to side, still not looking at them. The drugs were inhibiting his motor responses, but they couldn't entirely cut out his agitation.

"Don't try to move," said Lisa. "You have to conserve all your strength. The more time it takes, the more strength you waste. For God's sake, Morgan, tell us *now*, and then you can rest."

But all Morgan said in reply, his words heavy with drug-sodden anguish, was: "Nobody knows. Nobody knows."

"Then you must tell us now," said Lisa, soothingly. "You *must* tell us. You have to tell someone, Morgan. You can't carry secrets to the grave."

Smith frowned at her, obviously uncertain how sensible it was to let Miller know he was dying, but he said nothing. He was apparently content to defer to her judgment.

But Morgan Miller didn't respond to her plea. When Lisa had come into the room she had not been sure that Miller had anything to tell them, but what was happening now was bewildering. She felt herself growing angry— angry because Morgan Miller *was* nursing some secret which he had never shared with her, and which he *still* would not share, even though he was on his deathbed. The security angle, if there was one, did not distress her overmuch; what she felt was a sense of *personal* betrayal.

"Professor Miller," said Smith, sternly, when he saw that Lisa wasn't going to get any reply. "You have to tell us everything. It's absolutely necessary."

Miller looked at him, and curled his wrinkled lip. His eyes seemed very bright. "What will you do?" he asked, hoarsely. "Torture me?"

"What the hell is going *on* here?" demanded Smith of Lisa. "What is he playing at?"

It was Lisa's turn to frown. "We don't understand, Morgan. We don't understand why you won't talk to us. We're trying to catch the people who shot you—the people who bombed the mice. Was it Stella Filisetti, Morgan? Has she any reason to do this?"

Miller tried again to shake his head, and managed to move his right hand from beneath the blanket on the bed. He tried to wipe the tears from his eyes, but he had great difficulty controlling his hand.

"Stella?" he said, more as if he were talking to himself than answering the question. "*Must* be Stella. How . . . nobody knows! *Nobody knows*."

There was a sharp rap on the door, and Smith turned to open it. Lisa couldn't see who it was, nor could she hear what was rapidly whispered. When Smith turned round, though, he was clearly in an agony of indecision. He beckoned her over to the door.

"They've located Filisetti," he said. "She's under observation. We've got to pick her up. We need to find out how many others are involved, nip the whole thing in the bud even if we don't know what it's all about."

"Let me stay here," she whispered. "I think I can get him to explain, if there's time. I stand a better chance alone—if there's anyone in the world he trusts . . ."

Smith hesitated, but then nodded. He crossed swiftly to the bed, leaning over the plastic tent to look at Morgan Miller, who had closed his eyes. There was no way to be sure that he would open them again. Smith turned back, nodded curtly at Lisa, and then left.

Lisa went back to the bedside, and pulled up a tattered old armchair, over whose worn back she had deposited her clothing on so many occasions. She sat down, and now that she was unobserved, she began to weep. She had not wept for many years, and hoped that she never would again.

Lisa would not have said, had she been asked—or even if she had posed the question secretly to herself—that she loved Morgan Miller. She *had* loved him, long ago, but had long since outgrown it, as she had outgrown all passion and almost all affection. There remained, however, a sense in which Morgan Miller was closer to her than any other human being, and he was dying on *their* bed, where an assassin had shot him while he slept —as he almost always did—alone. If this was not an occasion for tears, there could surely be no other.

For several minutes, she was content to let the silence last, to secrete herself within her grief. Then she stood up again, went to the bedhead and removed the bug that Smith had planted on its rear side. She wrapped it carefully in a handkerchief, and put it in her pocket.

"You bastard, Morgan," she said, in a low tone. "You have to tell me. You hear me? You *have* to tell me. I'm surely entitled."

Morgan Miller opened his eyes again.

"Jesus, Lisa," he said, faintly. "They really did it. They really killed me."

"Yes they did," she said, levelly. "It's a miracle you've got the time you have. Whatever it is, someone knows about it. *I* want to know. I've never asked you for anything else. Never. But I want to know, Morgan. *I want to know.*"

Morgan Miller smiled a kind of smile that she had seen on his faded lips a hundred times before—a smile of superiority. She had never liked it. She sat down in the armchair again, and waited.

"Lisa," he said, quietly, "you're *not* going to like it."

"Tell me anyway," she said, in a cold, sardonic tone that *he* must have heard a hundred times before, and probably liked no better. "You wouldn't want to go to your grave keeping secrets from the only woman you ever really loved, now would you?"

"Hell no," he said. "Now how could I do a thing like that to you?" His voice, as he said this, was little more than an icy whisper.

He paused for some time, while Lisa waited, calmly.

Theirs had always been a relationship which had made many demands on her patience and insensitivity.

"It was a pure fluke," said Miller, keeping quite still and relaxed. His voice was faint, but no longer hoarse—his state seemed almost trance-like. "A shot in a million. I've tried to work out the biochemistry, but I never could. The key protein is some kind of controller, like the ones which determine the switching on and off of selected genes in different kinds of specialized cell.

"It was a bullet virus—one of those I adapted specifically to infect oöcytes. It was intended to preserve the egg-cells, cut the wastage rate. It preserved them, after a fashion. It stopped them dying off so fast, so that the infected mice were born with something like ninety per cent of the egg-cell store intact. There was no somatic transformation—at first I didn't think I'd achieved anything at all, except that the oöcytes could be preserved in any infected female. I kept a number of the mice alive, to track the oöcytes through the lifespan. When they reached the right age, puberty didn't happen. No ovulation. The mice were sterile. Seemed even more useless, then, but I kept monitoring, just in case.

"I sectioned a lot of tissue, just to track the rate of degeneration, without seeing anything unusual. The rate was still very slow. Then I caught the anomaly—an oöcyte that had started dividing, forming what looked like a tumour. Not a virgin birth, you understand. It wasn't forming an ordinary embryo, and the new cells looked to be dispersing, like a cancer in metastasis. It looked then as if the virus was a killer, and I kept the remaining live mice under observation to see what would happen. I waited for them to show external symptoms, but they didn't. I waited, and waited, and the damn things didn't die.

"They didn't die at all. Ever.

"Eventually, I figured it out. The oöcytes which were developing were producing new juvenile cells which gradually displaced the maternal cells in the *mother's body*. They were producing new individuals, all right, but not *separate* individuals. As the mother got older she became a mosaic, except that the new cells weren't genetically different: these freak oöcytes were diploid clone-daughters of the original. They were rejuvenating the host body, over and over again. Instead of living the one lifetime programmed into its originating egg-cell, each mouse was living a whole series of lifetimes, cannibalizing her own egg-cells. I'd infected the damn things with immortality.

"You probably remember the old joke about the chicken just being an egg's way of making another egg. DNA has always been immortal; our chromosomes live forever, they just use organisms as a way of swapping their individual genes around. Bacteria and protozoans generally don't bother—their cells just keep on dividing. It only needed a little genetic nudge to put the mouse chromosomes on a new track, so that they express their immortality through a series of individuals who would just grow up to displace one another inside the same body, shedding the aged cells just as a growing snake periodically sloughs its skin.

"I had a complete gene-map of the bullet virus that had done the trick. Its infective capacity was mouse-specific but the active DNA wasn't. I knew that I could tailor a virus to do the same thing to human egg-cells. Two or three misses, maybe, but the problem wasn't difficult. Armed with that gene-map, anyone with a decent lab could do it. But without the map, even knowing that it could be done, it would be impossible. You know how many ways there are to perm four bases into a string of DNA a hundred units long. I knew it would be hundreds of years before anyone else turned up another fluke like it. So I hid the map."

Lisa had listened in silence, not wanting to break the rhythm of his speech, fearing that if the flow were once switched off, it might be very difficult to get it going again. Now, though, Morgan Miller had stopped of his own accord, and he was watching her with his bird-bright eyes, waiting for her reaction, as if challenging her to work out the pattern of his motives for herself.

"You discovered immortality?" she queried. "And you decided to keep it a secret between you and the mice?"

He nodded slightly, but said nothing.

She realized that she had left something out. "You discovered a way to make *females* immortal," she corrected herself. "*Only* females."

He nodded again.

"What have you been doing?" she asked. "Trying to find a magic bullet that would transform sperm-cells the same way? In the interests of fair-play?"

"It wouldn't have worked," he said, softly. "A sperm-cell doesn't have the supporting biochemical apparatus. It's just a bundle of chromosomes. Its genes can only become active after invading another cell. Like a virus, in a way. In biochemical terms, males have always been parasitic on females. When oöcytes can do it on their own, a species doesn't really need males."

Lisa thought about the implications of what Morgan Miller had discovered, and what he had done—or not done—about it.

"How long ago, Morgan?" she asked, eventually.

He tried to shrug his shoulders, but couldn't. "Forty years," he said.

Forty years ago, thought Lisa, coldly. *I was in love with Morgan Miller then, and my body contained hundreds of thousands of egg-cells. Hundreds of thousands of potential lifetimes. And he knew—even then, he knew.*

*   *   *

She had known, of course, that Morgan Miller had not loved her, and that he never would. He would never have given her a child. Why should she be shocked because he had known a way by which he might have made her an elixir of life, and had not even tried?

Whatever happens now, she thought, *it's too late. I'm too old, and there are no more egg-cells left.*

Stella Filisetti, she remembered, was young enough still to be carrying viable egg-cells.

"Why did you tell Stella?" she asked.

"I didn't. Must be cleverer than I gave her credit for. A dozen immortal mice in a population of a thousand, all looking alike. I thought they were well enough hidden even in plain view. She always liked the mice, though—had a curious silly fondness for them. Sentimentality is so out of place in a biologist."

"You bastard, Morgan," said Lisa, levelly. "If she hadn't set you up, I swear I'd shoot you myself." She was surprised, as she said it, how tempted she was. It was odd, in a way, because she felt no white heat of passionate rage. If, as she felt tempted to, she were to rip aside the sterile tent, pick up the pillow and smother him, she would be doing it quite coolly. She knew, though, that there was no point.

"Well," he said, softly, "it's out now. Once she knew there was something hidden, she must have gone through my files *very* carefully. I had too many copies of the map, I guess. Maybe I should have destroyed it, if I really wanted to save mankind." He put a faint stress on the word "mankind," to emphasize that he meant just that, and no more.

"Did you?" asked Lisa. "Want to save mankind, that is?"

He grinned. "I rather liked the world as it was," he said. "In spite of the greenhouse crisis, in spite of the plague wars, in spite of the energy shortage, in spite of the economic collapse. Not a bad world, for one such as I. I'm glad I had no sons, though—Stella's people will make sure that the future's very different."

"Smith's men have found her," Lisa told him. "There's every chance that they'll get the map back, if she hasn't already run off and distributed a thousand copies. I don't suppose she has. The fact that they bombed the lab and tried to kill you suggests that they don't intend making their little discovery public. I think they want to keep it to themselves. Not so sentimental after all, you see."

He grinned again. "So much for sisterhood," he said.

Lisa studied his face carefully. "Why didn't you tell Smith?" she asked.

"Didn't have time."

"Yes you did. You held back. You waited for him to go, and then you told it all to me. Why?"

"Why'd you wrap up the bug?" he countered..

"It was making me self-conscious. I thought I'd like us to have a little privacy."

"I don't like men from the Ministry," said Miller. "My first inclination is always to tell them nothing."

"It seems," observed Lisa, "that your first inclination is to tell *everyone* nothing."

"I told you."

"Forty years too late."

"Too late for *you*, perhaps. But I never thought of you as a selfish person, Lisa. It was something I always admired in you. Authentic altruism. A sense of duty. You've always been my favourite."

Lisa watched him, knowing that he was playing a kind of game. He was teasing her, playing cat and mouse. There he was, on his deathbed, enjoying the idea that the future of the world might be still his to determine, his to play with, his to dispose.

She still felt a little like killing him, but didn't intend to.

Instead, she knew, she would wait, and listen, and see what he decided to do. If he wanted to, he could tell her where to find another copy of his map. If he wanted to, he could die silent, leaving it for the painstaking Mr. Smith to seek out with his fine-toothed comb. She didn't need three guesses to know what Mr. Smith would do with it.

There was a long pause while they watched one another, waiting to find out which one of them would break the silence, and what he, or she, would say.

Agents of the Ministry of Defence arrested Stella Filisetti later that day. Within a matter of hours, thay had made seven more arrests. Following a trial—which was held in secret because of its implications for national security—eight women were eventually sentenced to indefinite imprisonment in an unspecified location.

When Peter Smith returned to Morgan Miller's house the professor was still alive, and he remained alive long enough to repeat all that he had told Lisa Friemann. Smith's men then began a very careful and exhaustively thorough search of Morgan Miller's data-discs, looking for the crucial gene-map.

AVRAM DAVIDSON
The Odd Old Bird

For many years now Avram Davidson has been one of the most eloquent and individual voices in science fiction and fantasy, and there are few writers in any literary field who can hope to match his wit, his erudition, or the stylish elegance of his prose. His recent series of stories about the bizarre exploits of Doctor Engelbert Esterhazy (collected in his World Fantasy Award-winning *The Enquiries of Doctor Esterhazy*) and the strange adventures of Jack Limekiller (as yet uncollected, alas), for instance, are Davidson at the very height of his considerable powers. Davidson has won the Hugo, the Edgar, and the World Fantasy awards. His books include the renowned *The Phoenix and the Mirror, Masters of the Maze, Rogue Dragon, Peregrine: Primus, Rork!, Clash of Star Kings,* and the collections *The Best of Avram Davidson, Or All the Seas with Oysters,* and *The Redward Edward Papers*. His most recent books are *Vergil in Averno,* and, in collaboration with Grania Davis, *Marco Polo and the Sleeping Beauty*.

Here he gives us an affectionate, eccentric, and tasty look at a very odd old bird.

▼

The Odd Old Bird

AVRAM DAVIDSON

"But *why* a canal?"

"Cheaper, more, and better victuals."

"Oh."

Prince Roldran Vlox (to cut his titles quite short, and never mind about his being a Von Stuart y Fitz-Guelf) had "just dropped in" to talk to Doctor Engelbert Eszterhazy about the Proposed Canal connecting the Ister and the Danube . . . there were, in fact, several proposed canals and each one contained several sub-propositions: should it go right through the entirely Vlox-held Fens ("The Mud," it was fondly called . . . "Roldry Mud," the prince sometimes called himself)? should it go rather to the right or rather to the left? should it perhaps not go exactly "through" them at all, but use their surplusage of waters for feeder systems? and—or—on the one hand This, on the other hand That—

"What's that new picture over on the wall, Engly?" Guest asked suddenly. Host began to explain. "Ah," said Guest, "one of those funny French knick-knacks, eh? Always got some funny knick-knacks. . . . The British for sport, the French for fun. . . ." Still the guestly eyes considered the picture over on the wall. "That's a damned funny picture . . . it's all funny little speckles. . . ."

"Why, Roldry, you are right. What good eyes you have."

Promptly: "Don't soil them by a lot of reading, is why. Lots of chaps want to know about a book, 'Is it spicy?' Some want to know, 'Is it got lots of facts?' What *I* want to know is only, 'Has it got big print?' Shan't risk spoiling my eyes and having to wear a monocle. One has to be a hunter, first, you know." He made no further reference to the fact his host himself sometimes wore a monocle.

522

Eszterhazy returned to the matter of canals: "Here is a sketch of a proposed catchment basin—Yes, Lemkotch?"

"Lord Grumpkin!" said the Day Porter.

There followed a rather short man of full figure, with a ruddy, shiny, cheerful face. There followed also a brief clarification, by Lemkotch's employer, of the proper way to refer to Professor Johanno Blumpkinn, the Imperial Geologist; there followed, also, an expression on the Porter's face, indicative of his being at all times Doctor (of Medicine, Law, Music, Philosophy, Science, and Letters) Eszterhazy's loyal and obedient servant and all them words were not for a ignorant fellow like him (the day porter) to make heads or tails of; after which he bowed his usual brief, stiff bob and withdrew. He left behind him a slight savor of rough rum, rough tobacco, rough manhood, and rough soap . . . even if not quite enough rough soap to erase the savor of the others. The room also smelled of the unbleached beeswax with which they had been rubbing—polishing, if you like—the furniture's mahogany; of Prince Vlox, which some compared to that of a musty wolf (not perhaps to his face, though); of Eszterhazy himself (Pears soap and just a little bay rum) and of Professor Blumpkinn (Jenkinson's Gentleman's Cologne: more than just a little). Plus some Habana segars supplied by the old firm of Freibourg and Treyer in the Haymarket—London was a long way from Bella, capital of the Triple Monarchy of Scythia-Pannonia-Transbalkania (fourth largest empire in Europe) but so was Habana, for that matter. "Gentlemen, you have met, I believe," Eszterhazy said, anyway adding, "Prince Vlox, Professor Blumpkinn."

Further adding, "I am sorry that my servant did not get your name right, Han."

Blumpkinn waved his hand. "Calling me by the old-fashioned word for the smallest coin in his native province really helps me to remember a proper value of my own worth.—Ah. *Canal* plans. I hope that when the excavations are in progress you will be sure to keep me in mind if any interesting fossils turn up." It was not sure that Prince Vlox would be able to identify an interesting fossil if one hit him in the hough or bit him on the buttock, but Eszterhazy gave a serious nod. *He* knew how such things were to be done. Offer a small gift for reporting the discovery of "any of them funny elf-stone things as the old witch-women used to use"—they used to use them for anything from dropped stomach to teaching a damned good lesson to husbands with wandering eyes: but now all that had gone out of fashion—should certainly result in the reporting of enough interesting fossils, uninteresting fossils, and, indeed, non-fossils, to provide copingstones for the entire length of the Proposed Canal . . . if ever there was actually a canal. . . .

"And speaking of which," said Blumpkinn, and took two large sheets out between covers large enough to have contained the Elephant Folios; "I have brought you, Doctor 'Bert, as I had promised, the proof-sheets of the new photo-zinco impressions of the *Archaeopteryx*, showing far greater detail than was previously available . . . you see. . . ."

Doctor 'Bert did indeed now thrust in his monocle and scanned the sheets, said that he saw. Prince Vlox glanced, glanced away, rested a more interested glance at the funny French knick-knack picture . . . men, women, water, grass, children, women, women . . . all indeed composed of multitudes of tiny dots, speckles, . . . points, if you liked . . . a matter easily noticeable if you were up close, or had a hunter's eye.

"Yes, here are the independent fingers and claws, the separate and unfused metacarpals, the un-birdlike caudal appendage, all the ribs non-unciate and thin, neither birdlike nor very reptilian, the thin coracoid, the centra free as far as the sacrum, and the very long tail. . . ." His voice quite died away to a murmur, Professor Blumpkinn, perhaps thinking that it was not polite to lose the attention of the other guest, said, "This, you see, Prince Vlox, is the famous *Archaeopteryx*, hundreds of millions of years old, which the sensational press has rather inadequately described as the so-called 'no-longer-missing-link' between reptiles and birds . . . observe the sharp teeth and the feather . . . this other one unfortunately has no head . . . and this one—"

Here Prince Vlox, perhaps not an omnivorous student of paleontology, said, "Yes. Seen it."

"*Ah* . . . was that in London? or Berlin?"

"Never been in either place."

Blumpkinn gaped. Recovered himself. Looked, first amused, then sarcastic, then polite. Eszterhazy slowly looked up. "What do you mean, then, Roldry. 'seen it'? What—?"

Prince Vlox repeated, with a slight emphasis, that he had *seen* it. And he bulged his eyes and stared, as though to emphasize the full meaning of the verb, *to see*.

"What do you—Ah . . . 'Seen it,' seen it when, seen it where?"

"On our land. Forget just when. What do you mean, 'Am I sure?' I don't need a monocle to look at things. Why shouldn't I be sure? What about it?"

Blumpkinn and Eszterhazy for a moment spoke simultaneously. What about it? There were only two known *Archaeopteryx* specimens in the world! one in London, one in Berlin—think what a third would mean! Not only for science, but for Scythia-Pannonia-Transbalkania and its prestige.

Vlox, with something like a sigh, rose to his feet; clearly the subject no longer much engaged him . . . possibly because his own family and its prestige was incomparably older than the Triple Monarchy and *its* prestige. "Well, I'll have it looked for, then. Must be off. Things to do. My wine-merchant. My gunsmith. My carriage-maker. A turn of cards at The Hell-Hole. See if they've finished re-upholstering my railroad car. Tobacconist . . . new powder scales. . . . Can I execute any commissions for you, as they say? Haw haw! Tell you what, Engly, damned if I know what you want with this odd old bird, but tell you what: trade it for that funny French painting." And he donned his tattered seal-skin cap (so that he should not be struck by lightning) and his wisent-skin cape (also fairly tattered, but wisents weren't easy to get anymore), picked up his oak-stick, nodded his Roldry-nod, neither languid nor brisk, and went out into Little Turkling Street, where his carriage (as they say) awaited him. Some backwoods nobles kept a pied-à-terre in Bella in the form of a house or apartment, Prince Roldran preferred to keep a stable and to sleep in the loft. With taste and scent, no argument.

Silence for some seconds. Such was the prince's presence, that his immediate absence left a perceptible hole.

Blumpkinn: What do you say, Doctor 'Bert, is the prince *quite*, [a hesitation] . . . dependable?

Eszterhazy [removing his monocle]: In some things, instantly. He would think nothing of striking a rabid wolf with bare hands to save you. In others? well . . . let us say that fossils are not quite in his line. We shall see. Any kind of fossils from out that way should be interesting. If the old witch-women have left any.

The Imperial Geologist blinked. "Yes . . . if they've left any—Though I suppose . . . imagine, Doctor, they used to grind up dinosaur bones and feed them with bread and oil to pregnant women!!"

"That's what they did to my own dear Mother. Well, why not? Calcium, you know."

The Imperial Geologist (the King-Emperor, Ignats Louis, in authorizing the position, had hoped for gold and, no gold being found, had shrugged and gone out to inspect the new infantry boots)—the Imperial Geologist blinked some more. "Yes," he said. "Well, why not. Calcium . . . I know."

Some years before there had appeared the book *From Ram's Head to Sandy Cape on Camelback, by a New Chum* (Glasscocke and Gromthorpe, No. 3, the Minories, 12/-), and Eszterhazy had translated it into Modern Gothic, as he had its successors, *Up the Fly River by Sail and Paddle*, and *In Pursuit of Poundmaker, plus a General Survey of the Northwest Territories* (available at Szentbelessel's Book House near the New Model Road at two ducats *per* or all three for five ducats, each with eleven half-tone illustrations and a free patriotic bookmark; write for catalogue). From these translations a friendship had developed. Newton Charles Enderson was not really a "new chum," far from it: he was a "currency lad"; and now he was on holiday from the University of Eastern Australia and hoped to explore some more, in the lands of the Triple Monarchy.

There were a number of not-very-well explored (not very well explored by any scientific expeditions, that is; they had all been very well explored by the River Tartars, the Romanou, and by all the other non-record-keeping peoples who had gone that way since the days of (and before the days of:

caches of amber had been found there, and Grecian pottery) the Getae, who may or may not have been close of kin to the ancient Scythian Goths) and rather languid waterways disemboguing into the Delta of the Ister. And New Chum Enderson had wanted Eszterhazy to go exploring with him, in a pirogue. And Eszterhazy had very much wanted to do so. There were several sorts of bee-eaters which had never been well engraved, let alone photographed; skins of course were in the museums, and several water-colors had been made by someone whose identity had been given simply as *An Englishwoman*, long ago; still semi-impenetrably wrapped in her modesty, she had withdrawn into her native northern mists, leaving only copies of the watercolors behind.

"But I am afraid that our schedules don't match. Really I do regret."

New Chum regretted, too. "But I must be back for the start of term."

"And I for the meeting of the Proposed Canal Committee. Well . . . I know that your movements are as precisely dated as those of Phileas Fogg, so just let me know when you'll be back, and I'll give you a good luncheon to make up for your privations. There's a person in the country who's promised me a fine fat pullet, and the truffles should be good, too, so—"

New Chum gave a bark, intended for a laugh, of a sort which had terrified Pommies and Aboes alike. "I'm not one of your European gourmets," he said. "Grew up on damper and 'roo. Advanced to mutton, pumpkin, and suet pud. More than once ate cockatoo—they'd told me it was chook— 'chicken' to you—and I never knew the difference. Still, of course, I'll be glad to eat what you give me, with no complaint. . . . Ah, by the way. Don't depend on me much or at all to identify and bring back your bee-eaters. Know *nothing* of ornithology. Officially I'm Professor of Political Economy, but what I am, actually, is an explorer. Glad to give you a set of my notes, though." And on this they parted.

Two pieces of news. The country pullet would be on hand the next day. Also alas the sister-in-law's sister of Frow Widow Orgats, housekeeper and cook, had been Taken Bad with the Dropped Stomach—did she require medical advice?—an elf-stone?—no: she required the attentions of her sister's sister-in-law. The house, with the help of its lower staff, might keep itself for a little while. "And Malta, who I've hand-picked meself, will cook for you very well till I gets back, Sir Doctor." Malta, thought the Sir Doctor, had perhaps been handpicked so as to prevent the Sir Doctor from thinking of her as a suitable full-time replacement—she was not perhaps very bright—but merely he said, "Tomorrow they are bringing up a special pullet for the luncheon with the foreign guest and it may not look just exactly as the sort they sell here at the Hen Mark in town; so mind you do it justice."

Malta dropped several courtseys, but not, thank God, her stomach; said, "Holy Angels, my Lard, whatsoe'er I'm given to cook, I shall cook it fine, for Missus she's wrote out the words for me real big on a nice piece of pasteboard." Malta could read and she had the recipe? Well, well. Hope for the best. New Chum would perhaps not mind or even notice if the luncheon fell short of standard, but Eszterhazy, after all, would have to eat it, too.

However.

The roof of the Great Chamber did not indeed fall in on the meeting of the Proposed Canal Committee, but many other things happened, which he would hope had rather not. The chairman had forgotten the minutes of the last meeting and would not hear of the reading being skipped, *pro hac vice*, so all had to wait until they had been fetched in a slow hack, if not indeed a tumbril or an ox-cart. Then the Conservative delegation had wished to be given assurances the most profound that any land taken for the Canal would be paid for at full current market value; next, well before the Conservoes were made satisfied with such assurances, the Workingchaps' delegation had taken it into its collective head that Asian coolie labor might be employed in Canal construction and demanded positive guarantees that it would not. Then the Commercial representation desired similar soothing in regard to brick and building-stone—not only that it would not be imported from Asia, but from anywhere else outside the Empire—"Even if it has to come from Pannonia!"—something which the Pannonian delegation somehow took much amiss. Cries of *Point of order*! and *Treason*! and *What has the Committee got to hide*? and *Move the Previous question*! were incessant. And Eszterhazy realized that he was absolutely certain to miss anyway most of his luncheon engagement with Enderson.

So he sent word that the meal was to proceed without him, and his apologies to his guest, and he (Eszterhazy) would join him as soon as possible.

"As soon as" was eventually reached, though he had feared it wouldn't be. As he was making his way out of the Great Chamber he encountered Professor Blumpkinn, almost in tears. "I have missed my luncheon!" said the Imperial Geologist (he did not look as though he had missed many) dolefully. "They have prepared none for me at home, and in a restaurant I cannot eat, because my stomach is delicate: if anything is in the least greasy or underdone or overdone, one feels rising, then, the bile: and one is dyspeptic for days!"

"Come home with me, then, Johanno," said Eszterhazy.

"Gladly!"

One might ask, How far can a pullet go? but the pullet was after all intended merely as garnish to only one course of several; also a cook in Bella would sooner have suffered herself to be trampled by elephant cows rather than fail to provide a few Back-up Entrances, as they were called, in case of emergencies. A singularly greedy guest might become an Untoward Incident in a foreign *pension*: but not in a well-ordered house in Bella: What a compliment! God—who gives appetite—bless the man! and the order would be passed on, via an agreed-upon signal, to bring out one of the back-ups.

Going past the porte-cochère of the Great Hall, which was jammed with vehicles, Eszterhazy held up his hand and the red steam runabout darted forward from a nearby passage; almost before it had come to a stop, Schwebel, the engineer, had vaulted into the back to stoke the anthracite: Eszterhazy took the tiller. His guest, an appreciative sniff for the cedar wood-work (beeswax "compliments of Prince Vlox"), sat beside him.

"Who's *that?*" asked an Usher of a Doorkeeper, watching the deft work with the steering-gear.

"He'm Doctors Eszterhazy, th' Emperor's wizard," said Doorkeeper to Usher.

"So *that's* him!—odd old bird!" And then they both had to jump as the delegations poured out, demanding their coaches, carriages, curricles, hacks, and troikas. None, however, demanded steam runabouts.

"It will not offend you if we enter by way of the kitchen?" the doctor (although his doctorate was plural, he himself was singular . . . very singular) asked the professor.

Who answered that they might enter by way of the chimney. "Cannot you hear my stomach growling? Besides, it is always a pleasure to visit a well-ordered kitchen." Blumpkinn rang with pleasure the hand-bell given him to warn passers-by—the steamer was almost noiseless—and drivers of nervous horses.

"A moderate number of unannounced visits help keep a kitchen well-ordered." Besides, with a temporary cook and a guest with a very delicate stomach, an inspection, however brief, might be a good idea: and, in a few minutes, there they were!—but what was this in the alley? a heavy country wagon—and at the door, someone whose canvas coat was speckled with feathers—someone stamping his feet and looking baffled. "I tells you again that Poulterer Puckelhaube has told me to bring this country-fed bird, and to git a skilling and a half for it! 'Tain't my fault as I'm late: the roads about the Great Chamber was filled with kerritches."

But, like the King of Iceland's oldest son, Malta Cook was having none. "You's heard I'm only temporal here," she said, hands on hips, "and thinks to try your gammon on me!—but you'll get no skilling and a half at this door! The country chicking has already been delivered couple hours ago, with the other firm's compliments, and the foreign guest is eating of it now. Away with ye, and—" She caught sight of Eszterhazy, courtseyed, gestured towards the deliveryman, her mouth open for explanation and argument.

She was allowed no time. Eszterhazy said, "Take the bird and pay for it, we'll settle the matter later.—Give him a glass of ale," he called over his shoulder. Instantly the man's grievance vanished. The money would, after all, go to his employer. But the beer was his . . . at least for a while.

At the table, napkin tucked into his open collar, sunburned and evidently quite content, sat Newton Charles ("New Chum") Enderson, calmly chewing. Equally calmly, he returned the just-cleaned-off bone to its platter, on which (or, if you prefer, whereon) he had neatly laid out the skeleton. Perhaps he had always done the same, even with the cockatoo and the kangaroo. Eszterhazy stared in intense disbelief. Blumpkinn's mouth was opening and closing like that of a barbel, or a carp. "Welcome aboard," said New Chum, looking up. "Sorry you've missed it. The journey has given me quite an appetite." At the end of the platter was a single, and slightly odd, feather. Malta had perhaps heard, if not more, of how to serve a pheasant.

"My God!" cried Blumpkinn. "Look! There is the centra free as far as the sacrum, and the very long tail as well as the thin coracoid, all the ribs nonunciate and thin, neither birdlike nor very reptilian, the un-birdlike caudal appendage, the separate and unfused metacarpals, the independent fingers and claws."

"Not bad at all," said Enderson, touching the napkin to his lips. "As I've told you, I don't know one bird from another, but this is not bad. Rather like bamboo chicken—goanna, or iguana, you would call it. Though a bit far north for that . . . but of course it must be imported! My compliments to the chef! By the way. I understand that the man who brought it said that there weren't any more . . . whatever that means . . . You know how to treat a guest well, I must say!"

Contentedly, he broke off a bit of bread and sopped at the truffled gravy. Then he looked up again. "Oh, and speaking of compliments," he said, "who's Prince Vlox?"

"I see the French picture is missing," said Eszterhazy.

JOHN CROWLEY

Great Work of Time

One of the most acclaimed and respected authors of our day, John Crowley is perhaps best known for his fat and fanciful novel *Little, Big,* which won the prestigious World Fantasy Award. His other novels include *Beasts, The Deep, Engine Summer,* and, most recently, the critically acclaimed *Ægypt.* His most recent book is *Novelty,* a collection. His short fiction has appeared in *OMNI, Isaac Asimov's Science Fiction Magazine, Elsewhere, Shadows,* and *Whispers.* His story "Snow" was in our Third Annual Collection. He lives in the Berkshire Hills of western Massachusetts.

In the intricate, subtle, luminous, and mysteriously evocative story that follows, Crowley examines an eternal and all-encompassing British Empire on which the sun will never be *allowed* to set—unless, that is, something goes very seriously wrong.

▼
Great Work of Time

JOHN CROWLEY

I: THE SINGLE EXCURSION OF CASPAR LAST

If what I am to set down is a chronicle, then it must differ from any other chronicle whatever, for it begins, not in one time or place, but everywhere at once—or perhaps *everywhen* is the better word. It might be begun at any point along the infinite, infinitely broken coastline of time.

It might even begin within the forest in the sea: huge trees like American redwoods, with their roots in the black benthos, and their leaves moving slowly in the blue currents overhead. There it might end as well.

It might begin in 1893—or in 1983. Yes: it might be as well to begin with Last, in an American sort of voice (for we are all Americans now, aren't we?) Yes, Last shall be first: pale, fattish Caspar Last, on excursion in the springtime of 1983 to a far, far part of the Empire.

The tropical heat clothed Caspar Last like a suit as he disembarked from the plane. It was nearly as claustrophobic as the hours he had spent in the middle seat of a three-across, economy-class pew between two other cut-rate, one-week-excursion, plane-fare-and-hotel-room holiday-makers in monstrous good spirits. Like them, Caspar had taken the excursion because it was the cheapest possible way to get to and from this equatorial backwater. Unlike them, he hadn't come to soak up sun and molasses-dark rum. He didn't intend to spend all his time at the beach, or even within the twentieth century.

It had come down, in the end, to a matter of money. Caspar Last had never had money, though he certainly hadn't lacked the means to make it; with any application he could have made good money as a consultant to

531

any of a dozen research firms, but that would have required a certain sub-jection of his time and thought to others, and Caspar was incapable of that. It's often said that genius can live in happy disregard of material circum-stances, dress in rags, not notice its nourishment, and serve only its own abstract imperatives. This was Caspar's case, except that he wasn't happy about it: he was bothered, bitter, and rageful at his poverty. Fame he cared nothing for, success was meaningless except when defined as the solution to abstract problems. A great fortune would have been burdensome and useless. All he wanted was a nice bit of change.

He had decided, therefore, to use his "time machine" once only, before it and the principles that animated it were destroyed, for good he hoped. (Caspar always thought of his "time machine" thus, with scare-quotes around it, since it was not really a machine, and Caspar did not believe in time.) He would use it, he decided, to make money. Somehow.

The one brief annihilation of "time" that Caspar intended to allow himself was in no sense a test run. He knew that his "machine" would function as predicted. If he hadn't needed the money, he wouldn't use it at all. As far as he was concerned, the principles once discovered, the task was completed; like a completed jigsaw puzzle, it had no further interest; there was really nothing to do with it except gloat over it briefly and then sweep all the pieces randomly back into the box.

It was a mark of Caspar's odd genius that figuring out a scheme with which to make money out of the past (which was the only "direction" his "machine" would take him) proved almost as hard, given the limitations of his process, as arriving at the process itself.

He had gone through all the standard wish-fulfillments and rejected them. He couldn't, armed with today's race results, return to yesterday and hit the daily double. For one thing it would take a couple of thousand in betting money to make it worth it, and Caspar didn't have a couple of thousand. More importantly, Caspar had calculated the results of his present self ap-pearing at any point within the compass of his own biological existence, and those results made him shudder.

Similar difficulties attended any scheme that involved using money to make money. If he returned to 1940 and bought, say, two hundred shares of IBM for next to nothing: in the first place there would be the difficulty of leaving those shares somehow in escrow for his unborn self; there would be the problem of the alteration this growing fortune would have on the linear life he had actually lived; and where was he to acquire the five hundred dollars or whatever was needed in the currency of 1940? The same problem obtained if he wanted to return to 1623 and pick up a First Folio of Shake-speare, or to 1460 and a Gutenberg Bible: the cost of the currency he would need rose in relation to the antiquity, thus the rarity and value, of the object to be bought with it. There was also the problem of walking into a bookseller's and plunking down a First Folio he had just happened to stumble on while cleaning out the attic. In any case, Caspar doubted that anything as large as a book could be successfully transported "through time." He'd be lucky if he could go and return in his clothes.

Outside the airport, Caspar boarded a bus with his fellow excursionists, already hard at work with their cameras and index fingers as they rode through a sweltering lowland out of which concrete-block light industry was struggling to be born. The hotel in the capital was as he expected, shoddy-American and intermittently refrigerated. He ceased to notice it, forwent the complimentary rum concoction promised with his tour, and after asking that his case be put in the hotel safe—extra charge for that, he noted bitterly—he went immediately to the Hall of Records in the government complex. The collection of old survey maps of the city and environs were more extensive than he had hoped. He spent most of that day among them searching for a blank place on the 1856 map, a place as naked as possible of buildings, brush, water, and that remained thus through the years. He discovered one, visited it by unmuffled taxi, found it suitable. It would save him from the awful inconvenience of "arriving" in the "past" and finding himself inserted into some local's wattle-and-daub wall. Next morning, then, he would be "on his way." If he had believed in time, he would have said that the whole process would take less than a day's time.

Before settling on this present plan, Caspar had toyed with the idea of bringing back from the past something immaterial: some knowledge, some secret that would allow him to make himself rich in his own present. Ships have gone down with millions in bullion: he could learn exactly where. Captain Kidd's treasure. Inca gold. Archaeological rarities buried in China. Leaving aside the obvious physical difficulties of these schemes, he couldn't be sure that their location wouldn't shift in the centuries between his glimpse of them and his "real" life span; and even if he could be certain, no one else would have much reason to believe him, and he didn't have the wherewithal to raise expeditions himself. So all that was out.

He had a more general, theoretical problem to deal with. Of course the very presence of his eidolon in the past would alter, in however inconsequential a way, the succeeding history of the world. The comical paradoxes of shooting one's own grandfather and the like neither amused nor intrigued him, and the chance he took of altering the world he lived in out of all recognition was constantly present to him. Statistically, of course, the chance of this present plan of his altering anything significantly, except his own personal fortunes, was remote to a high power. But his scruples had caused him to reject anything such as, say, discovering the Koh-i-noor diamond before its historical discoverers. No: what he needed to abstract from the past was something immensely trivial, something common, something the past wouldn't miss but that the present held in the highest regard; something that would take the briefest possible time and the least irruption of himself into the past to acquire; something he could reasonably be believed to possess through simple historical chance; and something tiny enough to survive the cross-time "journey" on his person.

It had come to him quite suddenly—all his ideas did, as though handed to him—when he learned that his great-great-grandfather had been a commercial traveler in the tropics, and that in the attic of his mother's house (which Caspar had never had the wherewithal to move out of) some old journals and papers of his still moldered. They were, when he inspected them, completely without interest. But the dates were right.

Caspar had left a wake-up call at the desk for before dawn the next morning. There was some difficulty about getting his case out of the safe, and more difficulty about getting a substantial breakfast served at that hour (Caspar expected not to eat during his excursion), but he did arrive at his chosen site before the horrendous tropical dawn broke, and after paying the taxi, he had darkness enough left in which to make his preparations and change into his costume. The costume—a linen suit, a shirt, hat, boots—had cost him twenty dollars in rental from a theatrical costumer, and he could only hope it was accurate enough not to cause alarm in 1856. The last item he took from his case was the copper coin, which had cost him quite a bit, as he needed one unworn and of the proper date. He turned it in his fingers for a moment, thinking that if, unthinkably, his calculations were wrong and he didn't survive this journey, it would make an interesting obol for Charon.

Out of the unimaginable chaos of its interminable stochastic fiction, Time thrust only one unforeseen oddity on Caspar Last as he, or something like him, appeared beneath a plantain tree in 1856: he had grown a beard almost down to his waist. It was abominably hot.

The suburbs of the city had of course vanished. The road he stood by was a muddy track down which a cart was being driven by a tiny and close-faced Indian in calico. He followed the cart, and his costume boots were caked with mud when at last he came into the center of town, trying to appear nonchalant and to remember the layout of the city as he had studied it in the maps. He wanted to speak to no one if possible, and he did manage to find the post office without affecting, however minutely, the heterogeneous crowd of blacks, Indians, and Europeans in the filthy streets. Having absolutely no sense of humor and very little imagination other than the most rigidly abstract helped to keep him strictly about his business and not to faint, as another might have, with wonder and astonishment at his translation, the first, last, and only of its kind a man would ever make.

"I would like," he said to the mulatto inside the brass and mahogany cage, "an envelope, please."

"Of course, sir."

"How long will it take for a letter mailed now to arrive locally?"

"Within the city? It would arrive in the afternoon post."

"Very good."

Caspar went to a long, ink-stained table, and with one of the steel pens provided, he addressed the envelope to Georg von Humboldt Last, Esq., Grand Hotel, City, in the approximation of an antique round hand that he had been practicing for weeks. There was a moment's doubt as he tried to figure how to fold up and seal the cumbersome envelope, but he did it, and gave this empty missive to the incurious mulatto. He slipped his precious coin across the marble to him. For the only moment of his adventure, Caspar's heart beat fast as he watched the long, slow brown fingers affix a stamp, cancel and date it with a pen-stroke, and drop it into a brass slot like a hungry mouth behind him.

It only remained to check into the Grand Hotel, explain about his luggage's being on its way up from the port, and sit silent on the hotel terrace, growing faint with heat and hunger and expectation, until the afternoon post.

The one aspect of the process Caspar had never been able to decide about was whether his eidolon's residence in the fiction of the past would consume any "time" in the fiction of the present. It did. When, at evening, with the letter held tight in his hand and pressed to his bosom, Caspar reappeared beardless beneath the plantain tree in the traffic-tormented and smoky suburb, the gaseous red sun was squatting on the horizon in the west, just as it had been in the same place in 1856.

He would have his rum drink after all, he decided.

"Mother," he said, "do you think there might be anything valuable in those papers of your great-grandfather's?"

"What papers, dear? Oh—I remember. I couldn't say. I thought once of donating them to a historical society. How do you mean, valuable?"

"Well, old stamps, for one thing."

"You're free to look, Caspar dear."

Caspar was not surprised (though he supposed the rest of the world was soon to be) that he found among the faded, water-spotted diaries and papers an envelope that bore a faint brown address—it had aged nicely in the next-to-no-time it had traveled "forward" with Caspar—and that had in its upper right-hand corner a one-penny magenta stamp, quite undistinguished, issued for a brief time in 1856 by the Crown Colony of British Guiana.

The asking price of the sole known example of this stamp, a "unique" owned by a consortium of wealthy men who preferred to remain anonymous, was a million dollars. Caspar Last had not decided whether it would be more profitable for him to sell the stamp itself, or to approach the owners of the unique, who would certainly pay a large amount to have it destroyed, and thus preserve their unique's uniqueness. It did seem a shame that the only artifact man had ever succeeded in extracting from the nonexistent past should go into the fire, but Caspar didn't really care. His own bonfire—the notes and printouts, the conclusions about the nature and transversability of time and the orthogonal logic by which it was accomplished—would be only a little more painful.

The excursion was over; the only one that remained to him was the brief but, to him, all-important one of his own mortal span. He was looking forward to doing it first class.

II: AN APPOINTMENT IN KHARTOUM

It might be begun very differently, though; and it might now be begun again, in a different time and place, like one of those romances by Stevenson, where different stories only gradually reveal themselves to be parts of a whole . . .

The paradox is acute, so acute that the only possible stance for a chronicler is to ignore it altogether, and carry on. This, the Otherhood's central resignation, required a habit of mind so contrary to ordinary cause-and-effect thinking as to be, literally, unimaginable. It would only have been in the changeless precincts of the Club they had established beyond all frames of reference, when deep in leather armchairs or seated all together around the long table whereon their names were carved, that they dared reflect on it at all.

Take, for a single but not a random instance, the example of Denys Winterset, twenty-three years old, Winchester, Oriel College, younger son of a well-to-do doctor and in 1956 ending a first year as assistant district commissioner of police in Bechuanaland.

He hadn't done strikingly well in his post. Though on the surface he was exactly the sort of man who was chosen, or who chose himself, to serve the Empire in those years—a respectable second at Oxford, a cricketer more steady than showy, a reserved, sensible, presentable lad with sound principles and few beliefs—still there was an odd strain in him. Too imaginative, perhaps; given to fits of abstraction, even to what his commissioner called "tears, idle tears." Still, he was resourceful and hardworking; he hadn't disgraced himself, and he was now on his way north on the Cape-to-Cairo Railroad, to take a month's holiday in Cairo and England. His anticipation was marred somewhat by a sense that, after a year in the veldt, he would no longer fit into the comfortable old shoe of his childhood home; that he would feel as odd and exiled as he had in Africa. Home had become a dream, in Bechuanaland; if, at home, Bechuanaland became a dream, then he would have no place real at all to be at home in; he would be an exile for good.

The high veldt sped away as he was occupied with these thoughts, the rich farmlands of Southern Rhodesia. In the saloon car a young couple, very evidently on honeymoon, watched expectantly for the first glimpse of the eternal rainbow, visible miles off, that haloed Victoria Falls. Denys watched them and their excitement, feeling old and wise. Americans, doubtless: they had that shy, inoffensive air of all Americans abroad, that wondering quality as of children let out from a dark and oppressive school to play in the sun.

"There!" said the woman as the train took a bend. "Oh, look, how beautiful!"

Even over the train's sound they could hear the sound of the falls now, like distant cannon. The young man looked at his watch and smiled at Denys. "Right on time," he said, and Denys smiled too, amused to be complimented on his railroad's efficiency. The Bulawayo Bridge—longest and highest span on the Cape-to-Cairo line—leapt over the gorge.

"My God, that's something," the young man said. "Cecil Rhodes built this, right?"

"No," Denys said. "He thought of it, but never lived to see it. It would have been far easier to build it a few miles up, but Rhodes pictured the train being washed in the spray of the falls as it passed. And so it was built here."

The noise of the falls was immense now, and weirdly various, a medley of cracks, thumps, and explosions playing over the constant bass roar, which was not so much like a noise at all as it was like an eternal deep-drawn breath. And as the train chugged out across the span, aimed at Cairo thousands of miles away, passing here the place so hard-sought-for a hundred years ago—the place where the Nile had its origin—the spray *did* fall on the train just as Cecil Rhodes had imagined it, flung spindrift hissing on the locomotive, drops speckling the window they looked out of and rainbowing in the white air. The young Americans were still with wonder, and Denys, too, felt a lifting of his heart.

At Khartoum, Denys bid the honeymooners farewell: they were taking the Empire Airways flying boat from here to Gibraltar, and the Atlantic dirigible home. Denys, by now feeling quite proprietary about his Empire's transportation services, assured them that both flights would also certainly be right on time, and would be as comfortable as the sleepers they were leaving, would serve the same excellent meals with the same white napery embossed with the same royal insignia. Denys himself was driven to the Grand Hotel. His Sudan Railways sleeper to Cairo left the next morning.

After a bath in a tiled tub large enough almost to swim in, Denys changed into dinner clothes (which had been carefully laid out for him on the huge bed—for whom had these cavernous rooms been built, a race of Kitcheners?) He reserved a table for one in the grill room and went down to the bar. One thing he *must* do in London, he thought, shooting his cuffs, was to visit his tailor. Bechuanaland had sweated off his college baby fat, and the tropics seemed to have turned his satin lapels faintly green.

The bar was comfortably filled, before the dinner hour, with men of several sorts and a few women, and with the low various murmur of their talk. Some of the men wore *white* dinner jackets—businessmen and tourists, Denys supposed; and a few even wore shorts with black shoes and stockings, a style

Denys found inherently funny, as though a tailor had made a frightful error and cut evening clothes to the pattern of bush clothes. He ordered a whiskey.

Rarely in African kraals or in his bungalow or his whitewashed office did Denys think about his Empire: or if he did, it was in some local, even irritated way, of Imperial trivialities or Imperial red tape, the rain-rusted engines and stacks of tropic-mildewed paperwork that, collectively, Denys and his young associates called the White Man's Burden. It seemed to require a certain remove from the immediacy of Empire before he could perceive it. Only here (beneath the fans' ticking, amid the voices naming places—Kandahar, Durban, Singapore, Penang) did the larger Empire that Denys had never seen but had lived in in thought and feeling since childhood open in his mind. How odd, how far more odd really than admirable or deplorable that the small place which was his childhood, circumscribed and cozy—gray Westminster, chilly Trafalgar Square of the black umbrellas, London of the coal-smoked wallpaper and endless chimney pots—should have opened itself out so ceaselessly and for so long into huge hot places, sub-continents where rain never fell or never stopped, lush with vegetable growth or burdened with seas of sand or stone. Send forth the best ye breed: or at least large numbers of those ye breed. If one thought how odd it was—and if one thought then of what should have been natural empires, enormous spreads of restless real property like America or Russia turning in on themselves, making themselves into what seemed (to Denys, who had never seen them) to be very small places: then it did seem to be Destiny of a kind. Not a Destiny to be proud of, particularly, nor ashamed of either, but one whose compelling inner logic could only be marveled at.

Quite suddenly, and with poignant vividness, Denys saw himself, or rather felt himself once more to be, before his nursery fire, looking into the small glow of it, with animal crackers and cocoa for tea, listening to Nana telling tales of her brother the sergeant, and the Afghan frontier, and the now-dead king he served—listening, and feeling the Empire ranged in widening circles around him: first Harley Street, outside the window, and then Buckingham Palace, where the king lived; and the country then into which the trains went, and then the cold sea, and the Possessions, and the Commonwealth, stretching ever farther outward, worldwide: but always with his small glowing fire and his comfort and wonder at the heart of it.

So, there he is: a young man with the self-possessed air of an older, in evening clothes aged prematurely in places where evening clothes had not been made to go; thinking, if it could be called thinking, of a nursery fire; and about to be spoken to by the man next down the bar. If his feelings could be summed up and spoken, they were that, however odd, there is nothing more real, more pinioned by acts great and small, more clinker-built of time and space and filled brimful of this and that, than is the real world in which his five senses and his memories had their being; and that this was deeply satisfying.

"I beg your pardon," said the man next down the bar.

"Good evening," Denys said.

"My name is Davenant," the man said. He held out a square, blunt-fingered hand, and Denys drew himself up and shook it. "You are, I believe, Denys Winterset?"

"I am," Denys said, searching the smiling face before him and wondering from where he was known to him. It was a big, square, high-fronted head, a little like Bernard Shaw's, with ice-blue eyes of that twinkle; it was crowned far back with a neat hank of white hair, and was crossed above the broad jaw with upright white mustaches.

"You don't mind the intrusion?" the man said. "I wonder if you know whether the grub here is as good as once it was. It's been some time since I last ate a meal in Khartoum."

"The last time I did so was a year ago this week," Denys said. "It was quite good."

"Excellent," said Davenant, looking at Denys as though something about the young man amused him. "In that case, if you have no other engagement, may I ask your company?"

"I have no other engagement," Denys said; in fact he had rather been looking forward to dining alone, but deference to his superiors (of whom this man Davenant was surely in some sense one) was strong in him. "Tell me, though, how you come to know my name."

"Oh, well, there it is," Davenant said. "One has dealings with the Colonial Office. One sees a face, a name is attached to it, one files it but doesn't forget—that sort of thing. Part of one's job."

A civil servant, an inspector of some kind. Denys felt the sinking one feels on running into one's tutor in a wine bar: the evening not well begun. "They may well be crowded for dinner," he said.

"I have reserved a quiet table," said the smiling man, lifting his glass to Denys.

The grub was, in fact, superior. Sir Geoffrey Davenant was an able teller of tales, and he had many to tell. He was, apparently, no such dull thing as an inspector for the Colonial Office, though just what office he did fill Denys couldn't determine. He seemed to have been "attached to" or "had dealings with" or "gone about for" half the establishments of the Empire. He embodied, it seemed to Denys, the entire strange adventure about which Denys had been thinking when Sir Geoffrey had first spoken to him.

"So," Sir Geoffrey said, filling their glasses from a bottle of South African claret—no harm in being patriotic, he'd said, for one bottle—"so, after some months of stumbling about Central Asia and making myself useful one way or another, I was to make my way back to Sadiya. I crossed the Tibetan frontier disguised as a monk—"

"A monk?"

"Yes. Having lost all my gear in Manchuria, I could do the poverty part

539

quite well. I had a roll of rupees, the films, and a compass hidden inside my prayer wheel. Mine didn't whiz around then with the same sanctity as the other fellows', but no matter. After adventures too ordinary to describe —avalanches and so on—I managed to reach the monastery at Rangbok, on the old road up to Everest. Rather near collapse. I was recovering a bit and thinking how to proceed when there was a runner with a telegram. From my superior at Ch'eng-tu. WARN DAVENANT MASSACRE SADIYA, it said. The Old Man then was famously closemouthed. But this was particularly unhelpful, as it did not say who had massacred whom—or why." He lifted the silver cover of a dish, and found it empty.

"This must have been a good long time ago," Denys said.

"Oh, yes," Davenant said, raising his ice-blue eyes to Denys. "A good long time ago. That was an excellent curry. Nearly as good as at Veeraswamy's, in London—which is, strangely, the best in the world. Shall we have coffee?"

Over this, and brandy and cigars, Sir Geoffrey's stories modulated into reflections. Pleasant as his company was, Denys couldn't overcome a sensation that everything Sir Geoffrey said to him was rehearsed, laid on for his entertainment, or perhaps his enlightenment, and yet with no clue in it as to why he had thus been singled out.

"It amuses me," Sir Geoffrey said, "how constant it is in human nature to think that things might have gone on differently from the way they did. In a man's own life, first of all: how he might have taken this or that very different route, except for this or that accident, this or that slight push—if he'd only known then, and so on. And then in history as well, we ruminate endlessly, if, what if, if only . . . The world seems always somehow malleable to our minds, or to our imaginations anyway."

"Strange you should say so," Denys said. "I was thinking, just before you spoke to me, about how very solid the world seems to me, how very—real. And—if you don't mind my thrusting it into your thoughts—you never did tell me how it is you come to know my name; or why it is you thought good to invite me to that excellent dinner."

"My dear boy," Davenant said, holding up his cigar as though to defend his innocence.

"I can't think it was a chance."

"My dear boy," Davenant said in a different tone, "if anything is, that was not. I will explain all. You were on that train of thought. If you will have patience while it trundles by."

Denys said nothing further. He sipped his coffee, feeling a dew of sweat on his forehead.

"History," said Sir Geoffrey. "Yes. Of course the possible worlds we make don't compare to the real one we inhabit—not nearly so well furnished, or tricked out with details. And yet still somehow better. More satisfying. Perhaps the novelist is only a special case of a universal desire to reshape, to 'take this sorry scheme of things entire,' smash it into bits, and 'remold it nearer to the heart's desire'—as old Khayyám says. The egoist is continually doing it with his own life. To dream of doing it with history is no more useful a game, I suppose, but as a game, it shows more sport. There are rules. You can be more objective, if that's an appropriate word." He seemed to grow pensive for a moment. He looked at the end of his cigar. It had gone out, but he didn't relight it.

"Take this Empire," he went on, drawing himself up somewhat to say it. "One doesn't want to be mawkish, but one has served it. Extended it a bit, made it more secure; done one's bit. You and I. Nothing more natural, then, if we have worked for its extension in the future, to imagine its extension in the past. We can put our finger on the occasional bungle, the missed chance, the wrong man in the wrong place, and so on, and we think: if I had only been there, seen to it that the news went through, got the guns there in time, forced the issue at a certain moment—well. But as long as one is dreaming, why stop? A favorite instance of mine is the American civil war. We came very close, you know, to entering that war on the Confederacy's side."

"Did we."

"I think we did. Suppose we had. Suppose we had at first dabbled—sent arms—ignored Northern protests—then got deeper in; suppose the North declared war on us. It seems to me a near certainty that if we had entered the war fully, the South would have won. And I think a British presence would have mitigated the slaughter. There was a point, you know, late in that war, when a new draft call in the North was met with terrible riots. In New York several Negroes were hanged, just to show how little their cause was felt."

Denys had partly lost the thread of this story, unable to imagine himself in it. He thought of the Americans he had met on the train. "Is that so," he said.

"Once having divided the States into two nations, and having helped the South to win, we would have been in place, you see. The fate of the West had not yet been decided. With the North much diminished in power— well, I imagine that by now we—the Empire—would have recouped much of what we lost in 1780."

Denys contemplated this. "Rather stirring," he said mildly. "Rather cold-blooded, too. Wouldn't it have meant condoning slavery? To say nothing of the lives lost. British, I mean."

"Condoning slavery—for a time. I've no doubt the South could have been bullied out of it. Without, perhaps, the awful results that accompanied the Northerners doing it. The eternal resentment. The backlash. The near genocide of the last hundred years. And, in my vision, there would have been a net savings in red men." He smiled. "Whatever might be said against it, the British Empire does not wipe out populations wholesale, as the Americans did in their West. I often wonder if that sin isn't what makes the Americans so gloomy now, so introverted."

Denys nodded. He believed implicitly that his Empire did not wipe out populations wholesale. "Of course," he said, "there's no telling what exactly would have been the result. If we'd interfered as you say."

"No," Sir Geoffrey said. "No doubt whatever result it *did* have would have to be reshaped as well. And the results of that reshaping reshaped, too, the whole thing subtly guided all along its way toward the result desired—after all, if we can imagine how we might want to alter the past we do inherit, so we can imagine that any past might well be liable to the same imagining; that stupidities, blunders, shortsightedness, would occur in any past we might initiate. Oh, yes, it would all have to be reshaped, with each reshaping. . . ."

"The possibilities are endless," Denys said, laughing. "I'm afraid the game's beyond me. I say let the North win—since in any case we can't do the smallest thing about it."

"No," Davenant said, grown sad again, or reflective; he seemed to feel what Denys said deeply. "No, we can't. It's just—just too long ago." With great gravity he relit his cigar. Denys, at the oddness of this response, seeing Sir Geoffrey's eyes veiled, thought: *Perhaps he's mad.* He said, joining the game, "Suppose, though. Suppose Cecil Rhodes hadn't died young, as he did. . . ."

Davenant's eyes caught cold fire again, and his cigar paused in midair. "Hm?" he said with interest.

"I only meant," Denys said, "that your remark about the British not wiping out peoples wholesale was perhaps not tested. If Rhodes had lived to build his empire—hadn't he already named it Rhodesia?—I imagine he would have dealt fairly harshly with the natives."

"Very harshly," said Sir Geoffrey.

"Well," Denys said, "I suppose I mean that it's not always evil effects that we inherit from these past accidents."

"Not at all," said Sir Geoffrey. Denys looked away from his regard, which had grown, without losing a certain cool humor, intense. "Do you know, by the way, that remark of George Santayana—the American philosopher —about the British Empire, about young men like yourself? 'Never,' he said, 'never since the Athenians has the world been ruled by such sweet, just, boyish masters.' "

Denys, absurdly, felt himself flush with embarrassment.

"I don't ramble," Sir Geoffrey said. "My trains of thought carry odd goods, but all headed the same way. I want to tell you something, about that historical circumstance, the one you've touched on, whose effects we inherit. Evil or good I will leave you to decide.

"Cecil Rhodes died prematurely, as you say. But not before he had amassed a very great fortune, and laid firm claims to the ground where that fortune would grow far greater. And also not before he had made a will disposing of that fortune."

"I've heard stories," Denys said.

"The stories you have heard are true. Cecil Rhodes, at his death, left his entire fortune, and its increase, to found and continue a secret society which should, by whatever means possible, preserve and extend the British Empire. His entire fortune."

"I have never believed it," Denys said, momentarily feeling untethered, like a balloon: afloat.

"For good reason," Davenant said. "If such a society as I describe were brought into being, its very first task would be to disguise, cast doubt upon, and quite bury its origins. Don't you think that's so? In any case it's true what I say: the society was founded; is secret; continues to exist; is responsible, in some large degree at least, for the Empire we now know, in this year of grace 1956, IV Elizabeth II, the Empire on which the sun does not set."

The veranda where the two men sat was nearly deserted now; the night was loud with tropical noises that Denys had come to think of as silence, but the human noise of the town had nearly ceased.

"You can't know that," Denys said. "If you knew it, if you were privy to it, then you wouldn't say it. Not to me." He almost added: *Therefore you're not in possession of any secret, only a madman's certainty.*

"I *am* privy to it," Davenant said. "I am myself a member. The reason I reveal the secret to you—and you see, here we are, come to you and my odd knowledge of you, at last, as I promised—the reason I reveal it to you is because I wish to ask you to join it. To accept from me an offer of membership."

Denys said nothing. A dark waiter in white crept close, and was waved away by Sir Geoffrey.

"You are quite properly silent," Sir Geoffrey said. "Either I am mad, you think, in which case there is nothing to say; or what I am telling you is true, which likewise leaves you nothing to say. Quite proper. In your place I would be silent also. In your place I was. In any case I have no intention of pressing you for an answer now. I happen to know, by a roundabout sort of means that if I explained to you would certainly convince you I was mad, that you will seriously consider what I've said to you. Later. On your long ride to Cairo: there will be time to think. In London. I ask nothing from you now. Only . . ."

He reached into his waistcoat pocket. Denys watched, fascinated: would he draw out some sign of power, a royal charter, some awesome seal? No: it was a small metal plate, with a strip of brown ribbon affixed to it, like a bit of recording tape. He turned it in his hands thoughtfully. "The difficulty, you see, is that in order to alter history and bring it closer to the heart's desire, it would be necessary to stand outside it altogether. Like Archimedes, who said that if he had a lever long enough, and a place to stand, he could move the world."

He passed the metal plate to Denys, who took it reluctantly.

"A place to stand, you see," Sir Geoffrey said. "A place to stand. I would like you to keep that plate about you, and not misplace it. It's in the nature of a key, though it mayn't look it; and it will let you into a very good London club, though it mayn't look it either, where I would like you to call on me. If, even out of simple curiosity, you would like to hear more of us." He extinguished his cigar. "I am going to describe the rather complicated way in which that key is to be used—I really do apologize for the hugger-mugger, but you will come to understand—and then I am going to bid you good evening. Your train is an early one? I thought so. My own departs at midnight. I possess a veritable Bradshaw's of the world's railroads in this skull. Well. No more. I will just sign this—oh, don't thank me. Dear boy: don't thank me."

When he was gone, Denys sat a long time with his cold cigar in his hand and the night around him. The amounts of wine and brandy he had been given seemed to have evaporated from him into the humid air, leaving him feeling cool, clear, and unreal. When at last he rose to go, he inserted the flimsy plate into his waistcoat pocket; and before he went to bed, to lie a long time awake, he changed it to the waistcoat pocket of the pale suit he would wear next morning.

As Sir Geoffrey suggested he would, he thought on his ride north of all that he had been told, trying to reassemble it in some more reasonable, more everyday fashion: as all day long beside the train the sempiternal Nile—camels, nomads, women washing in the barge canals, the thin line of palms screening the white desert beyond—slipped past. At evening, when at length he lowered the shade of his compartment window on the poignant blue sky pierced with stars, he thought suddenly: But how could he have known he would find me there, at the bar of the Grand, on that night of this year, at that hour of the evening, just as though we had some long-standing agreement to meet there?

If anything is chance, Davenant had said, that was not.

At the airfield at Ismailia there was a surprise: his flight home on the R101, which his father had booked months ago as a special treat for Denys, was to be that grand old airship's last scheduled flight. The oldest airship in the British fleet, commissioned in the year Denys was born, was to be—mothballed? Drydocked? Deflated? Denys wondered just what one did with a decommissioned airship larger than Westminster Cathedral.

Before dawn it was drawn from its great hangar by a crowd of white-clothed fellahin pulling at its ropes—descendants, Denys thought, of those who had pulled ropes at the Pyramids three thousand years ago, employed now on an object almost as big but lighter than air. It isn't because it is so intensely romantic that great airships must always arrive or depart at dawn or at evening, but only that then the air is cool and most likely to be still: and yet intensely romantic it remains. Denys, standing at the broad, canted windows, watched the ground recede—magically, for there was no sound of engines, no jolt to indicate liftoff, only the waving, cheering fellahin growing smaller. The band on the tarmac played "Land of Hope and Glory." Almost invisible to watchers on the ground—because of its heat-reflective silver dome—the immense ovoid turned delicately in the wind as it arose.

"Well, it's the end of an era," a red-faced man in a checked suit said to Denys. "In ten years they'll all be gone, these big airships. The propeller chaps will have taken over; and the jet aeroplane, too, I shouldn't wonder."

"I should be sorry to see that," Denys said. "I've loved airships since I was a boy."

"Well, they're just that little bit slower," the red-faced man said sadly. "It's all hurry-up, nowadays. Faster, faster. And for what? I put it to you: for what?"

Now with further gentle pushes of its Rolls-Royce engines, the R101 altered its attitude again; passengers at the lounge windows pointed out the Suez Canal, and the ships passing; Lake Mareotis; Alexandria, like a mirage; British North Africa, as far to the left as one cared to point; and the white-fringed sea. Champagne was being called for, traditional despite the hour, and the red-faced man pressed a glass on Denys.

"The end of an era," he said again, raising his flute of champagne solemnly.

And then the cloudscape beyond the windows shifted, and all Africa had slipped into the south, or into the imaginary, for they had already begun to seem the same thing to Denys. He turned from the windows and decided—the effort to decide it seemed not so great here aloft, amid the potted palms and the wicker, with this pale champagne—that the conversation he had had down in the flat lands far away must have been imaginary as well.

III: THE TALE OF THE PRESIDENT *PRO TEM*

The universe proceeds out of what it has been and into what it will be, inexorably, unstoppably, at the rate of one second per second, one year per year, forever. At right angles to its forward progress lie the past and the future. The future, that is to say, does not lie "ahead" of the present in the stream of time, but at a right angle to it: the future of any present moment can be projected as far as you like outward from it, infinitely in fact, but when the universe has proceeded further, and a new present moment has succeeded this one, the future of this one retreats with it into the what-has-been, forever outdated. It is similar but more complicated with the past.

Now within the great process or procession that the universe makes, there can be no question of "movement," either "forward" or "back." The very idea is contradictory. Any conceivable movement is into the orthogonal futures and pasts that fluoresce from the universe as it is; and from those orthogonal futures and pasts into others, and others, and still others, never returning, always moving at right angles to the stream of time. To the traveler, therefore, who does not ever return from the futures or pasts into which he has gone, it must appear that the times he inhabits grow progressively more remote from the stream of time that generated them, the stream that has since moved on and left his futures behind. Indeed, the longer he remains in the future, the farther off the traveler gets from the moment in actuality whence he started, and the less like actuality the universe he stands in seems to him to be.

It was thoughts of this sort, only inchoate as yet and with the necessary conclusions not yet drawn, that occupied the mind of the President *pro tem* of the Otherhood as he walked the vast length of an iron and glass railway station in the capital city of an aged empire. He stopped to take a cigar case from within the black Norfolk overcoat he wore, and a cigar from the case; this he lit, and with its successive blue clouds hanging lightly about his hat and head, he walked on. There were hominids at work on the glossy engines of the empire's trains that came and went from this terminus; hominids pushing with their long strong arms the carts burdened with the goods and luggage that the trains were to carry; hominids of other sorts gathered in groups or standing singly at the barricades, clutching their tickets, waiting to depart, some aided by or waited upon by other species—too few creatures, in all, to dispel the extraordinary impression of smoky empty hugeness that the cast-iron arches of the shed made.

The President *pro tem* was certain, or at any rate retained a distinct impression, that at his arrival some days before there were telephones available for citizens to use, in the streets, in public places such as this (he seemed to see an example in his mind, a wooden box whose bright veneer was loosening in the damp climate, a complex instrument within, of enameled steel and heavy celluloid); but if there ever had been, there were none now. Instead he went in at a door above which a yellow globe was alight, a winged foot etched upon it. He chose a telegraph form from a stack of them on a long scarred counter, and with the scratchy pen provided he dashed off a quick note to the Magus in whose apartments he had been staying, telling him that he had returned late from the country and would not be with him till evening.

This missive he handed in at the grille, paying what was asked in large coins; then he went out, up the brass-railed stairs, and into the afternoon, into the quiet and familiar city.

It was the familiarity that had been, from the beginning, the oddest thing. The President *pro tem* was a man who, in the long course of his work for the Otherhood, had become accustomed to stepping out of his London club into a world not quite the same as the world he had left to enter that club.

He was used to finding himself in a London—or a Lahore or a Laos—stripped of well-known monuments, with public buildings and private ways unknown to him, and a newspaper (bought with an unfamiliar coin found in his pocket) full of names that should not have been there, or missing events that should have been. But here—where nothing, nothing at all, was as he had known it, no trace remaining of the history he had come from—here where no man should have been able to take steps, where even Caspar Last had thought it not possible to take steps—the President *pro tem* could not help but feel easy: had felt easy from the beginning. He walked up the cobbled streets, his furled umbrella over his shoulder, troubled by nothing but the weird grasp that this unknown dark city had on his heart.

The rain that had somewhat spoiled his day in the country had ceased but had left a pale, still mist over the city, a humid atmosphere that gave to views down avenues a stageset quality, each receding rank of buildings fainter, more vaguely executed. Trees, too, huge and weeping, still and featureless as though painted on successive scrims. At the great gates, topped with garlanded urns, of a public park, the President *pro tem* looked in toward the piled and sounding waters of a fountain and the dim towers of poplar trees. And as he stood resting on his umbrella, lifting the last of the cigar to his lips, someone passed by him and entered the park.

For a moment the President *pro tem* stood unmoving, thinking what an attractive person (boy? girl?) that had been, and how the smile paid to him in passing seemed to indicate a knowledge of him, a knowledge that gave pleasure or at least amusement; then he dropped his cigar end and passed through the gates through which the figure had gone.

That had *not* been a hominid who had smiled at him. It was not a Magus and surely not one of the draconics either. Why he was sure he could not have said: for the same unsayable reason that he knew this city in this world, this park, these marble urns, these leaf-littered paths. He was sure that the person he had seen belonged to a different species from himself, and different also from the other species who lived in this world.

At the fountain where the paths crossed, he paused, looking this way and that, his heart beating hard and filled absurdly with a sense of loss. The child (had it been a child?) was gone, could not be seen that way, or that way—but then was there again suddenly, down at the end of a yew alley, loitering, not looking his way. Thinking at first to sneak up on her, or him, along the sheltering yews, the President *pro tem* took a sly step that way; then, ashamed, he thought better of it and set off down the path at an even pace, as one would approach a young horse or a tame deer. The one he walked toward took no notice of him, appeared lost in thought, eyes cast down.

Indescribably lovely, the President *pro tem* thought: and yet at the same time negligent and easeful and ordinary. Barefoot, or in light sandals of some kind, light pale clothing that seemed to be part of her, like a bird's dress—

and a wristwatch, incongruous, yet not really incongruous at all: someone for whom incongruity was inconceivable. A reverence—almost a holy dread—came over the President *pro tem* as he came closer: as though he had stumbled into a sacred grove. Then the one he walked toward looked up at him, which caused the President *pro tem* to stop still as if a gun had casually been turned on him.

He was known, he understood, to this person. She, or he, stared unembarrassed at the President *pro tem*, with a gaze of the most intense and yet impersonal tenderness, of compassion and amusement and calm interest all mixed; and almost imperceptibly shook her head *no* and smiled again: and the President *pro tem* lowered his eyes, unable to meet that gaze. When he looked up again, the person was gone.

Hesitantly the President *pro tem* walked to the end of the avenue of yews and looked in all directions. No one. A kind of fear flew over him, felt in his breast like the beat of departing wings. He seemed to know, for the first time, what those encounters with gods had been like, when there had been gods; encounters he had puzzled out of the Greek in school.

Anyway he was alone now in the park: he was sure of that. At length he found his way out again into the twilight streets.

By evening he had crossed the city and was climbing the steps of a tall town house, searching in his pockets for the key given him. Beside the varnished door was a small plaque, which said that within were the offices of the Orient Aid Society; but this was not in fact the case. Inside was a tall foyer; a glass-paneled door let him into a hallway wainscoted in dark wood. A pile of gumboots and rubber overshoes in a corner, macs and umbrellas on an ebony tree. Smells of tea, done with, and dinner cooking: a stew, an apple tart, a roast fowl. The tulip-shaped gas lamps along the hall were lit.

He let himself into the library at the hall's end; velvet armchairs regarded the coal fire, and on a drum table a tray of tea things consorted with the books and the papers. The President *pro tem* went to the low shelves that ran beneath the windows and drew out one volume of an old encyclopedia, buckram-bound, with marbled fore-edges and illustrations in brownish photogravure.

The Races. For some reason the major headings and certain other words were in the orthography he knew, but not the closely printed text. His fingers ran down the columns, which were broken into numbered sections headed by the names of species and subspecies. *Hominidae*, with three subspecies. *Draconiidae*, with four: here were etchings of skulls. And lastly *Sylphidae*, with an uncertain number of subspecies. Sylphidae, the Sylphids. Fairies.

"Angels," said a voice behind him. The President *pro tem* turned to see the Magus whose guest he was, recently risen no doubt, in a voluminous dressing gown richly figured. His beard and hair were so long and fine they seemed to float on the currents of air in the room, like filaments of thistledown.

" 'Angels,' is that what you call them?"

"What they would have themselves called," said the Magus. "What name they call themselves, among themselves, no one knows but they."

"I think I met with one this evening."

"Yes."

There was no photogravure to accompany the subsection on Sylphidae in the encyclopedia. "I'm sure I met with one."

"They are gathering, then."

"Not . . . not because of me?"

"Because of you."

"How, though," said the President *pro tem*, feeling again within him the sense of loss, of beating wings departing, "how, how could they have known, how . . ."

The Magus turned away from him to the fire, to the armchairs and the drum table. The President *pro tem* saw that beside one chair a glass of whiskey had been placed, and an ashtray. "Come," said the Magus. "Sit. Continue your tale. It will perhaps become clear to you: perhaps not." He sat then himself, and without looking back at the President *pro tem* he said: "Shall we go on?"

The President *pro tem* knew it was idle to dispute with his host. He did stand unmoving for the space of several heartbeats. Then he took his chair, drew the cigar case from his pocket, and considered where he had left off his tale in the dark of the morning.

"Of course," he said then, "Last knew: he knew, without admitting it to himself, as a good orthogonist must never do, that the world he had returned to from his excursion was not the world he had left. The past he had passed through on his way back was not 'behind' his present at all, but at a right angle to it; the future of that past, which he had to traverse in order to get back again, was not the same road, and 'back' was not where he got. The frame house on Maple Street which, a little sunburned, he reentered on his return was twice removed in reality from the one he had left a week before; the mother he kissed likewise.

"He knew that, for it was predicated by orthogonal logic, and orthogonal logic was in fact what Last had discovered—the transversability of time was only an effect of that discovery. He knew it, and despite his glee over his triumph, he kept his eye open. Sooner or later he would come upon something, something that would betray the fact that this world was not his.

"He could not have guessed it would be me."

The Magus did not look at the President *pro tem* as he was told this story; his pale gray eyes instead wandered from object to object around the great dark library but seemed to see none of them; what, the President *pro tem* wondered, did they see? He had at first supposed the race of Magi to be blind, from this habitual appearance of theirs; he now knew quite well that they were not blind, not blind at all.

"Go on," the Magus said.

"So," said the President *pro tem*, "Last returns from his excursion. A week passes uneventfully. Then one morning he hears his mother call: he has a visitor. Last, pretending annoyance at this interruption of his work (actually he was calculating various forms of compound interest on a half million dollars) comes to the door. There on the step is a figure in tweeds and a bowler hat, leaning on a furled umbrella: me.

" 'Mr. Last,' I said. 'I think we have business.'

"You could see by his expression that he knew I should not have been there, should not have had business with him at all. He really ought to have refused to see me. A good deal of trouble might have been saved if he had. There was no way I could force him, after all. But he didn't refuse; after a goggle-eyed moment he brought me in, up a flight of stairs (Mama waiting anxiously at the bottom), and into his study.

"Geniuses are popularly supposed to live in an atmosphere of the greatest confusion and untidiness, but this wasn't true of Last. The study—it was his bedroom, too—was of a monkish neatness. There was no sign that he worked there, except for a computer terminal, and even it was hidden beneath a cozy that Mama had made for it and Caspar had not dared to spurn.

"He was trembling slightly, poor fellow, and had no idea of the social graces. He only turned to me—his eyeglasses were the kind that oddly diffract the eyes behind and make them unmeetable—and said, 'What do you want?' "

The President *pro tem* caressed the ashtray with the tip of his cigar. He had been offered no tea, and he felt the lack.

"We engaged in some preliminary fencing," he continued. "I told him what I had come to acquire. He said he didn't know what I was talking about. I said I thought he did. He laughed and said there must be some mistake. I said, no mistake, Mr. Last. At length he grew silent, and I could see even behind those absurd goggles that he had begun to try to account for me.

"Thinking out the puzzles of orthogonal logic, you see, is not entirely unlike puzzling out moves in chess: theoretically chess can be played by patiently working out the likely consequences of each move, and the consequences of those consequences, and so on; but in fact it is not so played, certainly not by master players. Masters seem to have a more immediate apprehension of possibilities, an almost visceral understanding of the, however, rigorously mathematical logic of the board and pieces, an understanding that they can act on without being able necessarily to explain. Whatever sort of mendacious and feckless fool Caspar Last was in many ways, he was a genius in one or two, and orthogonal logic was one of them.

" 'From when,' he said, 'have you come?'

" 'From not far on,' I answered. He sat then, resigned, stuck in a sort of check impossible to think one's way out of, yet not mated. 'Then,' he said, 'go back the same way you came.'

" 'I cannot,' I said, 'until you explain to me how it is done.'

" 'You know how,' he said, 'if you can come here to ask me.'

" 'Not until you have explained it to me. Now or later.'

" 'I never will,' he said.

" 'You will,' I said. 'You will have done already, before I leave. Otherwise I would not be here now asking. Let us,' I said, and took a seat myself, 'let us assume these preliminaries have been gone through, for they have been of course, and move ahead to the bargaining. My firm are prepared to make you a quite generous offer.'

"That was what convinced him that he must, finally, give up to us the processes he had discovered, which he really had firmly intended to destroy forever: the fact that I had come there to ask for them. Which meant that he had already somehow, somewhen, already yielded them up to us."

The President *pro tem* paused again, and lifted his untouched whiskey. "It was the same argument," he said, "the same incontrovertible argument, that was used to convince me once, too, to do a dreadful thing."

He drank, thoughtfully, or at least (he supposed) appearing thoughtful; more and more often as he grew older it happened that in the midst of an anecdote, a relation, even one of supreme importance, he would begin to forget what it was he was telling; the terrifically improbable events would begin to seem not only improbable but fictitious, without insides, the incidents and characters as false as in any tawdry cinema story, even his own part in them unreal: as though they happened to someone made up—certainly not to him who told them. Often enough he forgot the plot.

"You see," he said, "Last exited from a universe in which travel 'through time' was, apparently, either not possible, or possible only under conditions that would allow such travel to go undetected. That was apparent from the fact that no one, so far as Last knew, up to the time of his own single excursion, had ever detected it going on. No one from Last's own future, that is, had ever come 'back' and disrupted his present, or the past of his present: never ever. Therefore, if his excursion could take place, and he could 'return,' he would have to return to a different universe: a universe where time travel *had* taken place, a universe in which once-upon-a-time a man from 1983 had managed to insert himself into a minor colony of the British Crown one hundred and twenty-seven years earlier. What he couldn't know in advance was whether the universe he 'returned' to was one where time travel was a commonplace, an everyday occurrence, something anyway that could deprive his excursion of the value it had; or whether it was one in which one excursion only had taken place, his own. My appearance before him convinced him that it was, or was about to become, common enough: common enough to disturb his own peace and quiet, and alter in unforeseeable ways his comfortable present.

"There was only one solution, or one dash at a solution anyway. I might, myself, be a singularity in Last's new present. It was therefore possible that if he could get rid of me, I would take his process 'away' with me into whatever future I had come out of to get it, and thereupon never be able to find my way again to his present and disturb it or him. Whatever worlds I altered, they would not be his, not his anyway who struck the bargain with me: if each of them also contained a Last, who would suffer or flourish in ways unimaginable to the Last to whom I spoke, then those eidolons would have to make terms for themselves, that's all. The quantum angle obtended by my coming, and then the one obtended by my returning, divorced all those Lasts from him for all eternity: that is why, though the angle itself is virtually infinitesimal, it has always to be treated as a right angle.

"Last showed me, on his computer, after our bargain was struck and he was turning over his data and plans to me. I told him I would not probably grasp the theoretical basis of the process, however well I had or would come to manage the practical paradoxes of it, but he liked to show me. He first summoned up x-y coordinates, quite ordinary, and began by showing me how some surprising results were obtained by plotting on such coordinates an imaginary number, specifically the square root of minus one. The only way to describe what happens, he said, is that the plotted figure, one unit high, one unit wide, generates a shadow square of the same measurements 'behind' itself, in space undefined by the coordinates. It was with such tricks that he had begun; the orthogons he obtained had first started him thinking about the generation of inhabitable—if also somehow imaginary—pasts.

"Then he showed me what became of the orthogons so constructed if the upright axis were set in motion. Suppose (he said) that this vertical coordinate were in fact revolving around the axle formed by the other, horizontal coordinate. If it were so revolving, like an aeroplane propeller, we could not apprehend it, edge on as it is to us, so to speak; but what would that motion do to the plots we were making? And of course it was quite simple, given the proper instructions to the computer, to find out. And his orthogons— always remaining at right angles to the original coordinates—began to turn in the prop wash of the whole system's progress at one second per second out of the what-was and into the what-has-never-yet-been; and to generate, when one had come to see them, the paradoxes of orthogonal logic: the cyclonic storm of logic in which all travelers in that medium always stand; the one in which Last and I, I bending over his shoulder hat in hand, he with fat white fingers on his keys and eyeglasses slipping down his nose, stood even as we spoke: a storm as unfeelable as Last's rotating axis was unseeable."

The President *pro tem* tossed his extinguished cigar into the fading fire and crossed his arms upon his breast, weary; weary of the tale.

"I don't yet understand," the other said. "If he had been so adamant, why would he give up his secrets to you?"

"Well," said the President *pro tem*, "there was, also, the matter of money. It came down to that, in the end. We were able to make him a very generous offer, as I said."

"But he didn't need money. He had this stamp."

"Yes. So he did. Yes. We were able to pick up the stamp, too, from him, as part of the bargain. I think we offered him a hundred pounds. Perhaps it was more."

"I thought it was invaluable."

"Well, so did he, of course. And yet he was not really as surprised as one might have expected him to be, when he discovered it was not; when it turned out that the stamp he had gone to such trouble to acquire was in fact rather a common one. I seemed to see it in his face, the expectation of what he was likely to find, as soon as I directed him to look it up in his Scott's, if he didn't believe me. And there it was in Scott's: the one-penny magenta 1856, a nice enough stamp, a stamp many collectors covet, and many also have in their albums. He had begun breathing stertorously, staring down at the page. I'm afraid he was suffering, rather, and I didn't like to observe it.

" 'Come,' I said to him. 'You knew it was possible.' And he did, of course. 'Perhaps it was something you did,' I said. 'Perhaps you bought the last one of a batch, and the postmaster subsequently reordered, a thing he had not before intended to do. Perhaps . . .' But I could see him think it: there needed to be no such explanation. He needed to have made no error, nor to have influenced the moment's shape in any way by his presence. The very act of his coming and going was sufficient source of unpredictable, stochastic change: this world was not his, and minute changes from his were predicated. But *this* change, this of all possible changes . . .

"His hand had begun to shake, holding the volume of Scott's. I really wanted now to get through the business and be off, but it couldn't be hurried. I knew that, for I'd done it all before. In the end we acquired the stamp. And then destroyed it, of course."

The President *pro tem* remembered: a tiny, momentary fire.

"It's often been observed," he said, "that the cleverest scientists are often the most easily taken in by charlatans. There is a famous instance, famous in some worlds, of a scientist who was brought to believe firmly in ghosts and ectoplasm, because the medium and her manifestations passed all the tests the scientist could devise. The only thing he didn't think to test for was conscious fraud. I suppose it's because the phenomena of nature, or the entities of mathematics, however puzzling and elusive they may be, are not after all bent on fooling the observer; and so a motive that would be evident to the dullest of policemen does not occur to the genius."

"The stamp," said the Magus.

"The stamp, yes. I'm not exactly proud of this part of the story. We were convinced, though, that two *very* small wrongs could go a long way toward making a very great right. And Last, who understood me and the 'firm' I represented to be capable of handling—at least in a practical way—the awful paradoxes of orthogony, did not imagine us to be also skilled, if anything more skilled, at such things as burglary, uttering, fraud, and force. Of such contradictions is Empire made. It was easy enough for us to replace, while Last was off in the tropics, one volume of his Scott's stamp catalog with another printed by ourselves, almost identical to his but containing one difference. It was harder waiting to see, once he had looked up his stamp in our bogus volume, if he would then search out some other source to confirm what he found there. He did not."

The Magus rose slowly from his chair with the articulated dignity, the wasteless lion's motion, of his kind. He tugged the bell pull. He picked up the poker then, and stood with his hand upon the mantel, looking down into the ruby ash of the dying fire. "I would he had," he said.

The dark double doors of the library opened, and the servant entered noiselessly.

"Refresh the gentleman's glass," the Magus said without turning from the fire, "and draw the drapes."

The President *pro tem* thought that no matter how long he lived in this world he would never grow accustomed to the presence of draconics. The servant's dark hand lifted the decanter, poured an exact dram into the glass, and stoppered the bottle again; then his yellow eyes, irises slit like a cat's or a snake's, rose from that task toward the next, the drawing of the drapes. Unlike the eyes of the Magi, these draconic eyes seemed to see and weigh everything—though on a single scale, and from behind a veil of indifference.

Their kind, the President *pro tem* had learned, had been servants for uncounted ages, though the Magus his host had said that once they had been masters, and men and the other hominids their slaves. And they still had, the President *pro tem* observed, that studied reserve which upper servants had in the world from which the President *pro tem* had come, that reserve which says: Very well, I will do your bidding, better than you could do it for yourself; I will maintain the illusion of your superiority to me, as no other creature could.

With a taper he lit at the fire, he lit the lamps along the walls and masked them with glass globes. Then he drew the drapes.

"I'll ring for supper," the Magus said, and the servant stopped at the sound of his voice. "Have it sent in." The servant moved again, crossing the room on narrow naked feet. At the doorway he turned to them, but only to draw the double doors closed together as he left.,

For a time the Magus stood regarding the doors the great lizard had closed. Then: "Outside the City," he said, "in the mountains, they have begun to combine. There are more stories every week. In the old forests whence they first emerged, they have begun to collect on appointed days, trying to remember—for they are not really as intelligent as they look—trying to remember what it is they have lost, and to think of gaining it again. In not too long a time we will begin to hear of massacres. Some remote place; a country house; a more than usually careless man; a deed of unfamiliar horridness. And a sign left, the first sign: a writing in blood, or something less obvious. And like a spot symptomatic of a fatal disease, it will begin to spread."

The President *pro tem* drank, then said softly: "We didn't know, you know. We didn't understand that this would be the result." The drawing of the drapes, the lighting of the lamps, had made the old library even more familiar to the President *pro tem*: the dark varnished wood, the old tobacco smoke, the hour between tea and dinner; the draught that whispered at the window's edge, the bitter smell of the coal on the grate; the comfort of this velvet armchair's napless arms, of this whiskey. The President *pro tem* sat grasped by all this, almost unable to think of anything else. "We couldn't know."

"Last knew," the Magus said. "All false, all imaginary, all generated by the wishes and fears of others: all that I am, my head, my heart, my house. Not the world's doing, or time's, but yours." The opacity of his eyes, turned on the President *pro tem*, was fearful. "You have made me; you must unmake me."

"I'll do what I can," the President *pro tem* said. "All that I can."

"For centuries we have studied," the Magus said. "We have spent lifetimes—lifetimes much longer than yours—searching for the flaw in this world, the flaw whose existence we suspected but could not prove. I say 'centuries,' but those centuries have been illusory, have they not? We came, finally, to guess at you, down the defiles of time, working your changes, which we can but suffer.

"We only guessed at you: no more than men or beasts can we Magi remember, once the universe has become different, that it was ever other than it is now. But I think the Sylphids can feel it change: can know when the changes are wrought. Imagine the pain for them."

That was a command: and indeed the President *pro tem* could imagine it, and did. He looked down into his glass.

"That is why they are gathering. They know already of your appearance; they have expected you. The request is theirs to make, not mine: that you put this world out like a light."

He stabbed with the poker at the settling fire, and the coals gave up blue flames for a moment. The mage's eyes caught the light, and then went out.

"I long to die," he said.

IV: CHRONICLES OF THE OTHERHOOD

Once past the door, or what might be considered the door, of what Sir Geoffrey Davenant had told him was a club, Denys Winterset was greeted by the Fellow in Economic History, a gentle, academic-looking man called Platt.

"Not many of the Fellows about, just now," he said. "Most of them fossicking about on one bit of business or another. I'm always here." He smiled, a vague, self-effacing smile. "Be no good out there. But they also serve, eh?"

"Will Sir Geoffrey Davenant be here?" Denys asked him. He followed Platt through what did seem to be a gentlemen's club of the best kind: dark-paneled, smelling richly of leather upholstery and tobacco.

"Davenant, oh, yes," said Platt. "Davenant will be here. All the executive committee will get here, if they can. The President—*pro tem.*" He turned back to look at Denys over his half-glasses. "All our presidents are *pro tem.*" He led on. "There'll be dinner in the executive committee's dining room. After dinner we'll talk. You'll likely have questions." At that Denys almost laughed. He felt made of questions, most of them unputtable in any verbal form.

Platt stopped in the middle of the library. A lone Fellow in a corner by a green-shaded lamp was hidden by the *Times* held up before him. There was a fire burning placidly in the oak-framed fireplace; above it, a large and smoke-dimmed painting: a portrait of a chubby, placid man in a hard collar, thinning blond hair, eyes somehow vacant. Platt, seeing Denys's look, said: "Cecil Rhodes."

Beneath the portrait, carved into the mantelpiece, were words; Denys took a step closer to read them:

> To Ruin the Great Work of Time
> & Cast the Kingdoms old
> Into another mould.

"Marvell," Platt said. "That poem about Cromwell. Don't know who chose it. It's right, though. I look at it often, working here. Now. It's down that corridor, if you want to wash your hands. Would you care for a drink? We have some time to kill. Ah, Davenant."

"Hullo, Denys," said Sir Geoffrey, who had lowered his *Times*. "I'm glad you've come."

"I think we all are," said Platt, taking Denys's elbow in a gentle, almost tender grasp. "Glad you've come."

He had almost not come. If it had been merely an address, a telephone number he'd been given, he might well not have; but the metal card with its brown strip was like a string tied round his finger, making it impossible to forget he had been invited. Don't lose it, Davenant had said. So it lay in his waistcoat pocket; he touched it whenever he reached for matches there; he tried shifting it to other pockets, but whenever it was on his person he felt it. In the end he decided to use it, as much to get rid of its importunity as for any other reason—so he told himself. On a wet afternoon he went to the place Davenant had told him of, the Orient Aid Society, and found it as described, a sooty French-Gothic building, one of those private houses turned to public use, with a discreet brass plaque by the door indicating that within some sort of business is done, one can't imagine what; and inside the double doors, in the vestibule, three telephone boxes, looking identical, the first of which had the nearly invisible slit by the door. His heart for some reason beat slow and hard as he inserted the card within this slot—it was immediately snatched away, like a ticket on the Underground—and entered the box and closed the door behind him.

Though nothing moved, he felt as though he had stepped onto a moving footpath, or onto one of those trick floors in a fun house that slide beneath one's feet. He was going somewhere. The sensation was awful. Beginning to panic, he tried to get out, not knowing whether that might be dangerous, but the door would not open, and its glass could not be seen out of either. It had been transparent from outside but was somehow opaque from within. He shook the door handle fiercely. At that moment the nonmobile motion reversed itself sickeningly, and the door opened. Denys stepped out, not into the vestibule of the Orient Aid Society, but into the foyer of a club. A dim, old-fashioned foyer, with faded Turkey carpet on the stairs, and an aged porter to greet him; a desk, behind which pigeonholes held members' mail; a stand of umbrellas. It was reassuring, almost absurdly so, the "then I woke up" of a silly ghost story. But Denys didn't feel reassured, or exactly awake either.

"Evening, sir."

"Good evening."

"Still raining, sir? Take your things?"

"Thank you."

A member was coming toward him down the long corridor: Platt.

"Sir?"

Denys turned back to the porter. "Your key, sir," the man said, and gave him back the metal plate with the strip of brown ribbon on it.

"Like a lift," Davenant told him as they sipped whiskey in the bar. "Alarming, somewhat, I admit; but imagine using a lift for the first time, not knowing what its function was. Closed inside a box; sensation of movement; the doors open, and you are somewhere else. Might seem odd. Well, this is the same. Only you're not somewhere else: not exactly."

"Hm," Denys said.

"Don't dismiss it, Sir Geoffrey," said Platt. "It *is* mighty odd." He said to Denys: "The paradox is acute: it is. Completely contrary to the usual cause-

and-effect thinking we all do, can't stop doing really, no matter how hard we try to adopt other habits of mind. Strictly speaking it is unthinkable: unimaginable. And yet there it is."

"Yes," Davenant said. "To ignore, without ever forgetting, the heart of the matter: that's the trick. I've met monks, Japanese, Tibetan, who know the techniques. They can be learned."

"We speak of the larger paradox," Platt said to Denys. "The door you came in by being only a small instance. The great instance being, of course, the Otherhood's existence at all: we here now sitting and talking of it."

But Denys was not talking of it. He had nothing to say. To be told that in entering the telephone box in the Orient Aid Society he had effectively exited from time and entered a precinct outside it, revolving between the actual and the hypothetical, not quite existent despite the solidity of its parquet floor and the truthful bite of its whiskey; to be told that in these changeless and atemporal halls there gathered a society—"not quite a brotherhood," Davenant said; "that would be mawkish, and untrue of these chaps; we call it an Otherhood"—of men and women who by some means could insert themselves into the stream of the past, and with their foreknowledge alter it, and thus alter the future of that past, the future in which they themselves had their original being; that in effect the world Denys had come from, the world he knew, the year 1956, the whole course of things, the very cast and flavor of his memories, were dependent on the Fellows of this Society, and might change at any moment, though if they did he would know nothing of it; and that he was being asked to join them in their work—he heard the words, spoken to him with a frightening casualness; he felt his mind fill with the notions, though not able to do anything that might be called thinking about them; and he had nothing to say.

"You can see," Sir Geoffrey said, looking not at Denys but into his whiskey, "why I didn't explain all this to you in Khartoum. The words don't come easily. Here, in the Club, outside all frames of reference, it's possible to explain. To describe, anyway. I suppose if we hadn't a place like this, we should all go mad."

"I wonder," said Platt, "whether we haven't, despite it." He looked at no one. "Gone mad, I mean."

For a moment no one spoke further. The barman glanced at them, to see if their silence required anything of him. Then Platt spoke again. "Of course there are restrictions," he said. "The chap who discovered it was possible to change one's place in time, an American, thought he had proved that it was only possible to displace oneself into the past. In a sense, he was correct. . . ."

"In a sense," Sir Geoffrey said. "Not quite correct. The possibilities are larger than he supposed. Or rather will suppose, all this from your viewpoint is still to happen—which widens the possibilities right there, you see, one man's future being as it were another man's past. (You'll get used to it, dear boy, shall we have another of these?) The past, as it happens, is the only sphere of time we have any interest in; the only sphere in which we can do good. So you see there are natural limits: the time at which this process was made workable is the forward limit; and the rear limit we have made the time of the founding of the Otherhood itself. By Cecil Rhodes's will, in 1893."

"Be pointless, you see, for the Fellows to go back before the Society existed," said Platt. "You can see that."

"One further restriction," said Sir Geoffrey. "A house rule, so to speak. We forbid a man to return to a time he has already visited, at least in the same part of the world. There is the danger—a moment's thought will show you I'm right—of bumping into oneself on a previous, or successive, mission. Unnerving, let me tell you. Unnerving completely. The trick is hard enough to master as it is."

Denys found voice. "Why?" he said. "And why me?"

"Why," said Sir Geoffrey, "is spelled out in our founding charter: to preserve and extend the British Empire in all parts of the world, and to strengthen it against all dangers. Next, to keep peace in the world, insofar as this is compatible with the first; our experience has been that it usually is the same thing. And lastly to keep fellowship among ourselves, this also subject to the first, though any conflict is unimaginable, I should hope, bickering aside."

"The Society was founded to be secret," Platt said. "Rhodes liked that idea—a sort of Jesuits of the Empire. In fact there was no real need for secrecy, not until—well, not until the Society became the Otherhood. This jaunting about in other people's histories would not be understood. So secrecy *is* important. Good thing on the whole that Rhodes insisted on it. And for sure he wouldn't have been displeased at the Society's scope. He wanted the world for England. And more. 'The moon, too,' he used to say. 'I often think of the moon.' "

"Few know of us even now," Sir Geoffrey said. "The Foreign Office, sometimes. The PM. Depending on the nature of H.M. Government at any moment, we explain more, or less. Never the part about time. That is for us alone to know. Though some have guessed a little, over the years. It's not even so much that we wish to act in secret—that was just Rhodes's silly fantasy—but well, it's just damned difficult to explain, don't you see?"

"And the Queen knows of us," Platt said. "Of course."

"I flew back with her, from Africa, that day," Davenant said. "After her father had died. I happened to be among the party. I told her a little then. Didn't want to intrude on her grief, but—it seemed the moment. In the air, over Africa. I explained more later. Plucky girl," he added. "Plucky." He drew his watch out. "And as for the second part of your question—why you?—I shall ask you to reserve that one, for a moment. We'll dine upstairs . . . Good heavens, look at the time."

Platt swallowed his drink hastily. "I remember Lord Cromer's words to us when I was a schoolboy at Leys," he said. " 'Love your country,' he said, 'tell the truth, and don't dawdle.' "

"Words to live by," Sir Geoffrey said, examining the bar chit doubtfully and fumbling for a pen.

The drapes were drawn in the executive dining room; the members of the executive committee were just taking their seats around a long mahogany table, scarred around its edge with what seemed to be initials and dates. The members were of all ages; some sunburned, some pale, some in evening clothes of a cut unfamiliar to Denys; among them were two Indians and a Chinaman. When they were all seated, Denys beside Platt, there were several seats empty. A tall woman with severe gray hair but eyes somehow kind took the head of the table.

"The President *pro tem*," she said as she sat, "is not returned, apparently, from his mission. I'll preside, if there are no objections."

"Oh, balls," said a broad-faced man with the tan of a cinema actor. "Don't give yourself airs, Huntington. Will we really need any presiding?"

"Might be a swearing-in," Huntington said mildly, pressing the bell beside her and not glancing at Denys. "In any case, best to keep up the forms. First order of business—the soup."

It was a mulligatawny, saffrony and various; it was followed by a whiting, and that by a baron of claret-colored beef. Through the clashings of silverware and crystal Denys listened to the table's talk, little enough of which he could understand: only now and then he felt—as though he were coming horribly in two—the import of the Fellows' conversation: that history was malleable, time a fiction; that nothing was necessarily as he supposed it must be. How could they bear that knowledge? How could he?

"Mr. Deng Fa-shen, there," Platt said quietly to him, "is our physicist. Orthogonal physics—as opposed to orthogonal logic—is his invention. What makes this club possible. The mechanics of it. Don't ask me to explain."

Deng Fa-shen was a fine-boned, parchment-colored man with gentle fox's eyes. Denys looked from him to the two Indians in silk. Platt said, as though reading Denys's thought: "The most disagreeable thing about old Rhodes and the Empire of his day was its racialism, of course. Absolutely unworkable, too. Nothing more impossible to sustain than a world order based on some race's supposed inherent superiority." He smiled. "It isn't the only part of Rhodes's scheme that's proved unworkable."

The informal talk began to assemble itself, with small nudges from the woman at the head of the table (who did her presiding with no pomp and few words) around a single date: 1914. Denys knew something of this date, though several of the place names spoken of (the Somme, Jutland, Gallipoli—wherever that was) meant nothing to him. Somehow, in some possible universe, 1914 had changed everything; the Fellows seemed intent on changing 1914, drawing its teeth, teeth that Denys had not known it had—or might still have once had: he felt again the sensation of coming in two, and sipped wine.

"Jutland," a Fellow was saying. "All that's needed is a bit more knowledge, a bit more jump on events. Instead of a foolish stalemate, it could be a solid victory. Then, blockade; war over in six months . . ."

"Who's our man in the Admiralty now? Carteret, isn't it? Can he—"

"Carteret," said the bronze-faced man, "was killed the last time around at Jutland." There was a silence; some of the Fellows seemed to be aware of this, and some taken by surprise. "Shows the foolishness of that kind of thinking," the man said. "Things have simply gone too far by then. That's my opinion."

Other options were put forward. That moment in what the Fellows called the Original Situation was searched for into which a small intrusion might be made, like a surgical incision, the smallest possible intrusion that would have the proper effect; then the succeeding Situation was searched, and the Situation following that, the Fellows feeling with enormous patience and care into the workings of the past and its possibilities, like a blind man weaving. At length a decision seemed to be made, without fuss or a vote taken, about this place Gallipoli, and a Turkish soldier named Mustapha Kemal, who would be apprehended and sequestered in a quick action that took or would take place there; the sun-bronzed man would see, or had seen, to it; and the talk, after a reflective moment, turned again to anecdote and speculation.

Denys listened to the stories, of desert treks and dangerous negotiations, men going into the wilderness of a past catastrophe with a precious load of penicillin or of knowledge, to save one man's life or end another's; to intercept one trivial telegram, get one bit of news through, deflect one column of troops—removing one card from the ever-building possible future of some past moment and seeing the whole of it collapse silently, unknowably, even as another was building, just as fragile but happier: he looked into the faces of the Fellows, knowing that no ruthless stratagem was beyond them, and yet knowing also that they were men of honor, with a great world's peace and benefit in their trust, though the world couldn't know it; and he felt an odd but deep thrill of privilege to be here now, wherever that was—the same sense of privilege that, as a boy, he had expected to feel (and as a man had laughed at himself for expecting to feel) upon being admitted to the ranks of those who—selflessly, though not without reward—had been chosen or had chosen themselves to serve the Empire. "The difference you make makes all the difference," his headmasterish commissioner was fond of telling Denys and his fellows; and it was a joke among them that, in their form-filling, their execution of tedious and sometimes absurd directives, they were following in the footsteps of Gordon and Milner, Warren Hastings and Raffles of Singapore. And yet—Denys perceived it with a kind of inward stillness, as though his heart flowed instead of beating—a difference *could* be made. Had been made. Went on being made, in many times and places, without fuss, without glory, with rewards for others that those others could not recognize or even imagine. He crossed his knife and fork on his plate and sat back slowly.

"This 1914 business has its tricksome aspects," Platt said to him. "Speaking in large terms, not enough can really be done within our time frames. The Situation that issues in war was firmly established well before: in the founding of the German Empire under Prussian leadership. Bismarck. There's the man to get to, or to his financiers, most of whom were Jewish—little did they know, and all that. Even Sedan is too late, and not enough seems to be able to be made, or unmade, out of the Dreyfus affair, though that *does* fall within our provenance. No," he said. "It's all just too long ago. If only . . . Well, no use speculating, is there? Make the best of it, and shorten the war; make it less catastrophic at any rate, a short, sharp shaking-out—above all, win it quickly. We must do the best we can."

He seemed unreconciled.

Denys said: "But I don't understand. I mean, of course I wouldn't expect to understand it as you do, but . . . well, you *did* do all that. I mean we studied 1914 in school—the guns of August and all that, the 1915 Peace, the Monaco Conference. What I mean is . . ." He became conscious that the Fellows had turned their attention to him. No one else spoke. "What I mean to say is that I know you solved the problem, and how you solved it, in a general way; and I don't see why it remains to be solved. I don't see why you're worried." He laughed in embarrassment, looking around at the faces that looked at him.

"You're right," said Sir Geoffrey, "that you don't understand." He said it smiling, and the others were, if not smiling, patient and not censorious. "The logic of it is orthogonal. I can present you with an even more paradoxical instance. In fact I intend to present you with it; it's the reason you're here."

"The point to remember," the woman called Huntington said (as though to the whole table, but obviously for Denys's instruction), "is that here—in the Club—nothing has yet happened except the Original Situation. All is still to do: all that we have done, all still to do."

"Precisely," said Sir Geoffrey. "All still to do." He took from his waistcoat pocket an eyeglass, polished it with his napkin, and inserted it between cheek and eyebrow. "You had a question, in the bar. You asked *why me*, meaning, I suppose, why is it you should be nominated to this Fellowship, why you and not another."

"Yes," said Denys. He wanted to go on, list what he knew of his inadequacies, but kept silent.

"Let me, before answering your question, ask you this," said Sir Geoffrey. "Supposing that you were chosen by good and sufficient standards—supposing that a list had been gone over carefully, and your name was weighed;

supposing that a sort of competitive examination has been passed by you—would you then accept the nomination?"

"I—" said Denys. All eyes were on him, yet they were not somehow expectant; they awaited an answer they knew. Denys seemed to know it, too. He swallowed. "I hope I should," he said.

"Very well," Sir Geoffrey said softly. "Very well." He took a breath. "Then I shall tell you that you have in fact been chosen by good and sufficient standards. Chosen, moreover, for a specific mission, a mission of the greatest importance; a mission on which the very existence of the Otherhood depends. No need to feel flattered; I'm sure you're a brave lad, and all that, but the criteria were not entirely your sterling qualities, whatever they should later turn out to be.

"To explain what I mean, I must further acquaint you with what the oldest, or rather earliest, of the Fellows call the Original Situation.

"You recall our conversation in Khartoum. I told you no lie then; it is the case, in that very pleasant world we talked in, that good year 1956, fourth of a happy reign, on that wide veranda overlooking a world at peace—it is the case, I say, in that world and in most possible worlds like it, that Cecil Rhodes died young, and left the entire immense fortune he had won in the Scramble for the founding of a secret society, a society dedicated to the extension of that Empire which had his entire loyalty. The then Government's extreme confusion over this bequest, their eventual forming of a society—not without some embarrassment and doubt—a society from which this present Otherhood descends, still working toward the same ends, though the British Empire is not now what Rhodes thought it to be, nor the world either in which it has its hegemony—well, one of the Fellows is working up or will work up that story, insofar as it can be told, and it is, as I say, a true one.

"But there is a situation in which it is not true. In that situation which we call Original—the spine of time from which all other possibilities fluoresce—Cecil Rhodes, it appears, changed his mind."

Sir Geoffrey paused to light a cigar. The port was passed him. A cloud of smoke issued from his mouth. "Changed his mind, you see," he said, dispersing the smoke with a wave. "He did not die young, he lived on. His character mellowed, perhaps, as the years fell away; his fortune certainly diminished. It may be that Africa disappointed him, finally; his scheme to take over Tanganyika and join the Cape-to-Cairo with a single All-Red railroad line had ended in failure . . ."

Denys opened his mouth to speak; he had only a week before taken that line. He shut his mouth again.

"Whatever it was," Sir Geoffrey said, "he changed his mind. His last will left his fortune—what was left of it—to his old university, a scholarship fund to allow Americans and others of good character to study in England. No secret society. No Otherhood."

There was a deep silence at the table. No one had altered his casual position, yet there was a stillness of utter attention. Someone poured for Denys, and the liquid rattle of port into his glass was loud.

"Thus the paradox," Sir Geoffrey said. "For it is only the persuasions of the Otherhood that alter this Original Situation. The Otherhood must reach its fingers into the past, once we have learned how to do so; we must send our agents down along the defiles of time and intercept our own grandfather there, at the very moment when he is about to turn away from the work of generating us.

"And persuade him not to, you see; cause him—cause him not to turn away from that work of generation. Yes, cause him not to turn away. And thus ensure our own eventual existence."

Sir Geoffrey pushed back his chair and rose. He turned toward the sideboard, then back again to Denys. "Did I hear you say 'That's madness'?" he asked.

"No," Denys said.

"Oh," Sir Geoffrey said. "I thought you spoke. Or thought I remembered you speaking." He turned again to the sideboard, and returned again to the table with his cigar clenched in his teeth and a small box in his hands. He put this on the table. "You do follow me thus far," he said, his hands on the box and his eyes regarding Denys from under their curling brows.

"Follow you?"

"The man had to die," Sir Geoffrey said. He unlatched the box. "It was his moment. The moment you will find in any biography of him you pick up. Young, or anyway not old; at the height of his triumphs. It would have been downhill for him from there anyway."

"How," Denys asked, and something in his throat intruded on the question; it was a moment before he could complete it: "How did he die?"

"Oh, various ways," Sir Geoffrey said. "In the most useful version, he was shot to death by a young man he'd invited up to his house at Cape Town. Shot twice, in the heart, with a Webley .38-caliber revolver." He took from the box this weapon, and placed it with its handle toward Denys.

"That's madness," Denys said. His hands lay along the arms of his chair, drawing back from the gun. "You can't mean to say you went back and *shot* him, you . . ."

"Not we, dear boy," Sir Geoffrey said. "We, generally, yes; but specifically, not we. You."

"No."

"Oh, you won't be alone—not initially, at least. I can explain why it must be you and not another; I can expound the really quite dreadful paradox of it further, if you think it would help, though it seems to me best if, for now, you simply take our word for it."

Denys felt the corners of his mouth draw down, involuntarily, tightly; his lower lip wanted to tremble. It was a sign he remembered from early childhood: what had usually followed it was a fit of truculent weeping. That could not follow, here, now: and yet he dared not allow himself to speak, for fear he would be unable. For some time, then, no one spoke.

At the head of the table Huntington pushed her empty glass away.

"Mr. Winterset," she said gently. "I wonder if I might put in a word. Sit down, Davenant, will you, just for a moment, and stop looming over us. With your permission, Mr. Winterset—Denys—I should like to describe to you a little more broadly that condition of the world we call the Original Situation."

She regarded Denys with her sad eyes, then closed her fingers together before her. She began to speak, in a low voice which more than once Denys had to lean forward to catch. She told about Rhodes's last sad bad days; she told of Rhodes's chum the despicable Dr. Jameson, and his infamous raid and the provocations that led to war with the Boers; of the shame of that war, the British defeats and the British atrocities, the brutal intransigence of both sides. She told how in those same years the European powers who confronted each other in Africa were also at work stockpiling arms and building mechanized armies of a size unheard of in the history of the world, to be finally let loose upon one another in August of 1914, unprepared for what was to become of them; armies officered by men who still lived in the previous century, but armed with weapons more dreadful than they could imagine. The machine gun: no one seemed to understand that the machine gun had changed war forever, and though the junior officers and Other Ranks soon learned it, the commanders never did. At the First Battle of the Somme wave after wave of British soldiers were sent against German machine guns, to be mown down like grain. There were a quarter of a million casualties in that battle. And yet the generals went on ordering massed attacks against machine guns for the four long years of the war.

"But they knew," Denys could not help saying. "They did know. Machine guns had been used against massed native armies for years, all over the Empire. In Afghanistan. In the Sudan. Africa. They knew."

"Yes," Huntington said. "They knew. And yet, in the Original Situation, they paid no attention. They went blindly on and made their dreadful mistakes. Why? How could they be so stupid, those generals and statesmen who in the world you knew behaved so wisely and so well? For one reason only: they lacked the help and knowledge of a group of men and women who had seen all those mistakes made, who could act in secret on what they knew, and who had the ear and the confidence of one of the governments—not the least stupid of them, either, mind you. And with all our help it was still a close-run thing."

"Damned close-run," Platt put in. "Still hangs in the balance, in fact."

"Let me go on," Huntington said.

She went on: long hands folded before her, eyes now cast down, she told how at the end a million men, a whole generation, lay dead on the European battlefield, among them men whom Denys might think the modern world could not have been made without. A grotesque tyranny calling itself Socialist had been imposed on a war-weakened Russian empire. Only the intervention of a fully mobilized United States had finally broken the awful deadlock— thereby altering the further history of the world unrecognizably. She told how the vindictive settlement inflicted on a ruined Germany (so unlike the wise dispositions of the Monaco Conference, which had simply reestablished the old pre-Bismarck patchwork of German states and princedoms) had rankled in the German spirit; how a madman had arisen and, almost unbelievably, had ridden a wave of resentment and anti-Jewish hysteria to dictatorship.

"Yes," Denys said. *"That* we didn't escape, did we? I remember that, or almost remember it; it was just before I can remember anything. Anti-Jewish riots all over Germany."

"Yes," said Huntington softly.

"Yes. Terrible. These nice funny Germans, all lederhosen and cuckoo clocks, and suddenly they show a terrible dark side. Thousands of Jews, some of them very highly placed, had to leave Germany. They lost everything. Synagogues attacked, professors fired. Even Einstein, I think, had to leave Germany for a time."

Huntington let him speak. When Denys fell silent, unable to remember more and feeling the eyes of the Fellows on him, Huntington began again. But the things she began to tell of now simply could not have happened, Denys thought; no, they were part of a monstrous, foul dream, atrocities on a scale only a psychopath could conceive, and only the total resources of a strong and perverted science achieve. When Einstein came again into the tale, and the world Huntington described drifted ignorantly and inexorably into an icy and permanent stalemate that could be broken only by the end of civilization, perhaps of life itself, Denys found a loathsome surfeit rising in his throat; he covered his face, he would hear no more.

"So you see," Huntington said, "why we think it possible that the life— nearly over, in any case—of one egotistical, racialist adventurer is worth the chance to alter that situation." She raised her eyes to Denys. "I don't say you need agree. There *is* a sticky moral question, and I don't mean to brush it aside. I only say you see how we might think so."

Denys nodded slowly. He reached out and put his hand on the pistol that had been placed before him. He lifted his eyes and met those of Sir Geoffrey Davenant, which still smiled, though his mouth and his mustaches were grave.

What they were all telling him was that he could help create a better world than the original, which Huntington had described; but that was not how Denys perceived it. What Denys perceived was that reality—reality, the world he had come from, reality sun-shot and whole—was somehow under threat from a disgusting nightmare of death, ignorance, and torture, which could invade and replace it forever unless he acted. He did not think himself capable of interfering with the world to make it better; but to defend the world he knew, the world that with all its shortcomings was life and sustenance and sense and cleanly wakefulness—yes, that he could do. Would do, with all his strength.

Which is why, of course, it was he who had been chosen to do it. He saw that in Davenant's eyes.

And of course, if he refused, he could not then be brought here to be asked. If it was now possible for him to be asked to do this by the Otherhood, then he must have already consented, and done it. That, too, was in Davenant's silence. Denys looked down. His hand was on the Webley; and beside it, carved by a penknife into the surface of the table, almost obscured by later waxings, were the neat initials *D.W.*

"I always remember what Lord Milner said," Platt spoke into his ear. *"Everyone can help."*

V: THE TEARS OF THE PRESIDENT *PRO TEM*

"I remember," the president pro tem of the Otherhood said, "the light: a very clear, very pure, very cool light that seemed somehow potent but reserved, as though it could do terrible blinding things, and give an unbearable heat, if it chose—well, I'm not quite sure what I mean."

There was a midnight fug in the air of the library where the President *pro tem* retold his tale. The Magus to whom he told it did not look at him; his pale gray eyes moved from object around the room in the aimless idiot wandering that had at first caused the President *pro tem* to believe him blind.

"The mountain was called Table Mountain—a sort of high mesa. What a place that was then—I think the most beautiful in the Empire, and young then, but not raw; a peninsula simply made to put a city on, and a city being put there, beneath the mountain: and this piercing light.

"Our party put up at the Mount Nelson Hotel, perhaps a little grand for the travelers in electroplating equipment we were pretending to be, but the incognito wasn't really important, it was chiefly to explain the presence of the Last equipment among the luggage.

"A few days were spent in reconnaissance. But you see—this is continually the impossible thing to explain—in a sense those of the party who knew the outcome were only going through the motions of conferring, mapping their victim's movements, choosing a suitable moment and all that: for they knew the story; there was only one way for it to happen, if it was to happen at all. If it was *not* to happen, then no one could predict what was to happen instead; but so long as our party was there, and preparing it, it would evidently have to happen—or would have to have had to have happened."

The President *pro tem* suddenly missed his old friend Davenant, Davenant the witty and deep, who never bumbled over his tenses, never got himself stuck in a sentence such as that one; Davenant lost now with the others in the interstices of imaginary pasthood—or rather about to be lost, in the near future, if the President *pro tem* assented to what was asked of him. "It was rather jolly," he said, "like a game rather, striving to bring about a result that you were sure had already been brought about; an old ritual, if you like, to which not much importance needed to be attached, so long as it was all done correctly . . ."

"I think," said the Magus, "you need not explain these feelings that you then had."

"Sorry," said the President *pro tem*. "The house was called Groote Schuur—that was the old Dutch name, which he'd revived, for a big granary that had stood on the property; the English had called it the Grange. It was built on the lower slopes of Devil's Peak, with a view up to the mountains, and out to sea as well. He'd only recently seen the need for a house—all his life in Africa he'd more or less pigged it in rented rooms, or stayed in his club or a hotel or even a tent pitched outside town. For a long time he roomed with Dr. Jameson, sleeping on a little truckle bed hardly big enough for his body. But now that he'd become Prime Minister, he felt it was time for something more substantial.

"It seemed to me that it would have been easier to take him out in the bush—the *bundas*, as the Matabele say. Hire a party of natives—wait till all are asleep—ambush. He often went out into the wilds with almost no protection. There was no question of honor involved—I mean, the man had to die, one way or the other, and the more explainably or accidentally the better. But I was quite wrong—I was myself still young—and had to be put right: the one time that way was tried, the assassination initiated a punitive war against the native populations that lasted for twenty years, which ended only with the virtual extermination of the Matabele and Mashona peoples. Dreadful.

"No, it had to be the house; moreover, it had to be within a very brief span of time—a time when we knew he was there, when we knew where his will was, and *which* will it was—he made eight or nine in his lifetime —and when we knew, also, what assets were in his hands. Business and ownership were fluid things in those days; his partners were quick and subtle men; his sudden death might lose us all that we were intending to acquire by it in the way of a campaign chest, so to speak.

"So it had to be the house, in this week of this year, on this night. In fact orthogonal logic dictated it. Davenant was quite calmly sure of that. After all, that was the night when it had happened: and for sure we ought not to miss it."

That was an attempt at the sort of remark Davenant might make, and the President *pro tem* smiled at the Magus, who remained unmoved. The President *pro tem* thought it impossible that beings as wise as he knew the one before him to be, no matter how grave, could altogether lack any sense of humor. For himself, he had often thought that if he did not find funny the iron laws of orthogony he would go mad; but his jokes apparently amused only himself.

"It was not a question of getting to his house, or into it; he practically kept open house the year round, and his grounds could be walked upon by anyone. The gatekeepers were only instructed to warn walkers about the animals they might come across—he had brought in dozens of species, and he allowed all but the genuinely dangerous to roam at will. Wildebeest. Zebras. Impala. And 'human beings,' as he always called them, roamed at will, too; there were always some about. At dinner he had visitors from all over Africa, and from England and Europe as well; his bedrooms were often full. I think he hated to be alone. All of which provided a fine setting, you see, for a sensational—and insoluble—murder mystery: if only the man could be got alone, and escape made good then through these crowds of hangers-on.

"Our plan depended on a known proclivity of his, or rather two proclivities. The first was a taste he had for the company of a certain sort of a young man. He liked having them around him and could become very attached to them. There was never a breath of scandal in this—well, there was talk, but only talk. His 'angels,' people called them: goodlooking, resourceful if not particularly bright, good all-rounders with a rough sense of fun—practical jokes, horseplay—but completely devoted and ready for anything he might ask them to do. He had a fair crowd of these fellows up at Groote Schuur just then. Harry Curry, his private secretary. Johnny Grimmer, a trooper who was never afraid to give him orders—like a madman's keeper, some people said, scolding him and brushing dust from his shoulders; he never objected. Bob Coryndon, another trooper. They'd all just taken on a butler for themselves, a sergeant in the Inniskillings: good-looking chap, twenty-three years old. Oddly, they had all been just that age when he'd taken an interest in them: twenty-three. Whether that was chance or his conscious choice we didn't know.

"The other proclivity was his quickness in decision making. And this often involved the young men. The first expedition into Matabeleland had been headed up by a chap he'd met at his club one morning at breakfast just as the column was preparing for departure. Took to the chap instantly: liked his looks, liked his address. Gave him the job on the spot.

"That had worked out very well, of course—his choices often did. The pioneer column had penetrated into the heart of the *bundas*, the flag was flying over a settlement they called Fort Salisbury, and the whole of Matabeleland was in the process of being added to the Empire. Up at Groote Schuur they were kicking around possible names for the new country: Rhodia, perhaps, or Rhodesland, even Cecilia. It was that night that they settled on Rhodesia."

The President *pro tem* felt a moment's shame. There had been, when it came down to it, no doubt in his mind that what they had done had been the right thing to do: and in any case it had all happened a long time ago, more than a century ago in fact. It was not what was done, or that it had been done, only the moment of its doing, that was hard to relate: it was the picture in his mind, of an old man (though he was only forty-eight, he looked far older) sitting in the lamplight reading *The Boy's Own Paper*, as absorbed and as innocent in his absorption as a boy himself; and the vulnerable shine on his balding crown; and the tender and indifferent night: it was all that which raised a lump in the throat of the President *pro tem* and caused him to pause, and roll the tip of his cigar in the ashtray, and clear his throat before continuing.

"And so," he said, "we baited out hook. Rhodes's British South Africa Company was expanding, in the wake of the Fort Salisbury success. He was on the lookout for young men of the right sort. We presented him with one: good-looking lad, public school, cricketer; just twenty-three years old. He was the bait. The mole. The Judas."

And the bait had been taken, of course. The arrangement's having been keyed so nicely to the man's nature, a nature able to be studied from the vantage point of several decades on, it could hardly have failed. That the trick seemed so fragile, even foolish, something itself out of *The Boy's Own Paper* or a story by Henley, only increased the likelihood of its striking just the right note here: the colored fanatic, Rhodes leaving his hotel after luncheon to return to Parliament, the thug stepping out of the black noon shadows with a knife just as Rhodes mounts his carriage steps—then the young man, handily by with a stout walking stick (a gift of his father upon his departure for Africa)—the knife deflected, the would-be assassin slinking off, the great man's gratitude. You must have some reward. Not a bit, sir, anyone would have done the same; just lucky I was nearby. Come to dinner at any rate—my house on the hill—anyone can direct you. Allow me to introduce myself; my name is . . .

No need, sir, everyone knows Cecil Rhodes.

And your name is . . .

The clean hand put frankly forward, the tanned, open, boyish face smiling. My name is Denys Winterset.

"So then you see," the President *pro tem* said, "the road was open. The road up to Groote Schuur. The road that branches, in effect, to lead here: to us here now speaking of it."

"And how many times since then," the Magus said, "has the world branched? How many times has it been bent double, and broken? A thousand times, ten thousand? Each time growing smaller, having to be packed into lesser space, curling into itself like a snail's shell; growing ever weaker as the changes multiply, and more liable to failure of its fabric: how many times?"

The President *pro tem* answered nothing.

"You understand, then," the Magus said to him, "what you will be asked: to find the crossroads that leads this way and to turn the world from it."

"Yes."

"And how will you reply?"

The President *pro tem* had no better answer for this question, and he gave none. He had begun to feel at once heavy as lead and disembodied. He arose from his armchair, with some effort, and crossed the worn Turkey carpet to the tall window.

"You must leave my house now," the Magus said, rising from his chair. "There is much for me to do this night, if this world is to pass out of existence."

"Where shall I go?"

"They will find you. I think in not too long a time." Without looking back he left the room.

The President *pro tem* pushed aside the heavy drape the draconic had drawn. *Where shall I go?* He looked out the window into the square outside, deserted at this late and rainy hour. It was an irregular square, the intersection of three streets, filled with rain-wet cobbles as though with shiny eggs. It was old; it had been the view out these windows for two centuries at the least; there was nothing about it to suggest that it had not been the intersection of three streets for a good many more centuries than that.

And yet it had not been there at all only a few decades earlier, when the President *pro tem* had last walked the city outside the Orient Aid Society. Then the city had been London; it was no more. These three streets, these cobbles, had not been there in 1983; nor in 1893 either. Yet there they were, somewhere early in the twenty-first century; there they had been, too, for time out of mind, familiar no doubt to any dweller in this part of town, familiar for that matter to the President *pro tem* who looked out at them. In each of two lamp-lit cafés on two corners of the square, a man in a soft cap held a glass and looked out into the night, unsurprised, at home.

Someone had broken the rules: there simply was no other explanation.

There had been, of course, no way for anyone, not Deng Fa-shen, not Davenant, not the President *pro tem* himself, to guess what the President *pro tem* might come upon on this, the first expedition the Otherhood was making into the future: not only did the future not exist (Deng Fa-shen was quite clear about that), but, as Davenant reminded him, the Otherhood itself, supposing the continued existence of the Otherhood, would no doubt go busily on changing things in the past far and near—shifting the ground therefore of the future the President *pro tem* was headed for. Deng Fa-shen was satisfied that that future, the ultimate future, sum of all intermediate revisions, was the only one that could be plumbed, if any could; and that was the only one the Otherhood would want to glimpse: to learn how they would do, or would come to have done; to find out, as George V whispered on his deathbed, "How is the Empire."

("Only that isn't what he said," Davenant was fond of telling. "That's what he was, understandably, reported to have said, and what the Queen and the nurses convinced themselves they heard. But he was a bit dazed there at the end, poor good old man. What he said was not 'How is the Empire,' but 'What's at the Empire,' a popular cinema. I happened," he always added gravely, "to have been with him.")

The first question had been how far "forward" the Otherhood should press; those members who thought the whole scheme insane, as Platt did, voted for next Wednesday, and bring back the Derby winners please. Deng Fa-shen was not certain the thrust could be entirely calculated: the imaginary futures of imaginary pasts were not, he thought, likely to be under the control of even the most penetrating orthogonal engineering. Sometime in the first decades of the next century was at length agreed upon, a time just beyond the voyager's own mortal span—for the house rule seemed, no one could say quite why, to apply in both directions—and for as brief a stay as was consistent with learning what was up.

The second question—who was to be the voyager—the President *pro tem* had answered by fiat, assuming an executive privilege he just at that moment claimed to exist, and cutting off further debate. (Why exactly did he insist? I'm not certain why, except that it was not out of a sense of adventure, or of fun or curiosity: whatever of those qualities he may once have had had been much worn away in his rise to the Presidency *pro tem* of the Otherhood. A sense of duty may have been part of it. It may have been to forestall the others, out of a funny sort of premonition. Duty, and premonition: of what, though? Of what?)

"It'll be quite different from any of our imaginings, you know," Davenant said, who for some reason had not vigorously contested the President's decision. "The future of all possible pasts. I envy you, I do. I should rather like to see it for myself."

Quite different from any of our imaginings: very well. The President *pro tem* had braced himself for strangeness. What he had not expected was familiarity. Familiarity—cozy as an old shoe—was certainly different from his imaginings.

And yet what was it he was familiar with? He had stepped out of his club in London and found himself to be, not in the empty corridors of the Orient Aid Society that he knew well, but in private quarters of some kind that he had never seen before. It reminded him, piercingly, of a place he did know, but what place he could not have said: some don's rich but musty rooms, some wealthy and learned bachelor's digs. How had it come to be?

And how had it come to be lit by gas?

One of the pleasant side effects (most of the members thought it pleasant) of the Otherhood's endless efforts in the world had been a general retardation in the rate of material progress: so much of that progress had been, on the one hand, the product of the disastrous wars that it was the Otherhood's chief study to prevent, and on the other hand, American. The British Empire moved more slowly, a great beast without predators, and naturally conservative; it clung to proven techniques and could impose them on the rest of the world by its weight. The telephone, the motor car, the flying boat, the wireless, all were slow to take root in the Empire that the Otherhood shaped. And yet surely, the President *pro tem* thought, electricity was in general use in London in 1893, before which date no member could alter the course of things. And gas lamps lit this place.

Pondering this, the President *pro tem* had entered the somber and apparently little-used dining room and seen the draconic standing in the little butler's pantry: silent as a statue (asleep, the President *pro tem* would later deduce, with lidless eyes only seeming to be open); a polishing-cloth in his claw, and the silver before him; his heavy jaws partly open, and his weight balanced on the thick stub of tail. He wore a baize apron and black sleeve garters to protect his clothes.

Quite different from our imaginings: and yet no conceivable amount of tinkering with the twentieth century, just beyond which the President *pro tem* theoretically stood, could have brought forth this butler, in wing collar and green apron, the soft gaslight ashine on his bald brown head.

So someone had broken the rules. Someone had dared to regress beyond 1893 and meddle in the farther past. That was not, in itself, impossible; Caspar Last had done it on his first and only excursion. It had only been thought impossible for the Otherhood to do it, because it would have taken them "back" before the Otherhood's putative existence, and therefore before the Otherhood could have wrested the techniques of such travel from Last's jealous grip, a power they acquired by already having it—that was what the President *pro tem* had firmly believed.

But it was not, apparently, so. Somewhen in that stretch of years that fell between his entrance into the telephone box of the Club and his exit from it into this familiar and impossible world, someone—many someones, or someone many times—had gone "back" far before Rhodes's death: had gone back far enough to initiate this house, this city, these races who were not men.

A million years? It couldn't have been less. It didn't seem possible it could be less.

And who, then? Deng Fa-shen, the delicate, brilliant Chinaman, who had thoughts and purposes he kept to himself; the only one of them who might have been able to overcome the theoretical limits? Or Platt, who was never satisfied with what was possible within what he called "the damned parameters"?

Or Davenant. Davenant, who was forever quoting Khayyám: *Ah, Love, couldst thou and I with Him conspire To take this sorry scheme of things entire; Would we not smash it into pieces, then Remold it nearer to the heart's desire . . .*

573

"There is," said the Magus behind him, "one other you have not thought of."

The President *pro tem* let fall the drape and turned from the window. The Magus stood in the doorway, a great ledger in his arms. His eyes did not meet the President *pro tem*'s, and yet seemed to regard him anyway, like the blind eyes of a statue.

One other . . . Yes, the President *pro tem* saw, there was one other who might have done this. One other, not so good at the work perhaps as others, as Davenant for example, but who nonetheless would have been, or would come to have been, in a position to take such steps. The President *pro tem* would not have credited himself with the skill, or the nerve, or the dread-nought power. But how else to account for the familiarity, the bottomless *suitability* to him of this world he had never before seen?

"Between the time of your people's decision to plumb our world," said the Magus, "and the time of your standing here within it, you must yourself have brought it into being. I see no likelier explanation."

The President *pro tem* stood still with wonder at the efforts he was apparently to prove capable of making. A million years at least: a million years. How had he known where to begin? Where had he found, would he find, the time?

"Shall I ring," the Magus said, "or will you let yourself out?"

Deng Fa-shen had always said it, and anyone who traveled in them knew it to be so: the imaginary futures and imaginary pasts of orthogony are imaginary only in the sense that imaginary numbers (which they very much resemble) are imaginary. To a man walking within one, it alone is real, no matter how strange; it is all the others, standing at angles to it, which exist only in imagination. Nightlong the President *pro tem* walked the city, with a measured and unhurried step, but with a constant tremor winding round his rib cage, waiting for what would become of him, and observing the world he had made.

Of course it could not continue to exist. It should not ever have come into existence in the first place; his own sin (if it had been his) had summoned it out of nonbeing, and his repentance must expunge it. The Magus who had taken his confession (which the President *pro tem* had been unable to withhold from him) had drawn that conclusion: it must be put out, like a light. And yet how deeply the President *pro tem* wanted it to last forever; how deeply he believed it *ought* to last forever.

The numinous and inhuman angels, about whom nothing could be said, beings with no ascertainable business among the lesser races and yet beings without whom, the President *pro tem* was sure, this world could not go on functioning. They lived (endless?) lives unimaginable to men, and perhaps to Magi, too, who yet sought continually for knowledge of them: Magi, highest of the hominids, gentle and wise yet inflexible of purpose, living in simplicity and solitude (Were there females? Where? Doing what?) and yet from their shabby studies influencing, perhaps directing, the lives of mere men. The men, such as himself, clever and busy, with their inventions and their politics and their affairs. The lesser hominids, strong, sweet-natured, comic, like placid trolls. The draconics.

It was not simply a world inhabited by intelligent races of different kinds: it was a harder thing to grasp than that. The lives of the races constituted different universes of meaning, different constructions of reality; it was as though four or five different novels, novels of different kinds by different and differently limited writers, were to become interpenetrated and conflated: inside a gigantic Russian thing a stark and violent *policier*, and inside that something Dickensian, full of plot, humors, and eccentricity. Such an interlacing of mutually exclusive universes might be comical, like a sketch in *Punch*; it might be tragic, too. And it might be neither: it might simply be what is, the given against which all airy imaginings must finally be measured: reality.

Near dawn the President *pro tem* stood leaning on a parapet of worked stone that overlooked a streetcar roundabout. A car had just ended its journey there, and the conductor and the motorman descended, squat hominids in greatcoats and peaked caps. With their long strong arms they began to swing the car around for its return journey. The President *pro tem* gazed down at this commonplace sight; his nose seemed to know the smell of that car's interior, his bottom to know the feel of its polished seats. But he knew also that yesterday there had not been streetcars in this city. Today they had been here for decades.

No, it was no good, the President *pro tem* knew: the fabric of this world he had made—if it had been he—was fatally weakened with irreality. It was a botched job: as though he were that god of the Gnostics who made the material world, a minor god unversed in putting time together with space. He had not worked well. And how could he have supposed it would be otherwise? What had got into him, that he had dared?

"No," said the angel who stood beside him. "You should not think that it was you."

"If not me," said the President *pro tem*, "then who?"

"Come," said the angel. She (I shall say "she") slipped a small cool hand within his hand. "Let's go over the tracks, and into the trees beyond that gate."

A hard and painful stone had formed in the throat of the President *pro tem*. The angel beside him led him like a daughter, like the daughter of old blind Oedipus. Within the precincts of the park—which apparently had its entrance or its entrances where the angels needed them to be—he was led down an avenue of yew and dim towers of poplar toward the piled and sounding waters of a fountain. They sat together on the fountain's marble lip.

"The Magus told me," the President *pro tem* began, "that you can feel the alterations that we make, back then. Is that true?"

"It's like the snap of a whip infinitely long," the angel said. "The whole length of time snapped and laid out differently: not only the length of time backward to the time of the change, but the length of the future forward. We felt ourselves come into being, oldest of the Old Races (though the last your changes brought into existence); we saw in that moment the aeons of our past, and we guessed our future, too."

The President *pro tem* took out his pocket-handkerchief and pressed it to his face. He must weep, yet no tears came.

"We love this world—this only world—just as you do," she said. "We love it, and we cannot bear to feel it sicken and fail. Better that it not have been that it die."

"I shall do all I can," said the President *pro tem*. "I shall find who has done this—I suppose I know who it was, if it wasn't me—and dissuade him. Teach him, teach him what I've learned, make him see . . ."

"You don't yet understand," the angel said with careful kindness but at the same time glancing at her wristwatch. "There is no one to tell. There is no one who went beyond the rules."

"There must have been," said the President *pro tem*. "You, your time, it just isn't far along from ours, from mine! To make this world, this city, these races . . ."

"Not far along in time," said the angel, "but many times removed. You know it to be so: whenever you, your Otherhood, set out across the timelines, your passage generated random variation in the worlds you arrived in. Perhaps you didn't understand how those variations accumulate, here at the sum end of your journeyings."

"But the changes were so minute!" said the President *pro tem*. "Deng Fa-shen explained it. A molecule here and there, no more; the position of a distant star; some trivial thing, the name of a flower or a village. Too few, too small even to notice."

"They increase exponentially with every alteration—and your Otherhood has been busy since you last presided over them. Through the days random changes accumulate, tiny errors silting up like the blown sand that fills the streets of a desert city, that buries it at last."

"But why these changes?" asked the President *pro tem* desperately. "It can't have been chance that a world like this was the sun of those histories, it can't be. A world like *this* . . ."

"Chance, perhaps. Or it may be that as time grows softer the world grows more malleable by wishes. There is no reason to believe this, yet that is what we believe. You—all of you—could not have known that you were bringing this world into being; and yet this is the world you wanted."

She reached out to let the tossed foam of the fountain fall into her hand. The President *pro tem* thought of the bridge over the Zambezi, far away;

the tossed foam of the Falls. It was true: this is what they had striven for: a world of perfect hierarchies, of no change forever. God, how they must have longed for it! The loneliness of continual change—no outback, no *bundas* so lonely. He had heard how men can be unsettled for days, for weeks, who have lived through earthquakes and felt the earth to be uncertain: what of his Fellows, who had felt time and space picked apart, never to be rewoven that way again, and not once but a hundred times? What of himself?

"I shall tell you what I see at the end of all your wishings," said the angel softly. "At the far end of the last changed world, after there is nothing left that can change. There is then only a forest, growing in the sea. I say 'forest' and I say 'sea,' though whether they are of the kind I know, or some other sort of thing, I cannot say. The sea is still and the forest is thick; it grows upward from the black bottom, and its topmost branches reach into the sunlight, which penetrates a little into the warm upper waters. That's all. There is nothing else anywhere forever. Your wishes have come true: the Empire is quiet. There is not, nor will there be, change anymore; never will one thing be confused again with another, higher for lower, better for lesser, master for servant. Perpetual Peace."

The President *pro tem* was weeping now, painful sobs drawn up from an interior he had long kept shut and bolted. Tears ran down his cheeks, into the corners of his mouth, under his hard collar. He knew what he must do, but not how to do it.

"The Otherhood cannot be dissuaded from this," the angel said, putting a hand on the wrist of the President *pro tem*. "For all of it, including our sitting here now, all of it—and the forest in the sea—is implicit in the very creation of the Otherhood itself."

"But then . . ."

"Then the Otherhood must be uncreated."

"I can't do that."

"You must."

"No, no, I can't." He had withdrawn from her pellucid gaze, horrified. "I mean it isn't because . . . If it must be done, it must be. But not by me."

"Why?"

"It would be against the rules given me. I don't know what the result would be. I can't imagine. I don't *want* to imagine."

"Rules?"

"The Otherhood came into being," said the President *pro tem*, "when a British adventurer, Cecil Rhodes, was shot and killed by a young man called Denys Winterset."

"Then you must return and stop that killing."

"But you don't see!" said the President *pro tem* in great distress. "The rules given the Otherhood forbid a Fellow from returning to a time and place that he formerly altered by his presence . . ."

"And . . ."

"And I am myself that same Denys Winterset."

The angel regarded the President *pro tem*—the Honorable Denys Winterset, fourteenth President *pro tem* of the Otherhood—and her translucent face registered a sweet surprise, as though the learning of something she had not known gave her pleasure. She laughed, and her laughter was not different from the plashing of the fountain by which they sat. She laughed and laughed, as the old man in his black coat and hat sat silent beside her, bewildered and afraid.

VI: THE BOY DAVID OF HYDE PARK CORNER

There are days when I seem genuinely to remember, and days when I do not remember at all: days when I remember only that sometimes I remember. There are days on which I think I recognize another like myself: someone walking smartly along the Strand or Bond Street, holding the *Times* under one arm and walking a furled umbrella with the other—a sort of military bearing, mustaches white (older than when I seem to have known him, but then so am I, of course), and cheeks permanently tanned by some faraway sun. I do not catch his eye, nor he mine, though I am tempted to stop him, to ask him . . . Later on I wonder—if I can remember to wonder—whether he, too, is making a chronicle, in his evenings, writing up the story: a story that can be told in any direction, starting from anywhen, leading on to a forest in the sea.

I won't look any longer into this chronicle I've compiled. I shall only complete it.

My name is Denys Winterset. I was born in London in 1933; I was the only son of a Harley Street physician, and my earliest memory is of coming upon my father in tears in his surgery: he had just heard the news that the R101 dirigible had crashed on its maiden flight, killing all those aboard.

We lived then above my father's offices, in a little building whose nursery I remember distinctly, though I was taken to the country with the other children of London when I was only six, and that building was knocked down by a bomb in 1940. A falling wall killed my mother; my father was on ambulance duty in the East End and was spared.

He didn't know quite what to do with me, nor I with myself; I have been torn all my life between the drive to discover what others whom I love and admire expect of me, and my discovery that then I don't want to do it, really. After coming down from the University I decided, out of a certain perversity which my father could not sympathize with, to join the Colonial Service. He could not fathom why I would want to fasten myself to an enterprise that everyone save a few antediluvian colonels and letter writers to the *Times* could see was a dead animal. And I couldn't explain. Psychoanalysis later suggested that it was quite simply because no one wanted me to do it. The explanation has since come to seem insufficient to me.

That was a strange late blooming of Empire in the decade after the war, when the Colonial Office took on factitious new life, and thousands of us went out to the Colonies. The Service became larger than it had been in years, swollen with ex-officers too accustomed to military life to do anything else, and with the innocent and the confused, like myself. I ended up a junior member of a transition team in a Central African country I shall not name, helping see to it that as much was given to the new native government as they could be persuaded to accept, in the way of a parliament, a well-disciplined army, a foreign service, a judiciary.

It was not after all very much. Those institutions that the British are sure no civilized nation can do without were, in the minds of many Africans who spoke freely to me, very like those exquisite japanned toffee-boxes from Fortnum & Mason that you used often to come across in native kraals, because the chieftains and shamans loved them so, to keep their juju in. Almost as soon as I arrived, it became evident that the commander in chief of the armed forces was impatient with the pace of things, and felt the need of no special transition to African, i.e., his own, control of the state. The most our Commission were likely to accomplish was to get the British population out without a bloodbath.

Even that would not be easy. We—we young men—were saddled with the duty of explaining to aged planters that there was no one left to defend their estates against confiscation, and that under the new constitution they hadn't a leg to stand on, and that despite how dearly their overseers and house people loved them, they ought to begin seeing what they could pack into a few small trunks. On the other hand, we were to calm the fears of merchants and diamond factors, and tell them that if they all simply dashed for it, they could easily precipitate a closing of the frontiers, with incalculable results.

There came a night when, more than usually certain that not a single Brit under my care would leave the country alive, nor deserved to either, I stood at the bar of the Planters' (just renamed the Republic) Club, drinking gin and Italian (tonic hadn't been reordered in weeks) and listening to the clacking of the fans. A fellow I knew slightly as a regular here saluted me; I nodded and returned to my thoughts. A moment later I found him next to me.

"I wonder," he said, "if I might have your ear for a moment."

The expression, in his mouth, was richly comic, or perhaps it was my exhaustion. He waited for my laughter to subside before speaking. He was called Rossie, and he'd spent a good many years in Africa, doing whatever came to hand. He was one of those Englishmen whom the sun turns not brown but only gray and greasy; his eyes were always watery, the cups of his lids red and painful to look at.

"I am," he said at last, "doing a favor for a chap who would like your help."

"I'll do what I can," I said.

"This is a chap," he said, "who has been too long in this country, and would like to leave it."

"There are many in his situation."

"Not quite."

"What is his name?" I said, taking out a memorandum book. "I'll pass it on to the Commission."

"Just the point," Rossie said. He drew closer to me. At the other end of the bar loud laughter arose from a group consisting of a newly commissioned field marshal—an immense, glossy, nearly blue-black man—and his two colonels, both British, both small and lean. They laughed when the field marshal laughed, though their laugh was not so loud, nor their teeth so large and white.

"He'll want to tell you his name himself," Rossie said. "I've only brought the message. He wants to see you, to talk to you. I said I'd tell you. That's all."

"To tell us . . ."

"Not you, all of you. *You:* you."

I drank. The warm, scented liquor was thick in my throat. "Me?"

"What he asked me to ask you," Rossie said, growing impatient, "was would you come out to his place, and see him. It isn't far. He wanted you, no one else. He said I was to insist. He said you were to come alone. He'll send a boy of his. He said tell no one."

There were many reasons why a man might want to do business with the Commission privately. I could think of none why it should be done with me alone. I agreed, with a shrug. Rossie seemed immediately to put the matter out of his mind, mopped his red face, and ordered drinks for both us. By the time they were brought we were already discussing the Imperial groundnut scheme, which was to have kept this young republic self-sufficient, but which, it was now evident, would do no such thing.

I too put what had been asked of me out of my mind, with enough success that when on a windless and baking afternoon a native boy shook me awake from a nap, I could not imagine why.

"Who are you? What are you doing in my bungalow?"

He only stared down at me, as though it were he who could not think why I should be there before him. Questions in his own language got no response either. At length he backed out the door, clearly wanting me to follow; and so I did, with the dread one feels on remembering an unpleasant task one has contrived to neglect. I found him outside, standing beside my Land-Rover, ready to get aboard.

"All right," I said. "Very well." I got into the driver's seat. "Point the way."

It was a small spread of tobacco and a few dusty cattle an hour's drive from town, a low bungalow looking beaten in the ocher heat. He gave no greeting as I alighted from the Land-Rover but stood in the shadows of the porch unmoving: as though he had stood so a long time. He went back into the house as I approached, and when I went in, he was standing against the netting of the window, the light behind him. That seemed a conscious choice. He was smiling, I could tell: a strange and eager smile.

"I've waited a long time for you," he said. "I don't mind saying."

"I came as quickly as I could," I said.

"There was no way for me to know, you see," he said, "whether you'd come at all."

"Your boy was quite insistent," I said. "And Mr. Rossie—"

"I meant: to Africa." His voice was light, soft and dry. "There being so much less reason for it, now. I've wondered often. In fact I don't think a day has passed this year when I haven't wondered." Keeping his back to the sunward windows, he moved to sit on the edge of a creaking wicker sofa. "You'll want a drink," he said.

"No." The place was filled with the detritus of an African bachelor farmer's digs: empty paraffin tins, bottles, tools, hanks of rope and motor parts. He put a hand behind him without looking and put it on the bottle he was no doubt accustomed to find there. "I tried to think reasonably about it," he said, pouring a drink. "As time went on, and things began to sour here, I came to be more and more certain that no lad with any pluck would throw himself away down here. And yet I couldn't know. Whether there might not be some impulse, I don't know, traveling to you from—elsewhere. . . . I even thought of writing to you. Though whether to convince you to come or to dissuade you I'd no idea."

I sat, too. A cool sweat had gathered on my neck and the backs of my hands.

"Then," he said, "when I heard you'd come—well, I was afraid, frankly. I didn't know what to think." He dusted a fly from the rim of his glass, which he had not tasted. "You see," he said, "this was against the rules given me. That I—that I and—that you and I should meet."

Perhaps he's mad, I thought, and even as I thought it I felt intensely the experience called *déjà vu*, an experience I have always hated, hated like the nightmare. I steeled myself to respond coolly and took out my memorandum book and pencil. "I'm afraid you've rather lost me," I said—briskly I hoped. "Perhaps we'd better start with your name."

"Oh," he said, smiling again his mirthless smile, "not the hardest question first, please."

Without having, so far as I knew, the slightest reason for it, I began to feel intensely sorry for this odd dried jerky of a man, whose eyes alone seemed quick and shy. "All right," I said, "nationality, then. You are a British subject."

"Well, yes."

"Proof?" He answered nothing. "Passport?" No. "Army card? Birth certificate? Papers of any kind?" No. "Any connections in Britain? Relatives? Someone who could vouch for you, take you in?"

"No," he said, "None who could. None but you. It will have to be you."

"Now hold hard," I said.

"I don't know why I must," he said, rising suddenly and turning away to the window. "But I must. I must go back. I imagine dying here, being buried here, and my whole soul retreats in horror. I must go back. Even though I fear that, too."

He turned from the window, and in the sharp side light of the late afternoon his face was clearly the face of someone I knew. "Tell me," he said. "Mother and father. Your mother and father. They're alive?"

"No," I said. "Both dead."

"Very well," he said, "very well"; but it did not seem to be very well with him. "I'll tell you my story, then."

"I think you'd best do that."

"It's a long one."

"No matter." I had begun to feel myself transported, like a Sinbad, into somewhere that it were best I listen, and keep my counsel: and yet the first words of this specter's tale made that impossible.

"My name," he said, "is Denys Winterset."

I have come to believe, having had many years in which to think about it, that it must be as he said, that an impulse from somewhere else (he meant: some previous present, some earlier version of these circumstances) must press upon such a life as mine. That I chose the Colonial Service, that I came to Africa—and not just to Africa, but to that country: well, *if anything is chance, that was not*—as I understand Sir Geoffrey Davenant to have once said.

In that long afternoon, there where I perhaps could not have helped arriving eventually, I sat and perspired, listening—though it was for a long time very nearly impossible to hear what was said to me: an appointment in Khartoum some months from now, and some decades past; a club, outside all frames of reference; the Last equipment. It was quite like listening to the unfollowable logic of a madman, as meaningless as the roar of the insects outside. I only began to hear when this aged man, older than my grandfather, told me of something that he—that I—that he and I—had once done in boyhood, something secret, trivial really and yet so shameful that even now I will not write it down; something that only Denys Winterset could know.

"There now," he said, eyes cast down. "There now, you must believe me. You *will* listen. The world has not been as you thought it to be, any more than it was as I thought it to be, when I was as you are now. I shall tell you why: and we will hope that mine is the last story that need be told."

And so it was that I heard how he had gone up the road to Groote Schuur, that evening in 1893 (a young man then of course, only twenty-three) with the Webley revolver in his breast pocket as heavy as his heart, nearly sick with wonder and apprehension. The tropical suit he had been made to wear was monstrously hot, complete with full waistcoat and hard collar; the topee they insisted he use was as weighty as a crown. As he came in sight of the house, he could hear the awesome cries from the lion house, where the cats were evidently being given their dinner.

The big house appeared raw and unfinished to him, the trees yet ungrown and the great masses of scentless flowers—hydrangea, bougainvillaea, canna—that had smothered the place when last he had seen it, some decades later, just beginning to spread.

"Rhodes himself met me at the door—actually he happened to be going out for his afternoon ride—and welcomed me," he said. "I think the most striking thing about Cecil Rhodes, and it hasn't been noticed much, was his utter lack of airs. He was the least self-conscious man I have ever known; he did many things for effect, but he was himself entirely single: as whole as an egg, as the old French used to say.

" 'The house is yours,' he said to me. 'Use it as you like. We don't dress for dinner, as a rule; too many of the guests would be taken short, you see. Now some of the fellows are playing croquet in the Great Hall. Pay them no mind.'

"I remember little of that evening. I wandered the house: the great skins of animals, the heavy beams of teak, the brass chandeliers. I looked into the library, full of the specially transcribed and bound classics that Rhodes had ordered by the yard from Hatchard's: all the authorities that Gibbon had consulted in writing the *Decline and Fall*. All of them: that had been Rhodes's order.

"Dinner was a long and casual affair, entirely male—Rhodes had not even any female servants in the house. There was much toasting and hilarity about the successful march into Matabeleland, and the foundation of a fort, which news had only come that week; but Rhodes seemed quiet at the table's head, even melancholy: many of his closest comrades were gone with the expeditionary column, and he seemed to miss them. I do remember that at one point the conversation turned to America. Rhodes contended—no one disputed him—that if we (he meant the Empire, of course) had not lost America, the peace of the world could have been secured forever. 'Forever,' he said. 'Perpetual Peace.' And his pale opaque eyes were moist.

"How I comported myself at table—how I joined the talk, how I kept up conversations on topics quite unfamiliar to me—none of that do I recall. It helped that I was supposed to have been only recently arrived in Africa: though one of Rhodes's band of merry men looked suspiciously at my sun-browned hands when I said so.

"As soon as I could after dinner, I escaped from the fearsome horseplay that began to develop among those left awake. I pleaded a touch of sun and was shown to my room. I took off the hateful collar and tie (not without difficulty) and lay on the bed otherwise fully clothed, alert and horribly alone. Perhaps you can imagine my thoughts."

"No," I said. "I don't think I can."

"No. Well. No matter. I must have slept at last; it seemed to be after midnight when I opened my eyes and saw Rhodes standing in the doorway, a candlestick in his hand.

" 'Asleep?' he asked softly.

" 'No,' I answered. 'Awake.'

" 'Can't sleep either,' he said. 'Never do, much.' He ventured another step into the room. 'You ought to come out, see the sky,' he said. 'Quite spectacular. As long as you're up.'

"I rose and followed him. He was without his coat and collar; I noticed he wore carpet slippers. One button of his wide braces was undone; I had the urge to button it for him. Pale starlight fell in blocks across the black and white tiles of the hall, and the huge heads of beasts were mobile in the candlelight as we passed. I murmured something about the grandness of his house.

" 'I told my architect,' Rhodes answered. 'I said I wanted the big and simple—the barbaric, if you like.' The candle flame danced before him. 'Simple. The truth is always simple.'

"The chessboard tiles of the hall continued out through the wide doors onto the veranda—the *stoep* as the old Dutch called it. At the frontier of the *stoep* great pillars divided the night into panels filled with clustered stars, thick and near as vine blossoms. From far off came a long cry as of pain: a lion, awake.

"Rhodes leaned on the parapet, looking into the mystery of the sloping lawns beyond the *stoep*. 'That's good news, about the chaps up in Matabeleland,' he said a little wistfully.

" 'Yes.'

" 'Pray God they'll all be safe.'

" 'Yes.'

" '*Zambesia*,' he said after a moment. "What d'you think of that?'

" 'I beg your pardon?'

" 'As a name. For this country we'll be building. *Beyond the Zambesi*, you see.'

" 'It's a fine name.'

"He fell silent a time. A pale, powdery light filled the sky: false dawn. 'They shall say, in London,' he said, ' "Rhodes has taken for the Empire a country larger than Europe, at not a sixpence of cost to us, and we shall have that, and Rhodes shall have six feet by four feet." '

"He said this without bitterness, and turned from the parapet to face me. The Webley was pointed toward him. I had rested my (trembling) right hand on my left forearm, held up before me.

" 'Why, what on earth,' he said.

" 'Look,' I said.

"Drawing his look slowly away from me, he turned again. Out in the lawn, seeming in that illusory light to be but a long leap away, a male lion stood unmoving.

" 'The pistol won't stop him,' I said, 'but it will deflect him. If you will go calmly through the door behind me, I'll follow.'

"Rhodes backed away from the rail, and without haste or panic turned and walked past me into the house. The lion, ocher in the blue night, regarded him with a lion's expression, at once aloof and concerned, and returned his look to me. I thought I smelled him. Then I saw movement in the young trees beyond. I thought for a moment that my lion must be an illusion, or a dream, for he took no notice of these sounds—the crush of a twig, a soft voice—but at length he did turn his eyes from me to them. I could see the dim figure of a gamekeeper in a wide-awake hat, carrying a rifle, and Negroes with nets and poles: they were closing in carefully on the escapee. I stood for a moment longer, still poised to shoot, and then beat my own retreat into the house.

"Lights were being lit down the halls, voices calling: a lion does not appear on the lawn every night. Rhodes stood looking, not out the window, but at me. With deep embarrassment I clumsily pocketed the Webley (I knew what it had been given to me for, after all, even if he did not), and only then did I meet Rhodes's eyes.

"I shall never forget their expression, those pale eyes: a kind of exalted wonder, almost a species of adoration.

" 'That's twice now in one day,' he said, 'that you have kept me from harm. You must have been sent, that's all. I really believe you have been sent.'

"I stood before him staring, with a horror dawning in my heart such as, God willing, I shall never feel again. I knew, you see, what it meant that I had let slip the moment: that now I could not go back the way I had come. The world had opened for an instant, and I and my companions had gone down through it to this time and place; and now it had closed over me again, a seamless whole. I had no one and nothing; no Last equipment awaited me at the Mount Nelson Hotel; the Otherhood could not rescue me, for I had canceled it. I was entirely alone.

"Rhodes, of course, knew nothing of this. He crossed the hall to where I stood, with slow steps, almost reverently. He embraced me, a sudden great bear hug. And do you know what he did then?"

"What did he do?"

"He took me by the shoulders and held me at arm's length, and he insisted that I stay there with him. In effect, he offered me a job. For life, if I wanted it."

"What did you do?"

"I took it." He had finished his drink, and poured more. "I took it. You see, I simply had no place else to go."

Afternoon was late in the bungalow where we sat together, day hurried away with this tale. "I think," I said, "I shall have that drink now, if it's no trouble."

He rose and found a glass; he wiped the husk of a bug from it and filled it from his bottle. "It has always astonished me," he said, "how the mind, you know, can construct with lightning speed a reasonable, if quite mistaken, story to account for an essentially unreasonable event: I have had more than one occasion to observe this process.

"I was sure, instantly sure, that a lion which had escaped from Rhodes's lion house had appeared on the lawn at Groote Schuur just at the moment when I tried, but could not bring myself, to murder Cecil Rhodes. I can still see that cat in the pale light of predawn. And yet I cannot know if that is what happened, or if it is only what my mind has substituted for what did happen, which cannot be thought about.

"I am satisfied in my own mind—having had a lifetime to ponder it—that it cannot be possible for one to meet oneself on a trip into the past or future: that is a lie, invented by the Otherhood to forestall its own extinction, which was however inevitable.

"But I dream, sometimes, that I am lying on the bed at Groote Schuur, and a man enters—it is not Rhodes, but a man in a black coat and a bowler hat, into whose face I look as into a rotted mirror, who tells me impossible things.

"And I know that in fact there was no lion house at Groote Schuur. Rhodes wanted one, and it was planned, but it was never built."

In the summer of that year Rhodes—alive, alive-oh—went on expedition up into Pondoland, seeking concessions from an intransigent chief named Sicgau. Denys Winterset—this one, telling me the tale—went with him.

"Rhodes took Sicgau out into a field of mealies where he had had us set up a Maxim gun. Rhodes and the chief stood in the sun for a moment, and then Rhodes gave a signal; we fired the Maxim for a few seconds and mowed down much of the field. The chief stood unmoving for a long moment after the silence returned. Rhodes said to him softly: 'You see, this is what will happen to you and all your warriors if you give us any further trouble.'

"As a stratagem, that seemed to me both sporting and thrifty. It worked, too. But we were later to use the Maxims against men and not mealies. Rhodes knew that the Matabele had finally to be suppressed, or the work of building a white state north of the Zambezi would be hopeless. A way was found to intervene in a quarrel the Matabele were having with the Mashona, and in not too long we were at war with the Matabele. They were terribly, terribly brave; they were, after all, the first eleven in those parts, and they believed with reason that no one could withstand their leaf-bladed spears. I remember how they would come against the Maxims, and be mown down like the mealies, and fall back, and muster for another attack. Your heart sank; you prayed they would go away, but they would not. They came on again, to be cut down again. These puzzled, bewildered faces: I cannot forget them.

"And Christ, such drivel was written in the papers then, about the heroic stand of a few beleaguered South African police against so many battle-crazed natives! The only one who saw the truth was the author of that silly poem —Belloc, was it? You know—'Whatever happens, we have got/The Maxim gun, and they have not.' It was as simple as that. The truth, Rhodes said, is always simple."

He took out a large pocket-handkerchief and mopped his face and his eyes; no doubt it was hot, but it seemed to me that he wept. Tears, idle tears.

"I met Dr. Jameson during the Matabele campaign," he continued. "Leander Starr Jameson. I think I have never met a man—and I have met many wicked and twisted ones—whom I have loathed so completely and so instantly. I had hardly heard of him, of course; he was already dead and unknown in this year as it had occurred in my former past, the only version of these events I knew. Jameson was a great lover of the Maxim; he took several along on the raid he made into the Transvaal in 1896, the raid that would eventually lead to war with the Boers, destroy Rhodes's credit, and begin the end of Empire: so I have come to see it. The fool.

"I took no part in that war, thank God. I went north to help put the railroad through: Cape-to-Cairo." He smiled, seemed almost about to laugh, but did not; only mopped his face again. It was as though I were interrogating him, and he were telling me all this under the threat of the rubber truncheon or the rack. I wanted him to stop, frankly; only I dared say nothing.

"I made up for a lack of engineering expertise by my very uncertain knowledge of where and how, one day, the road would run. The telegraph had already reached Uganda; next stop was Wadi Halfa. The rails would not go through so easily. I became a sort of scout, leading the advance parties, dealing with the chieftains. The Maxim went with me, of course. I learned the weapon well."

Here there came another silence, another inward struggle to continue. I was left to picture what he did not say: *That which I did I should not have done; that which I should have done I did not do.*

"Rhodes gave five thousand pounds to the Liberal party to persuade them not to abandon Egypt: for there his railroad must be hooked to the sea. But then of course came the end of the whole scheme in German Tanganyika: no Cape-to-Cairo road. Germany was growing great in the world; the Germans wanted to have an Empire of their own. It finished Rhodes.

"By that time I was a railroad expert. The nonexistent Uganda Railroad was happy to acquire my services: I had a reputation, among the blacks, you see . . . I think there was a death for every mile of that road as it went through the jungle to the coast: rinderpest, fever, Nanda raids. We would now and then hang a captured Nanda warrior from the telegraph poles, to discourage the others. By the time the rails reached Mombasa, I was an old man; and Cecil Rhodes was dead."

He died of his old heart condition, the condition that had brought him out to Africa in the first place. He couldn't breathe in the awful heat of that summer of 1902, the worst anyone could remember; he wandered from room to room at Groote Schuur, trying to catch his breath. He lay in the darkened drawing room and could not breathe. They took him down to his cottage by the sea, and put ice between the ceiling and the iron roof to cool it; all afternoon the punkahs spooned the air. Then, suddenly, he decided to go to England. April was there: April showers. A cold spring: it seemed that could heal him. So a cabin was fitted out for him aboard a P&O liner, with electric fans and refrigerating pipes and oxygen tanks.

He died on the day he was to sail. He was buried at that place on the Matopos, the place he had chosen himself; buried facing north.

"He wanted the heroes of the Matabele campaign to be buried there with him. I could be one, if I chose; only I think my name would not be found among the register of those who fought. I think my name does not appear at all in history: not in the books of the Uganda Railroad, not in the register of the Mount Nelson Hotel for 1893. I have never had the courage to look."

I could not understand this, though it sent a cold shudder between my shoulder blades. The Original Situation, he explained, could not be returned to; but it could be restored, as those events that the Otherhood brought about were one by one come upon in time, and then not brought about. And as the Original Situation was second by second restored, the whole of his adventure in the past was continually worn away into nonbeing, and a new future replaced his old past ahead of him.

"You must imagine how it has been for me," he said, his voice now a whisper from exertion and grief. "To everyone else it seemed only that time went on—history—the march of events. But to me it has been otherwise. It has been the reverse of the nightmare from which you wake in a sweat of relief to find that the awful disaster has not occurred, the fatal step was not taken: for I have seen the real world gradually replaced by this other, nightmare world, which everyone else assumes is real, until nothing in past or present is as I knew it to be; until I am like the servant in Job: *I only am escaped to tell thee.*"

March 8, 1983

I awoke again this morning from the dream of the forest in the sea: a dream without people or events in it, or anything whatever except the gigantic dendrites, vast masses of pale leaves, and the tideless waters, light and sunshot toward the surface, darkening to impenetrability down below. It seemed there were schools of fish, or flocks of birds, in the leaves, something that faintly disturbed them, now and then; otherwise, stillness.

No matter that orthogonal logic refutes it, I cannot help believing that my present succeeds in time the other presents and futures that have gone into making it. I believe that as I grow older I come to incorporate the experiences I have had as an older man in pasts (and futures) now obsolete: as though in absolute time I continually catch up with myself in the imaginary times that fluoresce from it, gathering dreamlike memories of the lives I have lived therein. Somewhere God (I have come to believe in God; there was simply no existing otherwise) is keeping these universes in a row, and sees to it that they happen in succession, the most recently generated one last— and so felt to be last, no matter where along it I stand.

I remember, being now well past the age that he was then, the Uganda Railroad, the Nanda arrows, all the death.

I remember the shabby library and the coal fire, the encyclopedia in another orthography; the servant at the double doors.

I think that in the end, should I live long enough, I shall remember nothing but the forest in the sea. That is the terminus: complete strangeness that is at the same time utterly changeless; what cannot be becoming all that has ever been.

I took him out myself, in the end, abandoning my commission to do so, for there was no way that he could have crossed the border by himself, without papers, a nonexistent man. And it was just at that moment, as we motored up through the Sudan past Wadi Halfa, that the Anglo-French expeditionary force took Port Said. The Suez incident, that last hopeless spasm of Empire, was taking its inevitable course. Inevitable: I have not used the word before.

When we reached the Canal, the Israelis had already occupied the east bank. The airport at Ismailia was a shambles, the greater part of the Egyptian Air Force shot up, planes scattered in twisted attitudes like dead birds after a storm. We could find no plane to take us. *He* had gone desperately broody, wide-eyed and speechless, useless for anything. I felt as though in a dream where one is somehow saddled with an idiot brother one had not had before.

And yet it was only the confusion and mess that made my task possible at all, I suppose. There were so many semiofficial and unofficial British scurrying or loafing around Port Said when we entered the city that our passage was unremarked. We went through the smoke and dust of that famously squalid port like two ghosts—two ghosts progressing through a ghost city at the retreating edge of a ghost of empire. And the crunch of broken glass continually underfoot.

We went out on an old oiler attached to the retreating invasion fleet, which had been ordered home having accomplished nothing except, I suppose, the end of the British Empire in Africa. He stood on the oiler's boat deck and watched the city grow smaller and said nothing. But once he laughed, his dry, light laugh: it made me think of the noise that Homer says the dead make. I asked the reason.

"I was remembering the last time I went out of Africa," he said. "On a day much like this. Very much like this. This calm weather; this sea. Nothing else the same, though. Nothing else." He turned to me smiling, and toasted me with an imaginary glass. "The end of an era," he said.

March 10

My chronicle seems to be degenerating into a diary.

I note in the *Times* this morning the sale of the single known example of the 1856 magenta British Guiana, for a sum far smaller than was supposed to be its worth. Neither the names of the consortium that sold it nor the names of the buyers were made public. I see in my mind's eye a small, momentary fire.

I see now that there is no reason why this story should come last, no matter my feeling, no matter that in Africa he hoped it would. Indeed there is no reason why it should even fall last in this chronicling, nor why the world, the sad world in which it occurs, should be described as succeeding all others—it does not, any more than it precedes them. For the sake of a narrative only, perhaps; perhaps, like God, we cannot live without narrative.

I used to see him, infrequently, in the years after we both came back from Africa: he didn't die as quickly as we both supposed he would. He used to seek me out, in part to borrow a little money—he was living on the dole and on what he brought out of Africa, which was little enough. I stood him to tea now and then and listened to his stories. He'd appear at our appointed place in a napless British Warm, ill-fitting, as his eyeglasses and National Health false teeth were also. I imagine he was terribly lonely. I know he was.

I remember the last time we met, at a Lyons teashop near the Marble Arch. I'd left the Colonial Service, of course, under a cloud, and taken a position teaching at a crammer's in Holborn until something better came along (nothing ever did; I recently inherited the headmaster's chair at the same school; little has changed there over the decades but the general coloration of the students).

"This curious fancy haunts me," he said to me on that occasion. "I picture the Fellows, all seated around the great table in the executive committee's dining room; only it is rather like Miss Havisham's, you know, in Dickens: the roast beef has long since gone foul, and the silver tarnished, and the draperies rotten; and the Fellows dead in their chairs, or mad, dust on their evening clothes, the port dried up in their glasses. Huntington. Davenant. The President *pro tem*."

He stirred sugar in his tea (he liked it horribly sweet; so, of course, do I). "It's not true, you know, that the Club stood somehow at a nexus of possibilities, amid multiplying realities. If that were so, then what the Fellows did would be trivial or monstrous or both: generating endless new universes just to see if they could get one to their liking. No: it is we, out here, who live in but one of innumerable possible worlds. In there, they were like a man standing at the north pole, whose only view, wherever he looks, is south: they looked out upon a single encompassing reality, which it was their opportunity—no, their duty, as they saw it—to make as happy as possible, as free from the calamities they knew of as they could make it.

"Well, they were limited people, more limited than their means to work good or evil. That which they did they should not have done. And yet what they hoped for us was not despicable. The calamities they saw were real. Anyone who could would try to save us from them: as a mother would pull her child, her foolish child, from the fire. They ought to be forgiven; they ought."

I walked with him up toward Hyde Park Corner. He walked now with agonizing slowness, as I will, too, one day; it was a rainy autumn Sunday, and his pains were severe. At Hyde Park Corner he stopped entirely, and I thought perhaps he could go no farther: but then I saw that he was studying the monument that stands there. He went closer to it, to read what was written on it.

I have myself more than once stopped before this neglected monument. It is a statue of the boy David, a memorial to the Machine Gun Corps, and was put up after the First World War. Some little thought must have gone into deciding how to memorialize that arm which had changed war forever; it seemed to require a religious sentiment, a quote from the Bible, and one was found. Beneath the naked boy are written words from Kings:

> Saul has slain his thousands
> But David his tens of thousands.

He stood in the rain, in his vast coat, looking down at these words, as though reading them over and over; and the faint rain that clung to his cheeks mingled with his tears:

> Saul has slain his thousands
> But David his tens of thousands.

I never saw him again after that day, and I did not seek for him: I think it unlikely he could have been found.

AFTERWORD

Much of the impulse and many of the details of the preceding come from the second and third volumes of Jan Morris's enthralling chronicle of the rise and decline of the British Empire, *Pax Britannica* (1968) and *Farewell the Trumpets* (1978). I hope she will forgive the author the liberties he has taken, and accept his gratitude for the many hours she has allowed him to spend dawdling in a world more fantastical than any he could himself invent.

The story of Rhodes's death and many details of his character and conversation are taken from Sarah Gertrude Millin's elegant and neglected biography *Cecil Rhodes* (London, 1933).

The story of Rhodes in Pondoland, along with much else that was suggestive, comes from John Ellis's book *The Social History of the Machine Gun* (1975).

For an introduction to that book, for his convincing analysis of the possibilities and limits of what I have called orthogonal logic, and in general for his infectious enthusiasm for notions, the author's thanks to Bob Chasell (hi, Bob).

HONORABLE MENTIONS
1989

Brian W. Aldiss, "North of the Abyss," *F&SF*, Oct.

———, "Three Degrees Over," *Dark Fantasies*.

———, "Three Evolutionary Enigmas," *New Pathways*, May.

Ray Aldridge, "Blue Skin," *F&SF*, March.

———, "The Flesh Tinker and the Fashion Goddess," *Pulphouse Four*.

Poul Anderson, "Death Wish," *The Microverse*.

———, "Statesmen," *Time Gate*.

Patricia Anthony, "Bluebonnets," *Aboriginal SF*, July/Aug.

———, "Eating Memories," *Aboriginal SF*, May/June.

Kim Antieau, "Windows," *Pulphouse Four*.

Yoshio Aramaki, "Soft Clocks," *Interzone*, Jan./Feb.

Isaac Asimov, "The Smile of the Chipper," *IAsfm*, April.

———, "Too Bad!" *IAsfm*, Mid-Dec.

A.A. Attanasio, "Atlantis Rose," *Journal Wired*.

J.G. Ballard, "The Enormous Space," *Interzone*, July/Aug.

———, "War Fever," *F&SF*, Oct.

John Barnes, "Restricted to the Necessary," *Amazing*, March.

Neal Barrett, Jr., "Tony Red Dog," *Razored Saddles*.

Greg Bear, "Sisters," *Tangents*.

Doug Beason, "A Reasonable Doubt," *Pulphouse Four*.

M. Shayne Bell, "Bangkok," *IAsfm*, July.

Gregory Benford, "All the Beer on Mars," *IAsfm*, Jan.

———, "Mozart on Morphine," *F&SF*, Oct.

———, "We Could Do Worse," *IAsfm*, April.

R.P. Bird, "The Soft Heart of the Electron," *Aboriginal SF*, July/Aug.

Michael Bishop, "The Ommatidium Miniatures," *The Microverse*.

James P. Blaylock, "Unidentified Objects," *OMNI*, July.

T. Coraghessan Boyle, "King Bee," *Playboy*, March.

Bruce Boston, "Headed for Prime Time," *Pulphouse Four*.

R.V. Branham, "The Color of Grass, The Color of Blood," *IAsfm*, Mid-Dec.

Alan Brennert, "Healer," *F&SF*, Feb.

F. Alexander Brejcha, "Viewpoint," *Analog*, April.

Edward Bryant, "A Sad Last Love at the Diner of the Damned," *Book of the Dead*.

———, "Good Kids," *Blood Is Not Enough*.

Algis Budrys, "What Befell Mairiam," *F&SF*, Oct.

Lois McMaster Bujold, "The Mountains of Mourning," *Analog*, May.

Pat Cadigan, "Dirty Work," *Blood Is Not Enough*.
——, "The Power and the Passion," *Patterns*.
Richard Calder, "Mosquito," *Interzone*, Nov./Dec.
Orson Scott Card, "Pageant Wagon," *IAsfm*, Aug.
Jonathan Carroll, "Mr. Fiddlehead," *OMNI*, Feb.
Lenore Carroll, "Eldon's Penitente," *Razored Saddles*.
Susan Casper, "A Child of Darkness," *Blood Is Not Enough*.
Michael Cassutt, "Passages," *Synergy Four*.
Suzy McKee Charnas, "Boobs," *IAsfm*, July.
Ronald Anthony Cross, "The Front Page," *IAsfm*, Nov.
——, "Two Plotting Pods," *IAsfm*, May.
John Crowley, "Novelty," *Novelty*.
Scott A. Cupp, "Jimmy and Me and the Niggerman," *The New Frontier*.
——, "Thirteen Days of Glory," *Razored Saddles*.
Jack Dann "Kaddish," *IAsfm*, April.
Avram Davidson, "Events Which Took Place a Day Before Other Events,"
    IAsfm, Sept.
——, "Waiting for Willie," *IAsfm*, October.
Charles de Lint, "The Drowned Man's Reel," *Pulphouse Three*.
——, "Romano Drum," *Pulphouse Five*.
Bradley Denton, "The Sin-Eater of the Kaw," *F&SF*, June.
Thomas M. Disch, "The Happy Turnip," *F&SF*, October.
Gardner Dozois, "Solace," *OMNI*, Feb.
Judith Dubois, "Etoudi's Monkey," *F&SF*, Feb.
J.R. Dunn, "The Gates of Babel," *OMNI*, May.
Scott Edelman, "Is This a Horror Story?" *Pulphouse Five*.
George Alec Effinger, "Everything but Honor," *IAsfm*, Feb.
——, "Marîd Changes His Mind," *IAsfm*, May.
——, "Maureen Birnbaum After Dark," *Foundation's Friends*.
Greg Egan, "The Cutie," *Interzone*, May/June.
Harlan Ellison, "The Few, the Proud," *IAsfm*, March.
Christopher Evans, "Lifelines," *Dark Fantasies*.
Sheila Finch, "Ceremony After a Raid," *Amazing*, July.
——, "The Old Man and C," *Amazing*, Nov.
Marina Fitch, "Pieces of the Sky," *Pulphouse Three*.
Michael Flynn, "On the Wings of a Butterfly," *Analog*, March.
——, "Soul of the City," Analog, Feb.
John M. Ford, "The Hemstitch Notebooks," *IAsfm*, August.
Karen Joy Fowler, "Duplicity," *IAsfm*, Dec.
——, "Game Night at the Fox and Goose," *Interzone*, May/June.
Esther M. Friesner, "Poe White Trash," *F&SF*, Dec.
Gregory Frost, "Divertimento," *IAsfm*, Dec.
Mary Gentle, "The Tarot Dice," *IAsfm*, Mid-Dec.
Lisa Goldstein, "City of Peace," *Interzone*, July/Aug.

Colin Greenland, "The Traveller," *Zenith*.

Peni Griffin, "The Goat Man," *IAsfm*, May.

Eileen Gunn, "Computer Friendly," *IAsfm*, June.

——, "The Sock Story," *IAsfm*, Sept.

Joe Haldeman, "Time Lapse," *Blood Is Not Enough*.

Karen Haber, "A Plague of Strangers," *Full Spectrum II*.

Rory Harper, "Monsters, Tearing Off My Face," *IAsfm*, May.

Harry Harrison & Tom Shippey, "Letter from the Pope," *What Might Have Been, Vol. 2*.

Nina Kiriki Hoffman, "A Legacy of Fire," *Amazing*, Jan.

Elizabeth Hand, "The Boy in the Tree," *Full Spectrum II*.

——, "On the Town Route," *Pulphouse Five*.

Alexander Jablokov, "The Ring of Memory," *IAsfm*, Jan.

Phillip C. Jennings, "Five Letters," *Amazing*, May.

——, "Martin's Feast," *IAsfm*, July.

Janet Kagan, "Naked Wish Fullfillment," *Pulphouse Three*.

——, "The Return of the Kangaroo Rex," *IAsfm*, Oct.

Richard Kadrey, "The Kill Fix," *IAsfm*, May.

John Keefauver, "Uncle Harry's Flying Saucer Swimming Pool," *The New Frontier*.

James Patrick Kelly, "Dancing With the Chairs," *IAsfm*, Feb.

——, "Faith," *IAsfm*, June.

John Kennedy, "Encore," *IAsfm*, July.

Garry Kilworth, "White Noise," *Zenith*.

William King, "Skyrider," *Zenith*.

Nancy Kress, "People Like Us," *IAsfm*, Sept.

——, "Renaissance," *IAsfm*, mid-Dec.

Marc Laidlaw, "His Powder'd Wig, His Crown of Thornes," *OMNI*, Sept.

——, "Kronos," *IAsfm*, May.

Geoffrey A. Landis, "Sundancer Falling," *Analog*, March.

R. A. Lafferty, "Gray Ghost: A Reminiscence," *Strange Plasma*.

David Langford, "The Facts in the Case of Micky Valdon," *Dark Fantasies*.

Joe R. Lansdale, "The Job," *Razored Saddles*.

——, "On the Far Side of the Cadillac Desert with Dead Folks," *Book of the Dead*.

Ian Lee, "Driving Through Korea," *Interzone*, Jan./Feb.

Tanith Lee, "The Janfia Tree," *Blood Is Not Enough*.

——, "The Rakshasha," *Forests of the Night*.

——, "Zelle's Thursday," *IAsfm*, October.

Jonathan Lethem, "The Cave Beneath the Falls," *Aboriginal SF*, Jan./Feb.

Megan Lindholm, "A Touch of Lavender," *IAsfm*, Nov.

Duncan Lunan, "In the Arctic, Out of Time," *IAsfm*, July.

Bruce McAllister, "Little Boy Blue," *OMNI*, June.

Paul J. McAuley, "Jacob's Rock," *Amazing*, March.

Jack McDevitt, "Leap of Faith," *IAsfm*, May.

——, "Tracks," *IAsfm*, Dec.

——, "Whistle," *Full Spectrum II*.

Ian McDonald, "Listen," *Interzone*, March/April.

Maureen McHugh, "Baffin Island," *IAsfm*, August.

——, "Kites," *IAsfm*, Oct.

Tom Maddox, "Baby Strange," *OMNI*, April.

Barry N. Malzberg, "Another Goddamned Showboat," *What Might Have Been, Vol. 2.*

Phillip Mann, "An Old-Fashioned Love Story," *Interzone*, May/June.

Lisa Mason, "The Oniomancer," *IAsfm*, Feb.

Francis J. Matozzo, "Why Pop-Pop Died," *Pulphouse Five*.

Victor Milán, "The Floating World," *IAsfm*, April.

Judith Moffett, "Not Without Honor," *IAsfm*, May.

——, "Remembrance of Things Future," *IAsfm*, Dec.

Pat Murphy, "How I Spent My Summer Vacation," *Time Gate*.

——, "Prescience," *IAsfm*, Jan.

Jamil Nasir, "Not Even Ashes," *Interzone*, Sept./Oct.

Resa Nelson, "The Next Step," *Aboriginal SF*, Jan./Feb.

Kim Newman, "Twitch Technicolor," *Interzone*, March/April.

Chad Oliver, "Old Four-Eyes," *Synergy Four*.

Paul Park, "Carbontown," *Strange Plasma*.

Steve Perry, "Willie of the Jungle," *Pulphouse Three*.

Frederik Pohl, "The Reunion at Mile-High," *Foundation's Friends*.

Steven Popkes, "Rain, Steam and Speed," *Full Spectrum II*.

Paul Preuss, "Half-Life," *The Microverse*.

Keith Roberts, "Kaeti and the Village," *Weird Tales*, Winter.

Kim Stanley Robinson, "The Part of Us That Loves," *Full Spectrum II*.

——, "Remaking History," *IAsfm*, March.

——, "The True Nature of Shangri-La," *IAsfm*, Dec.

Rudy Rucker, "As Above, So Below," *The Microverse*.

——, "Drugs and Live Sex—New York City, 1980," *Journal Wired*.

Kristine Kathryn Rusch, "Fast Cars," *IAsfm*, Oct.

——, "Phantom," *F&SF*, June.

Richard Paul Russo, "Lunar Triptych: Embracing the Night," *IAsfm*, mid-Dec.

——, "More Than Night," *IAsfm*, April.

Robert Sampson, "A Plethora of Angels," *Full Spectrum II*.

——, "Magician in the Dark," *Weird Tales*, Winter.

Al Sarrantonio, "The Trail of the Chromium Bandits," *Razored Saddles*.

Aaron Schutz, "Small," *IAsfm*, Dec.

Charles Sheffield, "Dancing with Myself," *Analog*, August.

——, "Destroyer of Worlds," *IAsfm*, Feb.

——, "Nightmare of the Classical Mind," *IAsfm*, Aug.

——, "Serpent of Old Nile," *IAsfm*, May.

Rick Shelley, "The Sylph," *Analog*, March.

Lucius Shepard, "Bound for Glory," *F&SF*, Oct.

——, "The Father of Stones," *IAsfm*, Sept.

——, "Surrender," *IAsfm*, August.

Lewis Shiner, "Gold," *Razored Saddles*.

——, "Steam Engine Time," *The New Frontier*.

John Shirley, "I Live in Elizabeth," *Heatseeker*.

Robert Silverberg, "A Sleep and a Forgetting," *Playboy*, July.

——, "Chiprunner," *IAsfm*, Nov.

——, "In Another Country," *IAsfm*, March.

——, "To the Promised Land," *OMNI*, May.

Martha Soukup, "Dreams of Sawn Ivory," *Amazing*, May.

Brian Stableford, "The Will," *Dark Fantasies*.

Allen M. Steele, "Free Beer and the William Casey Society," *IAsfm*, Feb.

——, "John Harper Wilson," *IAsfm*, June.

——, "Red Planet Blues," *IAsfm*, Sept.

Michael Swanwick, "Snow Angels," *OMNI*, March.

Judith Tarr, "Roncesvalles," *What Might Have Been*, Vol. 2.

Melanie Tem, "The Better Half," *IAsfm*, mid-Dec.

Lisa Tuttle, "In Translation," *Zenith*.

——, "Skin Deep," *Dark Fantasies*.

Harry Turtledove, "Counting Potsherds," *Amazing*, March.

——, "Departures," *IAsfm*, Jan.

——, "Pillar of Cloud, Pillar of Fire," *IAsfm*, mid-Dec.

Steven Utley, "My Wife," *IAsfm*, Feb.

——, "The Tall Grass," *IAsfm*, June.

Howard Waldrop, "The Passing of the Western," *Razored Saddles*.

Sage Walker, "Indian Giving," *IAsfm*, April.

Ian Watson, "Nanoware Time," *IAsfm*, June.

Lawrence Watt-Evans, "Real-Time," *IAsfm*, Jan.

——, "Windwagon Smith and the Martians," *IAsfm*, April.

Don Webb, "Rex," *New Pathways*, Dec.

Deborah Wessell, "As We Forgive Those Who Trespass Against Us," *IAsfm*, Sept.

——, "The Last One to Know," *IAsfm*, April.

Dean Whitlock, "Iridescence," *IAsfm*, Jan.

Kate Wilhelm, "Children of the Wind," *Children of the Wind*.

Walter Jon Williams, "The Bob Dylan Solution," *Aboriginal SF*.

——, "No Spot of Ground," *IAsfm*, Nov.

Chet Williamson, "Yore Skin's Jes's Soft 'n Purty . . . He Said. (Page 243)," *Razored Saddles*.

——, "To Feel Another's Woe," *Blood Is Not Enough*.

Connie Willis, "Dilemma," *IAsfm*, mid-Dec.

——, "Time-Out," *IAsfm*, July.
Gene Wolfe, "How the Bishop Sailed to Inniskeen," *IAsfm*, Dec.
Thomas Wylde, "Black Nimbus," *IAsfm*, March.
Jane Yolen, "Feast of Souls," *IAsfm*, Jan.
——, "The Sea Man," *F&SF*, March.